# THE AWAKENING COMPLETE SUPERNATURAL THRILLER SERIES

---

THE AWAKENING, THE UNBELIEVERS, THE CONFLAGRATION, THE ILLUMINATION

LISA M. LILLY

# THE AWAKENING

---

BOOK 1 IN THE AWAKENING SERIES

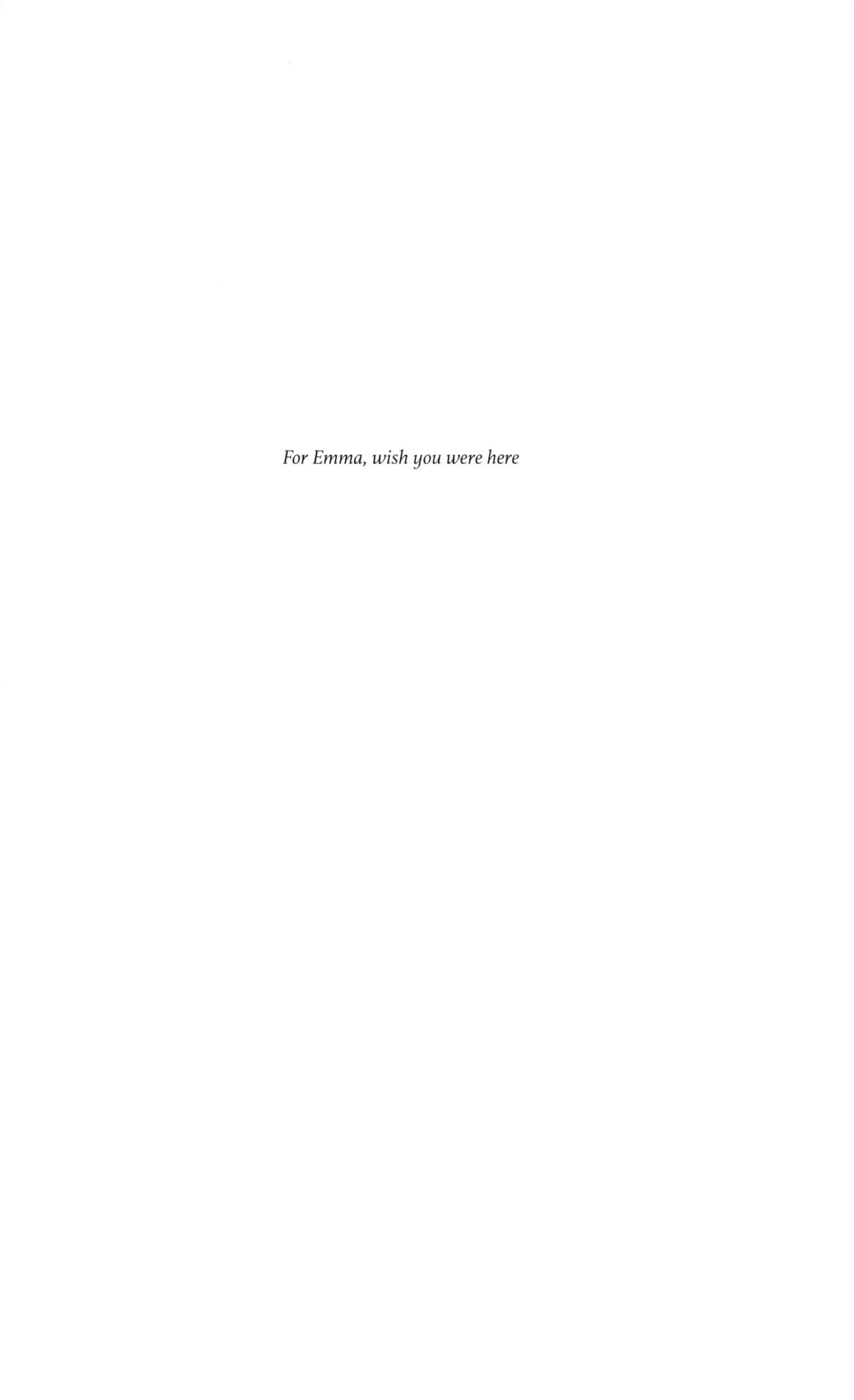

*For Emma, wish you were here*

# 1

Tara folded and unfolded the pink referral slip. Her fingers made sweat marks on the paper. "I can't be pregnant. I haven't had sex."

But her first pregnancy test had been positive, too, and now instead of telling Tara it was a mistake, her family doctor had gotten the same result.

Dr. Lei closed Tara's chart. Vivaldi played softly from the Bose Wave system on the credenza behind her. "You're still with Jeremy?"

"Yes."

"Still planning to get married?" Dr. Lei said.

"We haven't set the date, but eventually. After college, before med school."

Tara had over a year of college left, then med school, then an internship. That's why she'd insisted on waiting. So she would never have a conversation like this. She understood Dr. Lei needed to ask these questions, but it wouldn't lead to anything useful.

"And you're not sexually active?" Dr. Lei asked.

"We haven't had intercourse."

"It's possible to be a virgin and become pregnant," Dr. Lei said. "It's rare, but it can happen if there's contact and sperm travel to an ovum."

"We're careful. We're always careful."

Dr. Lei's cinnamon scented potpourri highlighted rather than masked the office's alcohol-peroxide smell, making Tara slightly nauseated and adding to her unease about what might be happening in her body. But this was better than the University's medical services unit, where the nurse practitioner talked to Tara while Tara sat wrapped in a paper gown, her bare legs dangling over the exam table's edge.

"Have you engaged in mutual masturbation?" Dr. Lei asked.

"Yes."

"Has there been any time when, as a result of any activity, Jeremy's sperm came anywhere near your vulvar area?"

"No. Never."

Long ago, Tara had promised herself she'd never repeat her mother's life. Her parents never complained about having five kids, but they hadn't planned it, either, and Tara felt sure her mother would feel less angry and frustrated, and be happier all around, if she hadn't gotten pregnant at nineteen.

"Some young women feel it's not really intercourse if the man penetrates her but doesn't ejaculate. Have you and Jeremy ever tried that?"

Tara shook her head.

"Is there anyone else you've engaged in any sexual activity with?"

"No one."

The miniature grandfather clock on the wall ticked. Tara tried not to let her thoughts race ahead of her. *You don't know what's going on yet.* Dr. Lei tapped her fingers on her desk. "None of what you've described could lead to pregnancy. Still, it's unlikely you'd get two false positives in a row."

"But both labs could have made mistakes, couldn't they?"

Already knowing the answer, Tara twisted the referral slip into a pink string. It was possible, but unlikely, that both labs erred in the same way for the same patient.

Leaning back in her chair, Dr. Lei folded her hands across her diaphragm and stared at the ceiling. Tara started to speak, then stopped, pressing her hands against the chair arms. Dr. Lei was a thorough physician, she asked a lot of questions before proposing courses of action. *Just answer her questions, let her think it through.* Unlike Tara, Dr. Lei hadn't spent the last two weeks turning over all these points in her head.

Dr. Lei looked at Tara again. "I'm sure you've considered this, but could something have occurred you're unaware of? A night you drank too much and someone, not necessarily Jeremy, forced himself on you?"

"No. I drink, but I've never passed out or had a blackout."

Dr. Lei pursed her lips. "I don't know what to tell you. Let's schedule an ultrasound and go from there."

"What do you think you might see?"

"I don't know," Dr. Lei said. "But whatever we see or don't see, that will tell us what to do next."

"Is it –" Tara's throat tightened, but she had to talk about what weighed on her most. She took a breath. "Could it be a tumor? I mean, with Megan—"

Dr. Lei reached across her desk to touch Tara's hand. "Tara. Nothing in the medical literature suggests your sister's brain tumor is hereditary. You don't have a predisposition to cancer."

"But you need to rule it out."

"I need to rule out all potential causes, even remote ones. But remember, there are many reasons your cycle may be off, including something as simple as stress." Turning to her laptop, Dr. Lei accessed her schedule, something she normally left to her assistant. "Let's get you in as soon as possible. Thursday morning at ten?"

Hands shaking, Tara almost dropped her backpack as she fished out her planner to check the date. "I'm still hoping it's all just a mistake. Two mistakes."

"It may be," Dr. Lei said. "But we need to find out."

THE RED-HAIRED MAN scanned the student lounge from his corner armchair, deliberately slumping despite the tension coursing through him. He fingered the photo in his pocket, then took it out and cupped it in his hand to shield it from anyone else's view. He'd cut it from a Webster Groves High yearbook, so it was a few years old.

In the photo, Tara Spencer's blonde hair hung straight past her shoulders. Her blue-green eyes, wide and almond shaped, were the focal point of her face. He saw no mark in the photograph, but it could be anywhere on Tara's body.

Unlike the other students, Tara looked as if she were having fun, as if she and the photographer had just discovered they both loved the same type of music or played the same sport. The man guessed most other students thought Tara friendly and kind. A good person.

Appearances could deceive.

Three girls walked in. He peered at them, looking for a match, reminding himself Tara's hair color or cut could be different now. A brunette leaning against a vending machine bragged to her friends about last Friday's beer bash, and how much she would drink this Friday, and how devastated she felt that this was only Wednesday. Two boys flipped a mini-Frisbee near the back of the lounge while they complained about a professor who refused to let them use notes in their open-book exams.

The man doubted anyone serious about studying came to this place. But he'd been told he'd find her here. And he had to see her in person.

Then he'd decide what to do to her.

AT EIGHT-THIRTY WEDNESDAY NIGHT, Tara pulled into the driveway. She planned to run in, grab her laptop, and head back to school to finish her ancient history paper. She could work at home, but she focused better with noise and activity around her, the effect of growing up with four younger siblings. All morning during Advanced Physics, which she loved, and all afternoon during work, all Tara could think about was what Dr. Lei would see on the ultrasound tomorrow. Tara pressed her fingers into her abdomen, searching for masses. Then she thought of Megan, hooked up to IVs for chemo, vomiting for hours in the middle of the night, thinning to a near skeleton, then ballooning months later from the steroids.

*Please don't let it be cancer,* Tara thought, then felt guilty for thinking it. If Megan, who was nine, had to face radiation and chemo without flinching, who was Tara to demand a reprieve? But if it wasn't cancer, what could it be? A benign cyst maybe. Which still didn't explain the positive pregnancy tests.

*It's nothing, don't think about it. It's all a mistake.*

Tara climbed the outside back stairs to the attic, fumbled for her keys in the dark.

"Hi, Tara."

Her brother Bailey's piping voice came before Tara had pushed her door all the way open.

"Hey, squirt."

Tara dropped her backpack on the floor and hung her parka on the coat rack. She'd fixed up the attic into a studio apartment with her grandfather's help, and neither had thought to build a coat closet. "What's up?"

Bailey sat cross-legged on Tara's futon, a Batman comic book open on his lap. One of Dad's Buddy Holly CDs played in the background.

"Hospital. Megan's white count is low." Bailey was only eleven but, like the rest of the family, had gained an encyclopedic knowledge of medicine in the last five years.

"Really bad?" Tara said, and thought, *what if I'm in the hospital next? What will that do to Bailey?*

"It's just for an IV. She might come home tomorrow. Want to play a game?"

Tara plopped down at her tiny kitchen table and flipped on her laptop to check e-mail before she headed out again. "I've got to finish a paper. And don't you have school tomorrow?"

"A quick one?" He grinned at her, crinkling his nose.

Bailey was blonde, like Tara, with light freckles barely visible across his cheeks, and blue eyes. Already he had a bunch of little girls calling him, but he was true to SueLyn, the trumpet player he'd had a crush on since kindergarten. Tara caught herself wondering whether, if she really were pregnant, the baby would look like Bailey, and how she could keep taking care of Bailey and the other kids if she became a mother herself.

*But that's crazy. I'm not pregnant.*

Thoughts about pregnancy kept jumping into Tara's mind. She couldn't understand it. Her friend Vicki told Tara she worried if she was only a day late because her birth control pills might have failed. That made sense to Tara, birth control pills did fail. So did condoms and diaphragms and everything else. But not abstinence.

"No one's been home at all," Bailey said, giving Tara his sad eyes. "Mom left me a note for when I got back from school, and Kelly's at rehearsal."

He was hamming it up, but he really did get lonely when everyone was out. Sometimes even when everyone was around. Bailey was healthy and mostly happy, and Megan needed so much. It was why Bailey came to Tara's, even if she wasn't there.

Tara ran her fingers through her hair. She needed to get up early and wash and dry it, and her doctor's appointment was at ten, which didn't leave much time for writing. Still, she could barely think about anything except the ultrasound anyway. And she felt superstitious about disappointing Bailey, as if it somehow would be bad luck for Megan. "What d'you want to play?"

"Stratego?"

"That's not short, buddy."

But she closed the laptop. She'd set her alarm two hours early and finish her paper in the morning.

~

THE PIANO PLAYED in the living room – *The Bread of Life* for the third time. A door slammed somewhere upstairs and Tara's mother's yelled, "I don't care whose turn it is. You know how the dryer works."

*She's in a good mood.* Tara's stomach tightened. She hadn't done anything wrong, yet it felt like she had. Sliding the ultrasound photo back into her anatomy text, Tara looked at the clock on the microwave. She'd told her mother and stepdad at breakfast she needed to talk to them about something important, and it was already almost eleven. Her shift at Dirty Things Laundry started in an hour, and she still needed to change out of her sweats and T-shirt. Probably just into jeans and a T-shirt, but she'd like time to get calm again, too, after the way she expected this conversation to go.

Bailey wandered into the kitchen, trailing a Wiffle Ball bat behind him. He pressed his nose to the sliding glass doors, peered out at the snow and sleet, and sighed.

"Are you just passing through?" Tara said.

He turned around. "Should I be?"

"Yeah. Scram."

Bailey frowned. "Jeez. Everyone's crabby today. Some Saturday."

He left as Tara's mother, Lynette Spencer, walked into the kitchen. Already wearing her trench coat over corduroys and a blazer, she ran a comb through her short, bobbed hair, a bottle of Clinique's palest foundation shade in her other hand. Lynette stood nearly a half a foot shorter than Tara, but about twenty-five pounds heavier. Her figure was round and curvy, while Tara's was angular, and she always looked polished.

"So what's all the drama?" Lynette said. "I've got Weight Watchers in twenty minutes."

Tara tried to slide her chair back, but the kitchen table was so large, and the room so small, she had nowhere to go. "Sorry. I forgot."

"Of course you did. It's not like you need to go." Lynette peered at herself in the microwave's glass window, touching up her foundation. "So?"

"Can we wait for Dad?"

Lynette turned toward the doorway to the living room. "Pete!"

The piano cut off. A moment later, Tara's stepfather came in and sat down next to Tara. He smelled like the dark-roasted coffee he always drank, and he sat perfectly straight, shoulders back, a holdover from being raised by an Army colonel. "What's going on, honey?" Pete and Lynette had married when Tara was three. He was the only father Tara remembered.

"It's complicated." Tara crinkled the corner of a page in her book, then made a conscious effort to stop and look at her dad. He smiled, deepening the faint lines around his eyes she'd noticed only recently. His hair had gone gray years before, he was fifteen years older than Lynette, but somehow he hadn't seemed to be aging to Tara until recently. "I don't know how to explain it, but Dr. Lei thinks I'm pregnant."

"What?" Pete's smile disappeared.

"That figures." Lynette dropped the foundation bottle on the counter with a thunk. "Though I really thought Jeremy was more responsible than that."

"Jeremy? You thought Jeremy was more responsible?"

After all the times Jeremy had tried to persuade Tara to have sex, with or without a condom, she couldn't believe her mother thought he was the one who was more responsible.

"You must have known this could happen. What do you expect me to say?" Lynette crossed her arms and stared at Tara.

Tara glared back. "I just thought you'd want to know."

Pete touched Tara's arm. "Of course we want to know." To Tara's relief, though her dad looked a little pale, he didn't seem angry.

"You and Jeremy were planning to get married anyway, right?" Lynette said.

"Yeah, but—"

"So it'll be a little sooner than you planned. You're better off than I was." Lynette fluffed her hair with her fingers. "You can even finish college if that's what you want."

Lynette started buttoning her coat, but Pete shook his head at her. She stayed put, but picked up her car keys.

"If that's what I want?" Her mother's deliberate blindness to Tara's ambitions was not the point, but it sidetracked Tara all the same. "Have you not noticed me studying my eyes out for the MCAT?"

"Of course I have. But that's not for sure, is it?"

"Where I go is not for sure. That I'm going is."

"Not anymore, apparently."

Lynette didn't smile, but her words had a lilting, sing-song quality that made Tara feel her mother was happy, or at least pleased, on some level, at the idea that Tara had stumbled. Sometimes Tara thought it was her resemblance to her biological father, who was olive-skinned and wiry like Tara, that set her mother on edge. Other times Tara figured it was what Jeremy's mom had told her. It was hard for mothers when their daughters surpassed them professionally, and Tara was on the way. Lynette had never graduated college. Despite a 4.0 GPA, she'd dropped out after her third semester when she met Tara's biological father, and he persuaded her to chuck everything and travel the country with him and his rock band. Then she'd gotten pregnant with Tara, and that had ended the relationship.

Pete Spencer cleared his throat, glancing between Lynette and Tara. "We're getting off track. Tara, you're sure you're pregnant?"

"That's what I was about to say when Mom interrupted." Tara glared at Lynette. "Dr. Lei says I am, but Jeremy and I never had sex."

"Define sex," Lynette said. "Because you wouldn't have to actually have intercourse, as you should remember."

In her senior year of high school, Tara, who'd been seeing the same boy for three years, had missed a period. Worried because her friend Vicki told her it was possible to get pregnant without intercourse, she'd asked her parents detailed questions. Her mother answered matter-of-factly. Her dad, on the other hand, turned a pasty shade and had never really liked Tara's high school boyfriend after that.

"I remember. And I've been over that with Dr. Lei."

"Then which is it, Tara? Pregnant or not?" Lynette said.

Tara swallowed hard. "The ultrasound shows I'm pregnant, but I can't be. Dr. Lei can't explain how this happened."

Lynette put her hands on her hips, her keys still folded in one fist. "I think we're all pretty clear how these things happen."

Pete shot Lynette a look. "Lyn."

"What? It's not some big mystery. You're acting like I'm the one being irrational."

"Dr. Lei says there must be something I don't remember, like at a party, or something I'm repressing, but there's nothing like that."

"Or maybe you were a little more intimate with someone than you're willing to admit, even to yourself," Lynette said. "That seems more likely."

"It might be more likely, but I'm telling you it didn't happen."

"I don't know, Tara. I'd come up with a better story for Jeremy, if I were you."

Tara stood, bumping the kitchen table with her thighs so it screeched forward. "Story? A better story? I'm telling the truth and you want me to come up with a better story?"

Pete put a hand on Tara's arm. "Tara."

Tara pulled away. "No. She's fucking accusing me of lying."

"Language," Pete said.

"All I'm suggesting is maybe you're having a little trouble taking responsibility for your actions," Lynette said.

"I can't believe you. I've always been up front with you, especially about Jeremy. You're the one always saying I tell you too much." Tara put her hands to her ears, mimicking her mother. "'Too much information, Tara.' So why do you think I'm lying now?"

"Because what you're saying is absolutely ridiculous."

# 2

He crept from the elevator. His dark hair and clothing helped him blend into the shadows between the hallway emergency lights. Yesterday, he'd seen Dr. Lei under a false name, claiming a history of migraines. It gave him a chance to see the office layout. And steal a building keycard.

When he reached the door to the office suite, he put on his gloves, struggling when the latex stuck to his sweating hands. When he fished out his lock-picking tools, the pick dropped on the carpet with a thunk. He snatched it, started again. Pushed away thoughts of the years he'd waited, the disappointment that could lie beyond the heavy glass door. He was right about this time, this girl.

At last the lock released. On entering the waiting room, the smell of rubbing alcohol assaulted him. His body stiffened.

*Focus.*

Moving away from the frosted glass door, he flicked on his flashlight. Charts from previous days' visits stood in wire racks on the desk corner, ready for filing. He flipped through any chart with a patient name that might be female, checking age and marital status, then glancing through the notes.

The tenth chart must be it, but he skimmed the others before he read that one more closely. The office notes were practically hieroglyphic, between the doctor's rushed handwriting and the medical abbreviations. But he'd studied enough to pick out what he needed – *twenty-one year old white female...two positive pregnancy tests...denies sexual activity...return for ultrasound.* He made his way to the back hall, read more as he waited for the copier to warm up. So much information.

Tara Spencer would be easy to find.

## Field Report 1.2: Tara Spencer

Since initial report and review of medical records, the following has been determined:

Subject's mother (Lynette Spencer) and stepfather (Peter Spencer) devote their time primarily to subject's youngest half-sibling, Megan, who was diagnosed with a brain tumor five years ago. Subject often attends half-siblings' school and sporting events, supervises their homework, and collects half-brother Bailey from school. Subject attends classes at St. Louis University ("SLU") and works evenings and Saturdays at Dirty Things Laundromat one half block from campus.

Boyfriend, Jeremy Turano, 22, manages family-owned restaurant, Trattoria Alleata, in Rock Hill. Subject sees Turano one to two times per week, speaks to him often by phone, and appears unaware of his sexual relationship with Suzanne Freeman, a hostess at Trattoria Aleata. It is unknown whether Turano's sister, Vicki, who is also subject's friend, is aware of the Turano–Freeman relationship.

Subject drives to school and work through populated neighborhoods, parks in lighted areas, and carries cell phone. Subject jogs occasionally, but always with friends. Subject is frequently accompanied by other students while on campus. She plays intramural basketball and Frisbee.

At night, subject is isolated, as she sleeps in what appears to be a partially finished attic apartment in her mother and stepfather's home. Apartment can be accessed through exterior or interior stairway. The latter poses a danger, as family members might be alerted if subject were approached or might be inside apartment without this investigator's knowledge.

Most promising venue appears to be Dirty Things Laundromat from eleven p.m. to midnight, as few patrons enter establishment during that time period.

Having determined subject's schedule, this investigator will act as soon as opportunity presents, unless otherwise advised.

# 3

Tara's best friend Vicki reached across the coffee table and tapped Tara's arm. "Cute guy at eleven o'clock totally checking you out." Vicki nodded toward the coffee bar in the far left corner of Common Grounds.

A wiry man wearing new-looking blue jeans and a stark white T-shirt averted his eyes when Tara looked. His dark hair stood straight in a long crew cut that sharpened the angles of his face.

"Sure, 'cause I'm gorgeous today." Tara ran her hand through her hair, pulling out a few tangles in back. Her olive skin tended toward dark circles under her eyes even when she was sleeping well, and lately she barely slept at all.

"Yeah, you look a little dragged out." Vicki sipped her latte. "And thinner. You're not dieting, are you? That would be nuts."

Tara and Vicki met every Wednesday evening at the Common Grounds coffeehouse/Internet cafe to study and catch up. Flute music played over the speakers and incense scented the air, but tonight neither made Tara feel relaxed.

"No. But I have to tell you something." Tara shut her laptop. "I didn't before because I haven't said anything to Jeremy yet, but I'm talking to him tonight."

Vicki was Jeremy's sister, and much as Tara had wanted to spill everything to Vicki, she'd felt it wasn't right to ask Vicki to keep secrets from her brother.

"You're breaking up with him, aren't you?" Vicki said.

"What? Of course not."

"Because the whole medical school thing, you know I could never see that working."

Tara frowned. She'd never guessed Vicki felt that way about how Tara's school plans fit or didn't fit with Jeremy, and she thought she and Vicki talked about everything. "I'm not breaking up with him."

"Then what – Oh my God. It's that pregnancy test, isn't it?" Vicki leaned forward, almost tipping her latte onto her interior design workbook. "It wasn't a mistake."

A girl reading by the windows looked over at them, apparently finding the conversation more intriguing than *A Tale of Two Cities*. For the first time, Tara wished Common Grounds played hard rock. Loud. She didn't care what strangers thought, but that didn't mean she wanted to announce her private life to the world at large. And she was pretty sure she knew the girl from Calculus last year.

"It's not what you're thinking," Tara said.

"I'm thinking you finally did it with Jeremy and didn't even tell me. I'm your best friend – how could you not tell me?" Vicki wagged her finger at Tara.

"No, we didn't. We haven't."

"You did it with Roger and didn't tell me?"

Roger, Tara's lab partner, had asked Tara out once and she'd said no.

"Of course not. Not with anyone."

"So, what, you got artificially inseminated and didn't tell me?"

"No. I can't be pregnant. There's some mix-up. I'm seeing a specialist tomorrow." But Tara's face flushed and her hands shook. The oncologist she'd seen had confirmed all Dr. Lei's findings and ruled out a tumor. Which was a relief, yet Tara didn't feel as relieved as she'd thought she would.

*If I am pregnant,* Tara thought, *how can I take care of a baby and finish college? And forget med school. But this is insane. I'm not pregnant.*

Tara had spent every waking moment since she'd seen the oncologist searching her memory for unaccounted-for time, or for some place where she could have been drugged and assaulted, for any way she could have gotten pregnant without knowing what was happening.

There was nothing.

"What'd your parents say?" Vicki asked.

"They made me talk to Father Saur, then insisted I see a shrink. The shrink interviewed me and gave me all these personality tests. He couldn't find anything suggesting I suffered any sexual abuse or was repressing, so he decided I must be lying."

"Nice." Vicki sat straighter and set her drink on the coffee table. "So what are you going to – that guy is really staring. It's not him, is it? Is he the other guy?"

"There is no other guy." Tara clenched her fists in her lap. "And I don't know who that is."

Tara glanced again at the man with the crew cut, who still sat reading his newspaper. Something about him looked familiar, the rigid, squared way he held his shoulders, maybe. She guessed him in his late twenties, possibly a grad student.

"How'd you find the specialist?" Vicki said.

"He wrote an article on conditions that appear as pregnancy but aren't. It's more focused on psychosomatic issues, like hysterical pregnancy, but I figure he's the best person to see."

The wind chimes over the front door jangled, but it wasn't Jeremy, just a couple teenage boys in baggy jeans and backwards baseball caps, snow coating their jackets.

Tara had no idea what to say to Jeremy when he did arrive. *Gosh, honey, my doctor thinks I'm pregnant, but I can't be. You believe me, don't you?*

Because that had worked so well with her parents.

Jeremy got there about 8:30. He stopped at the coffee bar just inside the door to brush the snow from his dark hair and take off his leather jacket. Tara wanted to tell him not to order anything, that she'd rather talk somewhere else, but she felt frozen in place on the couch.

"You're up." Vicki stuffed her books into her backpack.

Tara looked at her friend. "Hang out, will you? Not right here, but around?"

Vicki squeezed Tara's hand. "Sure, I'll go sit with soldier boy."

The man at the coffee bar did have something of a military look, though Tara couldn't put her finger on why. It might be his neatness, or his ramrod posture. Maybe Vicki would talk to him, find out he had nothing to do with Tara, and believe Tara about the pregnancy. Or lack of pregnancy.

Jeremy crossed the room and hugged Tara. His jacket chilled her cheek. She shivered, but leaned into him anyway. He smelled of winter air and white Dial soap. Her eyes burned. *What if it's the last time he ever hugs me?*

"Hey. What's wrong? Is it Megan?"

Tara sat on the sofa. Jeremy sat next to her, keeping his arm around her.

"No, she's better," Tara said. "We just brought her home from the hospital."

"So what did you want to talk about?" Jeremy glanced at the clock over the windows. Outside, the wind whipped snowflakes sideways and in circles. "I promised Mom I'd come back for closing tonight, we're short-handed."

"Maybe we should talk another time. Somewhere private." Even as she suggested it, Tara knew she couldn't wait to talk to Jeremy. If only the temperature were less arctic, they could have at least taken a walk.

Jeremy shook his head. "I've got the trade show this weekend. We won't see each other 'til next Saturday."

"Oh, yeah."

Tara picked up a granola bar she'd bought earlier but hadn't opened yet. She pulled the brown tab at the back. It caught under her fingernail. She didn't want to talk to Jeremy in the middle of Common Grounds, but she couldn't wait another week and a half. And she couldn't do it on the phone by text message.

"Tara?"

Tara took a deep breath. She wasn't pregnant, but something very bad was happening, and if she ever wanted a decent night's sleep again, she had to tell Jeremy.

*It's not like I did anything wrong.*

She shifted a little to face him.

"Okay. I missed a couple periods and figured it was all the stress from the extra classes and my work schedule this semester. But I was kind of concerned, so I went to my doctor."

"Are you all right?"

Tara ran her hand through her hair. "I don't know. See, Dr. Lei thinks I'm pregnant, which of course I can't be, but she can't find anything else wrong."

She felt Jeremy's body tense, but he didn't pull away. "But she knows you're not pregnant. You had a pregnancy test, right?"

"Well, yeah. But it was positive." Tara still held the granola bar, and she squeezed it. "Two tests were, actually, and I just don't know what's happening and I'm really scared."

Jeremy pulled away and stood, glaring down at Tara. "Who was it?"

"What?"

"I knew the second you said you missed your period. Who was it? Roger? I'll fucking kill him."

"Not Roger. No one. It's a mistake."

"So your doctor's just wrong."

"She must be."

Past Jeremy, Tara saw a guy she knew from SLU join the girl with *A Tale of Two Cities*. They held hands across the table, smiling.

Tara longed to be that girl, wished she could sit at that table and drink chai tea and talk with Jeremy about her chem class and his day at the restaurant and whether he wanted to pursue an MBA while she went to med school. She ought to be that girl. She had been that girl. And yet instead she was telling Jeremy she'd had a positive pregnancy test when she couldn't be pregnant.

Someone opened the front door, and icy air swept through the room.

"What about other doctors?" Jeremy said.

"They said the same thing." Tara slid to the end of the couch and shifted so she sat on its arm, closer to eye-level with Jeremy.

"And they're all wrong." Jeremy's voice grew louder, and the SLU couple peered at him.

"Can we talk about this somewhere else?" Tara set the granola bar on the coffee table and reached for Jeremy's hand. "Please?"

Jeremy jammed his hands in his jeans pockets. "Talk about what? You tell me sex is too risky and we need to wait, then you fucking do it with someone else. What's to talk about?"

"I'm telling you I never had sex with anyone." Tara stood, clenching her fists, her eyes filling with tears. "This is a mistake. Just because no doctor's figured it out yet doesn't make it not a mistake. I don't know what's wrong with me, or how this could be happening, and I'm scared –"

"Stop it. Stop lying." Jeremy turned away, then pivoted back. "It was never going to work anyway. You'll be off to medical school, at least you would have been. You didn't have any place for me. Now you have to find a place for a baby. Good luck."

Tara grabbed his arm, even as she thought that Vicki had been right about medical school and Jeremy. "I'm telling you the truth."

Jeremy jerked away. "Right." He stalked across the room and out the door, not even glancing at Vicki, who still sat at the counter.

When Tara looked around, most people appeared intent on reading, clicking laptop keys, or listening to their iPods, but she felt sure they'd all been staring a second before.

She kicked the coffee table, making it shake. "Show's over." Tara sank down onto the couch and bent forward, elbows on her knees, head on her arms. "It's over."

Vicki sat and put her arm around Tara. "That didn't go well."

"He didn't believe me," Tara said. "He didn't care how I feel, or how this happened, or anything."

"That sucks. Look, why don't we get out of here? I've got an early class tomorrow, but I've got time for a beer."

"Yeah, okay." Tara wiped her eyes. Then it hit her. If she were pregnant, she couldn't have a beer. It was only one of many things that would change. If she were pregnant. *But I'm not.*

Vicki zipped her jacket. "What?"

Tara shook her head. "Nothing. I just, it hit me that if I were pregnant, I wouldn't drink."

"But you don't think you are."

"I can't be. But Jeremy's definitely assuming the worst."

"Try to see it from his point of view." As they crossed the room, Vicki's boot heels clunked on the coffee house's hardwood floor. "It must look like you strung him along, telling him you didn't want to have sex until you at least finished college, because you might get pregnant, then you go off with someone else."

"Is that what you think?"

"I don't know what I think, really. It's all so weird. I mean, you said you've already had confirming tests and seen specialists. What else could it be?"

"Have you ever known me to lie to Jeremy? Or you for that matter?"

"Everybody lies."

Tara paused at the door. "I don't know what's going on any more than Jeremy does. Or you do."

"You can see where it would be hard for him to believe that, though, can't you?"

The door chimes clanked as they stepped outside. The wind smacked Tara's face. "Yeah. I can see that."

~

AT ELEVEN THAT NIGHT, once she was home, Tara tried Jeremy on his cell phone. He hung up on her. Answered the phone just to hang up, apparently, because he had Caller I.D. The whole night, Tara lay awake, imagining what else she could have said to explain things, and what she might say when they talked again. In the morning, exhausted, she stumbled through a shower and grabbed a granola bar and banana for her drive. She left her knapsack on the kitchen table.

The heavy outside door slammed shut behind her, and Tara started down the stairs. It was only when she remembered the knapsack and turned back that she saw the blood.

# 4

It dripped from the doorknob onto the landing's chipped gray paint. Clutching the railing, Tara scanned the door, the side of the house, the steps, but couldn't see any source for the blood. No wounded or dead animal. Nothing. Zigzag heel prints behind her on the landing reproached her. She'd stepped in the blood without even realizing. More of it trailed down the stairs and pooled on the second-floor landing. Tara hurried down.

A lump half the size of Tara's fist lay in the reddish-brown puddle, a reed-like black stick jabbed into it. Tara sank to a sitting position on the stair just above the landing, arms crossed over her stomach. She leaned forward for a closer look, and the twin smells of formaldehyde and latex paint hit her. Tara jerked back.

*Not blood.* Which she would have realized sooner, if she'd been thinking clearly. Blood would have clotted and smeared, not dripped, unless it was still flowing from a living being.

The lump lay still. Though she knew what it must be, Tara fumbled through her knapsack for a pencil to slough some of the paint away. Her efforts revealed a head twice the size of the body. The skin, under the paint, was grayish and dull. A nub of a hand poked up. Stringy legs curled inward toward the bulging stomach. The knitting needle pierced where the right eye would have grown.

"Jesus."

Based on what she'd learned in Anatomy, Tara guessed the age about sixteen weeks in utero. She pressed her palms together and struggled not to vomit.

Who could do this? The only people who knew were Jeremy, Vicki, Tara's parents, the doctors, and the parish pastor.

Then there was the question of why.

A screeching sound behind her nearly stopped her heart.

It was just her dad opening the window. Tara's parents' room looked out onto the lower landing.

"Tara? Oh my God."

"Mom, seriously, it's okay. Go," Tara said.

Lynette stood fast in the doorway between the kitchen and living room, eyeing the police detective, who sat at the kitchen table, arms crossed over his chest.

"Harold can get someone else to finalize his brief." Lynette was a legal secretary, and because of Megan's illness, she was allowed to be on flex-time. The partners she worked for were understanding, but Tara knew her mom worried one day they'd decide they couldn't deal with her absences and odd hours. And she'd long since used all her paid time off for the year, so every day she missed cost the family money.

"No, really. You were out all last week already. I'll be fine."

"Honey, I know I was hard on you about this whole pregnancy thing, but I want to be here for you. I'll call in."

"Mom, you go. I'll let you know what happens. It's okay."

Gripping the back of a kitchen chair, Tara watched her mom head down the stairs, then turned toward Detective Mallard. She wished she'd asked one of her parents to stay, she knew either would have. But Tara's dad's job was even more demanding, and if he lost it, the family lost its health insurance.

The detective flipped a page on his notebook. He was a big man, and he perched precariously on one of the wooden chairs, his legs jammed under the kitchen table, his neck nearly bursting from his collar.

"You were about to give me your boyfriend's full name."

"Jeremy Robert Turano. But I told you, he wouldn't do something like this. No matter how mad he is."

The detective hadn't said so, but Tara felt sure he must know Jeremy. Fewer than four thousand people lived in Rock Hill, and Trattoria Alleata, the Turanos' restaurant, was the closest, and best, Italian restaurant around.

"And his address?"

"58 Plant Court, Webster Groves."

Mallard nodded. "Two and a half miles away."

"But he had no idea I was pregnant before last night around 9 p.m. Where would he even get a fetus between then and this morning? It's not like they sell them at the grocery store."

Mallard drummed his pencil on the table while Tara spoke, then said, "His sister lives at the same address?"

"No, she lives with their parents." Tara gave him Vicki's address. "But she'd –"

"I know. Never do anything like this."

"She wasn't even mad at me."

Mallard peered at Tara, his eyes flat ovals. "She didn't believe it, though. Your story about not knowing how you got pregnant."

"My story – no, she probably didn't believe me."

"Um-hm."

Tara pressed her lips together. She needed the police to figure out who did this, so the least she could do was be polite, even if Detective Mallard wasn't showing her the same courtesy. And she couldn't entirely blame him for being skeptical. If her own mother and friends didn't take her at her word, she couldn't expect a stranger, and a police detective at that, would. But, somehow, she did expect it.

From outside came the sound of a garbage truck rumbling to a halt at the driveway, then cans scraping the asphalt.

"Shouldn't we be looking at motive?" Tara said. "At who would want to scare or threaten me?"

"You see this as a threat?"

"What else?" Tara shivered, picturing the needle through the fetus' eye space. "I mean, I'm supposedly pregnant, and someone leaves a fetus with a knitting needle and what looks like blood on my porch. What is that but a threat?"

Mallard leaned back and crossed his arms over his sloping belly. "Yet you refuse to tell me about the potential fathers."

"Because there are none. When I said I can't be pregnant, I meant it. It's not that I can't pick one guy out of all the guys I've been with. There are no guys. That's the whole problem."

"When did you tell Vicki Turano you were getting a pregnancy test?"

"Weeks ago. So, what, you think she ran out and got a fetus and some paint just in case it turned out I was pregnant, and it wasn't Jeremy's?"

Mallard slapped the notebook on the table. "Look, Miss Spencer, I don't know what you expect. Something like this, the most likely perpetrator is the father, but you won't tell me who it is. The next most likely are your boyfriend and his sister, and you say it can't be them. The remaining people who know you're pregnant – excuse me, supposedly pregnant – I'm sure you'll tell me didn't do it. Your mother, your dad, your doctor, your shrink and your pastor." He ticked them off on his fingers as he spoke. "Am I right?"

"Yes. But maybe someone at my school. I am PreMed. The students would know where to get fetuses."

Mallard raised his eyebrows. "Anyone at school know you're pregnant?"

"Only if they overheard last night."

"Other than random overhearers, did I miss anyone who knows you're pregnant?"

"No." Tara clenched and unclenched her jaw. "I know this sounds crazy. I'm not trying to be obstructionist, I just can't think of anyone who could have done this."

"I did miss someone."

Silently, Tara ran through the people she'd told. "I don't think so."

"You."

"What?"

Pointing at Tara, Mallard stood. His head nearly touched the light shades on the ceiling fan above him. "You know you're pregnant. And what do I know about you? You're pregnant and you don't know who the father is. You're trying to sell your parents on a bullcrap story about never having sex. You announced your pregnancy in the middle of a crowded coffeehouse. Your sister's been ill for years and, as I saw today, everything revolves around her. Your parents probably never have time to spend with you, never make you a priority. Well, welcome to real life." Mallard snapped his notebook shut. "Here's some free advice. You want attention, go back to the shrink."

Tara stood, too. "So you're not going to do anything."

Mallard shoved the notebook in his pocket and walked around the table. "I'll file a report. In triplicate. I'll interview the 'suspects.' I'll find out if any fetuses were stolen from the medical schools at SLU or Washington University or anywhere else. I'll fill out a supplemental report. In triplicate. I'll update you and my supervisors regularly. I'm sure it'll be a grand use of the taxpayers' money."

TARA ATTENDED HER AFTERNOON CLASSES, struggling to focus, clenching her hands into fists whenever she thought about the detective's words, fighting back tears when she remembered the things Jeremy – and Vicki – had said. It was one thing to understand in her mind why they would doubt her, it was another to feel it. She wasn't positive she'd believe either of them if the situation were reversed. The more Tara's mind spun, the harder she found it to sit still, and only her lab partner Roger's desperate plea for help with the Advanced Chemistry problems kept Tara from bolting from class. It wasn't as if she could do anything at home but look at the red paint on the landing. At least the police evidence technician had taken away the fetus.

In all three classes that day, Tara studied every other student. She wondered if any of them knew she was supposed to be pregnant, and what sort of person sent a message via fetus and knitting needle, and why. Mallard was right that Jeremy and Vicki were the only ones with motives, but she couldn't accept them doing such a thing. Would someone strongly anti-abortion? People who called themselves pro-life had thrown a pipe bomb into the Planned Parenthood in St. Louis the year before, even though there were people working in it at the time. The pro-lifers considered it justified – it was war. But if this was war, Tara couldn't figure out the message. The stabbed fetus seemed to suggest she have an abortion, not forgo one.

Tara tried to remember if any of her classmates had been at Common Grounds the night before, or if any had talked to her about abortion issues. And she tried to assess if any were cruel enough to consider a bloody-looking fetus a funny prank. No one seemed likely, or even possible. But, then, she spent most of her time working and taking care of the kids, not hanging out. Most of her fellow students liked Tara, but other than the friends she played basketball with a couple times a month and classmates she studied with, she didn't know any of them that well.

Work that evening at the Laundromat was easier to get through than school at first. It took less concentration. But by nine, the Laundromat emptied and the darkness outside began to unnerve Tara. She stood at all times with her back to the machines or the checkout counter, watching the door, just in case anyone planned a repeat performance. Her dad called to be sure she was okay, and so did her sister Kelly, but otherwise it was a quiet night.

At 11:45, she folded the last T-shirt, holding it by the edges so she touched it as little as possible. She knew it was clean – she'd washed and dried all of this particular frat boy's laundry herself – but emblazoned on the front was the question part of the disgusting joke about the difference between a freshman girl and a toilet seat.

The clock ticked over the double exit doors and the Pepsi machine hummed, but the washers and dryers stood silent. The phone rang, startling Tara, and she dropped the T-shirt. She hurried to the counter, telling herself even as she reached for the receiver that it was probably her dad again. Not Jeremy. But she'd told Vicki about the fetus, maybe Jeremy was calling to see if she was okay. Or to yell at her if the police had questioned him. She hesitated, then answered.

"Is Eric Williams there?" a young woman said.

Tara wasn't sure if she was relieved or disappointed it wasn't Jeremy. "Nope." She didn't know an Eric Williams, and she couldn't see into all the Laundromat's corners because a third of the overhead light bulbs needed replacing, but it didn't matter. She was alone.

"Are you sure? He told me he'd be studying while he did his laundry. He promised. He might be back by the double load dryers."

"No one's here. Sorry."

"OK, thanks."

Tara hung up. At least every other week she got a call from some girl looking for her boyfriend. Dirty Things Laundromat was a popular place for guys to claim they were hanging out while spending time elsewhere. Why it never crossed their minds how easy it was for their girlfriends to figure out amazed her. Then again, as the frat boy's laundry proved, these guys weren't candidates for either the brightest bulb or the sensitivity to women award. Or the marginally decent human being award, for that matter.

The folded T-shirt had landed on the floor, backside up so she could see the punch line to the joke: "The toilet seat doesn't follow you around after you use it." Tara stamped on the shirt, then jumped on it, then kicked it toward the dryers.

"Too bad. He'll need to wear something else."

Tara retrieved the T-shirt and tossed it under the counter, feeling slightly better. Maybe she'd wash the shirt the next time the frat boy brought in his laundry and give it back to him. Maybe. She bet he wouldn't miss it in the meantime, or even remember when he last wore it. She glanced again at the clock. Ten more minutes and, if no one came in, she could lock the doors and go home. Otherwise, if even one person scurried in before closing, Tara would have to wait for him or her to finish. Normally she didn't care, it was an extra hour and a half of pay for doing more homework, but tonight was different. She wished she'd tried to get someone to cover for her.

Tara switched off the lights toward the front – nothing said she couldn't at least make it look like the place was closed – and bent down to put the paper money from the cash register into the safe.

When she straightened up, a man stood on the other side of the counter, directly in front of her.

"You look different up close," he said.

# 5

Kali Kerkorian woke, sure she'd heard a noise. Fluorescent light from the trailer park's community center seeped in around her blinds, but she saw nothing out of place.

There. Again. An inhale and exhale. From the kitchen. Kali eased onto her side – she couldn't sit up in her lofted bed or her head would hit the ceiling – then swung her legs around and climbed down the ladder. Logic told her the sound was Grandmother crying, but she'd only heard that once before in all seventeen years of her life.

The floor chilled Kali's bare feet, even through the carpet. She tiptoed the five paces to the kitchen. Grandmother sat at the far end of the table, still dressed in her gray sweat suit and black Reeboks. Her chest rose and fell. A tear trailed down each side of her face, reflecting the moonlight that shone through the window over the sink.

"Grandmother? Are you ill?"

That, too, seemed impossible. At seventy-four, Grandmother still jogged every afternoon after services. She'd never broken a bone, never even caught a cold for as long as Kali could remember. She read the *New York Times* every morning and the Qu'ran and the Bible every evening.

Grandmother shook her head. "I am not."

Kali sat next to Grandmother and took her hands, which felt like ice. An owl hooted outside. "What is it? The anniversary tomorrow?" Kali glanced at the clock on the under-cabinet microwave. "Today, now."

"I was certain," Grandmother said. "I saw the pattern of the stars. I dreamed about the Mayan ruins."

"Probably because you were thinking of her," Kali said.

Grandmother had named her oldest daughter – Kali's aunt – Maya, for the ruins, though it wasn't a traditional Armenian name. Grandmother had visited the ruins with Grandfather the year Maya was born. She said they'd spoken to her.

Years later, Grandmother chose Kali's name as well, after the Hindu mother goddess of resurrection and creativity. By the time she entered junior high, Kali had read enough to know how mistaken American culture's view was of the goddess Kali as a bringer of destruction and death. Still, she often wished she were named after some goddess no one ever pictured wearing skull necklaces or drinking demon blood. Or, even better, she wished she were named Jenny or Anne or Laura.

Grandmother shook her head. "Every year, this day comes and goes. Always I watch for signs. Only this year did I see them. When your cycle was off, I felt certain. Perhaps my age gave me hope where there is none. I was so sure I'd be part of the great battle, so sure you would lead it. But I may be wrong. Or I may not live long enough."

"I'm sorry," Kali said, feeling guilty. She didn't want to lead any battle. She felt sorry her grandmother was so sad, and sorry for what had happened to her aunt.

But very grateful not to be pregnant.

HE PACED in front of the hotel room's west window. He needed to go out, do something, celebrate. Or mourn. Contact was being made in this moment. It only remained to be seen what the true story was with the girl, which would tell him the path to take. He paused, rested his forehead against the glass, his energy suddenly drained. At times, this fight seemed endless. At times, he wished it would pass to someone else.

Below him, the lights of St. Louis strung out into the night. He always stayed at the Westin's highest available floor, wanting what he thought of as a God's eye view. It gave him perspective. One needed perspective to get through life, especially a life of service.

The sound of squealing brakes penetrated the room, though muffled by the glass and distance. He shut his eyes, but couldn't shut out the memory. The passing decades never dimmed it.

The rain. The winding California road, the steep drop. The young woman's face, white in the glare of his headlights through her open driver's side window. Had he really seen her eyes dilate in terror as he swerved his Corvette into her lane? Surely he'd been too far away, surely it happened too fast. But, in memory, her eyes widened, her mouth formed a scream. *Why?* He always imagined she screamed *Why?* in that last moment, when her tiny hatchback careened toward the edge, streaking across the wet, shining road. Screams melding with the shrieking tires.

But she knew why. And he knew. She might appear lovely, but she carried evil. And evil must be stopped. History attested to that. The crusades, the holy wars, the preemptive strikes.

But evil never died, never truly was vanquished. It returned. And he stood ready. Exhausted, but ready.

# 6

Tara gripped the checkout counter's edge. Her eyes swept the Laundromat for escape routes.

"What do you want?"

This was the guy with the crew cut who'd stared at her in Common Grounds. Tonight he wore a gray T-shirt and cargo pants. He stood straight, and his arms hung at his sides, not tensed or bent as if he were about to reach for a weapon. Still, his pants had large side pockets that could conceal a knife or gun. Or both.

Tara put her hand in her pocket and felt for her cell phone's On button.

"Just to talk," the man said. "My name is Cyril Woods. I'm here to help."

"Help how?"

Unlike most retail establishments, the laundry didn't keep much cash on hand, except what was locked in the washers, dryers, and vending machines, so the owners had never installed a silent alarm.

"With your baby."

"Baby?" Tara stepped back in surprise and used the movement to edge slightly to her left.

To reach the front entrance, she would have to dart under the counter and race out. Tara felt sure Cyril, who was nearly half a foot taller than she was, and muscular and wiry, could stop her. He didn't seem poised to spring, but he kept his eyes riveted on her, as if he physically couldn't look away. At a party, it might have been flattering. Alone at midnight in the Laundromat was something else entirely.

"I don't have a baby."

"But you're pregnant."

"Why do you say that?" Then it hit Tara. Of course. He'd overhead the conversation with Jeremy in Common Grounds. And, maybe, hours later, left the fetus on her back steps. Tara's stomach and diaphragm tightened, making it hard to breathe.

The cell phone finally buzzed in her pocket. She coughed to cover the sound, even as her fingers fumbled over the buttons. Tara pressed what she thought was the Nine, trying not to move her hand much so Cyril wouldn't guess what she was doing.

"You can call someone," he said, "but I'll just leave and come back another time."

Tara pressed one twice and poised her finger over the Send button. "Look. If you're trying to help, then you'll let me close for the night, and we can meet somewhere public and talk."

Cyril's dark eyebrows arched. "Of course. I'm not trying to scare you."

"Really," Tara said. "You're doing a damn good job."

Holding up his hands, Cyril backed away until he bumped the industrial-sized dryer behind him. "I only want to talk where we won't be overheard."

"Uh-huh." Still holding the phone, Tara ducked under the counter and walked toward the door. Cyril didn't try to stop her, didn't even move closer. "And the present you left on my back steps this morning?"

"What?"

"The preserved fetus, the red paint, the knitting needle. Very subtle."

"Fetus? What are you talking about? What happened?" Cyril reached toward her, then dropped his arm to his side. "Are you all right?" He seemed truly puzzled, and worried about Tara, but he could just be a good actor.

"I'm fine."

"Did you see who did it?"

"No."

Tara pulled her cell phone from her pocket. The screen showed she had dialed 911. Her breath came a little easier. One touch and she'd be connected. She wished she had a smartphone, so she could take Cyril's photo. But her phone was a hand-me-down from her dad, who'd bought an inexpensive flip phone years ago. "The Loca Mocha."

"What?" Cyril said.

"It's a student-run coffee house two blocks south on Grand." Tara opened the glass door. The cold air and traffic sounds lessened the claustrophobia she'd felt inside with Cyril. "Get in your car first and start driving. I'll meet you there. After I make a call."

To Tara's surprise, Cyril headed for a newish-looking Toyota Corolla. She'd expected an SUV. He looked the type to make believe he lived in the mountains and took hazardous off-road trails while driving I-64 every day.

"You'll really come?" he said.

"Like I want you popping up on me again," she said. "Might as well hear what you have to say."

Tara memorized the Toyota's license plate and scribbled it down as soon as she got into her Saturn. Her first instinct was to call Jeremy. She tried Vicki's cell instead. She got the voicemail and left a detailed message, including the license number, Cyril's name and description, and where she'd be. She phoned her brother Nate and, amazingly, he answered and agreed to drive over to the Loca Mocha, park, and watch through the windows until she got done.

"What is it, a blind date?" he said. "You finally gave up on Jeremy?"

"Right. I'll explain later."

"Whatever you say. You're paying me by the hour, you know."

"Deal."

TARA PERCHED on an overstuffed chair in front of the Loca Mocha's glass window. Four quick strides would get her out the door. Cyril had frowned when she took the seat facing the door, and after he sat, he glanced several times behind him, then around at everyone else in the place. A few highly caffeinated SLU students tapped away on their laptops at desks against the far wall, and a group of theater majors sat in a circle in the corner running lines. The smell of burnt coffee hung in the air.

Cyril's expresso stood, untouched, on the table. Aside from his stiff posture, he didn't appear much different from the SLU students. Buzz cuts weren't popular at the moment, but a few guys Tara knew – and at least one girl – wore their hair that way. Cyril's clothes were too pressed and clean – who ironed cargo pants? – but that just signaled neat-freak. Or smothering mom. Or maybe obsessive-compulsive.

"So what makes you think I'm pregnant?"

"It's a long story." Cyril cleared his throat. "I'm an aspirant. Which means I just started studying to become a deacon. This is part of my Ministry of Service."

"Spooking people is part of your Ministry of Service?"

"Helping people is part of it."

Tara sipped her chai and studied Cyril's face. He'd unnerved her in the darkened laundry, but in the warm, recessed lighting of the Loca Mocha, he seemed less threatening. His mouth formed a straight line, but not as if he were angry, more like he was concentrating. His eyes, a light gray that contrasted his black eyebrows, had a hopeful look.

*He's probably some pro-lifer who's afraid I'm going to have an abortion. If he starts lecturing, I'm out of here.*

"And what does all this have to do with you thinking I'm pregnant?"

"My superiors told me a doctor in the St. Louis area had a patient who claimed to be a virgin and pregnant." He held up his right hand. "I don't know how they knew that. But I was sent to investigate."

Her chair squeaked on the hardwood floor as Tara edged it back. If Cyril were a normal person and he'd merely overhead her conversation, he would just say so. Either he was creating an elaborate story on his own, or he really belonged to some strange religious group. That had access to people's medical records. "Investigate how?"

"I broke into your doctor's office and looked at charts until I found the patient with an unexplained pregnancy. The records provided your address, where you attend school. I found your parents' house and watched it." Cyril kept his gaze steady as he spoke, though a few times the muscles below his eye twitched, as if he longed to break eye contact with Tara and stare at the floor, or the coffee bar, or anywhere but at her.

Tara glanced sideways, but could only see her and Cyril's reflections superimposed on the darkness on the other side of the window. She knew Nate's van idled outside, she'd waited to enter the Loca Mocha until he parked, but she wished she could see him.

"I asked people questions, and I followed you," Cyril went on. "I'm sorry, but it was for a good cause."

"No one told me anyone asked questions."

Tara didn't know what would make him more dangerous – if he'd really been investigating her, or if he was making all this up to freak her out. She ought to just leave, but the idea of being pregnant was so impossible and scary that she needed to know what Cyril had to say, no matter how crazy it might be.

"I gave plausible reasons for my questions." Cyril shifted in his chair, bending his arms, but he kept his hands planted on his knees. "No one suspected anything unusual."

"So you're good at lying."

Tara shivered. Yet, she felt drawn to Cyril. He was the only person she'd spoken to, other than perhaps Dr. Lei, who didn't think she was lying or deluded.

Cyril clasped his hands together. "My superiors needed to know certain things before I approached you."

"And who are your superiors?"

"Leaders of the Brotherhood of Andrew of Crete. Andrew was a monk in the late seven hundreds, during the reign of the Emperor Kopronymos. The Emperor tortured and killed him for defending Christians who revered the cross and other icons."

"And that relates to me how?" Tara said. *He's crazy. Someone finally believes me and he's crazy.*

"The Brotherhood of Andrew was formed to pass on what Brother Andrew learned from visions he had before he died. Visions about you."

Cyril's pupils were normal, not dilated, and the whites of his eyes were clear, not reddened, like Tara imagined they might be if he were taking some mind-altering drug. But that didn't make him sane. "A monk thirteen hundred years ago had visions about me?"

"Not you personally, not by name or a vision of what you look like or anything like that. That would be crazy."

"Yeah, wouldn't it?"

"The visions gave Andrew of Crete insight into Chapter 12 of the book of *Apocalypse*. A revelation about *Revelation*, so to speak." Cyril started to lean forward, then pulled back, as if afraid to invade her private space. "Chapter 12 speaks of the first and second signs of the Apocalypse. The first: a woman wearing a crown with twelve stars gives birth to a child destined to rule the earth."

"And the second sign?"

"The Beast – the Antichrist – comes forth and fights to devour the child, plunging the world into chaos," Cyril said. "Andrew of Crete's visions tell us more about what both signs mean."

Despite the absurdity of it, Tara held her breath.

"The woman's crown has twelve stars that represent infants' eyes. Six infants can be born – six chances to save the world. And with each pregnancy, the Beast arises, vowing to stop the birth of the new Christ. This happened at least four times so far, possibly five, in the last two thousand years. Each time the Beast prevailed.

"Tara, you and your baby may be the world's last chance. And that's why I need you to come with me."

# 7

"You think my baby is the next Christ? Is that like the next Toyota?" Even as she spoke, it hit Tara that she'd said "my baby" for the first time. *My baby. Really?* Tara glanced at her watch. It was only thirty hours from when she'd told Jeremy about the positive pregnancy tests. It felt like that had been decades ago.

Cyril frowned. "This isn't a joke."

"Not a joke. A delusion," Tara said. "A very detailed delusion."

But Cyril acted in a normal way, other than his words. He'd been keeping his distance from her, speaking clearly and in a logical order. He wasn't overly charming, either, which she'd read many psychopaths were.

"Are you deluded?" Cyril asked.

Tara shook her head, remembering the shrink's view of her. It did make it hard for her to judge Cyril. Yet, he had to be lying or crazy. No other options existed. Which must be exactly how Vicki and Jeremy felt. Tara felt a moment of sympathy for them. But they knew her, supposedly loved her, and didn't believe her. Cyril was a stranger to Tara.

"I assure you," Cyril said, "we aren't the only group who believes this about your child, or that fetus wouldn't have been left at your door. You need protection."

"You think – who do you think did that?"

She ought to be careful not to be drawn into Cyril's delusion. But perhaps he did know something about whoever had left the fetus.

"Those who want to stop the next Messiah, who might have hoped to scare you into an abortion. Or miscarriage. Or others, men who believe the woman bears not the next Messiah but the anti-Christ himself."

"The anti-Christ."

Head spinning, Tara glanced toward the coffee house's glass door, reminding herself Nate was right outside. And plenty of people were in the coffee house with her.

Cyril was the most likely person to have left the fetus. But he had let her leave the Laundromat, which would have been the place to harm her if he'd meant to. And Tara couldn't risk not hearing the rest of Cyril's story. Because maybe someone else believed it, someone who wanted to harm her and her baby. If, she added quickly to herself, there was a baby.

"How could anyone even know about me?" Tara asked. "How could this Brotherhood have found out about me, known enough to send you here?"

"There are writings that suggest the location and time where the Messiah may be born. The Brotherhood monitors those places. Consults with local priests, hospitals, doctors. I'm told one of our members is a computer guru. Most likely, your doctor researched your condition on-line and he traced her." Cyril spread his hands out. "This is only speculation. I know only those persons with whom I work directly. "

Hoping it would calm her, Tara sipped her tea. Her hand shook so much she set the cup down immediately. It clinked in the saucer.

"I'm not religious. I'm not sure I even believe in God."

Cyril raised his eyebrows. "But you're Catholic."

"My parents are. I'm not. Much to my dad's dismay."

Cyril thought for a moment. "Have you noticed anyone watching you lately?"

"Besides you? No."

"May I show you something?"

"I guess."

Tara's muscles tightened as Cyril unsnapped one of the larger pockets of his cargo pants. But he only withdrew a laminated photograph about the size of a postcard. He passed it to her.

The photograph showed a stone vase with chipped edges and fine cracks criss-crossing its body. A face had been carved into the vase's surface. A woman's face. She had large, almond-shaped eyes and a smallish nose like Tara's, and long hair.

"What is this?" Tara said.

"A follower of Brother Andrew carved this vase in the ninth century after meeting a woman the follower believed would give birth to a new messiah. You see the resemblance?"

A cappuccino machine buzzed and burbled as Tara studied the photo. "To me? The nose, maybe, but this could be anyone. What happened to her?"

"No one knows. She disappeared a month before she would have given birth."

Tara tried to give the photo back, but Cyril shook his head.

"I have many more. You may keep that."

Tara set the photo next to her teacup, not sure what to think or how she felt. "Okay."

"Andrew foresaw a great battle between the Beast and God for each woman's child. If the Beast is vanquished, the child rules the earth for the good of all mankind."

Tara stared at the photograph. The woman on the vase appeared sad, her eyes cast downward. Her smile was so faint as to be almost non-existent. An echo of a smile.

It took a few seconds for Cyril's words to filter into Tara's mind. She looked at him. "What if the Beast wins?"

"The child dies, perhaps the woman dies." Cyril stared at her, his gray eyes steady, as if making sure his words sunk in. "And if you're the last woman, as I suspect, and the Beast prevails, darkness will descend over a third of the earth and the world will plunge into chaos."

On the other side of the coffee house, the cappuccino machine still whirred, coins jangled into the tip jar, and people at other tables studied and laughed and talked. The scent of cinnamon mingled with the burnt coffee smell. Tara gripped her chair's seat cushion, feeling its worn ribbing against the insides of her fingers. Cyril had to be insane, or at least badly mistaken, but no one else had explained her apparent pregnancy.

"That's crazy." Tara stood, but she moved too quickly and dizziness hit her. She grabbed the chair back to keep from swaying.

Cyril stood, too, grasped Tara's arm to steady her. "I know how it sounds. But please don't go. You need my protection."

Tara pulled away. "It's late. My brother's waiting for me." She added the last so he would know she wasn't alone. She started for the door.

Cyril reached it first.

Tara tensed, but he opened it for her. "Let me take you somewhere safe," Cyril said.

"No. Thanks."

"Then take this. Please." He pushed a paperback copy of the New Testament at her. Tara took it to forestall any more conversation. "I'll keep watching over you," Cyril said.

In the parking lot, Tara gulped the exhaust-tinged night air, hurried to the van, and climbed in.

Nate, who'd been slumped in the driver's seat, straightened up. "What about your car?"

"I'll get it tomorrow. Just go."

# 8

Tara peered into the passenger sideview mirror as they drove toward the highway. She couldn't tell if any of the headlights behind them were the Toyota's. She supposed it didn't matter. Cyril already knew where she lived.

"You gonna tell me what the deal is with this guy?" Nate accelerated and the van's valves chattered as it merged onto the expressway.

"His name is Cyril Woods, and he says he knows why I'm pregnant."

Tara filled him in as they drove toward Rock Hill.

"So the dude's crazy," Nate said.

"Must be."

"Are you going to check it out?" Nate nodded at the New Testament Tara held. "The *Revelation* passage?"

"Oh. Yeah." Tara clicked on the overhead dome light and opened the book. The photo depicting the stone vase fell out. Tara retrieved it off the floor mat and handed it to Nate. "He showed me this. He must have slipped it into the book."

Nate held the photo close to his face, glanced at it, then gave it back and focused on the road again. "What's it supposed to prove? It doesn't even look like you."

"I thought the nose maybe."

"Please. Everyone's got a nose."

Tara noticed something else in the book. "There's a card in here, too, with Cyril's name and a phone number on it."

"I'm sure you'll be calling him right up."

"Yeah."

"I don't remember the priests reading *Revelation* in mass," Nate said.

"That's because it's called *Apocalypse* in the Catholic Bible." Tara turned to the table of contents. Fortunately, *The Apocalypse of John* wasn't very long. "But you're right, it wasn't read much."

Unlike Nate, Tara had paid attention during mass when she was growing up, often trying, without much success, to figure out the point of the readings. The one where God told Abraham to kill his son, and Abraham agreed, particularly troubled her. How could the same god who later issued a commandment against murder demand his most faithful follower kill his son to prove his loyalty? And then say, "Oh, just messing with you" and it was all supposed to be okay?

"Then why'd this guy call it *Revelation*?" Nate slowed the van and changed lanes as they neared their exit. "I thought he was a deacon."

"Maybe he's a deacon in some other church," Tara said. "Do other churches have deacons?"

"You got me."

Tara flipped pages, trying to remember which chapter Cyril had mentioned. "Here it is." She closed her eyes, feeling suddenly nauseated. "Better wait until we're home."

The van's bouncing and the lemony smell from Nate's air freshener didn't help her stomach, but Tara felt comforted by both. Of all her siblings, she felt closest to Nate, despite their differences. Tara was outgoing, talked a lot, and laughed easily. Nate kept to himself, would barely crack a smile for anyone but Tara until he was three or four, and was the least likely to pry into anyone else's business. Yet, they'd both decided to apply to SLU instead of going away to college because of Megan's illness. They scrapped about who would babysit or make dinner or mow the lawn, but when it came down to it, Tara knew Nate would be there for her, no questions asked.

When they reached the house, they hesitated together at the front stoop, debating going upstairs, where Bailey might be sleeping in Tara's attic apartment, or to the basement, where Nate had created a room for himself that was part beneath the basement stairs and part carved from the laundry room. It was unlikely anyone else would be sleeping in Nate's space, but the heat vents carried sound directly to and from their parents' room, and Tara wanted her conversation private for a while.

"Why don't we grab some ice cream," Nate said.

Ice cream had been a late night ritual for Tara and Nate when they'd babysat the younger kids. It sounded good despite the season.

"Why not?"

The kitchen felt warmer than outside, but the Spencers kept the thermostat at sixty-five at night to cut the gas bill. Tara chose the chair closest to the heat register. Nate rummaged in the freezer. "So go ahead."

Tara found her place in the New Testament. "Chapter 12, in verses one through five, talks about the woman with the crown of twelve stars. She's pregnant, and when she delivers, a great red dragon – sometimes called the Beast – appears, and his tail drags a third of the stars down onto the earth." Tara turned the page. "'And the dragon stood before the woman who was about to bring forth, that when she had brought forth he might devour her son.'"

Nate scooped three different ice cream flavors into bowls. "That's why I like Bible stories. They're so upbeat."

"So the child is born and ascends to heaven, and the woman flees to the wilderness. The Beast creates a river of spit to drown her, but it doesn't work, because the earth opens and swallows the spit."

"Whoever wrote that had to be on some serious hallucinogens," Nate said as he set the bowls and spoons on the table.

Tara read through the passage again silently. "I don't see why Cyril thinks I'm this woman."

"You mean besides you claiming you're a virgin and pregnant?"

"I'm not 'claiming' anything. Not even that I'm pregnant – the doctors are the ones telling me that. And nothing here says the woman giving birth is a virgin. It makes no sense."

"So where'd the virgin thing come from?" Nate said.

"Andrew of Crete's interpretation of the text."

"Well, that's serious Catholics for you. All women should be both virgins and mothers if at all possible."

"What do you think it means that the only person who believes me is a religious nut? And I'm not even religious?" Tara said.

"You used to be." Nate retrieved a jar of fudge topping from the cabinet and popped it into the microwave. The machine whirred, and the smell of chocolate filled the room. "And I believe you."

"You mean you're like Dad – you believe I'm not lying, I just don't remember what happened. I'm repressing."

"Well, yeah. What else could it be?"

"Right." Tara slammed the book shut. Nate was only being logical, but she wished someone would take her at her word. Someone other than Cyril Woods, who thought she was going to end up the dead mother of a messiah.

The microwave dinged. "You think Cyril's dangerous?" Nate said.

"I don't know. They always say to trust your gut in these situations, and I felt pretty freaked out when he appeared like that."

"But you felt okay about him later."

"Yeah. When we got into the light."

Nate poured steaming hot fudge on their ice cream and slid one bowl across the table to Tara, then sat down. "What if he's right?"

"Right that I'm carrying a future messiah?"

"Well, if you believe it happened two thousand years ago, why not now? Why not you?"

Tara eyed her brother, not sure if he was making fun of her. But it wasn't like Nate to be mean, at least not unless he was really annoyed, and usually that was with Bailey. "But I don't believe it. At least, I have serious doubts. The earliest written gospel is Mark, and it starts with Jesus when he's, like, twelve. My comparative religion professor said the virgin birth story was circulated much later, probably to make it seem like Jesus' life conformed with Old Testament prophecies."

Nate shrugged. "Just trying to keep an open mind. You're the one who got mad when I said you were repressing."

"Because I'm not."

# 9

Dr. Lei applied the leads to Tara's lower abdomen.

"You can't really blame Vicki," Tara's mother said. Lynette had driven Tara to the office for her follow up ultrasound when Vicki failed to show. She'd even held Tara's hand in the waiting room. Only one other woman had been there, and a red haired man Tara assumed was waiting for his wife or girlfriend. He looked familiar to Tara, but she couldn't place him. "After all, Jeremy is her brother."

"I know."

Tara clenched her hands, forgetting for the moment about Vicki as she stared at the monitor. She'd conceived, if she had, in some bizarre, unknown way, who knew what floated in her uterus? A malignant tumor? A horned creature with a tail? Horror movie images had flooded Tara's mind when she'd awakened sweating and shivering at two that morning, and no amount of thinking how ridiculous she was being had banished them. She'd finally gotten out of bed at four-thirty and studied for next week's Anatomy exam.

Lynette, standing at Tara's side, took Tara's hand again. "I remember how cold the jelly felt when I was at the Planned Parenthood clinic and pregnant with you."

Crackling filled the air as the monitor blinked, showing only static. Dr. Lei pressed a few keys and a fuzzy white form appeared. The image blurred further when Tara shifted to try to get more comfortable on the exam table.

"It wasn't cold with the other kids?" Tara said to her mother, trying to get her mind off her fears even as she peered at the screen. "Just with me?"

"I don't remember. Maybe I was just prepared for it the next time. The next four times." Lynette glanced at Dr. Lei. "I was nineteen with Tara, and so sure my boyfriend would be thrilled once he got used to the idea of a baby, he might even want to get married."

Dr. Lei reached for her mouse and clicked a few times. "It'll be just a moment, I'm having a little trouble with the scanner."

Her first ultrasound hadn't shown much at all, she'd basically taken Dr. Lei's word for it that it confirmed her pregnancy. Now Tara closed her eyes, afraid of what she might see when the image of the being inside her became clear.

*That's crazy.*

"I take it he didn't?" Dr. Lei said.

"What? Oh, hardly," Lynette answered. "He demanded I get an abortion. I never saw him again."

Tara had heard the story before. What a way to find out your boyfriend didn't love you or want a future with you. At least Jeremy had an excuse – he really thought Tara had cheated on him. It went a long way toward explaining why her mom was so cynical. Though Tara always found it difficult to imagine her mother young and in love and deluded.

"See?" Dr. Lei said. Tara forced herself to open her eyes. Dr. Lei pointed. "There's the arm. And here, that indentation you see, that's an eye."

Tara's heart stuttered as she peered at the tiny being, traced in her mind the curve from forehead to nose, the hand smaller than her fingertip, the bent legs. "It's a baby." She let her breath out. She really was pregnant. As much as she'd thought about the concept, realized it must be so given the tests and the later doctor visits, it hadn't seemed real until now.

"What else would it be?" Looking at Dr. Lei, Lynette rolled her eyes. "She's so dramatic."

Tara craned her neck. She studied the form's forehead and rounded stomach. It looked like her brothers' and sisters' second trimester ultrasounds, like an infant, if a disproportionate one. The fetus seemed normal, though Tara didn't know what to look for in an ultrasound to tell. "Everything looks okay?"

Dr. Lei moved the scope slightly for a different view, from the front rather than the side. "She looks fine."

"She?" Wonder swept through Tara. However it had happened, a baby girl grew inside her. *When she's born, will she look like me?*

"It appears so. And based on your last period and the size of the fetus, I'd say you're about seventeen or eighteen weeks along."

That was over four months, so she was due in October.

"Are there other tests I should have to make sure nothing's wrong?" Tara asked.

Lynette's grip on Tara's hand tightened. "Why would anything be wrong?"

Dr. Lei clicked a few keys on the keyboard next to the monitor. The printer in the corner whirred. "You could have an amniocentesis. But that entails some risk to the fetus. Absent suspecting anything in particular, I advise against it. Your baby looks normal and healthy." She touched Tara's arm. "Why don't you get dressed and we can talk in my office?"

Tara hesitated to ask her mother to come into the office with her, but she'd always shared things with her parents. And even if her mom didn't believe her about the baby's conception, she knew a lot about being pregnant. And giving birth.

Tara and Lynette sat side-by-side in the soft suede chairs in front of Dr. Lei's desk. Tara liked the chairs. They made her feel as if Dr. Lei really wanted her patients to relax and talk.

"You're in excellent health," Dr. Lei said.

"What about diet?" Lynette said. "I read in *Time* that a lot of pregnant women are undernourished, even in our country, because so few people eat fresh food anymore. I know Tara never sits down to a full meal, she's always running around."

"Nutrition is important." Dr. Lei spoke for a few minutes about diet, exercise and the changes Tara should expect in her body. She took foil vitamin packets from her desk drawer and started counting them out.

Tara fingered Cyril's card, which was in her jeans pocket. She'd taken to carrying it, along with the laminated photo showing the vase. She wasn't sure why, except it reassured her she hadn't imagined Cyril, that there was someone who didn't think she was lying, even if his explanation was impossible. She found herself studying the carving on the vase at odd times, between classes, or during a long lecture, trying to figure out whether the woman's face really looked like hers or if the power of suggestion made her think so.

"Is there any way someone could see my medical records?" she asked Dr. Lei.

Dr. Lei stopped counting. "Only my staff, unless you authorize me to send copies somewhere."

"What about just in general? Could someone find out you have a patient who doesn't know how she got pregnant?"

"I consulted with other doctors, but that would be confidential. And I've searched medical databases." Dr. Lei frowned. "But those searches shouldn't be accessible to anyone else."

Dr. Lei's sleek white laptop sat behind her, closed, on her mahogany credenza. She must be connected to the Internet to be running searches. Which fit with Cyril's guess that someone in the Brotherhood had traced Dr. Lei by computer.

Lynette looked at Tara. "What's this about? The laboratory fetus?"

"Fetus?" Dr. Lei asked.

"Someone left what looked like a bloody fetus on my steps," Tara said. "It turned out it was paint, not blood, but the fetus was real. A specimen from a lab somewhere." The incident seemed almost unreal in retrospect, especially told in the ordered, professional atmosphere of Dr. Lei's office with piano music playing in the background.

"What a horrible thing. Were you harmed?"

"It shook me, but I'm fine. We still don't know who did it."

Dr. Lei's forehead creased. "Do you have reason to believe someone in my office is involved?"

Tara shook her head. "Not at all."

"The police questioned Jeremy," Lynette said.

"That does not seem like him." Dr. Lei was also the Turanos' family doctor. "Though people do strange things when distraught."

"That's not why I'm asking about your records." Tara took a deep breath. She hadn't mentioned Cyril to her parents. She kept thinking – wishing – it would turn out she wasn't pregnant. Then nothing Cyril said would have anything to do with her. But now, she couldn't deny her pregnancy. And maybe her mother would behave a little more reasonably with Dr. Lei there. "About two weeks back, this guy approached me. He claims he's part of a religious order, the Brotherhood of Andrew. The Brotherhood thinks my pregnancy is fulfilling some Biblical prophecy."

"What?" Lynette said.

"Prophecy?" Dr. Lei said.

Tara explained Cyril's story and showed them the laminated photo of the carved vase.

"What is this supposed to prove? It doesn't even look like you." Lynette threw the photo on the desk. "Why didn't you mention this when it happened?"

"I was freaked out. I needed to think."

Dr. Lei examined the photo. "It may bear a slight resemblance, but it's not striking. Yet this man says it shows something about you?"

"He says a follower of Brother Andrew carved it. Of a woman who was a pregnant virgin, and she disappeared."

Lynette grimaced. "My God, Tara. A stranger approaches you in the Laundromat alone at night, and the more he talks, the crazier and the more threatening he sounds, and you don't tell us or call the police?"

"I didn't feel scared of him."

"You didn't feel scared." Lynette stared at Tara, eyes traveling over Tara's face.

"Not really. Not after we talked. And that police officer who came out before wasn't exactly overflowing with concern."

"Hm."

Dr. Lei handed the photo back. "I must agree with your mother to some extent, Tara. This man may have been involved in the incident with the fetus. And if he broke into my office – and I'll do everything in my power to find out if he did – he obviously has little regard for the law."

Lynette turned toward the doctor. "I'm not sure Cyril is dangerous after all."

"Because?" Dr. Lei said.

"Because I'm not sure there is a Cyril."

# 10

The space between Dr. Lei's eyebrows creased, as if in puzzlement, but Tara knew right away where her mother was going and felt steam rise through her body.

"Only Tara has seen this Cyril," Lynette said. "Even Nate, who drove the van to get her when she was supposedly meeting with him, never saw him. Only Tara."

"So, what, now I'm a pathological liar? I can't believe this shit." Tara stood and paced behind the chairs to keep from screaming loud enough for every patient in every exam room in the entire office complex to hear.

"That's not what I'm saying." Lynette's voice sounded low, steady. It incensed Tara even further.

"You just can't stand that Dad's supporting me in this, can you? That he believes me that I don't know how it happened."

The real issue, Tara thought, was the same as it always was. Tara had more of her biological father's disposition, his accepting, open way with people. Lynette always said Pete's parents couldn't stand Lynette, but when they met Tara, they couldn't stop talking about what a sweet, pretty, happy little girl she was and how much they looked forward to being grandparents. And Tara always sensed her mother felt hurt underneath that her future in-laws liked Tara on sight and took longer to warm to Lynette.

Dr. Lei reached her hands toward both of them, as if she could calm them by her touch, though the desk was too wide for her to connect. "Lynette, I've been treating your family for over ten years. Until now, I did not get the impression you'd had difficulty with Tara prevaricating. I think we must assume, for safety's sake, and in the absence of other evidence, that Tara is telling the truth."

Lynette frowned but stayed silent.

"You really think Cyril could be dangerous?" Tara asked Dr. Lei.

"This is beyond my area of expertise, but that a young man – a potential stalker – has apparently fixated on you concerns me."

Tara stopped pacing. "He hasn't contacted me again." She knew she ought to be more worried about Cyril, but she'd paid close attention to his body language and words, and she felt fairly sure he really did want to help her, however strange his story was.

"That's something," Dr. Lei said. "But I urge you to talk to the detectives who investigated the fetus incident."

Lynette started to say something, then stopped, and tapped her fingers on the arm of her chair.

"Lynette?" Dr. Lei said.

"My father was psychotic."

"What?" Tara said.

All Tara knew about Grandpa Tieg was that, before he died, he used to call asking Tara's parents for money, with outlandish reasons why he needed it. Lynette never sent it, because she knew he'd spend it on alcohol.

"He used to disappear for days and claim he'd met famous people," Lynette said, "or made a major archeological discovery when it'd been a decade since he'd been on a dig or even taught."

Tara stared at her mother. "So I'm crazy? Make up your mind, Mom. Is your daughter a lunatic, a liar, or in denial? Or maybe it's all three. It could be all three."

"I'm just saying, delusional thinking could run in the family. You've always been very imaginative."

Tara turned to Dr. Lei. "Is there anything else? Because I prefer to wait outside while my mother theorizes about my mental health."

"Lynette, I'd like a few minutes with Tara."

After Lynette left, Dr. Lei motioned Tara to sit, then walked around the desk to sit next to her.

"I know this is difficult. You must be very confused and concerned about how this pregnancy occurred, and now this man approaches you. I wish I had answers. But I can tell you, you are very healthy, your fetus appears healthy, and I have no questions about your mental state."

"At least someone doesn't." Tara squeezed her hands into fists. "I can't believe her. After I even went to that shrink like she and my dad asked. At least he didn't think I was crazy, even if he didn't believe me."

Dr. Lei touched Tara's hand. "Your mother has a difficult family history. She may feel guilty, thinking she could have passed on a predisposition to mental illness to you. Or fearing that, because of her upbringing, she's been a poor parent and somehow caused your current troubles. So it comes out as anger toward you."

"Maybe." Tara wasn't convinced, but she recognized Dr. Lei was a little more objective.

"Have you considered what I mentioned on our last visit?" Dr. Lei said. "I thought you might prefer to discuss it privately, away from your mother."

"Not really." Tara pressed her hands together. They felt clammy. "I just couldn't believe I was pregnant, so I pushed the idea out of my head." Tara swallowed hard. She'd always assumed she'd never consider abortion, even if she got pregnant without being married. But she couldn't have imagined a situation like this.

"I do not want to pressure you, but Missouri law only allows a woman to choose an abortion within twenty-two weeks from her last menstrual period, unless her life or health is threatened," Dr. Lei said.

"But I didn't even know for sure I was pregnant until about fourteen weeks after. And I didn't believe it until now."

"Such circumstances make no difference under the law. I'm sorry. Three weeks, four at most, are left to decide."

TARA OPENED her apartment door to find Vicki sitting on the futon.

"Tara, I'm so sorry."

"What happened?" Tara tossed her keys on the table and dropped her backpack on the chair. "I waited twenty minutes, and my mom decided to go with me." Not that Tara had been that surprised by Vicki's absence. Ever since Tara had told Vicki about the pregnancy tests, Vicki was always on her way into class or work or the store when Tara called, and then she didn't return the call for days. Before, they'd talked nearly every twenty-four hours.

"Well, that's good. At least you had someone there."

"It's not good. It gave her more chances to yell at me, and now she thinks I'm crazy because I was an idiot and told her about Cyril."

Tara opened her backpack and took out the vitamin samples Dr. Lei had given her, slamming them on the table. Behind her, the refrigerator buzzed on.

"Cyril?"

"That guy I've been trying to tell you about, but you never have time to talk. He says he's a deacon in a religious order, and he knows why I'm pregnant, and he gave me this."

Tara dug out the photograph of the vase and handed it to Vicki.

Vicki studied it. "What's he giving you things for? Is he a stalker?"

"That's what Dr. Lei thinks."

After Tara poured Cokes for both of them, she told Vicki about the Brotherhood of Andrew and Chapter 12, and everything Cyril had said. She could tell by the way Vicki's eyes narrowed and her chin jutted that she didn't believe a word, maybe not even that someone named Cyril existed, until Tara described how Cyril dressed.

Vicki's eyes widened. "He's the guy from the coffee shop."

"That's right – you saw him." For an instant, Tara felt like running downstairs and telling her mother that Vicki had seen Cyril, too. But that wouldn't prove anything, and Vicki's next words made that even clearer.

"I knew he was involved. But you're saying you're not seeing him, and he's not the baby's father, and he thinks you're the next virgin Mary?"

"Forget it." Tara took the empty glasses to the sink. They clunked when they hit the stainless steel. She ought to put them in the dishwasher, but it seemed like too much effort. "You obviously don't believe me, and you don't want to hear what's going on. I don't know why you even came here."

"Can you blame me?"

Tara turned back toward Vicki. "Yeah, I can blame you. Friends are supposed to be there for each other." Tara had been friends with Vicki since first grade at St. John of the Cross, but in the last month she'd come to feel she didn't know Vicki at all. No matter how confused Tara might be about something going on with a friend, Tara would never abandon that person.

"You're asking an awful lot, Tara."

"How do you figure? How many times since junior high have I held your hair when you puked, or driven out to get you when you got pissed at Chad or Raul or Billy or whoever, or covered for you when your mom or your latest boyfriend asked questions you didn't want to answer? Now I need help, now I need support, and you can't even pick up a fucking phone and text me that you're not going to show?"

"What is this shit?" Vicki stood. "I screw up all the time and tell you. Now you screw up, but do you tell me what really happened? No. First you say you don't know how you got pregnant, and now it's a divine conception."

Tara stood, too, staring at her friend. That was the problem? "So if I slept with Roger, or some bonehead I never met before at a party, that'd be okay, that'd be better?"

"It'd be normal at least. Human. Like the rest of us."

"What are you talking about? I'm human. I make mistakes."

"Please." Vicki waved her hand. "I'm not talking about getting a C on a term paper or your mom catching you when you snuck out and met Danny Parker at the mall."

"What about – no. This is insane. I'm not doing this." Tara stomped to the windows and stared out at her Saturn parked in the driveway. Maybe she'd pack her things and drive away. Get as far as she could from here, from her family, from everything. She pressed her palms against the cool glass.

"Just tell me what happened, Tara. You don't have to tell anyone else. And I won't say anything to Jeremy. He's such an asshole, it's not like he can complain about what you did."

Tara spun around. "What?"

"I—nothing. I didn't mean anything." Vicki took the photo from the table. "This woman looks a little like you."

"What about Jeremy?"

Vicki sighed. "I didn't mean to get into it. But maybe it'll show you it's okay to admit you cheated. Jeremy was – is – fooling around with Suzanne. The evening hostess at the restaurant. Since last fall."

Tara felt like someone kicked her in the gut. She gripped the window sill behind her. "He's been seeing her all this time?"

"Not seeing her, really. It's just for sex."

"Just sex."

*Just sex.* Images of Jeremy with Suzanne, a pretty brunette who always took a few minutes to chat with Tara at the restaurant, ran through Tara's mind. Jeremy holding Suzanne, Jeremy kissing Suzanne. Jeremy making love with Suzanne, when Tara never got to feel that, never got to know what it would be like. And now Tara was pregnant, her life ruined, and Jeremy would go off and maybe marry Suzanne, and have a family with her, and the Turanos would love her, and play with Jeremy and Suzanne's kids, and think of Tara as that awful girl who cheated on their son.

"Goddamnit." Tara brought her fist down on the window sill, barely noticing the pain.

"I only found out after you guys split," Vicki said. "But, see, so you cheated on him. He cheated on you, too. It's no big deal. You can admit it."

"Right. No big deal." Tara looked away from Vicki, holding back tears.

*It only means I'll never get Jeremy back, and he's not who I thought he was anyway. And neither is Vicki.*

Vicki walked over to Tara and touched her shoulder. The scent of Vicki's light, citrusy perfume brought Tara back for an instant to the sleepovers they'd had in junior high. It seemed like a century ago.

"I really am sorry about blowing off your appointment," Vicki said. "It was lousy of me."

"It doesn't matter."

Tara didn't care anymore that Vicki had missed the ultrasound. Vicki would never believe Tara didn't know how she got pregnant. Neither would Tara's mother, or anyone, probably, other than Cyril, who might very well be crazy. As for other friends, Tara had made a lot of friends in grade school and high school. But between work and college and helping take care of the other kids since Megan had been diagnosed, she hadn't really stayed that close with anyone outside the family other than Vicki and Jeremy. Not close enough that anyone would believe her.

"I have to tell you something else." Vicki clasped her hands together in front of her. "And I'm sorry about this, too, but I'll be gone all summer. My mom finally agreed I could do the internship in my aunt's art gallery."

"She changed her mind?"

Vicki had been lobbying for the New York trip for months, but Mrs. Turano was against it, and Vicki's aunt wouldn't let her come without her mother's agreement.

Vicki looked down.

"Oh." *Mrs. Turano must hate me.* "It's a great opportunity. Have a good time."

Tara unlocked the door and held it open for Vicki to leave.

"You're mad," Vicki said.

"What difference does it make – whether you're here or there, how can I talk to you about anything when you won't believe me?" Tara said.

"And how can I talk to you when you keep lying?"

Vicki stormed out and slammed the door behind her.

The phone rang as Tara watched Vicki run down the stairs, get in her car and drive away. The answering machine clicked on, and Tara's classmate Heather spoke.

"Tara, where are you? Did you forget the cram session? We'll be here at least 'til eleven. Hope everything's okay."

Tara sank to a sitting position on the floor and put her head in her hands. She couldn't see how anything would be okay again.

# 11

Tara's shoulders ached. She slipped her backpack off and stepped down into the locker pit, a rectangular area off the lecture halls. Metal lockers lined the walls and stood back-to-back in two rows down the middle. Tara squeezed to the right. She was starting to show, even with loose clothes on, if someone looked closely, but it wasn't enough to make her very large. Still, she felt awkward, as if she inhabited a different body than the one she'd known all these years.

For each question on her ancient history final, Tara'd written a detailed response, but she never felt sure what the professor was getting at. All that work for the last two and a half years to keep her GPA near a 4.0 – it was 3.96 as of last semester – so she'd have a choice of medical schools and maybe get a scholarship. Now this semester would sink it.

*And what does it matter? I can't raise a baby, attend medical school and earn enough to support us all at the same time.*

Every night during the past week, Tara had lain awake thinking about what Dr. Lei said about terminating the pregnancy. She hadn't seen abortion as a black and white issue since her days at Catholic grade school when she'd believed everything the Church taught. But Tara had never felt sure, either, that it was something she could feel right about for herself, Church or no Church, God or no god. In the middle of the night, the idea beckoned her. She could return her life to how it ought to be. Not this world where everything she'd worked for slipped away because of some bizarre event she had no control over.

This morning Tara had punched in two numbers of Dr. Lei's line. Then she hung up.

*It's so unfair.* Tara felt childish thinking that because she'd understood long ago, even before Megan's diagnosis, that fair had very little to do with life. But she'd worked hard, she'd been careful, she'd even lost Jeremy to Suzanne because she wouldn't have sex with him, and now she was pregnant anyway. It was beyond not fair. She pressed her forehead against her closed locker door.

"There you are."

Tara turned. Cyril stood near the pit's back exit, dressed in a gray tank top and black work pants. His arms were muscular, but lean, his face clean-shaven. He seemed serene, which irritated her even more.

"What are you doing here?" Tara said.

"You paged."

"I thought you'd call me, not show up."

"I was near."

Tara's stomach rumbled. She turned back to her locker – she had an apple inside – and spun her combination lock. She hadn't been able to keep down breakfast, and for lunch she'd managed only half a protein bar. That probably contributed to the exhaustion she felt so often these days. She couldn't understand how she could feel starving and sick to her stomach at the same time. No wonder her mother had been crabby during her pregnancies.

Books and computer printouts cascaded from the locker when Tara opened the door. She'd researched last night at the University library instead of studying. Watching the cascade, she sagged against the locker behind her. Just the thought of putting all those papers back in order seemed overwhelming.

Cyril bent to help retrieve everything. "Commentaries on *Revelation*?"

"Yeah." Tara took the top book from him and shoved it on the shelf. It slipped forward again, and Tara slammed her hand against it so it banged to the back of the locker.

"You seem disturbed."

"You think?" Tara said.

Cyril handed her the printouts. "Something in particular?"

"I may have just flunked a final for the first time ever. I can't imagine I can finish college in a year anyway, with a baby on the way that I can't possibly be pregnant with. I no longer have a boyfriend, and now I have no best friend, because she thinks I'm lying." Tara rearranged her books with the largest on the bottom so the stack wouldn't tumble again. She put the computer pages on top. She ought to take everything home, she only had another week for the locker rental, but the physical effort seemed overwhelming.

"Then she wasn't much of a friend. But I'm sure that doesn't make it easier."

Another student entered the locker pit. Cyril scrutinized her as she opened her locker. She glared over her shoulder at him.

"I at least thought she'd, I don't know, suspend her disbelief, as they say in the movies. Although I don't know if I'd believe her if the situation were reversed," Tara said.

Cyril gave Tara the last of the books. "Of course you would. You trust people."

*Like Jeremy*, Tara thought. *Cyril probably knows all about him and Suzanne.* But she didn't feel like discussing it. Her throat ached, and if she started crying, she wasn't sure she could stop. Last night she'd driven by the restaurant and seen

Jeremy's car. She'd pulled to the curb, letting the car idle for a few minutes, but then she'd driven on. She couldn't think of anything to say if she'd stopped. She could yell at him, but it wouldn't solve anything, and he'd just accuse her of cheating just as he had.

"Well, the fact that I'm even talking to you probably tells you that," Tara said. "No big points for observation there."

The other student shut her locker and left. The locker area fell silent. Everyone rushed out after the last final of the day, including the professors, and for a moment it seemed Tara and Cyril were the only ones on the floor.

"Why did you call me?" Cyril said.

Tara sighed. "I had an ultrasound, I saw the baby. I'm definitely having a baby."

And, though she didn't say it, she'd wanted to see Cyril again. The week after the ultrasound had been harder, rather than easier, when it came to her family, because now it was beyond doubt Tara was pregnant, and they found it incomprehensible that she wouldn't admit to having sex or at least to the possibility of someone assaulting her.

"At least you're convinced of that." Cyril walked past the center row of lockers and peered around, then rechecked the row where he and Tara stood. "I was coming to see you anyway when you paged. I may know who left the fetus with the knitting needle on your stairs."

"Who?"

"Did I talk to you before about the agents of the Beast?" Cyril said.

"Really not." Tara thought of Dr. Lei's concerns about Cyril. *But who else am I going to talk to?* "Who are they? What are they?"

Cyril glanced behind him again, as if he expected to see something other than lockers. "We should talk somewhere else. Somewhere you wouldn't usually be."

"As long as it's in public." Tara wasn't planning to call the police on Cyril as Dr. Lei had suggested, but she'd heed the warning to be cautious.

"Wherever you want," Cyril said. "Let's go."

Tara slammed her locker door, and the lights went out.

# 12

Pete refilled his and Lynette's sangria glasses. Just the two of them were out tonight. Lynette looked beautiful, her hair swinging in clean lines toward her chin, the restaurant's candles and colored lights highlighting her pale complexion. Pete smiled, feeling his neck and shoulder muscles relax. Megan had been feeling better, her blood tests were good, the steroids seemed to be working, and she was excited about a night home with just her siblings. She and Bailey had been debating which DVDs to watch and what flavor popcorn to make since Monday. Which meant Pete and Lynn, with minimal parental guilt, could enjoy a night where they ate food that was still hot, engaged in dinner conversation without anyone complaining about who ate whose tacos, and didn't need to tip extra to make up for the Pepsi spilled on the terrazzo floor. Pete loved the chaos involved in having five kids, it contrasted the rigid, controlled way he and his brother had been raised. But he longed for time alone with his wife too, something that hadn't happened for longer than Pete cared to think about. Neither he nor Lynn had much energy left for anything beyond making ends meet and getting to doctors and the hospital.

But Lynette was holding out a spiral-bound notebook she'd pulled from her shoulder bag. "Look at this."

Pete leaned forward. On the notebook's cover, a phoenix rose from flames. "That's Tara's journal." Pete had bought it for Tara at a local independent book store she liked.

Lynette set the notebook between them on the varnished wood table. "I know. I read it."

"Lynn." Pete drew back.

"She left it in the family room."

A band in the back of the restaurant started playing cheerful Mexican music, contrasting the set of Lynette's jaw.

"That doesn't make it all right to read it," Pete said.

Before Lynette could answer, the waiter, Eddie, appeared with chips and two bowls of salsa. He slid the spicy salsa nearer Lynette's plate, the mild near Pete. Most of the wait staff at *La Hacienda* remembered and liked Lynette and Pete. Even though when Nate was ten he'd run full speed into a waitress toting a tray of strawberry margaritas, and a year later Bailey threw up on the maitre d's shoes.

After Eddie left, Lynette said, "I read it because I'm worried."

"About something more than her being pregnant?"

Tara had finally admitted to Pete and Lynette that she really was pregnant, but still insisted she didn't know how it had happened. Pete believed her, but almost wished he didn't, because it meant she'd either had some sort of blackout or was in total denial. Tara wasn't a drinker so far as Pete knew, but he was trying to face that there must be a lot he didn't know about her. He'd always felt proud of his relationship with Tara, felt sure she confided in him about the things that mattered to her. Now it seemed she'd hidden whole parts of her life, so well he'd had no idea he was missing major parts of the narrative.

"Tara never crammed for finals," Lynette said. "The rest of this semester she worked and saw Jeremy – at least until they broke up – and played basketball and Frisbee, and barely studied. The usual. But then she never crammed."

"Maybe she didn't need to." Pete took a chip and broke it in half, then split the halves into quarters. He stared at the pieces. "Maybe she finally developed better study habits."

Lynette just looked at him.

"Okay." Tara had always done well in school, but she wasn't one to prepare for things. "But she's old enough to make her own decisions. If she didn't study, she'll see it in her grades and do better next time."

"Medical school means more to Tara than anything," Lynette said, "especially now that Jeremy's out of the picture, and she says she's determined to find a way to go, even with a baby. But she's reading a bunch of strange books instead of studying."

"What kind of books?"

Pete hoped Tara had just started reading sci fi or romance or some other genre Lynette felt wasn't serious enough. That probably wouldn't warrant this much discussion, but Lynette and Tara knew how to set one another off. Pete tried to stay out of it, but his sympathies were more often with his stepdaughter than his wife. Lynette had always been especially hard on Tara. Pete had never understood exactly why.

"Not ones she got in her comparative religion class." Lynette flipped the notebook to the first page. "Here's a few from her reading list. *Jesus and the Lost Goddess. When God Was a Woman. The Goddess, The Grail, and The Lodge.* See a pattern?"

"Tara's always been interested in religion."

Pete encouraged Tara's inquiries, though the Church seemed clear enough to him without outside reading. In a childhood that involved moving every other year, the Catholic mass had been an anchor for Pete, a predictable ritual he could participate in even if he didn't know the language the priest spoke.

"She doesn't even go to mass," Lynette said.

"The two don't have to go hand in hand." Pete wished Tara would start attending mass again, but he had drifted away from the Church during his early college years, so he remained optimistic about Tara rediscovering her faith. "At least she's reading."

"Here's another," Lynette said. "*The Feminine Face of God* by some former nun, Sophia Gaddini."

"That doesn't sound too disturbing."

"But what's this obsession about God being a woman?" Lynette said. "God is God. The only reason Tara would care about this is her pregnancy."

"A lot of people have issues with the way God is consistently referred to as male."

"But listen to what Tara wrote."

"Lynn, I wish you wouldn't. I kept journals all my life, I'd be appalled if anyone read them." Pete kept his locked in his tiny study.

"It's important. I'm not reading to invade her privacy. Listen – 'Gaddini thinks the Garden of Eden story reflects an attempt to stamp out Goddess worship by using symbols of feminine creativity and knowledge – such as the serpent and the Tree of Life – as props in a drama casting women as evil.'" Lynette read. "As if there's some big male conspiracy to take over religion."

"So you're worried Tara's starting to see herself as some sort of female icon?"

Pete found the idea troubling, but Tara's musings about religion might not be that unusual for a young woman trying to find her path.

"There's more." Lynette leaned forward. "Notes about the goddess Isis and her son Houras, supposedly precursors of Mary and Jesus. And about Demeter and her daughter Kore. According to some myths, Demeter was a virgin mother. This is what I've been worried about since she started talking about this Cyril person. Tara's not lying. She really thinks she's conceived in some divine way."

The music's volume and tempo increased, and someone started playing maracas. Pete rubbed his forehead, unconsciously tracing the lines that seemed to deepen with every passing week, and stared at the bright red salsa in its yellow bowl. He'd read about children with terminally ill siblings wishing they were sick, too, so they could get some of their parents' attention. Was this a version of that? But Tara was well-adjusted. Happy. At least, she had been before getting pregnant.

*Or you just want to believe that.*

"What exactly did she say?"

Lynette pushed Tara's notebook toward Pete.

Pete hesitated, then took it. He believed in privacy, but not if one of his children was in danger. And he might well have missed signs that Tara was troubled. In the years since Megan's tumor had been discovered, almost all his and Lynn's energy had gone to seeking out doctors and treatment, struggling to pay the bills, and hanging onto their jobs. It wasn't fair, but they counted on Tara to take care of the other kids – not of Nate, who was nearly an adult himself – but Kelly and Bailey and even the day-to-day, non-medical parts of Megan's life. If Tara was falling apart, who could be surprised, given how she'd been rushed into adult responsibilities when she'd still been in high school. Pete didn't know what else he and Lynette could have done, how they could have managed without Tara and later Nate taking on many of the parenting burdens, but he felt he ought to have figured out something.

"Check out the bottom of that page," Lynette said. "I don't know how this happened without us seeing it. Even before she got pregnant, there must have been signs."

Pete read the last paragraphs, written in Tara's loopy scrawl, aloud.

> How can I believe I'm the mother of the next messiah when I'm not sure I believe there was a first one? But I'm really pregnant, and I never did anything to get pregnant. Unless I forgot, but how can you forget something like that? I barely slept this month. All I can think about is why this happened and what I'll do. And about Jeremy, and Vicki, and my family. Am I being punished for something? So bizarre that I don't feel sure I believe in any god, yet I'm afraid the Catholic God is punishing me. For some unknown thing since I actually stayed a virgin like you're supposed to, even if not for the "right" reason.
>
> Maybe I am crazy. All I can think is if this really happened to Mary, I don't know how she stayed sane, how she didn't just jump off a cliff somewhere or hang herself because I bet everyone reacted to her, if that story is real, the same way they are reacting to me. But, then, Mary supposedly had an angel who came to talk to her. I bet some guy just wrote that into the story so people wouldn't think about how hard it was for Mary, and so they didn't have to talk about how mad and scared she was.
>
> I think about what Cyril said, and sometimes I just feel exhausted and overloaded, like I'm sinking. Into what I don't know. Grayness. Darkness. All I wanted was to take care of the kids, finish college, start medical school, marry Jeremy. I've been doing everything I'm supposed to do, whatever Mom thinks. And yet here I am. And who knows about Cyril and these other religious people who supposedly believe all these things about this prophecy. Who knows if they are dangerous to me or a child if I had one. Am I doing this baby a favor carrying it to term? How am I supposed to know? And all Cyril's talk about a great battle. I don't want a battle. It is enough of a battle to get out of bed each morning and keep moving through the day with all this going on, and without Jeremy, and without Vicki. Some days I don't think it's worth it. Sometimes I'm afraid I'll just sink into nothingness or, worse, send myself there. Get some of the serious painkillers Megan had last year and just float away to nothingness.

Pete reread the passage, willing the words to be different, trying to quell the rolling in his stomach. The words raised more fears than he could face – that he might be close to losing his oldest daughter as well as his youngest, that Tara was imperiling her soul, both by what she believed about her child and by contemplating suicide.

He gripped Lynette's hands. "We need to call the psychiatrist."

# 13

"That figures," Tara said when the lights blinked out. "It's the third time it's happened this month. And I so don't feel like walking down nine flights of stairs."

Though Tara felt a little better after talking with Cyril – who knew why given that he'd only said things that were disturbing, but maybe it was just having someone to talk with – the mild nausea she experienced nearly all the time now worsened with bouncing. As she'd discovered when she'd played basketball the night before at one of SLU's gyms, trying to work off mid-finals stress and shake the dark mood she'd been in.

"Shhh." Cyril touched her elbow. She could barely see him. The locker pit lacked emergency lights.

Tara heard students swearing and people bumping into one another on the other side of the wall.

"Where's the closest stairway?" Cyril said.

Tara tensed at the urgency in Cyril's voice, though she couldn't see why the power outage disturbed him.

"Back the way you came in."

Cyril took her hand. "Lead me."

Tara felt her way along the metal lockers, which still held the cold from the recently-ceased air conditioning. The pulse in Cyril's thumb pounded against the inside of her wrist. "What is it?"

"Maybe nothing," Cyril said.

Tara's free hand hit open air, and she eased around the corner out of the pit. Cyril followed. An exit light glowed above the west stairway entrance across the hall, illuminating a few stragglers chatting near the elevators.

"And if it's something?" she said.

The stairwell door banged open. A man charged at Tara. His hooded sweat-shirt half-hid his face, making it a whitish blur. A knife glinted in his hand. Adrenalin surged through Tara.

"Run!" Cyril shoved Tara out of the way. Her shoulder and the side of her leg hit the door jamb. Pain shot through her knee, but she managed to stay on her feet.

Cyril bolted forward and shoulder-checked the assailant in the stomach. The man doubled over Cyril, groaning, but kept his grip on the knife. The two grappled, then the man broke away and lunged toward Tara. She sidestepped, but not quickly enough, and the knife slashed a line above her elbow. She spun, aiming a kick at the back of the man's knees and hitting his right calf instead. It threw him off balance. He stumbled into the wall and hit his forehead. When Tara kicked again, this time on target, he dropped to his knees, and his hood fell away. His hair looked red in the exit light's glow.

Cyril slammed his fists down on the back of the man's neck and knocked him to the floor.

Cyril looked at Tara. "There could be more."

Tara pushed past Cyril through the darkened locker pit, then into the east stairwell. In the emergency lighting, she could barely see the stairs. Blood trickled down her arm.

*That guy stabbed me. He stabbed me.*

No one had ever assaulted Tara. She felt outraged and vulnerable at the same time. And scared. At the same time, she felt more alive than she had in weeks. She did care what happened to her. And to the baby, wherever it had come from.

At the door to the stairwell, Tara hesitated, then jerked it open. She ran down three flights, gripping the railing, Cyril on her heels. A door screeched above them. Footsteps pounded. At the fourth floor, they exited near the language labs. Cyril scanned the lab, spotted a door stop, and wedged it under the door from the stairwell.

"Might slow him down for a minute," he said.

Tara led Cyril around the corner, past the administrative offices, and into the Women's Room. She knew the way, even in semi-darkness, because Vicki loved to sneak cigarettes here during class breaks. Stale smoke and the smell of chlorine hung in the air. Gray light bled through the frosted glass window at the far end of the restroom.

Banging came from the hallway behind them, like a body slamming into the door. Tara raced toward the window shoved it open, and climbed onto the fire escape. Cyril followed and shut the window.

They ran along the metal escape, down two flights, and across construction scaffolding into a service entrance of the building next door. With Cyril's footsteps clanging on the metal behind her, Tara couldn't tell if they were still being pursued, but she didn't pause or look back to find out.

Darkness shrouded this building's interior, too, but Tara found the side door that led to a musty hallway housing professors' mailboxes. Cyril grabbed Tara's hand from behind her and paused, listening. The sounds of voices and slamming doors came from other areas of the building, but no footsteps sounded nearby.

"Did we lose him?" Tara whispered.

"I hope so." Cyril wasn't breathing as heavily as Tara, but his words were clipped, as if it took extra effort to speak. "Let's go."

The early evening sun hit Tara's face when they exited the building into a courtyard. She wiped sweat from her forehead and the back of her neck. Her heart slowed some. The cut on her arm had started to scab, forming a sticky line about an inch long.

She turned to Cyril. "I've seen that guy. Around campus."

"But you never met him?"

"No. Who is he?"

Cyril shook his head. "Don't know. He seemed familiar to me, too. We should keep moving."

They hurried toward the trees along the courtyard's perimeter. Despite the foliage, Tara felt exposed. "You must have a guess as to who he is, where he's from."

"Brother Andrew foretold the Beast would take the form of man. So it could devour the virgin and her child before it was born," Cyril said.

A car alarm blared from the parking lot ahead, and Tara jerked her head toward it. She didn't see anything unusual.

"You think that was the Beast from Chapter 12, turned into a man?" Tara's doubts about Cyril's sanity flew back. She searched his face. Clear eyes, thin lines around his mouth, the faintest stubble across his chin and cheeks. He slowed his steps slightly and met her gaze, as if he knew what she was thinking.

"Do I think the Beast literally turned into a man? No. But do I think some men serve the Beast's purposes? No doubt they do."

Tara shivered. "And you think that was one of them."

"I don't know what else to think. The attack can't have been random." He glanced around. "Where's your car?"

"In a lot two blocks away."

"Good. That's where your attacker will wait. Can we get a bus?"

"To where?"

"Anywhere you're not expected to be."

Skirting the parking lot, they cut behind the auditorium/theater and emerged on Ninth Avenue. The plexiglass-enclosed bus stop did nothing to shield them from view. All around, Tara saw other people who looked like students. They wore jeans or khakis and toted backpacks.

Which didn't mean they were harmless.

Tara turned back to Cyril. "Suppose I believe there is a Beast. Or at least people who believe they serve a Beast. How can I fight that?"

"You don't. You can't, not now. You need to find holy ground. The prophecy says only on holy ground can you safely bear your child and vanquish the Beast."

"Holy ground? Where's that?"

"It's unknown. Some portions of Brother Andrew's papers were lost."

"Big help." Tara scanned the street again. The air seemed more humid and heavier than earlier in the day, and she struggled to take a deep breath. "If no one knows where it is, how can I find it?"

"Finding the holy ground is my job. That and helping you safely reach it, so you can have your child."

"And if we don't find it?"

"If the birth takes place elsewhere, it's foretold the Beast will position itself near the Virgin, perhaps in disguise, to devour her offspring after it's born."

Dizziness swept through Tara. She grabbed Cyril's arm to steady herself. Black spots danced in front of her eyes.

"Are you all right?"

She shook her head and blinked twice. Her vision cleared. "Sort of."

A bus churned to a stop in front of them. Without checking the route number, Tara and Cyril boarded. It smelled of greasy french fries and spilled coffee. Tara gripped the seat backs as she made her way to the rear of the bus where she'd be able to see everyone who got on. The bus bounced into a pothole and her nausea returned. She stumbled toward the last row. She felt as if her whole brain were about to short-circuit with everything Cyril had told her, not just today, but since the first time she'd met him.

Cyril sat next to her, back straight, head up. "I should have informed you of all this sooner. But I was afraid to upset you. Which was unprofessional of me. Your safety is most important."

The bus stopped. None of the new passengers even glanced Tara's way. "Are you a professional?" she asked Cyril. "And if you are, a professional what?"

"A soldier. First for our country, and now for the Lord."

The words sounded strange, but, at the same time, Cyril seemed more human than before. She liked his confidence that his chosen path made a difference in the world. That it was right for him. It was how Tara had felt about becoming a doctor. Still felt, she realized, even now when it seemed that goal had been pushed so far off. Whatever else Tara thought about Cyril, he believed in what he was doing.

"What does being a soldier for the Lord mean?" Tara asked.

"For the present, that I protect you."

"Because people want to kill me." Despite the burning where the knife had cut her, the words felt like lines in a play to Tara. She felt more removed than if she were acting, as if she were only watching herself speak instead of playing a part.

"Perhaps it'll reassure you to know I've been keeping surveillance on you, and this is the first attempt I've seen."

"It's reassuring. And somewhat creepy."

Tara peered out the window, trying to catch a street sign or building number. She wanted to be inside somewhere familiar, surrounded by walls, not windows, and people she knew, not strangers. Yet Cyril said that's exactly where she shouldn't be.

*Still, I barely know him, even if he did protect me back there.*

The bus jerked to a stop, and Tara's stomach lurched. Folding doors opened. Tepid air and exhaust swept in.

14th Street was the next stop. Tara had no idea what type of area that was, but acid was rising in her throat, and her stomach rumbled. Pretty soon her vomit would add to the French fry/coffee/exhaust ambience. She couldn't just ride the bus all evening anyway.

She stood. "I need to get out of here. I'm due at work at seven."

Cyril grabbed her hand. "You can't go there. Or anywhere familiar."

Tara pulled away. "I at least need to call in. And I need to talk to my family." A shadow passed over Cyril's face. "What? What's that look?"

"Don't count on your family to understand."

"My parents are all right."

"In Luke 12:51-53, Jesus said he came not to unite but to divide. 'They will be divided, father against son and son against his father; mother against daughter and daughter against the mother.'"

"Another Chapter 12." Tara pulled the cord to request a stop. Her throat felt dry, but she'd left her water bottle in her locker.

Cyril touched her arm. "At least let me stay with you. Keep you safe." His hand felt warm on Tara's skin. Comforting. But years of her mother's warnings about not being so trusting flashed through Tara's mind. When Tara was being fair, she had to admit her mother was more often right than wrong. It was part of what made her so annoying.

"I can't just take off with you. I hardly know you."

"Others will pursue you."

The bus swayed and slowed. Tara gripped the overhead bar. She felt too warm and was having trouble getting enough breath. A surge of anger toward Cyril flashed through her. She didn't know if it was pregnancy hormones or the entire bizarre situation, but all her warmth toward him for saving her life was burned away by anger over his cryptic words and his whole message. "How do I know you're any better than them? I have only your word on all this."

"My word and God's."

"Your word and what you say is God's."

They exited the bus. The area was filled with warehouses, some of which were empty, others under construction, being converted to condos. Despite the heavy traffic, Tara saw only two other pedestrians. *I should have gotten off somewhere more residential.* They crossed the street to the stop on the other side. Tara stared at the route map taped to the glass, looking for a place to go where she'd know her way around, but where she didn't spend a lot of time, so that no one would expect her to be there. But she couldn't concentrate on the map, the lines and words seemed to jump around.

"At least don't go home," Cyril said. "Go to a mall, or a movie theater, or a restaurant. Make your calls from a pay phone. I'll stay out of your way if you prefer. I'll just keep watch."

*Just pick somewhere.* Ignoring Cyril, Tara decided on the No. 7. It would take her to the public library on Olive Street. She loved the library, the smell of paper and books, the wooden carrels with the finish rubbed away from years of people resting their elbows on the desks and reading. With her school and work schedule so busy, the last time she'd visited was two years ago, so no one would expect her there. And there was a convenience store next door. She could buy some Gatorade and something to eat.

She looked at Cyril, the way he stood, straight, alert, gray eyes scanning the area, then returning to her. Did he really want to help? Was he crazy? Or both?

An SUV screeched around the corner. A gunshot cracked through the air, and Tara dropped to the ground.

# 14

Something pinched the back of Tara's hand. She tried to jerk away, but her arms seemed stuck to her sides. Her throat and chest felt tight. *Oh, God, I can't breathe.*

Tara's eyes felt glued shut. She opened her mouth and dragged in air. Smelled rubbing alcohol. She struggled to open her eyes. Could she be at a lab? Her back ached, but no sharp pains. Shoes clacked on a tile floor somewhere.

Flashes of the afternoon. Cyril following her onto a bus. Then nothing. Had Cyril done something to her? But there had been someone else, a man with a knife. Tara moved to sit, but her body felt weighted. She tried again to open her eyes. They fluttered. Bright light seeped in. She wasn't blindfolded then.

*C'mon, c'mon.* At last, Tara could see. A needle stuck into the back of her hand. Metal bars beyond her arm. *Bars?* She swung her head to the left. Pain. Harsh light. Then to the right. Bailey. Against a pale green background. Bailey. She must be okay, be somewhere safe. She let her breath out.

"Hey."

Bailey leaned close and whispered. "I talked the nurse into letting me come in even though visiting hours are over and she only wanted to let Mom and Dad in."

Tara licked her parched lips as relief surged through her. A hospital. Not great, but she wasn't a prisoner somewhere.

"Why am I here?" Something nagged at Tara, but she didn't know what. Some reason she shouldn't be in a hospital. She peered at the doorway beyond Bailey. It led to a white-walled hallway.

"You fainted," Bailey said. "At the bus stop."

"But I got on the bus." Tara pictured herself boarding the bus. But then what?

"The doctor said you have low blood sugar and you're dehydrated. Oh, yeah, and you're pregnant."

"I knew that."

"Are you and Jeremy getting married?" Bailey practically bounced in excitement.

Tara smiled, some of her tension ebbing despite the circumstances. "I doubt it, squirt. I don't even know how I got pregnant."

Bailey rolled his eyes. "Everyone knows how you get pregnant."

"No, I mean I don't remember doing anything I could get pregnant from."

"So it just happened? Out of nowhere?"

"More or less. No one believes me, though. Almost no one."

"I do," Bailey said. "Weird things happen all the time."

A shadow fell across Bailey, and Tara's eyes darted to the doorway again. Her heart thumped. But it was only her parents. They wore their work clothes – Pete in a collared gray shirt and dress pants, Lynette in a sweater and A-line skirt. Tara ought to be reassured seeing them, but she still felt anxious.

*Father against son and son against his father; mother against daughter and daughter against the mother.*

Where had the words come from?

"Honey. You're awake." Pete crossed the room and kissed Tara's forehead. She breathed in the combined scents – Safeguard soap, mint, and a hint of coffee – she always associated with her dad, and her eyes filled with tears.

Tara cleared her throat. "Bailey's keeping me company."

Handing Bailey two singles, Lynette said, "Why don't you get some soda."

Bailey snatched the bills and ran for the door. "Cool."

"How do you feel?" Lynette asked Tara.

"Not so bad," Tara said.

"What happened?"

"I don't remember everything. But Cyril met me at school."

"Cyril." Lynette frowned.

"Yeah. I wanted to ask more about the things he'd said. And the power went out and this guy – something happened." Tara shut her eyes, picturing the darkened hall, and felt her heart speed up. "This guy attacked us. But we got away somehow, and we got onto a bus."

The moment at the bus stop came back to Tara. She could hear the gunshot. Her eyes snapped open. "Oh my God. Someone shot at me. Did the police arrest anyone? Was it a man with red hair?"

Lynette stared at her. "Why would you think someone shot at you?"

"I heard it. It's the last thing I heard."

Pete rested his hand on her arm. His fingers felt warm. "The man who called the emergency room said he had a blowout when he turned the corner. He skidded past the bus stop and saw you faint. That's all."

"Really? Oh." Relief flooded through Tara. "Cyril was telling me people would come after me, and right then I heard the sound—"

"So this Cyril person was still with you?" Lynette asked.

"He was right next to me at the bus stop."

The bed sagged slightly as Pete sat down on its edge. Worry turned the corners of his mouth down. "I don't know anything about anyone named Cyril. The man who had the blowout said a school friend was with you, but he left for class when he saw you would be all right."

"That was Cyril."

"So you know Cyril from school?" Lynette said.

"No, no. He probably just said that. He's very secretive."

"I see." Lynette moved the Kleenex box aside and grabbed the Styrofoam pitcher on the bedside table. She poured Tara another cup of water. "He's not a very good friend if he took off right after you fainted."

"He's not a friend. I told you. I only met him once before. But he says people are after me, people besides this Brotherhood of Andrew."

Pete brushed Tara's hair away from her face. "You need to rest. And drink more water. We'll take care of everything."

"I don't see how you can." Ignoring the water, Tara hit the button to raise her bed. "Shouldn't we call the police? That guy at school stabbed me." Tara bent her arm to show them. A narrow bandage made a horizontal line above her elbow. "And Cyril was pretty adamant there would be others after me."

"The doctors said whatever it was didn't go very deep," Lynette said.

"You haven't seen anyone hanging around here, have you? In the waiting room, or the hall? A man with red hair?"

"No one," Lynette said.

Distorted voices from the hospital PA system came from the hall, and something banged the wall in the room behind Tara, making her bed shudder. It occurred to her that Cyril probably lurked somewhere in the hospital, keeping an eye out for her. Suddenly, that didn't seem so creepy.

"No one else at school saw anything unusual," her dad said.

"How do you know?"

"We talked to the dean."

"Well, the lights went out," Tara said. "What would anyone see?"

Pete opened his mouth, but Lynette shot him a look. "We'll figure it out," he said. "Don't worry. We need to go now, though. Nate's watching Megan, and he's got work in an hour."

After her parents left, Tara muted the TV in the hope she'd hear better if anyone approached her room, though she didn't know how she'd tell if it was a nurse or doctor or someone coming to harm her. She kept glancing toward the doorway whenever she heard footsteps, which happened often. Around eight-thirty, the lights dimmed, and the hospital noises dampened, but didn't disappear.

Dr. Lei, white coat open over her gray pin-striped pants suit, stopped in around nine. She told Tara she was on an IV with nutrition and hydration and took Tara's pulse. Her fingers felt warm around Tara's wrist.

"Tell me what happened," Dr. Lei said.

"It started at school."

Dr. Lei pulled the vinyl visitor chair closer to the bed and listened as Tara told the story. When Tara finished, Dr. Lei said, "So you feel Cyril is the only one who believes you?"

"He is the only one. Well, other than Bailey." Tara sipped water from her paper cup. She felt less parched than when she'd awakened, and she had more energy. "You and my parents believe I'm telling you what I think is the truth, but it doesn't make sense to you. Of course it doesn't."

"And it does to you?"

"No. But I'm not lying, and I'm sure I haven't repressed anything, and everyone else thinks it's one or the other."

Dr. Lei shook her head. "I don't."

"You don't?"

"No. I think we have an unexplained phenomenon, but we'll find an explanation." Dr. Lei leaned back in the chair and tapped her pen on Tara's chart. "This Cyril person concerns me, though. I'm not a psychiatrist, but he sounds delusional."

Tara kept an eye on the open doorway, half-expecting Cyril to appear at the mention of his name. Half-wishing he would, so she could hear his version of what happened after she passed out. And so someone would be watching out for her, and she could let herself sleep.

"Wouldn't you think I sounded delusional, too, if you didn't know me?"

"No. You harbor appropriate questions and doubts. And you are not threatening anyone, or prying into medical records, or spying on people."

Tara sighed. "I know. But I'm starting to think Cyril is trying to protect me, whatever else is going on."

"But what do you think of his theories?" Dr. Lei asked.

"At first I thought he was crazy. But until that second ultrasound, I just couldn't believe I was pregnant. I know, all those tests and everything, but it didn't seem real. Now it does, and he's the only one offering an explanation, even if it's a bizarre one."

"But you are not religious, am I correct?"

Tara stared at the blank TV anchored to the wall across from the bed and tried to order her thoughts. "No. Not in any traditional way. But there could be – I don't know – forces at work. I know that sounds ridiculous or New Agey, but I don't know what else to think."

Dr. Lei leaned forward. "This Cyril is Catholic, correct? Or at least Christian? He believes you're some kind of latter-day Mary, mother of Jesus."

"He's Christian. But he could be wrong and right at the same time, you know? Maybe some of what he knows is accurate, and some of it is wrong because it's so colored by his own beliefs."

A television clicked on next door and canned laughter filtered into Tara's room. Tara hit the button to raise the bed further and pulled her knees to her chest. It eased her sore back.

"So where does that leave you?"

"I wish I knew. I mean, let's say Cyril is crazy. There obviously could be other crazies focused on me, right, who are dangerous? And if he's not crazy, then there really are people trying to get me."

*Great, I don't sound too paranoid*, Tara thought. But it made her feel better to share her thoughts out loud, and she trusted Dr. Lei.

Dr. Lei sighed. "This is very complicated. Will you speak to the police?"

"They'll probably call me nuts. Even my parents don't quite believe anyone tried to stab me. But I think I need to."

"I've put down no visitors beyond your family and asked the nurses to keep watch for you." Dr. Lei stood. "I'm sorry I can't do more."

"You've been great. Thanks. I'm really glad you could come see me."

"Of course." Dr. Lei glanced at her chart. "One other thing. Your parents requested I send a report to Dr. Weggner, the psychiatrist who evaluated you when you first discovered your pregnancy. As an adult, it's up to you what I send him, or even whether I tell your parents anything."

Cyril had said something about family that Tara wished she could remember, but she couldn't bring it to mind. She still felt woozy. "Did they say why? The Dr. Weggner part, I mean?"

"They want to update him about your condition and see if it changes his opinion."

Tara frowned. "I doubt it will. According to my mother, his opinion is I'm lying."

"Did you read his report?"

"Sure. He concluded I wasn't suffering from repressed memory syndrome or any sexual trauma, so in the absence of other evidence, he thought a fabrication was the most likely explanation. Isn't that doctor-speak for 'She's lying'?"

Dr. Lei smiled. "Actually, it's doctor-speak for 'I can't explain it.' But it's up to you if you want me to send him a report."

"If it'll make my parents feel better, that's fine. They're really upset."

Dr. Lei gave Tara a form to sign, then said, "Your mother seemed quite anxious. I will fax it."

# 15

**Exhibit A to Petition for Appointment of a Guardian of the Person of Tara Spencer**

Mark Weggner, M.D., Ph.D.
St. Louis Psychiatric Associates
4800 Professional Drive, Suite 603
Kirkwood, MO 63119

Via Facsimile
St. Louis County Circuit Court
5th Floor, 7900 Carondelet
Clayton, MO 63105

Re:Tara Spencer

To the Honorable Presiding Judge:

I was asked to provide an opinion, to a reasonable degree of medical certainty, regarding whether the above patient presents a danger to herself and others. I reviewed the following records to form my opinion:

Admission notes from current hospitalization
Attending physician's report from current hospitalization
Copies of journal pages (provided by parents) from the date patient claims she first discovered her pregnancy through the present

Notes from patient's initial office visit at St. Louis Psychiatric Associates
Results of psychological testing performed by St. Louis Psychiatric Associates

Patient was hospitalized because, while waiting at a bus stop, she heard a car backfire, believed the sound to be a shotgun blast, and fainted. This most likely was precipitated not only by a fear-induced adrenalin surge, but also by low blood sugar and dehydration.

It appears the patient continues to be completely unable to accept responsibility for her pregnancy. While initially I interpreted her insistence that she knew nothing about how she became pregnant as a fabrication to protect her "good girl" image, it now appears to have progressed to a full-blown delusion. Patient believes that one of her school friends belongs to a secret religious society devoted to protecting her as the virgin mother of the world's next Messiah. In her journal, she expresses anxiety about this belief, and recognizes that the belief may mean that she is, in her words, "crazy." She particularly expresses concern that she will prove unequal to the task of protecting herself and her fetus and hints she may obtain an abortion or commit suicide. Her parents and medical providers report paranoid tendencies, including the belief that various unknown persons wish to harm her.

The patient also has expressed the view that she is "unworthy" to be the mother of a messiah, which may reflect a real fear that she is unworthy to be alive, given that she failed to meet her self-stated goal of completing college and marrying before engaging in sexual intercourse. Her actual actions are so contrary to her idealized image of herself that she may wish to rid herself of her physical being – the literal "flesh" that was weak.

Further, the patient claims she was assaulted during a power outage at St. Louis University, where she is a student. No one was able to verify this alleged assault. The admitting physician reports an inch-long cut on the patient's right arm consistent with a slash by a sharp implement such as a knife, scissors, or razor. Self-infliction of the wound, either to corroborate the patient's story or to alleviate inner turmoil, could not be ruled out. Also troubling is the patient's assumption that the sound of a car backfire actually was gunshot. This suggests the patient's inability to distinguish reality from fantasy.

Recommendation: Psychiatric hospitalization to evaluate patient's condition and rule out any self-destructive ideation.

I am available to testify in court if needed, but due to the demands of my practice, would prefer to provide an affidavit or sworn responses to interrogatories if that would be sufficient.

Very truly yours,
Mark Weggner, M.D., Ph.D.

# 16

"I think I'm doing it wrong." Megan struggled to her feet, pressing her hands on the bed for balance. Once tiny for her age, over the last two months, Megan's face and body had bloated from steroids, and she'd gained a third of her body weight, making her one of the largest eleven-year-olds in her class. Her whole left side had weakened from the tumor's growth.

Tara reached over when it looked like Megan might totter, then pulled back. Megan liked to do things herself.

"What do you mean?" Tara asked.

Nate had picked Tara up at the hospital when she was discharged and driven her to school for her second and third finals. Tara got through them, sucking down two liter bottles of water to make sure she stayed hydrated. Then she retrieved her car and drove home in time to sit with Megan while she said her prayers.

"Mrs. Morgan said she read about a boy with cancer who prayed every day and got cured. So she said I should try praying. And I do, all the time, but it's not working."

Tara felt a surge of anger at Mrs. Morgan and everyone who said such things, but she pushed the thought aside and hugged her sister. "Sweetie, I don't think it works that way. Like Dad told you, lots of people are sick and lots of them pray, and they don't all get better."

Megan eased herself onto her bed and looked at Tara. "Why not?"

"No one really knows. Some people get better and some don't, and it's not because of what prayers they say. That wouldn't be very fair, would it, when you think about it? I mean, what if some little kid didn't know how to pray, a good God wouldn't hold that against the kid, right?"

"Maybe God doesn't like me."

Throat tightening, Tara tucked Megan under the blankets, pretending to fuss with the folds of the sheet so she could move Megan's arm for her without it seeming like she thought Megan couldn't do it. "If there's a god, I'm sure he – or she – likes you fine. Maybe God just doesn't have that kind of power, but is rooting for you all the same."

It was a question Tara struggled with constantly. Was it better to reassure Megan there was a God with a capital G, a God who cared about her and could help her but just wasn't interceding for some mysterious reason? Or to suggest that maybe there was no god, that sometimes things just happened, and they all had to do their best to help each other?

"Like when I watch a Cardinals game and really hope they win? And cheer?"

"Yeah, maybe like that."

"That would be okay. God cheering for me."

"So no more worries about if you're praying right, okay? What book do you want?"

Megan chose *The Marvelous Land of Oz,* her favorite of the Oz series because the boy Tip turned out to be Princess Ozma, the proper ruler of Oz. Sitting in Megan's rocking chair, Tara read until Megan fell asleep, then switched on the nightlight, turned out the bedside lamp, and watched Megan sleep curled around her Snoopy doll. Her sister's even breathing soothed Tara, and she dozed.

Later, the sound of her parents' raised voices woke her. Tara blinked, unsure where she was until her eyes fell on the Oz book.

Her dad's voice sounded higher-pitched than usual, like it did when he felt nervous, or angry, or both. "We've talked about this. It's the only way to be sure Tara's safe."

Tara sat straight in the chair and set the book on the nightstand without a sound.

"I don't like the idea of the sheriff knocking on Tara's door tomorrow morning," Lynette answered. "I know the lawyer said that's how the petition has to be served, but it seems so cold."

*Sheriff?*

Tara crossed the room, inched the door open, and pressed her ear against its edge. The wood felt cool against her skin.

"What else can we do?" Pete said. "Nothing, and she goes somewhere and has an abortion? Or what if she slits her wrists? We can't risk that. We can't lose Tara, too. I won't take that chance."

"But we could talk to her first. Figure out if she's really at risk for suicide, really contemplating an abortion."

"And what if she lies and says she's fine, then takes off? After she's served, we can explain," Pete said. "She'll know we love her, she'll know we're doing what's best for her."

Tara put her hand on the doorknob. She needed to tell them she wasn't suicidal, or seriously contemplating abortion, just overwhelmed and scared. But her mother's next words made her freeze.

"Not many people go to a psych ward voluntarily."

"All the more reason not to talk to her until the process is started," Pete answered. "She'll understand eventually. But if we tell her now, she'll say whatever she thinks will change our minds, but we won't know for sure if she's all right or not." A chair scraped across the floor. "I'd better check on Megan. I promised I'd say goodnight when we got home."

Tara scurried to the corner and crouched behind Megan's stuffed animals, breathing in their dusty scent with her head down, struggling not to sneeze. Her dad cracked the door a few inches, then retreated. Tara stayed still until she heard both her parents head down the hall to their bedroom and bath.

The sound of running water started, and Tara rushed into the kitchen, heart racing as she searched the room for papers that might have come from a lawyer. Her parents kept Megan's medical records and all their tax and work files in a file cabinet in the corner, but she found nothing there. She didn't know anything about the law, but it sounded like they needed the sheriff to see her, to tell her something or do something.

How could her dad do this? Tara was used to her mother making unilateral decisions, but her dad was always willing to talk things through first. He'd hated how little input he'd had into his life as a child, how his parents had been unable to consider his feelings when it came to moving to advance his father's career. He must be panicked, overloaded with everything with Megan and Tara's pregnancy and hospitalization. But that did not make this all right. No way was Tara going into a psych ward somewhere.

Tara ran up the back stairs and through the inner door to her apartment. Someone sat at her table. She gasped, then realized it was Nate. He wore his jeans jacket and held folded papers.

"Where've you been?" Nate said.

"In Megan's room."

"Look, here's the thing. Mom and Dad— "

"I know, they want to send me to some hospital," Tara said.

"They're calling it a treatment facility." Nate handed her the papers. "Mom read your journal, and now they think you're a total loon and the only way to keep you and the baby safe is to get guardianship of you, then of the baby when it's born."

"She read my journal? That's so – how could she – and how could Dad –" Tara sank down at the table, then stood again. "This is insane."

"No shit. I looked for the papers after they left for their extraordinary ministers' meeting. Mom put them in the roll top desk."

"How can they do this? Yeah, okay, it's bizarre I'm pregnant and don't know how I got this way, but it doesn't make me crazy. And I might have been bummed when I wrote in my journal, but that's what a journal's for. You write when you feel bad, you write all the things you wouldn't say. It doesn't mean that I always feel that bad."

"They think you can't take care of yourself."

Tara unfolded the pages. "There's a hearing in 35 days." She flipped to the end of the petition. "Supposedly I'm unable to manage my affairs due to recent emotional trauma."

"Yeah, it says there's an Exhibit A, which is supposed to be that psychiatrist's report, but it's not there."

"At least I know what they're basing it on. And it doesn't say they're going to put me in a hospital." Tara looked through the pages again. Maybe her parents weren't planning to confine her right away, maybe that was a last resort.

Nate leaned forward. "But they said that was the point. I was about to start the drum machine, so I had the headphones on and they thought I couldn't hear them, and that's what they said."

Tara paced between the table and her kitchen counter. "I need to think. If I was put in the hospital, would I be able to get out? And just because they want to do this doesn't mean they'll be able to, right?"

"I guess. It says you have a chance to testify at the court hearing."

"So maybe I need a lawyer." Tara put one hand against the refrigerator to steady herself. She felt faint and short of breath. She needed to eat something, and drink something, though her stomach was churning. "But how am I going to sound? And who's going to take my case? I got pregnant and I don't know how it happened, this religious guy thinks it's some prophecy and I'm half-convinced by him. And I seriously doubt he'll come into court and testify. Crazy, that's what the judge will say."

"For what it's worth, I don't think they can lock you up just because you're crazy. You have to actually be a danger to yourself or someone else."

"Like a fetus? Could they say I'm endangering the fetus?"

"I don't know."

Tara got out a carton of orange juice. "Do we know any lawyers?"

"I don't."

"I'm trying to think who would." Tara drank her juice, then found some celery and cut it into pieces. It seemed like the easiest thing to get down. She offered some to Nate, but he shook his head.

"The rabbit food's all yours. Are you better? You look pale."

"I'm fine physically." Tara started pacing again. "I should make some calls. You should go, that way you won't have to hold back from Mom and Dad if they ask what I've been up to."

Nate hugged her and left down the back stairs. Tara reached for the phone and found six rolled up fifty dollar bills next to it. Tears came to her eyes. That was nearly two paychecks for Nate.

Tara paged Cyril, who called back in a few minutes.

"You said you can keep me safe," she said.

# 17

Construction sawhorses blocked one lane of Manchester Road, creating a steady stream of cars that meant it took Tara an eternity just to turn right. She kept glancing in the rear view mirror, afraid she'd see her mother's or dad's car behind her. Her backpack and duffel bag rested on the seat next to her. She'd divided Nate's cash and three hundred dollars of her own between her jeans pockets and her bags. Her wallet contained a driver's license Vicki had gotten for her when Vicki was twenty-one and Tara was twenty and they wanted to get into clubs. The license belonged to a girl named Laura Summers from Kansas who looked a little like Tara. She'd waitressed at the Turanos' restaurant one summer, and she'd let Vicki have the license in exchange for trading work nights a few times, saying she'd report it lost and get a new one. Tara didn't know if she'd need it, but it seemed like a good thing to have if she had to be anonymous for a while. Which seemed like a crazy thing to be thinking about, but lately everything in her life was crazy.

Tara checked the mirror again after she turned onto McKnight to head toward the expressway. The second or third time she looked, she noticed a green sedan behind her. It kept two cars back, but changed lanes when she did.

*I'm getting paranoid. But just because I think people are out get me...*

Instead of merging onto I-64/US-40 to go to the airport, Tara continued north on McKnight. The sedan followed. Afraid to pull over, Tara fumbled her cell phone out of her backpack, keeping her eyes on the road. She didn't like making calls while driving, but she dialed anyway. Cyril answered immediately.

"No, don't come here," he said after Tara told him about the car. "We need somewhere you can leave your car and get lost. Without being too obvious that's what you're doing."

Tara thought for a minute. "I know where."

After she and Cyril hung up, Tara took a side road, made a U-turn, and headed back for the expressway. The green sedan didn't follow, it kept driving north on McKnight. But after a few minutes, Tara saw it again behind her. If she hadn't been so nervous about having her fears confirmed, she would have felt insulted. Did whoever was following her think she was that unobservant? But maybe the person didn't care about being seen, either because the purpose was to scare Tara, or because of an overwhelming confidence that Tara couldn't get away. Which did scare her.

She finally reached downtown St. Louis, the sedan still behind her. She pulled the car in front of the Marriott hotel entrance to Union Station. The old train station housed not just the hotel but dozens of stores and restaurants. Many had closed during the recent economic slowdown, but enough people would be around to make the place fairly safe and public. And, even better, given her bags, whoever followed might believe Tara was actually staying at the hotel.

The valet took Tara's car and gave her a ticket. Inside, Tara hurried through the hotel's restaurant/foyer with its vaulted ceilings. Cyril had promised to make a reservation for her on line and, thankfully, when she asked at the desk, he'd been able to get a room. Tara trusted the clerk would not give out her room number, but she acted quickly once inside anyway.

"Even people who know each other well recognize one another mainly by clothes, hair, posture, mannerisms," Cyril had told her over the phone. "So change as much as you can."

Tara changed from sweats to khaki pants, from a purple T-shirt to a long-sleeved front-buttoned white shirt. She only had one pair of shoes, the gym shoes she wore, so she couldn't change those. But she transferred as many items as possible from her duffle bag to the hotel dry cleaning bag, then switched the straps on her backpack so she could carry it like a briefcase. Her last action was to twist her hair into a double-looped pony tail using rubber bands she'd gotten from the desk clerk.

Tara left her empty duffle bag in the room. Then she took the elevator to a higher floor and wandered the halls, not wanting to stay in her room, but not wanting to leave earlier to be obvious about it. When an hour had passed since she'd checked in, she called Cyril, gave it five more minutes, then took the elevator down past the lobby floor to the level with the bagel shop. From there, she strolled to the other side of the mall, glancing in store windows, but resisting the urge to look around and behind her to see if anyone followed. The mall was fairly empty, as it was past nine, but a few people wandered through.

Outside, Tara headed toward the MetroLink entrance. The train could take her to the airport, but she spotted a sporty looking car that blinked its lights three times. Tara headed for the car and hopped in.

"I didn't see anyone following you," Cyril said.

"Nice car." Tara felt her shoulders relax a bit as Cyril clicked the locks. The car's interior smelled of leather and air freshener. "What kind is it?"

"Monte Carlo. I rented it. After your experience, I figured my vehicle might be known." Cyril looked her over. "And you look different. Good."

"Everything you know about intrigue – what branch of the service were you in?"

Cyril laughed. "Just the regular army. But I joined a private security firm after my discharge."

"I guess studying to be a deacon doesn't pay much."

"It doesn't pay anything."

The Monte Carlo accelerated smoothly. Tara looked in the side view mirror and saw no one behind them.

"So do you finally believe the origin of your pregnancy is divine?" Cyril asked.

Tara pulled out the rubber bands, wincing as strands of her hair got caught. "It's the most plausible explanation anyone's offered. But I don't buy it, not really. Because it wouldn't be me. If there were a mother of a divine messiah, it wouldn't be me."

"Why not?"

"I'm pretty sure I'm an atheist."

Cyril shook his head. "You're still finding your path. Nothing's wrong with that."

"That's so condescending." Tara frowned. It was the same thing her dad insisted on saying all the time. "If I said I was religious, you wouldn't tell me I'm still finding my path. But if I'm an atheist, I must still be searching."

"I didn't mean it that way. I'm always searching." Cyril touched her hand. Tara felt surprised, but she didn't pull away. After a second, Cyril returned his hand to the wheel.

"Looks like we're still alone," he said, glancing in the rear view mirror.

Tara looked over her shoulder. "Looks like it."

She studied Cyril as he drove. He was good-looking, especially with those intense eyes, and Tara appreciated his help, but she wasn't sure about his motives. Or what she thought of Cyril overall. Maybe if they'd met some other way, if Jeremy hadn't just broken up with her.

*Or if I wasn't pregnant. But then we never would have met in the first place.*

It was too strange to think of Cyril in a romantic way, and she felt sure he hadn't meant it that way. He was just reassuring her. It was only that it was uncharacteristic. Other than when they'd been running through the school, Cyril had kept his distance from her physically.

"Your actions are what matters," Cyril said. "Not what you believe. The way you care for your brothers and sisters shows the type of person you are. And that you've had the strength of character to stay a virgin despite a sex-saturated world."

"That wasn't a religious thing. When I was like, eleven, my mom sat me down and gave me the birth control talk. And part of it was which method of birth control she and my dad were using – or, in my case, she and my biological father – when they conceived each one of us kids."

Cyril raised his eyebrows. "Your parents didn't want children, and they had five?"

"No, they wanted kids. Obviously." Tara stretched her arm, working out a kink in her elbow from carrying her backpack at an odd angle. "They just meant to space them out more. Or maybe not have so many, I don't know. But I got her point –if you really don't want children, if you want to be sure, you either do something permanent about it, or you don't have intercourse."

The green Lambert sign, its airplane symbol glowing white in the headlights, loomed ahead. Cyril followed the exit and looped into the main terminal.

Inside the terminal, Cyril suggested they stop for something to eat, as it would be a while before they would have time to eat anywhere again. Plus, he needed time to figure out the best next step. Tara's stomach didn't feel ready for real food, but she thought Starbucks might work.

As they ordered, Tara kept glancing behind her. One whole side of the Starbucks was open, so twenty people could rush in as easily as one, and she'd never even hear a door open. She and Cyril sat side-by-side at a table near the condiments stand, backs to the wall, watching the terminal.

Cyril took the top off his expresso, but his eyes kept scanning the terminal. "So, if you're not sure about the divine nature of the pregnancy, why come to me?"

"I've got nowhere else to go."

He smiled. "That's not saying much for my powers of persuasion."

"You should do that more," Tara said. "It makes you look younger. And nicer."

Cyril's expression went flat again.

"I meant that as a good thing." Though she didn't feel hungry, Tara ate the apple slices from her fruit and cheese plate. She couldn't afford to pass out again. "Anyway, Vicki's in New York, and even if she wanted me to visit, that's the first place my parents will look. Jeremy's not speaking to me. My friends away at school don't even know I'm pregnant. It'd be a lot to throw at them."

"You have credit cards?"

"Card. A Visa with too much on it already."

"Paying your Visa bill is the least of your worries."

"Somehow, that's not very comforting."

Tara glanced around the Starbucks again, not sure what she was looking for. She hadn't seen the face of the man who'd charged her in the hall, or of the driver of the green sedan. And how much her appearance changed based on her clothes and hair showed just how hard it would be for her to recognize the red-haired man again if he made even a minimal effort to change his appearance.

"So your parents would expect you to stay with Vicki?" Cyril said.

"Yeah." Tara stirred her Chai latte, inhaling its spicy cinnamon scent. "Or my aunt in Iowa. Or my grandparents, but they're right here in town."

"All right," Cyril said. "Here's what you do."

# 18

"Maybe I should try again to explain to my parents," Tara said as she and Cyril left the Starbucks. "You could help."

"Too much risk," Cyril said. "A moving target is harder to find, harder to hit. If you land in a hospital, anyone determined enough can get to you."

"Did someone really try to shoot me on the street?" Tara said. "My parents said it was a tire blowout."

"The car really had a blown tire. Whether that was meant to be a distraction so someone could abduct you, I don't know."

They walked outside, and Cyril squeezed Tara's shoulder. "You're on your own for a while. Be careful."

Tara looked all around and behind her as often as she could as she made her way to the Southwest Terminal. There, she bought a ticket to New York with a stop in Chicago. In the security line, she almost took out the Laura Summers license, then thrust it back into her wallet at the last minute, giving the guard her own license with her boarding pass.

Clutching the boarding pass inside the gate area, Tara slipped into the Ladies' Room. A few minutes later, in her sweats and T-shirt again, with her hair pulled back, she exited the other door. She didn't notice anyone following her or even watching her, but she felt uneasy.

The Monte Carlo idled in the ten minute parking area. Cyril popped the trunk as she approached, and Tara dropped her hotel laundry bag and backpack inside and hurried to the passenger side to get in. Another chai latte sat in the cup holder. Tara wasn't sure when Cyril had found time to get it, but she sipped the sweet drink, calmed by the taste and its warmth.

"Where are we headed?"

"Branson." Cyril swung the car into traffic and drove toward the expressway.

Tara stared at him. "Where the country music is? And the theme parks?"

"It's a good place to get lost."

As Cyril turned onto the main road, Tara peered through the rear window. No one behind them. Tara felt her shoulders loosen a little, and she leaned back in her seat and cracked the window.

It had rained the day before, and the breeze brought in the smell of wet dirt and field grass. Cyril set his GPS. "Watch for the Tulsa exit."

"You know it's over 250 miles to Branson."

Cyril shrugged. "It'll take about 4 hours."

"What happens when we get there?" Tara asked.

"We hide," Cyril said. "I stay with you, keep you safe, and we figure out where the holy ground is."

"Hiding was pretty much my plan. I was hoping you had something more specific." Tara spotted the Tulsa exit. "There it is."

Cyril changed lanes. "I know how to hide. And how to search."

"You do have actual maps, right? Because I've found GPS not that reliable in some areas."

"I have actual maps."

As they drove, the vehicles around them and the streetlights on either side of the highway grew farther apart. Soon, blackness flanked the road. Tara felt safer then, as if she'd be harder to find in the dark. One set of headlights glowed far behind them.

"Was it your sister?" Cyril said.

Tara shifted her eyes away from the side view mirror and looked at Cyril. "What?"

"Many people drift away from their church, but they don't stop believing in God altogether unless there's some particular reason. I was wondering if it's because of what happened to Megan."

"You mean how could there be a god who would let a little kid get a brain tumor?" Tara said.

"It's a legitimate question."

"It wasn't exactly that. My parents never raised us to believe that having faith in God meant everything would go your way if you just prayed or were a good person."

"But?" Cyril said.

"I started thinking. I used to reconcile terrible things happening with the idea that maybe God was all powerful, but sort of hands off. You know, created the world, then stepped back to see what we could do in it, cheering us on from the sidelines."

A flatbed truck loaded with lead pipes closed in on the Monte Carlo, then moved to the left.

Cyril glanced out the side window and slowed the car slightly so the truck could pass more easily. "That's not being an atheist."

"No, it's not. And that's not what I believe now. After Megan was diagnosed, and I watched her hair falling out, and then saw her get all swollen with the steroids, I started being more aware of the awful things that happen to kids. I must always have heard things, but now it really caught my attention. Like that news story last year about a father dropping his son in a tub of boiling water as a punishment. And I thought, at least Megan knows the people around her love her, and she knows what happened to her was chance or bad luck, which sucks, but no one gave her a brain tumor on purpose. Then I would read about kids in Africa being born HIV positive and dying within a few months of AIDS. I mean, what is the point of that?"

The flatbed truck moved in front of Cyril.

"I couldn't reconcile it," Tara said. "An all-powerful god, who is good, couldn't not step in. Because you can't justify that as the child's free will, and there can't be anything those children could have done that brought those horrible things on themselves. And, if a god existed and was perfect, that god couldn't create a world where those kinds of things happen. I'd rather think no god than one that is okay with this world."

Another truck rumbled behind them.

"I see these things as the work of the Beast," Cyril said.

Tara shook her head, flicking her eyes between the truck in the mirror and the one ahead of them. *It's just two trucks on a highway. Nothing to worry about.*

"But if God's all powerful and all good," she said out loud, "he could knock out Satan. Or wouldn't have created a Satan in the first place."

"Satan is meant to challenge us. To test us."

"What kind of god sets up tests by destroying babies and letting Satan influence a father to boil his kid alive? Not one I want to worship."

Cyril rubbed his forehead. "God's ways are different than ours."

"Okay, but I could say that about anything. I could say—"

The truck behind them accelerated. The car swerved as Cyril jerked the wheel to the left. Tara gripped the armrest with one hand and pressed the other against the dashboard. The flatbed moved in front of Cyril's car, jettisoning pipe onto the freeway.

"Shit." Cyril swung the Monte Carlo across two of the opposite lanes of traffic to avoid the truck and the pipes. An SUV bore down on them, horn blaring, brakes screeching. Cyril maneuvered to the shoulder just in time, the Monte Carlo rattling across the rough pavement. In the other lanes, the smaller truck skidded, trying to avoid the pipes, but the flatbed truck kept rolling. As soon as traffic allowed, Cyril made a U-turn and sped back the way they'd come. Tara watched taillights of the two trucks diminish in the side view mirror.

"Deliberate, that had to be deliberate, right?" Tara said.

"It didn't look accidental. We need to get off this road."

"But to where?"

"I'll figure something out."

"You think they knew we were heading to Branson?"

Cyril shook his head. "I don't see how. That was entirely my idea, I didn't tell anyone. Not even my superiors. But we were spotted. We need a different car."

"Can you get one?"

"It'll slow us down, but yes."

Cyril's jaw was clenched, his neck stiff as he gripped the wheel. Tara didn't want to distract him, so she stared out the window, heart still pounding. Orange mile markers along the side reflected the Monte Carlo's headlights, flashing hypnotically. The rear view mirror showed only empty road behind them.

Cyril turned on the radio. A violin and oboe concerto filled the car. Tara didn't care for classical music, and she felt too wired to imagine she'd ever sleep again. But the music soothed her, and she'd been awake over twenty hours. After a time, she drifted off, hunched against the passenger door.

About an hour later, she woke with a cramped neck, alone. The car stood still. Tara peered out the window. They were on a stretch of road lined with warehouses. Cyril – she hoped it was Cyril – was about half a block from her, exiting a car a little smaller than the Monte Carlo. Tara opened her door, hearing nothing but crickets. She wondered how far they were from the highway. Cyril waved her over.

"Where'd you get this?" Tara asked, getting into the front passenger seat. It was a Toyota and it smelled like new leather.

"Don't ask," Cyril said. "Lock the doors, I'll be right back."

He drove the Monte Carlo into a loading dock of a warehouse, jumped back in with Tara, and started the Toyota. Tara studied Cyril as he piloted the car back to the expressway. He stared forward, eyes on the road. Even in profile, he looked so sure about everything, so focused, though he must have been shaken by the truck incident.

"Maybe I should call my parents," Tara said. "Tell them I'm okay."

"They won't be missing you yet," Cyril said. "And it's a bad idea. The location of a cell phone can be traced."

"Right, but my parents won't know how to do that."

"They're not the ones I'm worried about."

"Who are these people who are after me? The red haired man, the trucks."

"Agents of the Beast."

"But who are they specifically? And what do they want?"

Cyril sighed. "I don't know. Whoever left that fetus seemed to be trying to spook you, not harm you. The man with the knife probably wasn't trying to kill you or a gun would have been used. But now it seems things have escalated. Though the trucks also could be more for show."

"All to scare me?"

"Possibly. Perhaps into ending this all by having an abortion."

Tara looked back at the window and saw nothing but her own ghostly reflection. "That would solve so many things."

"But you never considered it."

"Of course I did. The pregnancy didn't even seem real to me, so terminating it would just be putting things the way they should be."

Cyril turned the radio down. "Do you still feel that way?"

"No. Whatever the reason for this baby, I love it. And my brothers and sisters will love it, and my parents will, even if I'm pissed at them right now. So it – she – won't be alone and unloved."

"She?"

The car swerved.

Tara tensed, peering out the windows to see if any another truck had come near them, but no one else was on the road. "What happened?"

"Nothing. Hit a bump." Cyril gripped the wheel with both hands and straightened the car. "You said 'she'?"

"Yeah. At the ultrasound, the doctor could tell, the baby's a girl."

"He was certain?"

"The doctor's a she, too. She was certain, yeah. Why?" Tara studied Cyril. His expression seemed more grim than usual, his mouth a straight line.

"That can't be," he said.

"Of course it can. It is."

Cyril changed into the center lane. "I didn't expect this."

"What? That I'd have another ultrasound?"

A sign notified them the next exit was twelve miles away.

"That your baby would be a girl."

"So?"

Cyril glanced in the rear view mirror, then merged into the right lane. "If your child is a girl, I can't help you."

# 19

Cyril forced his expression to remain flat as he considered what Tara had just told him. He longed for time to think this through without Tara in the car with him, but that was impossible.

"Let me get this straight," Tara said. "First you convince me I'm part of this ancient prophecy, and my life is in danger, and you're the only one who can protect me, and I tell my family and they think I'm crazy and want to lock me up, and it looks like my life really is in danger, and now, because I'm having a girl, you're saying 'oops, sorry, it was a big mistake'?"

"I don't know. This was never covered. We never discussed whether the – " Cyril stopped, uncertain what he could tell Tara now. If she wasn't the Virgin, she shouldn't know anything about the Brotherhood. Which meant he'd already said far too much.

He took the off ramp for St. Clair.

"What are you doing?" Tara said.

The ramp led to an unlit local road. Cyril focused on the white lane markings shining in his headlights, glancing away only to check the mirrors for other vehicles. There were none. He didn't look at Tara. He'd miscalculated. His mentor and immediate superior, Thomas Stranyero, had warned Cyril not to talk to the girl too soon, not to reveal anything until the Brotherhood was sure. But Cyril had felt sure.

He shouldn't say any more, but he owed it to Tara at least to explain what was happening. Or, more accurately, what wasn't.

"Chapter 12 is clear," he said. "The woman shall have a male child who shall rule the earth."

A green and yellow BP sign cast the only light in an expanse of darkness.

The unpaved frontage road leading to it made the Toyota shudder. Cyril tightened his grip on the steering wheel.

"It also says the woman will wear a crown with twelve stars, and it doesn't say the woman's a virgin," Tara said. "Obviously, there's some room for interpretation."

"Twelve stars is figurative. The virgin is part of Brother Andrew's prophecy. But male is male. There's nothing figurative about that."

Cyril gripped the steering wheel. *Why did I assume her child was a boy?*

But he knew the answer. Tara fit his image of the messiah's mother. Of any mother, the perfect mother. In taking evasive action at the university, she'd shown quick wittedness, intelligence, strength and courage. Knowing how she cared for her siblings, he harbored no doubt she could and would protect any child she bore, and herself, which would be vital in the coming months. Or would have been, if she'd been the one. She'd stood firm in the face of her boyfriend's disbelief, had gone her own way rather than shading the truth or having an abortion.

*Thomas put so much trust in me.*

"This is crazy," Tara said. "I'm not in a rush to be part of an apocalyptic prophecy, but you were convinced."

"I didn't know the facts. I'm sorry. I can't tell you how sorry."

The air inside the car had become stifling. Cyril buzzed his window down and a damp hay and manure smell swept into the car.

"And what about these people coming after me?"

The smell of gasoline mixed into the air as the car approached the station.

"It may be unrelated. Or they're mistaken, too." Cyril gritted his teeth. To his own ears, his explanations sounded forced. And false. But the prophecy was clear, the Virgin's child was to be a boy. And now not only had he failed in his duty to find the true Virgin, he might have put Tara in danger by focusing on her. "Or they followed me and believed what I believe. I put you in danger."

Once Cyril pulled into a parking spot, he couldn't avoid looking at Tara any longer. She'd twisted sideways in her seat and was glaring at him, her shoulder belt still strapped across her.

"Are you leaving me here?" she said.

"Of course not. I'm reporting for instructions."

Cyril didn't want to leave her alone, not when others seeking to harm her might still be near, yet she must not hear his conversation. He asked her to wait in the car with the engine on, windows closed, air running. He stepped outside, and clicked on his cell phone. Cyril suspected he'd be told to take Tara home or to the airport to get her car. *But maybe she's right*, he thought, as he punched in his mentor's private number. The text's specification of the child's gender might not be crucial. It might be an outgrowth of the times when it was written, when no one imagined a female ruling the earth.

Only one other car idled in the station lot, a red Honda Accord in front of the premium pumps. Cyril watched the driver, a middle-aged woman in sweats and a windbreaker, reholster the gas nozzle and unlock her vehicle. The woman appeared harmless, but appearances could be deceiving.

Thomas Stranyero answered on the second ring. Cyril explained the situation, keeping his voice neutral. A soldier, at least one at his level, must want what's best for the world and express no desires of his own. Better still, he must harbor no desires. Or fears.

"I'll discuss it with the Order," Thomas said. He raised his voice, but he sounded tired. Cyril had known Thomas fifteen years, since the day Cyril approached Thomas about becoming an altar boy, and he heard disappointment in his mentor's tone. "Find somewhere safe to pass the night. I'll contact you in the morning."

"Yes, sir." Hoping Thomas would offer encouragement or consolation, as he so often had through the years, Cyril waited to see if Thomas would say something more. But the line went dead.

Cyril closed his phone. At least Thomas hadn't rejected Tara out of hand. So Cyril still had a chance. If Tara was the new messiah's mother, he'd be with her, on the front line of battle. He'd help her rise, and he'd prove his worth to Thomas, repay him for everything he'd done.

*Please God. Let her be the One,* Cyril prayed, then realized what he'd said. *Your will be done*, he amended. *Now and forever.*

Cyril opened the car door and leaned in. "Nothing will be decided until tomorrow. We'll need to find a motel." He nodded toward the mini-mart. "Do you need anything?"

"I'll come in with you."

The night had grown warm enough that Cyril pulled his sweatshirt off. His body relaxed slightly at the feel of the humid air across his bare arms.

"So you just take orders." Tara walked through the door to the mini-mart. "You don't make decisions?"

"I'm not at that level."

Cyril also didn't trust himself to decide, but he didn't tell her that, just followed her through the door. And tried not to think how much he'd miss her if Stranyero ordered him to cut contact tomorrow.

THE RINGING WOKE TARA. She sat bolt upright and peered into the dark. Gray light filtered through the closed blinds, barely illuminating the chest of drawers and the fifteen inch TV on top of it. Cyril's muffled voice came from the adjoining room. Tara glanced at the clock radio. 5:30. She felt amazed she'd fallen asleep at all. Cyril's sudden change of heart not only left her nowhere to go, it hurt. She hadn't realized how much he'd begun to matter to her until now, when he seemed ready to bail.

As quietly as she could, Tara slipped out of bed, crept across the room, and pressed her ear to the door that separated her room and Cyril's. She'd left most of her things packed. If Cyril refused to help her further, Tara would find answers some other way. Cyril could drop her off at the nearest bus or train station, because she wasn't going home.

"Yes, sir," Cyril said. "I understand. Straight to the house."

*Damn*. Tara reached for the light switch, then stopped. The light would filter under the door and Cyril would know she was awake. And it didn't sound like he'd be willing to take her anywhere but home. She couldn't believe he was agreeing to that. He was no more trustworthy than Jeremy. Or Vicki, whom she'd thought was her friend.

She waited to see if Cyril said anything else.

"Where do I report after....I see...Does that mean there's still hope... No, sir. If the order later is to terminate, it won't be a problem ...But, sir, I must report that I cannot see her as an agent of...Of course...Yes, sir, I know, sir. Satan appears in many pleasing guises."

Tara backed from the door. *Terminate? Me? The pregnancy?* Tara stumbled toward the armchair next to the bed, feeling her way. She couldn't hang around to find out what Cyril's organization meant to do, whether it now saw her as an agent of Satan or of the Beast, or just as a liar. Still wearing her T-shirt and underwear from the night before, she yanked on her jeans and sweatshirt.

Cyril knocked on the door.

Tara froze.

He knocked again.

She had to buy time. "Hm??"

"Wake up."

"Huh?" She slid her hand along the nightstand, ran into her cell phone, and stuffed it into the front pocket of the backpack.

"I need to take you back home."

"Why?" She pulled on her socks and tennis shoes.

"I made a mistake. I'm sorry. I shouldn't have gotten so carried away without knowing all the facts."

*He couldn't sound so calm when he'd just been told he might have to kill me, could he? Maybe he just meant terminate the mission to protect me.*

"You're sure it's a mistake?" Tara tiptoed into the bathroom and grabbed the sample shampoo, soap and conditioner, still wrapped. Who knew when she might need them. She took a washcloth and hand towel, too.

"The Brotherhood is sure. We need to go back."

"All right. I guess. Give me a few minutes."

*The Brotherhood is sure. So he's not. But he'll do what they say. He said it himself. He doesn't make the decisions.*

Tara turned on the lamp and scanned the room, looking for anything else she'd unpacked, but she'd been too tired the night before to do much more than brush her teeth and drop into bed. She scurried back to the bathroom and turned on the shower. Cyril might not like waiting for her to finish bathing, but she was pretty sure it would be some time before he barged in.

Outdoor fluorescent lights cast a greenish glow over the parking spaces outside the Super 8 Motel, but left the walkways in darkness. A generic looking silver Toyota Camry sat in the spot right in front of Cyril's room, so she guessed that was the car they'd ridden in the night before. She hadn't gotten a good look at it in the dark. It did Tara no good regardless without the keys.

The air chilled her hands and neck. She zipped her sweatshirt and hurried toward the street. It seemed to be a main road, with two lanes on each side and one and two-story buildings lining it. Tara paused at the intersection. She couldn't believe all the things that had happened in the last two days, in the last two months.

*Don't think about it. Just move.*

A bus or train was what she needed, but she had no idea where to find one. Nothing looked open except a restaurant two doors down, and she bet that would be the first place Cyril would look, after the motel office to see if she'd asked any questions.

A truck barreled past. Tara had never hitchhiked and, as much as she wanted to get away from Cyril, she didn't risk it now. She'd rather take her chances with disappearing from her parents' house again, or even from a mental hospital, than getting picked up by a rapist or murderer. But she couldn't just stand here.

Tara tried to think where Cyril would expect her to go. Toward the highway, probably. She jogged the opposite direction for five blocks, her plastic hotel bag and backpack over her shoulders, then turned down a tree-lined side street. After another block, she turned again, onto a road with no streetlights. At least she was away from the main thoroughfare if Cyril drove along it looking for her, but she had no destination. Pushing down panic, Tara slowed to a brisk walk and felt in her backpack for her cell phone, a pen, and her notebook. She sat on a curb, shielding herself between a parked pickup truck and a sedan, and dialed 411 to get the phone numbers for the closest Greyhound and Amtrak stations.

If Tara had a newer phone with web access, she could have accessed MapQuest. Instead, she called both stations and asked for directions, thinking the whole time about Cyril's comments on tracing cell phones. Both stations were too far to walk to, though she was in good shape. She could take a local bus line to the Greyhound. Tara half-walked, half-jogged toward the stop that would take her there, thoughts racing. She stayed on side streets instead of the main road so she wouldn't be as visible, but kept looking over her shoulder for Cyril's Camry. A few houses had lights on, and now and then she heard a car starting or doors slamming. Birds, hidden by the tree branches overhead, chirped as the sky turned from black to sooty gray.

Tara didn't plan to get on a Greyhound, just make an appearance, buy a ticket for whatever bus left next, and let Cyril think that's where she was going. Then she'd come back later and get a ticket to her real destination. She'd covered four blocks when she heard an engine accelerate as if the car had just turned a corner and was picking up speed. While Tara couldn't see any headlights, she scrambled to the side of the road. The sound grew louder, and she dived under a parked SUV, pulling her bags after her.

The smell of asphalt in her nose, Tara peered at the street. A silver Camry, lights off, cruised toward her.

# 20

The car had to be Cyril's, though Tara couldn't see the driver in the gray morning light and didn't remember the license plate number. She couldn't imagine why anyone else would drive so slowly, lights off. Frozen, Tara watched the Camry approach, wondering if Cyril had some sort of portable device for tracking her cell phone. It seemed crazy, but at the moment, damp street under her belly, nothing seemed impossible.

The seconds Tara lay under the SUV stretched to infinity. But the Camry passed her at last, and she let out her breath as she listened to it continue down the street. The bus station was out, Cyril probably had come this way figuring that might be her destination. She needed a better plan. Or any plan.

When Tara'd started college, her mother had given her a book about avoiding dangerous people and situations. Annoyed as she was that her mother didn't think she could figure these things out for herself, she'd read it. It said that, if a person needed help, it was better to ask someone at random than rely on anyone who offered, because the likelihood that a random person wanted to cause harm was small. The other advantage to random was Cyril wouldn't be able to anticipate her actions.

After another fifteen minutes under the SUV, Tara eased out and hurried back the way she'd come. She stayed near parked cars so she could hide underneath again, listening for any engine noises. The growing sunlight made her nervous.

As she walked, she examined the houses around her. What she needed was someone who would let her call a cab or, even better, drive her a few towns over so she could catch a bus or train, because cab fare would use so much cash. Which meant someone who didn't have to rush off to work. Or, if she could stowaway in someone's car, she could catch a ride to that person's office and hope she could get a cab from there. That seemed iffy, though, and what if the office turned out to be near the motel? Cyril might circle back there and see her.

Houses with kids' toys in the driveway or swing sets in back seemed promising. Tara looked, too, for ones with pretty curtains, neat lawns, and uncluttered porches. She guessed those were most likely to have moms home during the day.

For a while she crouched near a station wagon in front of a brick ranch, the dew on the grass seeping into her tennis shoes and jeans, chilling her skin. The clock on her cell phone read 6:30, a little early to wake anyone she hoped would be a Good Samaritan, though she couldn't wait much longer. Tara could call Nate or Kelly, either would be willing to pick her up, but it would be a six hour drive round trip and neither could pull that off without her parents noticing. The only friend close enough to drive that far, no questions asked, was Vicki, and she was gone. And Jeremy, obviously also out of the question.

Tara's phone rang, this time showing her parents' number. Tara muted the ring and clicked off the phone.

At quarter to seven, Tara rang the doorbell of the ranch house. No answer. At a second house, the babysitter expressed sympathy for Tara, but said she couldn't let anyone in or take the kids anywhere.

A woman about ten years older than Tara answered the door of the bungalow on the corner. She wore an ironed white T-shirt and gray running pants. Beyond the woman, Tara saw a black lacquer bookcase with glass shelves. That and the foyer's sage green walls reminded Tara of her father's meditation room. She hoped that was a good omen.

"Hi, um, my name's Tara Spencer, and I'm wondering if I could use your phone to call a cab." Tara figured it was a risk to share her name, in case Cyril somehow tracked her to this house, but if someone asked her for help, she'd feel better if the person at least introduced herself. "I'm a SLU student and I was on a car trip to Branson with a guy I've known for a while, and I discovered he's kind of violent. So I took off when he thought I was showering, and now I need to get to a train or bus station. We were driving in his car."

The woman looked Tara up and down. "Did he hurt you?"

Tara shook her head. "No. But from some of the things he said, I felt like he was going to." Tara's throat tightened as she spoke. She still couldn't believe she was talking about Cyril.

"You were smart to leave." The woman opened the screen door. "Come on in. My name's Shevawn Garner." Shevawn gestured to Tara to follow her through the front room. "Did he figure out you're gone yet?"

"Yeah. He called my cell phone, but I didn't answer." Tara crossed the dining room's polished hardwood floors. The mahogany table and built-in buffet stood uncluttered.

*She must not have kids*, Tara thought. But twin girls wearing identical Cardinals caps and jerseys sat eating Cheerios at the kitchen's gleaming Corian breakfast bar. Tara guessed the girls about four. They smiled at her.

"Have you had breakfast?" Shevawn opened the stainless steel refrigerator door. "I have plenty of juice, and I can make you some toast."

"That'd be fantastic. Thank you." Tara sank onto a counter stool. Her legs had been shaking, probably since she'd run from the hotel room. She gulped the glass of orange juice Shevawn handed her.

"This guy sounds like bad news."

"Yeah, I'm getting that idea. Which is why I need to get as far from him as possible."

Shevawn set a plate of whole wheat toast in front of Tara. One of the girls pushed the butter across the counter.

"You're not planning to take a cab all the way to your dorm, are you? Or is your semester over?" Shevawn asked.

Her semester was over, Tara realized. Without her finishing it. Her last two finals had been scheduled for today. School seemed like years ago. At the same time, Tara didn't feel quite real sitting in this clean, bright kitchen instead of a windowless lecture hall with her laptop, notebooks, and Diet Coke arrayed in front of her.

"My thought is to go somewhere random on the train or bus, then hook up with one of my friends or family and figure out what to do next. Whether to go to the police, or just try to stay out of his way after this."

"There's an Amtrak stop in Washington, but it's sixteen or seventeen miles away. The girls and I can give you a lift, otherwise it'll cost a fortune to cab there. But I'd feel better if I knew you had somewhere specific to go."

"I'll be fine." Tara tried to sound more confident than she felt.

"Let's look at the train schedule. Girls, get your shoes."

A flat screen desktop sat on a computer cart in the corner. Shevawn pulled up the Amtrak website.

"Not a lot of choices," she said. "The only line that runs through any time soon is the Ann Rutledge."

"What's the closest major city?"

"Besides St. Louis? Chicago one way, Kansas City the other. Kansas City's closest."

"I could get a train or bus from either of those to just about anywhere. But I'm a lot more familiar with Kansas City. Do you mind if I look at the schedules?"

Shevawn stepped away from the keyboard. "Sure. Print if you want." She glanced at Tara's hotel bag. "Do you want something more sturdy to put your things in?"

"I don't want to cause you trouble."

"No trouble. I must have twenty bags from different promotions."

A few minutes later, Shevawn returned with a large red Estee Lauder tote bag. "There's probably still some cosmetic samples in there, the ones I don't use, you might as well take those too in case you want to freshen up. "

Tara started transferring her things. "Thank you so much. Do you by any chance have an old sweater you don't need, maybe in an unusual color, something I could put over my clothes? Just in case he's scoping out the station?"

Shevawn frowned. "I wish you'd just call the police now."

"What would I tell them? It really comes down to I've got a bad feeling about him. He hasn't done anything to me."

Once alone, Tara clicked the schedule for trains to Chicago and memorized the departure times. Then she bookmarked and printed the schedule to Kansas City. In case Cyril, or anyone else, ever found Shevawn, it was better Shevawn think she'd taken the train the opposite direction. Because Cyril had her buy the plane ticket through Chicago, Tara hoped he'd assume she wouldn't go there. At the station, she'd pay cash and get a ticket in Laura Summers' name.

Tara signed on to Yahoo to check her mail. One from Nate with the subject line "hope you're okay" and no other text. Tara hesitated, then typed back "still alive, more later," and shut off the computer.

THE FLOORBOARDS CREAKED when Tara stepped off the elevator in DePaul's building at Jackson and Wabash in downtown Chicago. She wore Shevawn's long-sleeved pink button-down shirt over her jeans. When Tara had peered at herself in the cracked mirror over the sink in the Women's room at Union Station, only her eyes had looked familiar. Even the shape of her face seemed different, between Shevawn's Cardinals' cap, the barrettes pinning her hair back, and the rose-colored lipstick she'd applied from Shevawn's bag.

The hall smelled like old paper. No one sat behind the wood-veneer reception desk, but it was after five, so Tara wasn't that surprised. As she followed signs to the professors' offices, the Estee Lauder bag slipped off Tara's shoulder. She yanked it back in place. Two steps later it slipped again and thunked onto the floor. Tara's eyes teared as she grabbed it by its handles. *I can do this. I can.* She hadn't slept much during the seven hour train ride, and she felt exhausted and scared. But she needed to pull it together. This was her one chance to convince Professor Gaddini she wasn't crazy.

Tara stopped in front of a plaque that read *Sophia Gaddini, PhD*. Her stomach tightened as she stared at the closed, off-white door. She had no Plan B if Professor Gaddini turned her away.

She made herself knock.

"Come in." Professor Gaddini's voice sounded low and warm.

The small office had sunrise-colored walls and plants sending vines across the bookcases. Professor Gaddini read at an antique desk to one side, a bottle of sparkling water in front of her, her long black hair swept into a gleaming, gold-edged clip. She smiled and swiveled her chair toward the door as Tara entered.

"Can I help you?"

"Professor Gaddini? I know you must be very busy, and I don't have an appointment, but there's something I need to ask you related to *The Feminine Face of God*." Tara's lips felt chapped, making it hard to form words. "At least, somewhat related."

Tara had rehearsed her opening line so often during the train ride the words sounded stilted to her. She carried the book with her in her backpack, and she felt almost as if she ought to take it out, as if owning it would prove something about her.

"You're a student?"

"No. That is, yes, but not here. At St. Louis University." Tara crossed the room in three steps and held out her hand. "My name's Tara Spencer."

Professor Gaddini's handshake was firm, her hand warm. Tara hoped hers wasn't too sweaty.

"Please. Sit down. And you can call me Sophia. My students do."

Tara perched on the futon along the wall opposite Sophia's desk.

"You came here from St. Louis?" Sophia asked.

"Yes." Tara took her cap off and pushed strands of hair out of her eyes. "I know I should have called first. But some things happened unexpectedly, and I just came here."

Sophia glanced at her watch. "I only have five minutes or so now, but if you tell me what this is about, perhaps we can make an appointment for Friday."

*Five minutes?* Tara had known she'd need to be quick, that a full professor at a university at the end of a term must be busy, but she didn't know what she could say in five minutes.

"It's complicated."

The phone on the desk rang, and Sophia glanced at it, but didn't answer. "I take it this is about something more than a research paper?"

"Well, I am researching, but for personal reasons. I've had some strange things happen to me. And this person, this man, told me it had to do with an organization called The Brotherhood of Andrew. Andrew of Crete."

Sophia looked at the ceiling for a moment. "I don't believe I've heard of a religious order relating to him. What's the connection to you?"

Exhausted despite her nerves, Tara willed herself to sit straight. The pink shirt stretched across her belly, but she didn't look very pregnant yet.

*This is it.*

"I found out two months ago, very unexpectedly, that I'm pregnant. This guy Cyril came to me, saying my baby fulfills a prophecy Andrew saw in visions before he died." Dr. Gaddini's face stayed calm, no frown, no raised eyebrows, so Tara kept going. "I thought Cyril was crazy. And then, when I finally started to consider what he said, he found out my baby is female and suddenly changed his mind. Completely."

Because of her writing on women, the Church, and divinity, Tara hoped the last part might catch Sophia's interest most.

"What do you mean when you say 'unexpectedly' pregnant?"

"I've never had sexual intercourse."

Now Sophia's eyebrows arched, but only slightly. "You're a virgin."

"Yes." Tara clasped her hands together and leaned forward. "I know it sounds crazy, or else you're thinking I'm a drinker or on drugs and something happened I don't remember, and there's no way I can prove to you otherwise. I've been to specialists. My pregnancy is perfectly normal, except no one can tell me how it happened. My family doctor is still researching, but the others say I must be lying or repressing. Which I don't exactly appreciate, but I probably would think the same thing if I were a doctor. Cyril is the only person who offered any other explanation."

*And then took off on me.*

Sophia rocked back in her chair. "That your child is divine?"

"He said Andrew had visions before his death based on the signs in Chapter 12 of Apocalypse."

"The woman with the crown of twelve stars brings forth a male child to rule the earth." Sophia paused to sip her water. "The passage doesn't indicate the woman is a virgin, but traditionally Catholic theologians view her as the Virgin Mary. In other words, not as a prophecy about a messiah to come."

Tara nodded. "Cyril said Brother Andrew's visions clarified the prophecy."

"And why come to me?"

Tara sensed this was the litmus test.

"I'm hoping you might know, or could help me find out, something about this Brotherhood of Andrew and Andrew's visions. If anyone else ever heard of the visions or shares these beliefs, how big the Brotherhood is, what its purpose is. Anything that would help me figure out why Cyril fastened on me, and why he changed his mind."

"I've no special expertise in apocalyptic prophecies."

Voices filtered through the door as other people passed the office.

"But you're a former nun and a professor of religious studies," Tara said, "so you'll know whether anything Cyril told me has any basis in the religious literature. And you're not religious yourself, at least, according to your books, so I thought you might not be as uncomfortable with exploring the topic as someone who was, who might either be offended I'd even ask about this or else assume it was true and view it more from a religious standpoint."

"You want someone objective."

"Yes. I mean, if we look at everything and you get to know me, and you think Cyril's a nut, or even I'm a nut, I want you to tell me."

Sophia glanced at her bookshelves, then back at Tara. "You say this Cyril changed his mind just like that? As soon as he found out your fetus is female?"

"Just about. He talked to his superiors first, and they agreed."

"It'd be interesting to know who his superiors are." Sophia closed her laptop. "I'm sorry. I need to go. I'd like to hear more, though."

"Thank you – that's so great. Because I'd understand if you just thought I was crazy and didn't want to, but I really would appreciate it if you could help."

"I'm not sure I can. But there's no harm in talking further. Where are you staying?"

"I don't know. I just got off the train. I figured I'd look on line for a hotel that's not too expensive."

"I doubt the inexpensive hotels are very safe for a young woman. And they're not really inexpensive." Sophia stood. "I'll only be gone a few hours. Why don't you stay here for now? There's a ladies' room down the hall and vending machines if you're hungry. When I get back, we'll figure something out."

"But you'll have to come back just to see me."

"It's no trouble. I live close by, and it's not as if anyone's using the office."

"Thank you so much, Professor."

"Sophia. My students call me Sophia."

# 21

Cyril pulled into the rectory parking lot and shut off the Monte Carlo, which he'd retrieved. No reason not to drive it now. He let his head fall back against the head rest. The sun hung just beyond St. John of the Cross' church steeple, tinting the metal cross atop it amber. He'd spent three hours cruising the streets of St. Clair. Nothing in the Order's or Cyril's own research suggested Tara knew anyone in the town. And, of course, he couldn't contact her parents. If things had gone according to plan, all would have been explained to them, but because Tara could not be the chosen one, they must learn nothing more than they already knew about the Brotherhood. From what Tara had told him, they most likely believed it part of a complicated delusion Tara constructed. Cyril felt sorry she had to face that, but he couldn't jeopardize his mission by explaining.

He'd interviewed persons at the Amtrak and Greyhound stations and called all the cab companies. He'd even walked through every public building he could find – library, grocery stores, strip malls – in case she'd decided to hide out in plain sight in town. Nothing. Tara had disappeared. Or she was hiding in someone's back yard or garage, and he couldn't check every one of those. Not alone, anyway, and Thomas said it wasn't time to call the cavalry yet, the girl would surface eventually.

Other than that, Thomas said little about Cyril's approach to Tara, which in itself was telling. Nothing about Cyril continuing to search for the true virgin mother, nothing about how Cyril had carried out his duties to the best of his abilities. Cyril understood. Cyril hadn't done his best, he hadn't exercised caution, in what he'd told Tara or in not anticipating her disappearance. Yet, he kept wanting to say – *you see, she's resourceful, she's smart, she's strong. How can you be so certain she's not the one?*

But he couldn't say that. Not just because he'd be questioning authority, or because he'd never before considered Thomas might be wrong about anything relating to the Brotherhood. But because he didn't trust his own motives. Between him and Thomas, he knew who had the best grasp of the situation, who could still think objectively. Which summed up the whole trouble with emotion, attachment. The whole reason Cyril needed to avoid it.

*Which is why I ought to leave. Now. It'd be better for me. Better for Tara.*

But Cyril got out of his car, slammed the door. The sound cracked through the empty lot.

The scent of lilacs from St. John of the Cross' garden filled the air. Cyril strode toward the sidewalk dividing the rectory and the church, determined to see if Tara's pastor, Father Saur, knew anything that might change the Brotherhood's collective mind.

# 22

"I hope I'm not putting you in danger staying here." Tara tucked the top sheet under the mattress corner. Sophia's guest room smelled of lavender and vanilla from the scented candles on the night table. "Whoever attacked me at school, and even whoever left that fetus, could still be looking for me."

"Is there any chance Cyril or his superiors arranged those things to make you feel you needed his protection?" Sophia said.

"Oh, I don't think – " Tara broke off, feeling foolish the thought hadn't occurred to her. It had been the knifing incident that made her welcome Cyril's presence rather than feeling nervous around him. "I suppose that could be."

It surprised Tara how disturbed she felt that Cyril might have lied to her.

"Either way, you didn't tell anyone you planned to come here." Sophia folded a light green bedspread over the pillows. "I think we're safe enough."

A cedar trunk stood at the foot of the bed, and Sophia sat down on it. "Tell me, did you talk to anyone at your church about what's happened to you?"

Tara longed for a shower and sleep, but she was eager to share anything that might help Sophia help her. She sat on the just-made bed. "It's my parents' church, really, I don't belong any more. But I did talk to the pastor, Father Saur. That's who suggested I be evaluated by the psychiatrist."

"Because he didn't believe you?"

"He said I should be evaluated to cover all the bases."

"Did Cyril ever say whether the Brotherhood of Andrew is a Catholic Order?"

"No. Does it matter?"

"It might help me pin it down." Sophia wrote a note on her notepad. "Catholicism is a bit more women-focused than some forms of Christianity.

Early Christians persuaded some pagans to convert by using the Virgin Mary to replace some of the female gods."

"But the Church isn't exactly woman-focused now," Tara said.

The wind shifted and a warm breeze came through the open window, ushering in a fresh, green scent with an asphalt undertone from the parking lot beyond Sophia's postage stamp yard.

"Not to any great extent. There was a sect of early Christians known as Gnostics, who viewed God as neither male nor female, but as a Being with both male and female aspects. The Gnostics also believed that each person must come to knowledge – or *gnosis* – of the divine in her or his own way, not through orthodox teachings handed down by designated leaders. That wasn't a very helpful philosophy for those who wanted to build and run an organized religion, and the Gnostics were forced out.

"One text in particular shows the difference in the Gnostic view of women versus the beliefs that prevail today," Sophia went on. "Are you familiar with *The Nag Hammadi Library*?"

Tara shook her head and stifled a yawn.

"I'll be brief." Sophia smiled. "Which always makes my students suspect I'll run on forever. The *Nag Hammadi Library* is a collection of fifth-century manuscripts. It includes scribes' copies of religious texts the Roman Catholic Church rejected and attempted to eradicate. Someone buried the manuscripts in an urn, and the urn was found in Egypt in 1945, nearly two thousand years later.

"The *Trimorphic Protennoia* is one of those manuscripts. It refers to a three-part Thought, or divinity, as the Father, Mother, and Son. I've always thought this could mean three divine persons, Jesus the Son, God the Father, and Mary the Mother, rather than the Holy Trinity that survived – Father, Son and Holy Spirit."

## Field Report 2.10

This investigator returned to St. Clair, Missouri, as assigned, and again questioned personnel at the Super 8 Motel, the Rolla Greyhound station, and the Washington Amtrak station. No persons at those locations recalled meeting Tara Spencer or recognized her photograph. With the assistance of Special Investigator Mullin, this investigator questioned persons who live within a two-mile radius of the motel. An eight-year old child thought he recognized the photograph of Tara Spencer. Child stated he saw someone who looked like Spencer a few weeks ago knocking on doors in his neighborhood around sunrise. Residents had previously been questioned by SI Mullin, but this investigator recanvassed and spoke to Shevawn Garner on Emerald Lane.

Garner denied ever meeting Spencer and claimed not to recognize her photograph. However, one of Garner's children overheard this investigator and asked her mother if the girl they drove to the train station was named Tara. Garner again denied knowledge of Spencer and claimed she drove the daughter of a friend to the Amtrak station a few weeks ago.

After examining local and Amtrak train schedules, this investigator and SI

Mullin determined Spencer could have traveled directly to 28 different cities. (See attached Exhibit A1.) Cross-referenced with names of Spencer's known friends and family, the list narrows to nine. (See attached Exhibit A2.) Despite a ticket purchased on Spencer's Visa to Kansas City, this investigator proposes focusing on Chicago and Los Angeles as target cities because Professor Sophia Gaddini teaches religious studies at DePaul University in Chicago and Professor Harold Heydeman teaches at UCLA at Berkeley. Spencer is familiar with the work of both professors and may seek them out for guidance. In fact, this investigator believes it is more likely Spencer would seek out such experts, given the response from her family and friends to her pregnancy.

Accordingly, this investigator requests permission to travel to Los Angeles and Chicago while SI Mullin begins traveling to the remaining cities.

# 23

"Nothing." Tara shut the book. Dust puffed into the air.

"Careful. " Sophia set down a stack of books. "The pages are fragile."

In the Rare Book Room, ten-foot high wooden shelves surrounded the two women, with only two openings – one that led to the exit, the other to the special collections. To enter, Tara and Sophia had to sign in and leave their shoulder bags and umbrellas locked behind the reference desk. They were only allowed to take in pencils and legal pads, no spiral-bound notebooks or laptops. A sweet, musty paper smell filled the air, along with latex from the gloves used to handle the most rare manuscripts.

"Sorry. It's just – this is so frustrating," Tara said.

The wooden chair Sophia pulled out from the library table squeaked on the gray and white tile floor. Sophia sat down. "What about the sermons?"

Before disappearing back into one of the collections, Sophia had pointed Tara to a book that included sermons by Andrew of Crete.

"There was a little," Tara said. "Andrew was devoted to the Virgin Mary. He even argued she should be considered divine, along with her son."

Sophia slid an open book across the table. It showed a photograph of a stone figurine woman holding a baby. "Some scholars draw parallels between Mary and Jesus and Isis and Houras. These figures could be the Virgin Mary and baby Jesus, except they were found in B.C.E. – Before Common Era."

"Isis was a goddess, right?" Tara said.

"Yes. In many myths, Houras grew to become a god, but then died, and Isis rebirthed or resurrected him. The stories represented harvest cycles."

"So resurrection isn't a new theme."

"Not at all," Sophia said. "But the female divinity's role has almost disappeared. The Goddess was immortal, divine, and more powerful than Houras. Most Christian sects attribute no special powers to Mary at all, other than becoming pregnant as a virgin, and that's supposedly an act of the Holy Spirit, not something she brought about."

"Is the virgin part meant to be anti-sex?"

Sophia shook her head. "I suspect it was simply to establish paternity. Until surrogate motherhood became possible, there was never a question who a child's mother was. The woman who carried and bore the baby. But the only way a man could be sure in Mary's time that he was the father of his wife's child was if she never had sex with anyone but him, either before or after marriage."

Shifting in her seat, Tara crossed her legs and tried to find a more comfortable position. Her body felt swollen and achy from the train ride and reading so long, though that would never have bothered her before she got pregnant. "So Mary being a virgin tells us Jesus isn't Joseph's child."

"Or any human male's child," Sophia said. "But as to Andrew – did the sermons say anything about Andrew's supposed visions?"

Tara shook her head. "Nothing."

Sophia bounced her pencil on the table. "Is it possible Cyril concocted this entire story?"

"It's crossed my mind," Tara said. "He seemed so sure of himself, though. And he talked to someone on the phone a couple times about me."

"I can't think what his motive would be to invent something like this," Sophia said. "If he meant to harm you, he could have kidnapped you or killed you easily enough in the Laundromat. Or even when you were running through your school."

Tara shivered. "That's cheery."

A door slammed somewhere in the stacks behind Tara and she jumped.

"This room isn't the town square," Sophia said, "but professors and students do come here occasionally."

Resisting the urge to look around, Tara forced herself to focus on Sophia. *If someone sneaks up behind me, she'll see it.* "I just keep thinking Cyril is going to jump out at me. Or that guy from the school."

"Cyril didn't say where that man might be from?"

"No. Just that other groups wanted to stop the birth. Maybe scare me into getting an abortion."

"Their methods seem a little extreme, if they just want to scare you." Sophia closed the book in front of her, leaned back in her chair, and stared at the ceiling. "On the other hand, I expect a well-organized group would not have difficulty killing one young woman who wasn't expecting it, assuming they were strongly motivated and cared more about achieving their purpose than being caught. So just frightening you probably was the intent. So far."

Crouching in an alcove in the Rare Book Room of the DePaul University Library, Kim Giddons did her best to take down the conversation between

Professor Gaddini and the blonde girl Kim assumed was a student. Kim had started listening while walking behind them on Fullerton Avenue. Eavesdropping was a socially unacceptable habit, but it wasn't one Kim had any desire to break. Some of her best story ideas came from overheard conversations. When the conversation started, Kim figured it was probably about nothing more than a research paper, but something about the girl's intensity kept Kim listening.

In the first week of the school year, Kim had gone to see David Lennard, the editor of DePaul's newspaper, about a staff position. David was the annoying artiste type, dressed in black with a beret, for God's sake. He informed her that freshmen needed to let their skills *develop* and *ripen*, because writing for a high school paper simply didn't prepare one for the intense world of college journalism. David suggested Kim wait and submit new writing samples in the spring. Instead, she'd called her friend who wrote features at *The Chicago Reader*, the city's most well-read alternative newspaper. She said if Kim brought her something original and exciting, she'd pass it on to her editor, which could lead to Kim's first payment for her writing. And her first opportunity to rub it in the face of David with the beret, who wouldn't know good writing if it were scrawled across a wall in front of him.

Kim was about to give up on the Gaddini thing – her knees were screaming – when the girl said, "So should I look for something on second messiahs, something that seems to directly relate to my pregnancy? Or about Andrew of Crete?"

Grinning, Kim eased into a sitting position on the floor and turned a fresh page on her pad. Pretty out there, but, after all, *The Reader* was an alternative paper.

~

SOPHIA WROTE SOMETHING IN SLANTED, even writing on her legal pad. "Who else knew about your pregnancy when Cyril approached you?"

"My parents. My former boyfriend Jeremy and his sister." Tara rubbed her fingers across a gouge in the table and thought. "And Father Saur."

For the first time, Tara wondered if Father could be connected to the Brotherhood. Or worse, the group that sent the man with the knife. She didn't want to believe the man she'd known since she was four, who stood outside St. John of the Cross every Sunday morning after 9:00 mass in his black robe, might want to harm her. But the idea of Father Saur being part of a conspiracy struck her as no more bizarre than anything else that had happened in the last few months.

"Any idea when the Brotherhood started?" Sophia said.

"Right after Andrew's death. Or maybe just before it, I'm not sure."

Both women returned to their stacks of books. Tara checked the index in her last one and found a reference to Andrew of Crete. She read the designated pages, then sighed. "This is like the others. Nothing about visions relating to Chapter 12 of Apocalypse. Or to pregnant virgins."

"Virgins?" Sophia said. "Plural?"

Tara slapped her hand on the table. "I'm an idiot. I didn't tell you. Cyril said the stars on the woman's crown form into the eyes of six infants, each a potential messiah. And that the Brotherhood believed there had been at least four of them already, maybe five, but each time the Beast prevailed."

"That's far from any interpretation of the text I've ever heard of. Were any of the pregnancies supposedly in our time?"

"I don't know." Sinking back in her chair, Tara said, "I feel like there are a million things I ought to have asked Cyril, but everything happened so fast."

Sophia reached across the table and squeezed Tara's hand. "I'd never expect you to have asked everything."

~

THREE DAYS LATER, Tara sat on the patio of the townhome next to Sophia's.

"Life can be strange." Sophia's neighbor, Julie, passed around a plate of cookies, her diamond rings flashing in the late-afternoon sunshine. A thin woman in her late fifties, with copper-colored hair, Julie had lived in four different countries and changed careers five times before she turned fifty. She'd just taken up mountain climbing. Tara found her fascinating. "Your pregnancy is puzzling. I wish I had an explanation for you. I'm sorry it's been so hard."

"Thank you," Tara said.

Julie and Sophia's friend Anne perched on the white wrought iron bench near Julie's outdoor fountain, her legs crossed under her flowing rose silk dress. "Are you planning to stay in Chicago for a while?" she asked.

"For a while," Tara said.

"You can stay with me any time," Anne said. "I might even have some part-time work in the studio. Sophia mentioned you were looking, and my receptionist is leaving for India at the end of the week."

"You're all so kind." Tara swallowed hard. These almost-strangers offered so much, when her family, at least her parents, had made things so difficult.

"I really wish you'd stay with Julie or Anne while I'm gone." Sophia was leaving the following Monday for a seminar in Merrillville, Indiana, on religion in the middle ages.

"I'll be okay on my own." Tara turned to Julie. "I promise I'll call you if I need anything."

Julie refilled Tara's tea cup. "You'd better."

The tea, which Anne had made to help Tara's morning sickness, tasted like the gingerbread men Grandma Spencer made every Christmas. Tara's throat ached. She wondered what her grandma thought of her pregnancy, if anyone had even told her.

The conversation turned to other things, and Tara listened and watched the changing sunlight play across the street outside as the sun set. The evening was warm, with just enough breeze to make Tara comfortable. She knew she needed to figure out what to do next, but she wished this evening could continue forever.

As they finished the tea and cookies, Sophia took a newspaper from her leather shoulder bag. "I almost forgot. I picked up a *Reader* on my way here. You said you wanted to look at the job ads. Though if Anne has something for you, maybe you won't need it."

Tara took the paper.

"You should come by tomorrow and see the studio," Anne said.

Caught by the front page of Section Two, Tara didn't answer.

Leaning forward, Sophia peered at the paper. "Tara? What is it?"

Numb, Tara turned the section toward Sophia so she could see the lead story, "The Second Coming?" by Kim Giddons.

# 24

**THE SECOND COMING?**
By Kim Giddons

St. Louis University student Tara Spencer claims she is a modern-day Virgin Mary, and DePaul University professor Sophia Gaddini may agree. Spencer discovered her pregnancy four months ago, but underwent two pregnancy tests and two ultrasounds before she accepted the truth. She insists she's never engaged in sexual intercourse, or in any sexual activity that could lead to pregnancy, nor has she been artificially inseminated. Individuals close to her suspect Spencer was assaulted and has simply blocked the memory of the event, but admit they never saw any sign she was seriously disturbed about anything other than the unexplained pregnancy.

Unfortunately for Spencer, God apparently didn't see fit to send an angel to explain things to her betrothed. Jeremy Turano, Spencer's boyfriend of one year, whom she expected to marry, ended the relationship on learning about the pregnancy. In a public scene, he accused her of infidelity. Only a month later, her parents filed a petition asking the St. Louis County Circuit Court to declare Spencer incompetent and appoint them as her legal guardians. This action appears to have triggered Spencer's flight to Chicago, where she met with renowned professor and former nun, Sophia Gaddini, PhD. Dr. Gaddini opened her home to the young woman, and is assisting her in researching the possible Biblical implications of her pregnancy.

The two started with the Book of *Revelation*, also known as *The Apocalypse of John*, based on reports regarding the visions of an eighth century martyr.

But a search for documents regarding the visions has so far been unsuccessful.

THE ARTICLE CONTINUED, adding background about Andrew of Crete. Nothing Tara and Sophia didn't already know. The article didn't mention anything about more than one virgin or even about The Brotherhood of Andrew, so Tara assumed the writer hadn't heard that part, and hadn't talked to anyone who had.

"So they probably didn't speak to my family. Nate and my parents both know about the Brotherhood of Andrew."

"I'm so sorry," Sophia said. "We should have been more careful what we discussed in public."

Tara rubbed her hands over her bare arms. Anyone could find her now. "How many people read this paper?"

"*The Reader's* available free all over Chicago." Sophia walked toward the wrought iron fence separating the patio from the street, then turned back toward the other women. "I don't know about elsewhere. It's also on the Internet."

"It won't take long before someone comes here." Tara paused to take a deep breath, trying to stay calm. "I wonder who said that about me being assaulted? Only my dad and maybe Nate thought that. Though I suppose if this Kim Giddons talked to people I knew at school, that might be the most logical answer anyone could figure about what might have happened."

"Could someone just fill me in?" Julie asked. She turned to Tara. "You said you didn't know how you got pregnant, but I didn't realize it was this complicated."

"Most of it is in the article," Sophia said.

The breeze had loosened some of Julie's hair, and she wound it back and resettled her pearl-edged bobby pins to fix it in place. Her eyebrows curved slightly as she looked at Sophia. "Do you believe Tara is pregnant with the next messiah?"

"I don't know," Sophia said.

Julie glanced at Tara.

"I don't either," Tara said, willing herself not to cry. She so longed for one quiet afternoon, one normal conversation that had nothing to do with her pregnancy.

Anne, who'd just finished reading the article, leaned over and squeezed Tara's arm. "Whatever's going on, Sophia will help you figure it out."

"Of course she will," Julie said.

Tara nodded.

"I wish I could be so sure." Sophia resumed pacing. "I'm afraid I haven't helped much so far."

"You've been a huge help," Tara said. "Are you kidding?"

Sophia half smiled. "I haven't found any answers."

Julie said, "Is there anything I can do?"

Sophia stared at the street for a moment. "Possibly." She sat again and took a notebook out of her shoulder bag. "You worked for a private investigator at one point, right? Could you find out about someone? His name is Cyril Woods." Sophia explained Cyril's connection.

"Will do," Julie said. "It's interesting this Kim Giddons didn't write anything about him, or the Brotherhood of Andrew, or Andrew's visions. She must have researched."

"Probably," Sophia said. "Which means she must not have found anything, which still leaves us with the possibility that Cyril Woods manufactured his entire story. Or someone fed it to him." She turned to Tara. "Do you know anything about his personal life? Or even how he first learned about the Brotherhood?"

"Nothing. I could call and see if he'd tell me. Everyone knows where I am now anyway." Tara thought of her parents. She'd put everything from home out of her mind the last few days, though she'd known she'd need to think about it all eventually. "Do you think my parents can have the legal papers served on me here?"

"I don't know. It's another state, so I imagine there's some sort of process that has to be gone through. I'll see if one of my colleagues at the law school can answer that."

Tara slumped, the metal chair back cool through her light blouse, unsure what to do now. Wait for Cyril – or worse, the man with the red hair – to find her? Or for her parents to send someone after her? Or take off again? Not that she had anywhere in mind to go. Or much money left to use for travel.

Anne leaned toward her. "This isn't all bad, Tara. If anyone means to harm you, in some ways you're safer with your story told. Potential attackers now know the police will pay attention if something happens to you, because the press will. And you may as well speak to your family, given it's not a secret where you are."

"That's true."

"And," Sophia said, "someone out there may know something about this prophecy and contact us."

"That'd be good." If the article helped her figure out what was going on, Tara might even be grateful for it.

When Tara started working at the yoga center the following day, no one mentioned the article. After a few days, she began to think few people read *The Reader*, at least few people who did yoga, or else everyone dismissed her as a crank. She attended two of Anne's classes, and walked through Millenium Park's gardens and across its silver, serpentine bridge. At Sophia's continued urging, she moved to Julie's when Sophia left for her seminar. It was more to make Sophia feel comfortable about leaving than because Tara felt nervous. If anything, she felt more relaxed than she had since her first pregnancy test.

Then, the first night at Julie's, the world exploded.

# 25

The bed shook, waking Tara. What sounded like hail pelted the townhome's walls as thunder boomed. Perfume bottles on the dresser rattled. Tara jumped out of bed in the dark, stumbled to the open window and peered out. No lightning or rain, but when she stepped away from the outside air, she smelled something sizzling inside.

The door to the hallway was shut. Tara touched it. Not hot, so she opened it. The hall was pitch dark, though a nightlight had been on in the bathroom when she'd gone to bed.

"Julie?"

The place had fallen silent, in stark contrast to the booming just moments before. Tara stepped on something sharp – glass? rocks? Heart racing, she retreated to the bedroom, felt on the floor for her sandals, put them on, and hurried back to the hall.

"Julie?"

The townhome's layout was the same as Sophia's, and Julie's bedroom shared a wall with Sophia's guest room. Running her hand along the wall as she moved, Tara found the bathroom. She'd seen matches on a shelf near the sink that held candles.

Tara lit one. Its light flickered over chunks of plaster, wood splinters, and glass strewn across the hallway floor, most of it clustered near Julie's bedroom. The bedroom door was gone, the doorframe splintered and cracked. Streaks of something dark spattered the walls, the floor, the debris. Tara's finger trembled as she pressed it against a streak on the wall. Her finger came away slick and sticky. The candle tipped sideways, spilling hot wax over her hand. She dropped the candle. It went out.

"Julie?" No answer.

Tara hurried back to the guest room in the dark and found the phone on the night table. The 911 operator answered immediately.

"There's been an explosion, something, I'm not sure."

"855 South Dearborn?"

"Yes. Yes, I think so." Tara felt grateful the address showed automatically, she was sure she couldn't have dredged the street name from her memory.

"Anyone hurt?"

"I don't know. I think so. She's not answering – Julie, the owner – she's not answering when I call to her, and it looks like it blew up in her room. The door's gone. I'm down the hall."

"Emergency personnel are on the way. Can you safely exit the building?'

"Maybe. I'm not sure."

"Can you take cover under a table or other furniture?"

"Not in this room."

*She's worried about other explosions*, Tara thought, remembering the procedures she'd learned at SLU for terrorist bomb attacks. But Tara didn't care. She needed to find Julie, who might be buried under rubble. Injured by a bomb that must have been meant for Tara.

"Is anyone else there?'

"No. Just us two. At least, that's all I know about. That's all that was here when I went to sleep around ten. I need to go. To find Julie."

The phone was old and used a cord, so Tara couldn't take it with her. She dropped the receiver on the bed. Sirens started somewhere nearby, maybe from the fire station a mile down the road. *Close, at least they're close.* Tara and Sophia had walked by the station on the way to Millenium Park the day before.

Tara stumbled over wood and drywall on her way back to the bathroom. She lit another candle and headed for the bedroom. She might be walking toward another bomb, but nothing felt real except the need to keep moving.

When Tara entered Julie's room, she fumbled for the light switch. Nothing happened. She held the candle high. A jagged hole cut through the wall along the bed. Drywall, wood, shoes, insulation, glass, everywhere. More dark streaks and spatters.

*Paint. It's just maroon paint, like on the fetus, that's all.*

Which of course Tara knew couldn't be right. But she peered around for Julie.

*Look under the rubble.*

Tara imagined she heard breathing. Julie breathing, the townhouse breathing. She moved toward the corner. A few strides from the rubble, her foot came down on something. She lowered the candle to see.

Hair. A length of clumped, coppery hair, shining in the candle light.

Bile rose in Tara's throat. "No." It came out a whisper, not a scream, and Tara refused to look closer, to bend down to see what else might lay on the floor, in the gloom. "No, no."

She eased back, but the hair stuck to the bottom of her sandal, pulling, pulling, until it dislodged something from the pile. Tara kept backing away, but the hair kept pulling, and the candle trembled, and something tumbled across the floor toward her. Candlelight glinted off two small, pale orbs. The face below them was missing, but the flickering light flashed on bone and flesh.

The candle flew from Tara's hand. Before it went out, it set the hair on fire. Shrieking, Tara stamped on the flames, her feet squishing hair and tissue, the smell of burning flesh assaulting her nostrils.

Blood filled the air, pulsing through the room. Tara kept stamping, though the fire was out. *Not blood*, she thought, *red light. The ambulance.*

Tara froze.

*They can fix this. I shouldn't move.*

The sirens cut. Only then did Tara realize how loud they'd become. The room fell silent. *I should have unlocked the door.* Her feet stung. The front door banged. Footsteps pounded up the stairs.

The red flashing light, like a strobe, made the three EMT's movements jerky.

"Help her." Tara pushed the female EMT away. "I'm fine. Julie needs help."

"My partners will." The woman's teeth looked orange in the red light. She grasped Tara's arm. "They'll take care of her. I need to get you out of their way, all right?"

"Yes."

The woman and another EMT put Tara on a stretcher and carried her downstairs.

"I'm pregnant," Tara said.

The woman took Tara's pulse. Tara closed her eyes. Her feet felt sticky from Julie's blood.

Rachel Fielding bandaged Tara's feet after taking out glass and wood splinters and wrapping Tara in a blanket. It was Tara's own blood on her feet, not Julie's, but the cuts had not gone deep. Technicians took blood, and X-rays, and did a pelvic exam, and asked questions. And took more splinters from Tara's right hand, where she'd grasped what was left of Julie's bedroom doorjamb. Tara couldn't remember touching the door frame. She couldn't think of anything but Julie's copper hair, and the upper half of Julie's face, open eyes staring....

Alone for a few minutes, Tara dressed in what she'd been wearing at Julie's – a tank top and cotton pajama pants, but her feet were bare because so much blood and glass had gotten into her sandals.

Dr. Fielding poked her head into the exam room. "Your father's here. Shall I send him back?"

"He is? I – Yeah."

Relief flooded Tara, despite the court papers. Her dad would be at her side when she talked to the police, his quiet calm helping her stay calm and stop picturing Julie's mutilated half-face, stop smelling singed hair and flesh, though it seemed the smell had burnt permanently into Tara's nostrils. He'd help her face her part in Julie's death and figure out what to do. And where to go. Home, or –

*How did Dad get here? How did he know what happened?*

The thoughts cut through the clutter in Tara's mind and adrenalin jolted through her body, temporarily driving out the numbness she'd felt since the explosion. She hadn't called, or told anyone to call, her parents. The news might have reported the explosion, but even if the press released her name, she doubted anyone would say what hospital she was in. And it would take her dad at least five hours to drive here, and three or four even by air.

Tara stood. The tile floor felt cool on the unbandaged parts of her bare feet. She glanced around, but the room had no exit except the door already opening.

A bulky red-haired man shoved Dr. Fielding into the exam room, then grabbed the doctor's forearm, just below the sleeve of her hospital greens. With his free hand, he pulled a gun from his windbreaker and held it to the doctor's left temple. The man's chest heaved, and the gun trembled. Tara thought he was the same man who'd assaulted her at the school, but she hadn't gotten a good look at his face then.

*He's afraid*, Tara thought. But she didn't know if that helped. It might make him more dangerous.

"Come here. Slowly." The man had a Brooklyn accent.

Focusing on the man's eyes, trying to read his intention, Tara inched toward him. When she reached him, he pushed Dr. Fielding aside, grabbed Tara's elbow with sweaty fingers, and pulled her against him. They faced each other. He was tall, his chin just above Tara's forehead. His breath smelled of onions. The revolver's tip against Tara's cheek felt warm from being against Dr. Fielding's skin. Tara felt as if the world had narrowed to just the few feet surrounding her and the man.

Dr. Fielding stepped toward the door. The man jerked his head to look at her. "Stay."

The doctor swallowed and nodded, long hair swaying.

The man turned back to Tara. "Do you have the mark?"

# 26

"I – what?"

Tara couldn't process the man's question.

He waved the gun away from Tara's head, then back. "The mark of the Beast. Of the serpent."

"The Beast? I don't have any mark."

He cleared his throat. "Show me. Take off your clothes."

"Uh, right here?"

Tara took in the way the man shifted from one foot to the other, and the slight deepening color of his neck. He was uncomfortable. She stepped back, hoping he would believe her uncomfortable, too, and not shoot her for it. She needed any extra second she could get to think. No one was behind her in the room, and Dr. Fielding stood to the side, poised to the man's right. Tara wondered if anyone in the ER heard what was going on, but she doubted it. Noise filled the place – voices, squeaking wheels, electronic beeps, ringing phones – echoing off the tile floors and bare walls.

The man's face flushed. "Yes, here."

Tara glanced around. Dr. Fielding flicked her eyes toward the man, and toward the open door beyond him, but Tara wasn't sure what Dr. Fielding meant, if anything. But at least it looked like Dr. Fielding was ready to help if Tara made a move.

"Okay."

If the man shot at Tara, it was unlikely he'd hit Dr. Fielding, given the angle, and the wall behind Tara was brick, though the sides looked like movable dividers.

"Hurry," the man said.

Tara pulled the drawstring on her pajama pants, twisting it so the string knotted. She looked down, bending forward, as if trying to see the knot. Instead, she crouched and bolted forward, the way she did when playing basketball in the driveway with the kids. She aimed for the door and the man instinctively moved to block her. At the last moment, she feinted right and rammed into his groin with her shoulder. Tara dropped to the floor and rolled away as he doubled over, then scrambled to her feet and ran out the door. Thumps and shouts sounded behind her, but no gun shots. Tara hoped someone had stopped the man, but she didn't pause. She darted around a gurney and several green-frocked interns, through double doors into the waiting room, and out to the street.

Too late it occurred to Tara that the man, with his long legs, probably could easily outrun her. She kept going, not sure what direction she was headed, but aiming for the busy street a few blocks away. Her breath strained her lungs. She longed to look back, but powered forward, bare feet slamming on the concrete. Her eyes teared when her feet hit rocks and debris, but still she ran.

When she reached what turned out to be Michigan Avenue, Tara darted right, through a small group of women wearing heels and short dresses. Only then did she glance over her shoulder. Other than the women, the sidewalk was deserted. Tara hurried on, covering five blocks in what felt like seconds. A few cars cruised the street, but Tara passed only one other pedestrian. At two in the morning, all the stores were lit but closed. She stopped in front of the alabaster and glass building –Water Tower Place – where Sophia had taken her only days before and crouched on the sidewalk near a giant concrete planter. A couple walked by but never glanced her way, despite her pajama bottoms and bloody, bandaged feet. Tara struggled to catch her breath and form a plan. Her whole body shook as images of the night leapt into her mind. Blood and debris in Julie's hallway, the clump of Julie's copper hair under her feet, the man with the gun.

Wrapping her arms around herself, Tara rocked forward and back.

*Think. I've got to think about what to do. Not about Julie, I can't, not now.*

Tara squeezed her eyes shut and patted where her pockets would be if she wore jeans. But her pajama pants had no pockets, and she had no money, no ID, no credit cards. Her wallet sat tucked in her backpack in Julie's guest room, along with her cell phone, and her clothes in Julie's guest closet. Tara couldn't go back there. The red-haired man would go directly there after the hospital, if he'd gotten away. And if he hadn't, one of his compatriots must be guarding the townhome.

She could call Sophia. But Tara had already brought so much destruction to her. She briefly considered Cyril, but he might only insist on taking her home. And now she had no question that others were after her. Whether they were agents of the Beast or just crazy she didn't know, but she couldn't go home.

*It's my fault. If I'd never come to Sophia, Julie would be alive.*

Tara ran through her list of who she could call again, but still came up with no one, except the police. She peered around the planter, scanning the sidewalks north and south on both sides of Michigan Avenue. She didn't see the red-haired man. Or anyone else at all nearby. Knees trembling, Tara stood. She spotted a church across the street and crossed. It might be open for shelter, or even have a phone.

When she reached it, though, the doors were locked. Tara walked the side streets until she found an all night fifties-style diner with a double-door entryway containing a payphone. She hurried in, relieved she didn't need to try to gain entry to the eating area dressed the way she was, and hoping no one inside would notice her and chase her out.

Hand shaking, she dialed the operator and started to ask for the nearest police station, then instead placed a collect call to Sophia's cell phone. The red-haired man hadn't followed her, and she owed it to Sophia to tell her what had happened, if she hadn't already heard.

Sophia answered on the first ring, which told Tara she must be awake and know what had happened. She accepted the charges.

"I'm so sorry," Tara said.

"Tara? Where are you?"

"I never meant for anything bad to happen to you, or Julie."

"Of course you didn't." Sophia's voice sounded choked, as if she were near tears. "It's a terrible, horrible thing. But whoever planted that bomb is responsible, not you."

The outer door swung open, and Tara jumped at the sound. She watched the people enter. None seemed interested in her. She'd found that one advantage of a crowded city. Less friendly, so less scrutiny.

Tara clutched the phone receiver. "Where are you?"

"In the car, on my way to the hospital to identify – to see Julie," Sophia said. "I'm her emergency contact person. The police found my number in her condo. Her brother can't be there until tomorrow morning, and I thought at least I could do this for him. So he doesn't have to see her until, well, maybe not at all. From what the police described, it will need to be a closed casket wake."

Tara swallowed hard. "She's not – her body's – " Tara couldn't finish, the vision in her mind was so vivid. She felt dizzy.

"Where are you?" Sophia said. "Still at the hospital?"

"No. This guy came after me." Tara told Sophia what had happened at the hospital.

"We've got to get you somewhere safe," Sophia said. "I'll come get you."

"No." Tara almost shouted. "They'll know to follow you and might hurt you, too. Everyone should think you don't want anything more to do with me."

"But you're stranded."

"I can't drag you into this further. I'll call the police. Maybe they can send someone to get me. And then I'm leaving town."

"To go where?"

"Anywhere away from here."

"Wait. Let me think." Someone turned up the juke box inside the diner, and upbeat Beach Boys' harmonies came through the glass door. Tara rested her forehead against the wall. The numbness was creeping in again, and Tara almost welcomed it. The land of not feeling seemed like a better place to be. But she couldn't allow herself the luxury. She needed to find somewhere safe.

Sophia said, "I'll call Anne. She can send one of her students, someone with no connection to you, to go shopping for some things for you if you're really set on leaving."

"It's too dangerous to get anyone involved."

"Not if it's someone who's never met you. No one will connect a stranger shopping at a twenty-four hour Target with what's happened. I'll arrange for all of us to meet at the police station, so you can tell the police everything that happened."

"They'll never believe this."

"They'll believe someone's trying to harm you, after everything that's happened, and that's what counts. We can figure out where you'll go after that. I'll bring your things to the station, if the police will let me into my townhome. Are you safe where you are?"

"I don't know. I don't see that guy anywhere. But someone's probably going to kick me out of the vestibule soon."

"Here's what you do. Go to Holy Name Cathedral. You can walk there." Sophia gave Tara directions. "I know the pastor. I'll call him now, he'll meet you there and give you cab fare to take to the police station on State Street. So you know it's safe I'll have him greet you by the name Lucina – the Roman goddess of childbirth."

In a small interview room at the station, a police detective listened to Tara's and Sophia's stories, taking notes without betraying his views on anything. Tara knew he must doubt she didn't know how she'd become pregnant, but he took seriously the threats against her, especially since he admitted that, so far, no one could see another reason anyone would target Sophia or Julie. He'd already talked to Dr. Fielding and the other hospital personnel. Tara's attacker had escaped after a struggle with two paramedics and a nurse, but they, and Dr. Fielding, had provided a detailed description.

Then Detective Gonsalves mentioned something that Tara realized had been at the back of her mind.

"I doubt the man who attacked you in the hospital set the bomb."

"That's probably right," Tara said. "He seemed so nervous with the gun."

"Dr. Fielding, the intern, thought he'd likely never handled one before. And whoever set that bomb had no questions for you, no hesitation. If that same person came after you in the hospital, you'd be dead now."

A door slammed somewhere in the facility, and the table shuddered. Tara rubbed her arms. Despite Cyril's warnings, and even the incident at SLU, she hadn't really felt in danger – except possibly from Cyril – until the explosion. The detective's flat tone, focused by the gray concrete walls around her, made it even more frightening.

*What could I have done that's so bad, that people want to kill me? Or so good that Cyril thought my baby would save the world, at least at first?*

Tara rested her forehead on her arms. Her head ached, and her body felt chilled from exhaustion. If only she could turn back time to before she'd become pregnant, whenever that had happened, and go in some other direction. Do something else, whatever she needed to do, to be somewhere else right now. Anywhere else.

*It must be too late for an abortion. And how could I do that when I don't know what the baby might mean for the world if she's born? Unless something about her really is evil.*

Sophia stroked Tara's hair, and tears sprang to Tara's eyes. More than anything, she wanted to call her mom and dad, hear their voices. But now she had to worry not only about whether they were still trying to commit her, but whether she'd endanger them, and her sisters and brothers, by going home.

"How sure are you the man at the hospital is the same one who attacked you at your university?" Detective Gonsalves said.

Tara wiped her eyes and straightened. Her tears kept coming, but she answered. "Pretty sure. Same hair color and body type. Plus, I just sort of feel like it was him. Maybe something about the way he moved, I don't know. But I didn't get a look at his face that night. And I was so scared this time I can't really remember his features. But I don't think it could be anyone else."

The detective looked at Sophia. "You said you've received hate messages."

"Some. After the article came out. Mostly by e-mail. I brought printouts."

"What?" Tara said.

Sophia handed a two-inch thick brown envelope to Detective Gonsalves, then put her hand on Tara's arm. "I didn't want to mention it until I returned, so you wouldn't worry while I was away."

After Detective Gonsalves told Tara to stay in touch and in town in case he had further questions, he let Sophia and Tara go. They met Anne's student, Lily, who'd waited for them on a bench near the exit. Lily was dark-haired and about Tara's height and weight. She brought a paper tote bag of her own clothes, including jeans, plus a new red backpack with Tara's things in it, cash Anne had put together, and a file folder with copies of the e-mails and letters since the *Reader* article. Tara changed in the handicapped-accessible stall in the police station's Ladies Room. Her shoulders ached and her arms shook with exhaustion. The effort required to tie tennis shoes felt overwhelming, so she put on flip-flops instead, even though she knew they'd be harder to run in. At the bottom of the paper bag was a wig made of long dark hair.

"I was a theater major," Lily said, from the other side of the stall door.

Tara stepped out and found Lily wearing one of Tara's long cotton skirts, a plain tank top, and a blonde wig. She didn't look just like Tara, but she'd pass if someone looked from across a street or drove by.

"Be careful." Tara hugged Lily. "Looking like me is dangerous."

"I'm only going out of the police station like this, in case someone's watching, then Sophia and I will find an open restaurant somewhere and I'll change."

Tara left the station first, wearing the dark wig. The sky had turned grayish-pink in the east, and the rising sun cast a purplish light on the battered cars in front of the station. Tara took the L to Union Station, where she bought an Amtrak ticket under the Laura Summers name. She chose Milwaukee because the train left in twenty minutes and she'd never been there, so it seemed as good a place as any.

Once there, Tara took a cab to the Motel 6 closest to the train station. In the room, she got undressed to shower. The jeans, a little large, slid off easily. The scar on the inside of her right thigh caught Tara's eye. It hadn't even crossed her mind when the red-haired man asked her about a mark. It was from surgery she'd had when she was fifteen to remove a benign bone tumor.

The whitish scar curved in the shape of an oblong S, and, when she flexed her muscle, it appeared to slither up her leg.

# 27

Cyril grasped the edge of the page with his gloved fingers. The paper smelled like dried leaves, and each time he turned a page he feared damaging it. Though not an original of Brother Andrew's writings, the translation, with subsequent commentary, was over five hundred years old. It had been stored in a safe in the back room of the Brotherhood's archives, a place Cyril had never gone before. He hadn't asked permission. Officially, he lacked any reason to be here. His efforts to change the Brotherhood's mind had been fruitless, and he'd been ordered to return to his regular job and search for a new ministry.

And he'd tried. But each night, Cyril imagined ways to redeem himself. When he saw the newspaper article, he'd rushed to Chicago. But Tara had evaded him.

Now, despite his blurring vision, a passage leapt out at Cyril. Heart racing, he grabbed a file of newspaper clippings, compared an article with the commentary, and with notes of a Brother Andrew scholar from only twenty years before. Now he understood. Now –

"You expect to fulfill your Ministry of Service requirements by huddling in a library?" Thomas Stranyero stood in the doorway, trench coat dripping, black umbrella at his side. Each strand of his thick, gray-flecked hair lay in place despite the weather. He removed his glasses and stared at Cyril. "Or do you no longer aspire to become Deacon Woods?"

Cyril swallowed hard and stood. He'd known his activities couldn't go unnoticed indefinitely.

"My aspirations remain the same. I believe I've found a Ministry of Service, that of proving the truth to the Brotherhood."

Thomas shrugged his coat off, folded it over a chair, and sat. "You remain convinced?"

"Of certain things."

Cyril showed Thomas the passages and articles and explained his theories.

Thomas shook his head. "I fear you will be disappointed. But I won't stop you, nor report your activities until I must. Act quickly. Act decisively. And be careful. Don't let this girl lead you astray again."

"I won't," Cyril said. "And I won't disappoint you."

THE RED-HAIRED MAN WAITED, knees bent, arms crossed over them, wedged between the file cabinets until Cyril and Thomas left and night fell. Unlike Cyril, he'd obtained authority to enter the Brotherhood's archives long ago, but he preferred not to be seen. Cyril had replaced the materials he'd reviewed, but they were easy enough for the man to pinpoint based on Cyril's and Thomas' conversation.

*This time, I won't ask if she bears the mark. I'll look for it on her dead body.*

# 28

Dear Tara,

I read about you on the Internet. I'm hoping Dr. Gaddini has a way to forward this letter to you even though the news articles say she lost contact with you.

This time must be scary for you. You must wonder how your pregnancy happened and what it means. It sounds like your family and friends feel confused, too, and worried about you. Even though they love you, they probably find it hard to believe you, which must make you feel lonely. We are strangers, but sometimes talking to a stranger helps more than talking to friends or family. Sometimes strangers understand our experiences and can help us find a new perspective.

If you'd ever like to talk, please e-mail me, or come and visit. Whether we ever speak or not, I wish you and your baby well and happy.

Kali Kerkorian-Lytle

klytle@uofseark.com

To:klytle@uofseark.com

From:thelittlestviking@mailmail.com

Re:Answer from Tara

Dear Kali,

Thank you for your letter. I noticed it includes drawings just like those on the Star Card in the Robin Wood Tarot deck. I've learned to read Tarot in my travels, it helps me sort through how I feel about things.

Do you read Tarot? Also, is there something particular you wanted to talk about? I appreciate your good wishes, especially since I've gotten plenty of angry letters cursing me. But I'm wondering if there's something more you're not saying. As I'm sure you can understand, I don't want anyone to know where I live, so please answer by e-mail. I check it every few days from public places.

Yours,
Tara

June 16, 1969 Los Angeles Times

MAYA KERKORIAN, AGE 19

Maya Kerkorian of Glendale, California, died Thursday evening when her car skidded over the side of Laurel Canyon Boulevard. According to police, no one witnessed the accident, but skid marks crossing the center line suggest an on-coming vehicle veered into Kerkorian's lane of traffic, forcing her off the road. Kerkorian planned to travel the next day to visit her grandmother in Armenia, her parents' country of origin.

A college student, Kerkorian had just completed her first year at UCLA. She planned to major in political science. She is survived by her mother, Nanor Kerkorian, her twin sister, Rozin (Rose) Kerkorian-Lytle, and her uncle, Emin Kerkorian.

Unitarian Universalist Church of North Hollywood, California
Hereby Ordains
Nanor Kerkorian, PhD
Minister of Care
and entrusts to her the sharing of faith
throughout this land
June 15, 1971

Please Join Us
For the First Sunday Service
at
The Willow Springs Community Center
Blue Springs, Arkansas
June 15, 1977
Pastor: Nanor Kerkorian

Dear Tara,

What the newspaper article omits is that Maya Kerkorian, my aunt, was nearly five months pregnant when she was killed. Everything I know about her came from other people, mainly my mother, who was Maya's twin, and my grandmother. Maya's planned visit to her grandmother in Armenia caused controversy in the family, as did her pregnancy.

It took Maya three months to admit her pregnancy to her mother – my grandmother, to whom I'll refer from here on as Grandmother. That's what I call her, and it will make this telling less confusing. Grandmother suspected the pregnancy, and she pushed Maya to tell her what was going on. Maya refused. From what I understand, Grandmother's way back then – though it's hard for me to imagine – was to try to make everyone what she wanted, on her timetable.

Finally, Maya blurted out she was pregnant, but claimed she was still a virgin. Grandmother accused Maya of lying. Grandmother said there was no shame in being pregnant, it was a mistake in judgment, but Maya must tell the truth and deal with it. (My sense is Grandmother was quite liberal for her times. Although in my history class, we learned of the sixties as a time of experimentation with sex and drugs, my mother assures me that adults, at least in Glendale, which had a large population of Armenian immigrants, still viewed a young woman becoming pregnant without being married as scandalous, unless she quickly wed. If not, she often left to stay with relatives or went away to a private school, and returned once she'd put the baby up for adoption. Of course, some girls obtained abortions, but no one spoke of that.)

Eventually Grandmother grew angry that Maya persisted in her story about being a virgin. Later, Grandmother realized she also felt angry that Maya, an A student at UCLA, took such chances with her education. Grandmother believed then, and does now, that all people – women and men – should do their best to use their talents and abilities for good in the world. And she believed women absolutely needed a college education to do this. She hoped Maya would become a professor, and Maya, so far as I know, wished to do so, though I wonder if she could be so certain at nineteen. I most certainly am not, and I'm only two years younger now.

Regardless, Maya felt betrayed by Grandmother's disbelief. Until that point, they'd gotten along well, more like good friends than mother and daughter. They sparred about curfews and boys, but that was about all. It was my mother, Rose, who clashed with Grandmother about everything, from religion to motorcycle riding to refusing to attend college right out of high school.

Rose told Maya she loved her, and didn't understand what was happening, and would help Maya figure it out. According to my mother, Maya longed for Grandmother to say just that, but Grandmother refused.

Grandmother was not particularly religious at that time. My family is from Armenia, the first country to adopt Christianity as its national religion, and Grandmother was born there. Armenians feel a strong sense of identity as Christians, and will occasionally visit churches. Also, you will see Khachkars (pronounced "hotchkars"), which are Armenian crosses, all over the country. Carved from wood, chiseled from stone. Yet people rarely attend church services, nor do they speak a great deal of religion, nor enforce many rules about it. It is considered rather personal, unlike here, where so many people insist that others must conform to or adopt their religious views. This perhaps is due to the many times other countries invaded Armenia, tore down the churches, killed Christians, and imposed their own religions.

Maya herself did not ascribe any religious significance to her pregnancy. Given the disputes with Grandmother, Maya wrote to her grandmother (my great-grandmother, Avids Kerkorian), who lived near Lake Sevan in Armenia, asking if she could live there until she had the baby. Grandmother had taken Rose and Maya to Armenia once, but Grandmother disliked visiting there, because she feared being unable to return. My great-grandmother was never able to get a visa out of the country to visit the United States.

When Maya announced her trip to Armenia, Grandmother raged that she hoped Maya never returned. Maya flew from the house, car keys in hand, slamming the back door so hard the screen came loose. My mother, Rose, hurried after Maya and persuaded her to take a walk rather than drive while so distraught. Together they paced the streets of Glendale as Maya yelled, then cried, then fell silent. Rose rarely played peacemaker, but she felt compelled to do so that night. She said it was as if her own heart were being shredded each time her mother and sister raved at one another, and she simply could bear it no longer. After speaking with Maya, Rose returned to speak to Grandmother, leaving Maya pacing in the yard, near the willow trees that grew along the lot line between our house and the neighbors'.

Rose convinced Grandmother that Maya truly believed she was a virgin and was very frightened, and that Grandmother might lose Maya forever if she insisted on casting her as a liar. Grandmother wept, the first time Rose can ever recall that happening, and hurried outside, under the stars, to embrace Maya. But Maya was nowhere to be found.

Maya's plane ticket, passport and visitor's visa still lay on her dresser in her room. Her flight wasn't for another week. (She'd used money from her college fund to buy the ticket, one can imagine Grandmother fuming over that.) Later, Rose and Grandmother guessed that Maya had decided to drive to a cousin's house in North Hollywood. It was where Rose often took refuge when feuding with Grandmother. Maya took Laurel Canyon Boulevard, which I'm told takes many sharp curves through the mountains. (I have not, myself, been to California.) You read in the article what happened.

At first, when the police told her another car had been involved, Grandmother assumed the driver was irresponsible and reckless, but had not meant to cause the accident. The local news station did a spot with her imploring the person to come forward and accept responsibility. But no one did. In cleaning out Maya's room, which Grandmother felt unable to do for nearly a year, Grandmother found a business card that included only a man's name – Thomas Stranyero – and a telephone number. The number was disconnected. Grandmother could find no listing for such a man in Los Angeles. The card bothered her, because Maya spoke to her about everything – at least until her pregnancy. She assumed Maya met the man during that time period.

The next night, Grandmother at last fell asleep after lying awake for hours, only to be started out of sleep by the wind rattling the windows. She got out of bed and, still in her nightgown, walked outside to the willow trees, certain she would rest no more that night. Rain had fallen earlier in the night, the grass felt damp between her toes, and the earth smelled fresh. As she neared the willows, a figure stepped out. It was Maya. She wore the clothes she'd worn the night she died, plain blue jeans and a floral gauze blouse.

Maya held out her arms, and Grandmother rushed to embrace her.

# 29

The bus jolted, and Tara changed position, rocking onto one hip, trying to shift the baby inside her. It rested high, pressing against her diaphragm and making it hard to breathe. Tara hadn't bothered trying to sleep. The seat next to her remained unoccupied, so she stretched her legs across it. Most of the Magic Bus was empty. The company was a new one, a competitor of Greyhound's that offered cheap overnight bus trips throughout the south.

As soon as she'd boarded the bus in Charleston, where she'd been living and working for the past month, Tara had examined her fellow passengers. She searched for signs of particular interest in her. Now, as the bus crossed the state line between Georgia and Alabama, she peered again at each of them again. Ever since she'd contacted Kali Kerkorian, Tara had been looking behind and around her more and more often. She doubted the motives of every person who spoke to her. Nothing rational prompted her actions, but a feeling persisted in Tara's gut that, somehow, by sharing her story with Kali, and leaving the city where she felt safe, she'd exposed herself and the baby to danger, even though she'd purchased the ticket under her assumed name, and she'd never told Kali where she was living.

Satisfied no one other than the bus driver was even awake, Tara leaned against the bus' inner wall to finish rereading the e-mails. She'd read them on the computer at the Charleston library, and several times since she'd printed them, and still felt at a loss as to what she believed. But tomorrow she would meet Kali and her grandmother, which she hoped would help her decide.

If it all turned out to be a farce, or if Kali was another religious fanatic, Tara decided that would end her quest for the meaning of her pregnancy until after she had the baby, even though she felt like she ought to keep trying. A true mother of a messiah or a miracle baby would. But Tara was tired. Tired of traveling on buses with worn out springs, and using dirty bathrooms, and wandering through unfamiliar towns, all to learn nothing.

In Charleston, Tara could stay anonymous, and could safely have her baby. She had rented a tiny room from a friend of a friend of Lily's. She kept photos of Megan, Kelly, Bailey, Nate and her parents under her mattress, so no one would see them, and she took them out every night to look at them. Afternoons and evenings, she worked for tips as a counter girl in a diner where the sweet, salty ocean breeze flowed in each time the door opened. Everyone in Charleston knew Tara only as Laura Summers. Her landlady, had she seen a photo of Tara from a few months before, would not have recognized her. Tara had cut her hair short, in an almost boyish-style, but wore blush and mascara every day, plus bangle bracelets and ruffled blouses and skirts she would have dismissed as too girlie the year before. When she looked in mirrors, she sometimes felt her real self had disappeared. But that was safer.

Tara planned to contact her parents soon. Much as she'd found what seemed to be a safe haven in Charleston, she felt lonely. She'd been hesitant to get to know anyone very well for fear she'd slip and reveal too much. Last week she'd e-mailed Nate and Kelly, and both felt sure their parents had abandoned the quest for guardianship of Tara. More important, they said Megan's tumor had turned malignant, and the doctors were treating her with more radiation and experimental drugs. Her hair was thinning again. Tara had sent Megan a Snoopy e-card, which Kelly promised to print on the color printer and give her if she wanted to hang a copy on her wall.

Tara looked down at the e-mail printouts from Kali again. Outside, the night was nearly black, for the bus traveled across farmlands and countryside devoid of streetlights. The pin light overhead illuminated only one paragraph at a time of the printing, but Tara read anyway.

Grandmother said later she half-expected Maya to disappear when Grandmother tried to hug her, or to be incorporeal, so that Grandmother's arms would simply pass right through her. But Grandmother hugged flesh and blood. Maya felt warm and alive. Her hair smelled of her honey-scented shampoo, her forehead felt smooth against Grandmother's cheek, and her breath felt warm on Grandmother's shoulder.

Grandmother heard rustling from above, and a little girl climbed down from the tallest willow tree. The girl wore no clothes, and her burnished skin suggested she'd bathed in the sun for many months. She moved nimbly, her feet and hands clinging to nitches in the bark. She jumped to the ground and smiled, her long, dark hair falling all around her, her eyes wide open and kind. Grandmother knew, without being told, that she beheld Maya's child. The child that would have been. She took the girl's small hand, and Maya's hand, and the three formed a circle under the willows. Tears filled Grandmother's eyes at the thought of the family she would have had.

The child said, "Despair not. Make a place for me at your table, and prepare the world for my return."

~

HE PULLED the SUV within a car-length of the corner and shifted into neutral, then positioned the customized passenger side view mirror so he could see the entrance to the Five and Diner. He'd followed Kali Kerkorian-Lytle for the last six days. After Tara escaped from Chicago, and his efforts to track her failed, he considered where she might turn next to learn about her baby. In her position, he would try to find the previous virgins. And if Tara was likely to find out about anyone, it would be Maya Kerkorian, the only one with living relatives.

Now, a week later, his work was about to pay off. He'd researched Willow Springs and, despite the security, infiltrated it by night. He knew the paths, the trailers, the deserted areas, and he knew where Tara would be vulnerable.

Adrenalin surged. It was almost time.

~

TAPPING one foot on the blacktop, Kali brushed damp strands of hair from her eyes and peered down the road, though she'd looked only a few seconds before. Still no sign of the Magic Bus, scheduled to stop at seven thirteen a.m. The same dusty SUV she'd seen ten minutes before cruised by again. Maybe the driver was lost.

Kali went into the Mini-Mart to cool off, and bought two chilled bottles of the cheapest water, Poland Springs. As she exited the store, the bus pulled into the lot. Kali's stomach tightened. As always, she wondered, and simultaneously felt guilty wondering, whether her family's belief that Maya became pregnant by some supernatural means amounted to nothing more than a shared exercise in denial.

Would Tara Spencer answer the question one way or the other? Was she the chosen one for whom Grandmother prayed? And, if so, would Kali be able to tell? She guessed Tara wouldn't have a halo over her head.

Kali tried to smile at the thought, so out of character for the traditions in which she'd been raised, but her mouth pulled tight as the bus doors hissed open. She'd barely slept the night before. Only six years old the last time Grandmother thought she'd found Maya's successor, Kali still remembered what had happened.

A young woman with chin-length blonde hair and olive-toned skin stepped off the bus, one hand against the small of her back. Her dress sloped over a melon-shaped mid-section. She didn't look all that far along.

Kali stepped forward. "Tara?"

The girl smiled, and it lit her face. "Kali? Thanks so much for meeting me."

Kali smiled back and held out one of the Poland Springs. "Would you care for some water?"

"Definitely. Thank you."

Kali sipped her own water, examining Tara. The lacy lavender dress and flowered duffel bag seemed out of place, not quite right with the athletic build that made it clear Tara was pregnant, not just heavy. "If you aren't too tired, I thought perhaps we'd get some breakfast and talk for a while before going to Willow Springs."

"Sure," Tara said. "Whatever's good for you."

Kali let her breath out. "Wonderful. You see, I haven't told Grandmother about you yet."

# 30

The two young women sat across from one another in a booth in front of The Five 'N Diner's front plate glass window.

"I'd appreciate if you wouldn't tell Grandmother why you're here when I introduce you. Just say you're interested in joining the community," Kali said. She had a narrow forehead and chin, and her face was a little too wide at the cheeks, but her eyes were so large and her lashes so heavy they made her look striking. Tara guessed Kali had been one of those girls who looked kind of funny in kindergarten, then turned into a beauty by the middle of high school. She wondered if, combined with living in her grandmother's unusual community, that had made Kali the odd girl out during school. Which made her feel for Kali, but it didn't mean Tara trusted her. And Kali asking Tara to lie about why she'd come to Willow Springs wasn't helping.

"Why wouldn't I tell her the truth?" Tara said. "Isn't that why you wanted me to come?"

"It's not so simple." Kali crossed her arms and leaned forward. "Before Grandmother started her own community, when she was a minister at the Unitarian church near Glendale, young pregnant women came to her. They'd heard about my Aunt Maya. Some claimed to be virgins. Grandmother knew they were lying, though one or two were psychologically disturbed and believed what they were saying. She gently drew their real stories from them."

"She sounds like a very kind woman."

"She is. She got jobs for some of the girls, helped others find housing. For others, depending how early they came to her and what they wanted, she helped them find doctors who did safe abortions."

"I take it something went wrong."

"Not with an abortion, but yes." A freight train rumbled by on the track behind the restaurant, rattling the window glass, tables, and dishes. Kali resumed when the noise died. "One young woman somehow convinced Grandmother she truly was a successor to Maya, or Maya reincarnated. It wasn't until she had the baby – and ten thousand dollars of Grandmother's money – that she told the truth. In a very hurtful way. I was quite young, but even at the age of seven I felt this girl appeared quite proud of her deception."

Kali had peeled the laminate from the edge of the table as she spoke, now she brushed the shavings to one side of her plate. "So, you see, while I'm not suggesting you're either mentally unwell or running a con game, I really don't know you, and I feel some responsibility to be more certain before I bring you into Grandmother's life."

The waitress plunked down Kali's and Tara's plates, making the table shake. "It'll be a few minutes for your milk," she said to Tara. "The market across the street's not open yet."

"Okay. Thanks." Tara poured syrup over her French Toast, then recoiled from the sweet, faintly maple scent. The bus' bouncing through the night had revived her morning sickness. She set down her fork, pushed her plate aside. "That's awful that anyone would use your Grandmother's faith against her like that. I didn't come to you, though. You came to me. Doesn't that reassure you that I'm not after something from your Grandmother?"

Tara felt sympathy for Maya's fears, but she also felt tired and hungry and slightly ill, and while she'd given up on going back to her real home, more than anything she wished to be back in Charleston.

"Please understand. It's not the loss of money that worries me, though that of course would be problematic," Kali said. "But Grandmother became severely depressed and had to be hospitalized. When I visited, she could barely walk across the room. My mother told me later she worried Grandmother might take her own life."

A fly buzzed past Kali and landed on her red plastic water glass. She shooed it away without glancing at it.

"I can see why you'd be concerned," Tara said. "But I don't know how I can prove to you I'm not crazy, or that I'm telling the truth. In fact, my parents think I am crazy, and they filed papers in court to try to get me declared incompetent, which is why I took off. One of the reasons, anyway."

Kali sat straighter. "What prompted them to do that?"

"Partly just my insisting I hadn't had sex, even after it was clear I was pregnant. Then there was this guy, Cyril Woods."

Tara paused to force down some plain toast, then told Kali about meeting Cyril, and what he'd said about the Brotherhood of Andrew.

"So your parents thought you just made up Cyril? Or imagined him?" Kali said. Tara couldn't tell from Kali's tone or expression whether she deplored Tara's parents' view or was tempted to agree with it.

"I guess. Or that I'd imagined what he said to me." Tara felt the usual hollowness when she thought about her parents or about Cyril. If she'd made him up, she would have made him more reliable. "I called them after the *Reader* article came out, and my mom just kept begging me to get help – psychiatric help –

even if I wouldn't come home. And my dad tried calling Sophia – Dr. Gaddini – to convince her I should be committed. She said even though she doesn't understand what's happening, she feels sure from knowing me that I'm sane and telling the truth. Which it'd be nice if my own parents would say."

"It's harder for parents, though, don't you think? They always seem to think the worst of their children."

"My dad never did before."

Kali smiled and touched Tara's arm, the first warmth she'd shown. "Well, I've only known you a short while, but you seem sane to me."

"Which leaves you with the 'is she lying?' question." Tara sighed. "It's okay. Everyone wonders that."

Everyone but Cyril. Who had still abandoned her.

Kali met Tara's eyes. "That must be hard. I'm sorry. My gut feeling is that you're truthful. But I don't remember much about the other girl. Maybe she would have fooled me, too. She fooled Grandmother, who has great insight into people, far more than I. So that's why at first I wish you'd merely say you're a visitor interested in joining the community. Let's see how it goes, then we can tell her."

The waitress returned with Tara's milk and the check.

Tara sipped her milk. It tasted fresh and sweet, and revived her a bit. "I've only got four days off from work. I needed to beg my boss to get that, and one has to be spent on the bus trip back."

Kali sighed and twisted her napkin. "I understand. And certainly Grandmother wouldn't approve of my advocating deception. I just – " Kali paused and cleared her throat. "I'm afraid she can't take any more disappointment. Everyone sees her as so strong, and she is strong, but she has a breaking point."

"What about this?" Tara said. "Let's spend the day with you showing me Willow Springs. When I meet your grandmother, I won't volunteer anything, I'll just tell her there are some complications in my life because of my pregnancy that I don't want to talk about yet, and I'm trying to work things out and hope visiting Willow Springs might help me do that."

Kali leaned forward. "That'll work. Grandmother will be curious, but she'll respect your desire for privacy." Kali drank half her tea and reached for the check. "Let's go."

Tara stood. "If she asks me something specific, though, and it seems like it's only right to answer, I will."

# 31

Kali drove Tara to a square frame house with no lawn at all, but a vegetable garden all around it. Behind it a winding dirt path led into a heavily wooded area. To one side of the house, a ten foot high chain link fence with barbed wire across the top surrounded rows of golf carts. Kali passed a keycard over a box with a tiny red light. The light turned green and the gate swung open.

"We can't drive an automobile into Willow Springs," she said. "The roads are too narrow. So each resident has a card to access a golf cart." The cart, too, started with the card rather than a key.

"You never wanted to create wider roads?" Tara said.

Kali shook her head. "The community started as a center for battered women, and it still functions as that to some extent. It's meant to be difficult to penetrate."

"Couldn't people walk in?"

"It's certainly possible. It is fifteen miles, though, to reach the housing area, and various alarms and trip wires are set randomly and moved periodically to make it difficult."

The gate clanged shut behind them, and Kali maneuvered the cart onto the dirt road. Tara braced herself against the jolting from the rough terrain.

"What about a bicycle or motorcycle?" Tara peered at the woods around her as she spoke. The tall trees blotted the sunlight despite the bright day, and in a just a few seconds, gloom descended around them.

"Any narrow vehicle can pass. And will be captured on video camera, so we'll at least be warned of any stranger approaching."

When the cart drove out of the woods and into the daylight, Tara let her breath out. Trailer homes with flower and vegetable gardens were scattered around the grounds, with trees and bushes everywhere, but spaced far enough apart to let sunshine through. Kali dropped Tara at a home about a mile from the edge of the woods.

The visitor trailer consisted of one large room and a bathroom. The kitchen area was tiled in large black and white squares with a breakfast counter, white cabinets, and counter stools for an eating area. The living room was carpeted in pristine short white shag. A built in day bed stood under the windows, plants all around it.

"Feel free to take a shower," Kali said, pointing toward the door off the kitchen. "Then rest for a couple hours. This is one of our guesthouses, where you'll stay during your visit."

"Shouldn't we go see your Grandmother first? I won't be here very long," Tara said.

"All the more reason to feel well while you are."

The hot shower felt wonderful, but all through it, the feeling nagged at Tara that she'd seen or heard something this morning that threatened her and the baby. It wasn't meeting Kali, she didn't think, or even the wooded darkness through with they'd traveled, though the security precautions made her feel nervous more than safe. It might have been something in the town of Blue Springs. Something she'd seen there, maybe, or overheard, but she couldn't imagine what.

Once out of the shower, she changed into a T-shirt and shorts and fell asleep almost the moment she lay on the crisp white sheets. Whatever she'd noticed that morning was forgotten.

~

THE LIGHTS, except those over the Exit signs, blinked out, plunging the Willow Springs Community Center into darkness. Tara grabbed the arm of the woman who stood next to her in their circle.

"Is that supposed to happen?"

A low, deep drumming started behind Tara. A spotlight clicked on, illuminating a woman with long dark hair poised on one leg, the other bent, as if she were about to leap forward. Tara relaxed, realizing this was part of the ceremony. The woman lifted a fiddle to her chin and swept her bow across the strings, sending a sweet high note into the air. Stringed instruments burst into sound from all around the room. Tiny white lights sparkled within and around each circle of women.

Everyone danced around the lights, and a chorus of voices rose in three part harmony. A little blonde boy took Tara's hands and started them both spinning. Tara felt almost weightless.

When the song ended, the room burst into applause.

A few moments later, Kali, dressed in a satin gown, made her way to Tara. She smiled. "So how do you feel?"

"Amazing," Tara said. "Happier than in ages. That's your service?"

Kali laughed. "It changes from month to month, but it generally involves music and dancing and lights."

"No sermons? No prayers?"

"None. We dance."

The lights brightened, revealing the windowless walls and carpeted floor with basketball markings on it. Kali explained that they'd learned this type of carpet worked as a basketball court floor, so the room could be used for all types of activities, and still function as a gymnasium for practices and games. The women slid out dividers for smaller events, and used wooden folding chairs, with pads for comfort, for meetings or plays. A low-rise stage at the far end was easily disassembled and stored, and the basketball nets were draped in black and barely noticeable during performances.

"The way we use space at Willow Springs inspired me to major in urban planning," Kali said. "I want to help all sorts of communities design better public spaces and homes."

The outer rooms Kali showed Tara included an arts room, a library with a reading porch overlooking a stream and garden, a row of sound-proofed music rooms with upright pianos, and workout rooms with hardwood flooring for dance, yoga and martial arts.

"One thing we can't afford is a pool," Kali said. "Nearly all the money went into this center, and the expense of putting in a pool and then maintaining it would have left nothing to develop the surrounding acres."

"This must have cost a fortune," Tara said, as she walked around the stair machines. She hadn't been on one in the months since she'd left home.

"Not as much as you might think. Grandmother sold her house in California when property values were quite high, and chose Arkansas, and this part in particular, because land was so inexpensive. One of the early founders was a real estate and tax lawyer. This land was unincorporated and undeveloped, and she negotiated deals with the town fathers and the state for favorable tax status and even some municipal funding, and with local contractors, who were starved for work. She really stretched Grandmother's dollars. The place is kept up by membership fees, which the women who live here can afford because they pay no state or municipal taxes. Janel explained it to me once. It's something like the deal the Amish have, since they take care of their own community services. We all still pay federal tax, though."

"Who makes the rules?" Tara said. "Your grandmother?"

Kali nodded. "If it relates to the funds, yes, because this whole space is her private property. She owns the land and leases to the women who live here at low rates. They build homes or rent or buy trailers. Whatever Grandmother makes, she puts back into the community. All the joint areas are equally available to everyone, however much or little she pays per month."

The next room featured floor-to-ceiling windows. The window glass was so clean it seemed to Tara she could step right through it into the grove of trees and plants outside, which were lit from beneath by uplights. About thirty woman of different ages and ethnicities filled the room, some at tables, some perched on floor pillows near the windows. Others gathered at the refreshment bar, chatting while their children tugged at their arms and begged for treats. It looked and felt like one of the moderately upscale bars near SLU, complete with soft piano jazz playing over the sound system, except for the lack of men.

Tara and Kali settled on counter stools at a tall square table, and Kali bought them sparkling black cherry sodas. "No men live here?" Tara said.

"You hadn't noticed before?"

Tara shook her head. "I guess not. I saw boys when we walked around during the day, so assumed I was mostly seeing moms home with their kids, and the men might be at work."

"No adult men live here. Since we started as a haven for abused women and their children, Grandmother felt it important that the community be women only."

Tara sipped her soda and found it darker and fizzier than any she'd bought in a grocery store.

"There's a phosphate fountain back there," Kali said. "One of our founders really loved soda fountains, and she runs all the concessions."

"That's so cool."

"It's part of the fun of a small community. And one of the drawbacks. We have certain wonderful things because someone here has an interest, then other things can't be had without a thirty-mile drive to the closest WalMart."

A small, smiling woman with gray and black hair piled on top of her head tiptoed toward them from the refreshment bar. Her fiery orange blouse shone above a long dark skirt. Wrinkles criss-crossed her face and neck. She carried a plate of star-shaped powdered cookies.

Meeting Tara's eyes, the woman put a finger to her lips and nodded toward Kali's back. Tara tried to keep her expression neutral, so as not to ruin the surprise by the woman who must be Kali's grandmother.

The woman put her free hand over Kali's eyes. "At last I find you."

Kali smiled. "I am not at all hard to find." She took her grandmother's hand and drew it away from her eyes. "This is my grandmother. And this is Tara."

"It's great to meet you," Tara said. "This is a wonderful place."

Keeping her eyes fixed on Tara, Nanor moved to the other side of the table and slid onto a chair. Tara caught an oaky, plum scent as she passed, almost like the red wine Sophia liked. The scent made her feel at home.

Nanor gestured toward the room around her. "A tribute to my daughter Maya. A safe place for women."

"Kali told me about Maya."

"Did she?" Nanor glanced at her granddaughter, and Tara wondered if she'd made a misstep in mentioning that. But surely everyone here knew about Maya.

"Yes."

The music changed to jazz with horns and a quick tempo, and Nanor raised her voice slightly. Her pitch was low but carried easily, and Tara wondered if she'd had vocal training. "While girls and women are raised to fear strangers – to worry about being raped, murdered, or assaulted in the street or in parking garages, which are real dangers – statistically, the most dangerous men are those they know and, particularly, those they live with. So Willow Springs started as a community for battered women, with only women."

"And now?" Tara asked.

"Before I was born," Kali said, "Willow Springs expanded to find space for any women and their children. But Grandmother still saw the advantages of a community where we can feel free to do and say as we like without male influence."

Tara took another drink of soda. "What advantages?"

"For one, more speech," Kali said.

The phrase rang a bell, and Tara searched her memory, vaguely recalling something from a political science course. "You mean, as in the best remedy for bad speech is more speech?"

Nanor smiled and touched Tara's elbow. Tara hadn't realized how tense she'd felt all day until that moment, because her tension drained and her shoulders dropped. She let her back rest against the chair.

"Indeed," Nanor said. "Many studies show that, in mixed groups, women speak far less than men. Even in settings like law school or medical school, where you'd expect the most assertive women might be."

"I didn't know that." Tara thought about her classes at SLU. The male students did seem to talk more, but Tara always assumed it was just that they liked to show off.

"Women – and girls – tend to take turns speaking, so they yield the floor to one another, and wait for the floor to be passed to them before speaking," Nanor said. "Men take the floor if they desire to speak, and assume that women will do the same. So, in a mixed group, most women wait their turn, and most men jump in and speak until someone interrupts them."

The bushes on the other side of the window swayed, and Tara tensed, until a rabbit bounded out. Tara watched the moonlight flash on its fur as it raced into the trees. When Tara looked away, she saw Nanor watching her.

Tara turned her mind back to the topic, though the moment had revived the uneasiness she'd felt earlier, the sense that she'd missed something important when she'd first arrived in Willow Springs. "But isn't it important for women and girls to learn to take the floor if that's what's necessary in a mixed group?"

"It is important," Nanor said. "Yet notice you assumed women must change and adapt, not men. Women constitute over the half the population and still, to the extent we are not like men, we are characterized as 'different' or as needing 'special' consideration. Men are as different from women as women are from men. Perhaps men should change. Learn to take their turns and to yield the floor at appropriate times."

"Will they, though? I mean, unless they have to."

Nanor nodded. "You've reached the heart of it. If women enter an area men traditionally control, being accepted means adapting to men, and this many women do constantly day in and day out. Which is exactly why I treasure a place designed around women, not men. Willow Springs is not utopia. But it is a place that women designed for women. Which, sadly, makes it—"

Sirens pierced the air, and a red light flashed above the door.

Nanor gripped Tara's arm. "Tara Spencer, what have you brought to our haven?"

# 32

The back of Tara's chair was wedged against the kitchen cabinets behind her, and her knees pressed against a table leg. In other circumstances, the shining black and white tile floor and the daffodils on the counter would have felt cozy, now Nanor's kitchen just felt claustrophobic. Nanor paced the six-foot section of floor space between the stainless steel refrigerator and the arched doorway to the living room, clutching her cell phone.

"Something set it off. You must be certain." Nanor clicked the phone shut and turned to Tara. "Did someone follow you?"

"No one. I took a bus. I was careful."

"Careful because you expected someone to follow?"

"Grandmother." Kali stood next to Tara, a hand on her shoulder. "You'll frighten Tara."

Nanor swung to face her granddaughter. "You keep things from me. You believe I do not see that? You believe I've become old and feeble?"

Kali stood straighter. "Of course not."

"Then why did you not tell me about Ms. Spencer?"

Tara's stomach rolled. She'd hadn't even had time to tell Nanor the truth about her visit before the sirens started, but guilt ingrained from years of Catholic grade school flared inside her all the same. Guilt that she'd been willing to lie by omission. Guilt that she might have brought danger to this community. And guilt that she might have endangered her baby by leaving Charleston, where she'd lived in safe anonymity.

"Sit," Nanor said to Kali. Then she turned to Tara. "Tell me your story."

"It may surprise you," Kali said.

"I think she knows the basics," Tara said.

"What?" Kali glanced between her grandmother and Tara. "Knows what?"

"You never told her my last name, but she called me Ms. Spencer."

Nanor nodded, her mouth set in a straight line. She stared at Kali. "You think I don't read the news? I know who Ms. Spencer is."

Kali sighed. "I'm sorry. I thought only to protect you."

"Knowledge is the best protection."

Tara started with her pregnancy, then described her meeting with Cyril. "He gave me this photograph." She handed Nanor the creased photo of the vase.

Nanor took reading glasses from her pocket and put them on. She drew in her breath.

"What?" Kali touched Nanor's arm, a worried expression on her face.

"A moment." Nanor jumped to her feet and hurried into her bedroom, her feet slapping the floor.

"I'm sorry," Kali said to Tara. Kali twisted her fingers together on the white Formica table. "I shouldn't have asked you to lie to her. It wasn't fair, especially after I asked you to come here."

"It wasn't," Tara said, feeling a little angry at Kali, but she knew she'd be as protective of anyone she loved.

Nanor returned, carrying a large brown envelope. She pulled photos from it and sorted them on the table. She pushed one toward Tara. Someone had clipped a business card to the top of it.

The refrigerator's hum grew louder as Tara stared at the photo. "It's the same vase."

The business card displayed the name Thomas Stranyero and a phone number, nothing more. The card was bright white, heavy, and textured, unlike the smooth grayish card Cyril had given her, but Tara couldn't ignore the similarity. She fished Cyril's out and handed it to Nanor.

"A connection must exist," Nanor said.

Peering at the two photos, Kali said, "Grandmother, why did you never tell me about the vase?"

"You are not the only one with concerns about my well being. I decided that, to protect myself after the last disappointment, I must keep some details to myself. Very few people know of the vase. Your mother is one, and only whomever she told." Nanor looked at Tara. "I took my photograph to an archeologist when I found it a year or so after Maya's death. As best as he can tell, the vase is Armenian, probably sixth century. I think perhaps my mother – Maya's grandmother – guessed that from Maya's description, which is why she wanted Maya to travel to Armenia. But my mother told us little in her letters and less over the phone. Armenia was part of the Soviet Union then, and one never knew who was listening, or what the KGB might deem subversive."

"But why Armenia?" Tara said. "I don't understand how that fits with Andrew of Crete's visions."

"Nor do I," Nanor said. "But we don't know if the Andrew of Crete story was told to Maya. Or if it has any basis in history."

A hot wind blew through the window, bringing in the scent of lilacs and rattling the blinds. Kali twisted around and raised them.

"Some of what Cyril told me must be true," Tara said. "At least, if Maya became pregnant as a virgin, and I did, that's two of us. I don't know about six."

"Or whether you are the last," Kali said. "I wish he'd told you more."

Tara looked at Nanor. "Maya never mentioned the vase to you? Or the Brotherhood or Thomas Stranyero?"

"She told me only she wished to go to Armenia to see her grandmother. I am not entirely surprised she held back, though. I reacted so badly in the beginning." Nanor took her glasses off and rubbed her forehead. "I felt so certain she must be lying."

Tara reached across the table and touched Nanor's hand. "My parents reacted the same way to me."

"And then they came to believe you?"

"No, then they decided I must be unbalanced. Which is why I left." Tara thought for a moment of the months she'd been away, wondered if everyone had gone on the yearly camping trip and if Bailey had insisted on burning everyone's marshmallows black over the fire.

"Strange, isn't it?" Nanor said. "We are all so willing to believe stories from the past, but not miraculous events in the present."

Tara shifted in her chair, pushed away her thoughts of home. Out the window over the kitchen sink, the night had turned completely black. "I don't know if my pregnancy is miraculous. Inexplicable, but not necessarily miraculous."

"Perhaps time will make it clear," Nanor said.

Kali filled a plate with shortbread cookies from a green glass jar on the counter and refreshed everyone's tea.

"Maybe." Tara shut her eyes, let her head rest against the counter behind her.

"You must stay with us," Nanor said.

"I don't know if that's safe for any of us."

"This is where you belong. Maya, and my granddaughter, charged me with a task. To prepare our world for a female messiah. Which must be the child you carry."

Tara swallowed hard, not much more comfortable with this type of statement from Nanor than she'd been when Cyril first spoke to her. And she'd thought about her baby's gender mostly in connection with Cyril abandoning her because of it, not as the possible reason for the baby to exist in the first place. She still didn't feel convinced a messiah had ever existed, let alone would return.

"But why a female messiah?" Tara said.

*My baby. We're talking about my baby. As a messiah.*

Nanor spread her arms wide. "She could change everything. End war. Usher in an age of compassion – real compassion, not lip service to the word while sending thousands off to slaughter others, then die themselves, while abandoning the poor and ill at home. Create real respect for families, based on love and companionship, not dominion and control. Care for our natural resources to ensure our descendants healthy, fruitful lives. Life, love, peace, cooperation. Rather than power, intolerance, destruction and competition."

"I – that's a lot to do."

"The religions of man are the tools rulers use to justify their actions and dominate others," Nanor said. "You have heard the saying – 'if God is a man, then man must be God?'"

Tara nodded. She'd read it in her studies the last few months, which Sophia had guided through email.

"In Willow Springs we believe in a divine being that is feminine and creative, rather than male and war-like. Which is why Maya's child – and yours – needed to be female. And it is why the world seeks to stop you. Maya's daughter came to end the three major male-centered monotheistic religions – Islam, Christianity, and Judaism."

Tara's hand, lifting her teacup, froze midair. "To end – How could you know that? I mean, why do you believe that was her purpose?"

"Is her purpose. It came to me over time, after much prayer and reflection, after years of working with the women here. I did not decide it or figure it out. I simply knew."

"A leap of faith." Tara's hands trembled, and her tea spilled. She set her cup back in the saucer.

Nanor nodded. "A leap of faith."

# 33

He expected she had locked the trailer's doors and windows, but he tried each anyway. So often people failed to do simple things to help ensure their safety. Tara, though, had been careful.

After each try, he faded back into the shadows of the surrounding trees, just out of the motion detector's range. Exactly two minutes later, he tried the next window, hoping anyone who saw the lights blinking would assume a malfunction, not an intruder. The open small square bathroom window, edged by glass blocks, appeared too small for a person to crawl through. But he removed the screen, gripped the trailer's side, and hoisted himself into the opening. Twisting so his shoulders aligned with the diagonal, he slithered through, praying he wouldn't be seen. He suspected the whole community attended the Friday night performance. He couldn't bring himself to call it a service, even in his mind.

Arms inside, he pressed his hands against the shower door to anchor himself. But the door swung and his upper body pitched down. His palms and forehead banged the tile wall. Everything went black, but he kept moving his hands down the tile to the floor, aware of every second his legs hung outside. His ankles made it through the window, but his feet caught on the window lip. He walked his hands across the shower stall floor for leverage, pulled one leg in and braced his foot. His body made a downward V as he inched his feet down the wall.

Sirens erupted outside. He froze, imagining in a moment he'd hear pounding on the door, shouts outside. Time stretched, the sirens kept blaring, but he heard no one near the trailer. At last he dropped to his knees, panting. Only then did his nausea subside. He crawled out of the shower stall, stood, and checked his weapons.

Now he needed only to hide, in case Tara brought anyone back with her. This time he wouldn't let her get away.

# 34

Nanor pressed her hand against Tara's cheek. "Your baby matters. She will change things. We must keep her safe."

The clanging bell sound of Nanor's phone made Tara's heart race. Kali covered Tara's hand with her own while they waited for Nanor to return from the living room, where she'd gone to take the call. Neither of them spoke.

When Nanor came back to the kitchen, some of the worry lines had disappeared from her forehead.

"It appears to have been a false alarm. A malfunctioning cart that somehow started down our paths and tripped alarms."

Tara leaned forward. "You're sure?"

"My security people are sure. But you are not?"

"I don't know. I keep thinking of what happened to Maya."

Tara imagined how frightened Maya must have felt on the dark, wet road when the car veered toward her. The man who'd come after Tara in the hospital was too young to have been the same man who drove his car into Maya's. But he could have been from the same organization.

"Did Maya have a scar anywhere?" Tara asked. "Or any other kind of mark on her skin?"

Nanor stared at the ceiling for a moment. "No birthmarks. When she turned three, she fell down the stairs and cut her chin open. The plastic surgeon at the hospital did a beautiful job, but left a very faint scar."

Tara gripped the edge of the table. "How was it shaped?"

"It curved into an S," Nanor said.

"What?" Kali asked Tara.

Shivering despite the hot kitchen, Tara told them about the red-haired man and what he'd said about the mark of the serpent.

To Tara's surprise, Kali laughed and squeezed Tara's arm. "A serpent's not negative. In Christian symbology it's linked with Satan. But in many cultures the serpent means healing, which is why the physician's symbol includes it. Also fertility and life. Then there's Kundalini, the serpent Goddess who sleeps at the base of the spine, coiled around the first charka."

Tara nodded. "I know the chakras from yoga. The body's eight energy centers."

"That's right. When you rouse Kundalini with yoga or meditation, she unfolds and rises through your body, awakening each chakra. Once she's risen to the crown chakra, you experience enlightenment."

The image of a serpent inside her made Tara squirm. "I'm not sure how I feel about a serpent inside me."

"Which just shows how deep our culture's view of the serpent goes," Kali said.

"At least I know there could be a positive side to the serpent mark."

"Or it could be just a scar," Nanor said. "The man you describe most likely would find some kind of mark on anyone he believed was evil."

Kali and Tara hugged just outside the guest trailer door.

"You don't need to decide anything now," Kali said. Her black hair shone in the floodlights around the trailer, and her teeth looked like pearls. "Grandmother can be a bit overwhelming, but I hope you'll seriously consider staying. We can help you."

"I can't see myself as the mother of the leader of a new type of religion."

"Not new," Kali said. "Old. But you're always welcome here regardless. Even if you completely disagree about your daughter's purpose, or even that she has a purpose."

Tears filled Tara's eyes. "Thanks."

From just inside the trailer's front screen door, Tara watched Kali walk toward the woods. The warm night breeze smelled like fresh, damp leaves. Talking to everyone today, she'd felt as if she were part of a family. She hadn't felt that wanted and accepted since before learning about her pregnancy. Maybe Willow Springs offered a haven where Tara could protect her child and be her real self, rather than Laura Summers.

Kali disappeared from view, and the motion detector lights outside blinked out. The trailer plunged into darkness. Tara froze just inside the door, listening, certain she'd turned on the living room floor lamp before she'd left that afternoon.

The instant she heard the footsteps, Tara reached in her pocket for her pepper spray and swung around so the screen door was at her back. She took a huge breath, kicked the door behind her open, and sprayed forward into the kitchen as she leapt backwards out of the trailer.

# 35

Tara stumbled on the uneven ground outside the trailer but stayed on her feet. Despite shutting her eyes, pepper spray got into them and her nose. What felt like fire seared her eyelids, nasal passages, throat. She coughed and gagged. Tears streamed down her cheeks. Inside the trailer, someone coughed and banged into things. Tara rifled through her pockets for her cell phone, then realized she didn't know anyone's number at Willow Spring well enough to dial by touch and memory, and she couldn't open her eyes yet.

A voice came from inside, between gasps. "Tara."

Despite his hoarseness and coughing, Tara recognized Cyril's voice. Her fingers, which had been gripping the cell phone, loosened, but she didn't let go. The last time she'd been with Cyril, he'd been plotting against her with his superior on the phone.

Backing away from the trailer until the motion detector lights blinked out, Tara held the pepper spray in one hand, finger on the trigger, and her cell phone in the other. She still heard Cyril coughing and choking, so she had some advantage over him if he did mean to harm her. And now at least she wasn't visible to him.

"What are you doing here?" she asked.

Cyril coughed again. "Talk. "Come in?"

"You come out."

"Don't want anyone to see." Cyril, doubled forward in pain, appeared in front of the screen door, a hunched silhouette. "Might throw me out."

"Which might be fine."

"Wait. Please." Cyril moved out of sight. Water ran and splashed in the trailer's kitchen, then a fan turned on. Cyril's shadow reappeared in the doorway, straighter now. "Not here to hurt you. But others might be." Cyril coughed, wiped his mouth with the back of his hand. "If I found you, the man who attacked you in Chicago could, too."

"What do you know about him?"

"What I heard on the radio. And through the Brotherhood."

"Does he belong?" Tara asked.

"To the Brotherhood? No."

Tara's back ached, her feet hurt, and she longed to sit. She stepped toward the trailer. Cyril was the first person who'd believed her about the baby, and she felt drawn to him after months of living in anonymity. But the very fact that she wasn't more uneasy made Tara uneasy. Maybe Maya Kerkorian had thought whoever ultimately ran her off the road meant her no harm, either.

"Back off," she told Cyril, still holding the pepper spray.

Cyril nodded and stepped away from the door.

"Turn on a light."

A moment later, the overhead kitchen light clicked on. Through the door, Tara looked at Cyril. He stood against the wall near the bathroom, hands at his sides, as far from the trailer's entryway as he could get without being out of sight. He wore jeans and a black long-sleeved T-shirt, and, for once, looked wrinkled and tired, with dark areas under his eyes. It made him seem more human, and less forbidding. A purplish bruise stood out on his forehead.

Tara clicked on her cell phone and found Kali's number, setting it to dial on one touch if she needed it. Then she approached the screen door. "Did you send that guy after me at the hospital?"

"Of course not. I would have protected you from him if I could have. I couldn't find you. You disappeared in St. Clair."

"Because you wanted to take me back home." Keeping her eyes on Cyril, Tara fumbled the door open and stepped inside. The air stung her eyes. It was good to know the pepper spray had probably hurt Cyril more than Tara, but she didn't think much of it as a self-defense measure now that she'd actually used it. "Or worse. I heard you talking to your boss, or whoever, about termination."

Cyril clenched his hands into fists at his sides. "I'm sorry. So very sorry. I knew you must have heard me, that it must be why you left. May I sit?"

Staying near the door, Tara nodded.

Sighing, Cyril sank down onto the daybed. His body sagged, but he looked up to meet Tara's eyes. "My mentor said if you were an agent of the Beast, we might need to terminate you, or make sure the pregnancy terminated. Even then, I knew I could never do either, but I felt certain you were not an agent of the Beast. So I said it wouldn't be a problem, because I knew I'd never need to do it."

"It's not a lot of comfort that the Brotherhood's willing to kill me, but you're not." But Tara sat on the armchair near the daybed. Her hands dropped onto her knees, but still she gripped the pepper spray in her right fist.

"It's not you personally the Brotherhood might consider eliminating," Cyril said. "It's an agent of the Beast, and only if they were certain."

"And that would make it okay? Killing me then would be okay?"

Cyril clasped his hands in front of him, almost as if in prayer. "No. I don't know. Killing a human being is wrong, but there are times, like times of war, when it must be done."

"And are these times of war?"

"I don't know. Maybe."

The religions of men, Nanor had said. But was it only men or all humans who tended toward wars?

"And could you do that? Kill someone?"

"If I were convinced that person was an Agent of the Beast and would set off Armageddon if I didn't."

"Have you ever killed anyone?" Tara asked.

"No." Cyril reached toward Tara, but stopped, his hand on the arm of her chair, inches from her arm. "I can't make up for turning on you the way I did, but I'd like to try to earn your trust again."

"And the Brotherhood?"

"They're convinced you're irrelevant to the prophecy. They're searching for someone else."

~

AFTER CYRIL HAD SHOWERED, he got back into his clothes, the only ones he had with him. He found oranges in the kitchen, peeled them and separated the pieces, then heated cream of chicken soup for him and Tara.

They ate at the fold-down table near the window. Cyril lifted a slat on the blinds and looked out, as if expecting guards from the community or a rogue member of the Brotherhood to peer in at him.

"When I last saw you," Tara said. "you were all about following orders."

Cyril stared at his hands. "I know. But when you disappeared, I realized if something happened to you, it was my fault. I told you about the prophecy, I may have led others who want to harm you to your door. Then I put you in a position where you felt you couldn't go home or stay with me. So I kept searching, and as I did, I spoke to more people who knew you. And I thought about you, meditated about you, remembered you." Cyril's hands rested on the table, centimeters from Tara's. He looked at her. "You're not lying about your pregnancy, or deluded, or any of the other explanations anyone has come up with. You're the one, that's the only answer."

"You can't know that."

"But I do." Cyril covered one of her hands with his. "Tara, if there's something more you need to do here, then do it, but please, come with me afterward."

"Come with you where?" Tara asked.

"To Armenia."

# 36

"It's where the first virgin – after Mary – was born in the seventh century." Cyril got the water pitcher from the kitchen and refilled their glasses as he spoke. "She was killed when Muslim armies from Caliphate attacked Armenia. It happened at Our Lady of Sorrows, a church dedicated to Mary." Cyril fished two photos from his jeans pocket and laid them on the table.

The first photo showed an oblong stone building with a small brown brick building in front of it, but Cyril explained they were connected.

"The front part," he said, "is a rebuilt entryway, constructed in the fourteenth century. The stone portion behind it was built in the ninth century. The whole church used to be larger, but the Turks destroyed it when they invaded, so the new entryway was added. All that's left of the original building is an inner sanctum you can't see in this photo that dates back to the sixth century."

"Is this it?"

Tara pointed to the second photo, which showed drawings and paintings of the Virgin Mary, and photos of statues of her, pasted onto sticks and stuck into hard-packed dirt in front of a stone wall. Thin white taper candles stood among them, some leaning against one another. Others had toppled and lay on the dirt. More photos were affixed to the stone wall at odd angles.

"Yes. That's part of the inner sanctum. The townspeople bring pictures and light candles in the hope that Mary will grant their petitions."

Tara scraped the bottom of her soup bowl. She hadn't thought she could eat any more tonight, but she craved the food to make up for her lack of sleep. "And going to this church will help me how?"

"My mentor, though he disagrees with me about you, told me if I feel certain you are the one, I should prove it. So I researched the Brotherhood's archives to learn about the earlier virgins. The first virgin belonged to this church and prayed there, and the meaning of her pregnancy was revealed to her and those with her at the time. If you go there, I'm convinced the same will happen to you."

"Why go to archives to find all that out? Didn't you learn about the earlier virgins as part of your training?"

Cyril shook his head. "Everyone is told only what he needs to know. Which is why I had to break into the archives just to do my research."

"But why keep it all so secret?"

"Because the more people know, the easier it is for someone outside the Brotherhood to find the virgin and kill her."

"Like the guy at the hospital." Tara set down her soup spoon, her appetite gone.

Cyril leaned toward her. "I'm sorry. I told you too much in the beginning, too fast. Somehow, from people you told, other forces must have figured out who you are. Or even from a leak within the Brotherhood."

"You had to tell me something," Tara said. "Otherwise, I never would have listened to you."

Cyril smiled. "You didn't anyway. Until your parents acted so rashly. Have they reconsidered?"

"Not so far as I know. It's been about a week since I checked e-mail. I'm paranoid about calling, ever since you told me even cell phones can be traced."

"Better paranoid than dead," Cyril said.

Tara licked her lips, which felt dry and cracked. "Right. But how can going to Armenia really help? Even if a sign is revealed, if only you and I see it, who else will believe it?"

"Something will be at the shrine." Cyril sat again. The eating area was so small his knees nearly touched Tara's under the table. "Documents, artifacts. People in the area who've heard legends. Or an apparition might explain why the next messiah is female, and I can use that reasoning to convince the Brotherhood. Because the more I think of it, the more I can't see why it couldn't be. The Catholic Church refuses to ordain women, but other Christian religions do so. And the refusal to allow women to be priests isn't based on scripture, it's a decision by the Church. So it is mutable. Or the shrine itself might be the holy ground."

Tara thought about sharing what Grandmother and Kali had told her about the vase originating in Armenia. It tended to validate his theory. But Cyril had abandoned her before, it might be better to keep some things to herself. Particularly Nanor's theory that the baby was meant to end all monotheistic religions.

"How long does it take to get there?" Tara asked.

"About fifteen hours by air, plus layover time in London."

"It seems like a long way to go on a maybe."

Cyril took her hands. "I know. And I know you've no reason to listen to me or trust me after what happened. But I'm telling you, this is where the answers are. And if you don't go soon, as your pregnancy gets more advanced, you might not be able to travel."

"What if this is the holy ground?" Tara said.

"Where?"

"Here. I've felt better here than I have since I got pregnant. Happier, safer, more at home."

Cyril glanced around the trailer as if she meant just that small area. Then he looked down at their clasped hands, and let go. "The holy ground isn't about feeling at home."

"Shouldn't it be?"

"Religion isn't about comfort."

"Sure it is," Tara said. "Why does everyone want to believe in heaven? So they're not afraid to die. So that when someone they love dies, they can believe they'll see that person again."

It was the same reason Tara and Nate and Bailey and Kelly never shared their doubts about religion with Megan, though they spoke freely with each other. They all wanted her to feel sure that, if she died soon, it didn't mean the end.

"But what about hell? The thought of that isn't a comfort," Cyril said.

Tara thought about it. "No. But churches need hell. If you can convince people, even really good people, that they might suffer eternal torment, they'll feel afraid and need the churches to 'save' them."

Cyril studied her face. "You really believe that?"

"I told you, if my pregnancy is about a new Jesus Christ for the Christian church, it makes no sense that I'm chosen to be the mother."

"Not necessarily." The wind rattled the front door, and Cyril glanced at it. "Jesus came to change things. He threw the moneychangers out of the temple, he ate with tax collectors and prostitutes, he said the spirit of the law is more important than the letter of it. Maybe your baby is about change, too."

Tara glanced at the photo of the Armenian church again, then leaned back into her chair and closed her eyes.

"You must be exhausted," Cyril said. "How are you feeling?"

"Tired. Achy. My back and feet hurt."

"Come here. If you want."

Cyril motioned her to the armchair, and he sat on the ottoman and rubbed her feet. It felt odd for a moment to Tara, then she just shut her eyes and enjoyed the massage. "What time is it?" she said, after what felt like a long time.

"Nearly midnight."

"Do you have somewhere to stay?"

"No. I don't think I should leave you alone. If I found you, and I got into this trailer so easily, so can someone else. Anyone else."

Cyril was right. Tara could lock the bathroom window, but there might be a hundred other ways to get in. Security didn't seem all that high here, despite this having been a haven for abused women early in its history. Cyril had gotten through it somehow, and tricked the security people into believing the alarm was a runaway cart. She'd need to ask him how he'd done that, so she could alert Nanor to it.

"I'll sleep on the floor," Cyril said. "Or on the ground outside the trailer, but I can't leave."

"You don't have to sleep outside."

Tara found an extra blanket and pillow in the cabinet above the daybed. Cyril arranged them on the carpet between the front door and the bathroom.

In the bathroom, after securing the window, Tara changed into an oversized cotton T-shirt and stretchy sweat shorts. Her return bus ticket to Charleston fell out of her pants pocket. She held it, almost smelling the salty sea air. She loved walking along the ocean, passing pastel colored buildings and sprawling Bed and Breakfasts on the coast. She could simply return to Charleston and give birth to the baby under her assumed name.

But what then? Tara turned on the cold water, splashed her face, and brushed her teeth. She would still need a safe place to live, and she didn't want to stay indefinitely where she knew no one, and she couldn't really get to know anyone if she kept pretending to be someone else. She and the baby needed some sort of normal life, with family and friends. If Tara could find more answers about the pregnancy, it might tell her how to raise her child, where to go from here. The holy ground, whether here or in Armenia, might offer more than just a safe place for the birth. And, through Cyril, perhaps the Brotherhood would decide to leave her alone. It was too much to think they would help her, especially since Tara felt Nanor was closer to the truth about her baby than they were.

It also felt good having Cyril here. He'd caused her a lot of trouble, but he'd helped her, too, and despite everything, she liked him.

In the living room, Tara turned off the lamp and climbed onto the day bed. "It's so far away."

Cyril already lay on the blanket on the floor. "It is," he said.

"And I don't know the language." Tara started to roll onto her stomach, but she couldn't sleep that way anymore. She settled onto her side, facing the room and Cyril, even though she couldn't see much in the dark. "I'd be crazy to go there just because the first virgin lived there, and there's a legend she had a vision in a church."

"And Maya Kerkorian planned to go there," Cyril said. "Didn't you say that?"

It struck Tara that she'd never lain in the dark, talking to a man outside her family, other than Jeremy.

"Yes."

"You don't really think that could be a coincidence?" Cyril said.

"Even if it's not, it doesn't mean Maya would have found answers there."

A rustling sound came from Cyril's direction, and Tara guessed he'd turned to face her in the dark.

"There's something else," he said. "Something else that bothers you about going there."

"You admitted the Brotherhood was willing to kill me," Tara said. "And you're part of the Brotherhood."

"It's not like a cult," Cyril said. "And I'm not bound by any vows to do what they say. Yes, I followed their orders, when I believed those were the right orders, but now I'm taking my own path, because I believe the people in charge are wrong."

"But you haven't quit. You're still working with them."

"Working to show them they're wrong. I'd never hurt you, Tara."

Rearranging her pillows, Tara tried to find a more comfortable position. "I find people only say that when there's some reason they think they're going to hurt me."

"I'd never hurt you," Cyril said. "I love you."

# 37

Tara opened the trailer door and stepped onto the flat stone path leading toward the dirt road. Cyril was showering. She'd responded to his declaration of love the night before by telling him she was surprised, and she wasn't sure he knew her well enough to love her. Tara had also felt pleased, though she didn't mention that. It was nice to be wanted after so much rejection – from Jeremy, Vicki, her family. And Cyril was certainly one of the most interesting people she'd ever met. Still, she didn't know if she could trust him, and she wasn't exactly looking for a boyfriend. Even the word seemed odd applied to Cyril, as if he lived somehow outside the day-to-day world. For her, he did.

All the times she'd seen Cyril had involved running away from someone – sometimes from him – or trying to figure out what was true or not about his information. Separating how she felt about him as a person from that seemed impossible. The undercurrent of excitement she felt might have more to do with associating him with danger and close calls, not with her feelings for him as a person.

Just as Tara reached the road, Kali walked out of the woods. Her long black hair was pulled into a ponytail. That and her magnolia print sundress made her look younger than seventeen, despite a frown that creased her forehead and circles under her eyes.

"Bad news," Kali said.

Tara stopped in the path. "What?"

"A man was detained early this morning trying to enter the grounds. He sounds like the one who attacked you at the hospital. Tall. Red hair. He will not say his purpose here."

Tara made herself take a deep breath. The man had been detained. He posed no danger right at this moment.

"What will you do with him?"

"We will call the police. Ours is private property and he trespassed. But Grandmother will speak to him first. She'd like to see you as well."

"I was about to look for her."

"She's at the chapel. I'll take you."

"Thanks." Tara's lower back twinged, and she put her hand on it. She'd woken feeling achy, and the baby hung lower than usual, putting pressure on her muscles.

"This way." Kali led Tara into the woods. "You must wish you could just put everything back to normal, before you got pregnant."

"I do," Tara said, trying not to think about the red-haired man. "Though some things I've really enjoyed, like meeting Sophia and her friends, and you and your grandmother, and the service last night."

Kali smiled. "It is really wonderful, isn't it?"

"Almost everyone I knew before this had such a similar life to mine," Tara said. "Sure, some families in my neighborhood had fewer kids, or maybe their dad wasn't around, but it was just accepted that the thing to do is get married and have kids at some point. That's what family is about, and community is about. So it's been cool seeing different kinds of families."

"Sometimes the families people choose work better than those they were born into."

The trees grew thicker and blocked more sunlight, except for a few shafts beaming through the leaves. Tara pulled her sweater around her. "Is that how it is for you?"

"Yes. My mom and I just never really connected, and Grandmother and I always have. Which I think my mom resents. Then Mom married a man with a nasty temper. He's not physically abusive, but he snaps at her and criticizes and undermines her. I always called him on it, and he'd back off a little, but I finally realized that made him more antagonistic to her when I wasn't around. So I told her I wanted to live with Grandmother here at Willow Springs, and she said all right. I try to convince her to come here, too, but she won't."

The trees grew sparse again, and the sun hit Tara's face, so she didn't see the building right away when they stepped into the clearing. She shaded her eyes. Gray stone walls rose out of the field as if they'd grown there. The stone made her feel stronger, safer, as if the Brotherhood could not reach her here, though obviously that wasn't so.

Inside, too, the chapel appeared to be an extension of the outdoors, with light yellow and green carpets laid across stone floors. Plain square windows, half the height of the walls, made the trees and sun seem part of the decor. Tara inhaled, and despite being indoors, the air tasted earthy and fresh.

"It's modeled after Frank Lloyd Wright's Unity Temple." Kali pointed to the ceiling. "The ceiling is low and has a skylight, to bring God's light into the chapel, rather than using a high ceiling and spires to make God seem far away and unreachable. The pews stand on three levels – below, above, and in line with the pulpit, so whoever speaks is neither above nor below the congregation as a whole. There are no images or statues of any god or goddesses, so that no one's conception of the divine will be limited."

"It's beautiful." Tara closed her eyes and listened to the silence.

Nanor sat in a pew at floor level near the far wall, five rows from where Tara stood at the chapel's center.

"I'll give you some privacy." Kali left, her bare feet barely making a sound on the moss-colored carpet.

"The man you detained, where is he?" Tara asked.

"In the perimeter building you saw with Kali yesterday. He did not get past there."

"What will you do when you talk to him?"

"I will attempt to ascertain his purpose here, but I doubt he'll tell me," Nanor said. "When you depart today, you should take a different exit from our grounds in case he's been released by the police at that point. Kali will show you. You are leaving, are you not?"

Tara moved to the center of the chapel. "I'm not sure."

"You're sure you're leaving," Nanor said, "or you wouldn't look worried. You're unsure you're doing the right thing."

"You're right. I'm unsure." With pews all around, both above and below, and sunlight shining through the skylight, Tara felt almost as if energy flowed into her from all points. "But I'm going to Armenia."

Nanor drew in her breath. "It's a mistake."

"I need to know why this happened to me. What it means."

Shaking her head, Nanor stood. "But I told you what it means." Her low voice carried through the open room. She held her shoulders square, but her face sagged from forehead to mouth, and Tara felt waves of sadness from her.

"I'm not your daughter," Tara said. "I wish I could bring her back for you, and your granddaughter. But I can't."

Nanor gripped the pew in front of her. "I know you are your own person, on your own path. But I truly believe that Willow Springs is where it leads. A place where women's values are honored. Where feeding children comes before building weapons, where art is valued as much as commerce, and compassion means caring for one another, not bending your neighbor to your will. We must convince the world to abandon their religions of destruction."

"You might be right. But I need to be the one to figure that out. Or maybe my daughter will, when she's old enough. Until then, I need to keep her safe, and to do that, I need to know more about why she's here."

"Your young man didn't want you when he learned your child was female."

"Jeremy? He didn't know the baby's gender."

Nanor shook her head. "Your young man now. His Church is against you. Can you be sure he's not as well?"

"I don't think – how did you –" Tara wondered if the trailer had a camera, or if Nanor had someone watching Tara. If so, why not warn Tara Cyril was inside before Tara encountered him? And for that matter, why had security been able to stop the red-haired man but not Cyril?

Stepping out of the pew, Nanor extended her hands toward Tara. "You and your baby have a purpose. To show people of faith a new way. A way of true love and creativity rather than death and power."

As Nanor's hands closed around Tara's, warmth and energy seemed to hum into Tara from the older woman's palms. It felt wonderful, but it didn't mean Nanor's mission belonged to her. And it didn't mean Tara could trust her entirely. Obviously, there was more to Willow Springs' security than it had seemed at first.

"Not everyone who believes in Christianity, or Judaism, or Islam is about death and power," Tara said.

"Not everyone, no. But the power structures are. Those who govern are. Think about it. What story is central to all three religions?"

Tara shook her head. "I don't know. I know the books in the Old Testament, most of them, are common to Christianity and Judaism. But I don't know anything about Islam."

"You mentioned the story yourself. How it disturbed you as a child."

"Abraham and Isaac?"

"Yes. The Akeedah. A voice Abraham believes is God tells Abraham to sacrifice his son. And Abraham willingly ties his son to an altar and raises his knife. He only stops when God stays his hand at the last second. And it bothers you. Why?"

"Because God supposedly does it as a test. He tells Abraham to do something that's wrong as a test, and Abraham does it. Which to me means he failed."

"When you first head the story, what did you think Abraham should have done?"

"Argued with God. Said it's not right to kill human beings, and you telling me to do it can't make it right. I thought that should be the test. Whether Abraham would do the right thing, even if someone appearing to be God told him it was all right to do something bad. Whether he'd show his faith and love for God by loving and protecting other human beings, and loving his son. It seemed all wrong that the way to show faith is to kill someone."

"And don't you think that's played out over and over? In every holy war, every time a nation's 'fathers' sacrifice their countries' sons – and now daughters – and those of other countries, in battle?"

"I never thought about it."

"The Akeedah is about obedience above all. Abraham and Isaac are not to question, not to examine the moral quandary and do their utmost to make the right choice, not to choose the path of love rather than murder/suicide. They are not to choose. They are to obey. This is what you can stand against. This is what your daughter can stand against. And this is the tradition your young man comes from."

If Nanor had raised her voice, if she'd demanded, if she'd paced and pounded her fists on a pulpit, Tara would have found it easier to refuse her. But Nanor spoke with quiet force, her voice trembling with love, not anger. Her eyes overflowed with warmth, and a glint of tears.

"That may be right. You may be right about all of it. But I need to find the meaning for myself, as best I can. And he's not my young man."

Nanor sighed and nodded. "Of course. You must find your own way." She frowned. "I can hardly demand you surrender your will to mine after that speech. But be careful, Tara. My daughter still comes to me. And she says he will not lead you to what you seek."

Tara squeezed Nanor's hands. "Maybe I don't need to be led."

# 38

The car idled two houses away from the end of the cul de sac, in a dark spot between streetlights. The Spencers' windows were darkened, even those in the basement, where Nate usually played his keyboards into the night. A twenty-five watt bulb burned in the faux lantern near the front door, light only to showcase a prowler obliging enough to step right onto the stoop.

Tara gripped her keys and her backpack, put her hand on the car handle.

"Twenty minutes," Cyril said.

"I know right where it is." Tara opened the door. Night sounds from the street – crickets, the buzz of the streetlights, the wind chimes from the neighbors' patio – flooded the car, making Tara homesick. She'd left here only months ago, but it felt like decades.

"Tara?"

"What?" Tara shut the door, and they sat again in shadowy silence.

"I hope you don't feel uncomfortable with me. After I told you how I feel." Cyril stared straight ahead as he spoke, as if afraid to look at her.

"I don't." Tara touched his hand. "I hope you don't."

Cyril turned toward her, his face half-hidden by darkness. "I wish we'd met some other way. And yet, there is no other way we could have met."

"Probably not."

"It's real, though. How I feel. It's not just about my ministry or my certainty that you're the mother of the next messiah."

"It's all a little hard to sort out," Tara said. "I think we'll just need to see how it goes."

Cyril touched Tara's cheek. His fingers felt rough, but warm. She closed her eyes for a second, liking just being with him without wanting it to be anything more.

"Yes." Cyril glanced at the dashboard clock. "You better hurry."

Tara got out of the Monte Carlo, heart racing. Getting involved with Cyril at this point would be a bad idea; she didn't need Nanor to tell her that. She tried to ease the heavy car door shut, but still its thunk echoed in the cul de sac.

Skirting the faint light in the front of the house, Tara circled to the back and climbed the stairs to her apartment. At the door, she fumbled getting her key into the lock. Finally, it opened. In the dim light from the streetlights, Tara made out the outlines of her kitchen area and her futon along the wall, blankets rumpled. The door slipped from her grasp and swung shut behind her.

Someone sat straight up on the futon.

"Shit!" Tara backed away, slamming her shoulders painfully into the door.

"Tara?"

"Nate? Jesus." Tara turned on the light over the sink. Not much looked different, other than a pile of Nate's clothes in the corner. "You're staying here?"

Nate shrugged. "Just when I've got so much equipment in the basement I can't get to my bed. Which you're more than welcome to have if you're staying, if you can unbury it."

When Nate hugged her, Tara's eyes filled with tears. "I miss you. And everyone. And being home. I don't know how things got this way."

Nate stepped back. "I take it you're not moving back in. I don't see any luggage."

"I just came for my passport."

"To go where?"

"Armenia. Long story."

"Mom and Dad are ready to give up the idea of getting custody of you or the baby."

"Really?" Tara felt a surge of relief, mixed with anger that it had taken them so long to figure that out. She wished more than anything she could take time to see them.

"They told me. You should talk to them."

"I will, eventually, I promise. How's Bailey? And Megan and Kelly?"

Nate filled her in on Bailey's latest baseball team and Kelly's latest play, and Megan's newest treatment, which was making her hair fall out again, but seemed to slow the tumor's growth. Tara found her passport in her chest of drawers and pulled out three pairs of sweat pants and every oversized T-shirt she owned. The skirts and dresses look was getting to her, and she figured sweats would work better for traveling anyway.

"You're not saying hi to anyone else?" Nate said. "Or good-bye?"

Tara glanced at the clock on the microwave, wishing she could check in on Megan, kiss her forehead; longing to sit with Nate and drink beer or soda and talk the way they had last summer on the rare occasions they were both home at night. Now it felt like she'd never even lived in this apartment.

"I can't. If we miss our connection, it'll be two days until the next one. But tell everyone I love them. And miss them. Here's the name of someone I'll be keeping in touch with, in case you need it."

A quick beep came from the street. Tara scribbled down Sophia's number for Nate. Someone at home needed to know how to reach her.

TARA SAT, legs extended, on the carpet in a cordoned non-smoking area of Heathrow Airport. She reached for her toes, or as close as she could get to them with the baby in the way, trying to stretch out the kinks in her knees. Her eyes felt gummy. On the flight to London, Cyril had persuaded the man next to them to take the aisle seat and give Tara the window, so she could lean against the wall and try to sleep, but she'd barely dozed. She and Cyril had played cards half the time to entertain themselves, and Cyril had read aloud to her from the in flight magazine when the only way she could fight her queasiness was to shut her eyes and take deep breaths.

Haze from the smoking areas across the corridor burned Tara's lungs. She longed for the clearer air in the U.S. She wished again she could have visited with her family before leaving. If she weren't afraid the call could be traced, Tara at least would have called to talk to everyone. Though one of the things she really wanted to talk about she wasn't sure she could have explained to any of them.

Cyril sat near her on a plastic chair in the row of chairs to Tara's right rather than on the floor.

"What about your vows?" Tara asked him.

Cyril glanced up from the guidebook he'd been reading about Armenia. "What?"

"Aren't you supposed to take vows of celibacy?"

"I haven't taken them yet."

"But deacons do, right?"

Cyril leaned forward, elbows on his knees. "Married men becoming deacons vow that, if something happens to their spouses, they'll stay celibate and not remarry. Single men take a vow of celibacy."

"And when are you supposed to take yours?"

"Two years from now at the earliest."

"So how does that fit? With telling me you love me?" Tara drew her knees toward her chest and wrapped her arms around them, rocking slightly. The movement helped her feel less weighed down by the baby.

Cyril looked at her, his gray eyes serious. "I don't know. I never thought I'd have to deal with that issue."

"So you've never had a girlfriend? Never fallen in love?" Tara wasn't sure she felt ready to consider a relationship with Cyril or anyone. But she wanted to know where he really stood. If loving her meant foregoing his religious path and he would resent that, it would never work no matter what either of them wanted.

"I had girlfriends," Cyril said. "I had sex. But I never fell in love."

"Never?"

"I always felt a few steps removed. Eventually the girlfriends felt it, too, and stopped seeing me. After a while, I figured I couldn't fall in love, that it just wasn't in me."

Static blared over a loudspeaker, then a muffled female voice read a list of gate changes. Tara got off the floor and sat next to Cyril.

"But what would make you think that?"

Cyril looked at the floor, then at her. "When I was eight, I first heard the word 'divorce,' and I asked my mother what it meant. She told me, and I asked why she didn't get one. At that point, my father had already put her in the hospital twice. The second time with a broken jaw and three cracked ribs. She just shook her head and said, 'Where would I go? How could I take care of you and your sister?' She seemed so sad. And so tired."

"How old was your sister?"

"Twelve. My dad never hit her, never yelled at her. I envied her when we were growing up. Sometimes hated her. But later, after I grew up, learned more, I realized why she was the favorite."

"He sexually abused her."

Cyril nodded and clenched his fists. "I didn't stop it. I didn't know, and I didn't stop it."

Tara put her hand on his shoulder. "You were a little kid."

"I finally stopped him from hitting my mother. When I was twelve, I started working out, and I learned how to fight. I was thirteen the last time he touched either of us."

"Are they still together?"

"I don't understand it, but they are. He mellowed, somewhat, when he retired. She says he doesn't hit her. I don't see any bruises. My sister says she doesn't see any."

Tara rubbed the back of Cyril's neck. "I'm sorry you grew up that way. It's something I always took for granted, that home was a safe place to be. At least it was until my parents tried to commit me."

"Your family loves you. And you love them."

"Don't you love your mother? Or your sister?"

"I don't know. I do the things I'm supposed to do for family. But the first deep love I really felt was for God. And now for you."

"I – that's – I'm not sure how to handle that. I care about you, I feel a lot for you, but I don't know how I feel exactly."

Cyril took her hand. "That's all right. You don't know how amazing it is to me just to love someone. To find out I can love someone. It's wonderful. Though I need to figure out what it means for my future." He shook his head. "This is the first time in four years I've considered not becoming a deacon."

# 39

The plane landed in Triblesi around four a.m. Tara's head had fallen on Cyril's shoulder while she dozed. Now she awoke and peered into darkness. The spires of a single sprawling building, the only source of light, twisted upward against the black sky. A few people shuffled off the plane. Tara stood in the aisle and stretched her arms above her head, then bent from the waist, first to one side, then the other. The London stopover had lasted six hours. The flight to Triblesi had been five.

When she sat again, Cyril handed her a green, rectangular piece of paper with adhesive strips on the back. "Paste it into your passport."

The printed lettering was unfamiliar to Tara, but handwritten answers were written on each line in English. One said "21 days."

"What is this?"

"A visa. You need one for customs in Armenia. And, more important, to get back out."

"You said all I needed was a passport."

"That's all you needed to get. I obtained this through Thomas' connections. Otherwise, it wouldn't have issued in time."

"Thomas?"

"My mentor."

The name tugged at Tara's mind. "Thomas Stranyero?"

Cyril stared at her. "How did you know his last name?"

"Nanor Kerkorian found his card in her daughter's things after she died. Just a card with his name and a phone number, a lot like the one you gave me." Tara's stomach tightened. She didn't know if Thomas Stranyero was connected to Maya's death, but it seemed like a good bet.

Cyril blinked, then looked over Tara's shoulder through the window, as if searching for the explanation on the tarmac outside the plane. "I knew someone from the Brotherhood contacted her. It makes sense it would have been Thomas. He'd just become a deacon himself then."

The seatbelt icon blinked on, and Tara sat and buckled her belt across her hips, below the swell of her stomach. "What else did he say about Maya?"

"Just that before he could verify her pregnancy was divinely-caused, she died in an accident."

The plane lurched, and Tara gripped the armrest. "It wasn't an accident. Someone ran her off the road."

"Thomas said it might have been intentional, that no one ever knew."

"Why didn't he contact her family?"

"Not much he could say I imagine."

"He never told you?"

"I didn't ask."

As the plane taxied, Tara shut her eyes. She'd flown a few times before this trip and never felt sick, but the pregnancy had changed that. Of course, an added cause now was the thought of Cyril telling Thomas Stranyero about them going to Armenia. She didn't trust the Brotherhood, though she'd begun to feel she could count on Cyril.

"What do you know about the other virgins?" Tara said. "When we met, you said there'd been at least four."

"The first I just found out about, the one from Armenia. Then there was one during the Inquisition, a Jew living in Spain. She was killed when she wouldn't convert, at least that's the story, but we suspect someone knew the origin of her child and made it look that way."

Tara's eyes flew open despite her queasiness. "So, basically, some religious group or another killed her. Either the Catholics because she was Jewish, or someone else because she might be carrying the next messiah?"

"I know how it sounds. That doesn't make all religious groups evil."

"It doesn't make them good."

Cyril sighed. "It doesn't. There are references to a girl in Syria in the twelfth century, who miscarried after an earthquake that almost destroyed her town. She lived, but there's no record of her having another child. Rumors exist of virgins in other areas, but none confirmed."

The plane lifted into the night air and swayed. "Did they all die?"

"I don't know." Cyril touched her arm just below the elbow. "But that's one of the reasons it's so important to be careful."

"You shouldn't have told Thomas about us going to Armenia. We could have found another way."

"You can't think he had anything to do with Maya Kerkorian's death?"

"He was ready to have me killed. Maybe he decided she was an agent of the Beast. Or someone he worked for did."

"He would have told me. Or the records would show it. The Brotherhood records don't show any of these women being determined to be fakes or agents of the Beast. Anyway, we couldn't spend a month getting you a visa. You wouldn't have been able to travel."

The last of Cyril's points was valid. Both Dr. Lei and Tara's doctor in Charleston had been hesitant about Tara flying at all but, when pressed, agreed that since she'd had no complications, she should be all right. Tara would never have taken a risk for any less of a reason, but she decided not going and remaining in the dark about the baby's origins presented more danger than traveling and possibly learning something that could save her and her baby's lives.

"I wish there'd been another way, that's all," Tara said. "If it comes down to it, and your Brotherhood disagrees with you about me, what will you do?"

Cyril squeezed her hand. "I'd stand by you. But it won't come to that."

Forty minutes later, the plane landed in Yerevan, Armenia's capitol, and the flight attendant herded them down metal stairs onto the tarmac. Floodlights lit the edges of the rectangular airport. Just one set of runway lights stretched behind the plane, disappearing into darkness. Unlike airports at home, with rows of planes, this plane appeared to be the only one expected tonight. Tara shivered despite the warm air all around her.

They rode a glass enclosed escalator to the baggage area. Bright orange scarred conveyor belts creaked and circled the room. Men with carts approached, gesturing toward the bags tumbling onto the conveyor, but Cyril shook his head. When they'd collected their duffel bags and Cyril's leather backpack of research materials, they started down a hall marked in three languages, including English, advising that anyone with medications needed to enter it. The guard waved them to the other lane without checking their bags. Their visas stamped, they took another escalator to the ground level and looked for taxis.

"There." Cyril pointed to a sign with an outline of a car on it. They exited the double doors and found one taxi.

The driver hopped out and waved.

"Where are we going?" Tara said.

"There's a hotel in the main business area of Yerevan," Cyril said. "It should be safe and it's not too expensive. I wrote down the address in English and Armenian."

The driver looked at the scrap of paper with the address and nodded. "American?" he said, gesturing to them. His accent sounded Russian to Tara.

"Yes," Cyril said. "You speak English?"

"Some."

Cyril got in the back seat of the cab with Tara, and the driver raised his eyebrows and pointed at the seat next to him. "In front," the driver said. "Men sit in front."

"It's okay. I'll stay back here," Cyril said.

Just off the exit ramp from the airport, a white car with what looked like gray clouds painted over it honked at them. The taxi driver pulled to the side of the road.

"Police," he said.

The driver got out. He and the policeman gestured and shouted. Other cars drove by, and the passengers stared at Tara, craning their necks to keep watching through their back windows as they sped down the street. Tara and Cyril clasped hands and waited.

After a few minutes, the driver poked his head in Tara's window. "We must pay. He sees Americans. If we don't pay, he will take us to the station. Many hours. I'll lose money."

"But what did you do wrong?" Tara said.

The driver shrugged. "No need for wrong. We must pay."

Cyril gave the driver a few bills.

After the driver disappeared, Cyril told Tara, "I read about this. It's the usual thing for police to collect bribes for minor infractions, but if they see Americans, they assume we can pay much more."

"But how could he know from outside that we're American?"

"Your hair. Not many blondes here."

After more shouting, the driver got back in the car, and the police car drove away.

"Why the smog on the car?" Tara asked. "The smoke?"

"To blend," the driver said.

"Camouflage?" Cyril asked.

"Yes," the driver said. "We often fight, are at war. The police cars must blend into the battle."

Tara wrapped her arms over her stomach. She'd never thought much about what it would be like to live with war at the doorstep, in the streets, all the time. Willow Springs, with its woods and arts and dance, had seemed so calm. It seemed much more likely to be the holy ground, the safe place to give birth, than here.

It took another thirty minutes to reach the hotel. The driver drove a mile out of the way to show them a spot off one of the main roads where four taxis were parked at odd angles. "Here you find taxis to take you anywhere," the driver said.

At the hotel, Cyril paid for the cab.

"I should get some Euros," Tara said. "In case we get separated."

Cyril handed her some. "Until we can exchange more."

They ate at a restaurant down the street from the hotel, started by a group of Armenians who'd taken a business class run by the Peace Corps. The waiter, who spoke fairly good English, said their goal was to provide American-style food at prices that were within the range of the average Armenian. Her stomach still wavering, Tara found it difficult to get down the stringy chicken, but the bottled water tasted good and the cooked carrots passable.

After, Tara and Cyril found an Internet Café. At a square table near the window, Tara opened email from Megan, who had just gotten back from the doctor. Megan wrote that she had trouble dressing and undressing the doll Tara had sent, but Mom helped. Nate added that the doctors were talking about trying to get Megan to a facility that offered proton treatment – like radiation but more targeted. A facility in Illinois offered it, but could only accommodate 2,500 patients a year out of over ten thousand who needed it. Tara closed her eyes, imagining hugging Megan and hoping her sister knew how much Tara loved her. She wrote back to her siblings, sent an email to Sophia, and signed off the computer.

The hotel Cyril had chosen reminded Tara of a student dorm. The manager took their money at the desk and led them up three flights and down a narrow but clean hallway to a room the size of a large walk in closet. Twin beds pressed lengthwise against opposite walls, a white chest of drawers between them. The attached bathroom was clean, too, but both rooms felt stifling, despite the open window over the chest. A small metal fan sat on the desk, and the manager turned it on. It barely stirred the air.

"I didn't want to get two rooms," Cyril said. "Obviously no one followed us, but I'm nervous leaving you alone."

"It's okay," Tara said. "Do you mind if I shower first?"

Tara washed what seemed like layers of oil off her face. When she finally felt clean, she closed her eyes and let the cool water run over her. The traveling had worn her out, but excitement surged within her, along with hope that, finally, she would find answers. She pushed away thoughts of her family and how long it had been since she'd seen any of them but Nate. If she started thinking of that now, she'd only sink into gloom, a feeling she'd found herself struggling with in the last months due to the pregnancy hormones – or everything going on in her life. When she got back home, she promised herself she'd find a way to stay in touch with her family without putting them in danger.

After she got out of the shower, Tara dug through her backpack and put on the gray tank top and Casper the Ghost boxer shorts she meant to sleep in.

Cyril sat on the narrow bed against the far wall, shoulders slumped, still in his jeans and T-shirt, the bed still made. He'd pulled the blinds against the bright sun, giving the room a half-lit, late evening feel, though it was only four-thirty in the afternoon local time.

"I lied," he said.

"About what?"

"I didn't ask Thomas' help, I just used his contacts and didn't tell him. And I feel guilty about it now."

Tara sat next to Cyril, tucking her legs underneath her. "Do you feel guilty because you used his contacts without telling him, or because you didn't trust him enough to tell him?"

"Because I don't trust him. And I didn't want to tell you that because I didn't want to admit it to myself."

"It's hard when you're doubting someone so important to you. Or even just doubting things that person believes." Tara thought of her dad and how hard forming her own views about religion had been given his strong feelings about it.

Cyril pressed the back of his head against the wall and closed his eyes as if shutting out pain. "It is."

"But it can't be wrong. Don't you have a right – maybe even a responsibility if you want to follow a religious path – to reexamine what you believe, and be sure the path you're on is one that's right for you?"

Cyril opened his eyes and looked at her. "But I owe Thomas so much. I was on the road to becoming my father. Drinking, fighting. Thomas showed me another kind of man to emulate. He encouraged me to go to a group for young adults whose parents abused them – he's the only one I told about my family. I never would have gone, never would have gotten any help." He swallowed. "So I hate to doubt him."

Tara took Cyril's hand, settling herself against the wall next to him. "I felt terrible when I started questioning Catholicism. It's so important to my dad. My mom's more practical about it. She more or less thinks if people do the right thing and are honest and treat each other well, that's what counts. Dad took it as a personal rejection when I stopped going to mass."

"What did you do?"

"I just kept talking with him about what I was thinking and how I was feeling, and emphasizing that it was about coming to my own beliefs, just like he did when he was younger. But I don't know if he'll ever get over it."

If she'd kept going to mass, Tara wondered if her dad would have been more likely to believe her now.

Sirens blared in the street below, and even those sounded different to Tara from those at home, lower pitched, with a slower rhythm.

When the noise faded, Cyril said, "Do you still feel bad about it?"

"Yeah. Especially now that I'm separated from the whole family. But I couldn't be Catholic just to make him happy. That seemed more disrespectful, going through the motions of something my dad sincerely believes."

"I don't think I could talk to Thomas about my questions."

"You're afraid he'll stop being there for you. Stop loving you," Tara said.

A tear formed in the corner of Cyril's eye, but he blinked and it disappeared. "I never thought of it that way. But I might be."

Tara touched his shoulder. "So there is someone else you love."

"Yes."

"I don't know if questioning his beliefs will hurt your relationship. I hope not. But some people really can't handle that type of thing." Tara thought of her grandmother, who had refused to speak to one of Tara's uncles for years after he stopped attending mass. Fortunately, she'd mellowed a bit over the years. She'd just frowned and snapped, "Don't be like Uncle Toby," when Tara said she'd stopped going to church. "But it doesn't make your love worth any less, or make you any less lovable."

Cyril sat straighter. "I'm sorry. I shouldn't feel like this. I need to keep my emotions controlled."

"How could you not feel bad? It's not just Thomas. So much of your life is about becoming a deacon, and now you're wondering if it's right. That's bound to be scary."

Cyril took her hand. "It is. And I don't want to let you down, telling you I'm not sure about my beliefs when I've dragged you all the way to a foreign country. But I don't have any doubts about you, about your place in all this."

"There's no way you've let me down. Are you kidding? You're the only person who believed me from Day One."

"But I abandoned you."

"You were struggling with doing the right thing. I get that. It's hard."

"Forgive me?"

"Of course."

"I'm sorry this is hard for you," Cyril said. "I can't even imagine it. Your friends, your family, not believing what's happening, not believing you."

"I keep feeling like they ought to, like I would if the situation were reversed, but this is a such an unbelievable thing, maybe I wouldn't. I still question it myself. Yet I want them to believe me anyway. Does that make sense?"

Cyril nodded. "Perfect sense." He reached for Tara and pulled her into his arms, resting her head on his shoulder. Tara relaxed against him, feeling his fingers run through her hair.

When Cyril kissed her, their lips fit perfectly. His tasted like tears. They pressed together, and Tara felt as if the narrow bed, the ailing fan, the humid air, fell away, leaving only the two of them.

When Cyril slid her tank top over her head, and took off his T-shirt, Tara closed her eyes to absorb the feeling of his skin against hers.

"Tara, maybe we shouldn't."

She looked him in the eyes, falling into the gray. "Let's just forget everything. Just for now."

CYRIL WOKE and jerked away from the warm body next to him. He got to his feet, sweating. As his eyes became accustomed to the night, he saw the outlines of Tara's body. Her chest rising with her breath, the swell of her womb, the lines of her legs, the dark space between them that he'd explored. He touched her naked thigh, face burning.

*How could I? Oh my God, I am heartily sorry for having offended – the Virgin, she was the Virgin, and now –*

Cyril shut his eyes, remembering how it felt to be so close to Tara, inside her. He staggered from the bed, away from her, fell to his knees, banging them on the tile floor. He welcomed the pain. He fumbled for his jeans, yanked them on.

*How could I, how could I, she was so pure, she was everything, she – she – She wanted me to.* The last thought hit him like icewater. She had unbuttoned his jeans, opened her lips, opened her legs. She had wanted him.

His eyes traveled over her naked form again.

"Whore."

# 40

Tara lay naked on her back on a rough concrete platform. Pain sliced through her. She screamed and strained to deliver the baby. The full moon glowed above – an amber disk against a black sky that lacked a single star. Sophia held Tara's head in her lap, and when Sophia leaned forward, blocking the moon from Tara's view, everything turned black. Tara heard footsteps approach, heavy, angry. She couldn't see, but somehow she knew it was Cyril.

"Whore," he said.

Tara opened her eyes. Sweat coated her body. She felt the soft bed beneath her, the fan's anemic breeze on her face. She felt stinging between her legs, but not from trying to give birth. As in the dream, Cyril stood over her. She could barely make out his features in the dark.

"Cyril?"

He turned away. "Slut."

"What?" Tara sat, pulled the sheet around her. Cyril's touch had so moved her, had seemed to convey all his love for her. When he'd finally been inside her, despite the initial pain, she'd felt a sense of connection she'd never known before. And she'd felt grateful she'd never shared this with anyone else. For even though Cyril said he'd had sex before, she knew on some level this was a first for him, too. The vulnerability, the closeness, the emotion. "Cyril, what's wrong?"

He spun to face her. "You. Coming on to me. Drawing me in. Convincing me to doubt my beliefs, to doubt the Brotherhood. Pretending to be a virgin, to be pure."

"I never pretended anything."

"You let me believe your child was conceived divinely, and now I know it couldn't have been."

"What are you talking about?"

Pulse racing, Tara turned on the lamp. Cyril glared at her, forehead creased, eyes wide. He wore only jeans. His feet and chest were bare.

"You want me to believe a woman who's truly pure, a woman truly worthy to be the mother of Our Lord, would fuck a man while she's pregnant, when she never did before?" Cyril turned his back on Tara, grabbed his shirt from the floor, and pulled it over his head.

"I never did. And I never claimed to be carrying 'Our Lord.'" Tara stood. Her mind felt sluggish, unable to process well enough to understand what had happened, what Cyril was saying. "I never asked you for anything, never lied to you."

"You lied with every word, every movement. Everything you did was to fool me."

"Fool you? What is the matter with you? You sought me out, remember? You convinced me. Then you came back again, begging forgiveness. You told me you loved me." Tara's stomach churned. Sweat soaked the sheet wrapped around her.

*How can he turn on me? Again? Again. And I let him back into my life. Welcomed him.* Nanor's words came back to her – *he will not lead you to what you seek.*

"I was weak. Blind." Cyril sat on the other bed, put on his socks and shoes without looking at her. "I sinned. You led me into sin."

"I led you. Unbelievable. I – where the hell are you going?"

Cyril threw his wallet and shaving kit into his duffel bag. "Away from you. Back to the states, where I belong, back to the Brotherhood."

"You're leaving me here? In a foreign country? What the fuck gives you the right to treat me this way?"

"You're a tool of the Beast. You're like Eve, like all women, holding out temptation."

"You're insane."

Cyril zipped his bag, threw it over his shoulder, and slammed out the door.

Cyril's New Testament still sat on the pressboard table between the beds. Tara flung the book against the door. "You forgot your fucking Bible."

It hit the floor with a thunk, and Tara grabbed it and ripped the pages out, swearing and stomping on the pages. When it was all shredded she sagged on the tile floor against the wall, crying until she had no breath.

*What the hell do I do now?*

SUN CUT THROUGH THE BLINDS, making the room steamier and waking Tara. Her eyes and throat ached. She stumbled toward the bathroom for a drink of water, then remembered the water might not be treated here and fished through her backpack for the half bottle of Evian she had left from the plane.

Paper shreds littered the floor. After a shower, which didn't make her feel much better, Tara pushed them into a pile and scooped as many as she could into the garbage, hoping a neater room would help her think more clearly. At first, though, she just sat on the bed, reliving the scene with Cyril. She didn't think he really meant the names he'd called her, but he clearly couldn't deal with his own sexuality. Or being with her.

*Which didn't give him the right to leave me here.*

But here she was. Cyril had taken all the information about the church with the shrine, including the photographs and his notes. Tara didn't remember the church's name, and didn't think he'd ever told her what part of Armenia it was in. Panic seized her – had Cyril taken both return tickets with him? She rifled through her things, shoving aside toiletries, tank tops, panties, cash. At the bottom of her bag, she found the blue and red envelope. Her ticket. She took a ragged breath, sat on the bed, and pulled out the cash again. She had two hundred ten dollars and fifty Euro.

Feeling light-headed, Tara rested her head on her knees for a few seconds. Her insides still felt raw from the sex. *At least I don't have to worry about getting pregnant.* But she hadn't even thought about AIDS or other sexually transmitted diseases. Cyril had made it sound like his sexual experience was limited, but she had no idea if that was true. Maybe he slept around all the time and was in denial about it. Tara's heart beat faster, and her chest tightened.

Closing her eyes, she took deep breaths. *I can't do anything about that now.*

After a few minutes, Tara opened her eyes again. What she could do was get something to eat, then find out where to change more of her money, then think about ways to find the church.

The desk clerk, a different one from the night before, gestured directions and drew a map showing how to get to a local store to buy food.

Tara showed him Euros and American dollars, then switched them from one hand to the other and said, "Bank?"

He shook his head, pointed to the map, then spread his arms.

"It's far?" Tara said.

"Yah, far. But okay." He pointed to the dollars.

"People will take dollars?"

He nodded. "Some take dollars."

"Thank you."

"Welcome," he said, smiling and looking her up and down, and stopping his gaze at her breasts. She hurried out.

The five-block walk took her nearly twenty minutes. The temperature felt near a hundred degrees, and though the air was dry, Tara was sweating and had to stop and rest twice. The store, on a corner, was half the size of the trailer she'd stayed in at Willow Springs. Tara found what looked like protein bars on a shelf toward the back, and bought two Fanta orange sodas. She really wanted orange juice, but wasn't sure if it had been made with local water. She found a map of the city under some old newspapers.

The clerk, a woman, didn't speak English, but she took dollars, to Tara's relief. Tara ate on the corner, watching cars half the size of those at home drive by. The heavy smog made it hard to breathe. Tara peered at her map, which showed drawings of different attractions and included some English explanations. She decided to try to find Old Republic Square, which looked like a shopping area. Tara wasn't sure exactly where she was in relation to the square, but after asking enough people, she figured out the way.

Once there, Tara was relieved to hear a number of people speaking English. Stopping at different merchants' kiosks and blankets, Tara looked at pottery, scarves, and toys, partly to be polite before asking questions, and also because she felt drawn to some of the brightly colored pieces. She wrote down what anyone told her about churches in the area. One man and two women had heard of churches with shrines to Mary like the one Tara described, but they said many shrines like it existed throughout Armenia, not just one. The display of photographs and candles that struck Tara as creepy and unusual apparently amounted to common practice in Armenia.

The rest of the day she traipsed from church to church in Yerevan, asking questions of whomever she could find. She spoke to two priests who could converse in English, but neither knew the church she meant. She asked about Avids Kerkorian, Kali's great-grandmother, on the off-chance she was well-known in the area, but got nowhere with that, either.

Back in the room that night, Tara struggled not to think about Cyril. She'd gotten used to living and traveling alone, but now she longed to be, not with Cyril, exactly, but with the person she'd thought he was. *This is a theme. Jeremy wasn't who I thought, Cyril wasn't who I thought. I need to work this out sometime.* She rolled onto her other side and counted her breaths, trying to clear her mind the way she'd learned in yoga. It helped some, though the last few days with Cyril still intruded on her thoughts as she tried to sleep. It seemed she wasn't much of a judge of character when it came to men. To anyone, perhaps? Which meant she might be wrong to trust Sophia as well, but she needed to trust someone. And she'd never had the types of doubts or questions about Sophia that she'd still harbored about Cyril despite coming here with him.

The second day Tara spent the same way as the first, and by mid-afternoon, feet swollen from her pregnancy and the heat, she sat in front of a statue of Mary in a small stone church. The chapel lacked air conditioning, but it was set a few feet below ground, and colorful stained glass blocked some of the sun's rays, so it felt cooler than outside. Tara wiped her forehead, then rubbed her hands on her sweat pants. She wished she'd packed more cotton skirts. She rested her head against the back of the pew, willing herself not to cry. If she started, she might never stop.

"Pardon me."

A woman's voice, with a Russian-sounding accent, came from behind Tara. Tara turned, straining her neck to look because it took too much effort to move her whole body. She saw a thin young woman with dark skin, short black hair, and blue eyes. The woman wore a blue dress that fell just past her knees, and stood with her hands clasped in front of her.

"Yes?" Tara said.

"Father Lawrence thought perhaps I may help you."

## 41

"He says you are trying to locate a church and a particular family, but don't speak Armenian. I may perhaps accompany you and translate."

"I – that'd be great. Except I have no idea where to go next."

It crossed Tara's mind that the offer of help might be an attempt to sabotage her, despite that the woman looked thin and delicate. Or she could be someone who might turn on Tara, the way Cyril had. *Twice*, Tara thought. *I've got to keep my eyes open.* But, unlike when she'd met Cyril, Tara didn't feel afraid of this woman.

The woman walked to Tara and sat. Her blue dress was frayed at the hem and along the neckline. "My name is Isabel."

"Tara. Why are you willing to help me?"

"I am a schoolteacher on holiday visiting relatives. I teach English and French to children near Ijevan, about three hours from here. With you, I will practice English. And perhaps you will tell me more about America, which I can tell my children. They love all things American."

"Really?" Tara was used to hearing that people in other countries despised Americans, especially since the latest developments in Iraq.

"Yes, particularly in our town. Few Americans travel there, so you would be a celebrity. I wish school were in and the children could meet you."

"I'm not that excited about celebrity." The *Reader* newspaper article had brought enough tragedy. Tara felt no desire for more attention. "But is that why people keep staring at me?"

"Most likely."

"At home, it's rude to stare."

Isabel nodded. "Here as well. But you are a foreigner," she said, as if that made the staring acceptable.

"Are you from here?" Tara asked.

"Yes, but I lived in Moscow for several years. One of my uncles had connections with the party and got me a job. Once Armenia became independent, I wished to return home. Would you like to meet my family before you decide if I should help you? You are welcome to join us for dinner."

"That would be wonderful."

Tara felt slightly less tired and more hopeful than before meeting Isabel. If nothing else, she'd eat dinner with someone nice, and learn more about Armenian culture, before starting over the next day. And she'd have a translator, which had to increase her odds of learning useful information.

As they walked, Isabel told Tara the history of the buildings they passed, and explained that her cousins lived nearby and worked in a restaurant.

Tara told her about the restaurant started with the help of a Peace Corps volunteer two years before.

Isabel nodded. "The United States has done much to help Armenia. But progress is so slow. We all wonder when things will improve."

"What in particular?" Tara asked as they walked through Old Republic Square, skirting the booths.

"Unemployment remains nearly 90%." Isabel gestured toward three men sitting on the steps of a boarded up storefront. "American aid is often diverted to politicians' pockets. Three times foreign governments sent money to rebuild the grade school in my town, and three times the contractors –friends of local government workers – abandoned the work half-way through and disappeared. My students meet in classrooms where chunks of ceiling fall on them and the heat works only half the time."

Isabel's cousins' restaurant was one of the few occupied buildings on the street where it was located. Eight round tables covered with white tablecloths crowded together in a dim room. All the curtains were drawn to keep out the sun. Standing floor fans blew on each table, making the heat somewhat tolerable. Tara lost track of the names of the family members, for within half an hour the room had filled with eleven people wanting to see the girl from America.

Over a salad of cucumbers – so fresh and crisp Tara nearly inhaled them – and sour cream, they peppered her with questions, keeping Isabel busy translating. The kids asked about American schools, and movies, and pop stars, the adults about prices, cars, and the government. Tara's energy returned as she answered, and she forgot her troubles. By the time the main course, chunks of barbecued meat, arrived, she was laughing and asking questions of her own about their day-to-day lives.

Isabel's aunt brought out biscuits and fresh cherry jam for dessert. The tartness completed the meal, and Tara closed her eyes for a moment to savor the taste. The aunt shooed the children away, then brought tea with condensed milk for Tara and Isabel.

"I'm trying to find a church," Tara said. She felt as good with these people as she had in months, and she'd decided that was the best gauge of whom to trust and who really wanted to help her. "I've only seen photos. There's a shrine to the Virgin Mary inside, and the outside is stone with what looks like three square separate sections kind of tacked together. If I can't find that, I'm looking for a woman named Avids Kerkorian, who must be in her nineties if she's still living. She lived somewhere near Lake Sevan thirty years ago."

"I'm not familiar with Avids, but some Kerkorians live about fifty miles from my village," Isabel said.

"And the church?"

Isabel shook her head. "That could describe many in the countryside. Do you know if it is a famous church? One likely to attract tourists? Or known only to locals?"

"I don't know. Except parts of it were built in the sixth century."

"We will go to the museum tomorrow and see if we can find more information." Isabel covered Tara's hand with hers. "We will find something. You will see."

~

THE BUS JOLTED. Chickens squawked. The road – which Isabel told Tara was called a switchback – zigzagged so close to the edge of the mountain that Tara shut her eyes and folded her hands over her stomach as if that would protect the baby should the bus pitch over the side. When she opened her eyes again, she focused on the stuffing that bulged from the seam of the seat in front of her and ignored the view.

Tara had seen as much of Armenia as possible in three days. Its beauty, once away from the traffic and crowds of Yerevan, struck her. Rock formations and clumps of trees decorated the countryside, and she'd seen statues and artwork at the museums, and dozens of stone churches. But nothing like the church in Cyril's photographs. Tomorrow she had to return to Yerevan, collect her things, and leave on an evening flight.

Wiping sweat from under her eyes, Tara shifted so the dry, hot breeze from the window hit her full in the face. The bus groaned across the last switchback, took a straightaway, then careened down the mountain's other side. A hen, accidentally let loose by its owner, screeched as it skittered into the aisle. Tara gripped the seat.

Isabel smiled. "The driver travels this route four times a week. Try not to worry."

Tara tried.

~

A BARN STOOD on the edge of the Kerkorians' land, with the house and outbuildings near it, but not connected. Hills and open fields stretched in all directions. After a large meal, most of which Tara skipped because Isabel warned her it was rinsed in local, untreated water, Tara helped wash dishes in metal basins with water from a pump. The father and brothers returned to the fields, and Tara helped the women shell peas and clean. The youngest daughter, Fimi, disappeared and returned to hand Tara a wood block with a cross carved into it.

"A Khachkar," Tara said. She'd seen them adorning doors of local churches and carved into stones on roadsides.

"Fimi wishes you to have it," Isabel said. "She started to carve three years ago. She pestered her brothers until they showed her how. Typically only boys carve. She says she knew it was special when she made it, and that she was meant to give it to someone who came from America. Her family laughed at her because no one visits. But she says here you are, and it is meant for you."

Tara thanked Fimi in Armenian and rubbed her fingers over the wood. She liked the Khachkars much more than the crucifixes in churches at home. The cross without Jesus hanging on it seemed more a symbol of hope and resurrection than one with his body nailed to it. Leaves and vines sprouted from the cross on this Khachkar.

"Please tell her it's beautiful. And that my sister Megan is her age, and I bet she'd love to learn how to carve wood." Tara felt a sudden longing for Megan, and for home.

The little girl clapped her hands and hugged Tara. When Tara looked at the Khachkar again later, she noticed a snake twining through the leaves.

That evening, as the sun set, the women took Tara to an outdoor stone kitchen. In the center, a cylindrical oven sank three feet into the ground. The mother and daughters rolled balls of dough into flat ovals, stretched the ovals over what looked like large cushions with a handle on the back, then slammed the dough-cushions into the sides of the in-ground oven.

"They make lavash," Isabel said. "The thin flat bread we've been eating all week."

The women let Tara and Isabel roll the dough for the next batch. The oven emitted a wall of heat.

The family claimed to be distantly related to Avids Kerkorian, but she'd died years before, and they knew nothing about a pregnant virgin. They could tell Tara only that Avids' daughter – Nanor – lived in America, and her son, the uncle Maya had mentioned – had been killed in a battle with Azerbaijan.

"I am sorry we've learned so little," Isabel said.

"It's all right," Tara said.

The dough felt soft and warm between Tara's fingers. She inhaled the smell of earth and animals. The hot wind brushed through her hair. Her muscles relaxed. The women chattered around her, and though she couldn't understand their words unless Isabel translated, Tara felt sure they enjoyed their work and one another's company. It reminded her of evenings when her dad made popcorn, and her mom let the kids drink as much soda as they wanted, and they played Monopoly and ate until they were exhausted.

"It is?" Isabel said.

"I came all this way to find answers, but maybe there aren't any. My best times since I got pregnant have been with the amazing people I've met, who've shared with me, and cared about me. Maybe that's what's holy. And if there's something I'm meant to do, or my baby is meant to do, we'll figure it out when the time comes."

Isabel rolled her wooden pin over her circle of dough one last time. "But you seemed so determined to find answers, and so frustrated by not getting them, when we met."

The mother watched Tara and Isabel speaking, her eyes warm, as if she understood the content.

"I can't say it wouldn't be nice if a voice from on high would just explain everything and tell me it's all going to work out. But I'm okay with not knowing. Really. With just being."

The mother bent and patted Tara's hand.

As she was getting ready for bed, Tara realized she'd misplaced the Khachkar. The last time she remembered seeing it was at the lavash pit, so when the full moon rose, Tara walked there. She took her journal with, wanting to write about Fimi. Stars scattered across the sky, brighter than she'd ever seen at home. She and Isabel were staying the night with the Kerkorians. In the morning, the brothers planned to drive them to the bus stop to return to Yerevan.

Tara found the Khachkar beneath the bench near the lavash pit. She sat, leaned back against the wood wall behind her, and breathed deep. The night air wrapped around her. Something rustled toward the other side of the pit, and a six-foot snake slithered from the grass onto the concrete. Its colors caught the moonlight, shifting as it swayed toward Tara.

# 42

The snake stopped a few feet in front of Tara. Its head rose toward the roof until the snake nearly stood on its tail. Tara shook her head, thinking she must have fallen asleep. But hot, dry wind chapped her lips. A dog barked from beyond the barn. Wood splinters from the bench beneath her thighs poked her flesh.

As the creature swayed, Tara shuddered, remembering the part of the Garden of Eden story which said the snake once walked on feet, but God punished it by making it crawl on its belly. But then she thought of Kali's explanation of the kundalini that rose through the body, opening each chakra, and relaxed a little.

The serpent's scales reflected the moonlight in violet and gold. Their light brightened until the hues obscured the snake, then diffused to reveal a woman. Her skin glowed mahogany brown under the moonlight. Her face reminded Tara of Sophia's, with her narrow nose and high forehead. Her eyes sparkled blue like Megan's, yet the lines around them etched deep into her skin, like Nanor's. Though Tara couldn't see the snake's colors any more, she felt them, their warmth and coolness, like sunlight and moonlight.

Tara forced herself to breathe, afraid she'd faint, and stared at the woman. "Who are you?"

"I am Protennoia, She who exists before the All. I am revealed in the immeasurable, ineffable things. I move in every creature, uttering a Voice by means of Thought. I am the real Voice."

The woman's lips moved when she spoke, yet Tara felt sure the vision before her was only a vision, not flesh and blood, not even the real form of what spoke. The voice flowed from word to word, syllable to syllable, in a register high enough to be feminine, yet low enough to be masculine.

"I walk uprightly. Those who sleep, I awaken, and I am the sight of those who dwell in sleep. Now the Voice that originated from my Thought exists as three permanences: the Mother, the Father, the Child. I am the image of the Invisible Spirit and it is through it the All took shape. I am the Mother as well as the Light which she appointed as Virgin."

"What does that mean?" Tara stretched her hand toward the woman, but her fingers passed through the image, as she'd thought they would. The hair on her arm stood, and her skin tingled. "Why are you here?"

"I came down before and reached into Chaos. I revealed myself to those who heard my mysteries. Now I come the second time in the likeness of a female to speak with them. And I shall tell them of the coming end of the Aeon and teach them of the beginning of the Aeon to come, the one without change, the one in which our appearance will be changed. We shall be purified with those Aeons from which I revealed myself in the Thought of the likeness of my masculinity."

Tara wished she had a recorder. Her mind couldn't move fast enough to process the words. "Can you help with what I should do? Is this the holy ground?"

"Tell all you can as soon as you can: the birth beckons, and hour begets hour, day begets day, the months made known the month. Time goes round succeeding time. I am the Word. The Word is a hidden Light, bearing a Fruit of Life, pouring forth a Living Water, the unreproducible Voice of the glory of the Mother, the glory of the offspring of God."

The woman disappeared, leaving Tara staring into the stone lavash pit. Tara looked around. The path to the house was deserted, silver grass stalks shone under the moonlight. The house and outbuildings stood dark.

The breeze rustled something at Tara's side. Her journal lay on the bench, open. As Tara stared at the blank pages, her own writing appeared.

Tara read the first line aloud. "I am Protennoia, She Who Exists Before the All."

# 43

To:thelittlestviking@mailmail.com
From:sophia.gaddini@DEPedu.org

Tara,

Do you know what this is? Do you remember my mentioning the *Trimorphic Protennoia* to you? It's one of the manuscripts that was found in Egypt, one the Catholic Church rejected and denounced as heresy back in the fifth century. The emphasis on God having both masculine and feminine aspects is consistent with the Gnostic point of view, which the Church abandoned. The text you forwarded, other than "tell all you can as soon as you can" is a combination of portions of the English translation of it in the Nag Hammadi library, with a few alterations.

Did you read the *Trimorphic Protennoia* at some point after we spoke? If not, that you'd have a vision or dream that incorporates it is truly amazing. (Even if you did, I'd be awed by the recall powers of your unconscious mind. I certainly could not quote so well from memory.)

I can't wait to talk about this with you. From the brevity of your e-mail, I assume you only had a few minutes and now have probably left the Internet café. If you do get this before you board your flight, please call me from the airport in Yerevan or as soon as you arrive in the U.S. If your flight stops in Chicago, please consider staying for a while. We can get a hotel room for you under another name.

And please, please take care of yourself. I should feel better knowing you are traveling with someone, but I have an uneasy feeling about it being Cyril Woods. If he's aware of the *Trimorphic Protennoia*, I doubt he'll view it as positive that text from it was apparently spoken to you, nor would his superiors. He may well try to talk you out of what you believe happened to you.

I hope you've written down everything you saw and felt and heard, not just the words spoken to you. If you share what's occurred, many people in the days and weeks to come will try to tell you what they believe your vision means or worse, what they think "really happened," and it will become harder and harder to sort out what you recall. For that reason, I'll say nothing of my own thoughts and interpretation and will wait to hear from you.

Love,

Sophia

# 44

"So it sounds like you and this serpent had quite a long chat."

Tara pressed her palms together in her lap. She wished she could see Sophia, who sat somewhere in the talk show audience beyond the bright lights. The studio's flat, electronic air reminded Tara of the time Bailey pressed and held all the buttons on Dad's CD player and it started to fry. Tara cleared her throat and turned toward Janet Stephanik, the program's host.

"Not a serpent. I saw a serpent first, but it became a woman who spoke to me."

Janet had a round, friendly face and soft, paunchy hands. She reached across her desk and patted Tara's arm. "Got it, snake turned into woman. Does that give you the sense that, uh, maybe this was a dream?"

"I wondered at the time if I was dreaming. All I can tell you is I don't have any sense of having fallen asleep, and I never had a moment where I woke up. I sat on a bench, I saw the snake slither toward me, it became a woman who spoke. When she was finished, I stood, looked around, and saw her words written in my journal. Then I walked back to the house."

"If it was a dream, does that change the meaning of what you experienced?"

Tara shook her head. "I don't think so. What the woman said is the same, whether she existed in the physical world or just in my mind."

"Any idea why this is all happening to you? The baby, the snake woman?"

"No."

"Are you very religious? Did you study theology in school?"

Tara shifted in her chair, trying to move the baby's weight so she could breathe more easily. "No to both. But since I got pregnant I've read a lot of books and papers about women and religion, and about the Apocalypse of John."

Nodding to the audience, Janet said, "There you go folks. Her qualification for receiving a message from the Almighty: She reads."

The audience laughed, and Tara felt her face burn. She reminded herself that even if Janet basically liked her, which Tara thought was the case, Janet's job, as the comedian/host, was to make everything a joke. But this was worth doing if it would somehow make the world safer for the people Tara loved.

"I'm not saying I was picked because I know something other people don't. I don't know why this happened, it just did."

"But what's it about, do you think? Some sort of serpent, Eve, Garden of Eden sequel? Because, I have to say, as sequels go, this one's pretty good so far."

This rated a few chuckles. Tara wondered if the show's producer cued the audience on when and how to laugh. Did the signs say guffaw, chortle, laugh uproariously?

"I don't think it's about the Garden of Eden, because a serpent's not necessarily a symbol of evil. In the goddess culture, the serpent meant life and healing. It was only when the male-dominated monotheistic religions took hold that the serpent, and other goddess symbols like the tree of life, were recast as evil."

"That's one of the things you read about?"

"Yes. And learned about from different people I met as I tried to figure out why I became pregnant."

"That's an age old question, isn't it, ladies?"

More chuckles.

*That's not even funny.*

Tara glanced toward stage right, wishing she could walk off. She'd only need to travel a few feet, the set was so small. But she needed to at least try to tell about her vision. The woman had told her to, at least that's how Tara interpreted Protennoia's words. Maybe a few people would hear and get something out of it.

"So let's get to it," Janet said. "I've asked an expert to join us and help interpret your vision. Folks, let's give a warm 'Janet' Welcome to the Reverend Frank McCoffell, professor of theology from the Brookings Christian University and author of *In God We Trust*."

"Expert?" Tara's stomach spasmed.

The audience's applause drowned Tara's question. She peered toward stage right again, wishing she could bolt from the set. But leaving would make her look like she was afraid to face questions.

She glanced at her watch. *Six minutes to go. Breathe.*

A husky man wearing a dark blue suit with padded shoulders, a white shirt, and a red tie strode on stage, sat down next to Tara, and pulled his chair forward.

"Thank you." His tenor voice seemed incongruous given his bulk.

"So." Janet gestured toward Tara. "Though we've got an expert here, let's start with your view. What does the message mean?"

"I've thought a lot about that. It probably means my baby will somehow help the world again emphasize feminine values and counteract the way the monotheistic religions focus on male values and approaches."

"'Feminine' meaning?" Janet said.

"Cooperation rather than competition, peace and conciliation rather than war and world domination, creation rather than destruction."

*I sound like I'm reading. Is anyone going to believe I'm speaking from my heart?* Sweat itched the skin under Tara's arms, and her mouth felt parched.

"Reverend?"

McCoffell turned so he faced the audience rather than Tara or Janet. "Those statements show Ms. Spencer's lack of knowledge of the New Testament – no offense, Ms. Spencer. But Jesus himself preached non-violence and cooperation. That's nothing new, nor are those values particularly 'feminine.' They're simply Christian."

Having discussed the issue with Sophia, Tara was ready. "But that's not exactly how Christianity's been practiced. Look at how many world leaders, including supposedly Christian leaders in our own country, say God wanted them to go to war. That's what I mean by masculine rather than feminine values. It's a traditionally masculine take on religion."

McCoffell started to respond, but Janet cut in. "Is it significant, then, that you got pregnant, and got this message, at a time when our involvement in the Middle East, and the turmoil there, is more intense than ever?"

"I didn't think of that, but it might be."

*Maybe she really is interested in the vision. I'm not just a novelty for her show.* And Janet might be right. Maya Kerkorian's pregnancy happened during the Vietnam war. But Tara hadn't said anything about Maya or Willow Springs, partly because it wasn't her story to tell, and partly because Nanor had opposed Tara going public before Nanor could meditate on the message. Tara considered waiting for Nanor's okay, but Protennoia's voice rang in her mind: *Tell all you can as soon as you can.* If the baby's and Tara's survival depended on the message getting out, Tara figured she'd better start talking.

"So if the next Osama Bin Laden points missiles at New York City, we're all supposed to sit around and sing *Kum Ba Yah* until he goes away?" Janet said.

"I'm sure it's more complicated than that."

McCoffell grunted. "But you said, Ms. Spencer, peace and conciliation rather than war."

"I don't think that means you can never act to defend yourself or someone else. Just that we shouldn't rush to try to solve everything by violence."

"So God might be on the side of a country that came to its own defense? And you might not consider that a 'male' rather than 'female' response?" McCoffell said.

"I'm not sure if a divine being would take sides in a war."

"Not even, say, when the Nazis killed millions in the concentration camps?"

"I don't have an answer to everything," Tara said. "I don't claim to, and I don't know exactly what the vision means. Janet asked me what I thought it meant and I answered."

"But you're writing a book about it," Janet said. "For which Warner Brothers gave you a hefty advance. So you must feel you know something."

"I'm writing a book, yes, with the help of Sophia Gaddini. To share the message with as many people as possible. Each person will need to decide what she or he thinks it means."

The book had been Sophia's idea. It sounded like a perfect way to get the message out. And to earn some money to help pay for Tara's medical expenses and, she hoped, eventually her tuition when she returned to school. But Tara wondered if appearing on talk shows made sense. Other than the laughs, the feeling she got from the audience was flat, as if they'd built a wall between themselves and her. She wasn't exactly making a good case for herself.

"You're sharing that message pretty darn quickly," Janet said. "You supposedly had this vision two weeks ago and already you've got a publishing contract, and you're doing the talk show circuit."

"The woman told me to tell people as soon as I could. So that's what I'm doing. I only was able to get the book contract so fast because of Sophia. I'm really fortunate to know her."

"She's pretty fortunate, too, don't you think?" Janet's eyebrows, thick and dark, arched. "I mean, her first two books were a success in the academic world, which means they were read by, what, five or six professors? But this book could be a best seller, if people buy into your story. Or even if they don't."

"It's not about the money."

"So you'll be donating the money to a worthy cause?" Janet said.

"I didn't think about it. That's a good idea. And I probably will use some of it for the baby. And, I hope, to finish school."

McCoffell crossed his right leg over his left and rested his hands on his knees. "Ms. Spencer raises an interesting point. She certainly is in a position where she needs money. As I understand it, your family's abandoned you, isn't that right, Ms. Spencer?"

The lights seemed to get hotter. "I wouldn't necessarily say they've abandoned me," Tara said, even though that was what she felt her parents had done.

"But you haven't seen them in some time?"

"No. Not all of them, anyway."

"And, in fact, your parents believe you're delusional? They sought to have you committed?"

The studio hushed.

Tara swallowed. "They did that months ago, when I kept saying I hadn't had sex, even though it was clear I was pregnant. They were worried about me. They've changed their minds now."

"Is that so? Did you know they never withdrew the papers from the court?"

"No, I didn't know that."

*That can't be right. They told Nate they didn't want custody any more.* Then again, she'd left her parents a voicemail when she got back from Armenia, and they'd never called.

"That's a very serious indictment, isn't it?" Reverend McCoffell patted his receding hairline, though every hair lay perfectly in place. "Your own parents believing you're delusional?"

Tara turned toward McCoffell and looked him right in his watery blue eyes. "What would you think? Your daughter comes home and says she's pregnant, but she never had intercourse and can't explain how it happened, and then she says her pregnancy might be divine?"

Hearing the words out loud, Tara knew what she'd said was logical. But in her heart, she couldn't understand why her Mom and Dad hadn't believed her, no matter how crazy she sounded. If Nanor and Kali, who barely knew Tara, believed her, why couldn't her parents?

McCoffell twitched the corners of his mouth up for an instant, as if in sympathy, then snapped them back into a straight line. "I imagine I might react just as they did. So you can understand why we all need to ask questions. One question being, if you're not delusional, what might be your motive in telling this story?"

"To get the message out."

"Or earn money. You admit you need it."

"I wouldn't need money if I'd gotten pregnant the regular way. I'd be marrying my boyfriend – former boyfriend – and our families would help us take care of the baby so we could both work and I could finish school. Believe me, if I could change this all so I could just have a run of the mill unplanned pregnancy, life would be so much simpler."

Janet clapped her hands. "Now we're getting into the juicy part. Tara, do you really expect people to believe you're a virgin?"

Though her lower back ached, Tara sat straighter, trying to look more adult and credible. "I don't expect people to believe or not believe anything. I just hope they'll listen to the message and try to keep an open mind."

"But you are a virgin?"

"I was when I found out I was pregnant. I was until recently."

Tara had decided in advance if asked she'd tell the truth. If she didn't, certainly Cyril would never believe her about anything again, and she was damned if she'd give him a basis for calling her a liar. Plus, she couldn't deliver Protennoia's message and lie about anything connected to it. It wouldn't be right, no matter how uncomfortable Tara felt.

Janet clasped her hands and leaned forward, eyes practically glowing. "Really? Until recently. So you have a boyfriend for a year, and you're talking about getting married, and you never have intercourse with him, but then you discover you're pregnant and you decide, what the heck, might as well have sex?" She looked at the audience. "I mean, it kind of makes sense, right? No birth control worries."

Tara bit her lip. *Live with Janet* wasn't exactly *Jerry Springer*, but she was starting to feel like today's show was.

"It didn't happen that way. The man who traveled to Armenia with me, he fell in love with me, and things just, they just happened."

"The deacon. Whose name you won't give us."

Tara'd seen no reason to share Cyril's name or the Brotherhood's name, any more than she'd shared Maya's or Nanor's.

"He was studying to be a deacon. It happened one night when we stayed together. And he got angry at me in the morning and blamed it on me."

"Quite the morning after, huh? Have you heard from him since?"

Tara swallowed hard. "No." She wondered if Cyril was watching, and whether he felt bad about how he'd treated her. And whether he'd told his superiors about what had happened. If not, they'd know now.

"So, Ms. Spencer," McCoffell said, "you're saying that, though you resisted temptation and kept yourself pure, once you became pregnant, you were lured into sex by a religious man?"

"That's not what I'm saying. I don't believe sex makes people impure. I waited because I feel pregnancy is very serious, and I wanted to finish college before taking any chances. Birth control isn't foolproof."

McCoffell nodded. "So once you were pregnant, who you had sex with didn't matter to you."

"I didn't say that either. I cared about Cy—this man, and he'd been there for me when no one else had. Was I using my best judgment? Obviously not. But I survived. And, who knows, maybe I never would have had the vision if he'd stayed around, because I never would have met Isabel."

Tara longed more than anything to be done with this show, to lie down somewhere quiet and speak to no one. Her watch told her she had two minutes left of taping.

McCoffell tilted his head and raised his eyebrows. "So you want us to believe this woman appeared to you because you had sex?"

"Again, not what I said. Things happened the way they did. I don't know why."

Janet smiled at the audience, showing even, bleached white teeth. "We've got another guest, someone Tara knows well but hasn't mentioned yet today. Please welcome Roger Mitchell, a former fellow student of Tara's from St. Louis University."

"Roger?" Tara gripped the arms of her chair, mind racing. *Why would Roger –*

From side stage, Roger sauntered in. In school, Tara had only seen her lab partner in faded blue jeans and cotton T's. Today, he wore black jeans and a charcoal blazer over a gray silk button down shirt. A silver earring glinted in his left ear, and his heavy cologne filled the air. Roger waved at the audience and sat next to Reverend McCoffell.

"Roger, tell us how you know Tara."

Roger smirked. "We took Advanced Chemistry together at SLU. We sat next to each other the first day, and she begged me to be her lab partner because she said she'd struggled with her freshman year chemistry class."

"What?" Tara said. "You were the one who wanted to be partners."

Janet held up her hand. "Let's let Roger talk. Folks, you want to hear from Roger, don't you?"

The audience roared a yes.

Tara knew what he'd say, the only thing he could possibly be here to say.

"I knew she had a boyfriend, but she always chatted and joked with me, even though I tried to keep things light. Then she kept inviting me to study with her, even though I told her I prefer to study alone. So I knew she had a thing for me."

"I invited you because you needed help."

Roger rocked back in his chair. "Really? Who failed Advanced Chem last semester?"

"I failed because I missed the final, not because I didn't know chemistry."

Roger shrugged. "Whatever you say. Anyway, one night in March I finally agreed to study with her, but she insisted we go to the Sigma Alpha fraternity bash first. We both got trashed, and ended the night in bed. Well, on the floor, actually. Of course, we should have used protection, but neither of us was thinking clearly. Or thinking, for that matter."

"I never slept with him. I've never even gone to a fraternity party. Find me one person who's ever seen me at a fraternity party, or out with Roger."

Janet scrunched her face as if she were puzzled. "But didn't your boyfriend, Jeremy, assume the baby was Roger's? Another classmate of yours heard him accuse you of that in a Kirkwood coffeehouse –" Janet made a show of looking at notes "—called Common Grounds."

Sweat dripped down Tara's face and coated her neck. She wondered if the audience could see it. Not that it mattered at this point.

"Because Roger asked me out once and Jeremy was jealous. And because Jeremy knew it wasn't his. Not because I ever slept with Roger."

Janet spread her hands. "Roger says you did. And Jeremy thought you did."

"That never happened. When the baby's born, we'll do the testing, and that'll show the baby's not Roger's. Or Jeremy's."

"That doesn't mean anything," Roger said. "She was all over me, who knows how many guys she's been with. Sounds like pretty much the same thing happened with this deacon guy. He probably never knew what hit him."

"You fucking liar."

"Looks like someone hit a bit close to home," Janet said. "On that note, folks, we need to call it a day and leave it for you to decide. A virgin birth or a great publicity stunt? Either way, you heard it here first. I'm rooting for the female messiah on the way, one who seems to like baking bread – damn the carbohydrates – isn't too concerned about sex outside of marriage as long as you're in a foreign country, and wants us all to live in peace. Sounds awesome to me. Thanks for watching *Live with Janet!*"

Afterward, Tara hunched on the couch in the green room, her head down to avoid looking at anyone as much as to combat the dizziness she'd felt when she'd stood after the show ended. She heard other guests talking and moving around her.

"Tara?" The couch sagged as Sophia sat. She put her hand on Tara's back.

"No one will believe me. I can't prove a negative."

"Someone's here to see you," Sophia said.

"Tara?"

Tara couldn't believe her ears. She lifted her head and stared at the figure in the doorway.

"Mom?"

# 45

When her mom hugged her, Tara started to cry. Though Lynette didn't say it, Tara knew she must be sorry, for Tara could count the times her mother had initiated a hug.

Lynette brushed Tara's tears away. "I'm so glad you're all right."

"You mean, from the show?"

One hand still resting on Tara's shoulder, Lynette sat next to Tara on the couch. "The last we heard, you'd gone to Armenia. Sophia told me you left a voicemail when you got back, but we never got it. So I thought you were still in Armenia when the coup happened yesterday, and I called Sophia."

Red edged the skin around the corners of Lynette's eyes, and more lines etched her forehead than Tara remembered seeing before.

"What coup?" Tara had no idea what her mother was talking about.

"It was on the news."

Sophia pulled a straight back chair closer to the sofa and sat across from them. "While the president was traveling, the opposition party surrounded parliament and shot everyone, then took over. Your mom called me last night because she thought you were still there. It was after you'd gone to sleep."

Tara shook her head, feeling any more information would make it explode. The soldiers she'd seen in Yerevan and in the rural areas had disconcerted her, but she hadn't realized the Armenian government was that volatile. And she'd assumed her parents hadn't called her back because they didn't want to, not that they'd not received her message.

"I told your mom about the show, and she decided to come," Sophia said. "We figured you had enough on your mind before you went on, so I didn't mention any of it."

Speakers near the door piped in the theme music for the next performer, though the sound on the monitor over the mirrors was turned down.

Tara looked at Lynette. "You were there? Watching?"

Lynette smiled, but it looked strained. "You did fine, honey. You held your ground and you obviously believe what you're saying."

"Of course I do," Tara said, exasperated. "You don't still think I'm making all this up?"

Her mother pulled back. "No, no. I'm just saying, you came across as credible."

"But what do you think? Are you still trying to get me locked away somewhere?"

"No. I told your brothers and sisters that long ago. When the process server couldn't reach you, we just dropped it. We didn't even think about having to withdraw anything from the court."

Tara longed to just go home with her mother, but she'd learned not to take things at face value. "And so are you back to thinking I'm lying?"

"Tara, I don't know what to think. I don't know what any of this means, but I don't believe you're lying or mentally unstable. And we really want you to come home. Your brothers and sisters miss you. We miss you."

An image of the clump of Julie's hair and what was left of her head on the bedroom floor flashed through Tara's mind. "I miss you, too. But I'd put you all in danger just being there."

"You could change your appearance again," Lynette said. "And stay at a hotel under another name."

Sophia nodded. "You could use some of the advance money to pay for private security."

"Maybe," Tara said. "But it's probably better I'm not in the St. Louis area at all. Especially after the show."

Lynette grasped Tara's hand. "Megan's having more trouble walking, and her headaches are more severe. Her brain swelled again. They brought the swelling down some in the hospital, and she's home now, but unless they can get her into that new drug trial, there's nothing else."

Tara cleared her throat. "Is it – is there a time frame?"

"The doctors won't say. The medical literature considers six weeks optimistic."

Sophia's Toyota smelled of new leather, though she said the car was four years old. Tara rode in the front seat on the way to Midway Airport, Lynette in the back. Tara's hair was black now, and short again. They'd spent the afternoon at the hotel dyeing and curling it, and applying self-tanner to Tara's face, arms and legs. Her skin felt greasy and a little irritated, but she looked different.

"What about Dad?" Tara said.

"He wants you to come home, too," Lynette said.

Tara pushed her shoulder belt aside and twisted in the seat to face her mother. "Yeah, but what does he think about my pregnancy?"

Lynette sighed. "It's hard for him, Tara. And you know your dad. He insists he's fine, and he just wants you to come home, and he's perfectly all right with not knowing why you're pregnant or what's going on."

"But you sense he's still angry with me."

"He says he's not."

"Then for sure he is." Tara sank back against the seat, starting to feel angry herself. What was more important to her father, her or the Church? Why did he assume she was the one who was wrong?

Sophia's cell phone played the first bars of *Ode to Joy*.

"Aren't you going to get it?" Tara said.

The Midway exit sign appeared, and Sophia eased the car into the right lane. "Chicago passed an ordinance against talking on cell phones while driving."

Tara reached for the phone. "Want me to answer?"

"We're nearly at the airport, I'll check voicemail after I let you out."

Fifteen minutes later, Sophia pulled into the drop off lane near Midway's main terminal. She and Tara hugged good-bye, then Tara got her and her mother's bags from the trunk.

Just as Tara and Lynette reached the sliding doors to the terminal, a horn blared behind them. Tara turned. Sophia's Toyota skidded to a halt in the No Parking/No Standing zone. A uniformed guard yelled as Sophia jumped from the car and hurried toward Tara.

"What is it?" Tara said. "What's wrong?"

"The voicemail," Sophia said. "It was the secretary to Cardinal John Phillipe Carruthers. The Pope wants to meet you."

## 46

"Something to drink before we take off?"

"What? Oh, no, thanks."

Tara ran her fingers over the seatback and footrest controls. She definitely liked first class. The seat size alone made her so much more comfortable than on the flight to Armenia. She stared out the window at JFK's tarmac, pressing her fingers to the glass. Excited as she was about seeing the Vatican and Pope Matthew I, Tara wished she could split herself in two. She'd barely hugged Megan and explained about the Pope's request before she had to leave for the connecting flight to New York. But she couldn't delay the trip. Dr. Lei made it clear flying became riskier the closer she got to her due date. And seeing the Pope might make people more likely to listen to her message, even if he didn't believe her.

At least the Vatican provided an extra ticket, so her dad could go with her. She'd half-expected to hear something from Cyril, he must have learned about the Pope's request, but she hadn't. Maybe he was embarrassed to speak to her. Or afraid she'd lead him back into temptation, even by phone. Tara hadn't tried to reach him.

"What will you say to him?" Pete asked.

"The Pope?" Tara said. "I don't know."

Pete frowned. "You should have something prepared."

The plane began taxiing, and Tara adjusted her seatbelt so it rested lower on her hips. She and her dad had spent the flight from St. Louis talking about what Tara had done since leaving home. Pete slammed his hand on the tray table when he heard the things Cyril said to Tara and how he'd left her in Armenia, but otherwise he just listened. He didn't say anything about how unwise it had been to have sex with Cyril. Tara figured he might feel that was pretty obvious at this point.

"The Pope heard my story on *Live with Janet*. It wasn't my ideal forum, but the facts pretty much got out there, even if I got made fun of."

"But you need a better answer," Pete said. "For why you were chosen. You can't just shrug and tell the Holy Father you have no idea."

"Why not?"

"He won't listen. Or believe you. You need an answer."

"Are you sure it's not you who needs one?"

The airplane accelerated, shuddered and lifted. "You should present your best case to the Pope," Pete said.

"Will what the Pope thinks change your mind? Will you believe me if the Pope does, is that it?"

Pete stared past Tara, out the window. "It's not a question of what I believe."

"It is to me. The Pope leads one religion out of a whole bunch of religions, and if he's willing to help get the message out, that's great, it's important. But not as important as you."

"I want to believe you, Tara," Pete said. "And I love you. I haven't handled this well, and I'm sorry. You can't imagine how sorry. I lie awake at night imagining doing things differently so you wouldn't have left home. But figuring out what I believe isn't only about you, it's about my faith."

"Is there some conflict between the two I don't know about?"

"How could there not be?" Pete waved his hand for emphasis and bumped the back of the seat in front of him. "The Catholic Church doesn't teach that another messiah will be born of a human woman. The Second Coming is when the Son of Man—Jesus—returns for the last judgment."

"But that's all open to interpretation, isn't it?"

Pete sighed. "I've never thought so. That's part of why I need to hear what the Pope says. Maybe I'm being too literal. I like the black and white answers the Church offers, or seems to offer. The Church is my home base. You know how much a part of our family it's been."

"I don't think it's going to ex-communicate you no matter what I do." Tara was half-joking, but felt that somewhere underneath, her dad might really fear that.

But Pete smiled. "I know that. But the other part of why I want to know what the Pope says is that I'm worried about you, Tara. Not just your physical safety. Your spiritual well-being. This is serious, what you're claiming, what you and this professor think your message means. It goes counter to thousands of years of Church teaching."

The flight attendant returned and gave them plates of fruit and cheese.

"I'm not so sure it does," Tara said, "or at least that it needs to. There are things you disagree with the Church on, and you don't think that puts your spiritual well-being in danger. Like getting a vasectomy after Megan was born because you and Mom couldn't see how you could take care of more kids."

Pete's forehead creased. "I struggled with that. And your mother shouldn't have told you about it."

"Why not? Being an adult is about learning to make decisions and take responsibility, right? And one of the ways to learn that is to see how other people do it."

"All right. But your pregnancy isn't just an issue where you or I might disagree with the Church. We're talking about the whole basis of Christianity. There's one Father, one Son, one Holy Spirit. One Holy Catholic Church. You're suggesting we didn't get the message right the first time. But we did get it right – we got the Church. Which is why there must be some other explanation. Not that you're lying or delusional, but something else. Something scientific maybe."

"If you look at it that way, there's no point in my seeing the Pope at all," Tara said. "He's supposed to be infallible, right, and so were all the other Popes? And he's the leader of the Church. So he's never going to agree the Church is wrong about anything."

"You talk about things being open to interpretation. What about your vision? Maybe it was a dream, and there was no message from anything divine at all. Or there was a message, but it's different from what you remember."

The plane tilted, and Tara squinted as sunlight blinded her for a moment. She remembered Sophia's e-mail about people trying to convince her the vision didn't really happen, or happened some other way. She'd expected it, but it hurt that her dad would do it. Given how he'd reacted when he'd read her journal, and how strongly he'd always felt about the Church, it shouldn't surprise her. Yet it did.

"The words are on the pages of my notebook." Tara cut the strawberry on her plate with the tiny airline knife and fork, not looking at Pete. "I might be wrong about what they mean. Everyone has to decide that for herself. Or himself. But those are the words."

Pete didn't answer. The plane climbed higher, and Tara finished her fruit and cheese, folded her tray table. She pulled the red felt blanket out of the seat pocket to wrap around herself, but she still felt cold.

DOZENS OF PEOPLE crammed into the Sistine Chapel, making the air humid and ripe. Tara stared at the ceiling. On first look, it had surprised her that it was made up of so many small paintings, rather than the just the one of God and Adam she'd seen on one of the art channels. But her mind wandered during the guide Marilene's explanation of when and why the artwork was commissioned. Tara appreciated the Cardinal's arranging the tour, and her dad was asking questions, but Tara wished she'd slept all morning instead. Plus, she kept feeling as if people were staring at her, though she never caught anyone in particular looking in her direction. For all she knew, the Brotherhood originated within the Vatican and might have agents – even the red-haired man – here. Cyril had insisted the Brotherhood wasn't connected with the Pope, but his word didn't mean much.

The air cooled and hushed despite the milling tourists as Tara and Pete followed Marilene into St. Peter's Basilica. The soaring ceiling seemed to lift the noise and heat from the atmosphere. Though wall sconces held white taper candles, none were lit, and no incense burned. Marilene said it was a rule, because the smoke would damage the artwork over time. The air felt pure, and charged.

Paintings hung everywhere, and statues stood throughout the Basilica. The *Pieta* was set back in the first alcove to the right. A plexi-glass wall fronted the alcove, sealing in the statue.

"This *Pieta* is the first of four Michaelangelo carved," Marilene said. "He was only twenty when he finished it. See how Mary's face appears unlined, even though this shows her holding Jesus' body after the crucifixion. She must have been in her forties, at least, because Jesus was supposed to be approximately thirty when he died."

Tara stepped closer to the plexi-glass. Mary looked younger than Tara was now. Perhaps the artist had meant to portray Mary at the age when Jesus was born, or how Mary looked and felt just after learning she was pregnant. Her head angled down, so her eyes appeared closed as she gazed at her son's prone body. She cradled him on her lap, one arm under his upper back, one under his knees. Marilene said art critics described Mary's expression as serene, but Tara felt sorrow emanating from her. Tara saw a young woman, full of faith and fear as she contemplated her newborn, projected forward thirty-some years to when she'd hold her grown son's corpse.

Tara pressed her hands over her belly. What might happen to her daughter because of the message Tara was determined to share? In the last few months, all she'd focused on was getting to her daughter's birth, as if that would ward off disaster and death. Now the fears she'd harbored and written about during the first weeks after the ultrasound came back full force. This was only the beginning.

*Why did I tell anyone about her? I should have pretended. Let the world think she was Jeremy's. Protected her.*

"It's hard to see Jesus' face." Marilene gestured with her left hand toward the Christ figure's head, which angled toward the back wall. "You used to be able to walk around the statute, but the Church erected this bullet-proof plexi-glass in 1972."

"Why?" Pete asked.

"A crazed geologist stormed in, shouting he was Jesus Christ, and took a hammer to it."

THE POPE's plain wood desk reminded Tara of the one her dad used in his home office before the room became a bedroom for Megan and Kelly. A worn white and green sofa backed against three large windows. Tara perched on the sofa, back straight, and Pope Matthew I sat in an oversized armchair. Sandalwood and lilacs scented the room, and early afternoon sunlight shone off the polished hardwood floor.

The Pope wore a black cassock and a skullcap, rather than the traditional papal robes and mitre. He was tall and wiry. Despite the heavy lines on his face and neck, Tara found it hard to believe he was eighty-nine years old. He moved with grace and speed, and his eyes, behind thick, black-framed glasses, danced.

The Pope poured Tara another Coke and settled back into his armchair. "You must wonder why I invited you." He had a slight Polish accent Tara recognized from her great-aunts on her mom's side.

"I am," Tara said. "It's wonderful to meet you, but there must be so many demands on your time."

For the last fifteen minutes, Pope Matthew had asked about Tara's college courses, Megan's health, and what Tara thought generally about politics, but nothing about the pregnancy or the vision. Tara answered, but couldn't relax.

"I want to show you something." The Pope sprung from his chair and retrieved a paper from his desk. He handed it to Tara. "My press secretary will release this tomorrow."

Tara had trouble reading the page because her hand trembled. She expected, despite how kind the Pope had been, a screed denouncing her and her vision. The typeface stood out, dark on a white page.

Pope Matthew I met with Tara Spencer yesterday. Ms Spencer, from the United States, claims to be pregnant through supernatural means and also claims she was told in a vision that her child's purpose is to bring a return to the values of peace and cooperation. No investigation has yet been conducted regarding Ms. Spencer's claims, and the Catholic Church takes no position regarding those claims. However, Pope Matthew found the young woman credible and well-meaning, and he wishes her well. As to her alleged vision, Pope Matthew commented that Jesus Christ called for peace and cooperation, and did not advocate violence as a means of achieving any purpose.

"You wrote this before meeting me?" Tara wasn't sure what to think. Maybe there was a catch, something she had to agree to before the Church would release this.

"I dictated it after watching you on television. I wanted to meet you to confirm what I felt." Pope Matthew smiled. "When you've been around as long as I, you learn about people."

"But I did terrible on that show. I couldn't answer the questions, I stumbled, and everyone laughed at me." Tara's face grew warm at the memory.

"Have you read Yeats, Ms. Spencer?"

"In my first-year literature class."

"Do you recall the poem *The Second Coming*?"

"Just the part about the rough beast slouching toward Bethlehem to be born."

"That poem includes two lines very apt for our time. Indeed, for any time. *The best lack all conviction, while the worst/are full of passionate intensity.*"

Tara remembered the lines when the Pope spoke the words. She liked Yeats, and she'd spent more time reading his poems than most others she'd been assigned. "So it's my uncertainty that convinced you?"

"Let's say your uncertainty about why you were chosen, and about the absolute meaning of your vision, convinced me of your sincere belief in the importance of the message, and the mandate that it be shared. As to its exact meaning, or your baby's role, I am as lost as you. More so, no doubt, because I didn't see what you saw, or hear what you heard."

"I'm still fairly lost. I mean, I know I need to get this message out, but I don't know what will happen next."

Pope Matthew leaned forward, elbows on his knees, hands clasped. "None of us do. But tell me about this man, the one studying to be a deacon who claimed to know the meaning of your pregnancy."

"You mean, about his religious order?"

"Yes." The Pope smiled again. "You need not discuss your personal feelings."

Tara gulped her Coke. Its cold sweetness was calming. "I'm not even sure what those feelings are."

The sounds of doors slamming, phones ringing, and footsteps hurrying down corridors filtered in from elsewhere in the building. It struck Tara again how unusual it was for the Pope to take time from his schedule for her. But, so far, he seemed to have no ulterior motive.

"You must be angry," the Pope said.

"I am. But I feel kind of sorry for him, too. He's confused about his faith, and himself, and what his feelings mean. I wish he'd realized that before telling me he loved me and having sex with me, but I don't believe he meant for things to happen the way they did. He didn't know he was going to react that way. I guess I said a lot about my personal feelings anyway."

*I'm talking to the Pope. About sex. Too weird.*

"And his religious order?"

"He said he worked for the Brotherhood of Andrew. Does that ring a bell with you?"

The Pope shook his head. "Not at all. What was the Brotherhood's mission?"

"Cyril said his was to protect me and help me find a safe place for the baby's birth." Tara told the Pope everything else she remembered about the Brotherhood, and about the attacks at SLU, in the hospital, and at Willow Springs, though she didn't describe Nanor's community in detail.

"Any incident since then?"

"No. Which almost makes me nervous in itself. Why would this guy – not Cyril, but the red-haired man – give up?"

"That can be answered only if you learn his objective."

"I don't even know who he is, let alone what he wants."

The Pope cocked his head. "But you suspect he may have been sent by the same Brotherhood that sent Cyril Woods?"

"Maybe." It was something that had occurred to Tara more than once. It explained why the red-haired man knew so much about her. "One hand not knowing what the other was doing. Or Cyril not knowing the real reason he was sent to me."

The sunlight shifted, shining right where the Pope sat. He crossed the room and shut the blinds partway, so the light fell in slats across the floor, and across his face when he sat down again.

"Religion certainly is not above politics. In fact, some would say it's all politics. We've been extremely cautious about your security. Guards surrounded you during your tour. You've been under our watch since you boarded the plane in St. Louis."

"Thank you."

"You should arrange private security at home."

"Sophia is working on that."

"Good. I will see if our archivists and researchers can find anything about this Brotherhood that might assist you."

The glass and gold wall clock near the door chimed three. The Pope glanced toward it, and Tara knew her meeting neared the end.

"What do you think about the suggestion in the message that the Church needs to focus more on feminine values?" she said. "Doesn't that suggest the Church is wrong to allow only men to lead?"

"Many will take it that way, I imagine. You'll notice I refrained from commenting on that, and I won't. There are certain procedures the Church follows to investigate an alleged apparition. To say more than I did before those take place would be improper."

"But what do you think personally?"

The Pope stood. "As the Pope, I lack the luxury of expressing personal opinions. But if you examine the history of my election, you'll see I was considered an unlikely choice. I advocated for an evolution of many Church teachings. But change is difficult in any organization, and as a new Pope, I move cautiously." Pope Matthew held out his hand and helped Tara to her feet. "We'll converse again in the future. Until then, I wish you well. The statement will issue tomorrow, before you arrive in St. Louis."

"Thank you." On impulse, Tara hugged Pope Matthew. He returned her hug.

THE PLANE LANDED in St. Louis at ten-thirty the next morning. Tara and Pete hurried through the jetway, anxious to get to Megan and see the rest of the family. Tara had told her dad about the conversation with the Pope, and he'd seemed relieved. That in itself upset Tara, that it should matter so much, but she focused on being reunited with her family and the Pope's kind words.

Flat screen TVs played in the gate area as they exited the jetway. Tara heard something about the Pope. She stopped in the middle of the boarding area.

"Maybe it's about the press release," Pete said, stopping next to her.

A brunette newscaster stared somberly into the camera. "Roman Catholics all over the world are in mourning today. Last night, the Vatican reported the death of Pope Matthew I. The Pope, age eighty-nine, suffered a heart attack and died just eleven hours ago."

# 47

Eyes fixed on the TV, Pete barely registered the thunk as Tara dropped her backpack in the carpeted gate area.

"The Pope had no history of heart disease," the newscaster said, "and was reputed to be in excellent health. Nonetheless, no autopsy has been conducted, as it is against Vatican law, and the Pope's body has been embalmed. Commentators already are speculating on which cardinal will next ascend to the papacy, and whether the short reign of this Pope – the shortest of any other than Pope John Paul I – is a sign from God that his election was an error."

Other passengers surged past Tara and Pete, but Pete stayed planted in front of the screen, even after the segment ended. He found it hard to breathe. He was not a superstitious person, but the Pope had died what must have been only hours after visiting with Tara, after speaking comforting words to her.

"Did he seem ill when you saw him?" he asked Tara.

Tara looked stunned, too, her face pale. "No. He was energetic. Fine. Healthy, like the newscaster said."

"I suppose at that age heart failure it always a possibility."

"I suppose."

Pete picked up Tara's backpack and turned toward the exit, running through his few moments meeting the Pope for signs of illness. Only the thought of Megan set his feet moving at last. She was supposed to be coming with Lynette to meet them, if she felt well enough. Going to Rome had been a difficult decision, with Megan's health so precarious. But after Tara had fled, Pete and Lynette had both realized they'd been living for years in a state of emergency, and while they wanted to be sure one of them was always with Megan, they needed to be there for their other children too.

"He was just so full of life," Tara said. They passed through the revolving door and headed for their baggage claim. "I feel bad thinking about it, but I wonder if he had the press release sent out before he died."

"Mom will know if anything's been on the news."

But no one from the family was in the baggage area. Pete turned on his cell phone. He'd meant to check as soon as they exited the plane, but the story about the Pope distracted him. He dialed and waited for his voicemail to engage, gripping the phone.

*So Megan didn't feel up to the drive. That's all.*

It was Lynette's tone of voice more than the message itself. She said was she was calling from the hospital. During the night, Megan's neck had started hurting, and her fever shot to one hundred four. Lynette, Nate, Kelly and Bailey were all with her.

Tara was watching the first suitcases dumping onto the conveyor belt. Pete snapped his phone shut and took her arm.

"Forget the bags."

~

"YOU DIDN'T NEED to talk to them." Pete threw his carry on bag onto the vinyl waiting room couch.

"It didn't slow us down," Tara said. But she felt like it had, though she couldn't quite admit it. The two reporters had converged on Tara and Pete in the baggage claim area. Tara pushed past them, and they followed her and Pete to the car. Tara answered questions as they hurried outside to the parking lot, only half aware of what she said.

Now, in the waiting room, Bailey ran to Tara, and she bent and hugged him. The alcohol-hospital smell was making her nauseous, and she held her breath for a moment. When she let go of Bailey, she sank into a chair near the vending machines.

Bailey hugged Pete and sat on the couch near him.

"It will feed the story," Pete said. "Passing on what the Pope told you."

"They asked me what he said. Was I supposed to lie? The story's supposed to keep going."

Pete unzipped his bag and slammed his wallet on the coffee table, making it shake. Bailey scooted to the far end of the couch. "We're stressed enough without reporters around, not to mention drawing the focus of whoever's been after you."

"After the *Janet* show, people are going to find me if they want to. That's the point of retaining the security company. I can't exactly hide out and tell people about my vision."

"Or your dream." Pete turned toward her. "What if it was just a wishful thinking dream telling you what you wanted to hear – that you're special, and your baby's special, and the Church is wrong about everything."

"You think that even with what the Pope said?"

"The Pope didn't say you were right about your message. And now he's dead."

"And you think that has to do with me?"

Lynette appeared in the doorway. "This is a hospital. I can hear you two down the hall."

Tara clenched her hands into fists, took a deep breath, and regretted it immediately when the smell made her stomach roll again. *Don't think about it now, don't think about any of it now.*

"I'm sorry," she said. "How's Megan?"

"Awake but groggy. She's back in her room."

They went to Megan's room. Megan was small for ten, her body barely a third of the length of the bed. Her head seemed to sink into the pillows.

Pete hugged Megan. Then Tara did, careful not to disarrange the tubes. "Hey, kiddo. I missed you like crazy."

Megan angled her head the least amount possible to still be able to look at Tara. "I missed you, too. How's your baby? Bailey said you had to leave to take care of her."

Tara touched the swell of her stomach. "She's good. Kicking right now."

"I'd like to meet her someday." Megan's eyes closed, and Tara reached under the sheet and held her sister's hand. It felt cool.

"I'd like that, too."

Megan didn't open her eyes again for over an hour. Pete and Lynette had walked down the hall with Bailey, leaving Tara and Megan alone.

"The tumor's blocking my cerebral-spinal fluid again," Megan said. Megan always asked the doctors a lot of questions. "My brain's swelling."

"Does it hurt?"

"Some. I'll die soon if the swelling can't be controlled."

Tara tightened her grip on Megan's hand and felt her throat closing. "The doctors might figure something out. They've done pretty good so far."

"Do you think Dave's in heaven?" Megan said.

The green line on the monitor over Megan's head spiked in rhythm. "You bet," Tara said. "He was a morally upstanding cat."

"Father Saur says animals can't go to heaven. They have no souls."

"Well, Father Saur's never been to heaven, so how can he know?"

"That's what Mom said."

"She's right. Dave was a good cat and you love him, so I say he's there."

Megan's eyes drooped again. "I hope so."

## SELF-PROCLAIMED MOTHER OF NEXT MESSIAH LIED ABOUT POPE, VATICAN CLAIMS

Pope Matthew II, elected just four days ago, asserts Tara Spencer lied about her meeting with Pope Matthew I. Spencer claimed on national television to be the mother of the next messiah two weeks ago. She visited Pope Matthew I just hours before he died and claimed on her return to the United States that he'd shown her a press release stating he believed her claims and wished her well. No such release ever issued.

It is clear now it never will. Based on Matthew I's notes of his meeting with Spencer, the Vatican published a statement denouncing Spencer as an opportunist intent on creating advance publicity for the book she's writing with controversial professor and former nun Sophia Gaddini. The Vatican further states the Pope evaluated Spencer as troubled and deeply suspicious of organized religion. Spencer, whose youngest sister remains hospitalized for treatment of a malignant brain tumor (continued on page A 23)

~

NO MIRACLES FOR ALLEGED VIRGIN'S SISTER

TARA SPENCER, the twenty-one year old SLU student who asserts she became pregnant last spring through supernatural means, was unable to procure any divine assistance for her youngest sister. Megan Spencer, age ten, died yesterday of a brain hemorrhage after a two-week hospitalization. Five years ago, following a routine eye exam which showed abnormalities, Megan Spencer was diagnosed with a cerebral astrocytoma. Such tumors are benign, and often can be removed surgically. Spencer's tumor, however, wound around her brain stem, and surgeons could excise only a small portion of it. Treatment over the last five years included aggressive chemotherapy and radiation, but the tumor turned malignant (continued p. A 19)

~

MEGAN SPENCER, Age 10

Megan Spencer of Rock Hill, Missouri, passed away yesterday at St. Joseph's hospital in St. Louis. Megan, ten years old, loved dancing, playing harmonica, and Snoopy. She is survived by her parents, Peter and Lynette Spencer, four siblings, Tara, Nate, Kelley and Bailey Spencer, as well as loving grandparents, aunts, uncles, and cousins. Visitation will be held at the Johnson Funeral Home Saturday evening only, from 4 p.m. until 9 p.m. Internment will be at Mary Queen of Heaven cemetery. In lieu of flowers, memorials can be made to the family or to the American Brain Tumor Association.

~

**Urgent: For Immediate Review: Field Report 3.3**

Tara Spencer's due date is seven and a half weeks away. New security precautions in the Spencer household, including an electronic alarm system and surveillance, preclude undetected approach despite that, as explained in Field Report 3.2, recent news coverage created ideal conditions. The Spencer vehicles are equipped with tracking, communication and alarm systems. All Spencer family members carry cell phones.

Given the importance of action before the birth, and the expectation that heightened security will continue, this investigator recommends the previously-approved action be taken at the visitation, funeral, or funeral luncheon for Megan Spencer. Grieving family members will likely be less alert, and the large number of guests will ease infiltration.

## 48

A lace collar hid Megan's tracheotomy scar. Highlights glinted in her curly pigtails. Her face looked full, not sunken or bloated. Pink tinged her cheeks, as if she'd been playing outside on a brisk day, yet the make up was barely noticeable, not like the thick pancake covering Tara had seen on other bodies.

*Bodies*. Tara shuddered as she knelt before the coffin. It was impossible to think of this as just Megan's body. Yet, the essence of Megan, whatever made her who she was, had disappeared. Her arm felt stiff under her blue dress when Tara touched it, despite how lifelike her face looked.

*No Megan here.*

Rather than a rosary, Megan's hands clasped the silver harmonica Nate had given her on her seventh birthday. A stuffed Snoopy Bailey had set in the coffin rested against her shoulder.

Tara stood and turned away. Bailey sat in the front row of chairs, where he'd perched after praying at the coffin. Tara had tried to persuade him to join Nate and Kelly in the kitchen area set aside for family, so he could eat a sandwich or at least some cookies, but he refused. Sophia, who'd driven in as soon as she heard the news, sat right behind him. At the back of the room, Pete and Lynette showed Grandma Spencer the poster boards the kids had put together with photos of Megan and the family. Tara took a step toward them, then stopped. Her dad had barely spoken to her since the return from Rome. He'd barely spoken at all, but it seemed to Tara less to her than to anyone.

Beyond her parents, a lone figure in a dark suit stood in the arched doorway. Tara watched Cyril inch into the parlor. He was watching her, as if ready to back out at the shake of her head. Tara clenched her hands into fists, inhaled the chilled floral-funeral air, and walked toward him.

Sophia rose as Tara passed her. "Tara? Who is that?"

"Cyril."

Voices buzzed around Tara, but she couldn't pick out the threads of any conversations. She'd felt that way since Megan's death, as if she were functioning in a thick fog that obscured not just her vision but sound and touch. Cyril stood out, the only black figure against a cloud of gray. He extended his hands, palms up, as she approached. He had no briefcase, no backpack that could conceal a weapon. Was he here to apologize? But that could accomplish nothing now.

They met between the last row of straight back chairs and the sitting area near the entrance. Cyril's hands felt cold and damp when he took hers. Tara pulled away.

"Tara." His eyes sunk into shadows. Dark stubble grazed his cheeks and chin.

"What do you want?"

"I'll leave if you prefer. But when I heard about Megan, I had to come. I'm sorry about her death." His voice cracked.

Tara glanced at Sophia, who stood a few feet away, ostensibly looking at the poster boards. Her presence comforted Tara, as did the fact that no one else knew what Cyril looked like. She lacked the energy to explain his presence or deal with anyone else's reactions to him.

While Cyril's sympathy struck Tara as genuine, it didn't change what he'd said and done in Armenia.

"All right. Thank you. Now I prefer you leave."

She turned to walk back toward the coffin, and he said, "Wait. I'm sorry about other things as well. I treated you badly."

Tara pivoted to face him. "Which treatment are you sorry for? Saying you loved me? Calling me a whore? Or abandoning me in Armenia?" Tara welcomed the anger surging through her. At least she felt something.

Cyril stared everywhere in the room except at her. "All of it. I wasn't in any position to start a relationship with anyone. I needed to work out my feelings about the Church, and becoming a deacon. And I probably need help dealing with my issues about sex. I took out my confusion on you. And my guilt. I blamed you because I couldn't accept my own behavior."

The words sounded right, echoed what Tara felt Cyril ought to recognize and say. But her gut told her he didn't mean – or feel – what he was saying.

"Why did you really come here?"

Cyril touched her arm, his fingers still clammy, and peered around the room again. "I really am sorry. I had feelings for you. I was sure I loved you, but I confused love and attraction. Or perhaps even what you said. Love for my ideal picture of a woman with love for you as a real person."

"So you're saying you said you loved me, and you thought you meant it, but now you realize you don't love me and never did."

"I – yes."

"Is there a reason you felt you needed to come here and tell me that in person? At my sister's wake? Because, believe me, I wasn't planning to track you down to try to start anything with you."

Cyril stepped back, bumped into the sofa behind him, and stumbled, almost falling. He righted himself. "I didn't think you were. I rambled, and I'm sorry. I only came here to express my sympathy."

"You've done that. Now you can go."

"Just one thing." Cyril reached into his inner suit jacket pocket.

# 49

"Everyone. May I please have your attention?"

Father Saur stood at the front of the parlor, hands raised, his back to Megan's coffin. The chatter in the room died. The priest's black cassock and white collar contrasted the wreaths of roses, daisies and daffodils behind him, some arranged with teddy bears and stuffed kittens.

"Wait," Tara said to Cyril. She harbored no strong desire to hear what Father Saur, who'd told Megan their cat Dave wouldn't be in heaven, would say, but she didn't want to interfere with anyone else hearing him.

"I've known Lynette and Pete Spencer since they came to St. John of the Cross for pre-marital counseling," Father Saur said. "On that day, I saw their commitment to each other, and to each child they've brought into this world.

"Parents have a job, perhaps the hardest job in the world. They not only must love their children, they must teach them. About the world, about doing what's right, about God's love. They must help them on their path to being the best human beings they can. Parents must live a life that provides a fine, loving example for their children to emulate. They must share their faith and values with their children and, by doing so, help their children find their way to God's love, and, eventually, to heaven's gate.

"All this, Pete and Lynette, you do every day for all your children. You did this for Megan. You did your job. It took a few less years than you expected. But anyone who knew and loved Megan can have no doubt that she learned faith, love, and kindness from you, her parents.

"Pete and Lynette, you helped your daughter along her path, you helped her be the best person she could be. You did your job, and now you're done. You helped your daughter to the gates of heaven."

Tears ran down Tara's cheeks. Who would have thought Father Saur would actually say something moving?

She turned back to Cyril. He held an envelope in his hand.

"Read it later," he said. "Please. After the wake is over."

"All right." Tara took the letter, thinking that she'd never said "all right" so many times in one conversation before.

"Good-bye." Cyril leaned in and kissed her cheek. His lips felt dry. He hurried out, not pausing when he reached the exit.

Sophia crossed the room, weaving through the other guests, and put her arm around Tara's shoulders. "What did he want?"

"To say he was sorry. About Megan and everything."

"But?"

"It didn't feel right. Any other time I've talked to Cyril, he's been so full of passionate conviction. One way or another. Tonight he sounded like he was delivering prepared speeches. And he barely looked at me."

"He probably felt nervous, which he should have, coming here. And you must be wrung out emotionally yourself."

Tara held up the envelope. "He asked me to read this after the wake is over."

"No reason you can't open it now."

"True. It's not like I owe him anything." Tara tore the envelope flap. Inside, she found a single sheet of paper with one line written across it.

"*There's a note in your mailbox*. What's the point of that?"

"Sounds like he wasn't sure you'd wait until after the wake, but he wanted to be sure you got his note."

Feeling light-headed, Tara sat on the sofa. For the last thirty minutes of the wake, she stayed there, hardly registering when people spoke to her. Sophia brought her a cold glass of water. When the last few friends and relatives trickled out, Tara and Nate held hands and approached the coffin together. Tara imagined the coffin lid closing, the coffin being lowered into the ground, dirt shoveled on top of it.

She gripped Nate's fingers. "We can't do this. It'll be so dark, and she won't have her nightlight. She won't know where she is."

Nate cleared his throat. "I know. Megan's gone – her spirit, her soul, whatever you want to call the essence of Megan – but it feels wrong to close the lid."

"And where did she go? Is she somewhere chasing Dave? Is she aware?" Tara breathed in the flowers, the cold, sweet scent. "That's what I wonder. Does Megan – not her body but who she is – still exist somewhere? Or did she just disappear?"

"Your vision or whatever doesn't make any of that clear?" Nate asked.

Tara shook her head. Her entire experience had never seemed so pointless. If she couldn't answer that question, if she couldn't comfort herself or her family, let alone save Megan, what did any of it serve? "Not at all."

"Tara?" Her mother's voice came from somewhere behind Tara, and Tara swung around. Lynette hurried toward her from the doorway to the kitchen area. "Tara, Nate, I can't find Bailey."

Tara looked around the parlor. "You checked the kitchen?"

"He's not there."

"Who saw him last?" Nate asked.

"I don't know," Lynette said.

"He was sitting right in front when – " Tara stopped as everyone began searching the funeral home.

*He was sitting right in front when Cyril came in.*

# 50

Bailey will survive if and only if you do as you are told.

1. Contact all major news outlets and arrange a press conference for the day after Megan's funeral.
2. Hold the press conference two days from now at the steps of the St. Louis Arch, at noon, seven minutes before the solar eclipse.
3. At the press conference, announce that your pregnancy is not divine and that you became pregnant through sexual intercourse while drinking at a party, and you do not recall who the father was.
4. Further announce your alleged vision was a hoax to raise money for your book, but you had an attack of conscience and feel you cannot carry out the hoax any longer.
5. Do not contact police, any other authority or any private security service.

Bailey will be in the audience. If you do as you are told, he will be released during the darkness of the eclipse.
To deviate from these instructions will be fatal.

# 51

No rain had fallen in days, and the concrete steps leading from the riverfront to the base of the Arch were dry. Even so, Tara, exhausted, slipped on the first step. She pitched forward, hands hitting the fourth stair. After regaining her balance, she brushed the dirt from her hands, tugged down the hem of her blue maternity sundress, and kept climbing. Sophia had helped her choose what to wear, and had sat with her through the night at Megan's grave. Tara didn't speak during the night, only stared at the freshly dug ground.

Now the baby kicked, first one spot and then another, as if somersaulting and flailing her legs. Tara touched her stomach, feeling the kicks in her palms.

*I can do this. I will do this.*

A microphone on a metal stand stood at the center of the concrete expanse below the Arch. Reporters and technicians pointed cameras at Tara from a makeshift wooden platform on the riverfront. In the grass on the other side of the Arch, kids gathered in small groups clutching cardboard boxes with pinholes punched through them so they could look at the shadow of the eclipse. Watching them, Tara felt less frightened for a moment. The kids didn't care about her or what she might say. They only cared about the eclipse.

Amateur photographers gathered on all sides, equipment set to capture the effect of the solar event on the silvery Arch. *They don't care about me, either*, Tara thought. *If only no one here did. We'd all be so much safer.*

When Tara had asked if Protennoia could protect her baby, Protennoia had answered: *Tell all you can as soon as you can.* But telling everyone the truth now meant sacrificing Bailey. And Tara had no assurance that some divine being – whoever or whatever that might be – would step in and save Bailey as Abraham's God saved Isaac after endangering him in the first place. Nor did Tara know whether Protennoia had been answering her question. Protennoia might have answered the same thing if Tara had said, *How did the world begin?* or *Did Jesus really rise from the dead?*

Telling the truth might not protect the baby at all. But it would surely kill Bailey. Tara paused at the base of the Arch and folded her hands over the baby. Her child would grow into a loving, kind person, whatever Tara said today, whatever the rest of the world thought about how she'd been conceived. Tara would see to it.

"I promise," she whispered. Her knees trembled, making her skirt sway. She hadn't saved Megan. But she could save Bailey.

Just west of the platform, a dark-haired man dragged a blonde boy through the gathering crowd toward the Arch. Tara shaded her eyes, peered down at them, almost certain based on the way they moved that it was Cyril and Bailey. As they walked closer, their features came into focus. Cyril's face looked blank, while Bailey's eyes appeared huge and his mouth twisted into a half-frown, half-gasp when he saw Tara.

*My fault. If only I'd stayed away from Cyril from the beginning, this wouldn't be happening.*

Cyril stopped a few feet from the steps, eyes trained on Bailey. His left hand crossed his body to hold Bailey against him, and he'd draped his right arm over Bailey's shoulders. As Tara watched, Cyril pressed his right hand, closed into a fist, against Bailey's neck, then opened his fingers slightly, showing Tara the needle poised at Bailey's neck.

The baby shuddered within Tara's womb. Tara pictured her child waving tiny hands, opening and closing her fingers, kicking her legs. At just past seven months in utero, if she were born, she could live, though she might need a little help. But her tiny heart would beat; her lungs could breathe.

That would need to be enough.

~

*I* TRUST *T*ARA.

Pete paced behind the camera crews, his heart pounding over the buzz of conversation and activity around him. He froze as Tara mounted the platform under the Arch. *She's just too young to decide what's right. And she doesn't trust anyone to help*. Which was Pete's own fault. Unconsciously, he gazed up at the five small windows at the top of the Arch, then forced himself to look away.

*It's right, it's right, I did the right thing.*

The time of the eclipse neared, and the blue sky deepened to violet, then to dark gray. As dark as the world had seemed to Pete since Megan's death. And now Bailey.

His fault. If he'd had been more supportive, Tara would never have turned to Cyril Woods or met Nanor Kerkorian or researched the Brotherhood. She'd never have come into contact with any of the people who might now be holding Bailey. If Bailey died, if anyone died....

*No one else will die.*

Pete had given the FBI as much information as he could, as much as he knew. He couldn't save Megan, but he could save Bailey. He would save Bailey.

The agent in charge agreed Tara and Lynette should be kept ignorant of the Bureau's involvement. That way, both would act as naturally as possible. Tara had insisted the authorities not be contacted, had insisted the instructions on the note be followed. Which Pete hoped meant she'd tell the truth about the baby's conception. Finally. Pete no longer believed there was a scientific explanation, and after all that had happened, he doubted the baby was divine. If it were, would Bailey be in danger because of this child? No, Tara had gotten confused, deluded. And now here they all were.

Father Saur had pointed out when Pete sought guidance that Tara couldn't face her mistake in becoming pregnant, so how could she face the harm that might come to Bailey if she stuck to her story? She really might have convinced herself her pregnancy was divine, despite Pope Matthew's death, despite Pope Matthew II's clear pronouncement. Father Saur urged Pete to help Tara tell the truth, to see the light. Pete had tried.

But Pete had also acted. The FBI agent assured him he'd done the right thing.

Pete suspected snipers watched from the top of the arch, poised with guns at the windows. But he didn't know. Better he didn't know, the FBI agent told him, so he wouldn't inadvertently tip off the kidnappers. Pete imagined other agents stood throughout the crowd. Perhaps the unshaven man to his right in jeans and Black Sabbath T-shirt, cell phone in his hand, was an agent in plain clothes. After all, who under the age of forty-five still listened to Black Sabbath? And the tall woman near the chain link fence strung in front of the Arch, with her brown hair twisted into a ponytail, hooked into her Ipod. Perhaps she was a specialist, ready to wrench Bailey away from whoever held him.

The one thing Pete had to admit was that the Brotherhood of Andrew Tara claimed existed probably was real. As was Cyril Woods. Sophia Gaddini had seen him at the wake. Or had at least seen a dark-haired young man with ramrod posture Tara later said was Cyril Woods. Pete wished he'd taken that part of what Tara'd said more seriously. No wonder she was convinced her pregnancy was divine, with someone like that feeding those beliefs.

*But what if I'm wrong? What if the baby is divine? Then I encouraged her to lie.*

Every night he'd been home in the last month, Pete had closed himself in his tiny study – what used to be his and Lyn's walk in closet – and read and reread the gospels. Nothing in the New Testament talked about the Virgin Mary's parents. Probably Mary had wisely told no one about her pregnancy, and she and Joseph married quietly and had a premature baby, like so many couples had done for thousands of years. If only Tara had done the same.

Tara cleared her throat, and the sound crackled over the PA system. Pete jerked his head toward the Arch. Tara looked small standing alone below it, and slender despite her pregnancy. The weight she'd gained settled low in front, all baby. Even from his vantage point on the riverfront, her eyes stood out in her pale face. She reminded him so much of Megan, how Megan might have looked if she'd grown. Something he'd never know.

Craning his neck, Pete looked for Bailey. But the dense crowd made it impossible to see the front rows, and if Pete forced his way through, he might only disrupt the FBI's plan, whatever that might be. So he stared at the ground, at the grass, trampled and bent from feet pounding across it all morning.

The crowd quieted. Wind rushed through the microphone.

"I have something to say," Tara said. Then she clutched her stomach and doubled over.

~

CYRIL TENSED his legs and gripped Bailey's arm, willing himself not to rush to Tara. *The Beast. She's an agent of the Beast, however sweet she looks. You know this.*

But, as he'd confessed to Thomas, he'd been weak. He'd let himself fall in love with her, or believe he had, he'd let himself question not just the Brotherhood, but his own vocation. Then he'd blamed her because he couldn't accept his own guilt.

"That doesn't make her blameless," Thomas had reminded Cyril as they faced each other in Father Saur's office at St. John of the Cross weeks later. The office smelled of incense and taper candles. "You sinned, yes. But you repented, and Tara Spencer never will. You heard her on television today. She believes sex before marriage is perfectly acceptable. She believes Jesus Christ – God himself – failed in delivering His message to the world. She believes the Holy Catholic Church failed in its mission, and the world needs a new Messiah. One in her own image. In the female image. She spreads lies and heresy, and, in her book, she'll tell whatever secrets you told her."

Cyril stared at the wood desk between him and Thomas. The desk filled three quarters of the room, with Cyril's chair wedged into one corner. The red-haired Investigator Mullin sat in the other corner. Cyril refused to look at him, though he'd assured Cyril that what had appeared to be attempts on Tara's life were merely attempts to capture her. He claimed not to know who had set the bomb that killed Tara's friend Julie. He and Thomas insisted that had been some faction outside the Brotherhood.

"What is my penance?" Cyril said.

"Stop her."

"The way – the way the imposter Maya Kerkorian was stopped?" Despite his remorse, Cyril pressed his palms together and offered swift, silent prayer this would not be necessary. He lacked Thomas' strength.

"No," Thomas said. "We'd only create a martyr and draw attention to the Brotherhood. We don't need a new Willow Springs community. That was my miscalculation. No, she must disclaim her story. Tell the truth."

"But she's been adamant so far."

"You know her." Thomas pointed at Cyril. "You must determine how to change her mind. That is your new ministry."

It took less than a minute's thought to pinpoint Tara's greatest weakness. And Bailey turned out to be a good choice for manageability as well. After Cyril and Investigator Mullin thwarted his first attempts to fight and run away, Bailey followed instructions and insisted Tara loved him and would cooperate. Now, at the foot of the Arch, Bailey remained motionless, not risking the needle plunging into his neck accidentally.

That Bailey didn't try again to escape worried Cyril. It made him think Bailey didn't really know Tara, that he was deluded. Tara loved Bailey, yes, but she had her own baby to consider, a baby she wanted to pave the way for. And a vision that told her to tell the world about the baby. If God told Cyril to make a sacrifice, even of a child, he'd have to follow Abraham's example and obey. Tara might do the same.

*But she didn't really have a vision*, Cyril reminded himself. She'd fabricated it or dreamed something that fit her grandiose imaginings of what her baby meant for the world.

Twilight settled around the Arch, and a gust of wind chilled the sweat on Cyril's back. He angled his left arm, the one holding Bailey, to see his watch. 12:03. The eclipse was starting early. How could that be? What did it mean?

On the platform, Tara straightened, her face twisted in pain. Cyril prayed she would speak before the eclipse, so Cyril could release Bailey and escape in the darkness. He squeezed Bailey's shoulder.

"Make your sister hurry."

Bailey waved his free arm. "Tara. Now."

WILL James saw Bailey's wave. The rifle twitched on his shoulder. Last week, Will had been called to a hostage situation at Union Station, just a mile west of here. He'd shot the hostage taker in the forehead. The man appeared to fall in slow motion. His body hit the plank floor with a deafening thud no one but Will seemed to hear. Will had barely slept since. Killing disturbed him – what kind of person would he be if it didn't– but it had never kept him awake nights other than during the early weeks of the first Iraq war. But something about that man, that hostage –

He peered through the scope, eyes fixed on the dark-haired man holding the needle.

PAIN SEARED THROUGH TARA, and she struggled to remain standing. She'd always imagined contractions, when they started, would begin gradually. A twinge. Then a jab. Then more intense pain. Instead, she'd beelined right to a vise clamped around her midsection.

Tara forced herself to breathe. Not to tighten her muscles against the pain. Whatever the cost, she needed to speak.

Wind whipped her hair around her face.

"I never –"

Feedback screeched. The audience cringed.

Cyril tightened his grip on Bailey's forearm. Tara's face had gone stark white. She suffered real pain then. That Cyril still longed to go to her told him how far he had to go. He'd prided himself on his spirit being stronger than his flesh. But he'd deluded himself. He was worse than most men, worse than his father. He'd had intercourse, not just with a woman, but with the woman he believed carried the next messiah. No matter that he'd been wrong about that, no matter her part in leading him into temptation. He'd believed it in the moment, and it hadn't stopped him.

In Cyril's right hand, the hypodermic trembled. Thomas had provided clear instructions. When the eclipse became total, if Tara had not recanted, Cyril must plunge the needle into Bailey's neck. It would kill him instantly, and Cyril would escape if he could. If not, he'd stand trial, denounced as a renegade from the Church. Another branch of the Brotherhood would capture Tara's sister Kelly and repeat its demands.

"But the Lord commanded, 'Thou shalt not kill,'" he'd said to Thomas, as he stared at the crucifix on the wall behind Father Saur's desk. The metal Jesus grimaced, his eyes peering up toward heaven.

Thomas shook his head. "That commandment doesn't apply to God's will. Look at the Old Testament. God killed many times, directly and through men who did His will. It's unfortunate, but it's necessary at times to protect not just the lives but the souls of others."

Cyril gripped the chair's arms. "But an innocent child?"

"What makes you think Bailey Spencer is innocent?" Thomas answered. "He's her sibling, after all. But even if he is, you're only sending him to God Our Father, who will reward him for his sacrifice. What's the life span of one child against the world's salvation?"

Cyril began to say God in heaven would never demand such a sacrifice. But God Himself had sacrificed His only son. And ordered Abraham to do the same centuries before. Knowing Jesus had been resurrected and God ultimately stayed Abraham's hand didn't comfort Cyril. The sacrifice of Bailey only worked if Bailey truly died, convincing Tara to recant before others she loved suffered the same fate.

*This only works if I kill Bailey.*

A shadow fell across the platform as Tara inched away from the microphone. The feedback died. Cyril tensed, the hypodermic slippery in his hand, his thumb on the plunger.

*Lord, let this cup pass from my lips.*

Standing a foot from the microphone, Tara tried again as the wind whistled around the Arch.

"I've never claimed my baby is divine." No whine from the equipment. The reporters on their platform leaned toward her. "I don't know that. What I did say – "

A barbed wire tightened around her uterus. When it eased, she continued. "My pregnancy began the usual way. Through sexual intercourse."

Feedback whined again, even as pain slashed through her. Tara dropped to her knees, barely aware of the concrete scraping her skin. She bent over, forehead pressed onto the rough platform. *Not here, it can't be here.* Cyril's words came back to her, what he'd said would happen if the baby wasn't born on holy ground: "If the birth takes place elsewhere, it's foretold the Beast will position itself near the Virgin, perhaps in disguise, to devour her offspring after it's born."

Contractions, seconds apart, forced screams through Tara's throat. She rolled into a fetal position. The gray around her deepened to near-black.

*The eclipse. My dream. The darkness. My baby, my baby...*

From the corner of her eye, she saw a flash of blonde hair.

"Bailey!"

The wind tore the word from her lips.

TARA'S DREAM.

Sophia, who'd stationed herself on the edge of the grass near the Arch, pushed through the crowd and raced up the steps, trying to recall everything Tara had told her about a recurring dream where she gave birth in darkness. *Soon it'll be like night. What does that mean?*

The microphone clattered down as Sophia pushed past it and knelt next to Tara. Lynette Spencer, who'd been standing with the amateur photographers, was there a moment later, Pete right behind her. Sophia eased Tara onto her back. Lynette positioned herself in between Tara's legs.

"It's already coming," Lynette said.

Sophia heard someone call Tara's name.

*Bailey.* Sophia'd forgotten the boy for a moment in her fears for Tara. She twisted and saw Cyril, the dark-haired man from the wake, gripping Bailey.

Sophia watched Cyril crouch, still holding Bailey's arm, so his head was near Bailey's ears. Bailey stepped forward. Behind her, Sophia heard Tara scream again, and then a baby's cry.

A shot rang out.

THE INSTANT TARA SCREAMED, Bailey yelled her name. In that one word, Cyril heard Bailey's love for Tara, and his fear of losing her. So like Cyril's love for his mother and sister, yet undiluted by the anger and contempt Cyril had felt toward both for the way they let his father treat them. Bailey's love was pure.

Cyril crouched and whispered to Bailey, "Go – you're free."

As Cyril released his grip, he heard the shot. The bullet hit his left ankle. He didn't know what happened at first. All he registered was losing his balance, then searing pain as he pitched sideways toward Bailey. The needle, in his sweating right hand, plunged into Bailey's neck.

Bailey plummeted forward. His head hit the concrete steps. Cyril reached for Bailey, and the second bullet tore into Cyril's midsection.

~

VOICES AND SOUNDS rushed past Tara, but made no sense. Stars shone in the sky, and the moon, a black disk, obscured the sun. The corona cast an orange twilight around Tara, Sophia and Lynette.

*Not so dark,* Tara thought, and the next pain shot through her.

"It's already coming," her mother said.

Tara grunted and pushed and clutched Sophia's hand.

"Her head's out," Lynette said.

The baby's cries cut through Tara's pain. Pete pulled his pocket knife out, and, moments later, Lynette handed Tara the baby. Tiny and slimy, dark hair plastered around her head, her mouth open. But she wasn't crying.

*She's laughing. I can't believe it. She's laughing.*

"Newborns can't laugh, Tara," Lynette said, though Tara was sure she hadn't spoken aloud. "They can't even smile."

Pete reached toward Tara and the baby. A shot rang through the air. Tara realized it was a second shot, that she'd heard one before but not recognized the sound. She turned her head.

Bailey lay face down at the base of the steps, forehead toward Tara. Cyril lay on his side a few feet away. Blood trickled from his mouth, glinting silver in the light from the corona.

"Dad. The baby."

Pete lifted the baby from Tara's chest, but said, "Tara, you can't –"

Tara rolled onto her side, then struggled to all fours. She needed to be near Bailey, to see him, to touch him. Maybe he was still alive. Her mother was already down the stairs. Sophia had her cell phone out and was shouting into it. Reporters crowded around in the semi-darkness.

Crawling sideways, Tara made her way down the stairs, the concrete scraping her knees and palms. Lynette got there first and pressed down on Bailey's chest, using the whole weight of her body, five times in rhythm. She listened, then breathed into his mouth, then repeated the process.

The next time Lynette lifted her head and did chest compressions, Tara kissed Bailey, then rubbed her fingertips, still sticky with blood and fluid from the birth, across his forehead.

Bailey gasped and opened his eyes.

Tears streamed from Tara's eyes. "Bailey? Are you all right?"

"He let me go, Tara. He let me go."

Lynette scooped Bailey into her arms. "Oh my God, thank God."

Cyril, a few feet away, groaned and extended his right hand toward Tara. "Forgive me," he whispered.

Before Tara could react, his arm dropped, and his head fell to the side. Tara dragged herself across the grass, dirt mixing with the blood on her hands. Cyril's face was alabaster, his eyes shut. Tara pressed her fingers to his neck. His pulse was so faint she barely felt it, and he didn't seem to be breathing. She needed to decide quickly, to speak before he was gone if she was going to speak. Tara gazed at Cyril's motionless face.

*He killed Bailey.*

But he'd tried to let him go. And to never forgive was the way of war, the way of violence, the way of hate.

"I forgive you." Tara kissed Cyril's forehead.

Cyril opened his mouth and drew in air, chest heaving. Startled, Tara drew back.

"Tara!"

Tara twisted at the sound of Bailey's voice. Bailey, pink-cheeked, ran toward her and threw his arms around her. The scrapes on his face had disappeared, and Tara saw no needle mark on his neck. His hug shot pain through Tara's insides, but she squeezed back. Moments later, her parents and Sophia surrounded her, and Pete handed Tara the baby.

"I'm naming her Sophia," Tara said to Sophia. "Because of my love for you, and because love is what brought her here. And because Sophia means wisdom. Which she'll need to fulfill her role in this world."

Shouts made Tara look over her shoulder. Police had surrounded Cyril and were leading him toward the street, leaving only patches of blood on the grass where he'd lain. Reporters followed, calling out their questions.

Overhead, the sun brightened.

ACKNOWLEDGEMENT

It's impossible to mention everyone who helped along the way as I wrote, rewrote, and published *The Awakening*. The instructors, lecturers, and participants at the Maui Writers' Workshops and Retreats I attended over the years provided invaluable advice and support. In particular, thriller writer Gary Braver generously answered my questions long after the formal workshops he taught finished. My friend Steve, a voracious reader of suspense and mysteries, commented on numerous drafts and later proofread more versions of *The Awakening* than I can count. He is the only person I know who can look at the 20th draft of a story and still spot the errors. (Any mistakes that slipped past his eagle eye are entirely mine.) Finally, thank you to my niece Emma, who loved to write and whose determination and courage continue to inspire me. Her time here was too short, and remembering that reminds me to appreciate every moment I have.

# THE UNBELIEVERS

---

THE AWAKENING, BOOK 2

# 1

Tara punched in the security code, resetting the alarm beneath the kitchen cabinets. Though she was already late, she peered through the small, square window over the sink. Gas lamps lit the path that bordered the house trailers nearest her temporary home. Holiday lights sparkled on bushes and around windows, creating shadows that darkened the spaces between the trailers.

Kali Kerkorian sat at the fold-down table behind Tara, tablet and textbook open in front of her. “Cyril can do nothing from jail,” she said.

“The people he works for can.” Tara turned away from the window to face her friend.

“And so?” Kali said. “You will stay in tonight?”

“Like every other night for the last four months, you mean?”

Kali shrugged and smiled. “I can make tea for us. Or return home to Grandmother.”

“No.” Tara zipped her jacket and resisted the urge to recheck the alarm. Her baby, who, by all natural laws, should not exist, slept on a blanket in the living room, unaware of any threats or of the controversy surrounding her. Tara longed to lie down and rest like that without at least part of her on the alert. She doubted she ever would.

Outside, dried leaves crunched under Tara’s gym shoes. She inhaled crisp night air. It smelled of pine. She exhaled a long breath. Kali knew about the death and damage caused by those who’d been after Tara while she’d been pregnant. She would take all security precautions. And Kali had watched Fimi before. But that had been during the day. Somehow, leaving the baby alone after dark felt more worrisome despite the protection the Willow Springs community offered.

The Friday night service at the Community Center, with its dancing and singing, helped Tara unwind and feel freer than she had since she'd discovered she was pregnant. The grown ups only hour after it added to her good mood. Most of her socializing in the last four months had been with Kali and Kali's grandmother, Nanor, the founder of Willow Springs. Both were people Tara loved, but it felt great to visit and laugh with others, too. A text from Kali at the start of the gathering reassured her that all was well and she could enjoy herself.

On the way back, Tara veered slightly off track toward her favorite section of Willow Springs – the lake that divided its residential area from the woods surrounding it. The night was hazy. Few stars dotted the sky, and the moon stayed hidden. When Tara reached the creek that fed the lake, she listened to its trickling water, her eyes scanning the landscape. Vigilance had become a habit.

Rustling came from the darkness to Tara's left. She froze, peering at silhouettes of bare trees. A rabbit, white tail bobbing in the faint starlight, darted across her path, startling her. A few minutes later, leaves skittered along the stones that edged the creek. More rustling in the distance.

"Another rabbit," Tara said aloud, her voice echoing. But she did an about-face. She'd been gone long enough for her first evening out.

The six trailers nearest Tara's stood dark, other than their holiday lights. No doubt her neighbors were still at the Community Center. All the lights glowed in Tara's trailer, just as she'd left them. But a John Fogerty song blared through the closed windows. She quickened her pace, hand dropping to the pocket where she kept her switchblade. While Fimi was a happy baby, rarely crying or fussing, Kali wouldn't crank the sound to that level to test Fimi's good nature.

Knife in one hand, Tara tried her cell phone with the other. No service. She ran for the front door. This couldn't be happening. The trailer she'd stayed in during her first visit to Willow Springs the year before had been broken into. By Cyril Woods. But he was in jail, and Tara had been assured all the security vulnerabilities had been fixed.

She burst through the door. Fimi's blanket, rattle, and stuffed monkey lay on the carpeted living area floor. But no Fimi.

*She's here, she's here, she's got to be here.*

The song changed to "Centerfield," and John Fogerty's cheerful voice sang "Put me in, coach." An undertone of sweat, acrid and unfamiliar, permeated the hall between the living room and bedroom. Strangers had been here. Or were here.

Tara forced herself to creep rather than race down the hall. She cracked the bedroom door. Kali lay on her side on the bed, wrists behind her back. Duct tape covered her mouth, and her eyes had swollen shut. Bruises purpled her forehead. Holding her breath, Tara eased the door open. She saw no intruders. And no Fimi. She rushed in.

"Kali?"

No response. Tara held her hand in front of Kali's nose and felt faint breath. She tried her phone again, then the landline. No dial tone. Tara rushed through the trailer, pausing only to yank open the few drawers and cabinets large enough to hold a baby. Outside, she banged on trailer doors until she found a neighbor with a working landline who called Security.

Tara circled her trailer looking for tire tracks, signs of the intruders, anything that might provide a clue. Aside from one emergency road, Willow Springs wasn't accessible by automobile. Only golf carts, bikes, and motorcycles fit through its gates, down the paths in the surrounding woods, and along the narrow residential roads. Tara found no tracks other than those leading to her own golf cart. She peered through the back window at Kali. She couldn't leave her friend. But how could she stay here when Fimi could be anywhere, with anyone?

At last, flashing red light flooded the front garden. The head of Security and the community doctor arrived in the first golf cart. Both women rushed inside. A second cart brought two more Security personnel. After Tara spilled out the story, search tasks were assigned.

Tara took her own cart and drove toward the closest wooded area. Someone from Security would be searching as well, but Tara had to do something. Residents jumped out of Tara's way as she drove, horn blaring. She saw no one who shouldn't be there.

*Where is she? Where is she? This was supposed to be a safe place. And Kali, what about Kali?*

When she reached foot trails, Tara pulled the cart to one side and hurried into the woods. She shone her smartphone's flashlight around, trying to think who would take Fimi. The obvious answer was the Brotherhood, the religious order Cyril Woods had belonged to. Probably still belonged to, despite being in prison awaiting trial for what he'd done to Tara's brother. But why now? News about Tara and Fimi had spread across the Internet. But after what Tara had said under the Arch for all the world to hear, few people believed what the press called Tara's "story" that she'd been shocked to discover her pregnancy because she hadn't had sex. Not many had believed even before Tara had spoken. So what threat could Fimi pose to the Brotherhood and its teachings?

Tara took a side path. She'd seen no trace of the Security person who was supposed to be here, but the woods spanned acres.

*Breathe. Panicking won't help.*

Fimi might have been taken by any of the hundreds of people who'd sent messages calling Tara evil, a liar, or a slut, or telling her God should have made her baby stillborn. But Tara thought if she were going to kidnap a child, she wouldn't send a warning first, she'd just do it.

Moving as quickly as she could, Tara examined each shadow, petrified she'd find Fimi's body on the ground or tied to a tree branch or bush. Twigs snapped behind her. Tara spun, her flashlight beam illuminating the trees around her.

Cyril Woods stood before her.

# 2

Cyril blinked, but otherwise stood motionless in the flashlight beam, shoulders rigid under his camouflage jacket. He still wore his hair in a buzz cut, but he was thinner than when Tara had last seen him, and pale. His jaw was swollen and bruised, and blood ran from a gash over his forehead. When she'd met Cyril, Tara had mistaken him for a college student, but the lines forming under his eyes made it unlikely anyone would do so now. His sharp cheekbones and the slant of his dark eyebrows over intense eyes made him striking. Tara remembered being attracted to him, but it was like remembering another person's emotions. Now she only wanted to wrap her hands around his neck and shake him until he told her what had happened to Fimi.

"Where is she? My baby. What did you do to her?"

"Nothing." Cyril lifted his hands in a surrender gesture, much like the one he'd made when he'd confronted Tara for the first time almost a year ago. Then she'd feared and distrusted him because she didn't know him. Now she feared and distrusted him because she did. "I did nothing," he said. "I came to help."

The flashlight beam jumped as Tara stepped toward him, and she willed her hand not to tremble. Cyril had been her first ally, and he'd turned on her in the worst possible ways. She couldn't believe he'd been released from prison after what he'd done to her little brother Bailey. Or had he escaped from jail? "Give. Me. My. Baby."

Despite her distress, Tara avoided Fimi's nickname. It might be pointless, but she hoped that when Fimi was older, answering to her nickname instead of her given name, Sophia Fiona, might protect her from those who didn't know her well enough to know better.

"I don't have her," Cyril said. "But I'll do all I can to help you find her."

Tara's cell phone still had no signal. She started toward the trail that led to her golf cart. The Security office had a landline and a police radio, if it came to that. Cyril kept pace with her, leaving as much space between them as possible on the narrow paths as if to emphasize that he meant no harm.

"Right," Tara said, "the Brotherhood of Andrew got you out of jail so you could help me."

"Someone made some kind of deal," Cyril said, "and the charges were dropped. No one takes credit for it. I returned to the Brotherhood to see what I could learn. I want to make up for what I've done."

"Sure you do. Where is she? Where's my baby?"

The Brotherhood had sent Cyril to Tara days after she'd learned of her pregnancy, supposedly to help her. At first, she'd been grateful despite that she couldn't accept the things he said about a prophecy and the Book of Revelation. He had been the only person who believed her that she didn't know how she'd become pregnant and that she hadn't had sex. Until he learned her child would be a girl.

"The Brotherhood sent two men," Cyril said. "Special Investigator Mullin, who attacked you before, and another I don't know. They want your child's DNA. Maybe I should have left them alone, maybe they would have just taken swabs and let her be if I had."

"Let her be? DNA? What are you saying?"

Tara felt a faint surge of hope. DNA could be tested without harm to Fimi. But then why take the baby at all, why not just swab her cheeks and be done? She couldn't trust anything Cyril said. She shifted from striding to jogging.

"The Brotherhood wants to analyze her DNA. To find out what she is."

"What she is? Human. She's human."

"You know what I mean – if anything makes her special or different," Cyril said. "If your child was conceived without sexual intercourse –"

"If? *If?*"

"I'm telling you how the Brotherhood sees it." Cyril breathed hard between words. Sitting in jail must have gotten him out of shape. "If she was conceived in some supernatural way, whose genes does she have? Yours? Your parents'? Entirely unique genes? You must have wondered about these things."

"I never wondered if she's human."

"You must have wondered if she's different."

Tara had, and before Fimi was born she'd harbored plenty of fears about what the baby might be like. One reason she hadn't sought DNA testing herself was concern that being different in any way would make Fimi a target. So far, Fimi behaved like any other baby and seemed healthy and happy. But obviously that and Tara keeping a low profile hadn't protected her. Or provided any answers on the question of why or how Fimi had been conceived. Tara had learned to live with that uncertainty as best as she could, and she'd made her peace with it, so long as Fimi had been safe.

The path became rougher, covered by tree branches not yet cleared from a recent freak winter storm. The debris forced Tara to slow her stride to pick around it. She felt like screaming in frustration at their slow progress.

"So what's the rest of your story?" she said.

Cyril frowned at Tara's use of the word "story," but didn't argue with her.

"I learned of the plot after it had already been put in motion. I broke in after the other two investigators, and it took me too long to get through the Willow Springs border fencing. They'd subdued your friend by the time I reached your trailer. I tried to intervene, but I was no match for them, though I landed some blows. Mullin stayed and fought me. The other ran with the baby. Mullin's last punch knocked me out. I don't know for how long, but long enough that I saw no one when I exited your trailer. I ran the way I believe they'd come in, with no luck, then circled back to find you, thinking it better to contact the authorities."

"So you're a hero."

"Clearly not, or I'd be handing you the baby right now."

They reached the golf cart. Tara's mind raced as she piloted it toward the Community Center, which housed the Security offices. "If you weren't in on it, how could you learn about the plan? Your superiors just told you? They can't trust you. Not any more than I do."

"I went to jail without saying a word about the Brotherhood or who instructed me to do what I did. And without turning in Mullin. But you're correct, I doubt they trust me. I failed to carry out their instructions many times. Now I'm pretending I'm back in the fold and most likely they're pretending, too. Perhaps they wanted me to follow them tonight for some reason, perhaps they wanted me to tell you what I'm telling you. You should take that into account."

"Take that into account?" Tara clutched the steering wheel to keep from taking a swing at Cyril. She forced herself to keep her eyes on the road. "Take that into account? How do you suggest I take that into account? Or figure out if you're here to help me or kidnap my child or call me a whore? What sort of mood are you in today? What's your sacred duty this time around?"

They reached a narrow street lined with gas lamps. On pavement instead of dirt, Tara pushed the cart to its top speed, as if the sooner she reached the Community Center the more likely there would be good news about Fimi. The wind whipped around them. Cyril gripped the side of the cart, face grim. "I know. I know I've failed. You, my mentor, myself. I tried to serve everyone and ruined everything. There's no forgiving me. But, Tara, you did forgive me. If only for an instant, you did."

In the intensity of the moments after giving birth, Tara had forgiven Cyril. He'd seemed genuinely remorseful. Cyril always seemed genuine, maybe he always said what he felt and believed. But what he felt and believed changed from moment to moment.

"I may have forgiven you, but I'll never trust you."

"So don't trust me, but use the information I gave you, if you can."

"Nothing you said is helpful."

Tara fought to stay calm despite the tightness in her chest and throat and her galloping heart. What had Cyril told her? Only that the Brotherhood had taken Fimi. The religious order would have been her first guess regardless, for while ministers on cable TV shows denounced her and late-night comedians made fun of her, throughout her pregnancy, no one outside the Brotherhood had tried to harm her or her family.

Floodlights illuminated all the grounds and gardens within a quarter-mile radius of the Community Center. The blinds had been drawn across the floor-to-ceiling windows, blocking any view from outside. No one had news of Fimi. Police from the nearest town, Blue Springs, Arkansas, took Cyril into custody. A detective questioned Tara at the coffee bar in the social room, which had been cleared of residents. She did her best to sound rational when she explained the controversy her pregnancy and Fimi's birth had stirred. At least the detective knew the parts about Cyril's previous criminal charges were true, as the Willow Springs Security personnel had provided copies of newspaper articles, police reports, and the indictment.

The detective looked little older than Tara, perhaps twenty-five or twenty-six, with a baby face and chubby fingers.

"Tell me you'll find her," Tara said.

# 3

Tara rose early the next morning to hike the woods and grounds of Willow Springs. Then she drove through the town of Blue Springs, hoping to see someone or something out of place, some sign of Fimi. She was unfamiliar with the town, though, so she didn't know exactly what "out of place" would mean. She'd ventured into Blue Springs only once during the last four months. It had been two weeks before. Because no one had contacted her at Willow Springs and no one had accosted her family in Missouri since Fimi's birth, Tara had decided it was safe to leave the secluded community for a short shopping trip with Fimi. Tara caught her breath. Had that been how the Brotherhood figured out where she and Fimi were staying?

*If only I'd stayed in, stayed safe.* But she couldn't have stayed within the confines of Willow Springs forever.

Her last stop was the hospital. When she reached Kali's room, the sound of blipping monitors and the smells of alcohol and antiseptic took Tara back to visiting her littlest sister Megan in the hospital in the days before Megan's death. Tara froze on the threshold, heart pulsing in her throat. Megan gone, Fimi missing, Kali unconscious. And little or nothing Tara could do to fix any of it. Hissing came from down the hall where respirators helped patients breathe. At least Kali was breathing on her own, the slight rise of her chest the only sign she was alive. Her forehead had swollen and her normally brown skin had turned putty-colored around purple and blue bruises.

"Her brain scans are not good. The doctors fear she will never awaken or, if she does, she'll be unable to speak or move."

Tara spun around, hand to her chest, startled though she recognized the voice. Nanor Kerkorian, Kali's grandmother and the founder of Willow Springs, stood in the hallway. Her black and gray hair was pulled into a bun, and her orange and red dress flowed around her, the bright colors jarring in the otherwise drab off-white corridor. In her mid-seventies, Nanor still practiced yoga, jogged three miles day, and oversaw the day-to-day functioning of Willow Springs. Today, though, she looked her age. Pink and red rimmed her eyes, and the wrinkles around them had multiplied.

"I'm so sorry." Tara hugged Nanor, comforted for an instant by the faint jasmine scent that hovered about the older woman, who quickly pulled away from Tara's embrace. "You warned me that staying silent about Fimi wasn't the way," Tara said. "And you warned me about Cyril. And I didn't listen."

The green vinyl chair near Kali's bed creaked as Nanor sank into it. "I did not foresee this. And I am to blame as well. I believed I knew best, that only I – I of all people in the world – could guide you and Fimi. Yet I failed to keep Willow Springs secure. And now Kali and Fimi suffer."

The hospital heating system was barely keeping pace with the unusually cold winter. Tara pulled her wool sweater tighter around her shoulders and stared at the gray sky and bare trees outside the window over Kali's bed.

"I thought if I lied about Fimi's conception that day under the Arch, and I dropped out of sight, the world would forget," Tara said. "But it didn't."

*Tell all you can as soon as you can.* The words had been said to Tara in a vision before Fimi's birth. They'd prompted her to speak about Fimi's conception on television, to the Pope, to everyone who'd asked. She and her mentor, Sophia Gaddini, for whom Fimi had been named, had started a book about Tara's experiences. But the publicity had brought nothing but threats and danger, so Tara had shifted instead to keeping silent.

Tara checked her phone to be sure the ringer was on and she hadn't missed any messages from the police or Security. Or her family members, whom she'd called during the night. Nothing.

"I don't understand how the kidnappers got in," Tara said. "I thought the weaknesses found after the break in last year were addressed."

"As did I," Nanor said. "I believed Willow Springs was safe." She looked at her granddaughter's battered face, at the tubes and lines running into her arms and under the sheets. "Now I understand. Nowhere is safe."

**Monks Struggle to Keep Temple and Ritual Afloat**

BANGKOK - Forty-eight hours after an unprecedented seven-day rainfall in Thailand, persistent floodwaters make cremating the dead in accord with local custom close to impossible. The main hall at the Lotus Temple in Bangkok remains under water. Monks must crowd into cramped spaces in the upper floors of the temple to perform chants.

**Californians Struggle Under Severe Water Restrictions**

LOS ANGELES - THE U.S. Drought Monitor announced yesterday that the Southern California drought reached Level D4 – Exceptional Drought Conditions. These conditions can be expected to cause severe water shortages and widespread crop and pasture losses. Following the announcement, over 3,000 protestors gathered at the Governor's mansion, demanding stronger limits on corporations they believe emit excess greenhouse gases that contribute to climate change.

At a recent talk at the Brookings Christian University, Reverend Frank McCoffell was asked about the drought emergency. The Reverend opined that climate change, if it is indeed happening, represents a message from God.

THE MAN who thought of himself as Raphael, after the angel who was a particular foe of the devil, highlighted the words "message from God" in the printout and tacked it onto his bulletin board. Old fashioned of him, he knew, to use cork and tacks rather than a computerized imitation of a bulletin board. But he'd been educated to take notes in ink on paper, and cut and paste with scissors and glue, before moving on to the digital world. He'd found working that way helped him focus. Alongside the articles – he had printed those from the Internet, no sense in wasting his limited time searching and collecting actual newspapers – he pinned his most recent photos of Tara Spencer and baby Spencer. His skin prickled. Signs, portents. He needed to interpret them correctly. Perhaps the extreme weather patterns since the child's birth amounted to coincidence. He'd monitor those developments and others. In matters of this type, erring on the side of caution was necessary, and his usual regard for human life remained paramount. So the question must be answered. Was baby Spencer human?

TARA ORDERED a cup of tea at the Five and Diner. After sitting with Kali, who remained unconscious, and Nanor for an hour at the hospital, Tara had driven to the local coffee shop. Partly because someone there might have seen or heard something unusual in the hours before or after Fimi's kidnapping, and more because it was where she and Kali had eaten breakfast together when they'd first met. As they'd talked, their initial wariness had given way to a wish to help one another, and when Tara had returned to Willow Springs following Fimi's birth, they'd become close friends.

*See how much I've helped her,* Tara thought, throat aching. *If I never came here, she'd be awake and safe right now.*

Her phone rang before the counter waitress returned with Tara's tea. A police officer told Tara a high school English teacher two towns over had entered his second period classroom and found a baby asleep in an infant seat. The baby appeared to be about four months old and wore a red and white sleeper, which matched what Fimi had been wearing, and she looked similar to the photos Tara had provided of Fimi. Paramedics had been dispatched to the school to bring the infant to the emergency room for examination. The teacher was being brought in for questioning, and the school had agreed to provide its security videos.

While the officer was still talking, Tara dropped a five dollar bill on the worn linoleum counter and hurried to the parking area without her tea. She arrived in the E.R. long before the ambulance. She paced the floor, ignoring the magazines, television, and patients awaiting treatment.

At last, the glass entryway doors whooshed open. Two paramedics came in, one on either end of what looked like a rolling crib. It had vinyl padding on three sides. An infant was strapped onto the mattress pad.

Tara rushed forward. "Fimi?"

~

For the next four days, Willow Springs kept a security guard stationed outside Kali's hospital room at all times. No other attempts to accost Tara or Fimi occurred. Tara offered to stay away from the hospital all the same. But Nanor insisted her granddaughter would heal faster with her closest friend nearby. Kali's bruises had mostly faded, but she hadn't so much as fluttered her eyelids.

Tara nodded at the guard as she entered the room, holding Fimi close against her chest. She'd barely set the baby down since being reunited with her, and at night she dozed with one hand wrapped around a crib bar. Cyril remained in the Blue Springs jail. He'd stuck with the story he'd told Tara.

"Remember, Kali may hear what you say even though she is unconscious," Nanor said. Her fuschia dress hung loose on her thin frame. She looked as if she'd lost weight over the past few days, and stray whitish-gray hairs hung around her face and straggled down her back, sprung loose from her usually neat bun. "There are studies showing coma patients are aware of what happens around them. She also may sense how you feel. So you must project peace and healing and calm. It will help her."

After some coaxing, Nanor left for a cafeteria break. Tara stood next to the bed, cradling Fimi in one arm, and held Kali's hand. It felt cool and too still. Tara rambled about the recent dusting of snow and the winter holiday events at Willow Springs for as long as she could. But fears about Cyril, the Brotherhood, and Fimi's DNA rushed through her mind. Her chest tightened and her pulse elevated. Projecting calm and relaxation didn't seem remotely possible.

Tara inhaled and shut her eyes. So far, she hadn't become adept at meditating. She'd tried during the past few months, but her thoughts had raced and when she tried to stop them, sadness over her sister Megan's death weighed her down, making her feel like she'd sunk into a hole as deep as the one that had been dug for the coffin. More recently, though, sessions with Nanor combined with yoga had helped Tara find peace now and then. She concentrated on her breath, then imagined the warmth she felt from holding Fimi flowing down her arms and through her hands to Kali. Tara's shoulders dropped, her knees unlocked, her eyes softened. The cool metal bedrail, the room's sterile alcohol scent, the crimson poinsettia on the bedside table, all dropped away.

*Breathe. In. Out. Breathe.*

When a thought intruded, Tara pictured it floating away in a bubble. The ventilators from the next room hissed rhythmically. The image of the deserted living room – no Fimi, no Kali – faded from Tara's mind for the first time since the attack.

*In. Out. Breathe.*

She had no idea how much time passed. It could have been a minute or an hour.

Tara opened her eyes.

Kali opened hers.

# 4

"Where am I?" Kali spoke clearly and looked far more alert than Tara ever would have expected for someone who'd been in a coma the instant before. "What's happening?" Kali's eyes darted around the room, taking in the monitors, the hospital bed, the metal tray with a box of tissues and a magazine on it.

"Kali?" Tara stared at Kali, unable to process that her friend had not only awakened, but spoken. "You're back."

Kali gripped Tara's hand. "How did I get here? The trailer – there were men – Fimi, did they take Fimi?" Her eyes fixed on Tara again, then dropped to the baby. "No, she's here, she's right here."

At the mention of her name, Fimi started to cry, the way she did when she got overtired. Tara opened her mouth to speak, but her brain felt sluggish as if she, and not Kali, had been in the coma.

"Tara, I'm sorry, I couldn't stop them. One of them hit me, and that's all I remember."

Tara shook her head to clear it. "Kali, it's fine. Fimi's fine. It's you we were worried about. I'll get Nanor." Tara let go of Kali's hand and stepped back. She lost her footing for an instant and grabbed the bed rail.

"Are you all right?" Kali said.

"I – sure, yes. Yes, don't worry about me." Tara breathed deep and, using all her effort, stood straight. The four days of worry had taken a greater toll than she'd realized. Her knees shook and the back of her head ached.

"Sit for a minute," Kali said. Color flushed the apples of her cheeks, and her hair seemed less matted, and more lifelike, than it had moments ago. The fluorescent lighting hit highlights in the black strands.

"Just for a minute." Tara dropped into the green armchair and rearranged Fimi against her. The baby quieted.

"What happened? Why am I in the hospital? Was I hit that hard?" Kali said.

"I"ll get the nurse. Or the doctor. They can fill you in."

"And they will. With all their medical jargon." Kali struggled to sit, and Tara fumbled for the button to raise the bed, but her fingers felt clumsy. It was Kali who found it. "And Grandmother will rush in frowning and directing what I'm to do and not do. So let us have some peace, just for a moment, and tell me why you seemed shocked when I spoke."

"It's been four days. We didn't know if you'd wake up."

Kali's forehead creased. "I feel fine." She flexed her hand, raised one leg under the sheet. "My head doesn't ache. My limbs don't feel stiff. I can't have been out four days." She put her hand through the bars on her bedrail to touch Tara's shoulder. "Not that I doubt you, my friend. Did the police find the men who broke in? There were two. At least, I think there were two. It's a bit fuzzy."

Tara summarized the events of the last few days, including her conversation with Cyril Woods, as quickly as possible. "Now I'm calling Nanor."

"One other thing before you do. Tell me – you believe Cyril was part of this plot?"

"Yes," Tara said. "Part of me wants to believe he wasn't, that he's changed and was trying to help. But how many times can I fall for that?"

"Still, from what you said, he could have escaped the grounds undetected. But he stayed to give you information. And Fimi is unharmed, so he may have told the truth about the reasons she was taken."

"Which only suggests he was in on it from the beginning."

Kali nodded. "Perhaps. I wish I could tell you if he was one of the men, but I don't know."

Tara longed to ask for details about the men, but she knew Kali would need to tell everything to the police, and she didn't want to exhaust her friend before that happened. Or before Nanor saw her.

"We can talk more another time," Tara said. "We can't leave your grandmother in the dark any longer. Or delay medical attention, though you look amazingly well." Tara hit the call button.

After Nanor saw Kali and the doctors examined her, the Blue Springs police detective questioned her. Kali described the two intruders. One had worn a ski mask and was medium height and stocky. The other, who wore a white face mask, had been tall and red-haired, broad-shouldered and solidly-built, like a football player.

*Mullin*, Tara thought. He'd attacked her twice when she'd been pregnant, so she knew what he looked like. His presence fit with what Cyril had said. But if Cyril had helped plan the kidnapping, he would have known Mullin was involved, so that didn't prove he'd told Tara the truth. Though neither man's description matched Cyril's wiry build.

The detective showed Kali photos. Tara couldn't see them, but assumed one of them was of Cyril. Kali didn't recognize any of them. She couldn't remember anything more.

~

"Releasing him?" Nanor put her hands flat on the metal table and rose from her chair, her violet skirt swaying. The clatter of plates and silverware filled the small hospital cafeteria. It was the middle of the lunch hour, and Tara had just returned from a meeting at the village hall. "That's impossible."

"It's possible. It's happening." Tara, a tray with a turkey sandwich and a Coke in front her, bounced Fimi on her lap. Too fast, as Fimi started to cry. Tara made herself sit still. Relieved as she was that Fimi and Kali were both fine, she wanted to pound the table in frustration over the lack of answers.

"You must not let that happen," Nanor said.

"I have no say. The assistant prosecutor claims she has no grounds to hold Cyril. Nothing contradicts his version of events. His fingerprints weren't found in my guest trailer. The two men Kali described don't match his physical build. The high school's security cameras weren't working – the detective told me they're spotty at best – so no one knows who brought Fimi there. The focus is on the teacher who found her. It turns out he has past domestic violence convictions the school missed in the background check."

"So very convenient." Nanor paced in the few feet of open space between their table and the vending machines. Despite her age, she still moved with a grace and fluidity Tara didn't think she'd ever match. "But there is the trespassing. Cyril Woods trespassed – that can be proven."

"Apparently he's cooperating with the prosecution, so that charge will be dropped too."

"Cooperating? Cooperating how?" Nanor said.

"He offered some type of information, and the prosecutor said if it bears fruit, she'll let us know. She wouldn't tell me specifics. But I talked to the detective, and he said he'd visited Thomas Stranyero. That name must have come from Cyril."

"Stranyero." Nanor froze, then sank back into her chair. Nanor's daughter, who'd been pregnant at the time, had been killed in a hit and run decades before. After her death, a card with Thomas Stranyero's name and a phone number had been found among her possessions. The name had meant nothing to Tara when Nanor had first shown her the card. But when she spent more time with Cyril, Tara had learned Stranyero was the man who'd recruited him into the Brotherhood. What it meant that Cyril had revealed his name to the police, Tara didn't know.

"Cyril must have known it would lead nowhere," Nanor said. "Which I assume is what occurred."

"You got it. The detective is convinced the Brotherhood of Andrew is nothing but a small religious group devoted to study and prayer."

"And Fimi's kidnapping?" Nanor said.

"The investigation is 'ongoing,' and the detective will keep us updated. And Cyril will be released later this week."

Tara's heart rate elevated at the thought. She breathed in the clean scent of

Fimi's baby shampoo and focused on the aquamarine colored wall behind Nanor. *At least Fimi's safe. For now. And Kali.*

Nanor clenched her fists and glared at the half-eaten brownie on her plate. "The laws of men. This is what happens under the laws of men."

LIGHTS GLITTERED like tiny ice crystals along the bare branches of bushes and up to the tops of shortleaf pine trees around the Community Center. Inside the entrance hall, a string quartet played, and volunteers packed baskets for the Blue Springs food pantries. The air smelled of peppermint hot cocoa.

Tara unzipped her jacket and Fimi's and checked the clock over the bulletin board. Kali was being released from the hospital in two hours. Tara planned to head to Nanor's for dinner after she met with Security. She hoped to be told it was safe to stay in the community, as much as anywhere could be safe. More than anything, she wanted to spend Christmas with her adopted family here at Willow Springs. Her mom and dad and siblings weren't celebrating this year. They couldn't bear it without Megan there to badger everyone into baking cookies for Santa on Christmas Eve, rather than leaving store-bought ones out, and to make the rounds at five a.m. the next morning, insisting her siblings get up with her to shake all the presents and try to guess the contents before opening them. No matter how sick she'd been, Megan had found the energy to celebrate each of her nine Christmases to the nth degree.

Tara's mom had also said that the stress of worrying about Tara and Fimi's safety might be more than Tara's dad could handle. Tara didn't know how to judge that for herself, for her dad rarely called her these days, or returned her calls, and when he did, he said little. Her mom said he was like that with everyone now. Tara didn't know if that made her feel better or worse. She still felt angry at her dad about the choices he'd made that day at the Arch and how he'd treated her. His refusal to talk to her added to her anger and worried her at the same time.

Sagun Halel, the newest Willow Springs Security associate, appeared in the entrance hall. A thin Indian woman in her late twenties, she wore olive green pants, hiking boots, and a waist-length fleece-lined vinyl jacket. She ushered Tara past the main social room to an interior room that smelled like mulled cider. Two upright pianos stood against one wall, bookcases overflowing with books and magazines against another. In the center, the two piano benches had been pushed together to serve as a coffee table, upholstered armchairs grouped around them.

"So I've closed the back doors the Brotherhood – if that's who it was – created in our computer system to override our alarms and cameras," Sagun said. Sagun had a computer programming degree and a reputation as a technology whiz. She'd started working at Willow Springs after Tara's first visit and before Tara had returned to live there following Fimi's birth, but she'd been filled in on all the threats to Tara and the unusual nature of Fimi's existence.

Tara let her breath out. "That's good news."

"Not entirely." Diedre Hartmann, the head of Security, sat across from Tara. A former police officer and bodybuilder, she was six-three and looked tall even sitting. Her mid-length curly hair seemed incongruous with the rest of her. Tara always expected her to have a Marine-style crew cut. "They shouldn't have been able to create them in the first place."

"So you're not sure you can keep them out in the future?" Tara asked.

"Oh, I'm sure," Sagun said. She glanced at Diedre, who nodded. "It's not that whoever got in was so skilled. It's that the system was too easy. Nanor delayed hiring someone with my expertise, and even once I got here, until this happened, she hesitated to spend what was needed to update our cyber defenses. It's new to her, and I don't think she understood the seriousness of the threat."

"So I've cost her a lot of money."

Diedre stretched one muscled arm across the back of her chair and onto the next. "It's good you did. Not good that Fimi was taken or Kali was harmed, but good that these issues were highlighted. If the Brotherhood found its way in, eventually others would have as well."

"What I don't understand is how the Brotherhood knew when I'd be away from Fimi. I hardly ever left her alone."

"They probably didn't know," Diedre said. "If you had been with Fimi, you would have been assaulted and subdued."

Tara's stomach rolled. If Diedre assessed the plan correctly, Tara, not Kali, had been the object of the attack. She'd put her friend in danger more directly than she'd realized.

The room's decorations, which had struck Tara as festive when she entered, now seemed oppressive, requiring a cheerfulness she couldn't match. The garland sparkled around the doorway, the ruby-red teapot and mugs glowed on a silver tray, the paper snowflakes strung above the piano seemed to dance. Looking at them, Tara understood her parents' decision not to celebrate this year.

"Which brings us to the point," Diedre said. "We took a vote."

Sagun poured herself more cider, keeping her eyes fixed on the teapot and cups. Her long black hair swung forward to hide her face.

"What kind of vote?" Tara shifted Fimi, who had started squirming, on her lap.

"The community – except Nanor and Kali, who were at the hospital – voted," Diedre said. She crossed her left leg so her ankle rested on the opposite knee, which pressed against the closest piano bench. "The issue was whether you and Fimi pose too much danger to keep living here with us."

Tara noted the "you" and "us" and guessed she knew the result of the vote. Her heart sank, but she could hardly have expected anything different. She pushed her cider aside. It had had grown cold, and the cinnamon had separated from the liquid, making it grainy.

"It was close," Diedre said. "But a majority voted you should stay."

"Oh." That should have made Tara feel better, but it didn't. She'd brought violence to Willow Springs, exactly what many women had come there to escape. "The ones who voted for me to leave were right. I need to find somewhere else to live."

Sagun straightened and met Tara's eyes. "Please don't feel that way. The last thing we wanted was to drive you away, but we felt the community should have a say."

"And it was close vote, which means a lot of people don't feel safe with me here. So it's right that I leave."

"At least Kali is almost completely recovered," Sagun said. "A miracle given what the doctors predicted."

Diedre frowned. "Doctors are wrong all the time. Which is a good thing in Kali's case. But we can't forget the danger to her."

Tara's mind flashed to the way she and Fimi had stood by Kali's bed. Had it helped? She didn't know. Fimi herself hadn't been ill once since she'd been born, not even sniffles, despite having been a preemie. But that could just mean she had a good immune system. Tara held her baby more closely against her stomach. It was probably coincidence that Kali had awakened when Tara and Fimi were there, or the normal healing effect of having people who loved her nearby.

"If you do plan to leave, we think it best you go right away. Tonight," Diedre was saying. Tara had missed the beginning of her statement.

"On Christmas Eve?"

Diedre leaned forward. "We're not trying to be cruel. But we're sure that if Nanor sees you, she'll insist on you staying, not just through the holiday, but indefinitely."

"It's true." Sagun played with her spoon. "She grows increasingly determined with age. If you truly wish to stay through the holiday, of course we won't stop you. But I believe you see that your presence here may be bringing great danger."

"Yes. And I'm sorry," Tara said. "I underestimated the Brotherhood."

"We're the ones who are sorry," Diedre said. "I'm embarrassed to say this is not a sanctuary. Not if it's so easily breached. We believe we've addressed any gaps, but I thought we'd done that before and it wasn't enough to protect Kali."

Tara nodded, closing her eyes to hold back tears. She didn't want to make either Diedre or Sagun feel bad.

Sagun disappeared for a few minutes and returned with a brown envelope she pressed into Tara's hand. "Take this. It's enough for a car rental and two weeks' hotel stay in case you need it."

The three of them stood. Diedre towered over the other two by almost a foot.

"What about Nanor and Kali?" Tara said. "They're expecting Fimi and me tonight."

"I'll stop by the hospital and tell them personally before I head to the airport," Diedre said. "My mom's taken a turn for the worse."

Tara had heard that Diedre's mom had some type of heart disease, and she felt bad that she'd never asked any more about it. She'd barely been keeping track of her own life. "I'm sorry."

*Seems like that's all I say these days.*

"Thank you." Diedre put her hand on Tara's back. "Your leaving is the best thing, Tara. I hope you know it's not personal. I have nothing against you, but I need to protect everyone, not just you and Fimi."

"Where will you go?" Sagun said.

# 5

"That is insane. Impossible. Intolerable."

Fenton MacNeil was not a huge man, only a large one, but he appeared enormous when he paced and waved his meaty hands. He never said anything, only shouted, either ecstatic or incensed. He punched words when he spoke, like a radio announcer.

Thomas Stranyero sat motionless in a wingback chair in MacNeil's two-story library, ignoring the older man's gesticulations. Instead, he studied the spiral staircase beyond MacNeil. It rose to a second level that had shining hardwood floors and rolling ladders resting against floor-to-ceiling bookcases. MacNeil's private collection rivaled the Brotherhood's, and he had a grander space to keep it in. Stranyero meant to own a house on this scale before he turned sixty-five. He had six years.

"Unacceptable." MacNeil poked his finger in Stranyero's face. "The parchment must be found and assembled. The Armenian section disappeared on your watch."

Stranyero pushed MacNeil's hand away from his face and stood. He employed a studied calm when dealing with MacNeil, who was used to people trembling and scrambling to appease him. Stranyero's approach both reassured and further angered his colleague. Stranyero liked keeping the man off balance. They held equal rank in the Brotherhood. But they depended upon one another, and either could derail the other's career. More important, MacNeil could prevent Stranyero from upholding the mission. Which, whatever others might believe of him, he desired above all things.

"Hardly," Stranyero said. "No one knows when that section was last consulted. We may be the first generation to actually need to piece together the message."

"Also thanks to you. The main investigators were your find, your responsibility."

Stranyero leaned against an antique credenza and spread his hands wide. "Cyril Woods performed perfectly."

"Not so the others," Fenton said.

"No, they're not perfect," Stranyero said. "But perhaps Mullin is still useful."

"Doubtful," MacNeil said.

Stranyero stared at the floor, weighing whether to speak. But MacNeil must harbor the same question. "You realize the entire document may never have existed in the first instance."

MacNeil pointed his finger in Stranyero's face again. "You'd better hope for your sake that's true." Then he stepped back of his own accord, something Stranyero had never seen MacNeil do. "For all our sakes."

Dr. Sophia Gaddini sipped her Shiraz and studied the man who sat in the black lacquer armchair on the other side of her fireplace. She suspected her colleague Jasmina Price had invited the visiting lecturer to Sophia's holiday eve gathering with an eye toward a bit of matchmaking. Sophia didn't mind. It distracted her from her worries about Tara, and her sense of helplessness at not being able to do more. Sophia had good research skills, but tracking down kidnappers lay beyond her area of expertise.

"Jasmina tells me you're the author of *The Feminine Face of God: Gender and the Divine*," Rick Gettleman said. His tweed blazer and pants looked custom tailored. Not so unusual for a professor, but he was an adjunct, which meant he likely got paid little more than a token amount for each class he taught. He was also an antiques dealer in New York; perhaps he did well at that.

"You know it?" Sophia said. Sales of her past books had increased since the publicity around her current collaboration with Tara Spencer, but it still surprised her when anyone outside the DePaul University community remembered a particular title.

"By reputation." Gettleman set his wine glass on the Chinese garden stool on his right and leaned forward. "One of my students raves about it."

"Always nice to hear."

Gettleman was certainly attractive, Sophia thought, especially the strong jawline, even features, and trim build. Perhaps too attractive. Sophia was nice enough looking – her father's dark Sicilian eyes and hair and her mother's fair Irish complexion and slim body type made a good combination. But men with Gettleman's looks usually paired with magazine cover-model types, which she was not.

"I understand your new work is about the Tara Spencer phenomenon," Gettleman said.

Sophia stiffened. "I don't know that I'd call her a phenomenon."

That she was working with Tara was well known. And Gettleman's slightly cocked head and the faint arch of his eyebrows showed nothing beyond ordinary curiosity. But given the recent break in and kidnapping, and the tragedy when Tara had stayed with Sophia last year, any mention of Tara set her on the alert.

"She spawned this wave of copycats, or copygirls, as the press is calling them," Gettleman said. "That in itself is a puzzling phenomenon."

"True."

The stories had begun appearing in the last few weeks. The media called it a mother-messiah complex. Psychiatrists were trotted out to assert that all the women, including Tara, found their lives difficult and dull and were trying to create some excitement and get attention by asserting they were virgins who discovered to their shock that they were pregnant. No story mentioned that Tara had been a pre-med student with a 4.0 GPA, close family relationships, a best friend, and a fiancé, and had lost nearly all of it because of her unusual pregnancy. Sophia had no doubt Tara's life would have been far happier had she kept silent about the unusual nature of her pregnancy. But Sophia said nothing publicly to contradict the media. Tara had asked her not to. After the frightening events surrounding Fimi's birth, Tara had decided disappearing from public view was the safer course. Sophia supported that decision, though it would mean returning the publisher's advance if Tara backed out of the book collaboration.

Sophia couldn't help thinking all the women might be disturbed or were being used by someone wanting to discredit Tara. On the other hand, if she believed Tara had become pregnant in some supernatural way, why automatically dismiss the others? And Sophia did believe, despite the growing overall agnosticism that had led her to leave the convent years before. She believed in Tara. She just didn't know what that meant.

"Will you do any field work?" Gettleman said. "For the book."

"I may." This ground should have felt safe, too; it was no more than what Sophia had discussed with the publisher and her colleagues. But she needed to know more about Gettleman before sharing. She smiled and refilled his glass. "Enough about work. Tell me, how do you like Chicago compared to New York?"

Gettleman said he liked it very well, but he was returning to New York for the spring semester. The conversation turned from there to books, always a way to Sophia's heart. A half an hour later, Sophia realized she'd been neglecting her other guests, but Jasmina had taken over pouring sparkling water, wine, or chocolate martinis and replenishing the appetizer trays.

*So Jasmina was plotting*, Sophia thought, but she smiled. A little romance now and then was a lovely thing.

"What about you?" she asked. "Have you published?"

Gettleman shook his head. "No. One benefit of being an adjunct – no 'publish or peril' for me," he said, referring to the requirement that full professors frequently author and publish scholarly works. "Though, certainly, in academia, there isn't much real peril, don't you agree?"

Firelight glinted through the Cabernet in Gettleman's glass, casting deep red shadows on the wall behind him, the one Sophia shared with the townhome north of hers. The wall had been rebuilt after Tara's visit, but the home beyond it remained vacant, and sometimes Sophia thought she heard the wind echo through it.

"I'm not sure I do," she said.

THE WIND HOWLED, cutting through Sophia's long wool coat and fleece-lined gloves as she exited River City. She walked north on Wells Street, the serpentine high rise complex looming behind her. She'd zipped credentials and credit cards under a false name for Tara into her shoulder bag. It was amazing what a former nun could arrange. Especially one who had counseled former convicts. She felt vaguely uneasy about what the powers-that-be would say if they learned of her activities. The current provost at DePaul, where she was a professor of religious studies, never shied from academic controversy. But obtaining forged documents was something else entirely.

As she passed the old brick office building near the intersection of Wells Street and Congress Parkway, Sophia glanced over her shoulder. A man in a black coat walked half a block behind her, hands in his pockets, head bent against the wind. It was after seven p.m. and dark, and the options and stock traders who parked in the area were long gone. Changing course, Sophia cut sideways through a deserted parking lot toward the bus stop.

A bus pulled in, ice sluicing off it and plummeting onto the salt-streaked street. Sophia hurried beyond it and up the concrete stairs that led to the LaSalle Street Metra station. No passengers milled about the open air railroad platform, though two trains sat, sending steam into the air. Disembodied female voices over a loudspeaker stated, "Track 2" and "Track 5" at alternating moments. As Sophia passed the glass-enclosed portion of the station, she checked for reflections. No one appeared to be behind her. She exited through the Chicago Stock Exchange plaza and took the most traveled way to her office. The city blocks struck her as bleak, but they always did in mid-January when frozen-over slush lined the streets.

The light orange walls, antique desk, and vanilla-scented candles in her University office lifted Sophia's spirits, though the wind made the building creak, as if someone crept through the faculty office hallways. She forgot the sounds as she finished planning her week. Her eighty-seven-year-old aunt, the woman who'd raised her while her musician parents traveled the country, would arrive in three days. Sophia bought theater tickets online and made reservations for dinner at *L'Oiseau*, a new French restaurant in Printers Row. Sophia feared it wouldn't last more than six months because nothing did in that particular location. Rick Gettleman would be in town as well. Sophia had invited him to join them for dinner.

It was the first time since her college years that she'd introduced a man to Aunt May. Sophia smiled as she thought of it, and turned to her mail. Usually it contained nothing more than advertisements, so she'd let it sit. The stack included an envelope marked personal and confidential. It contained a plain sheet of linen paper with *Pir Ferit* and an international telephone number printed on it. Farther down the pile was a letter post-marked two weeks earlier.

She read it. And wished she hadn't let her mail sit so long.

# 6

Dear Dr. Gaddini:

Forgive my writing you without introduction. You may be familiar with my family's businesses, but the matter about which I write is, I assure you, wholly unconnected with them. This endeavor is strictly my own. You and I share an interest in learning more about visions a particular young woman may or may not have experienced and about how those alleged visions are being used as a basis for certain activities and beliefs today. Through my inquiries, I've determined that a Sufi teacher connected with the Koca Mustafa Pasha Mosque in Istanbul may possess vital information that he would never share with me. I believe you will prove more capable of persuading him that you harbor good intentions. I will forward his name and telephone number to you under separate cover. You need not share whatever information you obtain with me or contact me, I merely wish to aid your efforts.

Very truly yours,

Erik D. Holmes

~

A bulb in Sophia's Tiffany lamp popped, startling her and interrupting her research. She pushed back from the desk.

She'd heard of Erik Holmes – it was hard to imagine anyone in the western world who hadn't. Holmes & Company, a wide-ranging but closely-held corporation, owned businesses selling everything from snack cakes to wind power technology. By twenty-five, Erik had earned an MBA with a concentration in Economics and a Ph.D. in Religious Studies, both from Harvard. At thirty, he'd become the youngest CEO of Holmes & Company. He delivered four years of stellar returns, then stepped down, succeeded by his brother, Henrik. The two were fraternal twins. Henrik, the older by two minutes, was known as a heavy drinker and gambler and was often in the press. It remained to be seen how the company would do with him at the helm.

Little was known about Erik Holmes' personal life, other than that he liked expensive cars and restaurants. Sophia's online searches failed to locate a photo of him, and she concluded he'd spent significant funds to keep his life private. She noted uneasily he'd resigned from his CEO position shortly after the news stories about Tara's pregnancy had issued.

Holmes' assurance that he merely wished to aid her didn't reassure Sophia. In her experience, people who took time to state they lacked an agenda had a very certain one. But that didn't mean she should ignore the contents of the letter.

After fishing a bulb from the bottom drawer of her antique credenza, Sophia pulled her notes on the Koca Mustafa Pasha Mosque. She'd researched it when Tara had first sought her help and told her about the Brotherhood of Andrew. The mosque had once been the monastery of St. Andrew in Krisei. So far as Sophia could tell, Andrew in Krisei was the same Brother Andrew whom Cyril Woods had spoken of. But the Brotherhood, which had interfered in Tara's life and her pregnancy, alternately friend and foe, seemed unconnected with the mosque. Apparently Holmes thought otherwise. She searched online for "Pir Ferit," the name printed above the phone number on the sheet of stationery she'd received in the plain envelope she assumed had come from Holmes. The only online reference that appeared was short on detail, identifying Ferit as a historian, Sufi, and visiting lecturer at the University of Istanbul.

After checking to see that it was a little after five a.m. in Istanbul, Sophia dialed the phone number. She didn't speak Turkish, but she'd found a translation site that gave her enough basic instruction to apologize for calling so early, and to ask if she'd reached Pir Ferit and if he spoke English. She had and he did.

"This is Dr. Sophia Gaddini."

"Professor Gaddini." Pir Ferit's voice sounded thin and wavery, but he seemed wide awake. "I've heard much of you."

"From someone in particular?"

"Ah, no, not from any individual, no. I am familiar with your scholarly work."

Sophia waited, but Pir Ferit said nothing more.

"I've heard you may be able to assist with my current research," Sophia said. Because Holmes had pointed her to Ferit, she assumed Holmes had also somehow brought her collaboration with Tara to Ferit's attention.

"Perhaps I may."

Sophia paced the width of her office, telephone cord trailing behind her, frustrated by the need for indirectness. But she knew firsthand the danger to those who became involved with Tara.

"Perhaps? What would you need to know to determine whether you can?"

"There is no way to make a determination through a telephone discussion," Pir Ferit said. "But, as you may have learned, I am a private collector, and one of my collections may include an item of interest to one of your students."

The website hadn't said anything about him being a collector, but it wasn't surprising in a historian. "What type of item?" Near her closed door, Sophia paused. Windows rattled down the hall.

"It must be seen in person to be appreciated," Pir Ferit said.

"You're suggesting I send my student overseas knowing nothing more about you or what might be in your collection?" Sophia crossed to her couch and sat, fingers pressed to her forehead.

"Oh, no. That would be most unwise. Especially as other students have traveled to seek my counsel and been most disappointed."

"Others? How many?"

Sophia hadn't realized any of the other young women had acted on their claims of being pregnant virgins beyond speaking to the press.

"Two visited me," Pir Ferit said. "Separately. Two others called but never visited."

"How did they learn of you?" Had Erik Holmes written to them as well?

"In different fashions."

"Why could you not help them?" Sophia asked.

"It is difficult to say."

Sophia paced the room again, struggling for some topic Ferit might be willing to discuss.

"Is your collection related to the Koca Mustafa Pasha Mosque?" she asked.

"Ah, you know its history, yes? That it was once the women's church?"

"Is that why you believe you can help?"

"I cannot say at this point."

*Wonderful. I'm learning nothing from a man I don't know about a collection that may not exist.*

"It seems you can't speak about anything," Sophia said.

"If you travel here, I will make myself available to speak with you in person and can be more informative."

"Travel there? When do you suggest I do that?"

"Immediately, as the window closes on its own time. And my age is advanced."

Sophia ran her fingers over Holmes' letter as if the feel of the heavy linen paper and the raised watermark could tell her what to do. Visiting the Sufi based on some cryptic comments could be fruitless. And not inexpensive. Sophia was reasonably comfortable financially thanks to the modest success of her books and her professor's salary, but her budget was far from unlimited.

"Come," Pir Ferit said, "and we will speak. If you believe I may help then perhaps you may send your student."

The calendar on the wall behind Sophia's desk nearly glowed in the lamplight, the dates of her aunt's visit highlighted in yellow. "It would be difficult to travel now."

"This is important work, yes?"

"Yes."

"So travel. And Dr. Gaddini? Tell no one of your plans."

Sophia asked the man a few more questions, to little effect. In the middle of one of his answers, her office door creaked behind her. She pivoted her chair.

Cyril Woods stood in her doorway.

Erik Holmes gripped the television remote and stepped closer to the grand piano. Tall, with a lean, muscular build and well-defined facial features, he wore a charcoal Armani suit and a light gray Dolce & Gabbana dress shirt with an open collar. Premature silver flecked his blond hair.

On the flat screen television above the piano, the St. Louis Arch loomed over a pregnant Tara Spencer. Erik froze the image as Tara clutched her mid-section and doubled over in pain.

*What were you thinking, Tara? Right that instant, after you told those lies?*

A chime sounded from the hotel suite's hallway. Erik's twin brother, Henrik, entered the sitting room. Erik hit the off button.

Henrik set his whiskey on the polished side table next to a vase of fresh lilies. "Ah, your obsession."

"Hardly."

Henrik lowered himself into an Art Deco armchair. Years of drinking and fine dining had puffed his nose and lips, and his jaw blurred into his neck. He looked years, rather than minutes, older than Erik. His suit, though clean and of good quality, looked as if he'd crumpled it at the bottom of his closet before putting it on. "Where is Ms. Spencer now?"

Erik shrugged.

"Oh, come, I'm not your competition. Or your enemy."

"That's debatable generally speaking." To Erik's frustration, his brother seemed determined to prove the truism Erik had learned in business school – the first generation earned the money, the second spent it, and the third became destitute. Erik intended that his nieces and nephews not become destitute, yet for now he had greater concerns. "But as to Tara Spencer, she's in a remote location."

Henrik took the remote and hit play. "But not too remote."

"Not at all," Erik said.

On screen, Tara crumpled to the ground.

"I'm sorry, what?"

Phone pressed to her ear, Tara maneuvered to a spot in front of Track 510 inside Chicago Union Station, angling between a woman pushing a double stroller and an older man walking with a cane. She'd spent the holiday season with her biological father, Ray Tigue, in Oklahoma City. His band had a two-week gig there at a bar and grill. Christmas lunch had included Fat Elvis Fries – sweet potato fries drowned in peanut butter sauce, topped with peppered bacon and dried banana chips. Not a traditional holiday, but fun. It was the first Christmas Tara had ever spent with Ray, the first time she'd spent more than a few hours with him, and the first time he'd met Fimi. At least something good had come from being exiled from Willow Springs. And she'd felt relatively safe, for Ray appeared nowhere in public records as her father. Her mom had listed "unknown" in that slot on the birth certificate, angry at Ray for deserting her when he learned she was pregnant. To the world, Tara's dad was Pete Spencer, who'd married her mom when Tara was three.

After the visit with Ray, Tara and Fimi had stayed with a friend of a friend of Sophia's in Kansas City. Now she was headed to Brookfield, Illinois, a near western suburb of Chicago, to a temporarily vacant apartment.

"This is why I thought we should speak in my office." Dr. Lei sounded tinny through the cell phone.

"I know. I really appreciate your doing this on the phone." Tara shifted Fimi, who was settled into a baby carrier wrapped around Tara's front, so she could put her right hand over her ear to block the overhead announcements and clanging train bells. "What were the results again? I don't understand."

Dr. Lei had handled the arrangements for Fimi's genetic testing. Tara wanted to know at least as much as the Brotherhood did about her child.

"Let me explain another way," Dr. Lei said. "Do you know how cloning works?"

"Cloning. No." Tara shifted her backpack, which sat on the station floor, so it wedged more tightly between her feet, making it harder for someone to swipe. She glanced at the clock above the departure monitors. She had twenty minutes until her train to Brookfield.

"A clone is created from the cell of the original animal," Dr. Lei said. "Or person, if we were advanced enough to clone an entire human being. The nucleus of the cell is placed inside a shell ovary and implanted in a female uterus. There, just like a being conceived naturally, it grows and divides into a zygote, an embryo, a fetus, etc., until it is born. No other being's cell is involved. So the clone, which refers only to how the being is created, not what it is – is really an identical twin of the original animal or person, just born however many years later."

"Okay."

"Fimi is like that. She is your twin."

"My twin. My twin? What does that mean, my twin?" Tara said.

"Genetically, she is your twin, but born twenty-one years later. It's as if she has no father, as if you were cloned."

Tara put a hand against the concrete block wall behind her as a wave of dizziness washed through her. She looked down at her baby. Her baby who was...herself?

"Tara? Are you well?"

Despite her shock, Tara felt a tiny bit of relief. *At least I'm not crazy. There really is no father.* Since she'd discovered her pregnancy, Tara had wondered if somewhere along the line she'd lost her mind. If she'd engaged in intercourse and become pregnant without remembering it. It seemed impossible, but no more impossible than her pregnancy in the first place.

"Tara?"

*But cloning?*

"I'm here," Tara said.

"I've never encountered such a thing," Dr. Lei said. "Though, of course, I never encountered anyone in your situation."

From the time Tara had learned she was pregnant, Dr. Lei had been supportive and reserved judgment regarding how the pregnancy had happened. Tara had never been sure what Dr. Lei personally believed, but she was grateful for her doctor's willingness to be open to some possibility other than that Tara was lying about never having had sex.

"There have been some experiments with animals and parthenogenesis – an ova generating a new being without fertilization," Dr. Lei said. "But nothing remotely applicable to humans."

"Could it – I mean, could someone have cloned me without my knowing it?" Tara felt grateful that the noise and people rushing around her helped her maintain a semi-private conversation.

"My knowledge of cloning is not vast," Dr. Lei said, "but I asked this of the geneticist with whom I spoke. First, to date, no one has successfully cloned a human, though progress has been made with animals and with individual human organs."

"But if someone's been working on it in secret, maybe it's possible," Tara said.

"My colleague said nearly any cell could be used to create a clone, so obtaining the necessary genetic material would not be difficult. But the cell, once it began to divide, would need to be implanted in your uterus. It is unlikely the implantation would take the first time – much as is the case with in vitro fertilization where many embryos are created, then a number implanted with the idea that most will not survive. I would have expected you to have several miscarriages before one pregnancy could be carried to term. And the actual implantation would be difficult to accomplish without your knowledge. If you were put to sleep and drugged so you would not remember, at the very least, you'd be aware of a gap in time. I won't say it's impossible, but it's highly improbable."

"Right." Tara felt her lunch rising in her esophagus. The station's mixed smells of diesel and floor wax weren't helping.

"There are other unexpected findings. We collected DNA samples from your mother, her mother, Ray Tigue, and Ray's parents. Ray Tigue is only a twenty percent match to your DNA. And to Fimi's, since hers is identical to yours."

Fimi fussed, and Tara bounced her a little. " Twenty percent. And that means?"

"Biologically, you are not the child of Ray Tigue."

"Not Ray's child?" Along with the confusion over what the results could mean, Tara felt overwhelmed with loss. She hadn't spent a lot of time with Ray over the years, but the recent visit had meant a lot to both of them. Ray had shown her a scrapbook he'd kept of all the important events in her life, including those that happened during the times when she'd thought he'd completely forgotten her.

"You are genetically related to him, but you are not his child. Based on the comparisons to him and his parents, he might perhaps be an uncle or cousin once removed."

"Oh."

"Tara, is anyone with you? I'm concerned about you receiving all this news alone."

"I'm in a train station."

"Is someone meeting you?" Dr. Lei asked.

"Yes. No. Eventually. At my next stop, after my next train, I mean." Tara felt too warm. She unbuttoned her heavy winter coat and pressed her hand, which felt cold, against her forehead. "Could we go back to this clone thing? I'm thinking it must be a mistake. The lab made a mistake." Tara had a sense of *déjà vu*, this was so much like the conversation she'd had with Dr. Lei the year before about her positive pregnancy tests.

"I had the samples rechecked, I had the tests rerun," Dr. Lei said. "Fimi is a clone."

# 7

After washing the dishes she'd bought in the Helping Hand Thrift Store down the street, Tara posted photos of her siblings, mom and dad, friends, and Fimi on the apricot-colored refrigerator, using magnets the previous tenant had left. She ran her fingers over one of Megan playing harmonica, a stuffed Snoopy at her side, wishing she could see her little sister just one more time. All the photos both made Tara smile and left a hollow feeling in her heart. After the attack on Kali, she felt afraid to visit home or encourage family to visit her, and she hadn't figured out what she and Fimi were going to do other than hide out in the tiny Brookfield apartment.

She wished she had baby pictures of herself to compare to Fimi. But, realistically, it probably wouldn't tell her much about whether Fimi was her clone. Baby photos were all over the family house in Rock Hill, and she and her sisters and brothers all looked nearly interchangeable, despite that genetically Tara was "only" their half-sister. She'd never thought of it that way, though. Pete Spencer had raised her since she'd been three years old. He was her dad. Ray Tigue's contribution was limited to occasional birthday cards and Tara having skin with an olive cast and hair a few shades darker than her sibs did. And now, perhaps, after she'd finally connected with him, it turned out he hadn't contributed that.

Tara turned away from the photos and tried Sophia's phone. She reached voicemail for the fifth time in two days. She wished she could talk through the test results with Sophia, who always offered a thoughtful, calming perspective, before sharing them with anyone else. Tara had started to worry something had happened to her. It wasn't like her not to respond.

Tara phoned her mom next. She had to talk to someone. She told Lynette how the holiday visit with Ray had gone, and then explained the results about Fimi's DNA and Ray being only a twenty percent match.

"How did Dr. Lei do this test anyway?" Lynette Spencer said. "She can't have that at her fingertips."

"She sent it to someone she works with at a genetic project."

"And that person did it free? Just as a favor?" Lynette said.

"She said it's not so expensive as it used to be." Tara cracked the window overlooking the railroad tracks. The apartment's steam radiators made it hot even on a below-zero January morning. "It was something she wanted to do for me after all these years of treating our family."

"So she's a philanthropist."

"You've never mistrusted Dr. Lei before, Mom."

"No, I haven't. But what she's saying is impossible."

"A little like when I told you I was pregnant, but I'd never had sex with anyone?" Tara had tried hard to get past her mother's initial reaction to her pregnancy, but it still bothered her, partly because, even now, she suspected her mother doubted her. Lynette's next words confirmed it.

"That's different. I know I never slept with anyone but Ray Tigue before I met your dad."

"Sure. And you don't know what I did."

"Tara, I know what you told me, and I don't necessarily not believe you."

"There's a ringing endorsement."

"But I know for certain I never had sex with anyone other than Ray," Lynette said. "Not a brother of his, which he didn't have, not a cousin of his, which he also didn't have, not anyone. Just him. So he has to be your biological father."

"Well, he's not."

Pete Spencer stared through the picture window at the snow mounds across the driveway. He needed to shovel, or hound his son Nate into shoveling, before tomorrow so he could drive to work. But that meant getting out of his sweats – the same ones he'd slept in – and putting on his down jacket and gloves. A lot to do before stepping outside. Though tracking down Nate might be harder. Pete's older son rarely appeared at home these days other than to sleep. The five years of Megan's illness had both taken forever for Pete and passed in an instant, and now he faced four remaining children, three of them adults or nearly so, whose lives no longer seemed to intersect his.

He thought again about the two-month paid sabbatical his company had offered him. But Pete needed the job to get him out of bed in the morning.

"Pete? Are you there?" his mother asked.

Greta Spencer called every Sunday. Pete usually let Lynette talk to his mother, but Lynette had insisted he be the one to explain the news about Fimi's DNA tests.

"Yes," he said. "And yes, I talked to Father Saur about it." Father Gregory Saur was the parish pastor. "He still believes Tara became pregnant in the usual way and just can't accept the mistake she made."

"But what about the test results?" Greta said.

"He said science is advanced but there are still mistakes. Or Tara misunderstood the doctor."

The oddity of Fimi's DNA made it seem more likely to Pete that Tara had been telling the truth about being a virgin when she'd discovered she was pregnant, making him a worse parent for not completely believing her. But what he'd done, he'd done. Nothing could change it. Or change anything that had occurred in the last year. He turned away from the window, which left him face-to-face with a stack of overdue medical bills on the dining room table.

"That doesn't seem likely," Greta said. "She was pre-med after all. She understands science. How long has Father Saur known Tara anyway?"

"Since she was baptized."

"Father Saur can't have baptized her," Greta said.

"He did. You were there." Tara had been baptized not long after Pete and Lynette had married, and Lynette had converted to Catholicism.

"Surely that wasn't the same priest."

"He's been in our parish forever."

"Pastors are rotated every ten years. The Diocese doesn't let them stay in one place that long."

"Maybe it's different in St. Louis, Mom."

After the call, Pete headed for the couch to lie down. But a few minutes later, he roused himself and walked to the computer. He pushed the unpaid bills and late notices with their huge red letters aside. And began researching "Roman Catholic, pastors, rotation."

The intercom squawked. The linoleum floor crackled under Tara's feet as she crossed the kitchen area in two quick strides. She pressed the discolored plastic button. "Hello?" She was hoping for Sophia, who'd sent a five-word message that she'd be in touch soon. Other than that, Tara knew only that Sophia had taken personal leave, which was all her teaching assistant would tell Tara. Sophia had an elderly aunt. Tara worried something had happened to her. Plus, it had been three days since Tara talked to anyone other than Fimi and the clerk at the local grocery store in person, so she longed for adult company. She'd been bundling up Fimi and taking walks just to get out of the apartment.

It was Tara's sister Kelly whose voice came through the intercom and who climbed the four flights to Tara's door.

Tara threw her arms around Kelly, her fears about having visitors momentarily eclipsed by joy. "Oh my God – what are you doing here? It's fantastic to see you."

"Merry Christmas. Really really late." Kelly set down a garbage bag full of presents.

"You're still in time." Tara waved toward the holiday lights she'd strung along the edges of the peeling kitchen cabinets and around the aging apricot-colored appliances to cheer the place. She didn't care that it was almost February, it made her feel a little bit at home. "You look awesome."

Her little sister also looked sophisticated. Kelly had gotten her hair cut into a bob similar to Tara's, but had done her makeup in a way that made her blue eyes pop and her cheekbones sharpen. The slouchy secondhand army coat she'd lived in throughout high school was gone. Now she wore a crimson wool coat with deep brown gloves, matching scarf, and close-fitting leather boots. Or faux-leather, Tara guessed, given the family's budget.

"Why didn't you tell me you were coming?" Tara said.

"I figured you might tell me not to." Kelly shrugged off her coat and brushed snow out of her hair. She'd lost a little weight, and now her build resembled Tara's, with none of their mother's plumpness. "And once I got on the road, I drove straight through. Made it in four-and-a-half hours."

Tara put her hands over her ears. "Don't tell me." Four-and-a-half hours meant Kelly had probably been speeding. In the snow and ice. And she'd only had her license for six months. "But, seriously, you just decided to come here?"

Kelly wedged her coat into Tara's tiny closet. "Yeah. It's just, it's not good at home, Tara. When Dad's not at work he just lies on the couch. Mom's hyper, Nate's out as much as he can be. Bailey's the closest to normal, but he spends a lot of time reading comic books in your attic apartment. He quit band, says he feels too sad to play his trumpet. All these presents have been in a bag for you by the door, and Dad keeps saying we'll ship them but no one ever does, and I just, well, I just had it."

That her dad had been okay with buying Christmas gifts, despite not otherwise celebrating the holiday, made Tara feel a little better. She got two mugs from the cabinet over the stove. "I'm sorry. Tea? I've got chai or lemon."

Kelly walked to the alcove where Fimi slept on her stomach in a playpen. "Coffee. She's beautiful. Has she been asleep long?"

"She just went down. She'll probably wake in an hour or so and you can say hi." Tara found her secondhand coffee maker and started a pot. She'd bought the coffee supplies in anticipation of Sophia visiting, she'd never gotten to like coffee herself. She hadn't known Kelly drank it.

Kelly checked inside the refrigerator. "Cream?"

"I usually have milk, but I just ran out."

"Black then." Kelly slid onto a counter stool next to Tara. "So what are you going to do?"

"About the milk?" Tara said.

Kelly punched her sister's upper arm. That at least seemed familiar. "Not the milk. Fimi. You. Life."

"I just got here a week ago."

"But you must have a plan. It's been more than a month since you left Willow Springs."

"Seriously?" Tara tried to adjust to the idea of her little sister drinking coffee and asking about her life plan. And felt at a loss as to how to answer. She hadn't been motivated to do anything during the last week. In the silence and solitude, it felt as if all the loss of the last year that she thought she'd dealt with–Megan's death, Cyril's betrayals, her ex-boyfriend and her best friend's rejection of her – had crashed in. "I don't, really. Before the break in Kali and I talked about getting an apartment together if SLU gave her enough of a scholarship, then I could finish school, too. Now the idea seems unbelieveably reckless, but at the time we both thought it might work."

"How much do you have left?"

"Of college?" The coffee had finished brewing, scenting the air with hazelnut. Tara put a cup of it and the sugar bowl in front of her sister, remembering Kelly's sweet tooth despite her insistence on black coffee. "A year, less the online class I'm taking now. I need to figure out the residency requirements though."

"But you haven't yet."

"No, I haven't, Mom. You have no idea what my life's been like."

Kelly stirred her coffee, though she hadn't added anything to it. "You haven't told me. You didn't tell me when you got pregnant. You told Nate, but not me."

"I never told Nate. He heard the way he hears things."

Nate was the second oldest of the siblings and was as quiet as the others were vocal, so he tended to be overlooked. Which resulted in people saying things around him without realizing he was listening.

"But you didn't talk to me about it. Ever," Kelly said.

"Of course I did."

"Not."

Tara tried to remember her conversations with Kelly the year before. Surely they'd discussed it at least once. But maybe they hadn't. With Megan so ill and needing so much from their parents, Tara had focused most of her attention on Bailey, who was the next youngest after Megan, when she'd been home.

"I'm sorry. Things spiraled out of control so quickly."

"I'm not trying to make you feel bad," Kelly said. "It was a crazy time. But I could stay with you and Fimi now. I'm done with high school. And I just, I really don't want to be at home. It's too hard."

"Done with school?" Tara stared at Kelly. "You're in your senior year. I couldn't have gotten that out of touch. You didn't drop out, did you? You didn't."

"Are you kidding? I finished half a year early. That's what I've been doing. Working on plays and taking extra classes and graduating early."

Tara squeezed her sister's hand. She'd always felt like a second mom to her sibs. Apparently she'd been just as clueless as mothers sometimes were about Kelly's life.

"Anyway, I'm not starting college until next fall," Kelly said. "I could stay with you for a while, help out. You're always changing your look. I can help with that – all my theater work was costumes and stage makeup."

"It's dangerous being with me. Look what happened to Kali."

"It's dangerous being your sibling," Kelly said. "Look what happened to Bailey. If I'm with you, at least I'll be in hiding. And I might be able to keep a better watch."

"It's cramped here. Wait'll you see the bathroom – when you sit on the toilet, your knees'll bump against the door."

"I'll fit in somewhere."

Tara's stomach clutched at the thought of everyone she loved in danger because of her. But Kelly was right, they already were. And no one outside the family knew where Tara lived now, other than Sophia. *Selfish, I'm being selfish.* But staying in one place, having her sister to spend time with, it would feel like a home. How good would that be?

Someone rapped on the door. Leaving the locks engaged and the chain on, Tara peered through the peephole, expecting a neighbor since she hadn't heard the vestibule buzzer.

This time it was Sophia. Her long black hair, which she usually combed out straight or gathered into a gold clip in the back, hung loose, the ends a bit ragged, and her skin, normally what Tara's grandmother would call peaches and cream, looked sallow.

"Are you all right?" Tara said as she opened the door.

"Yes, yes, I'm well." Sophia stripped off her gloves and laid them on the counter. "Kelly, good to see you." She turned back to Tara. "Tara, you must go to Istanbul."

# 8

From the third floor hotel window, with the dark sky beyond it, Busch Stadium looked bleak and cold. All the same, seeing it still made Tara smile, remembering when her Mom and Dad had taken her and her siblings to Cardinals' games before Megan's treatments had gotten too intense. After that, they'd still gone, but it was rare that the whole family could attend together.

Tara had the hotel room to herself. Kelly and Sophia had taken Fimi for a walk in the stroller through the Westin Hotel's wide and winding hallways. Tara held her cell phone, waiting for Dr. Lei to retrieve her file.

*So she's a philanthropist?*

Lynnette Spencer's words about Dr. Lei echoed in Tara's mind. Her mother often irked her, but she was often right, which irked Tara more. Tara knew from her genetics class that DNA analyses could run from a hundred dollars to a hundred thousand dollars.

"I asked only for comparisons to you, your parents and your grandparents," Dr. Lei said when she got back on the line, "and whatever other tests could be run given the budget. Happily, the request fell within a short-term grant covering children whose fathers were unknown, and who sought genetic testing at least in part to determine potential hereditary conditions. Be assured, no identifying information was provided with the samples."

"Where did this grant come from?" Tara asked.

"Not from government, if that's what concerns you. It's a relatively new private grant, funded last summer by the Genesis Foundation."

The name didn't mean anything to Tara, nor did the list of three trustees she later found on its website. She texted her brother Nate. He hardly qualified as a hacker, but he researched faster and found more information than anyone Tara knew, and he'd always helped her with computer issues.

Nate called back an hour later. Tara jumped out of the shower to answer. She sat on the edge of the tub, wrapped in a towel as they spoke, soaking in the warm steam that lingered in the bathroom.

"The IRS requires private foundations to make public disclosures about funding," Nate said, "but they don't need to do it on their websites. Genesis doesn't. The IRS also requires foundations to provide disclosures 'immediately' when you visit the office in person or within thirty days by mail."

"Where's the office?"

"About ten miles outside Scottsdale, Arizona."

Tara sighed.

"Don't freak," Nate said. "I got the info."

"How?"

"I'll tell you sometime when we're not on a cell."

Knowing about technology had made Nate slightly paranoid.

"So?" Tara said.

"The major, and only, contributor to the Genesis Foundation is the H.E.R. Holmes Company."

"A HAND." Thomas Stranyero pivoted on one heel to face the other two men in the small office. "One hand. That's the most the scrolls speak of."

Father Gregory Saur shifted in the straight-backed wooden chair, which was wedged in the corner. When Stranyero had arrived this morning he'd taken over the rectory, including Gregory's office, desk and dark leather armchair, but the silver-haired man from the Brotherhood of Andrew had spent most of the last hour pacing in the small area of open space in front of the desk. At least he'd allowed Gregory to sit in on the meeting this time rather than simply commandeering the space.

"This is barbaric. How could you lose control over this man, this deacon, or whatever his role is?" Gregory was finding it difficult to breathe. He liked Tara Spencer, though he doubted she'd believe that given the events of the past year. He didn't want to see her, or her child, suffer. And if the Brotherhood was so convinced she was deluded or lying about the conception of her child, he didn't see why they ought to suffer, and surely not on the scale that was being contemplated.

"For some, the line between devotion and fanaticism is thin," Stranyero said.

"Which is why orders like yours ought to be cautious."

"We are cautious," Stranyero said. "We're not perfect."

Gregory frowned. "And we're certain it will reach this point?"

"No, not certain," Stranyero said. "Not certain at all. Groups are predictable. Individuals are not."

A third man, Investigator Mullin, stood to the side of the desk. He held a long, narrow sword in one hand at his side, his broad shoulders stiff, his chin lifted in a way that set Gregory's teeth on edge, as if Mullin were challenging the world and felt certain he'd win. Throughout the meeting, Mullin had ignored Gregory completely and directed all his comments to Stranyero. Perhaps as it should be, as Gregory had a minor role in this matter and didn't belong to the Brotherhood. But Mullin's attitude did little to reassure him that Mullin, or the Brotherhood for that matter, had any real concern for Tara or her baby as people.

"I'm prepared." Mullin's orange-red hair seemed to blaze, giving him an evil look. Superstition, of course, this view of red-haired people, yet Gregory couldn't quite put it aside. Which probably had more to do with what he'd learned about Mullin's actions last summer than any lingering superstition. Gregory didn't need to wonder if Mullin was evil, he knew.

*No, I don't believe that, do I? He can't be evil if he's truly doing The Lord's work.*

The cynical side of Father Gregory Saur scoffed.

"You had better be," Gregory said. "I spoke to Pete Spencer. He's ready to do his part."

Since his daughter Megan's death, Pete had been visiting Gregory fairly regularly to talk about scripture. Understandably, Pete still seemed mired in grief, and Gregory had worried that he wouldn't be up to the task Gregory proposed. Instead, Pete had seized on the chance to act, though he'd been uncertain about what he'd say to his family.

Stranyero nodded. "Good."

Gregory turned his head away from the two men and stared at the giant crucifix hanging on the wall behind his desk. "How likely is it Mullin's skills will be necessary?"

Mullin raised his sword and looked at Gregory at last. "That depends."

"On what?"

"What Tara Spencer does next."

Like the converted warehouse condominiums in Sophia's Chicago neighborhood, the downtown St. Louis Westin had a loft feel, with large rooms and exposed high ceilings. The warm air blowing across her calves from the heat vent behind her took some of the chill from Sophia's body, but her hands still felt icy. She'd taken a walk after breakfast to clear her head before the meeting with Tara's family. Sophia felt certain visiting Pir Ferit could help Tara find the truth about her unusual pregnancy. But she didn't feel right advising Tara to do that without input from Tara's parents. At twenty-two, Tara didn't need their permission to travel, but they might offer valuable guidance.

*Or maybe I just want to share the responsibility with someone*, Sophia thought.

Tara's mother, Lynette Spencer, perched on an armchair near the dresser as Sophia explained about the letter from Erik Holmes. Lynette looked like she'd gained about ten pounds since Sophia had last seen her, making her face a bit rounder and her hips fuller. But she still had a soft, blond prettiness that contrasted Tara's olive complexion and wiry build. The only real similarity Sophia saw in the two women was in their almond-shaped, greenish-blue eyes and small, slightly tilted noses.

Tara's little brother Bailey sat on the bed farthest from Sophia, wearing headphones, absorbed in a computer game. He seemed to have recovered well from the trauma of the previous summer. Tara's college-aged brother Nate, thin like his sisters, drank coffee as he lounged in an armchair wedged into a corner, his feet resting on Bailey's bed. His casual pose didn't fool Sophia. When he'd come in, he'd scanned every inch of the room, and his eyes fixed intently on her when she described her reasons for traveling to Turkey.

In contrast, Tara's stepdad, Pete Spencer, stood with his back against one of the room's exposed concrete pillars, eyes fixed half a foot above Sophia's head, his mind clearly somewhere else. His hair, salt-and-pepper when Sophia had first met him at his daughter Megan's funeral, had turned stark white. Over the past five months his stomach had rounded slightly and his jawline softened. He still looked trim for a man in his late fifties, and he kept his shoulders squared, but the collar of his dress shirt had wilted, and the knees and bottom hems of his jeans were frayed, as if he were a college student rather than a CPA. Tara had mentioned that her grandfather on Pete's side was a military man who'd instilled in Pete a strong sense of discipline and order. That training seemed to be failing now.

"Pir Ferit claims to be a guardian of knowledge passed down from the time of Andrew of Crete, the martyr who supposedly had visions about pregnant virgins who lived and died after the time of Christ," Sophia said. "'Pir' is his title – loosely translated, it means 'old man' and often refers to a Sufi teacher. Pir Ferit says he can share that knowledge with one woman in his lifetime. He feels he must meet Tara in person to determine if she is the one."

Lynette leaned forward, her plump cheeks flushed. "So let him come here."

"He's quite old and in a wheelchair, and travel is difficult for him." Sophia had verified Pir Ferit's credentials, and that he suffered from disabling MS, through colleagues, taking nothing at face value. "Over the past four months, he says he met with two young women claiming to be pregnant virgins. He wasn't convinced either of them were the one he seeks."

Sophia had asked for the contact information for the women to confirm they'd returned home safely and to ask about their experiences, but the Sufi had refused to provide it. Which meant he'd likely protect Tara's privacy as well, but didn't help her confirm the visits.

"So what did you say that made him think Tara might be the one?" Lynette asked.

"I told him I believed she'd become pregnant in some supernatural way, but I didn't understand what that meant or why it had happened, and that I believed she'd been doing her best in an impossible situation. We also discussed my academic work, but I don't know if that had any influence."

Sophia suspected Pir Ferit simply followed his intuition upon meeting her.

Sufism included a high degree of mysticism, and he might very well trust his inner voice more than logic or reason. Or he might have ulterior motives for wanting to meet Tara, a possibility Sophia couldn't rule out, despite that nothing in his demeanor suggested it. In the end she, too, was relying on intuition, which made her uneasy. She was used to having more research upon which to base theories or recommendations.

Nate set his coffee on the nightstand. "How do you know he's not just some crazy guy with a thing about pregnant women?"

"I don't. But I've researched the writings of Andrew of Crete. Pir Ferit has documents that he's had quietly authenticated by experts, and those documents complement the ones I've seen. Together, the materials show Andrew devoted significant time to investigating reports, however ephemeral, of women who had allegedly become pregnant without intercourse."

"But Ferit didn't tell you anything concrete about what he could offer Tara." Lynette folded her arms over her chest and raised her chin.

"He insisted he needed to meet her first." Sophia glanced at Pete, but he stayed silent. Before this meeting, she'd been concerned about treading lightly so he wouldn't see her as a rival trying to usurp his, or Lynette's, role in Tara's life. Now she almost hoped he would become territorial or angry. It would show he felt connected to Tara. Sophia's own parents had been musicians who rambled from place to place and seemed perplexed at having a child to look after. They'd been kind but distant. Sophia had the impression Tara had been much closer to her mom and dad, and her dad's withdrawal must leave Tara feeling unmoored. On Tara's behalf, she hoped Pete would jump in.

But it was Lynette who spoke. "I don't see any reason Tara should go."

"It's her best – her only, at this point – chance to learn more about the origin of her pregnancy."

"It's true, mom." Tara said. She sat on the bed near Bailey, one hand resting on his ankle as he played his computer game. She shifted position to face her mother. "Nanor has theories, but staying at Willow Springs didn't do anything but endanger everyone there. I don't know how to build a life without knowing why this happened, why Fimi's here. I don't know if I can build a life. We'll always be looking over our shoulders, always be afraid. Of other people. Of the future. So it's worth it to me to talk with this man."

"And there's another reason," Sophia said, "that we believe Tara may be the one Pir Ferit seeks. It relates to the DNA finding that Fimi seems to be Tara's clone or twin. If that's so, and I recognize this is speculative, perhaps Fimi, like Tara, could or will become pregnant on her own. With another Fimi. Or a third Tara, if you look at it that way." Sophia twirled her grandmother's wedding ring, which she wore on the index finger of her right hand. She felt uncomfortable venturing so far into guesswork, but it did tie together what she'd heard from the Sufi.

Pete blinked and straightened. "That's a bit far-fetched. But if it's true, what does it have to do with Pir Ferit?"

Sophia felt relieved Pete at last had shown some interest in the discussion.

"He told me the truth could only be revealed in the presence of the one who will live forever. I didn't know about the DNA results then, so it made no sense. But now –"

Nate looked at his sister. "Tara to the infinite power. Sounds like living forever to me."

# 9

The news about the trip to Istanbul shocked Pete, though he thought he'd hidden it well. Based on what Father Saur had told him when they'd spoken two days ago, he'd expected this meeting to be about a completely different topic, one he'd done his best to force out of his mind so he could listen to Sophia. He wondered if Father Saur knew about Pir Ferit. If he did, Pete couldn't understand why the pastor hadn't shared the information.

"Unfortunately, I can't accompany Tara to Istanbul," Sophia said. "My teaching and conference schedule will not allow me to travel again until this summer. More important, my going would draw attention to her trip. But I've arranged with a colleague in Istanbul to be a guide and resource."

Pete stepped away from the concrete pillar, ready to offer to take a sabbatical from work. He didn't want Tara in a foreign country alone with the baby, no matter what he'd promised Father Saur.

"I might be able to get off work," Nate said.

"There's another wrinkle," Sophia said. "Pir Ferit can't reveal the truth to any woman who travels with men."

Lynette stood and made a dismissive gesture with one hand. "This is ridiculous. It's like a fairy tale. Or a cartoon."

Pete nodded. Part of what he loved about his wife was her bluntness. It wasn't always welcomed by others, but she often expressed his own view while he refrained, less willing to appear to step on viewpoints or beliefs different from his own.

Bailey glanced up from his game, noticing his parents' agitation. Tara smiled at him and mouthed, "It's OK, squirt."

Sophia nodded at Lynette. "I understand your reaction. I felt suspicious too, sure Pir Ferit was concocting conditions to suit himself. But the documents I read include instructions that the guardian must not reveal the truth to any woman who travels with men. My guess is this is due to fears about the Brotherhood of Andrew. Pir Ferit claims the Brotherhood – as opposed to Andrew of Crete himself – is unconnected with Pir Ferit's mission and poses a danger to Tara."

"And Pir Ferit doesn't," Nate said.

"I got no sense that Pir Ferit is dangerous," Sophia said, "though Tara must be cautious. Of the Brotherhood given what its people have done in the past, and of Pir Ferit because we don't know what agenda he might have. I argued at length with him about the difficulty his restriction might cause if Tara didn't want to travel alone. Pir Ferit remained polite but resolute to the end."

"I'll take some time from work." Lynette met Pete's eyes. "It'll be fine."

Pete and Lynette had taken out a second mortgage on the house to pay for experimental treatment for Megan. And Lynette had no paid time off coming. But Pete wouldn't protest if Lynette went. He owed Tara that, no matter what he thought about how she'd handled her claim of being a pregnant virgin. Or perhaps because of what he thought. The bills would just need to wait.

"Mom, no," Tara said. She moved to stand next to her mother. "You took off so much time the last five years with Megan, and so many bills still need to be paid. Anyway, I won't be alone. Kelly wants to go with me."

"What?" Pete moved further into the room, eyes shifting between his daughters, wishing they were small again and he could carry them away from harm. He knew it wasn't as if they were proposing to travel to a war zone. One of his coworkers had attended a family wedding in Istanbul the year before. But it wasn't as safe as the United States.

"High school and college students travel all the time to Europe to backpack or study there." Kelly put her hands on her hips and stared straight at Pete.

Lynette frowned. "Europe, not Turkey."

"Half of Istanbul's in Europe," Kelly said. "It's the only city on two continents."

Half an hour later, Pete and Lynette hadn't managed to change Kelly's mind. It turned out she could be every bit as determined as Tara had ever been. Perhaps more so, Pete thought, because for so long, as the middle child, she'd quietly gone her own way. She did as she pleased because she never caused any trouble and because the family had so many other concerns. He also failed in his efforts to persuade Tara to leave Fimi in the U.S. She didn't want the baby out of her sight. Pete understood. He had repeated dreams where he took Megan to the park and let her run to the water fountain without him, then never found her again. That being with a child didn't prevent danger was something Tara refused to hear.

He told himself that Kelly, Tara, and the baby would be fine. Sophia promised again to connect them with colleagues who could keep an eye out for them.

"There's one more thing to tell you," Sophia said. "Cyril Woods came to see me."

*At last*, Pete thought. This was what Father Saur had told him about. He tensed, uncertain what he'd say to his family to justify what he planned to do.

"Huh." Nate rocked his chair until its back rested against the wall. "So what's the doubting deacon got to say?"

"He's not a deacon." Tara's quick response surprised Pete. He'd assumed her feelings for Woods were gone. If they weren't, all the more reason for him to pursue the path he'd chosen. "Or maybe he is."

"He's not," Sophia said. "Yet. The Brotherhood plans to send him back to Armenia, to Our Lady of Sorrows. It's the church supposedly attended by a woman in the seventh century who was a pregnant virgin."

"That's why he took Tara there before, right?" Pete said. "Or started to."

"Yes, though – and Tara can correct me if I'm wrong – he was acting on his own then, without Brotherhood approval, and they never reached the church. The Brotherhood leaders supposedly are now convinced that hidden in or near the church is a document written to guide the young woman, and that she hid it before she was killed by an invading army."

Finally, Pete was able to ask what he'd been wondering during the entire meeting. "Could this relate to the information Pir Ferit claims to have?"

"I don't know," Sophia said. "I didn't mention either man to the other, as we don't know who is or isn't an ally."

"Why didn't the Brotherhood give Cyril that information last spring?" Lynette said.

"Maybe they did," Nate said, "and he held it back. What are the odds?"

"Why would Cyril share this with you?" Lynette asked Sophia.

"He claimed he wanted to tell Tara, but didn't know how to contact her directly," Sophia said. "He also said he'd tell her about whatever he finds before he tells the Brotherhood. If he informs them at all."

Pete nodded. Father Saur had said the Brotherhood didn't trust Cyril, and apparently that was for good reason. Pete didn't trust him either, but he asked Sophia, "Do you believe him? You're in the best position to judge. You've spent more time with him than any of us other than Tara." His eyes flickered toward Tara. "And you don't harbor any feelings for him to cloud your judgment."

Tara glared at Pete. He didn't flinch. If she felt angry at him, all the better, it might help her keep Cyril's past actions in mind.

"I don't know," Sophia said. "I only spent an hour or so with him. But I don't see what he gains from sharing the plans with me."

"Maybe he thought you'd convince Tara to go with him to Armenia again," Nate said.

"I'm not going anywhere with him," Tara said. "Which in a way is too bad, because we have no way to be sure he'll really pass on whatever he finds."

Pete saw the perfect opening. "I'll make sure," he said. "I'll go to Armenia."

# 10

"You need to stop him," Tara said. She and Lynette faced each other across the two queen sized beds. Everyone else had gone to the hotel restaurant for lunch, but Tara had asked her mother to stay and talk for a few minutes.

"How do you suggest I do that, Tara?" Lynette said. "I couldn't stop Kelly from going with you. Or you from taking Fimi."

Tara swallowed hard. Taking Fimi to Istanbul might not be the wisest idea, but she felt sure she needed to go, and she couldn't leave her baby alone after what had happened the last time she'd done so. She crossed her arms over her chest and focused on her mother. "How you always do." She felt sure her mom could change her dad's mind.

Lynette narrowed her eyes. "What's that supposed to mean?"

"You've always decided things," Tara said. "That we went to Catholic grade school, how much we got for allowance, what our curfews were."

Quick footsteps and kids' voices sounded from the hotel hallway. A family on vacation, probably. Tara wished she were here for a break from everything.

"First," Lynette said, "those are things that had to do with you kids, not with what your dad did. Second, those were joint decisions. I may have been the one who communicated them, but we worked them out together. And don't raise your eyebrows at me. Ask him if you don't believe me."

Tara had her doubts. Her mother had always been more vocal than her dad, and it seemed to her that her mother always got her way. But she didn't know what her parents discussed in private, and she'd certainly learned over the last year that relationships were rarely what they seemed, including to the people who were in them.

Tara leaned back against the wall and almost bumped her head on the bottom edge of the abstract framed print that hung there. "Fine, okay. But there must be something you can say. I don't want Dad going to Armenia with Cyril. Who knows what Cyril's planning to do there. Or what his intentions are overall."

"That's exactly your dad's point."

"But what if he threatens Dad or hurts him?" Tara said.

"Your dad can take care of himself."

"Really?" Tara walked around the beds to stand closer to Lynette. "Cyril's over thirty years younger and was actually in the military. Recently. At least, that's what he told me."

"And everything he tells you is true."

"Of course not. But seriously, Mom, if Cyril wanted to hurt Dad, could Dad stop him?"

A shadow crossed Lynette's face. "You think Cyril wants to harm your dad? Physically?"

"No. I don't know." Tara sank onto the bed. "Considering the things he's done..."

"Tara, if you believe he'd harm your dad, you need to tell me. Your dad's convinced that since Cyril let Bailey go, and he voluntarily went with the police, and he never attacked you, that he's not violent. Troubled, but not violent."

All her experiences with Cyril flipped through Tara's mind. If she said Cyril was violent, and certainly there were things he had done that would justify saying it, her dad might not go with him. But did she really believe it? Tara sighed. "I'm more worried about Cyril messing with his head."

If Cyril said he believed Tara's pregnancy was divine, that would contradict the Catholic Church. Tara resented that her dad's faith was more important to him than anything, including her, but she didn't know if he'd survive if he lost it. Yet for all she knew, the goal of the trip was to uncover something that could be twisted to make her look like a liar or delusional, which would confirm her dad's worst fears about her. Her stomach twisted into a knot.

Lynette sat next to Tara. "Your dad is struggling. With a lot. But this is the first time I've heard him say more than two or three sentences in a row since Megan died. It's the first time he's wanted to do anything. The plane ticket will be expensive, but he's been offered a paid sabbatical, and we'll manage."

"I don't trust Cyril."

"You trusted him enough to sleep with him."

Tara gritted her teeth. "Thanks, Mom. Thanks for pointing that out, it never occurred to me before how stupid I was to have sex with him."

"Tara, I'm just saying—"

"Yes, right. Got it."

Lynette took her hand. "I'm just saying that you must have seen something good in him. Maybe it's there somewhere, whatever you saw."

Tara stared at the gray sky outside the window. "Maybe. But with Cyril, I'm not sure that makes a difference."

~

"What is it you think you're doing?" Tara said. She'd called Cyril from the hotel room at the number he'd given Sophia. She figured if he had ways of tracing phones, he already knew where Sophia was, and would have guessed Tara would be with her, so there was no point in employing elaborate means to hide her location. It was the first time they'd spoken since the day of Fimi's kidnapping.

"Tara? Tara, how are you?" He sounded happy to hear from her despite her antagonistic tone.

"Thrilled," Tara said. "How else would I be with my dad about to spend who knows how long with you."

"What are you talking about?"

Tara walked to the window. Below her, a crowd of what looked like college students exited the subway at Pine Street. "My dad going with you to Armenia. What else would I be talking about?"

"You dad's coming with me?"

"You didn't know?"

"I – no, I never heard anything about that," Cyril said. "How did it come about?"

"He volunteered. When Sophia told us you planned to go."

"Then why would you think I knew about it?"

"It seems odd to me that my dad, who has barely gotten off the couch other than to go to work since Megan's death, now wants to travel to Armenia. I figured the Brotherhood of Andrew had something to do with it. Or you did."

"Why aren't you asking your dad?"

Tara pressed her forehead against the window. It felt cool against her skin. "He didn't want to talk about it. He doesn't talk to me much."

"I'm sorry."

"I didn't call to get sympathy. I called to see what you're planning to do in Armenia."

"Exactly what I told Dr. Gaddini. The Brotherhood finally believes me that there's some evidence or information, maybe a document, about the Armenian virgin mother at Our Lady of Sorrows church. I want to be the one to find it. For you. I can't say much more than that on the phone, but please believe me. I'm trying to make up for everything I did."

"I don't know if that's possible."

"I plan to try regardless."

"Did you suggest my dad come with you?" Tara said.

"I didn't. This surprises me as much as you."

Tara studied the people walking on the sidewalk below. People who probably had never had a conversation like this, though she knew she was far from the only person who didn't know whether to trust someone who'd betrayed her.

"Tara, think about it. Setting aside everything else and considering only our personal history, is your father someone I'd really want to spend a lot of time with? I couldn't think of anyone I'd feel more uncomfortable around."

"I'm sure it will be uncomfortable. He's going specifically to keep an eye on you."

"I don't blame him. But Tara, are you sure that's the only reason he's coming?"

SAGUN HALEL HAD the smallest of the Security offices at Willow Springs, with just enough space for a long computer table behind her and a shorter one in front of her with a visitor chair wedged between it and the door. Kali kept her arms close to her sides and her legs pressed together as she sat so she wouldn't knock over any of the stacks of materials next to her.

"Nothing's wrong with our server," Sagun said. "And I'm not finding any emails – sent or incoming – caught in the spam filter or any tracks showing anything's been deleted. Something could be going on at Tara's end. She's done her best to make her IP addresses untraceable, right?"

"Yes, I believe so." Kali held her tablet in her lap. Sagun had sent her a few test emails from different addresses to be sure she didn't have any issues. "She said something about her brother Nate rerouting communications or using proxies so it's hard to track her physical location through her email."

Sagun twirled a section of her long black hair around her index finger. "Given the way Tara left, maybe she's purposely staying out of touch. She seemed concerned about not exposing anyone at Willow Springs to more danger. The attack on you really shook her."

"What did she say exactly?" Kali asked.

"That she was sorry she'd underestimated the Brotherhood."

"I wasn't hurt that badly."

"As it turns out. But the doctors were full of doom and gloom the first day."

"So I've been told," Kali said.

Nanor had been strangely silent about Kali's injuries and recovery. The doctors had expressed amazement, as had the nurses. Kali believed them, because she had no reason not to, about how bad her condition had been. But since she'd awakened feeling good, with no awareness of being in a coma, she couldn't identify with the "miraculous" recovery. At Willow Springs, Nanor downplayed the extent of Kali's injuries to everyone, including Kali, and Kali didn't know why.

Kali twisted sideways in the chair so she could face Sagun more directly. "Did you see me? Right after the attack."

"I did. You looked very bad." Sagun glanced at her monitor, probably checking the time or thinking of some other task she needed to accomplish. Diedre's mother had improved somewhat after the holiday, but was in critical condition again, and Diedre had left for the hospital the day before. The Security staff was small, and their boss' absence left all of them with extra work, though no one complained.

Kali pulled on her jacket. "Thank you for taking the time to check. Each day, I grow more concerned. It's not like Tara to disappear with no word."

"Maybe she has a good reason." Sagun clicked a few keys, and the view on the monitor behind her changed to the Willow Springs gated parking area where residents left their cars and retrieved golf carts to drive within the community. "Maybe she doesn't want to share whatever it is she's doing."

"Maybe."

The weather was warm for early February – nearly seventy – and Kali left her jacket unzipped as she walked to the trailer where she lived with Nanor. It was possible Tara didn't want to share her current activities with Kali, Nanor, or anyone. But that didn't explain why she'd leave without saying anything. Kali wouldn't have asked her to share anything she didn't want to. It also didn't explain why she wasn't responding to email.

Which left Kali with the thought that Sagun was missing something. Or Sagun knew something she wasn't telling, and Kali was determined to figure out what it was.

~

"Scary," Kelly said.

Tara looked over her sister's shoulder. "Oh."

A thin, viscous film coated the faucets, and rust circled the drain of the pedestal sink in the closet-sized hotel bathroom. Grime streaked across the floor tiles, with what might be flecks of feces near the toilet. The sewage smell made both sisters gag. They backed away.

"I've never wished so much I could stand and pee," Kelly said.

"No kidding."

"We could stay with Sophia's friend," Kelly said.

Tara shook her head. They'd texted Sophia's colleague upon arrival and promised to check in periodically, but anyone looking for Tara would no doubt monitor Sophia's connections. Despite how dragged out she felt from the long flight, and that the bathroom turned her stomach, they couldn't risk it.

"I know, I know," Kelly said.

Kelly left to talk to the manager about getting the bathroom cleaned. Tara bounced Fimi, who'd been fussing, and stared out the window. It felt good to stand after so long in the cramped airplane seat. The amount of traffic in Instanbul surprised her. Mid-sized cars and small commercial trucks, which she'd learned were called LCVs here, crowded the streets. The skyline was a mix of old and new. It included domes, spires, and ancient buildings, but many of the office complexes and skyscrapers would have looked at home in downtown St. Louis.

The door slammed. Tara spun around, but it was only Kelly.

"They're sending someone," Kelly said.

"Good."

"Here, let me." Kelly took the baby and sat on one of the two twin beds. "You know, I was thinking on the flight. Fimi seems really normal."

"What?"

"I just mean, now I've spent a lot of time with her, and I see that she's a regular baby. Not a superbaby or anything. Seems stupid, right? Like I thought she might be performing miracles at five months old. But especially with this odd thing about her being your twin, I thought she might be extraordinary in some other way, too."

Tara sat next to her sister. "It's not stupid. Before she was born, I had nightmares that she'd come out and have horns or a tail or red eyes. I didn't really think that, but I was afraid there'd be something wrong with her. I loved her. And it felt like this unknown being had just taken over my life."

"Well, she did. In a way. Not her fault, but she did. So it must be a relief that she acts just like any other baby."

Tara took a breath. She'd told no one about the incident with Kali. But her sister had traveled all this way with her, she deserved to know whatever Tara knew. "There could be something. I'm not sure."

"What?"

"It's probably nothing." Tara's pulse raced, and the room, tiny and jammed with the two twin beds and a crib, seemed to close in on her. She trusted Kelly, but sharing her thoughts out loud made her half-formed fears more real.

"What's probably nothing?" Kelly said.

"Something might have happened." Tara explained about Kali's recovery. And then about how she'd felt a sort of power immediately after giving birth, and the effects it might have had before it faded.

"But that's good, right?" Kelly said. "If Fimi can help people heal? Either through you or by herself?"

"I don't know. She's different enough already. And if people thought she could heal injuries or illnesses, she'd never be left alone. If the Brotherhood wants to know her genetic makeup now, everyone would want to know it then."

Kelly gazed toward the window, eyes blank, not seeming to see the tall shiny buildings outside. "Still."

"What?" Tara said.

"Imagine if she could help someone like Megan. A child with cancer like Megan."

Sophia's colleague had suggested a café in the Fatih district where Tara and Kelly could meet Pir Ferit. By the time they arrived, he'd already maneuvered his wheelchair to a corner table and ordered tea. Intricate red and orange designs covered the bottom half of the teapot the waiter brought on a tray with matching clear tulip-shaped tea glasses that had no handles. Two sugar cubes came with each glass, but Pir Ferit told them they might want to add three, as he'd ordered the black tea *koyu* – very strong.

Tara kept her coat on, though unbuttoned, as did Kelly. The café looked warm, with its orange walls and sturdy wood tables and chairs, but the door to the street trembled from the wind, and cold air rushed in whenever anyone entered. Pir Ferit never shivered, despite wearing only heavy brown pants woven of textured cloth and a matching long-sleeved overgarment. His forehead was high due to a receding hairline, but not nearly as wrinkled as Tara had expected based upon him being in his nineties. He smiled at Tara, a smile that reached his eyes, which were clear and focused beneath grayish white eyebrows.

"So, tell me why you chose to travel so far to see this old man."

Tara strained to hear Pir Ferit's soft voice above the other patrons' conversations and the tinking of spoons against tea glasses.

"I'm looking for answers. About my baby." Tara held Fimi in her lap, bundled up and mostly hidden from view. "Whether she has any special role in the world. Why and how she was conceived."

Pir Ferit cocked his head to one side. "You feel the need for an explanation."

"Wouldn't you?"

"I do not always find explanation important." The Sufi elder drank his tea by holding the glass at the top, above the level of the hot liquid, with his thumb and index finger. If his MS made it difficult for him to keep his hand steady while doing so, he didn't show it. He returned his glass to the precise spot on the red table runner from which he'd lifted it. "If you learn something you believe is positive about your daughter or that ought to make others feel good about her, will that help you?"

"I think so."

"How?"

Tara wrapped one hand around her glass to warm it and inhaled the tea's bitter citrus marmalade fragrance. "Maybe by making other people less likely to want to harm her." As soon as she said it, though, Tara realized that raised the same issue as the chance that Fimi could heal people did.

Pir Ferit studied her face, as if waiting for her to complete her train of thought before he spoke again. Then he asked, "If you learn something positive, do you expect others will believe you?"

"I don't know," Tara said.

"And if you learn something that makes others fear her, will that help you?"

Tara tightened her hold on Fimi. "What could I learn that would make people fear her?"

"I do not suggest anything is to be learned of that nature. I merely wish you to consider whether it is always preferable to know than not to know. After all, your culture's creation story shows Adam and Eve being punished for eating from the tree of knowledge."

**Second Hurricane in as Many Weeks Hits Florida**

MIAMI - Just as residents of Boca Raton resettled into their city following Hurricane Harold, emergency broadcasts urged them to evacuate once more. Weary citizens hurriedly packed belongings, but many did not do so quickly enough and remained in the danger zone when Hurricane Isis hit. Multiple hurricanes within a short time in Florida are not unprecedented, but Boca Raton averages 5.42 years between direct hurricane hits.

The Deputy Director of the Center for Remote Sensing of Southeastern

Tropical Storms maintains that this unusual activity results from rising sea levels due to climate change. Experts at Southern Florida University reject that assertion. They argue that hurricanes that reach land represent one small – though highly publicized – type of high intensity storm, and that overall patterns do not link climate change to high intensity storms as a whole.

RAPHAEL ROSE FROM HIS PRAYERS. His back and knees ached, but he'd become used to that. He tacked the latest article to his board. Little cork showed between the printouts. The extreme weather reports presented no real surprise. Mark, Chapter 13, and Luke, Chapter 21, had predicted that in the last days the sun would be darkened, and there would be earthquakes in various places, terrors, and "great signs from heaven."

He eased his window open. City street sounds from below his small room washed over him. Soon, he'd be looking down at a different street, one in Istanbul. He knew what he'd see there. Merchants exhorting men and women to look, to feel, to buy. Some women would wear traditional garb for traditional reasons, keeping themselves shrouded. Others would cover their faces with scarves and their heads with hats only because the winter wind chilled their bones. In the summer, those same women would walk bare-headed, bare-faced. The Fatih district had changed. Old and new. Proper and what many liked to call modern. As if nothing more threatening than the passage of time had occurred.

Today, though, Raphael felt hope. The seeds had been planted. The tree soon would bear fruit. Poisonous perhaps, but fruit.

MULLIN STOOD behind a fruit stand in the Fatih district. A specially-made burqa that included an interior sleeve for his sword hid his hair, his whole body and the bottom two thirds of his face. He looked tall for a woman and too broad shouldered, but he'd practiced moving with a slight sway to his hips, and with his feet toed a bit inward, to counteract his usual stride. Using a magnifying mirror, he'd plucked his eyebrows into a thinner, more feminine line. Many soldiers would balk at such a disguise, but it didn't bother him. Unlike Cyril Woods, he had truly dedicated his life to service. He would do whatever he needed to do. He kept his left hand wrapped around the phone in his pocket. It remained still. No messages.

*They also serve who only stand and wait*, he thought. And waited.

# 11

Giant snowflakes drifted down outside the window, melting the instant they touched the brick sidewalk in front of the café. The waiter brought cucumber and yogurt salad and refilled their tea glasses.

"The woman who raised me was a guardian – perhaps the English word 'messenger' is more accurate – as was her mother, as am I," Pir Ferit said. "If you are the one I seek, I will be the first messenger in generations to truly fulfill our purpose."

"What purpose is that?" Tara said.

"As yet, I cannot say."

Tara pressed her lips together. "Are you the only messenger? The only one living now?"

"It may be there are more, but none of us knows the others."

Tara tried the yogurt and cucumber salad and thought about what to ask next. The cool sour cream-like taste contrasted the dark tea perfectly.

Kelly pushed her plate aside and leaned forward. "Was your mother a Sufi? Can women be Sufis?"

"Indeed. While in this world humans manifest in different forms, there ultimately is no female, no male, only Being."

"Then why no men for this trip?" Tara asked. "Sophia – Professor Gaddini – told my family I could only see you if I traveled with women."

Pir Ferit motioned the waiter and asked for something in Turkish before he responded. "My dear, you know the answer. Who pursued you with the most vigor when you were pregnant? Who seemed to wish you the most harm?"

"The Brotherhood."

"And do you imagine many women hold high positions with the Brotherhood? Hold any positions?"

Tara gazed out at the falling snow and thought about what Cyril had told her about the Brotherhood's overall structure. She'd never heard him mention a woman. But he had said something interesting to Sophia.

"I heard some of the women claiming now to be pregnant virgins may have been encouraged to do so by the Brotherhood," Tara said.

Pir Ferit nodded as the waiter set down a tray of Turkish shortbread cookies coated with powdered sugar. "This would not surprise me. But avoiding men is the best way to limit exposure."

"Except that there was no Brotherhood of Andrew in Andrew's time, right?" Kelly said. "So why would Brother Andrew create that requirement?"

"Truly, I do not know. I only know why it makes sense to follow it now." Pir Ferit turned to Tara. "You are aware that some early Christians did not view the divine being as male or female?"

"I've read that. It's how I found Dr. Gaddini in the first place." Tara wondered about Pir Ferit claiming not to know why the no traveling with men requirement had been created. He seemed intelligent and studious, she felt certain he must have researched it at some point.

"There existed some so-called heresies about Mary, the mother of Jesus," Pir Ferit said, "such as Collyridianism and Antidicomarianitism, that might interest you."

"Colly – Collyridianism and what?" Tara asked.

"No matter." Pir Ferit smiled at Kelly. "You asked about my mother. She was an artist. Quite well known. Her work can be found in the Basilica di Santa Maria del Fiore. In Florence." Pir Ferit glanced at Tara. "Have you ever visited Florence?"

Tara shook her head.

"It is a lovely city. One you must visit some day."

The tea had grown cold. White powdered sugar dusted the dark wood tabletop and table runner. Sophia hadn't been exaggerating when she'd warned that Pir Ferit tended to take the long way about to whatever he meant to say.

Kelly tapped her foot on the floor and jiggled her knee in a way she'd done since childhood when she became impatient. Tara put her hand on her sister's knee to still her.

Pir Ferit said, "I see I must reach the point at last." He motioned the waiter for more tea. "I suppose there is no harm in explaining my role and why I thought it worth meeting you. I told the other young ladies who came to see me, Miss Alma and Miss Zavia. It is not a secret."

Tara's shoulder sagged. After all the build up, he was just sharing what he'd share with anyone.

"The job of the guardian is to determine whom to entrust with a message from the past. I personally hope whoever that is will listen carefully to all that I say even before I pass on the message." Ferit gazed steadily at Tara, and she wondered whether he thought she hadn't been listening to him so far. "I do not know what the message says, only how it may be found."

"Don't you want to know?" Tara said. "What it says?"

"I believe sharing the message with the right person will be good for the world. That is all I need to know." Pir Ferit reached across the table and placed his hand on Tara's elbow. "If you wish to proceed, go the Yerebatan Sarayi – also known as the Basilica Cistern or Sunken Palace. You enter across from the Hagia Sophia. Both were built in the sixth century. See what you can see."

"What I can see? I'm not sure what you mean."

"It is foretold the One will have a vision. Perhaps something you see in the Basilica will trigger that. Once you've explored to your satisfaction, meet me at the Koca Mustafa Pasha mosque this afternoon. I study there and have a private space where we may speak."

Pir Ferit told them more about the Basilica Cistern, which he described as an underground cathedral originally built as a water container during the reign of Emperor Justinian I to meet the needs of the Great Palace of Constantinople.

"Am I looking for something in particular?" Tara said.

"Yes, but I cannot tell you what."

"Can I go with her?" Kelly asked.

"Yes and no," Pir Ferit said. "You may accompany her to the Basilica Cistern, but if she reaches what she seeks, you will not be with her."

ANDREA GUTZMAN PREFERRED the quiet stateliness of Florence to the glittering excesses of Rome. Roman cathedrals with their glossy marble floors, gilt-edged reliquaries, and soaring domes made of the finest and most expensive materials made her wonder how many starving people the Church could have fed by scaling back its supposed houses of worship. In contrast, Florence's outdoor sculptures, its churches with matte-finished tiled floors, its colorful chalk sidewalk art, gave her peace. At least some of the time.

At twilight each day after visiting the Basilica di Santa Maria del Fiore, Andrea stood on the Pont Vecchio, eating a vanilla gelato. It was her favorite indulgence, even in winter. The gold and rose sunset melted into the Arno River below her. She felt safe here. Lonely, true, but she would have felt lonely anywhere without her daughter. Three more months, and Andrea would see her again. That length of time ought to have seemed short compared to the six years she'd already endured, but it felt like an eternity.

Once both the sky and water had darkened into night, Andrea left the bridge and followed the winding streets back to her flat in the Duomo neighborhood. Her second bedroom served as her study. There, surrounded by favorite books and photos of her daughter, she spent hours at her antique desk, researching and writing. Her employer gave her great freedom to pursue lines of inquiry. He asked only that she tell no one else the results or the topic of her work. That was when she began to suspect she hadn't been hired despite her background, but because of it. That didn't bother her. She'd never anticipated obtaining any professional job again, or any job at all beyond waiting tables, so she wasn't about to quibble with working in obscurity.

Andrea had recently translated a particularly interesting passage, and she quickened her step. But when she reached the third floor of her building, she hesitated. Her door was shut, as she'd left it, but pushed slightly inward, as if she'd engaged the doorknob lock but forgotten the upper deadbolt. She paused. Listened. Nothing.

Inside the apartment, the atmosphere felt different. Less her own. Less peaceful.

Andrea kept her coat and gloves on. She eased a long black nightstick from behind the cabinet in her entryway and rounded the corner to her living room.

"Hands where I can see them." Andrea used her president-of-the-company voice. A voice that, oddly, had also come in handy in prison.

The stranger, who looked to be a woman, stood at the window, back to Andrea. Her dark, limp hair hung to her shoulders. About 5'6", she wore jeans, leather boots, and a wool sweater that hung loose around her upper body but snug at the hips. She was thin. Probably no threat, but Andrea never assumed. Not anymore.

"Turn slowly."

The woman looked skinnier from the front, with hollow cheeks and a narrow nose. And young. Perhaps only twenty-one or twenty-two. She held no weapons.

"Who are you and what do you want?" Andrea said.

"To talk," the young woman kept her hands in the air. "My name is Tara Spencer. I'm sorry about picking your lock, but I couldn't risk standing in the hallway. People are following me."

"Sit over there."

Andrea motioned to the far end of the sofa. Gripping the nightstick, she sat across from the young woman. She'd heard about the previous pope allowing Tara Spencer to visit him. It was hard to imagine anyone in Italy who hadn't heard about that. But nothing new had appeared in the mainstream news since then. That Andrea's research might relate to Tara's story had never occurred to her, and despite the young woman now in front of her, she still didn't see it.

All the same, she felt grateful she'd locked her current notes in her safe and had delivered her previous project on schedule the day before.

"I heard you're conducting research." The young woman eased her arms down until her hands rested, palms open, on her thighs. "I believe it relates to me."

"You're mistaken." Andrea wasn't about to confirm her activities by asking how Tara – if this young woman really was Tara Spencer – had learned about her.

"That your research relates to me or that you're researching anything?"

"Both. I'm here on a sabbatical," Andrea said.

The girl said nothing, probably hoping Andrea would fill the silence.

She didn't. She had lots of practice waiting.

In the Sultanahmet neighborhood of the historical part of Istanbul, Tara and Kelly sat on a wooden bench half a block from the Tourist Police Office, a tall yellow building. Down the street, a short squat structure housed the steps that led down into the Basilica Cistern. Nearby, the Hagia Sophia's domes soared, bounded by four minarets, three sandstone and one red brick. Automobile exhaust tinged the winter air. Many of the sedans on the multi-lane street looked like Fords. Tara hadn't expected to see so many American cars here.

The police presence and busy neighborhood made Tara feel safer than she had since the attack on Kali. Still, her heart raced at the prospect of finding answers. She took a deep breath and tried to ratchet down her expectations – it might all come to nothing.

Using a pre-paid phone bought from an airport shop, Tara texted Sophia's colleague to say where she and Kelly were going. Then she called her mom.

"The Basilica Cistern? Has he been reading too many Dan Brown novels?" Lynette said.

"What?"

"Never mind. You realize this monk is sending you to a tourist attraction. Does he get a cut on the tickets?"

"I know it seems weird, Mom." The snow had stopped, and what little of it that had stuck to the ground had melted. The sun shone. Tara felt less cold than in the café, despite that she'd taken her hat off. "Did Dad leave okay?"

"I dropped him at the airport. I couldn't tell if he was looking forward to the trip, but he shaved. He shaved and ironed his clothes."

"Ironing's good." Her dad was the only person Tara knew who ironed his jeans. If he'd gone back to that, he must be feeling more like himself. "I thought more about it, and I'm glad he'll be keeping an eye on what Cyril's doing. But I still don't get why he's willing to travel to Armenia to find out more about Fimi. He never talks to me about her. Or about anything lately."

The nearest stoplight changed. A sleek black Jaguar drove past, standing out among the tour buses and four-door sedans that crowded the street.

"He blames himself," Lynette said. "For all the bad things that happened in the last year. He's going with Cyril because he blames himself."

Pete Spencer blamed Cyril Woods. And the Brotherhood. And he feared he was now doing exactly what the Brotherhood wanted him to do, but he hadn't been able to resist being able to monitor and, he hoped, control Cyril Woods.

After stowing his carry ons in the top luggage rack, Pete flung himself into his aisle seat. The doors hadn't shut, but already the air had that stale, flat airplane smell that made Pete's head ache. Before Cyril Woods, Tara had claimed not to know how she'd become pregnant, but she hadn't suggested any sort of fantastical explanation. She'd seemed open to the idea that something might have occurred that she'd blocked from her mind. It was Cyril who'd put ideas into her mind, interpretations of her pregnancy that led Pete to question his daughter's mental state. Which started their estrangement. Every act by Cyril after that had placed him more and more at odds with the Church and the law, and endangered everyone around Tara. That the Brotherhood likely had manipulated Cyril didn't alleviate the man's guilt in Pete's mind. A man needed to decide for himself what he believed and what to do about it.

A flight attendant made the door-closing announcement, said the flight was expected to land in Chicago on time, and advised those connecting to international flights that further information would be available when they deplaned. The seatbelt light flashed. Pete popped his seat into the upright position and stared out at the tarmac. It didn't matter, he decided, whether or how much the Brotherhood had influenced Father Saur's request. Pete would do what he'd promised because it was the right thing. But he'd take care of his own agenda, too.

UPLIGHTS GLOWED at the bases of hundreds of columns supporting the Basilica Cistern's vaulted brick roof. The shadows at the top of and between the columns, especially those farthest away, deepened almost to black. The water at the Cistern's bottom reflected ripples of reddish light. Goldfish larger than a human hand swam there. To Tara, it appeared they darted through the wavering light itself. Cameras flashed every second or two, then the Cistern darkened again.

Voices and piped-in classical music echoed throughout the gigantic underground chamber. Tara's feet ached from walking multi-level concrete walkways, and her head felt fuzzy from jet leg. She and Kelly paused near a wooden railing. In the dim lighting, it was hard to distinguish facial features of anyone more than a few paces away.

"I keep feeling someone's following us," Tara said. "But I don't see anyone." Other than that feeling, nothing unusual had happened. Tara almost hoped a stranger would confront them. They'd examined nearly every part of the Cistern, and nothing had triggered a vision or any sort of revelation. She'd sat quietly on a bench for a while, staring at the water, hoping that would put her in the right frame of mind, but nothing had happened. In terms of safety, it was a relief that their trip so far had been uneventful, but it made Tara more anxious about the future. If she didn't find answers here, she had no idea what to do next.

"I know." Kelly turned her head from side to side, then glanced over her shoulder.

Tara pointed to a plain sign stating MEDUSA with an arrow below it. "Should we? It's the only part we haven't seen."

There were two stone Medusa heads, one positioned upside down and one sideways. Their faces, contrary to legend, didn't strike Tara as hideous or ugly, though stone snakes did grow out of them.

"Medusa was beheaded by Perseus." Tara ran her hand through her hair. "I hope that's not some sort of message for me since this is the only reference to a woman I've seen in this place."

Kelly consulted her folded paper guide, holding it under a light. "The heads are meant to ward off evil."

"Which doesn't give me anything to report to Pir Ferit." Tara's arms felt tired, and she shifted Fimi to her other side.

"Maybe it relates to the Cistern's history," Kelly said. "Whatever you're supposed to find or see."

"It was a reservoir," Tara said. "It supplied water to the nearby buildings, including the palace. I don't see what that could have to do with anything."

Kelly consulted the guide again. "It could hold twenty-one million gallons."

"So?" Tara started to think she'd dragged her sister and baby all the way to Istanbul for nothing, that Pir Ferit was just another crank. She'd gotten enough letters from people like him, both before and after Fimi's birth, that she ought to have recognized it, even if Sophia thought otherwise.

"It's two acres," Kelly said. "Which I feel like we've walked all of. It was restored in 1987."

They made their way to another bench and sat. "Maybe it's when it was built that matters." Tara felt like she was trying to convince herself more than Kelly, but the date could be significant. "Sixth century, right? That vase Cyril showed me a photo of when I met him, Nanor said it was from the sixth century. Though Cyril said the ninth, I think."

Kelly questioned Tara on everything Cyril had told her about the supposedly pregnant virgins who'd lived and died before Tara. They spoke quietly so the music nearly drowned their voices. Neither could figure out any connection to what they'd seen in the Basilica, but Tara was struck by how thoughtful Kelly had become, or perhaps always had been. She'd rarely had a one-on-one conversation with Kelly as they grew up. She'd talked most with her brother Nate, the next oldest after her, and after that with Bailey, whom she'd often cared for while her parents did their best to get Megan the right medical treatment and help her live a happy, full life while coping with cancer. The middle sibling in a big family probably often got overlooked, but that didn't make Tara feel any better about having missed getting to know her sister.

"I'm out of ideas," Tara said as their discussion wound down. The darkness and damp air pressed in on her with almost physical force. She shut her eyes. Disappointment, like gray fog on an autumn day, seeped into her bones. "I'd really hoped we could learn something."

"Maybe we can," Kelly said.

# 12

Pete and Cyril followed the purple Heathrow airport connection signs to the next terminal. They'd had seats at opposite ends of the Boeing 777 from Chicago to London, which had suited Pete fine. Now a six-hour layover loomed before them. After checking in for the next leg of the flight, Pete sat opposite Cyril in a lounge area and opened a book, *Zen at Work*. The sense of purpose that had propelled him to this point had ebbed during the long Chicago-to-London flight, replaced by the exhaustion that had plagued him for the last five months.

Cyril studied a spiral notebook, highlighting words and scribbling in the margins.

A group of students, some wearing plain shirts and pants or skirts and others in sport jackets and striped ties or blazers, hurried past. Their voices rose above the smooth, repetitive airline announcements. Pete caught snippets of their chatter about a Heathrow job fair.

*That's the kind of thing Tara should be doing*, he thought. *Not trekking through Istanbul.*

Pete pointed at Cyril's notebook. "What are you doing?"

"Research." Cyril stowed the notebook in his backpack. "The documents in the Brotherhood's archives are originals and sacred, not to be removed or copied, so these notes are all I could take with me."

"You don't believe in word processing?"

"Handwriting might be old-fashioned, but it can't be hacked," Cyril said.

"Research about Our Lady of Sorrows? The church in Armenia where we're heading? Where you planned to take Tara?"

Cyril nodded in answer to each question.

"So why didn't you? You knew about this church, you traveled all the way to Armenia, got her to travel all the way to Armenia."

"I made a mistake. Many mistakes." Cyril's chin trembled, but he met Pete's eyes. Pete couldn't tell if the appearance of unease was deliberate.

Tara had told Pete a bare bones version of what had happened in Armenia. Between that and what Cyril had done to Bailey, Pete could only stomach the man's presence by imagining shoving his rage into the back of his garage and slamming the door. He'd used that image often during Megan's illness, when anger over the unfairness of what his youngest daughter went through threatened to poison his life.

"Why take Tara there, why approach her in the first place, if you weren't sure she was the one Revelation referred to?" Pete had read and reread Chapter 12 of Revelation, the chapter Cyril had quoted to Tara when he'd first sought her out, and didn't see why anything Tara said or did fit with it.

"I exercised poor judgment," Cyril said.

"Poor judgment? Recklessness. Negligence. Criminal negligence."

The smell of Starbucks coffee filled the air as a young woman with long dark blond hair rushed past, clutching the trademark white and green cup. Another reminder of the Tara of years before. Now Tara changed her hair color and style frequently to be less recognizable, and she never left it long and straight the way she'd kept it during grade school and high school.

"I'd been told to approach her to find out more about her pregnancy," Cyril said, "and to give her as little information as possible, just enough to get her to share what she knew. But once we started talking, I could see she'd never believe me if I didn't tell her everything. And I wanted to tell her everything. I felt so sure about her, and I thought it would make her safer."

"Safer."

The skin around Pete's lips whitened. He stood and walked to the floor-to-ceiling windows. He wished he'd listened more closely when Tara began speaking of Cyril, instead of adopting Lynette's view that Tara was delusional. But Pete had really thought his daughter had lost her mind. And so he'd driven her to the very man who posed the most danger to the entire Spencer family.

"She's an atheist, you know," he said, watching a Boeing jumbo jet ease away from a jetway. "Or at least agnostic. That's what she claims."

"She told me," Cyril said.

"And you still filled her head with these stories about being the mother of the next messiah."

"I don't think you're giving her enough credit. I couldn't 'fill her head.' Tara has a mind of her own."

In two strides, Pete stood inches from Cyril, staring down at him. "Don't tell me about my daughter. Don't you try to tell me about my daughter."

Tara opened her eyes. Blood trickled down Kelly's wrist. "What did you do?"

"It's just a paper cut." The diagonal cut stretched three quarters of an inch across the fleshy right side of Kelly's palm. "A little deeper than I meant to do. But see. See if you and Fimi can heal me."

"This is crazy," Tara said.

Kelly's gray eyes fixed on Tara's. "This is the time to try. When no one but me will know. You need to find out what Fimi can do. Or what you and Fimi can do."

Tara fumbled in her backpack for her First Aid kit, part of the earthquake preparedness pack she'd put together based on tourist bureau recommendations. "It's not me. Nothing's ever happened with just me, only when I was holding Fimi. Or right after giving birth to her."

Kelly pushed the bandage Tara offered away. "Fimi's here now. So try."

A drop of blood fell on Tara's coat. She glanced around. Four people gathered near the Medusa heads, and more wandered along the walkways, pausing here and there to look at the columns or the goldfish. In the dim light, no one would notice what she and Fimi and Kelly did.

Tara's mouth felt dry. "I don't know what to do."

"What did you do with Kali?"

"I don't know. I didn't try to do anything. Just relax and send her good thoughts."

"So...."

"Okay." Tara reached around Fimi and grasped her sister's hands. "Keep an eye out. For what I don't know, but do."

She shut her eyes and breathed in for a count of four, held, then out, the way she did when trying to meditate. She listened to voices echoing in the Cistern, to faint strains of classical music featuring a choir that sounded like it sang far in the catacombs, to a thrum of a train from somewhere else underground, perhaps a subway, though she didn't think she'd seen one in Instanbul. She pushed that last thought from her mind and focused on Fimi's warmth against her body. The baby seemed to breathe with her. In. Hold. Out. In. Hold. Out. In....

"Tara."

"Huh?" Tara blinked, surprised to find she no longer held Kelly's hands. The biting odor of rubbing alcohol cut through the Cistern's damp stone smell.

"Look." Kelly held a hand-sanitizing wipe. She'd used it to clean her right palm and wrist, and they were now free of blood. And smooth. No trace of the paper cut existed.

"Fimi and I did that?"

"How else would it have happened?" Kelly said.

"You didn't – I mean, I know you wouldn't – it's not a prank or anything, like Nate might do?"

Tara hated to ask, but she'd needed to.

Kelly lowered her eyebrows and her forehead creased. "Yes, Tara, I'm playing a prank on you because we're here to have a wacky time. Or, actually, I want to rent you out as a sideshow attraction whenever I'm short of cash."

"Yeah, okay. It's just a little hard to take in." An ache started behind Tara's eyes and expanded into every inch of her head. Fimi began to cry.

"It's you or Fimi," Kelly said. "Or both you and Fimi."

Tara's shoulders rounded, and her back slumped. "But is this what Pir Ferit sent me here to do?"

"Probably not. He could have created some kind of test with his own body that'd mean more to him. And it wasn't a vision." Kelly glanced around the Cistern again. "Maybe there's nothing here for you, and he's, you know, he's just a little crazy."

Tara rocked side to side, trying to soothe Fimi, whose cries had turned to wails. She felt a little nauseous, and her head pounded. "Crazy or not, we said we'd meet him this afternoon at the mosque." The thought of visiting Pir Ferit rather than going back to the hotel to rest felt overwhelming.

"More walking," Kelly said.

"More walking."

A BUS TOOK them three miles from the Basilica Cistern to the Fatih District's traditionally Armenian Kocamustafapaş neighborhood. There, on the slopes of a hill near the Marmara Sea, the Koca Mustafa Pasha Mosque, with its domes, spires, and attendant buildings, sprawled. A low stone wall encircled its courtyard. Rather than sheltering Tara and Kelly from the wind, the wall seemed to catch the air and whirl it about. Tara raised Fimi's hood, though the sun still shone, keeping the temperature above freezing.

A man met them near the courtyard gate. He wore plain clothes like Pir Ferit, but was in his forties and tall, with a close beard and a long, narrow nose that angled slightly to one side. He said he'd been directed to give them a tour. His name was Ismail.

"This mosque was once known as the church of women." Ismail ushered them toward a long dead but sturdy-looking cypress tree with thick, bare branches. It stood near an octagonal wooden shelter and a column-shaped fountain with no water flowing from it. From the tree's lowest branch swung a chain the length of a tall man, with rusted, narrow links. "Which is one reason Pir Ferit was drawn here."

"I thought this used to be the Church of St. Andrew," Tara said.

"That was before." Ismail paused in front of the tree. "First, this was an Eastern Orthodox church dedicated to Andrew the Apostle, then to Andrew of Crete. Then it was the women's church. It became a mosque when the Ottomans captured Constantinople. That happened to many churches, though many others remained Christian. As you must have realized by now, Istanbul presents a unique crossover between Muslim and Christian, old and new. And it is the only city in the world that exists on two continents – Europe and Asia."

"It's more modern than I expected," Kelly said. "The city, not this mosque."

Ismail turned toward Kelly. He towered over her. "You thought us barbaric, living in the dark ages?"

Kelly flushed. "No, I didn't mean that. I just never thought that much about Istanbul."

"You should." Ismail pointed a finger at her. "It is a city vital to the world.

And perhaps to your sister. As is this very place. It is here that we will perform a test."

Tara stepped between Ismail and Kelly. "What kind of test?"

"You will see." A thin dark-haired boy wearing a woolen coat but no hat appeared from beneath archways along one side of the courtyard. Ismail waved him over. He looked to be about ten, not much younger than Tara's little brother Bailey. Ismail rested his hand on the boy's shoulder. "This is Hamed. He studies with Pir Ferit and will help us."

Hamed smiled at Tara, a quick, warm smile, then looked at the ground.

"Legend has it," said Ismail, "that where the chain is swung between two people who affirm contradictory propositions, it will circle, then hit the one who tells the truth."

The chain and the tree branches swayed in the wind, casting constantly moving shadows. Tara spread her feet a little wider and looked up at Ismail. "What do you mean, contradictory positions?"

Ismail smiled, but his eyes stayed cool. "My position is that this story you say the Brotherhood of Andrew told you – about Chapter 12 in the Book of Revelation foreseeing a second messiah – is merely that, a story."

"I don't necessarily disagree with you," Tara said. "That's part of what I'm trying to learn."

"Also, my position is that no virgin pregnancy ever occurred," Ismail said. "The earliest Christian gospel includes no claim the mother of Jesus was a virgin. The Qu'ran recognizes Mary as the mother of Jesus, but nowhere states his conception was supernatural."

"I don't know what happened to the Virgin Mary. I don't even know what happened to me."

Clouds shifted as they spoke, partially blocking the sun. The temperature dropped.

"Yet you claim you were still a virgin when you were told you were pregnant," Ismail said.

Kelly put her hands in her pockets, her gaze traveling from Ismail to her sister and back.

"I was," Tara said.

Ismail spread his hands. "So you see. I believe no virgin pregnancy occurred. Ever. For any reason."

"You mean you believe my sister's lying," Kelly said.

The sun disappeared completely. Cold settled into Tara's skin. She glanced at the aging tree, the fragile-looking chain. Rust flaked off it into the rising wind. "Did the other two women who came here do this?"

"They refused. As you are free to do."

*And they were sent home with no information*, Tara thought.

"Hamed will swing the chain," Ismail said, "or one of you may do so. You may choose where to stand."

# 13

Kali tightened her grip on the steering wheel when the road curved. That a hit-and-run driver had killed her aunt Maya always weighed on her. The most cautious driver in her high school class, she never truly relaxed behind the wheel.

She was on her way back from the hospital. Unknown to her grandmother, she'd seen her neurologist. For information, not treatment. Dr. Filkins described the severe trauma to Kali's brain that had disappeared within forty-eight hours. But he couldn't explain why that had happened. Spontaneous remissions of diseases sometimes occurred, but the doctor knew of no documented healings of head injuries as serious as Kali's in such a short time. As Kali's guardian, Nanor Kerkorian had been informed of that. But Dr. Filkins had told no one else, other than the medical team.

Nanor must suspect Tara or Fimi had something to do with the miraculous recovery. It was the only reason Kali could imagine for her grandmother to say so little about it. Kali understood the need for caution, but it hurt her feelings that her grandmother didn't trust her to be discreet. And that Tara didn't trust her either, as she still hadn't answered any of Kali's messages.

*Just let it go. For now,* Kali thought. She drove past the Village Hall. If she could talk to Tara, her best friend would tell her to concentrate on her studies. Mid-terms were approaching, and Kali needed to make certain her last semester high school grades didn't retroactively tank her college scholarship offers. After that, if she still hadn't heard from Tara, she'd find some way to reach her.

For the last ten minutes of the drive, Kali turned on music. The sweeping instrumentation of her favorite band, HEM, and the smooth, rich tones of the lead singer's voice helped Kali relax and clear her mind. Until she turned the corner and was within sight of the Willow Springs gated parking area.

Dozens of strangers stood in the private lot. Two people climbed the fourteen-foot chain link fence around the Willow Springs automobile parking area. The inner golf cart lot, which provided access to the community through a gate at its far end, was less accessible. A high brick wall topped with barbed wire – added after the attack on Kali – surrounded it. So far as Kali could see from the road, no one had gotten into the golf cart lot.

Kali pulled over once she was around a curve and out of sight. She called Security. Sagun answered.

"They're looking for clues," Sagun said.

"Clues?" Her Honda Civic's engine stuttered, and Kali tapped the gas pedal after making sure the car was still in park. It needed a tune up.

"It's a reality game played on-line and in the real world," Sagun said. "Called TARA2, loosely based on the events of Tara's life over the past year."

"You knew of this?" Kali said.

"I heard about it soon after Tara left Willow Springs. Perhaps the news of Fimi's kidnapping renewed interest in Tara."

"Why did you not tell me? One of these gamers could be interfering with my communicating with Tara."

"I told you," Sagun said, "I didn't find any interference. The game is its own world anyway – I've joined and check in periodically to monitor it – and Tara's real life emails aren't part of it."

"So why should all these players come here? Tara never spoke about Willow Springs to the news media." As soon as she'd said it, Kali realized that didn't matter. The Brotherhood knew.

"Perhaps she did tell someone," Sagun said.

A dark SUV sped past, its wake rocking Kali's smaller car. She put the phone on speaker and pulled farther off the road. "No, no. Tara would not do that. Cyril, though, he knew. And the other men who attacked me."

"I've seen no evidence they – or the Brotherhood as a whole – are involved in the game," Sagun said. "Though certainly they could be."

"What shall I do now?" Kali said. "I don't want anyone to follow me home."

The outer and inner parking lots required key codes to enter. But once the gates opened, a person on foot could follow behind or alongside a vehicle. The alternate police and fire entrance all the way on the other side of the community was an option, but both she and Sagun agreed it was better not to draw attention to it.

"You might want to check into a motel for the night," Sagun said finally. "The players won't leave until they find answers. Or until the police make them leave, but apparently there's a policeman's retirement dinner tonight, and no one is eager to leave given that nothing threatening is going on."

"What about the people climbing the fence?"

"I just saw that on the monitors. I'll try the police again."

Kali glanced at her backpack. It held some but not all the materials she needed to study. She hadn't expected to be away more than a few hours. "I will drive back into town and eat dinner there, then return. Surely even if the police are slow, these people will get tired. Or hungry."

"Some might," Sagun said, "but likely not all. I read about a game where a teenage boy stayed in an old phone booth during a hurricane waiting for a call that would provide a clue. But call me in an hour and we'll see."

"I will." Kali shifted the car back into gear and was about to hang up.

"Kali? I hate to say it, but this may be what Tara didn't want you to know."

"What?"

"If she's involved in this game, she won't want any of us to reach her to question her."

"She's not," Kali said and thought, *but I'm starting to wonder if you are.*

**"Virgin Pregnancies" All Part Of An Alternate Reality Game**

ST. LOUIS - "I LOVE IT! It's such a layered story," says Elena Gilbert, a non-pregnant twenty-something who plays the TARA2 alternate reality game. The identity of the Puppet Master, as the designers who run ARGs are referred to in the gaming world, is unknown, as is whether Tara Spencer willingly acted out a prewritten storyline to launch the game or is simply an unbalanced young woman whose delusions spawned the idea. Most participants favor the first theory, and none interviewed want to believe Spencer is delusional. A few contend she truly was blessed, or cursed, with a supernatural pregnancy. Those individuals believe that they are playing a serious game. Serious games are used for many real life purposes, such as business training, disaster preparedness, or harnessing the players' combined efforts to figure out a way to prevent climate change.

By playing TARA2, some gamers believe they will aid Spencer in real life. Players receive clues through "personal" messages sent to their devices, as well as by ferreting out hidden messages on websites, in special eBook editions, and at places significant to Spencer's narrative, such as the St. Louis Arch and the Vatican. Gamers then share information on line, enabling those who can't travel to learn of clues that otherwise require a live presence. Whether the additional ten young women who claimed in recent months to be pregnant virgins are part of TARA2 is unknown.

The stated goal of the game? Find the person who will explain the meaning and purpose of Spencer's pregnancy.

TARA AND KELLY stood under the stone arches near the courtyard's edge. The outdoor corridor, which had spires at either end, had been built only a year before to connect an outer building that housed studies and offices to the mosque.

"What if the chain hurts you?" Kelly said. "Or Fimi?"

"Keep Fimi far out of the way." Tara unhooked the baby carrier and handed Fimi, still nestled in it, to Kelly.

"I don't trust that guy," Kelly said.

"Ismail? I don't either," Tara said. "But it's not as if I have a vision to report to Pir Ferit."

Dense clouds formed just above the tree line. It was afternoon, but looked like dusk. The wind whistled as it whipped through the corridor. Kelly shivered and pulled the baby closer to her. "Maybe he would believe us about the cut being healed."

It took Tara only a few seconds to reject the idea. She'd trusted people way too quickly in the past. Especially Cyril, not to mention her ex-boyfriend. She didn't intend to repeat that mistake.

"I'm not telling strangers anything about Fimi that they don't already know," Tara said. "I came here to get information, not share it."

Kelly frowned. "But what if this test is dangerous somehow? In some way we aren't thinking of?"

"That could apply to this whole trip. I need to take some chances to try to keep Fimi safer later." Rumbling sounded in the distance. "Is that thunder?"

"Maybe blasting from a construction site. I'm not sure you can have thunderstorms in winter," Kelly said.

"Maybe." They'd passed two partially-constructed office buildings in the more modern section of the city. Perhaps a foundation for yet another was being created.

Hamed approached, peering at them from beneath dark straight bangs. "Yes?" he said. Tara wondered if he spoke any more English than that.

"Yes." Tara turned to Kelly. "Watch from the street. So Fimi has absolutely no chance of being hit if that chain flies off the tree or the branch breaks."

Hands sweating from nerves, Tara took her gloves off and lay them on the ground. Ismail stood ten paces from Tara, his back toward the corridor. From under the tree, Hamed flung the chain so it bisected the space between Ismail and Tara in a perpendicular line, then he darted out of its way before it swung back. Influenced by the wind, the chain arced toward Tara, then swung into a circle. Then it spiraled inward, appearing more likely to lose all momentum than to hit anyone.

The air hummed, and the skin on Tara's face and neck tingled. In Kelly's arms, Fimi started to cry. Lighting struck a spire, breaking it in two as thunder cracked. The top half of the spire plummeted toward Ismail. He froze, as if mesmerized by the flailing chain. Kelly scrambled farther from the courtyard, clutching Fimi and calling Tara's name.

Tara lunged into Ismail, sending them both out of the spire's path. It hit the ground where Ismail had stood a moment before, just missing the fountain but splintering the small wooden shelter. Tara and Ismail lay on the cold, hard ground. The wind blew the chain so that its bottom link grazed both of them.

Hail pelted down. Pir Ferit appeared at the mosque's entrance, having wheeled his chair there, and shouted at them all to come inside.

"So what about these other young women?" Pete said. Two tables away a fortyish man thumb-typed furiously on a handheld device. He was a bit on the heavy side and wore a baseball cap backwards, though otherwise his attire was business casual – khaki pants and a dark green long-sleeved LaCrosse shirt. Something about his posture bothered Pete. The man slouched, but his left foot was planted completely flat on the tile floor, his calf at an exact right angle to his thigh, and he held his arms rigid.

"The ones claiming to be pregnant virgins?" Cyril said. "At least two are Brotherhood plants."

"What for?"

"My best guess? To confuse the issue." Cyril's hands curled into fists. "Make Tara look like one of many disturbed young women so if she starts some sort of movement or talks about the Brotherhood, no one will find her credible."

Pete lowered his voice in case the backwards baseball cap man was listening. The seating area had gradually emptied while they'd been talking, leaving mostly vacant metal tables and chairs around them. "Your best guess? You don't know?"

"The Brotherhood doesn't trust me. That's why you were told to spy on me. I'm guessing by your pastor."

"I didn't need anyone to tell me to spy on you."

"So no one suggested you accompany me?" Cyril said.

"I chose to do so." Pete sipped his Pepsi, calmed by the syrupy taste that fizzed across his tongue. Not a drinker, or smoker, or one who normally indulged in sweets, Pepsi was as close as he got to a comfort substance. "How big is the Brotherhood?"

"Small. I've only met two colleagues, plus my superior, Thomas Stranyero. I heard the voice of one other who is in a dotted line to Stranyero, someone named Fenton. Which may be a first or a last name, I don't know."

The dotted line reference made Pete think the Brotherhood of Andrew must be larger than Cyril imagined. A dotted line relationship indicated two people who appeared at the same level on a company organizational chart, though one reported to the other indirectly. The large accounting firm where Pete worked used that terminology. Smaller companies, or organizations, didn't need such complex supervisory relationships. Or organizational charts.

If Cyril was telling the truth, he knew very little about the Brotherhood. If he was telling the truth.

"But you know the Brotherhood's mission," Pete said. "Find the mother of the new messiah – when you're not harassing and trying to discredit girls like Tara whom you believe are pretending to be that – see that the child is safely born and protected in life. A mission at which your order has failed at least five times over the past two thousand years, correct?" The words rolled out of Pete's mouth more easily than any he'd ever spoken in his life. He'd had nearly a year to consider them, since the time Tara shared that Cyril had approached her with his claims about the Book of Revelation and her pregnancy.

"That's the stated mission," Cyril said.

Pete raised his eyebrows. "It's not the real mission?"

"I harbor doubts. As I sat in prison, meditating on my part in the harm to your family, I asked myself whether that type of destruction could be justified by the stated mission. Perhaps, but it seems more likely there's an agenda of which I'm not aware."

"But you didn't question anyone."

"Your father was in the military," Cyril said. "Does a soldier question authority? Once you've joined, once you believe in the mission, you follow orders. The Brotherhood is like that, and I was well set for it after my time in the army. But I've realized that doesn't excuse me, that doesn't mean I'm relieved of the duty to make moral choices."

Out the window, cargo trucks trundled across the tarmac. Pete studied Cyril, trying to assess his sincerity. But he didn't know the man well enough, and the circumstances were too bizarre, to reach a conclusion. Pete wished he'd recognized that sooner, when he and Tara had begun clashing.

"So no one from the Brotherhood made the connection to this Armenian church before?" Pete asked.

"I was the first," Cyril said, "and it took me this long to convince anyone else it's important."

"So why send you? If no one trusts you?"

Cyril angled his chair away from the man with the backwards baseball cap, who'd finally stopped typing. Fluorescent light from the café counter hit Cyil's face, making his skin look too pale and his cheekbones too sharp, as if he'd lost weight in an instant. His arms hung loose at his sides. "As to why send anyone, hedging all bets I would guess. As to why me, my mentor may see this as a way I can redeem myself. Or he may believe my mistakes are so great since meeting Tara that I cannot be redeemed, so he's sending me where he knows I'll fail."

Pete narrowed his eyes. It had occurred to him that the Brotherhood might be sending Cyril on a wild goose chase to get him, or Pete, out of the way for some reason, but not that it had been done specifically to lower Cyril's standing in the order or demoralize him. "How could your mentor know you'll fail?"

"If he's traveled there already, explored every avenue, and knows there is nothing to be found."

"It's a long way to send someone to fail."

Cyril looked away. "Especially when I did so well at that right at home."

TEAK BOOKCASES LINED the walls of the study where Pir Ferit sat behind a desk in his wheelchair. Ismail hovered at his side. Tara tapped her fingers on the arm of her plain wood visitor chair, feeling as if electricity still charged the air.

Pir Ferit upbraided Ismail. Tara didn't understand the language, which she assumed was Turkish, but the tone came through. Ismail remained silent.

Switching to English, Pir Ferit said, "And what did you accomplish? What did you prove? Nothing." Pir Ferit looked at Tara. "My apologies. Some find it difficult to abandon old superstitions. I never intended the chain to be part of your experience here."

Ismail crossed his arms over his chest and said something else in Turkish. Tara wondered if Ismail thought, as she did, that it was difficult to know what to call superstition and what religion. She'd done all kinds of things, and considered all types of propositions, she would have dismissed in a second before her pregnancy. So she felt a twinge of sympathy for Ismail. Despite that he hadn't uttered so much as a thank you for her saving his life. Maybe he thought the spire would have missed him regardless, or he felt it indicated he was the one telling the truth.

Pir Ferit waved his hand. "It is over. Let us speak English from now on for the benefit of our guests. What did you see at the Cistern?" he asked Tara.

Tara took a deep breath to slow her racing pulse. The scent of the eucalyptus branches in the stone vase on the back bookcase helped calm her. "Tourists. All types of people, really. Water, dim light, columns. Fish. Nothing I wouldn't expect to see." Her voice sounded too loud to her own ears. It filled the tiny room.

"I see." Pir Ferit's forehead creased into multiple lines. He folded his hands on his desk. "You saw no symbol or sculpture with special meaning for you?"

"I kind of liked the Medusa head."

Pir Ferit shook his head.

As she shifted Fimi to her other side, Tara reconsidered whether she ought to share with Pir Ferit. He looked so concerned and kind. But Ismail, who still loomed next to the desk, glowered at her. She couldn't risk it. Especially when the Sufi hadn't asked if she or Fimi had manifested any hidden talents but instead what Tara had seen. "I wish I could tell you something more. I had so many hopes about meeting you."

Ferit wheeled around his desk and stopped next to Tara. "Then I'm afraid this may be the end of the line."

"I've come all this way." The adrenalin from the events in the courtyard had drained. Tara pressed her spine against the back of the chair, fighting to stay alert. "Can you offer any advice? Suggest another path I can pursue?"

Pir Ferit shook his head. He looked as weary as Tara felt. As if he and not Tara had spent the morning traipsing through the Cistern and the city. His shoulders and back sagged so that he almost slumped in his wheelchair. "I can suggest nothing. But I wish you well."

He reached out and rested his warm, dry palm against Tara's cheek.

PETE's spotless nylon duffle bag trundled toward him, and he grabbed it and swung it over his shoulder. His neck and knees ached from the two long flights. The lingering smell of stale smoke in the Zvartnots International airport baggage area irritated his nasal passages, already dry from the air travel.

A middle-aged man approached and spoke swiftly, gesturing toward their bags. Cyril shook his head. Pete understood most Latin-based languages. He'd taken French through college and spent much of his childhood in the different European cities in which his father had been stationed. But Armenian sounded part middle-eastern, part Slavic to Pete, and not at all familiar. It had its own alphabet as well, so Pete couldn't recognize any words on the posted signs.

Pete imagined Tara arriving here and, worse, traveling through this unfamiliar country alone. She'd never been out of the United States before that. She should have had someone to look out for her.

An hour later, a bus discharged them at the Armenian Opera House. During the day, the concrete circular building might have been unremarkable, but the silvery light shining on its first tier, and yellow-gold lights streaming up the columns of the second tier, made it glow against the night sky.

At a small café near the opera house, Pete and Cyril ate chicken and vegetable kebabs and lavash off square white plates. The portly owner told them that while they couldn't see it in the darkness, the wide street on which the café was situated afforded a view of Mount Ararat, the dormant volcanic cone reputed to be the final resting place of Noah's Ark. The owner poked his small, chestnut brown cigar toward the street and explained that the holy mountain no longer officially belonged to Armenia. The borders of Turkey had been extended to include it.

The owner brought tumblers of vodka, setting them carefully on the red placemats. Pete sipped, finding it too bitter for his taste, but it warmed his throat. Cyril drank half of his, started to say something, stopped.

"What?" Pete said.

"You won't believe me."

"Don't let that stop you. I don't believe most of what you say."

Cyril sat straighter. "I want you to know something. I never said a word to Tara against you, never tried to persuade her not to trust or listen to you. It's the nature of this situation. She told me of your strong faith. What happened to Tara couldn't help but challenge that. And it came in the midst of your daughter Megan's crisis. That you may not have responded ideally to Tara says nothing about you as a father."

Pete stared at this man – this criminal – who'd endangered Pete's entire family and devastated Tara. "You're telling me about being a good parent? You're offering me – what? Forgiveness? Understanding?"

"Not from me. You don't need forgiveness or understanding from me, but from yourself."

Pete slammed his glass down, making the table shudder. "You know nothing about me."

Outside, snow fell, blanketing the street, the parked cars, and the sidewalks in a glistening white layer.

"Then why are you here?" Cyril said. "To keep an eye on me, yes, but you could more easily protect Tara from me by staying at her side. So you must want to accomplish something else. It seems to me it must be redemption."

"I don't need redemption. I don't need analysis. I need one thing – knowledge." A group of five people, bundled in furs and large hats, entered and settled at a long table just beyond them. Pete lowered his voice. "I need to know what you know, what you learn, and what you find." Pete had also been charged with bringing whatever document he and Cyril found back to Father Saur, but he wasn't about to tell Cyril that. "And I want to know what you believe."

"About Tara?" Cyril said.

"Yes."

"I believe she's the kindest person I've ever known," Cyril said. "I'll never deserve her."

"And Fimi? Do you believe she's the new messiah? The Second Coming of Christ?"

Despite that he told himself he didn't care what Cyril thought or believed, that neither Cyril's nor the Brotherhood's views held any validity, Pete's breathing became shallow as he waited for the response.

Cyril looked straight at Pete. For the first time, Pete noticed the other man's eyes – clear light gray circled by black under dark, slanting eyebrows. Eyes that seemed honest, open. No wonder Tara had been taken in.

"No," Cyril said. "I don't."

# 14

Tara stared at the stone Medusa heads, the walkways, the tourists, looking for anything that might reveal special meaning. She and Kelly had decided to return to the Basilica Cistern after leaving Pir Ferit. Kelly sat alone near the entrance in case her presence during the first visit to the Cistern had interfered with Tara experiencing whatever vision she was meant to see. Tara studied the columns particularly carefully. Some were Doric, some Corinthian, some plain, some engraved. She'd read that they'd been gathered from defunct Roman sites. But none revealed any special meaning or, if they did, she was missing it.

*What am I supposed to find anyway? Secret passageway? Hidden message? Spirit guide?*

The glow from the uplights tinted Tara's hands, and Fimi's face, a deep orange-red color. Tara didn't remember that from the last visit. She glanced around to see if other people's exposed skin looked the same. But it was almost closing time, and the walkway around her had emptied.

To her far left, Tara noticed a stairway leading down to the water level. She inched toward it and put her hand on the wooden railing. It felt warm and textured against her palm. *This wasn't here before*, she thought. And despite the rough feel of the railing, the damp smell, and the echoing sounds of fish splashing below her, she felt sure she was dreaming.

When she'd been a teenager, Tara had begun having lucid dreams. At first, as soon as she'd realized she was in a dream, she'd felt frantic to get out, afraid she'd be stuck there and never return to real life. But she'd come to enjoy that sense of awareness while dreaming, eventually learning at times to control what happened. A book she'd read, recommended by Dr. Lei, had helped. She still remembered a line from it – *if you're falling in a dream, learn to fly.*

Tara had no idea what flying would mean now. And she didn't know what to look for in this dream Cistern any more than she had in the real one. The dim red light pressed in on her, and she felt the old fear that she'd never awaken. She opened her mouth to yell, which sometimes woke her, but forced herself not to. What if she was supposed to learn something here? She couldn't afford to leave too soon.

Fimi stayed almost completely still in the baby sling. Tara wondered if the baby was dreaming too, wherever the two of them were in real life. She felt unsure when exactly the dream had started. In the chilly mosque courtyard? During her first visit to the Cistern? Before that? Tara's chest tightened. Where were she and Fimi in real life? Were they in danger? She squeezed her hands into fists and released them, trying to let go of her anxiety and bring her mind back to the moment.

At the bottom of the staircase, instead of clear water and goldfish, Tara found a brackish swamp. She crossed it using stepping stones. *I'm walking on water*, she thought.

On the other side, Tara pushed through dense vegetation, some of it with prickles that scraped her arms, to a clearing. Dozens of combat jeeps and SUVs, all painted in camouflage colors, some draped with vines, had been parked there at odd angles. As Tara moved closer, she realized the largest wasn't an SUV at all, but an armoured transport vehicle. Its back doors had been flung open. Skeletons were harnessed to the ten empty seats that ran around the inside of the back module.

Heart pounding, Tara stumbled back. She no longer held Fimi. She peered around, but didn't see the baby.

*It's just a dream*, she thought, standing still and taking a few deep breaths. *She's fine in real life, she has to be.*

Beyond the transport vehicle, what appeared to be soldiers stood in a circle facing one another, motionless. Except they weren't real soldiers but dummies made of stuffed camouflage shirts, pants, and combat boots. Helmets with black visors served as heads, with nothing but empty space where their chins should be. They'd been propped so close together that their hands – stuffed brown leather gloves – touched one another's. In the center of the circle of faceless soldiers stood a platinum high chair. And in the high chair sat a miniatature version of the soldier dummies, the size of a six or seven-month old baby, elbows propped on the tray table.

Rather than a helmet, its head was a round, black bomb with a wick at the top.

~

"No, no, no, no, no—" Tara backed away from the soldiers and the baby bomb. "No."

Cold stone pressed against her back. Faces hovered over her. Kelly, her face pale, eyes large. Fimi, safe in Kelly's arms. An old man with a shaved head, face wide at the cheekbones, deep wrinkles below his eyes. Sitting in a wheelchair. A tall young man with a dark, close beard, a nose that tilted slightly to one side, and stern, thin lips.

"Tara? Are you all right?" Kelly gripped Tara's upper arm and helped her off the stone floor of the small study into a wooden chair.

The old man folded his hand over Tara's and pressed something into her palm. When he let go, she closed her fist around the object.

"Ms. Spencer," the old man said.

*Pir Ferit, his name is Pir Ferit.*

The object felt like a key made of soft wood.

The younger man stepped closer to Tara and said something in an unfamiliar language. Or perhaps her brain just wasn't working well enough to understand. The older man responded in English. "Let her alone."

The younger man stepped back, his mouth set in a grim, straight line.

*Ismail. He's Ismail. I'm in Turkey. But why did Pier Ferit give me a key and hide it from everyone?*

"Were we talking?" Tara asked.

Pir Ferit nodded. "You fainted."

Tara remembered the Basilica Cistern. The dream. The soldiers.

"It was so strange, I –"

Pir Ferit turned to Ismail. "Please fetch Ms. Spencer some ginger tea." He looked at Kelly. "Please go with him. The two of you can bring tea for all." Pir Ferit met Tara's eyes. "This tea will assist in regaining your bearings."

"Tara?" Kelly hesitated, her hand still resting on Tara's arm.

Looking at Pir Ferit, Tara said, "Yes, it's all right. That would be all right." She put out her arms for Fimi, keeping the key concealed.

Ismail, still frowning, spoke again in Turkish. One of his hands clenched in a fist at his side, the other remained in his pocket.

Pir Ferit said, "Would you be rude to our guest? After she traveled so far on a fruitless journey?"

Tara's heart fell at Pir Ferit's statement. It had been a fruitless journey, and a frightening one. Maybe Pir Ferit was only being polite in asking for tea and had nothing important to tell her.

Ismail spun on his heel and left the room. Kelly followed. Pir Ferit wheeled to the door and shut it, motioning Tara to stay seated.

"We must be quick." Pir Ferit returned to Tara's side, stopping only a few feet from her. "It takes a short time to brew tea, and Ismail harbors suspicions of me already."

"You don't trust him?"

"In this matter, I trust no one. Not even you. But still I hope."

Tara longed to ask why he kept Ismail with him if that was a concern, but she figured that wasn't the most important issue.

Pir Ferit leaned toward her. "What did you see?"

"I was back in the Cistern." Tara shuddered. "I stumbled into what looked like a jungle. Soldiers – or dummies that looked like soldiers, combat vehicles, a bomb. The bomb was part of a doll, a baby doll. All still. All a tableau, not the real thing." She opened her hand to see the key. It was carved from blond wood. "What is this for?"

Pir Ferit raised his hand in a stop gesture. "First, memorize the numbers and letters on the key. Before you speak further."

"Letters...." Tara turned the key over and saw nine letters and numbers carved into it. Using the mnemonics she'd learned for her medical school entrance exam to help remember formulae, she memorized it. Once she was certain it was fixed in her mind, and she'd repeated it three times to Pir Ferit's satisfaction, he took a metal file from his drawer and began filing. When he returned the key, the letters had been smoothed away.

"Now if it falls into anyone else's hands, they will believe they've obtained a secret, but they will hold only a useless piece of wood."

"And what do I do with the password?" Tara said.

"When you are alone and can access a computer, go to the official website for this mosque and look for a serpent icon. It is tiny in the bottom right corner. When you click, it will take you to a blank page. Type the password, though you will see no space for it. Simply type it. You will be taken to a portion of a document. At least, tomorrow you will be, as I will post it tonight."

"What kind of document?" Tara wondered if it was the same one Cyril believed would be found in the Armenian church.

"It is a third of a message from the past to the present. I learned it from the original, which is in ancient Armenian. You will need a translator, but one will likely appear when needed."

"Why not write it for me on paper? In English."

"I cannot risk paper being taken from you while you are in Istanbul, and I do not wish to lose nuance if I translate. Translation is not a great skill of mine. You must obtain at least two of the three original pieces of the document to see the ink and tear lines and fit it together. The text alone will not do. If you do not find the originals of the other portions, the original of mine is secured in a place of worship in Europe. There will be instructions on the site on how to find it."

Tara glanced at the round metal clock on the edge of Pir Ferit's desk. Ismail and Kelly had been gone nearly five minutes. "And the rest of the document?"

"Another part is reputed to be in a church in Armenia, I know not exactly where, but it interested me that you once traveled there."

So the document did connect to Cyril's claims. Which meant he had told the truth – maybe – about why he wanted to go there. "My dad and – someone else – are there now."

"Ah, wonderful. Someone you trust, I hope."

Tara hesitated. "I trust my dad." And she did. At least, she trusted him not to hurt her intentionally. But they'd been at odds since her pregnancy, and she could easily imagine circumstances where he might deliver the document to someone in the Church instead of her if he believed in his heart it was the right thing to do. And would Cyril stop that from happening? Or just take whatever they found to the Brotherhood?

"My piece and the Armenian piece should help you find the third," Pir Fert said. "Its whereabouts are unknown to me."

"Why did you send me to the Basilica Cistern?"

Pir Ferit smiled. "I sent each of the young women who visited me to a different historical site. Each returned, claiming to have had a vision. And perhaps each did, but if so, the visions had nothing to do with my message. Only you had no vision until I touched your face. That is what was foretold."

"So going there and reporting back was a test?"

"Yes and no. I did not mean to play games with you. But I needed reassurance of your integrity."

The sound of footsteps and Kelly's and Ismail's voices came through the door. Tara couldn't make out the words, only the tones. Kelly's pleasant and neutral, Ismail's consisting of what sounded like grunts.

Tara's mind raced as she tried to decide what she most wanted to ask Pir Ferit.

"My vision of the soldier and baby – what did it mean?"

Pir Ferit shook his head. "It was foretold that when the guardian's hand touched your face, you would see the echoes of a battle to come. What that means is unknown to me."

The door swung open. Icy air rushed in. Kelly carried a plain wooden tea tray. Ismail followed behind her, holding a book that he placed on Pir Ferit's desk. Hamed had joined them, and he served the tea, smiling at Tara.

"And what were you before, my dear?" Pir Ferit said to Tara, as if continuing a conversation.

It took Tara a moment to follow his lead. "Before I got pregnant?"

Pir Ferit nodded.

"I'd nearly finished college and was ready to take the MCAT. The exam for medical school." That seemed so far in the past to Tara, though it had been just a little more than a year before, that she felt almost as if she were talking about someone else's life. She loved Fimi, and she missed her life before Fimi.

"You were a good student?"

"I still am, I hope. I plan to go to medical school eventually."

Pir Ferit patted her shoulder. "I am certain you will if you are determined to do so. Do not lose heart. This trip has taken a different and unexpected turn. But life always does so. It will bring you many opportunities. Always remember the things you've heard from your elders, even if those things seem unimportant. That is the best advice."

Damp, chilled air rose from the stone floor. It seeped into Pir Ferit's feet through the soles of his shoes as they rested on his wheelchair's metal footrests. He unlocked his bottom desk drawer and slid out a small computer. Using a custom program, he typed Armenian characters, saving after every other word. Armenian was not his first language, and its alphabet had evolved over the years. Ferit had spent much time as a child learning its permutations. Nonetheless, his portion of the document had been particularly difficult to memorize. The original had been torn in jagged vertical lines. Ferit suspected the document was a letter, but it made little sense to him, and the sections that might contain a salutation, closing, and signature were missing. He again considered adding an English translation despite what he'd told Tara. But he feared changing the meaning if he translated Armenian to Turkish, then Turkish to English, without the entire text to help interpret. Better that Tara find a translator when the document was made whole, if that ever occurred.

Footsteps rang on the stone floor of the outside corridor. Pir Ferit smiled, though he knew he'd need to ask his friend to wait before they could visit, so that he could complete his task.

The knock came, and the door swung open.

"Ah, old friend, how lovely to –"

At ninety-two, Pir Ferit's reflexes remained sharp. When he saw the gun, he pressed two keys in tandem to run a sequence he'd programmed long ago. The sequence saved what he'd typed, posted it on the secure site, and exited the program, destroying his tracks. The computer blipped, indicating it had processed something, but Pir Ferit wasn't sure how much of what little text he'd typed had posted.

*Enough*, Pir Ferit thought as the first dart hit his shoulder. *I only hope I told her* –

# 15

The screen froze again. Tara swore at the computer, rebooting for the third time. Similar mutters came from other tables at the tiny Internet café.

Kelly peered over Tara's shoulder. "At least this time you actually got onto the website."

"Yeah, but I didn't see the symbol I'm looking for." Tara kept her words vague, wishing they weren't in a public café. But the hotel's Internet connection had been down all morning. She reached for her tea – the darkest, strongest brew the café offered. She'd felt headachy and drained all evening after leaving Pir Ferit. At night, she'd dreamed about sitting in her sister Megan's room reading Megan her favorite book in the Land of Oz series. She'd awakened at three in the morning in the dark hotel room with its iced-over windows and had trouble falling back asleep.

"We won't be able to read it anyway, right?" Kelly said.

"Not the document section. It'll be in Armenian. But there should be some other instructions there." Tara hoped the instructions about how to find the original of the document were more specific than Pir Ferit's usual comments.

After twenty more minutes of frustration, they decided to take a break, then look for another café to start over. They walked to a bazaar they'd seen from the bus the day before. It stood about a mile from the Koca Mustafa Pasha Mosque. Sellers hawked goods in what sounded like dozens of different languages, gesturing to designer shoes, costume jewelry, spices, pyramids of produce, pottery. A rich, savory smell led the sisters to a stand where women in starchy white garb sizzled goat cheese and parsley, a local specialty called *Gözleme*. Tara loved the jumble of colors around her – reds, greens, oranges, bright yellows, so much more vibrant and varied than in stores at home, and the spicy scents.

On the way out, Tara glanced at a group of traditionally-dressed women. She wondered how they felt about covering so much of their bodies every day, and whether they found it strange that American women sometimes walked around wearing so little. She turned to comment on it to Kelly.

The ground began to shake.

~

TEA GLASSES on the teak bookcase farthest from the desk clinked together, making a tinkling sound, like delicate bells, as Hamed removed his coat. He'd just entered Pir Ferit's study for his morning lesson. The earth's vibrations shifted the glasses toward the edge of the shelf until they crashed onto the floor. Glass shards flew.

The shaking stopped. Pir Ferit was nowhere to be seen, though the books he and Hamed were studying were stacked in the center of the desk. Hamed backed out of the room and ran for the mosque, afraid his teacher might be in the older building. If the tremors returned and became severe, it was more likely the mosque would sustain damage than the newer buildings. As he crossed the courtyard, skirting broken pieces of the spire that hadn't yet been cleared, Hamed told himself everything would be fine. The mosque couldn't be unfortunate enough to suffer earthquake damage when lightning had struck only yesterday.

He was wrong.

~

CLINKING, shattering, and smacking sounds came from everywhere as dishes, produce, and bottles tumbled off carts onto the pavement. Smells of overripe fruit and fish permeated the air. Horns blared. Tara and Kelly dropped to their hands and knees, Tara with one arm cradled across Fimi, who remained secure in the baby carrier. Tara had lived through minor earthquakes in St. Louis. Each time, after a minute or so, everything had stopped vibrating, and the aftershocks had been minor. Now, though, the trembling grew more intense, jarring her and sending bricks and boards falling from buildings. Rumbling, like that of an underground train, grew deeper and louder.

Down the street, the dome on a small, ancient mosque fell in upon itself at the center.

"Did you see that?" Kelly said. "It looked like an underbaked cake flopping."

"Pir Ferit," Tara said, imagining the same thing happening to the Koca Mustafa Pasha Mosque.

"Oh, no, you think? His mosque?"

They waited ten minutes after the shaking stopped to start for the mosque, picking their way through bricks, stone, and other debris strewn across the streets. To Tara's relief, the buildings they passed stood mostly intact. When they reached the mosque, though, it was a different story. While the outdoor corridor and its adjacent buildings had withstood the earthquake, the southeast corner of the mosque had collapsed.

Tara didn't see Pir Ferit anywhere. Near the mosque, Ismail hefted and shoved large sections of concrete out of the way, helped by two other men. A fourth man sat on the ground propped against pieces of broken spire from the lightning strike the day before, one arm cradled at his side, legs splayed out in front of him. He waved his uninjured arm, shouting and directing the men around him. Tara absorbed the frantic nature of his words though she didn't understand them. She ran to Ismail to ask about Pir Ferit.

"Someone saw him leave the mosque a few minutes before the earthquake started," Ismail said. "But we believe Hamed was searching for him when the earthquake hit."

More people from the area joined in clearing the debris. Despite wailing sirens and shouts from the street, all worked silently, straining to hear sounds from Hamed or anyone else who might have been buried. Kelly shoved bricks and medium-sized stones away from the edges of the pile to make more room for those who could lift larger pieces. Tara cleared whatever she could without dislodging Fimi, who was wrapped around her front in the baby sling. She couldn't imagine how Hamed could be alive under all the rock.

After what seemed like half an hour, but Tara guessed was more like five minutes, a young woman uncovered a small foot, wearing a boot, then the rest of the boy's body. Hamed lay motionless on his side in what might have been a kneeling position had he been upright. He'd folded his hand over his head as if to cover it at the last moment. His face was scraped from forehead to chin. A deep cut gashed the back of his head, and his right arm bent at an unnatural angle and was split open at the elbow, with bone, blood, and flesh showing through the torn shirt sleeve. Ismail pressed his fingers to Hamed's neck and nodded. But Hamed didn't open his eyes, and his face looked chalk white. Another woman handed Ismail a cloth, and he tied a tourniquet around the boy's upper arm. Two men ran toward the street, shouting. Tara guessed they yelled for a doctor.

Kelly, her face smeared with dirt and sweat, looked at Tara. "You and Fimi –"

Tara nodded and clambered over the debris to reach Hamed. Ismail watched her but didn't say anything or try to stop her. The last thing Tara wanted was to display any power Fimi might possess before any stranger, let alone a crowd of them, but she couldn't let Hamed die if there was a chance to save him. No one should die so young, and no parent should lose a child so young. Should lose a child ever. And unlike if she were trying to provide medical first aid, merely holding Fimi and meditating near Hamed could hardly put him in more danger. If a doctor arrived, she'd back away.

Tara rested one hand on Hamed's waist, the other on the side of his leg, both of which appeared uninjured, careful to barely graze him. Sweat slicked her palms, and her chest felt tight, as if an elephant stood on it. That Kelly's cut had healed in the Basilica Cistern seemed impossible and unreal, more like Tara's lucid dream than reality.

Tara's breath came faster. What was she thinking? She couldn't do this. The air felt gritty when she inhaled.

"Relax," Kelly said.

"Right."

Screeching sirens, horns, shouts. Kneeling on rubble that cut through her jeans, the baby pressed too tight against her, fussing. *Sure. Relax.* Tara shut her eyes, feeling foolish, as if she were a charlatan pretending to cure people to collect money. She breathed in the chalky air with its squashed fruit smell through her nose, let it out through her mouth. She heard Kelly yell something at the others. Tara pushed the sound of her sister's voice away until it blended with all the street sounds, and all the street sounds faded into a mass of white noise that no longer seemed connected to Tara and yet somehow absorbed her at the same time so that she became part of it.

*Breathe. In. Out. Hold. In....*

Time disappeared. Everything disappeared. Except for Tara's breath and the boy who lay under her hands, and Fimi, and then all that disappeared, too.

A woman's voice calling Hamed's name drew Tara back to the world. She opened her eyes. Hamed sat, his spine straight, his formerly broken arm moving easily, the wound closed. A row of small scabs along his elbow was all that was left amongst the blood smears. His face looked free of any marks, and the back of his head, still bloody, no longer gaped open.

Hamed grinned. It lit his whole face. Tara returned his smile and leaned forward to hug him, but before her arms went around him, her body seemed to melt into warm liquid. Still kneeling, she collapsed sideways. Kelly and Hamed grabbed her and eased her into a lying position. Kelly lifted Fimi from the baby sling around Tara's front and held her.

Two feet away, Ismail, jaw clenched and trembling, stared at Tara as she lay on the ground, rough pieces of debris knifing her back. Just beyond Ismail, a woman wearing a fuschia and pink headscarf and long coat pushed through the debris, embraced Hamed and rocked him, crooning his name. Then she hugged Tara, who'd struggled to a sitting position with Kelly's help. The woman's words spilled out, some Turkish, some English. She was Hamed's mother. She couldn't stop thanking Tara.

Hamed said something in Turkish.

"A miracle," his mother said. "He says you held him and Allah healed him. A miracle."

"I didn't do anything." Tara's legs and arms shook. She couldn't say any more, but she was able to shift to a clearer section of ground. The cold seeped into the backs of her thighs. She shivered.

A crowd gathered, and Hamed's mother spoke to them, gesturing to Hamed, Tara, and Fimi. People drew closer, some staring, some trying to touch Tara. Kelly blocked them and helped Tara, whose teeth were now chattering, to her feet, keeping an arm around her waist. An older woman thrust a child who had blood running down his forehead into Tara's path. A man staggered toward her, his twisted leg dragging behind him. Fingers plucked at her coat and at Fimi, brushed against the baby's face. Despite the chill, heat swept through Tara. She gasped for air. Kelly and Ismail pushed people away, Ismail shouting in Turkish.

Ismail turned to Tara. "Trouble. I told Pir Ferit that was all you would bring," Ismail said. "Get away from here."

# 16

Barely aware of the chaos around them, Tara stumbled past rubble, half-tumbled walls, and cars parked sideways or partially mired in cracks in the street. "Can't anymore. Rest."

"Just a little farther." Kelly held Fimi, who'd fallen asleep, against her right side. She put her left arm around Tara's waist, half-supporting her, half urging her forward.

Gradually, their path cleared, the worst of the damage behind them. Uninjured people trundled along the streets and sidewalks, looking for family members and gathering intact items and food where they could. Tara's legs felt like lead weights. She'd never been this tired in her life, including after Fimi's birth.

"Just a few minutes," she said.

Kelly glanced around. "It's not safe."

*Please, please, let me stop*, Tara wanted to tell her sister. But she also felt Kelly was right, though Tara didn't know exactly why. Everything that had happened at the mosque blurred in her mind. She pushed on, telling herself after each step that she'd take just one more. "The hotel is safer?"

"I hope so," Kelly said.

A tall burqa-clad figure on the other side of the street waved at them.

Father Gregory Saur hunched forward, lifting his black-framed glasses so he could peer without their aid at the screen. "They did it," he said, "Tara and the baby." Gregory could hardly believe his eyes. In fact, he wasn't sure he believed his eyes, despite his statement. If it were true, it meant he'd been completely wrong in what he'd told Pete Spencer.

"Unclear." The phone's speaker flattened Stranyero's voice so that it sounded steadier and colder than in person.

The radiator in a corner of Gregory's office hissed, struggling to keep pace with the dropping temperature outdoors. It had been below twenty – unusually frigid for St. Louis in February – throughout the last week.

"The people at the mosque believe it," Gregory said. "What else would make them flock to her? How else could the boy move his arm? And stand?"

"A trick," Stranyero said.

"Regardless, it will raise her profile." Gregory pushed his glasses higher on the bridge of his nose. "Now is the time we feared would come."

"Perhaps."

Gregory stared at the phone, perplexed. "Why send Mullin, if not for the aftermath of an event like this?"

"No need for concern," Stranyero said. "In an abundance of caution, I sent the order."

The line went dead.

Gregory walked to his window. It was situated directly above the radiator. A poor design that meant much of the heat rose and seeped out the ill-fitting window casement. He took out his pearl rosary, a gift from his mother on his ordination. Holding its gold crucifix, he recited: "I believe in God, the Father Almighty, Creator of Heaven and earth; and in Jesus Christ, His only Son Our Lord, Who was conceived by the Holy Spirit, born of the Virgin Mary, suffered under Pontius Pilate, was crucified, died, and was buried. He descended into Hell...."

Gregory trailed off, struck by the words he was in the habit of reciting in a meditative, almost automatic, way. How odd that the Apostles' Creed said Jesus had descended into Hell before rising from the dead and ascending into Heaven. Surely that had been discussed in the seminary, but it was so long ago he didn't recall. Why Hell first? Why Hell at all? The radiator hissed louder, as if chiding him for his questions. Turning away from it, Gregory finished the Creed and, ticking off each bead, said an Our Father, three Hail Marys, and a Glory Be. Then, because it was Tuesday, he recited the first Sorrowful Mystery.

EACH INSTANT FROZE, then clicked into the next, as if Tara were watching an old-fashioned slide show. A large burqa-clad figure on the other side of the street waved, then gestured to something behind them. Tara glanced over her shoulder, and a dark-haired woman was upon her. The young woman was pregnant enough that her shape showed through her quilted winter coat. She darted between Tara and Kelly, breaking them apart. Tara stumbled sideways, and took a few seconds to regain her balance. The pregnant woman spun around and swung her fist underhanded to hit Kelly's elbow from beneath. Kelly's grip on Fimi loosened. Adrenalin shot through Tara, erasing her exhaustion, and she lunged. But the woman had already snatched the baby and started running. She headed for a heavyset man wearing jeans, a parka, and a knit ski mask who had stepped out from behind a push cart. Something silver flashed at his side.

Tara ran after the woman, swerving around cars and people as if she were back in a college intramural basketball game.

*Oh my God, my God, I never should have brought Fimi here.*

A silver BMW Series 7 careened around the corner, directly into the pregnant woman's path. Tara grabbed hold of the woman's right arm from behind and flung herself backwards to stop the woman's momentum. The man in the parka and the burqa-clad figure, who'd both drawn swords, skirted either side of the car. As they circled, the burqa's face veil fell away, revealing a man's pale face. The BMW reversed, wheels spinning, and slammed into him. His body flew up and hit the roof of the vehicle, then bounced to the side of the road.

The pregnant woman shouted something on seeing the impact, but her words were lost as the car changed direction and roared toward the man in the parka. Kelly reached Tara and circled in front of the pregnant woman. From behind, Tara gripped both the woman's elbows and, using all her strength, squeezed them together. The woman's arms opened, and Fimi began to slip from her grasp. Kelly grabbed the baby, who was howling and squirming, nearly dropping her. Tara pushed the woman aside. She and Kelly cradled the baby between them.

The pregnant woman and the man in the parka ran west toward a row of houses across the street. The BMW halted, shimmering in the sunlight. The tall, pale man lay on his back five feet from it. Wisps of red hair stuck through his face veil.

"Mullin," Tara said, both horrified and relieved that he appeared to be dead, then horrified that she felt relieved about anyone's death. "It's Mullin."

The car's driver door swung open. A tall blond man in a tweed suit stepped out. Though the ground began shaking again, he kept his balance with seeming ease. In his left hand, he held a gun.

"Get in the car."

# 17

Tara scanned the street and sidewalks, pressing Fimi to her chest. Cyril had once told her it was hard for even a good marksman to hit a moving target, but she couldn't risk Fimi and Kelly on his advice. On the other hand, if this man was willing to kill them in the street, he'd certainly do it when he got them somewhere secluded, and they'd have less chance to escape.

"Now." The man gestured toward the BMW with his free hand, his mouth a grim line. He had the smooth good looks, perfectly-sized nose, and sharp cheekbones of the male models that sometimes came to SLU to pose for art classes, though he must be ten or fifteen years older than them.

"What do you want?" Eyes on the gun, Kelly moved closer to the man, as if she planned to step between him and Tara if necessary.

*Maybe she would.* Tears burned Tara's eyes. She blinked to clear them.

The man glanced down at the gun. "This isn't for you." He pointed to Mullin. "It's for his partner."

Tara slipped her hand in her coat pocket, finding her switchblade, though she couldn't imagine it would do her much good against a gun. Especially given that her hands and her legs had started shaking. Not from aftershocks, but from her returning exhaustion. "Who are you?"

The man drew himself up straighter. "Erik Holmes. I funded your trip. I guided you to Pir Ferit. And I stopped Mullin. Now I must insist you get in the car."

The man in the parka appeared between two houses across the street. Tara and Kelly both saw him and started toward Holmes' car. But Tara faltered. Her vision blurred. She felt Holmes' hands on her shoulders, and Kelly taking Fimi from her arms. A few moments later she lay on the back seat, knees bent to make room for an infant car seat belted behind the driver's seat.

She heard the BMW's front doors slam, then Kelly asking, "Where are we going?"

Then nothing.

~

"You're more of a target now," Holmes was saying when Tara became conscious again. She didn't know how long she'd been out, but Fimi was now strapped into the car seat near her feet in the back seat. The BMW's ride seemed smoother, so she guessed they'd gotten away from the worst of the earthquake damage. "Because that boy was healed, you're all more of a target."

"You think Tara should have let him die," Kelly said.

"If it meant saving herself and the baby? Yes."

Tara tried to sit. Dizziness and nausea swept through her, and everything went dark.

~

"We don't know anything about you," Kelly said.

Tara forced herself to focus on the conversation as her stomach churned. Afraid she might vomit and choke if she stayed on her back, she shifted to her side, keeping her eyes closed. The whole car seemed to revolve beneath her.

"I doubt that," Holmes said. "Professor Gaddini strikes me as a dedicated researcher."

"She said there's almost nothing available about you," Kelly said.

"True. But I'm sure she found nothing adverse."

Tara thought she smelled smoke, but it didn't seem to be in the car, as she had no trouble breathing. Had the earthquake started fires outside?

"Also nothing to tell us why you're interested in Tara," Kelly said.

"Be glad I am or your sister or niece would be missing a hand right now."

The car skidded around a corner. Tara pitched off the back seat onto the floor, landing on thick padding.

"Tara?" Kelly said.

"Okay," Tara mumbled. She pressed one hand against the padding, trying to push herself upright, but her arm gave way. She felt as if she'd used her entire store of strength earlier in the day. Her back was to Fimi, and she strained to hear any sound from the baby. "Fimi?"

"She's good." Kelly's voice sounded close; she must have leaned over the front seat to look. "Should we stop?"

"Tara will be safer on the floor," Holmes said. "It may be a rough ride, and there's padding there, so she'll bounce around less."

*A padded floor. A car seat installed and ready.*

"What did you mean 'missing a hand'?" Kelly said.

"It was a test," Holmes said. "An attempt at a test."

"What kind of test?"

"Within the past fourteen months," Holmes said, "Tara has spontaneously become pregnant, she and baby Sophia may have healed the maimed and raised the dead, and the baby may reproduce herself in perpetuity if her life follows Tara's."

"Are they testing for the messiah?" Kelly said. "No, that makes no sense."

Tara's hands grew cold. It didn't make sense. A religious order wouldn't maim anyone they thought might be their messiah. Though history suggested a government might.

"Not the messiah," Holmes said. The car swerved again. Tara pressed her body into the quilted padding, trying to keep still and avoid more dizziness. "Spontaneously regenerating a limb or digit if it's cut off is believed to be an attribute of the Antichrist. As is living forever. In addition, in the last two years, what some see as omens – earthquakes, tsunamis, droughts – all increased."

Tara's skin prickled. *The one who will live forever.*

"I don't know if the test was meant for Tara or the baby or both," Holmes continued, "but that's the purpose of those silver swords. If the finger or hand regrew, the Antichrist was found. If not, a human was injured, but could possibly be healed. A small price to pay for knowledge in the larger cosmic scheme."

ISTANBUL - THE BODY of a revered Sufi elder was found yesterday on the banks of the Bosphorus Strait near the Fatih Sultan Mehmet Bridge. Pir Ferit taught at the University of Istanbul and was last seen at the Koca Mustafa Pasha Mosque. The cause of death is drowning, but police in Istanbul believe foul play may have occurred.

"WHERE DID YOU GO LAST NIGHT?" Pete asked Cyril.

They'd shared a hotel room with two twin beds. Cyril had slipped out during the night, and Pete had been too exhausted to follow. In the morning, Cyril said nothing about his disappearance, just arranged transportation to Ijevan. Now, both of them rode in the back seat of an aging taxi that smelled of cigarette smoke.

"A walk," Cyril said. "I felt restless. I walked downstairs and back."

The hotel lobby had consisted of a narrow hall with a long reception counter. No chairs, no vending machines, no televisions. "You just ran up and down the stairs?" Pete said. "You didn't go outside?"

"I stepped out for a few moments. Nothing going on."

Cyril rummaged through his duffle bag, took out the British newspaper the *Times* he'd bought at a store near the taxi stand, and began to read, apparently unconcerned about Pete studying him or the taxi's jouncing ride. Pete had his book with him, but had never been able to read in cars without feeling sick. His mind was filled with questions for Cyril about the Brotherhood, but he didn't want to raise them with the taxi driver listening. He doubted the driver knew anyone who wanted to harm Tara, but after what his family had been through, Pete felt he couldn't be too careful. He remembered Tara passing on something Cyril had said to her – better paranoid than dead. Back then, he'd thought the comment a sign of Tara's delusions. Now he followed it.

As the drive continued, the terrain evolved. The boxy houses and faded brick Soviet-era apartment buildings became fewer and farther apart. Towering evergreens and bare-branched fruit-trees, poplars, and oaks covered the rolling hills.

"Pete." Cyril's hand shook as he held out the *Times*. He'd folded it open to an article reporting that Pir Ferit had drowned.

Pete's heart jumped, but he did his best to keep his face blank. He'd never told Cyril that Tara had traveled to Istanbul, let alone that she'd gone to see the Sufi teacher. "Why show me this?"

"The Koca Mustafa Pasha Mosque, where Pir Ferit was a visiting scholar, used to be a church dedicated to Andrew of Crete," Cyril said.

*The best thing I can do is keep searching for answers*, Pete thought. *It won't help Tara if I reveal too much to Cyril.* "I see," he said.

"And this." Cyril showed Pete another story, this one about an earthquake in western Turkey. The taxi's bouncing on the rough road made it almost impossible to read the print. But Pete saw that forty-four fatalities had been reported so far. Istanbul's Fatih District had sustained the most damage.

Pete unzipped his down jacket, sweating despite the taxi's barely functioning heater. He'd received a voicemail from Lynette earlier that day saying she'd tried Tara's and Kelly's phones and hadn't been able to reach them. Pete had assumed it was nothing more than poor cellular coverage.

"We could go there," Cyril said.

"What?"

"Change course. Go to Istanbul. Try to find out what happened. If you thought it would be helpful." Cyril looked at Pete.

"Why would I think it helpful?" Pete said.

*Tara's fine. Kelly's fine. Fimi's fine.* Pete pictured his granddaughter, remembered holding her in the Westin's lobby as she smiled and waved her hands at him. He ought to have spent more time with her, spent Christmas with her rather than withdrawing from everyone. *Please God, let them be fine.*

"Look," Cyril said, "I understand you don't want to share with me. You don't need to tell me anything about where Tara is or what she's doing. But I need to know that she's all right. Please."

Pete hesitated. "I don't know. Lynette hasn't heard from her in the last twenty-four hours."

Cyril paled. Beyond him, through the taxi window, Mount Ararat loomed in the distance, its snow-capped top nearly the same shade as the grayish-white winter sky.

"Should we go there?" Cyril said.

~

Tara jerked awake. She lay on her back in a bed, wearing a T-shirt, bra, and underwear, but her legs were bare. She windmilled her arms – no Fimi. Rolling onto her side, Tara reached out until she hit something. Sharp pain in her wrist cleared her mind. The air smelled like sandalwood and chai. The sheets felt soft and crisp. A hotel? A nightstand? Then there must be a lamp. She felt further, touched metal.

A light glowed on. Asian-sounding string music with chimes played quietly from an unseen music system. The bed was King-sized. Deep yellow-gold walls and drapes and bamboo wood floors warmed the spacious room. A telescope on a tripod stood in front of the shrouded windows to Tara's left.

A note on cream-colored paper lay on the nightstand. "I'm in the hotel business center. Fimi's with me. Holmes insisted on paying for the hotel suite. Back soon. Feel better. Everything's okay – relatively speaking." Beneath the words, Kelly had drawn a little happy face, something she'd done since she was a kid. The Four Seasons at Sultanahmet was printed in burgundy ink at the bottom of the notepaper.

Tara flexed her feet and jumped out of bed, relieved to find her muscles working well. She found her passport, money, and phone in her backpack, but the phone had no service. From the hotel's landline, she reached Kelly in the business center. At the sound of her sister's voice, Tara's breathing steadied and the knots in her shoulders and neck eased a bit.

A button opened the drapes to reveal a wide balcony and a panoramic view of the Sultanahmet neighborhood. The spires of the Hagia Sophia and the Blue Mosque soared above trees and shorter buildings. Through the telescope, Tara saw some blocked streets, crumbled portions of buildings, and broken tree limbs, but it didn't appear the earthquake had hit the area quite as hard as it had the Fatih District. Which made Tara think of Pir Ferit. They'd never found out what had happened to him.

When Kelly returned, the sisters sat at the polished round dining table in the hotel suite's sitting room, Fimi in the infant carrier near Tara. Tall windows trimmed in dark wood provided a view of the Sea of Marmara. The sun splashed off the deep blue water.

Kelly had printed out three pages. The staggered lines on the first page each included what looked like four to seven words, all in unfamiliar characters.

"Did you find a website that could translate it?" Tara asked.

"I tried. It spit back mostly junk – looks like the file got corrupted. Or free sites just aren't very good."

Kelly pointed to an English word in the midst of the keyboard symbols, numbers, and letters that littered the second page. "This is from the first screen after I clicked the serpent icon. It's the only word, or part of a word, that showed there. The rest was gibberish."

"'Collyridi' – Pir Ferit said something like that. When we were at the café. Related to early Christians."

"Yeah, I remember," Kelly said. "Kind of."

Tara retrieved a cellophane-wrapped fruit and cheese basket from the sideboard, hunger gnawing at her now that she felt sure she and her sister and daughter were safe, at least for the moment.

"He mentioned that word and another one I'd never heard. Shit." Tara struggled with the cellophane wrapping, which had stretched across the basket and twisted. "The last thing Pir Ferit said to me was to remember what my elders said, even if it seemed unimportant. And I don't remember." She dug in her pocket for her knife and cut through the cellophane.

As they talked through what Pir Ferit had said, and what Holmes had revealed in the car, Tara ate a golden-brown fruit shaped like an apple. It tasted like a pear instead, with a rough texture and a sweetness that complemented the pungent soft cheese Kelly had spread on crackers.

Their phones still had no signal. Tara guessed some of the cell phone towers were down.

"Why don't we call Sophia from the hotel's phone," Kelly said. "Holmes and Sophia both know we're here in the city, and probably other people do, too, if there have been stories about Hamed. So no need to worry about revealing our whereabouts."

"Hamed." Tara stopped eating. A little of the shakiness from the day before returned, and she sipped her bottled water. "I kind of blocked that out with everything else that happened."

"It was amazing," Kelly said. "Do you know how you did it?"

"I didn't do it." Tara set down the water bottle too hard, jarring her plate. "At least, not me alone. I never did anything like that before Fimi."

"I know," Kelly said. "I just meant, do you feel like you're learning to control it? Can you – you and Fimi – do that any time?"

Tara walked to the window and stared out at the Blue Mosque and the rolling waves. "No. I don't know."

"The way you sat there, you looked so calm, so peaceful. More than in the Cistern. And with so much going on around you. It must take a lot of focus."

"I said I don't know how it happened." Tara shut her eyes. She saw her sister Megan's body in the light pink casket, hair in blond pigtails, her stuffed Snoopy next to her. Maybe Tara had possessed some healing power starting when she was pregnant with Fimi. So why hadn't it revealed itself sooner? Or why hadn't she figured it out? There must have been some way she could have.

"It took a lot out of you," Kelly said. "Both of you. Fimi conked out too. She slept so long I started to worry, but she kept breathing fine and looked calm, so I just let her."

Tara turned back to her sister. "Let's call Sophia, see what she can figure out about these papers."

"But –"

Tara ignored her sister and dialed the phone.

PETE AND CYRIL sat on iron benches, Pete sipping Armenian coffee from a paper cup. On first taste, he'd found it too strong, but its slight cardamom flavor had grown on him. It helped keep him warm as the cold from the bench seeped into his skin through his jeans. They had at least half an hour to kill before the arrival of the bus that ran from Ijevan to the village near the church. The small park where they waited featured a larger than lifesized stone statue of a woman with an indistinct face. It was one of the city's one hundred sixteen sculptures.

Pete tapped his phone voicemail icon again. No messages. Though he hadn't admitted Tara was in Istanbul, he'd promised he'd keep checking in with Lynette and tell Cyril when he confirmed Tara was all right. Pete didn't know what he'd do if Lynette didn't hear from Tara or Kelly. He couldn't leave his daughters on their own in a foreign country if they were in trouble. But joining them would mean either leading Cyril to Tara or trusting Cyril to visit Our Lady of Sorrows alone, both of which were terrible ideas.

"What do you know about Pir Ferit?" he asked Cyril. "Seems like the Brotherhood must have checked him out at some point."

Cyril nodded. "The records show a deacon visited him over a decade ago when conducting research on Andrew of Crete's visions. Ferit refused to share what he knew, if he knew anything."

"Shouldn't Pir Ferit be on your side? If he's the curator of a private collection of Andrew's materials?"

"We've only his word that he has – or had – a collection." Cyril took off his gloves. The sun had come out at last and shone through the bare branches of the trees that shielded the statue and benches from the wind. "He never showed them to anyone. And he wasn't informed about the Brotherhood of Andrew. It was a secret to all except those who belonged to it – until I told Tara. Perhaps he would have shared the documents or information if he'd known."

*Perhaps not*, Pete thought. He saw no reason to tell Cyril that Sophia had seen the documents and that Pir Ferit knew about the Brotherhood.

Pete finished his coffee. A layer of dark sludge coated the bottom of the cup. He clicked his message icon again, wondering if Lynette had thought to try contacting Sophia. Then it occurred to him that he'd taken everything Sophia had said at face value. They all had. There was no reason not to, but now, sitting on this frigid bench with this man who'd done so much harm to his family, a man Tara had once trusted, Pete couldn't help second guessing. So much rode on the unsupported recommendations of a woman he'd never heard of a year ago.

What if Sophia had sent Tara into danger?

# 18

Shrieking came from behind Sophia. She spun, gripping the phone, and realized it was her teakettle. Her smartphone's chimes had awakened her at three in the morning. She'd called Kelly and Tara back from her landline, reaching them in a hotel business center where they said they'd found a deserted alcove. They'd been afraid their hotel room phone might be bugged. Their voices were so quiet the white noise from Sophia's forced air heating system drowned them out. She turned down her thermostat to shut off the blower as they told her what had happened in the last day. Kelly described Hamed's healing and how the people at the mosque reacted. Before Sophia could ask how Tara felt about it, Tara broke in to tell about an attack by two men with swords.

"And then Erik Holmes just appeared?" Sophia sat in the leather armchair near her fireplace, pulling her robe tighter over her chemise. She'd bought the chemise and some other silk lingerie in anticipation of Rick staying the night the next time he came into town – her first such purchase in a long time.

"It doesn't surprise me that Holmes would have people keeping tabs on what you're doing," Sophia said. "I am surprised he's there personally. It's fortunate. While you're both resourceful, it's hard to imagine you or Fimi could have survived that attack."

"I'm not so sure," Tara said. "About Holmes, I mean. If he knew so much, why couldn't he stop the attack before it started? Maybe he let it go forward to have an excuse to kill Mullin."

"Do you think he wanted to kill Mullin? Does he know Mullin?"

"I don't know," Tara said.

"We're sticking with him for now, though," Kelly said. "He seems less dangerous to us than the other swordsman. Which isn't saying much."

"You can leave Istanbul and return home any time," Sophia said. "With Pir Ferit missing and the attack on you, it might be the wisest course."

"But I haven't learned anything," Tara said. "Nothing useful that I can see, or at least not enough to put together answers."

Sophia stared at the flames in her fireplace, so yellow and bright in the dark room. Though she lived less than a mile from downtown Chicago, her street was tree-lined, dark, and dead silent in the middle of the night. For a moment, she felt as if she were the only person in the city, or perhaps the world. There was no one else she could ask to answer Tara's questions, to give her advice.

"It's your decision, Tara. I'm curious what Pir Ferit knows, or knew. I want answers for your well-being, but I have to admit, I also want them for my own intellectual and spiritual satisfaction. So I feel compelled to point out the dangers to you in case I overstated the case for your going there or underestimated the dangers you might face."

"I'd already gotten back on the Brotherhood's radar," Tara said. "This attack might just as easily have happened at home."

"Perhaps. But at home you'd have more friends and be more familiar with the area. I'm not saying you ought to return here or abandon your quest for answers, but it bears considering. I can have my colleague come and get you any time to take you to the airport if you don't trust Holmes to do it. She's a good friend, and if I tell her it's an emergency, she'll drop everything."

"I'll keep that in mind," Tara said, "and I'll think about whether I ought to come back."

"Did you learn anything from the website you mentioned?" Sophia asked.

Kelly explained the minimal information she'd retrieved and the partial word "Collyridi" on the printout. Sophia abandoned the fireplace for the much chillier office at the back of her townhome. Snow had fallen during the night, frosting her tiny yard. She set her lemon and seagrass tea on the desk and took a worn volume from one of her built-in bookshelves.

"Collyridians." Sophia ran her finger down the table of contents and flipped to the correct chapter. "They deified Mary, and the Catholic Church denounced them as heretics – meaning people who are professed believers but reject Church doctrine." The tightness in her chest eased a bit at having something helpful to offer Tara.

"That's it," Tara said. "That's what Pir Ferit was talking about. Heresies about Mary."

"The Collyridians saw Mary as a cocreator of Jesus with God, so something of a goddess in her own right." Sophia skimmed the sections on Marian heresies. She'd read them before, but it had been a while. "Her followers offered tributes in the form of bread left on a chair or throne. The only writings about the Collyridians that survived were written by their denouncers. So we're left with a skewed view of them."

"There are none left?" Kelly said. "No Collyridians?"

"New age goddess-worshipping groups exist that call themselves Collyridians, but none can be traced back to the original movement."

"Pir Ferit mentioned another heresy. A long word. Anti-something," Tara said.

Sophia turned pages. "Antidicomarianitism?"

"Maybe," Tara said.

"It's hard to say which heresy the Church found more troubling. The Antidicomarianites believed Mary had sex after giving birth to Jesus."

"So?" Kelly said.

"That contradicts the Catholic Church's teaching that Mary remained a virgin forever," Tara said. "You know all those songs and prayers saying 'ever-virgin'?"

"Okay, so I wasn't parsing out everything in mass the way you were," Kelly said. "I thought it was more a figure of speech."

"Seriously? I can't believe Mom and Dad didn't make you go to Catholic school. Or CCD."

"I guess they figured you and Nate suffered enough for all of us."

Sophia smiled at the sisters' back and forth, so sibling-like despite the tense circumstances. She felt glad that, despite all the trauma, they still had what she thought of as normal conversations with each other.

"The other Christian churches don't believe that," Kelly said. "About Mary staying a virgin forever. Do they?"

"It varies." Sophia returned to the armchair near her fireplace. "I'll research both heresies, see if I can find something that might relate to Pir Ferit."

"Should we tell Holmes about any of this?" Kelly said.

Sophia closed the aging book. Its side binding had loose threads. "I'm thinking no. If he truly wants to help, he should be willing to share whatever he knows without a *quid pro quo*. On the other hand, it might be worth telling him something if it seems it will help you decide what to do next. I wouldn't mention the website or document, though, given that Pir Ferit was so cautious about speaking to you alone and only posting it after he was sure you were the One."

"Yeah," Tara said. "I can't figure out if he was too cautious or not cautious enough."

TARA STOOD on the hotel room balcony with her coat on. Behind her, inside the spacious hotel sitting room with its gleaming furniture, Kelly and Fimi snuggled near the fireplace. Tara gripped the wrought iron balcony railing so hard her knuckles turned white as she stared at shifting clouds and the alternating light and dark shadows they cast on the Sea of Marmara. Until Sophia suggested it, she'd never considered abandoning her attempts to find answers in Istanbul. She felt angry at her mentor for not standing firm in her position that Tara needed to know more about Fimi to live in any sort of safety or peace. Yet Pir Ferit himself had said it might be better not to know.

For a moment, Tara felt a sense of relief at the idea that she could stop. Return with Fimi to the apartment Sophia had arranged in Brookfield, and if people discovered who they were, move somewhere else under false names.

While Tara couldn't finish college and go to medical school under a fake identity, if they remained under the radar long enough, people like the swordsman might become convinced she and Fimi weren't a threat.

But how likely was that? And, regardless, Tara still wouldn't know why all this had happened. Her stomach tightened as she recalled Pir Ferit's questions about whether it would really help her if she learned more about Fimi, especially if she learned something that made others fear her. But it was better to know than not to know. Without understanding why Fimi was on earth, Tara couldn't protect her child. Or take back the reins of her own life. And there was Hamed. An image of him smiling flashed in Tara's mind. How happy and healthy he'd been, how thrilled to be alive after near-death. If she and Fimi, or she or Fimi, could do that, Tara needed to understand how and why. It was too late to save Megan, but there might be a way to help other people through that healing power – without endangering herself or Fimi. If there was, Tara meant to find it.

She turned her back on the sea.

The nicest restaurant Tara had eaten in was Trattoria Aleata, an upscale Italian restaurant in St. Louis owned by her ex-boyfriend's family. The restaurant on the ground floor of the Four Seasons Sultanahmet made Trattoria Aleata look like a cheap diner. When she and Kelly arrived to meet Holmes for high tea, Tara felt like she'd wandered into a garden. Ficus trees stood at the entrance and framed the glass doors to the lanai. The floor was textured stone. Centerpieces with long narrow green leaves and lavender roses graced each table. Carved wood panels hung on the walls and created natural divisions between tables. The scents of lush foliage, chai, and Turkish coffee filled the air.

Tara ignored the splendor and studied the man across the table. Now that she'd decided to move forward wherever Pir Ferit's guidance, thin as it was, led, it was vital that she learn more about Holmes and why he'd become involved in her and Fimi's concerns. When she'd met Cyril, he'd struck her as tense, wiry, and vaguely military looking. Holmes, in contrast, appeared every inch the confident well-to-do young businessman, wearing a charcoal pinstripe suit, starched maroon shirt open at the neck, and a silver watch that looked pricier than Tara's Mom's Saturn. Cyril had kept his arms close to his body and stayed nearly motionless when he sat across from Tara the first time in a local coffeshop, careful not to invade her space. Holmes took up space, one arm across his chair arm, the other resting on the table, his feet set wide on the floor. He gave the impression of owning the restaurant. It was hard to look away from him.

After asking how she and Kelly were feeling, Holmes handed Tara a *Times*, pointing to an article about Pir Ferit.

"Oh no." Tara shut her eyes for a moment. She hadn't known Pir Ferit well, but she'd liked him and come to trust him. She passed the paper on to Kelly.

Holmes folded his hands in front of him, forearms resting on the table, and leaned forward. "It's odd for his body to be found in the strait. It's a heavily populated area, hard to haul a body there without anyone noticing."

"I suppose he could have gone there on his own and been attacked," Tara said, though she doubted Pir Ferit would have gone anywhere without uploading all the text for her. Her heart ached at the idea of the kind man becoming the victim of violence, possibly because of her.

"No one saw anything unusual at the mosque after you left," Holmes said.

Tara raised her eyebrows. "Are you asking me or telling me?"

"Telling you. I have sources there."

"So you know all about us and what we've been doing, " Kelly said, "but we don't know about you."

A server in dark pants and a long-sleeved white collared shirt brought champagne for everyone and took their tea order.

"What would you like to know?" Holmes said.

"What you want from me," Tara said.

Holmes met her eyes. His were perfectly symmetrical, with eyebrows that peaked just above his pupils, emphasizing his emerald green irises. His face was made of flat surfaces and straight lines, with just enough curve along his chin and cheekbones to keep him from looking harsh. Unlike with Cyril, Tara didn't feel uneasy around Holmes, and that in itself kept her on guard. He was an attractive man, a little too intense to be called charismatic, but definitely compelling. Another reason to remain wary.

"Nothing," he said, "but your attention and consideration. If you determine we're on the same side, perhaps we can work together."

"To do what?" Tara said.

"Defeat the Antichrist."

Tara folded her hands on the table in front of her, almost mimicking Holmes' confident pose, though her throat felt dry and her pulse pounded. "You don't think my baby is the Antichrist? Or I am?"

"Not at all. I said the swords were meant to test for the Antichrist, not that I believed you or the child *should* be tested."

The infant carseat, with Fimi settled in it, sat on a chair between Kelly and Tara. Kelly rested her hand on the top of it, above Fimi's head. "But you implied it," she said.

The server returned with a three-tiered silver tray. The bottom plate held scones, the middle tea sandwiches, and the top pink and yellow petit fours and miniature cream puffs. A second server set three small pots of tea on the table, one for each of them.

Using a sterling silver butter knife, Holmes spread clotted cream on a scone. "If you inferred that based on my comments, I apologize. It's not what I meant or what I believe. The Brotherhood believes the Antichrist is coming, or is here, and will take the form of a person. I believe it's here and is embodied in an institution." He shifted his gaze to Tara. "One you are perfectly poised to help me fight."

"An institution?" Tara said. "What institution?"

"The Roman Catholic Church."

~

A THREE FOOT tall rectangular stone stood near the entrance to Our Lady of Sorrows, a cross with wide beams carved into it, intricate designs etched along its edges. Pete had become used to seeing similar stone khatchkars of varying sizes throughout Armenia. They'd passed nearly a dozen during the two-mile walk to the church from the town where the bus had let them out.

The February day was brisk, but the sky was clear and the sun warmed the top of Pete's head. He'd finally heard from Lynette that his daughters and granddaughter were fine and at a hotel in Istanbul. The relief he felt, and the distance and time away from day-to-day life, had lifted some of the darkness that had weighed him down during the last five months. He hoped his renewed energy would last. He felt like he'd been granted a reprieve from a chronic illness – grateful, yet wary it might return.

Snow lined both sides of the stone and dirt path that led to the small brown brick section at the front of the church. "This entry area was constructed – or actually reconstructed – in the fourteenth century," Cyril said. He gestured toward the gray stone walls that rose above, and expanded on either side of, the brown brick. "That part of the building is from the ninth century and contains the main chapel. Somewhere inside it, toward the back, is an inner sanctum from the sixth century."

The main chapel held a few plain stained wood benches. The stone walls had discolored and crumbled in spots. Pete discerned a faded fresco of the Virgin Mary on the right side of an aging stone altar.

A man dressed in black handed them both unscented white tapers and matches.

"This is how people pray here," Cyril said. "They light candles. Rather than attending mass frequently or praying out loud in groups or alone with rosaries."

Pete lit his taper, breathing in the flat non-scent of paraffin. He missed the candle lighting in Catholic churches at home. Now, instead of flames, glass vigil cups featured tiny electric bulbs. Make a donation, turn on a light. Much less of a fire hazard, but it lacked the ritual flourish he'd found so beautiful, magical, and familiar as he'd moved from place to place during his childhood and teenage years.

Wax dripped onto the round white paper at his candle's base. Pete watched the flame flicker in the drafts from the arched windows. He felt unsure for what or whom to pray. Before Megan's death, he'd prayed for her health. Now she was gone. He knew he didn't need to pray for her soul. God could never turn Megan away from heaven.

But Tara was on a difficult path, one that made him fear for her safety and her soul.

*For Tara*, he thought, as the candle burned. *And for me. I pray for the courage to do what's right.*

At the back of the chapel stood a counter-height wood table filled with lit tapers and pictures of the Virgin Mary jumbled together. The mix included photos of statues of Mary, postcards of classical paintings featuring her, sketches done by artists with varying degrees of skill, and pages cut from prayer books or leaflets. The haphazard display made Pete think of the photo montages fictional serial killers in movies or on TV created. As if someone had stalked the Virgin Mary and tacked together images of her.

"Tara told me Armenia considers itself a very religious country," Pete said.

"Yes." Cyril held his candle so close to the paper images of Mary that Pete feared he'd light one on fire. "It was the first country to adopt Christianity as its national religion."

"When Lynette converted to Catholicism, she had a hard time getting used to the statues and stained glass windows of saints in Catholic churches," Pete said. "She was raised Protestant."

Cyril shoved aside two wire prayer card holders and grabbed a postcard-sized glossy photo that had been wedged behind them.

"What?" Pete said.

Hand trembling, Cyril handed over the photo of an ancient vase. On it was carved the face of a young woman, her features somewhat similar to Tara's, though Pete might perceive the similarity due to the power of suggestion. Cyril had given Tara a photo like this the first night he'd met her, telling her it was a carving of the first young woman after Mary to conceive a child without sexual intercourse. Tara had shared it with her parents later down the road, something Pete wondered if she ever regretted doing. If she'd never told them or anyone about Cyril or the supposed prophecy, maybe she'd be home raising Fimi with her parents' help and finishing school.

The photo looked clean and shiny, with no more than a tiny fold in the top right corner. "Doesn't look like it's been here long," Pete said. "How do you think it got here?"

Cyril shook his head. "No idea."

"Your Brotherhood companions?"

"I doubt it," Cyril said. "If they'd been here this recently, there'd truly be no reason to send me."

"Could be their way of taunting you," Pete said, but he didn't quite buy that. He presumed Father Saur had some connection to or information from the Brotherhood, and whatever motives Cyril attributed to the religious order, Pete doubted his pastor would send Pete on a wild goose chase.

The man who'd handed them the tapers approached. Cyril held out the photo and asked something in Armenian. The man answered, then started toward a door beyond the altar.

Cyril motioned Pete to follow. "I think he's taking us to the priest's wife."

"Priests get married here?" Pete said.

"The Armenian Church has both married and celibate priests."

In a tiny back office, a thin woman with steel gray hair hunched over a metal desk. She wore fingerless gray wool gloves. A thick rose-colored rug and fabric wall hangings gave the room a little warmth, but Pete still felt grateful for his jacket.

After ascertaining that the woman spoke some English, Cyril showed her the photograph. "We're looking for records about a young woman from the seventh century who became pregnant and claimed she was a virgin. She may have been baptized here. And died here. This may be a representation of her carved into the vase."

Pete felt surprised Cyril would be so forthright, but he couldn't think of a roundabout way to get the information.

The woman straightened her back. She swiveled her head to look first at Pete, then Cyril. Behind her gold wire-framed glasses, her eyelids drooped with age, but the eyes beneath them looked focused and alert. "And you are who?"

"I'm an aspirant," Cyril said. "Studying to be a deacon in the Roman Catholic Church. But this is not for the Church. It's a personal research project."

"And you?" the woman said to Pete. "Do you belong to Rome also?"

An odd way to put it. Pete wondered what she meant and how much her unfamiliarity with English influenced her word choice.

"No. That is, I'm Catholic, but I'm not a deacon. I'm here because of my daughter. Tara Spencer." Pete decided to follow Cyril's lead in being open. "She became pregnant, but she said she hadn't had sex and didn't know how it happened."

"Tara Spencer," the woman repeated.

"Yes," Pete said.

"She relates to these records you seek?"

This time Cyril answered. "Yes."

The woman took off her glasses and studied Pete. "How do I know you are who you say you are?"

"I have my passport."

Glasses on again, the woman inspected the passport, running her fingers over the stamps, checking the expiration date. The photo had been taken three years before when Pete and Lynette traveled to Mexico to meet a doctor who might have a new treatment to offer Megan.

"You are grayer," the woman said.

"I'm older." Pete felt older. More than three years older. Nearly all the gray had appeared during those years.

The woman snapped the passport shut. "Papers can be falsified." She pointed at Cyril. "I think probably he has done that. Or his organization has."

"I'm not with the – with his organization. Cyril's my guide, but I'm here for my daughter. Please. We've come a very long way, and this church is our only lead."

Hearing the words aloud, Pete realized on what a thin thread this quest hung. But at least he was doing something. At home he'd be grinding through the routine of work, bill paying, and sleep. Nothing he cared about missing, other than his family. And he'd felt almost as far from them while living in the same house as he did now. No doubt his own fault, but it was true all the same.

"How do I know you are who you say you are?" the woman said again.

"He was on TV," Cyril said. "On the news. With Tara."

Pete's first thought was that he'd never been on TV. But he had been. He'd been with Tara at the airport when they'd been ambushed by reporters. Pete had refused to answer questions and had been angry when Tara cooperated. He'd just learned Megan had been hospitalized while he was away visiting the Vatican with Tara. One of so many examples of how he'd failed to be there for one or another of his children.

*But there's only one of me*, he thought. *I couldn't be everywhere. And I couldn't do everything.*

Sadness washed through Pete, sweeping away some of the anger he'd felt, and replacing numbness with aching. His voice cracked as he said, "I have. Six or seven months ago. An interview at O'Hare airport when Tara and I returned from the Vatican."

Remembering the things he'd said to Tara at the hospital, Pete shuddered. If he could take them back now, he would. He didn't believe Tara wanted publicity for publicity's sake, though he still couldn't see how to reconcile Fimi's existence with the Catholic Church.

The woman pressed her lips together. "In the corridor behind this room is a pew. Sit. Wait."

The narrow rectangular room had a stone floor, but it felt warmer than the rest of the church. Pete and Cyril sat side by side, not speaking. Pete rested the back of his head against the wall. Within a few minutes, his hands and feet started tingling, and his whole body felt warm, but in a comfortable, relaxed way, not as if he had a fever or a sunburn. He tried to open his eyes, but it took too much effort. Besides, he felt wonderful. Free of worries. Free of responsibility. Free of pain.

Pete drifted into the dark.

He awoke hours later blindfolded, feet tied together, hands bound behind his back.

# 19

"The Catholic Church?" Tara set down the cucumber sandwich she'd been about to bite into. She wished someone supporting her was normal. Just a friend who wished her well. Someone like her biological father, Ray Tigue, with no agenda.

"Yes," Holmes said. "Did nothing Pir Ferit told you suggest that?"

"He didn't tell me much."

Holmes leaned back in his chair, studying Tara. "He must have told you something." As Holmes spoke, the conversations at the tables nearby hit a lull, making his voice sound loud. He lowered it. "You headed back to the mosque during an earthquake. You must have formed some bond with him."

"Why do you need to know?" Kelly said.

"It would help me understand the larger picture." Holmes waved his hand. "But if you must keep it to yourself, then do. For now. But understand, all the attention on you, all the concern, is a smoke screen to take the focus off the real issues – the evil the Church undertakes."

"What evil?" Tara asked.

"What do you mean smoke screen?" Kelly said. "Are you saying the men in the Brotherhood are just pretending to stalk Tara?"

Holmes shook his head. "Cyril Woods, for instance. He believes what he's told. Including that his mission is to seek out the mother of the next messiah and shepherd her to safety. In fact, the Brotherhood's mission has always been to find someone like Tara and stop her."

"Someone like me as in a woman who gives birth to a girl child?" Tara said.

Holmes stayed silent, waiting for the servers to pour fresh tea for everyone and replenish the finger sandwiches.

"A girl child, or perhaps any child, who appears to have a supernatural origin," Holmes said, once the servers had left. "The fear is always of an opposing force. The real members of the Brotherhood of Andrew, meaning those at the top of its hierarchy, don't want a new messiah. And they have no more connection to the man their underlings believe was the first messiah, Jesus Christ, than I do. They are simply protecting their base, and you are a threat. But they're a side show regardless. Not to diminish their power in the real world. They have it, use it, protect it."

Kelly glanced at Tara, then back at Holmes. "Are they part of the Catholic Church?"

"No. I suspect the Church views the Brotherhood as an annoyance, which is a serious underestimation. The Brotherhood, on the other hand, until recently, saw the Church as an organization too large and unwieldy to be helpful. Which meant it was out of the Brotherhood's control."

"Was?" Kelly said.

"The new pope," Tara said, thinking of her visit to the Vatican and the following events.

"It's a distinct possibility." Holmes sipped his champagne. "Your friend Sophia Gaddini, you trust her?"

"Yes," Tara said. "Why?"

"She was part of the Church for many years. She may still wish to protect it. Or she may never really have left."

"She left," Tara said.

Kelly pushed her plate and teapot aside. "So how is it you think Tara is in a position to help you 'defeat' the Church?"

"The Church's power lies in persuading people that the Church is the one way to God. Tara offers an alternative."

"I've never offered an alternative," Tara said. "I don't know why Fimi was conceived or how. I don't know what it means."

Holmes pointed with two fingers toward Tara. "Exactly – you don't know. People can make of it what they will, and you're not telling them what to think." Despite her skepticism, Tara found herself leaning in toward Holmes. His intensity seemed to draw her physically closer to him. "The major monotheistic religions – Christianity, Islam, Judaism – are about telling people what to think, how to behave, what to believe. You offer the option to not know. To be open to something new. For each person to decide for himself. Or herself."

"Look, Mr. Holmes," Tara said.

"Erik, please. You make me feel much older than I am with the 'Mr.'" Holmes smiled. He had even, white, perfectly straight teeth.

"Erik, then," Tara said. It felt a little odd to refer to him by his first name, but judging from his smooth skin and physique, she guessed him not much more than ten years older than she was, despite the silver in his hair. "You're entitled to your views, but I'm not on a mission to destroy anyone's religion. Other people have believed I was, and I told them just the same." Tara didn't mention Nanor in case Holmes didn't already know about Willow Springs, but she couldn't help thinking the two would get along well. Nanor believed Tara was meant to bring an end to Islam, Christianity, and Judaism – all three male-dominated monotheistic religions. "All I want is to find out as much as I can about why this happened and what it means for me and my daughter and then get on with our lives. So I don't think I can help you."

"First, I wish you the best in getting on with your lives, but if by that you mean living the type of life you would have had, a 'normal' life, yesterday's events make clear that will never occur. Pursue whatever leads you think you obtained from Pir Ferit if you must, but surely you realize nothing can give you back a normal life."

Past the restaurant's grandeur and greenery, the sliding doors showed bare trees and gray skies. Tara thought of Pir Ferit's body washed up on the banks of the Bosphorous Strait, of the death and destruction that followed her visit to Sophia the year before, of Kali, who hadn't answered any of Tara's recent emails, lying battered in the hosptial bed. Holmes was right. Nothing could put her life back together. Nothing.

"What's second?" Kelly asked Holmes. "You started by saying 'First.' What's second?"

Holmes kept his eyes fixed on Tara. "Second, I'm not asking for your help. I'm explaining why I seek to aid you. For in aiding you, I advance my own cause."

Tara met his eyes. "And if aiding me doesn't advance your cause?"

"I'm certain it will. So the real question is, how can I help you?"

THEY WORE loose-fitting abayas over their coats and hajibs that covered their hair and faces, leaving only their eyes visible. Fimi was hidden under Tara's abaya in the baby sling. Tara left the abaya's neck partially open to be sure Fimi got enough air. Away from Holmes, she and Kelly had decided that, as strange as his statements were, and whatever his real goal, for now they were safer with his help than without. After sifting again through everything Pir Ferit had said, Kelly suggested the Sufi teacher might have passed on what he knew to someone else, just as the message was passed down to him.

Tara decided if that were so, and Pir Ferit wanted her to figure it out, the only candidates were Ismail and Hamed. Hamed seemed more likely because Pir Ferit had said he didn't trust Ismail.

"Maybe I want it to be Hamed, since Ismail obviously didn't like me." Tara glanced both ways before they crossed an intersection, scanning for the swordsman or other threats as much as for vehicles.

"We had to start with one of them." Kelly took her sister's hand as they stepped into the street. "And it's not like we have other leads to follow."

"True. And Berna was nice."

Holmes had found out Hamed's last name, address, and telephone number. His mother, Berna, invited Tara and Kelly to visit when Tara telephoned. She said she'd wanted to thank Tara anyway and was glad for the chance to do so in person.

"I wish we could have Holmes drive us to the house," Kelly said. "I don't like walking on the street, even covered, even a short way, with that other guy still out there."

"I know."

They'd had Holmes drop them half a mile away so that his expensive car wouldn't attract attention. Both Tara and Kelly carried custom electronic devices that allowed them to contact Holmes in an instant. The devices also allowed Holmes to track them so he could stay within a few blocks at all times.

Rubble was strewn here and there along the cobblestone streets, but the earthquake hadn't caused as much damage in Hamed's neighborhood as it had near the mosque. It seemed strange to Tara to see any debris. It felt like weeks since the quake rather than just over twenty-four hours.

Berna brought out tea and pastries on a black and emerald inlaid tray. Hamed's father was away on business in London. Berna said she believed Tara had calmed Hamed and comforted him, helping him be open to a miraculous healing by Allah.

"We praise Allah and his messenger Mohamed for Hamed's safe recovery," she said.

Tara felt a surge of hope. Berna might mean exactly what she said and be using "messenger" to refer to Mohamed. But Pir Ferit had called himself a messenger.

It took a while for Hamed to feel comfortable talking with them. He spoke a small amount of English. When Tara asked, he said he felt well and held out his arm so she could see that it had healed perfectly.

"I'm very glad," Tara said. "Though sorry to hear about Pir Ferit."

"We are as well," Berna said. "He was a wise, kind teacher."

Kelly shifted in her chair to face Hamed. "Did you learn a lot from him?"

The boy nodded.

Tara sipped her sweetened tea. "What did you study?"

"Islam. History. Mathematics. Science." Hamed spoke slowly, as if translating each word in his mind before speaking.

Kelly and Tara exchanged glances, uncertain what to ask next.

"What did you like best?" Tara said. Hamed spoke of his love for mathematics. His words flowed more easily, but nothing he said suggested Pir Ferit had passed on information or a message to Hamed relating to Tara.

Someone knocked at the back door.

Berna flushed. "Excuse me."

She returned with a neighbor, an elderly woman whose sight was failing.

"I'm sorry," Berna said. "My neighbor says she does not wish to impose. But she says she heard that you and your baby helped Hamed."

Hand shaking, Tara placed her empty tea glass on the tray. She supposed she shouldn't be surprised word of Hamed's healing had spread, but it still unsettled her. "Please tell her it may have looked like that, but I have no special power to help or heal, and neither does my baby."

Tara told herself she wasn't lying. She didn't feel certain she could help. And if she didn't say no to the neighbor, then what about the neighbor's child, and cousin, and brother, and niece? She couldn't afford to collapse again, not with the other swordsman unaccounted for.

Berna and the neighbor spoke in Turkish.

"She asks if you would try," Berna said.

Kelly raised her hand in a Stop motion. "Tara and Fimi are still worn out from yesterday. It'd be dangerous for them to try anything now. And we need to return to our hotel."

The elderly woman touched Tara's lower arm.

"I'm sorry." Tara squeezed the woman's hand for an instant, then eased away from her and stood. The woman sighed, but said nothing more.

Half the sun, fiery orange, hovered above the horizon when they exited the house. A group of twenty to twenty-five people had crowded together in the narrow cobblestone street. They surged toward Tara and Kelly, calling out in Turkish and English. Some asked where the baby was.

"My apologies," Hamed's mother said. "This is my mistake. I told no one you were coming except my neighbor, but word has clearly spread."

Tara grasped her sister's hand, heart pounding, grateful Fimi remained hidden under Kelly's abaya.

A middle-aged man held out his hand. His index finger was missing. He spoke rapidly.

Berna barked something at him, but the man advanced, reaching for Tara's hand and Kelly's sleeve, apparently unsure which of them was Tara. Berna shooed him away, spoke to the crowd again.

Tara called Holmes.

"Walk west," he said. "I'm a quarter mile away."

The crowd surrounded them, moving as one unit, which at least carried them toward Holmes. Tara felt thankful for her full headdress, as she suspected otherwise people would pull her hair. But she felt hot under the abaya and her coat, with all the bodies pressing close. Sweat coated her underarms and dampened her back, and she found it hard to breathe when more people joined the group. A few of its members chanted in an unfamiliar language.

*A block, we just need to walk a block.*

A young man pushed between her and Kelly, breaking their hands apart.

"Kelly—"

Chanting drowned Tara's voice. The crowd pushed Kelly further west. Tara tried to follow, but someone grabbed her arm from behind and wrenched her sideways into a narrow passageway between houses.

PETE LAY on thin carpet over what felt like a metal floor that swayed beneath him. His shoulders ached. When he opened his eyes, he saw only black. No light seeped in around the edges of the blindfold. His hands were bound behind him.

Bouncing, rattling. *A van. I'm in the back of a panel van.* He tried to move his feet, but they, too, were tied together. At least he wasn't gagged.

"Cyril?"

No answer.

Pete kicked his feet in unison. They hit what felt like metal. A clanging sound echoed around him. He rolled along the carpeted floor until he banged into what must be a side of the van. It seemed too long to be the back. His body fit lengthwise against it. His head felt fuzzy. He had no idea how long he'd been out.

The van jounced, and his right knee smacked the floor at the perfect angle to shoot pain along his inner thigh. His shoulders and upper arms ached from having his hands behind him. Otherwise, though, his body didn't seem battered. Pete worked his wrists and felt the rope stretch. Whoever had bound him hadn't done so tightly. He considered whether Cyril had lured him to the church and set the trap. But much as he wanted to blame Cyril, he couldn't see what Cyril stood to gain. If he didn't want Pete to know anything about the church, he could simply have ditched Pete the way he had Tara, and there would have been little for Pete to do. He might have found Our Lady of Sorrows without Cyril, but surely long after him.

*But if Cyril's not part of this, where is he? And what could anyone else want with me?*

Pete froze, forgetting the ropes for a moment. *Tara. They want to get to Tara.*

# 20

### Canadian Military to Aid Alberta Residents

CALGARY, Alberta - The Alberta Premier deployed 1,000 troops to help recovery and rescue operations in Alberta, where torrential rains caused flooding. Nearly 70,000 people evacuated yesterday. To date, no deaths have been reported, but more rain is expected in the coming week.

~

### Flood Fixes Vex East Coast Cities

NEW YORK - BATTERED by increased rainfall and flooding on the east coast, mayors in cites from New York to Miami met last week to discuss solutions. Potential fixes include fortifying existing levees, adding floodwalls, and revamping sewer systems. Fiscal conservatives, however, charge that no new infrastructure is needed and decry what they see as unnecessary pork barrel spending. There is no evidence, they claim, that the series of storms that has wracked the east coast amounts to anything more than a temporary weather pattern.

~

RAPHAEL SHOVED THROUGH THE CROWD, pursuing the girl with the baby. He'd left his sword, which made him too conspicuous, in his tiny rented room. He hadn't expected another chance to take Tara off guard or alone now that Erik Holmes had intervened, so he'd decided to settle for following her to watch for other signs during the rest of her time in Istanbul. He could hardly complete his self-assigned mission if he suffered Mullin's fate. Mullin, whom Raphael hadn't known was in Istanbul. Had the Brotherhood at last taken Raphael's advice and decided the time to test the child had come? Or had Mullin been sent to stop Raphael? Hard to say. And no matter. He'd washed his hands of the Brotherhood with its bureaucracy and hesitancy and half-step maneuvers.

Being presented with this opportunity to seize the child showed he'd been correct in his action. He didn't know if the girl ahead of him was Tara or her sister, but he knew she carried the baby under her abaya. He'd seen the movement when the two exited the house.

A gift. It was a gift.

No, more than that. A sign from above. Manna from heaven.

*Wrong metaphor. Not manna. What is it? An omen. Or a directive.*

One part of his mind searched for the appropriate scriptural reference while another plotted the logistics of maneuvering the girl to the edge of the crowd and grabbing the baby despite the abaya. His mind always searched, spun, sorted through ideas and plans. Never resting. Never sleeping.

He felt certain that was why he'd been chosen.

HOLMES STARED at the dashboard screen, watching the icons representing Kelly and Tara fly apart. At least the baby's icon still blinked with Kelly. No one had separated them. But why had Tara veered away? Force? Choice? She'd seemed equally skeptical of him and drawn to him, so she might have left to do something she didn't want him to know about. The audio feed from his emissary had become nothing but the white/gray crowd noise. Tara's icon skidded north, off the street, into what must be a narrow passage between buildings. It didn't show on Holmes' GPS.

Holmes couldn't intercept Kelly and the baby and track Tara. In a split second, he made his decision. He stepped on the gas.

BRICKS SCRAPED TARA'S SHOULDER, but the abaya and coat protected her skin as a man yanked her into a narrow passageway between buildings. He pushed her against the wall behind her, his face only inches from hers. Little of the fading sunlight reached the passageway, but enough that Tara recognized Ismail. He pressed his hand over her mouth. The crowd's chanting grew more distant. Tara struggled to free herself, but Ismail had fifty pounds on her, all muscle. He blocked her attempted kick with his leg and knocked her phone from her hand when she pulled it from her pocket.

"Hold still," he said. "I mean you no harm, but I must speak with you. Understand?"

Tara nodded. Ismail was too strong for her to win a physical fight. Her only hope was to outwit him.

He took his hand from her mouth.

"I need to get to Kelly. And the baby." Despite her angst, Tara was careful not to say Fimi's name.

*Never, never, never should have brought her.*

"They will be fine. Your man will watch over them. I promise you."

"My man."

"Erik Holmes. Or whatever name he's given you."

"You know Holmes?"

"I work for him," Ismail said. "In a manner of speaking."

"What? I – what?" Tara didn't know if Ismail being connected to Holmes made her feel better about Ismail or worse about Holmes. Probably the latter. And she still didn't feel confident Fimi was safe.

"There's no time to explain," Ismail said. "If you are the One, I have information that may help you."

"A message? You're a messenger?"

"First prove to me you are the One who deserved Pir Ferit's guidance."

"Did you stop him from sending me what he knew?" Tara avoided mentioning the website in case Ismail didn't know about it.

He shook his head. "I don't know who stopped him. I don't know who killed him."

"But you believe someone killed him?"

Ismail's thin lips curled. "Of course. You believe he decided to take his wheelchair for a ride along the strait in winter?"

"So what can you tell me?" Tara said.

"Nothing until you prove to me you are the one who will live forever."

"When Pir Ferit put his hand on my face, I had a vision." Tara described the vision. Ismail shrugged and remained silent, unconvinced. Tara's mind spun. She could tell Ismail about the key, but she didn't feel safe disclosing it to someone Pir Ferit had said he didn't trust. She thought of Mullin's insistence when he'd pursued her while she was pregnant that she must have a mark. Of the Beast. And her fear when she'd realized what he must mean. But Nanor and Kali had told her that Nanor's daughter Maya had something similar, and it didn't mean anything evil.

"I have a mark. A scar in the shape of a snake. When I was pregnant, others seemed to think that mattered," Tara said. "You can't see it. It's on my leg."

"If a Muslim snake is found in a human home," Ismail said, "the human is to warn the snake three times to leave. If it doesn't leave, it is to be killed."

The light had faded too much for Tara to see Ismail's face, but his words chilled her. She resisted the urge to try again to run. "I don't know if that's a threat, and I don't care. Tell me what you can or let me go, one or the other."

Ismail folded his arms over his chest. "All right. I am no messenger, but I promised Pir Ferit that if anything happened to him, I would attempt to carry on his mission."

"And that is?"

"Pir Ferit was a guardian, meant to help the one who will live forever learn her role in the world. He had a portion of a document. I assume that's what he tried to pass on."

Tara's heartbeat quickened. Perhaps at last she'd find answers. Some sort of protection for herself and Fimi.

"And you have it? You have a copy?"

~

ERIK HOLMES WASN'T OFTEN surprised, and the rare times he was, it affected him only marginally. But he swerved the car when the feed cleared and he realized it was Ismail who'd pulled Tara aside. Ismail had only been supposed to follow her and keep watch on any developments near Hamed's house. Now it seemed he'd instigated them. Holmes braked to avoid a child who'd wandered into the street. He hit the gas again as soon as the path was clear.

More surprising was the revelation, if true, that Ismail had received a message from Pir Ferit. Holmes' research ought to have revealed that. It was a testament to the Sufi and his mentee that he'd managed to keep his secret. He felt pleased that Tara revealed so little, though it was more than she'd told Holmes. Of course, because Ismail had information to exchange with her. Apparently she'd learned from her experiences the year before.

Rounding a corner, Holmes screeched the car to a halt. He'd reached the crowd. He inched forward, and people spread out on either side of the street. Thankfully, most of the women weren't wearing burqas with veils. Holmes focused on those who were as he scanned the crowd for Kelly, hoping he could distinguish her by her short stature and by whose abaya billowed enough to hide a baby beneath it.

~

KELLY HEARD HONKING and struggled to move toward the sound, though she couldn't see through the crowd to be sure it was Holmes. She kept one arm crossed over Fimi, to protect her, and pointed the other in front of her in a fist to help push through the people blocking her path. She couldn't understand what they were saying, but their voices sounded like they were pleading, and they kept grasping her cloak. So far, no one had tried to hurt her, but they wouldn't get out of her way. Someone grasped the back of her burqa just below her neck. She yelled and bolted forward, jabbing her fist at the shoulder of the smallest woman in her path, who stepped aside.

Holmes appeared on foot. He grabbed Kelly's arm and muscled people out of the way as they ran for the BMW. He clicked a remote and the passenger door popped open. Kelly jumped in and pulled the door shut after her. An instant later, Holmes was in the driver's seat.

"Tara, what about Tara?" she said.

Ismail shook his head and crossed his arms over his chest. "He didn't trust me with a copy. He didn't trust anyone. He said there was no copy, that he'd memorized the text and would type it out for the One."

"Then how can you help?"

*Maybe he's stalling me while something awful is happening to Kelly and Fimi,* Tara thought. She scanned the ground for her phone, but couldn't see it in the shadows.

"He told me the original of his section of the manuscript had been preserved and passed down through the generations. Not by another guardian, but by a previous young woman who claimed to be a virgin despite being pregnant," Ismail said.

"Which you don't believe."

"Which I don't believe. But Pir Ferit did, and he has been good to me. He said the document is hidden in a house of worship and that he had traveled once to see it."

"That narrows it down. What house of worship? Where?"

"I don't know," Ismail said. "For the last decade, he's stayed in Istanbul. Who are the other women? In history?"

"You don't know?"

"He told me very little. You must know, or he would have been more specific."

"I know a little," Tara said. "But not much. What did Pir Ferit instruct you to tell me?"

Cyril had told Tara there had been at least four other women who claimed to be virgins and pregnant between the time of Jesus Christ and now, but he hadn't given her much information about them. Perhaps her dad could learn more while traveling with Cyril, without telling him why he needed to know.

"Not you," Ismail said. "The One Who Will Live Forever. Before the other women came to see him, he told me what I've told you. And he said that the One would know enough, combined with what he'd said to her, to find the original manuscript."

"But he hadn't spoken to any of us yet. How could he know that?"

"Perhaps he gave hints to each woman, knowing only the One could interpret them."

Tara rubbed her forehead. She'd always done well in school and had believed she was fairly smart, but she wondered if Pir Ferit had mistaken her for genius. Or a clairvoyant. "When did Pir Ferit tell you these things?"

"Two weeks ago. After the other young women visited, before you."

"All right," Tara said. "I'll think about all of it, try to remember everything Pir Ferit said, and maybe it'll give me an answer."

Ismail grabbed Tara's elbow again. "Now you must tell me. What you know."

"No, I don't think I must. This is for me to figure out and to find. Pir Ferit didn't tell me to share what I learn with anyone."

For a moment, Tara thought he wasn't going to let her go. At last, he stepped back. "I'll be watching," he said. "The world will be watching."

TARA FLUNG her hotel key card onto the marble shelf inside the door. Now that they were back at the hotel suite, anger and fear vied with her gratitude that Holmes had gotten Kelly and Fimi out of the crowd. She'd known Holmes had a great deal of power and influence, and that he'd been keeping tabs on her, but she hadn't grasped how thoroughly he had been doing that and how secretive he'd been. "You spied on me."

Kelly carried Fimi past both of them and settled her into the crib the hotel staff had brought.

"I spied on Ismail if I spied on anyone, but I didn't, because he knew I'd wired him." Holmes took a bottle of sparkling water from the mini-bar and twisted the cap off. His clothes looked freshly pressed and his hair swept back from his forehead in smooth waves. He appeared no more tense than if he'd spent the day in his office. "You'd prefer I hadn't?"

"I'd prefer you told me about Ismail working for you." Tara remained in the hallway between the entrance and the dining area, not wanting to encourage Holmes to settle in.

"We're all learning about one another. Deciding how much to share. Correct? You didn't tell me about this document. Or anything about what Pir Ferit told you. I didn't tell you about Ismail."

Tara pressed her hands against her sides, struggling for calm. "That's true."

"So perhaps what bothers you is that I have more ways than you do of finding out information."

"Of course that bothers me. Wouldn't it bother you?"

Holmes smiled. "I'm sure it would. So I apologize that I didn't tell you about Ismail. It's something I should have shared." He gave a slight bow, almost as if he were sweeping off his hat to her. "And now I'll leave, as I'm sure you have things to discuss that you don't want to share with me. I hope what Ismail said was helpful."

"Was it?" Kelly asked after Holmes had left. She handed Tara a handwritten note that said, "You think Holmes is listening now?"

"Maybe," Tara said, answering both questions.

Kelly reached into her knapsack and pulled out a deck of cards. She'd originally brought them to play during the long plane ride. "I have an idea. Crazy Eights." She set a pen and a stack of the hotel's stationery next to the cards on the dining room table.

"What?" Tara said.

"We need a break," Kelly said. "Crazy Eights, like when you used to let me stay awake all night with you and Vicki."

The mention of her former best friend filled Tara with longing. Right before Tara had left Willow Springs, Vicki had sent her an email apologizing for a lot of things, including how she'd reacted to the pregnancy. Tara had written back, but the two hadn't had the chance to connect otherwise. The exchange had made Tara feel only slightly better. She and Vicki needed to see each other in person to talk things through if they were to become friends again, and who knew when that could happen.

"OK," Tara said. "Crazy Eights."

While Kelly dealt the cards, Tara took the pen and started writing out what she knew about the other women Cyril had told her had supposedly become pregnant despite being virgins. As she finished each page, she slid it across the table to Kelly. The two of them discussed the cards as they wrote to each other. A day or two earlier, Tara might have felt foolish enacting such a charade on the off chance someone was listening through electronic devices, as if she were living in a spy movie.

*But I might as well be,* Tara thought. *Who knows who's listening. Holmes? The Brotherhood? Ismail?*

The first woman Tara knew of, after Mary, who'd claimed to be pregnant and a virgin had lived in Armenia. There'd been another during the Inquisition who was Jewish and lived in Spain in the late fifteenth century. Cyril had told Tara that the woman supposedly was killed during the time of the Inquisition because she wouldn't convert, but he suspected someone knew the origin of her child and murdered her. Another woman had lived in Syria in the twelfth century but suffered a miscarriage after surviving an earthquake. Then there was Nanor's daughter, Maya Kerkorian, who'd been killed on a wet winding road in California by a phantom vehicle.

"Pir Ferit knew you'd gone to Armenia, right?" Kelly wrote.

Tara nodded. She'd had the same thought. Pir Ferit knew she'd been to Armenia and, in fact, had said part of the document was reputed to be there – a different part from the one he spoke of. If another piece of the document had been in Willow Springs or connected to Maya, Nanor would have told her, Tara felt certain of it. Which left the virgins in Spain or Syria or one Tara knew nothing about.

"How many houses of worship do you think there are in Spain and Syria?" she wrote, thinking of Ismail's comment about where Pir Ferit had last seen the document section he'd meant to provide to Tara. "Plus Pir Ferit and I never talked about the other women who claimed to be virgins and pregnant. For all he knew, I was clueless about that."

Now it was Kelly's turn to nod. Tara slumped in her chair, feeling chilled despite the warmth of the fire. Without knowing where Pir Ferit had traveled, she didn't see any next step.

"I shouldn't have brought the baby here," Tara said aloud, pausing their written exchange and the card game.

"Maybe not," Kelly said. "But how could you have come without her?" She gestured toward the pages they'd written, then toward the fireplace, and Tara nodded. They didn't need these pages floating around.

"I don't know. But the danger seems worse here, so far from home away from anyone we know."

"You want to stop looking?" Kelly fed the pages into the fire. "For answers?"

"No. But I can't keep risking Fi—the baby."

As Kelly dealt a new hand of cards, Tara turned over in her mind different ways to get Fimi out of harm's way while still pursuing her goal.

Kelly slid a new note in front of Tara. "What about other things Pir Ferit said? Who first passed on the 'message' to him?"

Tara wrote underneath. "His mother. Right?"

"I thought he said something else," Kelly wrote.

Tara shut her eyes, picturing the café where they'd first met the Sufi, tracing the conversation in her mind. She picked up the pen again. "You're right – he didn't say 'mother,' he said something like 'the woman who raised me.' Might not be the same person. But he talked about his mother too."

Kelly wrote underneath Tara's lines. "Right. She was an artist."

"Florence. He said some of her works are in Florence."

# 21

forwarded message from lin210*8888845

<<forwarded from UNDER10xready >>

;; server unknown

;; multiple destinations

;; error msg from nskl@xtra.org

;; unable to recognize mailbox

Re: Hope you're okay

Tara, I've sent you three emails and gotten no response, and the phone number which I have for you is no longer good, so I don't know if you are receiving these or not. In case not, I'll say again that Grandmother and I feel that Sagun and Diedre unfairly pushed you to leave Willow Springs. I hope you know we always wanted you to stay.

Please email me if you can do so safely. It's better not to call, Grandmother's become wary about using the phone, though I'm uncertain exactly why. But I want to know that you're all right.

Also, I am curious about what happened when I was in the hospital. I don't want to say too much here, but I pulled my hospital records without Grandmother's knowledge. And there are discrepancies. All I remember is awakening and you and Fimi were there. I can't help wondering if a connection exists. And if it does, whether you've figured out what it means. I have an important reason for wanting to know, so please respond if you can and tell me if I'm off base. If so, I'll let this go and have some peace. If not, let's find a time to talk. I'm sorry to bother you but, again, it's important, otherwise I wouldn't ask.

Hope you are well.

Love,

Kali

<< forwarded message from lin210*8888845 >>

<< forwarded from UNDER10xready >>

;; server unknown

;; multiple destinations

;; error msg from nskl@xtra.org

;; unable to recognize mailbox

Re: re: Hope you're okay

Hey, Kali,

I'm so glad to hear from you! I never received your emails. Thanks for telling me you and Nanor wanted me to stay. I guessed that was so, but I recognized Diedre and Sagun had a point, even if I didn't quite like the way they went about things. The last thing I want is to endanger anyone there.

I'm sorry I don't know quite what you're trying to say about the hospital or anything happening. I'm relieved you're all right and obviously was thrilled when it turned out your injuries weren't as bad as the doctors at first thought. They definitely don't know everything. As soon as things calm down, I'll come visit and we can totally catch up and talk about whatever you like. I'll make it as soon as I can. Fimi is doing fine, and I am as well as possible under the circumstances.

Love to you and Nanor.

Tara watched Kelly and Fimi, followed closely by a security guard, inch through the İstanbul Atatürk Havalimanı airport screening lines. The guard, who was ex-FBI, had flown in solely to escort Kelly and Fimi home. Tara and Sophia had chosen the guard. Holmes had wired money to pay for it. Sending Fimi home was the hardest decision Tara had ever made, and up until Kelly and the baby were out of sight, she was tempted to change her mind. But she couldn't justify keeping the baby with her as she followed the trail of Pir Ferit's cryptic comments to Florence and who knew where else. Neither could she abandon her search for answers.

Kelly had promised to call when they were settled on the plane and when they landed in Heathrow, Chicago, and St. Louis, though Tara would be in the air by then, on her way to Florence with Holmes. At least she'd get a message on landing with an update about her daughter, which might help ease the emptiness in her heart.

*It's better this way, it really is*, she thought.

The news services had noted Fimi's presence when reporting Hamed's healing, so Tara hoped everyone would believe the infant was still with Tara overseas. To that end, she'd bought a lifesized baby doll, dressed it in Fimi's clothes, and settled it into a baby carrier wrapped around her. The doll's limbs felt cool and hard pressed against her diaphragm and made her miss Fimi more. The doll wouldn't fool anyone nearby, but if someone watched her from a distance as she traveled Europe, it might create the illusion that Fimi remained with her.

"Tara?" Holmes said.

Tara turned to him. His broad shoulders, calm manner, and vast resources made her feel a little more grounded than she had earlier in the trip, despite the ache she felt at separating from her sister and daughter. Holmes rested his hand on her shoulder, as if he sensed her distress.

"Sorry what?" Tara said.

"You said someone would be meeting us in Florence?"

"Sophia Gaddini. Neither of us wanted to say much over the phone, but as soon as I mentioned Florence she got really excited and said she'd been planning to tell me something about that city that she was sure I'd want to hear."

"I see." Holmes' voice had a flat tone. Tara hadn't told him what Pir Ferit had said or what she and Kelly believed it meant, only that she thought Florence was the next place to try. Probably he thought she ought to be more forthcoming. And if Sophia agreed it was a good idea, perhaps she would be.

Sophia's knees and neck ached. At thirty-five, her joints ought to withstand long flights. But seven plus hours in a middle seat did anyone in, and that's all she'd been able to get on short notice. To her relief, the plane landed in Florence half an hour early. The man in the aisle seat helped wrestle her large carry on bag from the overhead bin. It was her only luggage. She'd learned as the child of musicians and later as a nun to travel light.

She stopped at a convenience shop for a bottled water and a small box of Belgian chocolates, a brand she loved that she could only find in Europe. As she left the store, she thought she saw Tara walk past the sliding doors near the taxi stand. It was always a little hard to recognize Tara. She changed her hair color and style often and shifted her clothing choices. This young woman was slight and a little shorter than average, wearing a heavy dark gray winter coat. She carried a baby in a baby sling around her front.

Sophia started across the baggage area toward the young woman, her thoughts preoccupied with how much flack she'd get from her dean for her sudden absence. Now that she was a tenured professor, she had more leeway and security than in the past, but neither was unlimited.

A tall man walking at Tara's side came into view. Sophia froze.

What was Rick Gettleman doing in Florence?

A door slammed. From inside the panel van, heart hammering, Pete listened to footsteps crunch in snow. He simultaneously regretted that he'd stayed so distant from Tara since Fimi's birth and cursed her for not keeping quiet about her unusual pregnancy. Telling anyone beyond the family placed them all in danger.

"My name is Kerri Geiser, Mr. Spencer. I will open the doors in a moment. I apologize for the method of transport. It is important that you not know where you have been taken if you decide not to help us." A woman's voice, but not the priest's wife. The accent sounded Russian, with rolled R's, stressed syllables, and the W's pronounced like V's.

*Help you do what?* Pete thought, struggling with the ropes around his wrists. Was it a bad sign that Kerri Geiser had given him her name? If it was her real name. For the first time, he wished he'd taken boxing or martial arts like his father had wanted him to do. He might know something more about fighting, as Cyril no doubt did. He'd been in pretty good shape before Megan's death; he'd found a way to work out every other day, at least by swimming half an hour at the Y. But since then he'd let it slide, and he'd become softer and weaker. He'd let a lot of things slide.

He heard creaking as the doors opened, and a blast of icy air hit him. His down jacket had come most of the way unzipped, and he was sweating from his struggles, so he felt chilled and clammy. No light seeped in around the edges of the blindfold, so it must be after sunset.

"Slide forward until you sit at the back bumper of the van," Geiser said.

He inched his body through the dark toward the cold air, his shoulder joints protesting the unnatural position they'd been forced into. Based on her voice, Pete guessed the woman's age as mid-thirties. But he was probably wrong. He'd met many clients in person after speaking to them on the phone who looked nothing like he'd imagined.

"Why am I here?" He maneuvered into a sitting position, a challenge with his hands behind his back, and put his feet on the ground.

"Stand slowly, don't lose your balance. Now shuffle forward – there's enough play in the bonds for you to do so – until your feet bump the threshold. The door is open."

Pete did as he was told, swaying more than once and unable to pinwheel his arms for balance. The woman gripped his arm to steady him, her fingers like a vise around his bicep. He flushed at being at this stranger's mercy. At the same time, his mind struggled with the incredible nature of what was happening. He was an accountant, a father, a quiet man, not someone in an action movie. The events of the last year didn't seem real. He had no idea what to do when he got inside wherever it was he was being taken. Lash out at whoever stood nearest when his hands or feet were freed? Run? He'd never felt this physically helpless before. But how different was it from the last six years of his life? He'd been helpless to change any major event, and his efforts to do so had done nothing or created more pain rather than less. Dozens of specialists for Megan, sending Tara to the psychiatrist, contacting the FBI to try to save Bailey. His eyes burned with tears he refused to shed, and he squeezed his eyes shut beneath the blindfold.

"Stop." Geiser put her hand on his arm. "You are now at the threshold. Hop a bit to get over the doorjamb. I won't join you inside. I will wait in the van."

Pete hopped, feeling both ridiculous and apprehensive. The door swung shut behind him.

~

Andrea Gutzmann thought she knew the answer, but she wasn't about to give it to the well-dressed businessman sitting on the sofa across from her. He'd gained entry to her flat on false pretenses, claiming connections with some of her former colleagues in academia, and he'd told her of Pir Ferit's death. That had shaken her, but it hadn't left her devoid of common sense. First, she didn't know if the man told the truth about Pir Ferit being dead. Second, whether Pir Ferit were dead or alive, Andrea didn't believe for a second that this stranger had worked with him. The Sufi had said nothing about Andrea sharing information with someone new at any time, other than whoever knew the key. She'd sent the young woman claiming to be Tara Spencer away for the same reason. Plus, Pir Ferit had assured her that if she hadn't completed her work at the time of his death, her stipend would continue, so long as she abided by the terms of their agreement, including the confidentiality provision. She didn't need a new contact to whom to provide her written reports – she'd never sent anything directly to Pir Ferit. Her contact here in Florence was perfectly fine. They'd had gelato together that afternoon.

"I am taking his place," the man said when Andrea told him she didn't know anyone called Pir Ferit. "Carrying on the tradition, so to speak." He wore a steel gray business suit with an almost imperceptible hound's tooth pattern and a fairly expensive looking platinum watch, though not with a recognizable brand name. "How else would I know about your work for him?"

"I don't know what or whom you're talking about."

"I see you're good at keeping Pir Ferit's secrets. But it does not follow that others will keep your secrets."

"Are you threatening me?"

"Not at all. Simply making the point that the need for secrecy creates problems when people die."

Andrea thought fleetingly of her daughter. Could this man know the deal she'd made with her ex-husband? A deal with the devil if ever Andrea had made one, but one she'd abided by, and so had her ex. Andrea had three months left before she could see her daughter again, her daughter who knew nothing of Andrea's crimes or her imprisonment. The additional year of separation had taken every effort on Andrea's part, and now this man might make it all for nothing.

But she'd given her word to Pir Ferit. The word of a convicted felon, convicted for fraud, no less, but he'd accepted it at face value.

"I can't help you." Andrea picked up the china tea tray with its rose-patterned cups and saucers, the only thing of value she'd brought to Florence. Her ex had preserved it despite the bitter divorce and returned it to her on her release from prison. It had belonged to Andrea's grandmother, and it made her feel a little less lonely to keep it and use it. She planned to pass it on to her daughter.

The man rose from the couch, giving her a fleeting hope that he meant her no harm. An instant later, Andrea was on the floor, shards of china around her.

~

"Mr. Spencer." Another woman's voice. This one sounded older, an alto voice with a slight tremor. Her English sounded more British, less slavic.

"Who are you?" His arms ached from being tied behind him.

"A friend," she said. "Perhaps of your daughter's."

"Her friends haven't helped her much," Pete said.

"Nor have you."

Pete swallowed. "I've tried." The words sounded weak to Pete's ears. His father's voice rang in his head. The colonel didn't believe in trying, only succeeding.

"Have you?" He felt a faint stir of the air, smelled gardenias. A warm hand touched his cheek, and his shoulders relaxed for an instant before he tensed again. "You may call me Paulina, though it's not my name. Hold still and I'll untie you. I trust you won't try to hurt me, but if you do, my guard is right outside."

Pete didn't know if "guard" meant Kerri Geiser or someone else. But he decided he'd hear this second woman out. If he needed to start swinging, better to do it once he had an idea of the space around him and how many people were involved. Not that he had a great deal of confidence he'd be effective swinging at anyone.

When Paulina untied him and removed his blindfold, Pete discovered he stood in a narrow kitchen with a worn floor and metal cabinets. Gray light filtered through a tiny window over the sink. A plain white ceiling fixture added a bit of additional light.

Pete shook his hands to regain circulation. Paulina led him into the next room, a combination sitting and bedroom. A twin bed sat along the far wall, a desk with two chairs sat in one corner, serving as both a study area and a table, and bookshelves lined the opposite wall.

The air smelled of kerosene from a small heater in the room's center. It didn't seem to have much effect. The house felt only slightly less cold than outside.

Paulina had thin wrists and fingers, and her bones appeared fine beneath the faint wrinkles criss-crossing her skin. Small ruffles edged the collar of her parchment-colored blouse. Her pants were black and straight. She sat at the desk and motioned him to sit near the bookshelves.

Despite the circumstances, he couldn't help looking at the books. A few he'd read, one about Zen, one about St. Thomas Aquinas.

"Your daughter is Tara Spencer?"

"Yes."

"Not your biological child, though?"

"Does it matter?" Pete never made the distinction in his mind. Family was family. The only reason he'd never formally adopted Tara was out of respect for Ray Tigue and concern that Tara might feel her biological father didn't care enough to oppose it. But he and Lynette had changed her last name early on, so she'd feel at one with the family.

"Perhaps not. And no one knows who her biological father is, correct?"

He was determined not to blurt anything else out. It wasn't like him to do that. "Is that something you need to know?"

Paulina smiled. "It may be something no one will ever know. Tell me, when your daughter told you she was pregnant and still a virgin, did you believe her?"

Pete looked at his hands. "No."

"And do you believe her now?"

Pete hesitated. Cyril had never asked him this. Tara had not asked him. Perhaps because she didn't want to hear the answer. He hadn't asked himself, not in a long time, not since the day at the Arch. The darkness he'd lived with since then had kept him from re-asking the question, had kept his mind numb, his heart empty, even after the strange DNA test results. Then the activity with Cyril had kept his mind busy.

"I'm uncertain," he finally said.

"You've come a long way for answers to a puzzle that is no puzzle at all if you don't believe her."

And Pete realized it was true. For so long, he'd searched for an explanation for Tara's pregnancy. First, one consistent with the laws of nature and the Church. That Tara was lying, that she was delusional. But Paulina was right, he'd never have come so far if he believed either explanation applied. Tara had never been an attention-seeker, and other than attention, insisting her pregnancy had a supernatural origin had brought her nothing but pain and heartache, so he didn't believe she was lying. And if she was unbalanced or delusional, then so were Sophia Gaddini and Cyril Woods and the other members of the Brotherhood, an organization Father Saur acknowledged actually existed. Plus, the DNA test results showed something unusual about Tara's pregnancy. Dr. Lei could have falsified them, but to what end? It'd be easy enough to find out if she was lying. Lynette was already planning on seeking another opinion if Tara agreed.

So Pete was left with a daughter who'd become pregnant without sexual intercourse, yet who freely admitted to being a non-believer. She hadn't attended mass in years, and while she shared most of Pete's values, she rejected the church.

"I want to believe her."

Paulina smiled. "Ah. 'And the father of the child cried out, with tears in his eyes, "Lord I believe, help my unbelief."' Mark 9:24."

The phrase beginning "Lord I believe" was one Pete had heard before, but he'd never known from what part of the gospel it came. A woman in the visiting room at the pediatric cancer ward had quoted it. Her son, like Megan, had cancer, and she said the verse helped her stay a believer. Megan's illness had never shaken Pete's faith. He'd never thought that believing entitled anyone to a happy life or freedom from the trials that plagued others. One needed only to read the Book of Job to know that. But Tara's experience, that raised questions.

"You're Christian?" he asked Paulina.

"I'm not not Christian."

"Do you think Tara's child is a new messiah?"

"That presupposes a previous messiah, does it not? But my opinion does not matter. You believe you are here to help your daughter, correct?"

Pete shifted in his chair. These people had knocked him out, hauled him here, wouldn't tell him anything, and now were questioning his intent? "I am here to help her."

"And yourself as well."

Pete tensed. Did she know about Father Saur's instructions? "I don't know what you mean."

"You seek answers so you'll know how to behave with your daughter," Paulina said. "What to do. What to say. What attitude to take toward her. Your Church Father has rejected her, but you haven't, not entirely."

It took him a moment to realize by Church Father, she meant the Pope. He supposed that was as good a way to refer to him as any.

"And you sided with him," Paulina said.

"I did not," Pete said. But his face flushed, remembering the things he'd said to Tara at the hospital after the visit. He stood and turned away from Paulina and toward the bookshelves.

"If now you find Tara's lied all this time, or been mistaken about her role, whatever she believes it to be, will you feel justified in your doubt, in the times you feel you failed her?"

Some of Paulina's books had shiny, colorful bookjackets, others were old hardcovers, with faded print and textured bindings that gave the room a faintly musty old book smell. As Pete ran his hands over the spines, they felt solid. Reliable. Which was why he'd never quite become comfortable reading on electronic devices. He didn't like words that could disappear at the touch of a button. "Are you asking if I'll feel better if I find she was untruthful?"

"Won't you?" Paulina said.

Pete spun to face her. "That's ridiculous."

"You ask me if I'm Christian, you ask if her baby is the new messiah," Paulina said. "What are those but questions designed to make your daughter fit into your religious tradition, your beliefs, when already you know she does not fit."

"I don't know that."

"Your pope told you so."

"But he could be—" Pete stopped, seeing the trap. Church doctrine held each pope to be infallible. He doubted most Catholics, at least in the United States, believed that was literally so given that some popes had reversed positions from past popes, but it was the doctrine. Pete believed in doctrine.

"I've always been there for Tara. I may have been misguided when I did certain things, but I acted out of concern for her well-being and for her soul. That's why I'm here now, looking out for her."

"Are you? Looking out for her?" Paulina said

"Of course I am."

*"We're counting on you," Father Saur had said."To tell us what's really happening, to share with us whatever information you learn if Cyril Woods won't, to bring us any document you find. We can guide Tara in the right way to see what's happened to her. We can be sure there's no misunderstanding, no confusion, among the people about her role. The Church's survival may depend upon that, upon people not misinterpreting what's happening to her and her child. She herself may misinterpret her role, may misunderstand any information in that document. That's why we must see it first."*

Pete returned to his chair, sat, and squared his shoulders, his back straight enough to make the colonel proud. "Of course I am."

# 22

Andrea floated, buoyed by the heavy sea salt of the ocean inlet in Salt Lake City. She could almost taste the salt, and she felt it on her skin, soothing and warm. Like a sea salt scrub, the kind she'd gotten in the days *before*. Before she'd discovered her business partner's actions. Before she'd decided to cover rather than reveal his malfeasance and destroy her business. The business she'd built following leaving academia, proud to be an executive in one of the most lauded non-profits, proud of the example she provided for her daughter. Together they'd gone on a spa weekend, Andrea's one vacation in all those years. *I'm sorry, sweetie,* she thought, *not much of an example at all.* She ought to feel sad at that, but she didn't. She drifted, drifted, vaguely aware of a man's voice murmuring. Was she responding? She didn't think so, but she might be. The man was saying something about a woman who'd traveled from Spain centuries ago. To Florence. A beautiful city, Florence. And now numbers and letters swirled in the waves around her. Were they part of a formula? A password? Andrea didn't feel sure. An image of a silvery key floated past her.

The voice continued.

~

CYRIL AWOKE LYING on the wood bench in the narrow waiting room. He shivered and sat, confused. Had he fallen asleep? The only light in the corridor came from candles flickering on either side of the fountain; the only sound was the water trickling. He was alone. His watch said over five hours had passed.

He jumped to his feet, stumbled, and pressed his hand against the stone wall to right himself. Through his glove, the wall felt cold. He waited for the room to stop spinning, then made his way to the office. The computer remained on, casting a bluish light about the walls, cursor blinking on a password screen. The fountain's gurgling sounded fainter in here. A cloth bound book lay on the desk, its cover worn, the binding loose. It hadn't been there before, he felt certain. He grabbed it but didn't stop to read it. He needed to find Pete, who must have been drugged, too.

The rest of the church was deserted as well. Night had begun to fall, and the doors were locked from the inside. Cyril could leave, but no one could enter, at least not without forcing the locks. He stared out one of the small, square windows at the front of the church and saw only darkness. He fished out his phone, a little surprised to find it still in his pocket and holding a charge. Apparently whoever had knocked him out hadn't meant to cut him off from everything. Once he unlocked it, he found a message from Pete.

*Stay there.*

Sent an hour before. It might not be from Pete. If it was from Pete, it might not be a command Cyril should follow. But if he left here, he didn't know where to go, or where he might find Pete.

He found the light switches but decided against turning them on. Perhaps it was better that no one know anyone remained in the church, other than whoever had left him here. He unearthed a set of candles instead, lit them, and began to read.

SOPHIA'S and Tara's room at Hotel D'Art had dark, shining hardwood floors and windows that overlooked the Arno River. Another time, Sophia would have made a mental note to return there someday for a summer vacation, but too much else occupied her mind. Holmes set their luggage near the closet and said he'd meet them in the library off the lobby in two hours. He had business to take care of after he settled into his own room.

"Business as Eric Holmes or Rick Gettleman?" Sophia asked.

"Gettleman," he said. "I don't want anyone to know I'm here." Holmes shifted slightly, but otherwise didn't look uncomfortable. He'd spoken little at the airport after saying that he'd had reasons for failing to tell Sophia he was Erik Holmes. Other than to discuss directions, all three of them had stayed silent during the drive from the airport to the hotel in the rental SUV.

Sophia stared at the door after Holmes shut it behind him.

"Are you all right?" Tara said. "I got the impression you and Rick were pretty close."

"I'm not sure." Sophia took off her coat and hung it in the closet, draping her emerald-colored scarf around its collar so she'd be sure to remember it if they left in a hurry. It gave her a moment to collect her thoughts. "But how are you? Tell me what's been happening."

After ordering coffee and tea from room service – *it's going on Rick's bill, so why not*, Sophia thought – the two sat in armchairs at a small round table in front of the windows. Sophia put Rick/Holmes out of her mind as she listened to Tara's reasons for pinpointing Florence.

When she finished, Tara said, "But why did you think we should come here?"

Sophia sipped her cappucino, which was quite good. "There may be a connection to one of the previous pregnant women. You said one lived in Spain during the Inquisition. Many Jews fled to Florence to escape the Church's oppression."

Tara looked doubtful. "That's not much to go on."

"I've another reason, and I feel more certain it's significant now that you told me Pir Ferit hinted you should visit Florence. It relates to the doctrines he mentioned – Collyridianism and Antidicomarianitism. The only significant work I found linking the two was by a former professor who now lives here in Florence."

"Seriously?"

Sophia nodded. "Andrea Gutzman, Ph.D. She left academia to head a non-profit. Later, she was convicted of fraud in connection with the organization's finances, and after serving her prison term, she moved to Florence. No one knows what she's doing here or how she's paying for her stay. Or how she got a visa, for that matter, as Italy doesn't welcome felons. She hasn't published in many years."

"So maybe she's connected to or working for Pir Ferit." Tara's face clouded. "Or the Brotherhood. They'd have clout, I bet, to get her a visa."

"Perhaps. But given Pir Ferit's suggestion that you travel to Florence and his mentioning the subject of her work, it seems more likely to be him. Just in case, though, I think we ought to surprise her tomorrow rather than calling ahead."

Tara nodded. "Do we tell Holmes?"

Sophia stared through the window at the colors reflecting off the river and drained the last of her cappucino. She hadn't realized how much she'd invested in the relationship with Rick until finding he wasn't who he'd pretended to be. Now she didn't know what to tell Tara. "I'm not inclined to share anything with him. Though I can't imagine I'm objective on the topic."

"Do you buy his explanation for his Rick Gettleman persona?" Tara asked.

"To the extent he's given one?" Sophia took her empty cappucino cup to the room service tray near the door, then sat on the edge of one of the two queen sized beds. Each had layers of white sheets and coverlets with different shades of white stripes. "It's a good way to keep his real identity unknown. But becoming friends with me – dating me – and not telling me, that concerns me. I had no sense he was hiding anything. Someone who can lie that well – it's troubling." She ran her fingers over the coverlet, its fabric smooth and soft. "Then again, I'm sure my personal feelings color my view. I liked Rick Gettleman very much, and I thought he liked me, and now it turns out he doesn't exist." She glanced at Tara. "I'm sorry. I'm here to support you, not the other way around." Despite feeling that she and Tara had become friends, the age difference and her role as a teacher and advisor left Sophia feeling it was wrong to lean on Tara for emotional support.

"Maybe Rick does exist," Tara said. "Maybe he's who Holmes would be in a perfect world. Who he really feels like he is."

"I'd like to say anyone who lies like that can't be trusted. But you've lived and traveled under false identities for good reason, so I don't believe that's a measure of someone's character in certain situations." Sophia made a conscious effort to set aside her hurt feelings. The point here was Tara's and Fimi's safety. She tried to think objectively. "The question is, do we believe Holmes is on our side? Or, rather, that his goals align with ours, since we know he has a different reason for wanting the truth."

"I'm not sure that is the question," Tara said. "It's more whether he really wants the truth, even if it doesn't support his goals. And whether he's a danger to me and Fimi if we no longer align with his goals."

"Such as if it turns out you or Fimi are some type of continuation of the Christian faith."

"He doesn't have a problem with Christianity, I don't think. Just with the organized Catholic Church. Which it seems pretty clear I won't be part of."

"Tell me more about what he said to you," Sophia said.

Tara relayed her conversations with Holmes.

It felt odd to hear about Rick as if he were a stranger. *And he is*, Sophia thought. *Tara knows him better than I do.*

"He says he doesn't want to harm people. He wants to bring down the institution," Tara finished.

The hotel room had darkened as the sun sank toward the horizon. Sophia switched on a lamp. "If he's telling the truth."

"Yes," Tara said. "If he's telling the truth."

Dr. Andrea Gutzman looked to Tara to be twenty or so years older than Sophia, perhaps in her mid-fifties, with ash blond bobbed hair and a thin, straight up-and-down figure. She wore a tailored blazer and blue jeans that looked expensive but worn. Her flat was small. Books piled everywhere.

The three sat on worn upholstered furniture in a small sitting area in front of the windows, Gutzman closest to the door. After she'd set out tea in mismatched cups, she said, "I've read your books, Dr. Gaddini. They lean a bit toward popular culture for my taste, but excellent content."

"Thank you. Please, call me Sophia."

"Wonderful. And I'm Andrea. But I'm not sure what I can do for you. A young woman came to me before claiming to be Tara Spencer."

Tara leaned forward. "Really? How long ago?"

Already, Tara felt her decision to leave Holmes out of this meeting was justified. Until she knew more about why he'd lied to Sophia, she had no intention of telling him anything that wasn't necessary.

"Two weeks." Andrea described the woman, but nothing about her sounded familiar to Tara. She hadn't been visibly pregnant, so it couldn't be the same person who'd helped the swordsmen.

"I told her nothing, because I had nothing to tell. I'm on sabbatical. I don't know anything about any issues relating to Tara Spencer." Andrea looked at Tara. "Whether that's you or not."

"I've just been to visit a Sufi teacher, Pir Ferit. Maybe you know him." Tara studied Andrea, but didn't see any reaction to the name. "He gave me a key."

Tara handed over the wooden key, and Andrea ran her finger along the blade where Pir Ferit had filed off the symbols. "What do you want me to do with this?"

"Does it mean anything to you?" Tara said. "It used to have numbers and letters carved on it. I memorized them."

Andrea raised her eyes. "So?"

"If you know some type of key, too, some type of password, that might relate to your stay here in Florence, or why you came to Florence, we could separately write down part of the password we know – say the first three characters – and see if they match. If so, perhaps we should talk."

Tara had thought about it before they'd gone to see Andrea and decided that was the best away to avoid revealing too much of the key to someone who might be unconnected to Pir Ferit.

"I have a password I've used for various things," Andrea said. "Perhaps it is the same as the one you know, perhaps not."

Guarding their slips of paper, Tara and Andrea wrote, then lay the pages on the coffee table.

They matched.

"Why don't you both write three more characters?" Sophia said.

They continued until they'd confirmed both knew the entire password.

Andrea let out her breath. "I still don't see a connection between you and anything I'm doing. But the match makes me trust you enough to tell you that a man was here. After the other 'Tara Spencer' and before you. I'm afraid I told him the entire password."

She described the man as a bit on the heavy side and appearing to be in his mid-forties, with silverish hair and expensive clothes. Tara wondered if he might have been Thomas Stranyero, Cyril's supervisor from the Brotherhood, but she'd never met Stranyero herself, only heard about him from Cyril. She also wondered if it could have been Holmes, but the timing made it unlikely, and no one would call Holmes either heavy or fortyish.

"He drugged me," Andrea said. "Probably with sodium pentathol or something similar to get me to talk. Everything is fuzzy, and I don't know for sure what I said. But if I told him that someone who claimed to be Tara Spencer visited me, and I didn't tell her anything because she didn't know about the key, I can't believe he wouldn't ask what that meant. And I remember numbers and letters floating around me in a haze."

"Does it matter?" Sophia said. "Will he be able to use it for anything? Perhaps it was only meant to connect you and Tara."

"I don't know," Andrea said. "Pir Ferit told me that if he died, someone might come to see me who mentioned the key and could recite the password, and I should cooperate with that person. So if he told other people that, and now this man knows ...."

"Who else might he go see?" Tara said.

Andrea shook her head. "I've no idea."

Tara sipped the Orangina Andrea had given her and walked to the window. Holmes stood outside, surveilling the street. Tara and Sophia had decided it was no use trying to hide their movements from him. But they hadn't told him in advance where they were going, and they'd insisted he not accompany them inside Andrea's home. He hadn't disagreed, but he hadn't looked happy.

*Too bad*, Tara thought. *He can't expect us to trust him when he pretended to be someone else.*

She turned back to Andrea. "What did you tell this man about Collyridianism and Antidicomarianitism?" Tara stumbled over the pronunciations.

Andrea stared at Tara. "Why would I tell him anything about that?"

"Isn't it part of what you were researching for Pir Ferit?"

"No."

"Oh." Tara slumped against the wall. So they'd reached a dead end.

"It's my hobby," Andrea said. "I've always been fascinated by both groups. But Pir Ferit never asked me about that. Are those beliefs connected to you?"

"Maybe." Tara explained Pir Ferit's comments.

Andrea tapped her fingers on the arm of her chair. Her nails were short but filed into perfect ovals. "He mentioned both? In the same sentence?"

"Is that significant?" Sophia asked.

"The Church regarded the two as opposites. But that makes no sense to me. After all, in the mythology preceding Christianity, many gods and goddesses were depicted as sexual, even as what would be considered promiscuous in today's culture. So why couldn't people in the first century believe both that Mary was divine in her own right and that she'd had sex with her husband after giving birth to Jesus? Nothing about the latter inherently negates the idea of divinity."

"So you believe the two groups combined?" Sophia said.

"I believe they were never separate, and the Church simply preferred to portray them that way. Or purposely tried to set them out against one another."

"But why do that?" Tara said.

"To splinter the group. Or to make it appear fragmented or disorganized to those on the outside so it'd be less likely to gain members."

"Is there any religious order or group that holds either belief today?" Tara asked.

"Within the Church? Definitely not. Outside it? There might be. The more I researched, and the more information I found, the more convinced I became that an order that followed both beliefs went underground to avoid being wiped out."

"Does it still exist?" Sophia said.

"I never found it. But I suspect a cloister – a hidden religious order – exists somewhere in Appalachia. It's a fascinating area of the United States religion-wise. Faith healers, snake handlers, ancient orders. The cloister wouldn't stand out. If I'm correct, it's a quiet, academic type of order. Focused on history, ancient documents, research."

Tara's pulse quickened at the mention of documents. This must be what Pir Ferit had meant her to learn from Andrea. But Sophia said, "This is all a bit speculative."

Andrea nodded. "Yes. I hadn't found enough evidence to publish before I left academia. But I'm happy to share my work with you. It wasn't part of my agreement with Pir Ferit, and I don't plan to return to academia, so I've no reason to keep it secret. I'd like to see someone investigate further."

"What were you researching for Pir Ferit?" Tara asked.

Andrea listed topics relating to ancient Islam, Judaism, and Christianity, but neither Tara nor Sophia could see any connection between them and anything Pir Ferit had said to Tara.

"Also," Sophia said, "I don't see any reason you needed to be in Florence to research any of those areas."

"There is no reason that I can see," Andrea said. "But he paid me handsomely to remain in Florence until someone with the key appeared. The funds go directly to accounts for my daughter's education and then some. All my savings went to pay my lawyer's fees and restitution, and my ex-husband unfortunately was never much of one for holding a job. So if Pir Ferit wanted me to live in Florence, I decided I'd live in Florence. It meant lengthening the separation from my daughter, but it was my only chance to provide her a good start in life."

"I thought it might be worth Tara coming to Florence because of a possible connection to Jewish people who came here to escape the Inquisition," Sophia said. "Do you know anything about that part of Florence's history?"

Andrea shook her head. "I'm sorry, I don't."

"What did Pir Ferit ask you to do with your finished work?" Tara said.

"Keep it secret. And deposit my manuscripts periodically with a contact I meet at the Basilica di Santa Maria del Fiore. What happens after that, I've no idea."

"That name is familiar," Tara said. "I think Pir Ferit mentioned that cathedral. Maybe that's the Florence connection, the real reason he wanted you to be here."

"Would you have told the man who interrogated you about taking your work there?" Sophia asked.

"It's likely," Andrea said. "He came to see me about Pir Ferit, so I imagine he asked me everything you did, and I told him. I'll give you my contact's name, and you can find out if the man visited him as well."

An hour and a half later, Sophia and Tara sat at a wood table in a back office of a small gallery not far from the beautiful green and white marble Basilica with its swarms of tourists. Matte finished black and white checkerboard tiles covered the gallery's floors. The walls had been painted soft white, and contemporary artwork from local artists hung everywhere. Tara found the quiet inside soothing after the crowded streets. The curator, Oslo Lucchesi, was a young man. He didn't know anything about a key or about Pir Ferit's mother, whose artwork Pir Ferit had said could be found in the Basilica. He also couldn't provide any background on Andrea's research. All he did with her reports, per Pir Ferit's instructions, was compile them in a safe in his own gallery, then mail them once a month to the Koca Mustafa Pasha Mosque. He'd just sent a package by post when an American businessman came to see him about Andrea's work. Oslo told him nothing about it because he knew nothing.

Sophia asked the question about Jews and the Inquisition.

Oslo nodded. "The man who came to see me asked about that as well, though I don't understand why the sudden interest."

Tara's heart sank. If whatever the curator had to say led to the manuscript, the mysterious man would have found it by now.

"My great-great-great-grandmother's best friend," Oslo said, "was a woman who'd emigrated here during the Inquisition. Her descendants still live in the northern Apennines."

"Is there a synagogue near them?" Sophia asked.

"Yes. Not the easiest place to reach, but you can get there."

After the visit, they found the day had turned warm for mid-February. They paused outside the Palazzo Vecchio, Florence's city hall, and Tara lifted her face to the winter sun. She wished Fimi could be here to see the city with its cobblestone streets, Gothic cathedrals, and sidewalk chalk artists despite that the baby was too little to appreciate it. A stunning array of sculptures stood in an open air pavillion nearby, including one where Perseus held Medusa's severed head. Tara stared at it, mesmerized both by the detail with which the artist had sculpted Perseus' muscles and the recurring Medusa head theme.

"Tara?" Sophia said.

"What? Oh, sorry, right, you were asking about Holmes – uh, Rick."

Sophia half-smiled. "Holmes is fine. It's a little easier for me to think of him that way."

"Have you guys talked? I know there hasn't been much opportunity, but I thought maybe this morning, before I got up."

The only plus Tara had found about being without Fimi was sleeping late that morning, though as soon as she woke, she automatically looked for the baby and panicked when she didn't see her. But Fimi was safe. Kelly had called to say she'd reached the house and the alternating security guards seemed strong and smart.

Sophia nodded. "We met briefly for coffee. We agreed to set aside dealing with our personal relationship for now. If there is one to deal with."

"I'm sorry."

"Most certainly not your fault."

"I think it's time to officially part ways with him," Tara said. "I don't want to take him with us to the synagogue. The man, whoever it was, who saw Andrea and Oslo must have gone there already, so we're not in any danger from him. And if we learn something, I don't want Holmes to hear it. I might share with him later if it makes sense, but like with Andrea, I don't want him to hear first-hand. Just in case."

"You're not concerned with the swordsman?"

"I am, a bit. So I think we make a great show of leaving my pretend baby with Holmes tomorrow morning, if he's willing to play along. And tell the hotel staff and anyone who will listen that Holmes is taking my baby on a trip with him. When it comes down to it, the swordsman's got to be more interested in her. He and Mullin tried to grab Fimi first, not me, and when Kelly and I were separated in the crowd outside Hamed's, he went after Kelly, which had to be because she had the baby." Tara shivered. "I just hope he's not in the United States. And that the security guards staying with my family are as sharp as their resumes suggest."

**Field Report 5.42**

It has been learned by this Special Investigator that a young woman bearing a resemblance to Tara Spencer and a baby appearing to be approximately five to six months old, both accompanied by a guard, arrived in St. Louis a day and a half ago via a flight from Istanbul through New York. No recognizable names appear in the passenger manifest, but as subject frequently travels under an assumed name this absence presents no surprise. The source was unable to approach closely enough to verify the identity of the young woman. However, she traveled with the guard and baby to the Spencer home in a black towncar registered to Cambridge Car Services. A recommendation is made by this SI to resume surveillance if possible without raising alarms. Failing that, another decoy could be deployed.

"PLACIDA CLAIMED TO BE A VIRGIN, so the story goes, though she was unmarried and pregnant." Mareisa de la Vega, a small, quiet woman in her late sixties, spoke softly in English. "Her parents believed her. They held strong religious views and thought that she had always been a blessed girl, though her sister argued it was just a ploy on Placida's part to cover her sin. The parents believed Placida might give birth to a messiah – the first messiah, you understand, as the Jewish people do not believe Jesus Christ was the messiah."

Tara and Sophia sat in a bench toward the front of the small synagogue, their bodies angled toward Mareisa, who stood in the aisle on a deep red carpet. Late morning sunlight came through the leaded glass windows, and textured fabric wallpaper and hangings covered the walls.

"Before the pregnancy was announced, the whole family had been planning to flee Spain because of the Inquisition, and this news hastened their departure," Mareisa said.

"Did they make it to Florence safely?" Tara asked.

"The father and sister did. But not Placida and not her mother. The father remarried. I am one of his descendants."

Sophia typed notes into her phone. "So what happened to Placida? And her mother?"

"Just before the family was to leave, a woman came to Placida to give her a letter. She said an aunt of an Armenian woman who also claimed to be a pregnant virgin had written it. The aunt had figured out what was happening and explained it in a letter. Placida couldn't read it because it was written in Armenian, but she understood it to be dangerous."

"Dangerous how?" Sophia said.

Mareisa shook her head. "The legend does not say. But Placida was frightened enough about transporting the letter safely, or perhaps about being found with it, that she tore it into at least three pieces and distributed it among her family members. Placida was captured before boarding the ship. One story is that an angry mob heard about her assertions about her pregnancy and deemed her a witch, another is that the Inquisition punished her for refusing to convert to Christianity from Judaism. Whatever the reason, she was strangled and burned at the stake. No one knows if she kept part of the letter with her such that it was burned or taken by Church authorities or if she'd given it all away. Only two relatives – her father and sister – and one piece of the letter, made it to Florence."

"And it's here?" Tara said, trying not to visualize Placida's awful fate. "You kept it here?"

"Yes. Over a decade ago, a Sufi, Pir Ferit, visited and asked to see it. He gave information that satisfied my older sister, who was the caretaker at the time, and she allowed him to see it. He then created a code and said that he would send the spiritual heir of Placida to us and when he did, we should give her the original.

"And did anyone come?"

"The only woman to appear is you. Last week a man visited. I found it strange that a man would visit, and that he would know the code, but he did. I pretended ignorance because the Sufi told us specifically a woman would come, one who was not traveling with men. I told the man who came the story was a fable that had been passed down, and that we had no evidence of its truth."

"Did he believe you?" Tara said.

"He seemed to."

A lecturn Mareisa said was called a bimah stood at the center of the sanctuary. She manipulated an edge of it, and the shelf slid off the pedestal. On the underside of the shelf, Marisa removed a panel to reveal a papyrus section preserved between two sheets of polyester film. Tara's pulse quickened.

"This is not the complete piece," Mareisa said. "Somewhere along the line, before Pir Ferit came to see us, before I was born, someone broke into the synagogue where it was previously kept and stole it. It was recovered, but the thief had begun to cut it to pieces, perhaps to further disperse and hide it. We did not get back all of it. I have photocopies of this section here and in another location. I will retain one and give two to you with the original. I believe you will need the original to understand the entire document. But if it's lost, a copy may help."

It was late afternoon by the time they headed back toward Florence. Sophia had spent much of her youth in the Rocky Mountains and felt more comfortable than Tara did driving down the winding roads, so she took the wheel. They passed giant ancient trees, including fir and beech, some long dead but still beautiful. The sun shown through the bare tree branches, creating patterns on the narrow mountain road.

"These pieces of Placida's document," Tara said. "They can't be the three pieces I'm looking for, can they? Because burned at the stake, lost at sea, how would that fit? How would those pieces have survived?"

"Perhaps none of the document was lost at sea. That might have been a story circulated to keep others from continuing to seek it."

"Maybe."

"Have you heard anything from your dad? Or Cyril?"

The SUV bounced, knocking Tara's water bottle from the cupholder. She tightened its cap and held it between her knees. "I got a message yesterday from my dad that they'd gotten on the bus that would take them to the church. It was sent over a day before I got it. Nothing since then. My mom hasn't heard anything. But Fimi's fine."

"It sounded like the church was in a fairly rural area," Sophia said. "It wouldn't surprise me if there's no email or cell phone coverage there."

"So who do we think visited Mareisa?" Tara said.

"She didn't recognize the photo I took of Holmes. Though he was across the lobby when I took it."

At Tara's urging, Sophia had taken the picture as Holmes checked out. He hadn't objected to separating from them, making Tara believe he was still tracking them one way or another.

"Holmes could have sent someone else to the synagogue," Tara said. "He was keeping tabs on Pir Ferit through Ismail. He might have figured out the Florence connection before you ever met Pir Ferit."

Sophia took her foot off the gas as she approached a portion of the road where the decline steepened. "That's a point. It could also be someone we don't know about. You've been getting a lot of press in the States lately."

"I have?"

"Your 'miracle' has been reported pretty widely."

Tara settled back into her seat, not sure what to make of that development. She'd been subject to press coverage before, and little of it had been friendly. Once she'd sought to tell everyone about her pregnancy, but that hadn't resulted in anything good. Now the last thing she wanted was to draw more attention.

Twenty minutes later, Sophia glanced in her rear view mirror. "That car's following awfully close." Tara twisted and saw a Smart car behind them.

"I'm surprised it made it up the mountain." The car was a two-seater with a small engine, popular in Europe.

"It must have come out one of the side roads," Sophia said.

Tara tried to see the driver, but sun reflecting off the windshield blocked her view. "At least it can't catch us if you accelerate."

"No," Sophia said. "But those three can stop us."

# 23

From a side path, two more Smart cars pulled behind the first three, creating two layers of vehicles to block the narrow road. For Tara, the attack in Istanbul by the swordsmen had seemed to slow time. The appearance of the cars accelerated it. Sophia hit her brakes, and the small SUV's tires alternately skidded and rolled as momentum took them further down the mountain into the closest Smart car.

Four men leapt from the two compact vehicles behind them. All wore nylons over their faces and dark bodysuits. More poured from the Smart cars in front, providing a comically dramatic picture, like dark clowns emerging from a row of Volkswagens. They swarmed the SUV, breaking the glass in the rear window with tools Tara couldn't see as she ducked and covered her face to avoid the shards. Two grabbed her arms, pinning her. Her heart thumped in her chest, but the men didn't harm her. Their rough hands ran over her body and found the photocopy of the document section pressed between her shirt and her stomach. Another took the faux-leather portfolio where Sophia had stored the papyrus original.

After one of them shot out the SUV's tires, the men swarmed into their Smart cars. An army in tiny vehicles, they easily maneuvered around the stranded SUV and down the mountainside.

THE JOURNAL COVER had a horizontal grain. It had no designs stamped upon it. The side binding was plain as well, and worn, and its pages felt thick and textured, almost like cloth. Cyril's rudimentary Armenian didn't allow him to determine much more than that a woman named Rima Petrosyan had become pregnant at nineteen, somewhat old at the time to be unmarried and for a first pregnancy. The journal, which appeared to be a record of someone's research regarding the church's history in the seventh century, mentioned a vision and the girl's aunt. Cyril couldn't tell if the aunt had the vision or the girl had. Probably the aunt, as it seemed she'd traveled to distant lands to visit wise men and women who today might be called spiritual gurus. In 642, she or someone else had written a letter to Rima. From the research he'd done before the trip, Cyril knew Arabs invaded Armenia that same year, and an army had set fire to Our Lady of Sorrows and burned half of it. As best as Cyril could tell from the journal, Rima and her baby were trapped in the church and died in the fire. The letter arrived after Rima died. The last note in the journal about Rima was that a local artisan had carved her image into a vase. Which must be the vase in the photo the Brotherhood had given Cyril when he'd started his mission, the same photo he'd seen in the church earlier that day. Nothing indicated where the vase itself might be now or what had happened to the letter.

Cyril closed the journal and ran his fingers over the cover. It must have been placed on the desk for him, for surely the priest's wife they'd spoken to knew Cyril had been left alone in the church. Had he and Pete been separated so he would learn something Pete didn't know? Or was this unimportant, meant to distract Cyril from something else?

The regular church records he found in the office showed nothing unusual. Births, baptisms, deaths. After perusing those stored in file cabinets, he tried the computer. The unprotected files showed nothing other than records of donations and people who'd visited over the years. Cyril searched the rest of the church, opening cabinets, feeling for secret compartments, climbing to run his hands along high window ledges. He found nothing else of interest. When he returned to the office, the journal was gone.

Half an hour later, someone pounded on the door. Cyril climbed onto a pew to peer out the window. The shadowy figure looked enough like Pete that Cyril opened the vestibule. Pete had a bruise on his cheek, and the shadows under his eyes deepened in the candlelight, but otherwise he seemed fine. He described a long van ride and talking with a woman who called herself Paulina.

"I finally convinced her I meant to help Tara, and she gave me a document."

"Just like that?"

Pete nodded, and Cyril felt certain he was leaving out part of the story.

"What kind of document?" Cyril asked.

"I don't know. She just said I must bring the original to Tara."

"I see." Cyril had shown he couldn't be trusted to keep Tara's best interests at heart, so he understood why Pete didn't want to share all of what he'd learned. But Pete hadn't exactly proven himself trustworthy where Tara was concerned either. More than once, Cyril had wondered if the Brotherhood had persuaded Pete to work with it. It wouldn't be the first time the organization's left hand didn't know what the right was doing. It made sense that a member of Tara's family might have better luck obtaining information than anyone connected with the Brotherhood. Perhaps someone had figured that out and enlisted Pete.

Or Pete was only doing what he'd claimed he'd come along to do – keeping an eye on Cyril.

"I don't need to know what the document is or what it's for," Cyril said, "or to see it. In fact, I don't want to know. That way, you'll never wonder if I shared the contents with the Brotherhood. I just want to help you get it to Tara."

Pete started to say something, but Cyril raised his hands, palms out in a conciliatory gesture. "I don't expect you to believe me."

They decided they were better sleeping at the church than trying to travel anywhere that night. They lay on pews, their jackets on for warmth. Cyril moved a prayer book under his head, staring up into the dark.

"Paulina had me dropped where I could get a taxi with enough money to travel here or directly to the airport," Pete said.

"They didn't offer to take you? To the airport?"

"They thought I'd be more of a target with them."

"Why did you come back here?" Cyril asked. "After all I've done, I would never have expected you to come back for me."

Not only what he'd personally done, Cyril thought, but because of the Brotherhood itself. It had taken him far too long to accept it, but he realized now that the Brotherhood must oppose Tara not because she might be lying or misleading people but because she might be telling the truth.

"I didn't come back for you," Pete said. "I came back to see if you'd learned anything. But you say you haven't."

Cyril maneuvered onto his side, the pew hard beneath his shoulder. "The church records show nothing of interest."

"I also thought it'd be safer with two of us traveling home," Pete said.

The eves creaked overhead. "I hope so."

"A COPY IS BETTER THAN NOTHING," Sophia said.

They sat in their hotel library five hours after the attack by the men with the Smart cars. Tara still felt chilled, and her feet were sore and her knees aching. They'd walked more than two miles before reaching a spot with cell phone reception to call the rental car company. But they'd hung onto the second copy of the papyrus section. It had been folded and hidden in Sophia's boot.

Sophia buttoned the last two buttons of her cashmere sweater. "It's actually better than what Pir Ferit planned to provide, which was only the text. With the photocopy you can see the layout on the page along with the words. That's a lot to work with, especially if your dad obtained a section from Armenia. And if that cloister in the Appalachians has the last section, we'll be able to put together a nearly complete document."

Tara had received a message from Cyril that he and Pete were fine, and that Pete had something for her and would get in touch soon. Tara guessed Cyril was afraid of the message being intercepted, but she wished he'd been more specific. She also wished her dad had gotten in touch himself. While she doubted Cyril would bother to communicate with her at all if he'd abandoned her dad or doublecrossed him somehow, she felt uneasy relying on him for information. It was like mountain climbing in a thick fog and counting on Cyril to tell her where to find the next handhold.

"Who knows whether my dad has a document section or something else? Or if we can find that cloister or if they'll have part of the document if we do find it." Tara wrapped her hands around her hot chocolate. Her fingers still felt frozen.

"There are a lot of unknowns, and that's challenging, I realize," Sophia said. "Are you concerned Cyril will trick your dad and take whatever they found to the Brotherhood?"

Tara and Sophia assumed the men who'd accosted them on the mountain had come from the Brotherhood, but neither felt sure, and they hadn't ruled out the possibility that Holmes had organized the document theft.

"No. My dad definitely doesn't trust Cyril." Tara's drink had started to cool, and the chocolate had clumped. She set her cup on the square dark wood side table. The vision of Placida burned at the stake loomed in her mind. She could almost smell the smoke and feel the flames. "But my dad might think he should give the document to the Church. The more I think about it, the more likely that seems."

"That occurred to me as well," Sophia said.

"I know how much the Church means to him, and I feel like I ought to understand that, but I still take it personally. I'm his daughter, but the Church is more important to him. That maybe sounds childish, but it's how I feel." Tara shut her eyes to hold back the tears that threatened to overwhelm her. The things her dad had said and done after she'd insisted her pregnancy hadn't come about in any natural way – how could she not take that personally?

"It's not childish. Of course you feel that way." Sophia put her hand on Tara's shoulder. "It might help to think about his context. There's a large age gap between you and your dad, and your dad and his parents. Your grandparents grew up in a Catholic Church where the priest interpreted everything. It wasn't until the Pope in 1943 issued the *Divino Afflante Spiritu* that non-clergy were encouraged to study the Bible. And Bible-reading, at least in the U.S., for Catholics didn't truly take hold until Vatican II many years later. Think of that. The Bible, the official holy book, and many people felt they should not try to interpret it for themselves. Add that to your grandfather the colonel's reverence for authority and order, and it's easy to see why the Church's views are so important to your dad. If you need the Church to interpret the Bible, how much more so a newly discovered document, origin unknown, that may contain a message about a new messiah."

Tara rested her head against the back of the couch, breathed deep, and considered what Sophia had said. It gave some context not just for her dad but for some of the things her grandmother had said when Tara had stopped attending mass. "That makes me feel a little better about my dad in terms of our relationship. But more concerned he'll take the document to someone in the Church rather than to me."

"If you could talk to your dad, perhaps at the very least you can persuade him to keep a copy."

"If I can reach him."

Sophia walked to the open doorway between the library and lobby, glanced around, then returned to stand near the glass and metal bookshelves. "Going back to the portion of the document we found at the synagogue, I actually hope the Brotherhood, or someone from the Church, obtained it. Another group could be more dangerous."

"More dangerous?" Tara said.

Sophia nodded. "Yes. If the Brotherhood's goal was to kill you, or Fimi for that matter, you'd probably be dead by now."

"That's somehow not that encouraging." The idea ought to have sent a shock through Tara, but instead she felt weighed down and almost as tired as she had after she and Fimi had healed Hamed.

"It is in a way. However misguided, I believe the Brotherhood's foot soldiers today at least mean to follow the Ten Commandments, as do most people who serve the Church. They might kill the Antichrist because that would be the devil, Satan, however they frame it. But they would only kill humans for an extreme reason. Others, perhaps, would not have such restraint. Which is also to say, perhaps it's just as well whoever it is got the copy of the document. You've nothing else to provide, so you should be left alone."

"Can you read what we have?"

"I'm afraid not. I can read Greek and Hebrew, but I know only a bit of modern Armenian, and the Western variant of it at that," Sophia said. "This looks like the Eastern variant and, more important, the original written language."

The candles flickered in square blue vigil holders on the coffee tables, sending out a faint pomegranate scent. Tara stared at the flame on the one nearest her as she shivered. She felt as if her body would never be warm again. "So we need to risk bringing someone else in."

"Perhaps not," Sophia said. "From what Andrea told us, I suspect someone at the cloister in Appalachia might be able to translate. Given their scholarly bent and the focus on ancient writings, if they have a part of this document, it makes sense they have someone who can translate. Plus I have to think that's why Pir Ferit directed us, in his indirect way, to Andrea Gutzman."

Shifting her gaze from the candles, Tara stared at the ceiling as she tried to recall Pir Ferit's words. "He said something about that."

"What? About the women?"

"No, something about a translator might appear when I needed one. Why couldn't he just tell me everything I needed to know?"

"You said he didn't trust anyone. It's likely his last way of being sure you're the one he was meant to share with."

"So do we tell Holmes about any of this? He left you his contact number, right?"

"Yes," Sophia said. "It's up to you what we tell him. And what we do next."

A draft swept into the library area from the lobby as a late night guest arrived. Tara stared at the congealing chocolate in the cup. She needed to decide. Where to go next, who to believe, with whom to share what she'd learned. But all she really wanted was to go home, crawl into her own bed in her old attic apartment with her daughter, and sleep. Through the rest of winter, the rest of the year, maybe the rest of the decade. And not awaken until she was older. And wise enough to know what to do.

RAY TIGUE RINSED the silverware in the right side of his sink, his sweatshirt sleeves pushed to his elbows, exposing the tattoos on his wrists. He'd gotten them twenty-five years before. Over the years, they'd stretched and faded, the names of the bands and the designs a little less clear.

There was no reason to worry, he thought, glancing at the door as if it could reassure him about his just-departed visitor. The young woman, Alma Duttenhaver, had recently joined his church group and had stayed for an extra cup of coffee after a Bible study meeting. Alma knew Ray was a recovering addict, and she confided that she'd become hooked on painkillers after a high school sports injury. She was especially grateful to be in recovery because she was now pregnant. Her loose clothes had hidden the pregnancy, but once she mentioned it, Ray wondered how he could have missed it before. He told her his daughter had recently given birth and how excited he was to be a grandparent. He still thought of Tara as his child, no matter what the DNA tests – which were most likely wrong – said. Ray was an only child of only children, and even if he believed Lynette had been seeing someone else while dating him, and he didn't, he couldn't think of anyone she could have met who was related to him closely enough to fit the supposed DNA results. It seemed more likely to him that Tara's doctor had doctored the results, so to speak, for some reason of her own.

Alma had been surprised to hear Ray had a daughter because there were no family pictures in his tiny studio apartment. So he'd explained that he wasn't really part of Tara's life, that she'd been raised by her mother and stepfather. Alma asked how that felt. They talked for nearly an hour all together. It struck Ray as odd in retrospect that he'd discussed Tara in more detail than ever before. But he hadn't said her name, or anything that would identify her. To be safe, he'd be more careful about what he said about Tara in the future. Alma had said she hoped he wouldn't mind chatting with her occasionally after meetings. She said he reminded her of her dad, who had died when she was in grade school.

Ray looked at the two mugs in the sink. Had he rinsed those yet? He wasn't sure. He turned on the cold water.

PETE SHIFTED ON THE PEW. Uncomfortable as it was, it was his thoughts, not the physical discomfort, that kept him awake. Paulina had given Pete a document, which she said was a portion of a letter. Despite his own doubts, which he felt sure must have been apparent to her, she'd said, "I'm trusting you to do with it what's right."

*But what's right?*

Pete suspected somehow Paulina had known about the conversation with Father Saur – not that Father Saur himself existed, but that someone like him, someone from the Church or the Brotherhood, was counting on Pete every bit as much as Paulina was. But still she had entrusted him with the document. Not Cyril.

Though that was hardly a choice. Pete pulled his jacket tighter around his body. The church had grown colder throughout the night. Cyril had claimed to care about Tara, had claimed to love her, from what she'd said. Yet at every turn he'd chosen his religious beliefs over her. Someone like that couldn't be trusted. Or forgiven. Cyril had said he'd realized he was wrong, he said he felt remorse, but Pete couldn't think of any reason Tara would believe him or let him into her life again.

A rustling came from the other pew. Pete guessed Cyril must still be awake, perhaps wrestling his own demons.

"What happened between you and Tara at the Arch?" Pete said.

"Tara healed me." The answer came immediately.

"Why? Why would she do that?"

"I asked her to forgive me," Cyril said. "And she did."

"You really believe that?" Pete said.

"Yes. She may not trust me, she may never trust me. But she forgave me. And that's enough."

Pete remembered the panic he'd felt that day. The way his own heart had seemed to halt when he saw one of his children, white as chalk, pitch to the ground. The wind outside the church howled, rattling the heavy front door and making the bells in the tower clang. "I can't forgive you," he said. "And I don't understand how Tara could."

# 24

Kelly glanced sideways as she finished washing her hands. A young pregnant woman about Kelly's height, which meant she was a little on the short side, entered the movie theater restroom. Her cheeks had a slightly bloated look, as if she were retaining water, and she wore heavy gray tights, a parka that hung open, and a T-shirt dress that stretched tight across her middle, emphasizing her pregnancy. She looked like she might topple forward any moment given her slim shoulders and stick-like legs.

"Tara?" the girl said. "I need your help."

Kelly dried her hands in the hot air dryer, her mind racing with its highpowered whir. Fimi was safely at home with her mom, her brothers, and a guard from a security service. Kelly didn't know how her parents were managing to pay for that, probably by borrowing on credit cards, but they were. The last she'd heard, Tara had traveled through Florence and was heading to Pennsylvania. Tara hadn't said why.

"Who are you?" Kelly said

The girl stepped closer. "My name is Alma D—just Alma. You probably won't believe me, but I'm in the same situation you were."

*Let her talk*, Kelly thought. *And let her believe I'm Tara. She'll say more.*

"Okay."

"I don't know where to turn. My stepmother asked me to move out because she thinks I'm making this up. I actually stayed a little while with those weird guys from the religious order that's been plaguing you."

"How did you find them?" Kelly asked.

"I played that game, TARA2, for a while, and another player gave me a code that led me to a guy named Raphael."

Kelly's older brother Nate had told her about the game when she'd returned home from Florence.

"And what happened?" Kelly said.

"They ran some tests on me and said they don't believe you or me."

"What kind of tests?"

The two young women stood in the middle of the scuffed tile floor, the smell of popcorn wafting in. The restroom was deserted. Kelly had left in the middle of the movie to answer a text from Tara. This girl must have been following her most of the day.

"Like ESP-type tests. You know, to see if I could tell what other people are thinking or guess the next card or move marbles."

"Weird," Kelly said, not knowing what else to say. She felt sure Tara had told her everything that had happened with Cyril and the Brotherhood, and she hadn't heard anything about tests like that. Though Tara obviously had never cooperated with them.

Alma pushed her hair behind her ears. "Yeah, I couldn't do them. But I don't think it means, you know, that I'm not telling the truth."

"But they thought so."

"Yeah, I guess," Alma said. "They said they couldn't help me."

"What did you want them to do?"

"Give me answers. About why this happened and what I should do. Isn't that what you want?"

"Answers are always good." It occurred to Kelly that being alone with Alma, if that was really her name, might not be the best idea. She didn't look dangerous, but who knew if she had a weapon or was stronger than she looked. The woman in Istanbul hadn't had a weapon, but she'd caused plenty of damage. "Let's sit out in the lobby."

They sat on an orange suede bench not far from the concession counter, and Alma told Kelly that after taking tests in a conference room for three days, she'd been sent on her way by the Brotherhood, but a man had called her. He said he was a deacon in the Brotherhood and that he had some information that might help her.

"Did you meet him in person?"

"No he just talked to me on the phone."

Kelly wondered if it had been Cyril, but she'd never spoken to him and didn't know if there was anything distinctive about his voice.

"How do you know he was really with the Brotherhood?" Kelly said. "People aren't always who you think they are." *Like me*, she thought.

"He knew so many things about them," Alma said. "And about you. Where you lived, your whole family, your biological father, and how he's not really your biological father."

Kelly pressed her palms to the suede bench to keep her hands from shaking. Tara had hoped no one had connected her with Ray Tigue. Apparently they had. Though maybe not, Alma hadn't said Ray's name. She could be just fishing.

"And what did this guy Raphael want?"

"He said there's a place we can go to find out the truth. Somewhere the

Brotherhood isn't welcome. Then he sent me this. He said you might know what to do with it."

Kelly stiffened as Alma reached into an inner pocket of her parka, but all she pulled out was a page that appeared to be a photocopy of a strip ripped from a larger document. The characters on it were unfamiliar to Kelly. But she had to think they might be Armenian.

~

The taxi sputtered and jerked. The driver stayed in the center of the road because so many cracks and potholes covered the edges that no vehicle could safely traverse them. Whenever a car came from the other direction, it also traveled in the center, and one or the other veered to the side. Too much like a game of chicken for Pete. He kept his eyes on the countryside out the back passenger window, always conscious of the partial document he carried. He'd placed it among layers of parchment, then inside a plastic bag and pressed it against his body between his shirt and bare skin. At least they were making fairly good time on the trip to the airport. Cyril sat in front, shoulders stiff, staring straight ahead. It encouraged Pete that despite being decades younger, sleeping on the pews had made Cyril ache as well.

The taxi coughed and slowed. "Is there no vehicle in this entire country that runs right?" Pete said. He hadn't decided anything for certain until the early morning hours. Now that he'd made his choice, the four-hour drive to the airport seemed interminable.

A loud noise, like a car backfiring, came from behind them. Something seared into Pete's shoulder.

"Get down," Cyril said. He shouted in Armenian and pulled a gun from his jacket.

Pete dove for the floor and landed on the back seat. He clapped his opposite hand over his injured shoulder. His glove was thick enough that he couldn't feel the wound with his fingers, but blood gushed, soaking the wool. More shots, seemingly from a distance. A scuffle in the front, the sound of a door opening and slamming. More gunfire. The taxi rocked, its engine spasmed and roared, and it shot forward.

The initial shock wore off, and a hot poker speared Pete's shoulder. Everything went black except for fluorescent sparks behind his eyelids. Pain drove out all thought – who had started shooting, who was still shooting, who was driving.

The car jerked and bumped over the roads, careening one way, then the other. Each jolt sent sweat pouring down Pete's face.

He prayed he'd pass out, but while his grip on reality diminished, the white hot pain remained.

*Sorry Tara. So sorry.* Despite the blurring in his mind, Pete felt the plastic sleeve with the piece of the document inside against his chest, now slippery with blood. *I'm so sorry.*

Then he was gone.

CYRIL HAD SPOTTED the taxi driver's nervousness, the way he watched the rear and side view mirrors constantly. Cyril had bought a Glock the first night he and Pete spent in Armenia. When the driver slowed the vehicle, making the engine stutter, Cyril pulled the gun, made the driver stop, and shoved him out of the vehicle. Cyril didn't know if the driver shot at the taxi as it drove away or if the shots came from somewhere else. It didn't matter. He hit the gas and sped away as fast as the car would take him.

The back window had several bullet holes with starlike cracks emanating from them, and he knew from Pete's cries that he'd been hit. But Pete still moaned in the back, so he was alive. Cyril was afraid to stop, afraid to let anyone gain on them, but finally found a place to pull the taxi into the woods. He got out to check on Pete, who was unconscious. The bleeding, as bad as it looked, had slowed and clotted. Pete lay in a fetal position.

Being careful of glass fragments and shards, Cyril cut away Pete's jacket and shirt sleeves and examined, cleaned, and dressed the wound as best he could with the supplies in his travel First Aid kit. The bullet had grazed Pete's left upper arm but not penetrated it. When he finished, he unbuttoned Pete's shirt. Even unconscious, Pete tried to hold the clear plastic folder encasing the document he'd meant to bring to Tara.

With some difficulty, Cyril eased it out of Pete's shirt, wiped the blood off the plastic folder, and pressed it against his own chest.

PETE AWOKE ALONE, shivering. In the dark. He felt sweaty and chilled, but he knew where he was. In the taxi's back seat. His own down jacket was wrapped around him, and another coat lay on top of him. Cyril's?

He felt his chest with his right hand, slid it under the jacket. The blood, no longer damp, had hardened the fabric of his shirt. The document was gone. Pete shut his eyes, giving in to the hot pain that inflamed his shoulder, neck, and head. What had he expected from the man who'd nearly gotten Bailey killed? His cell phone was in his pocket, but when he managed to maneuver it out he found it was out of power.

Inch by inch, Pete raised himself to a sitting position. Each movement intensified the pain, sending spots swirling around his head and leaving him gasping. After what felt like an eternity, the pain settled into a heavy throb that made him nauseous. His left shoulder had been taped. Cyril must have provided the first aid, so perhaps he didn't mean to leave Pete after all. Pete fumbled for the door handle, then wondered what his goal was. He had no idea where he was and wasn't likely to be able to find a road in the dark. Instead, he unzipped his backpack and found a power bar and a bottle of water. It took forever to eat and drink, all he could manage were tiny bits and sips. He lay down again, resolved to try to flag a vehicle in the morning.

Some time later, he didn't know how long, he heard a motor approaching. His heart beat faster.

KELLY WASN'T sure what to make of Alma. After calling ahead, she brought her home to meet Lynette and Nate. Bailey stayed in Tara's old apartment with a security guard. After what had happened to him before, no one wanted him near anyone who might be connected to the Brotherhood.

Alma wouldn't let Kelly touch her photocopy, let alone make a copy of it.

"I want to go with you," Alma said. "Raphael said you'd figure out where to take it, you and Sophia Gaddini. And wherever you go, I want to go. I need to find out what's happening to me."

They sat in the living room, Alma in the armchair near the piano, Lynette and Nate on the couch kittycorner from Alma, and Kelly across from her. Kelly had tried to arrange it so they didn't seem like they were ganging up on the young woman. If Alma felt more comfortable, she might talk more.

Lynette took off her reading glasses, folded them, and used them to point at Alma. "So what do you think caused your pregnancy?"

"I don't know," Alma said. "I went to the doctor because my periods stopped, and I thought I was sick or something. I couldn't believe it when he said I was pregnant. I didn't know he was going to do that test. I'd told him there was no way I could be pregnant." She glanced at Kelly. "I guess you know what that's like."

Kelly fussed with Fimi's blanket, tucking it more tightly around her, wishing she could tell Alma the truth, but afraid to without talking to Tara. She didn't want to reveal where Tara was or what she was doing. "That's a scary situation. I guess your doctor took you through all the ways it could have happened."

Alma narrowed her eyes. "What do you mean?"

"You know, asked if you had any blackouts, or if someone could have drugged you and taken advantage of you, or if you'd engaged in any sex play short of intercourse that could have caused pregnancy."

"Now you sound like the Brotherhood guys."

"Well, they have to at least ask, don't you think? I thought a lot about what could have happened."

"But then you knew it was divine right? You know something amazing happened?"

"I wouldn't say that." Kelly had never heard Tara use the word "divine." And Kelly didn't think of Fimi that way, despite the healing powers Fimi might have. Fimi was Fimi. Her niece. A regular baby who needed her diapers changed and cried and smiled. "Something unusual is happening, but I don't know what."

"Well, I do," Alma said. "I'm sure my baby and yours are the new messiahs. There could be more than one, right? Why not? Or maybe it's just my baby, since you say you're not sure."

"Right," Kelly said, offended on Tara's behalf at what she took as Alma's implication that Tara might be lying.

After Alma had gone to sleep in Kelly's room, Lynette, Nate, and Kelly sat around the kitchen table with classical music playing and the doors shut so Alma couldn't hear them. The guard sat in an armchair wedged next to the linen closet so he could watch Kelly's room to be sure Alma didn't creep out and eavesdrop. Or do anything else.

"I don't believe her," Lynette said. "But I didn't believe Tara, and she's my daughter, so I don't know how much that means."

"Usually the simplest explanation is the right one," Nate said. "Yeah, Tara has had this bizarre experience, but what are the odds that someone else had it too, and someone from the Brotherhood just happened to give her this piece of paper that means something, and she just happened to decide to get in touch with Tara. More likely they're playing some kind of game, and Alma's their pawn. Or she's in on it."

Kelly tried again to reach her dad. In the last twenty-four hours, he hadn't responded to texts or phone messages. It worried all of them, though Lynette pointed out that cell phone towers weren't ubiquitous there as they were in the U.S., so he probably didn't have reception. That her mother said that three times within two hours told Kelly Lynette wasn't convinced.

# 25

"I don't like it." Sophia clicked the cell phone speaker off and ended the call. She and Tara sat in a campground near Altoona, Pennsylvania. They'd just heard about Alma from Kelly and Nate.

"I don't, either," Tara said. "I agree with Nate. I wish we'd hear back from my dad, both to know he's okay and to see if Cyril's heard anything about this woman Alma."

Sophia wanted to say that Pete was fine, but she feared hollow reassurances would only make her friend feel worse. She felt nearly as concerned about Pete's emotional distance from Tara as his physical safety. For every friend Sophia had kept from her days as a nun, there were ones she'd lost because her decision put too much stress on their own belief systems. She hoped Pete wouldn't let the possible conflict between the Church and whatever Fimi's existence meant become a permanent barrier to his relationship with Tara. But she'd known parents who'd withdrawn in far less challenging circumstances.

"Do you think Cyril would tell you the truth?" Sophia asked. The topic of Cyril seemed safer than Pete, though only marginally so. "If he knew something about Alma?"

"I don't know," Tara said. "When I was still hearing from both of them, it at least sounded like Cyril stuck with my dad."

"Which might only mean he needs to know what your dad finds." Sophia spoke softly, again not sure how Tara might react. She doubted she needed to remind Tara of Cyril's past actions, but the heart sometimes forgot what it wanted to forget. "If the strip Alma has a copy of is what's missing from the section we have, that means the Brotherhood has the original from the synagogue, plus the missing piece from it. And we have no original. So if the one in

Armenia falls into the Brotherhood's hands, it may be enough for them to learn whatever this secret is about you and Fimi before you do."

"Yeah." Tara stretched her hands toward the fire. "I'm not thinking Cyril's become a new person, if that's what you're worried about. And I'm sure my dad isn't thinking that."

An image of the afternoon she'd spent wandering through the Art Institute with Rick Gettleman and dining at Henri across Michigan Avenue flashed through Sophia's mind. "It's hard to know whom to trust."

"No kidding."

The fire began to die down, and Sophia added a log to it. She hadn't been camping in years, but most of her skills from traveling through folk and bluegrass festivals with her parents were merely rusty, not forgotten. The fire leapt and sparks flew. Tara and Sophia drew their feet back.

Sophia slid the map of the Appalachian mountains farther from the flames. After consulting again with Andrea Gutzman and talking with colleagues at the University of Pennsylvania, Sophia had pinpointed the area where she thought the cloister was located. It was a section of the mountains that included several Apostolic congregations rumored to practice snake handling. Which might not be a particularly good omen for the views those at the cloister might hold. But, as Andrea had pointed out, it was a good place to fly under the radar if your religious order was a bit unusual.

Unfortunately, Sophia's questions to colleagues, and her and Tara's visits to different churches and retreats, had probably broadcast their whereabouts, undercutting the efforts they'd made to cover their tracks by zigzagging across the country with different flights and trains and fake tickets.

Tara took the kettle from the fire, using a branch to lift it out of the flames. She poured tea for both of them. "Do you miss Holmes? Rick?"

"More than once, I've started to think, oh, Rick would be a great person to get some insight from on this. Or just to talk with. He was wonderful to talk with, such a good listener. Which, I suppose, makes sense."

"He wasn't necessarily only listening to get info," Tara said. "For the little bit we were all together, I watched him. He seemed pretty distraught that you were unhappy with him. And fairly smitten."

"I'm not sure that matters," Sophia said. "I doubt I'll ever feel I truly know him."

"Yes," Tara said. "I know exactly what you mean."

Seeing her dad's cell phone number on the display, Tara answered her phone on the first ring. The Jeep they'd rented whined as the road grew steeper. In the rear view mirror, the faith healer's tent shrunk to thumbnail size. She and Sophia had visited three faith healers, two convents, and a commune in the past day and a half.

"Dad?" Tara said.

"No. Sorry. Cyril."

"What are you doing with my dad's phone?"

"He's here, he's just a little weak," Cyril said. "But he's fine. I'll put him on."

"Wait – what?"

Sophia glanced at Tara. "Everything all right?"

"I don't know."

A few seconds later, Pete got on the line. His voice sounded soft, but Tara recognized it.

"I'm in the hospital in Yerevan," he said. "But I'm fine." Tara gripped the armrest, oblivious to the beauty of the glistening snow-frosted trees that covered the slopes outside the Jeep's windows, as her dad told her he'd been shot. He described how Cyril had gotten him help and reassured her he was fine.

"And I have something for you," Pete said. "I think it's a portion of something you've been looking for."

"I am looking for something," Tara said. "Piecing something together." She wasn't sure if her dad was being cautious because Cyril was within hearing distance or because he didn't trust the phones.

"Cyril helped me find it," Pete said. "In fact, he kept it safe for me while I was unconscious, and now he's returned it. I'll tell you more when I see you."

Tara let her breath out. "He's really helping you."

"I'm sure," Pete said. "We're helping each other."

"Okay. Good. Sophia and I are trying to find the last part of the – thing. When I know where it is, I'll let you know where to meet us."

"All right, honey. I'm putting Cyril back on. I need to rest and get my blood pressure down before they'll let me out."

In the second of silence while the phone was being handed back and forth, Tara's stomach tightened as she wondered if Cyril could be holding her dad captive, pointing a gun at him. But she rejected the idea. Her dad was smart, he would have said something to signal Tara.

"Tara?" Cyril said. "I'm stepping into the hall to give your dad some peace. Don't worry, I'll stay outside the door so no one gets in. I've been sleeping on a chair by the bed."

"He's healing all right?" Tara said.

"Yes, he should be released later today."

"I texted you before to ask where you both were. Why didn't you answer?" As much as it seemed Cyril was at last on her side, Tara didn't feel sure about his actions.

"I didn't want to tell you he was in the hospital before he was well enough to talk to you. But I didn't want to lie to you. So I waited."

"But you're sure he's fine now?"

"I'm sure. We'll be on a plane as soon as we can be. I need to fill you in on what else I learned at Our Lady of Sorrows. I didn't tell your dad because, well, I don't know if he's sharing everything with me. But I put it into an encrypted file, and I'll send you a code. Once you've read it, you can tell me if it's all right to share."

Tara hung up, relieved that rather than trying to get information from her, Cyril had provided it. And earlier she'd spoken to her mom, who'd put Fimi on the phone so she could hear Tara's voice. Fighting car sickness, Tara retrieved the file with Sophia's tablet and read aloud to Sophia what Cyril had learned about Rima Petrosyan from the journal.

"It seems to fit with the story Placida's descendant told us," Sophia said.

Tara buzzed the window down and breathed in crisp cold air. "It does. We just need to find the cloister to put it all together."

~

"It doesn't look like a chapel." Tara stopped at the crest of the hill, breathing hard. The day had warmed and she felt sweaty under her coat and gloves. She and Sophia had parked the rented Jeep at a clearing miles further down the mountain, then hiked winding trails to this spot. Since leaving the baby doll with Holmes in Florence, Tara had found herself missing its weight and the sense of security – probably false – it provided. She'd hoped anyone following her would believe she still had Fimi and not look for her elsewhere. But if she'd kept the doll, surely by now anyone tracking them would have figured out she didn't have a real baby with her.

A single-level cylindrical gray poured concrete building with narrow rectangular stained glass windows stood before them. Mountains loomed behind it, and stone walls extended on either side of it, disappearing into the woods that surrounded the building.

Sophia, also breathing hard, folded the map and stowed it in her bag. "If this is the place, I'm not sure it's technically a chapel anymore. But I know what you mean."

The path to the entrance consisted of stepping stones like those Tara had walked over in her vision at the Basilica Cistern. A small pond to one side of the path had frozen over. Beneath the top layer of ice, though, goldfish swam.

No one came to greet them, or stop them, as they approached the chapel. Its black Lucite doors opened easily. The vestibule, which was empty, had dark stone tiles and walls. Beyond it, the polished wood floor in the main room nearly glowed. At the center of that room stood a large round wood table, a basket filled with loaves of bread on it. Smaller tables and chairs – some armchairs, some oversized, some wooden folding chairs – were grouped around the room, low bookcases creating de facto room dividers without blocking any area from view.

Overhead, Art Deco fixtures provided soft light, making the room look warm despite the concrete walls. To Tara's left, a beam of light illuminated a pedestal with a back that curved to match the chapel wall. Upon it sat a stone vase that looked similar to the one in the photo Cyril had given her so long ago, though Tara couldn't tell if a face had been carved into it. She stepped through the archway that connected the vestibule and the main room.

Alarms shrieked.

## 26

Tara froze, heart pounding.

"Stay where you are." The woman's voice carried over the alarm, but Tara didn't see anyone. Speakers must be hidden in or near the archway where she and Sophia stood.

The smell of fresh bread filled the air. The comforting scent seemed incongruous given the wailing alarm.

"Show any weapons," the voice said.

*Weapons?*

Tara remembered her switchblade just as Sophia said, "Metal detector."

"Right. Yes." Tara unbuttoned her long coat so she could ease her hand into her jeans pocket. "It's a knife. That's all we have."

"Put it on the tray."

A wooden tray sat on a ledge on a tall cabinet just inside the hall. Tara set the knife there. The tray glided into the cabinet. It reminded Tara of something her grandfather would make, probably using a pulley system.

At last, the alarm stopped. Tara's ears pulsed, as if she could still feel the sound.

"Step back and step through again."

Sophia and Tara followed instructions.

Two women entered from the opposite side of the vast room. The first walked with a cane and wore a dark A-line skirt that ended past her knees, a white blouse, and a navy blue blazer. Not a traditional nun's habit, but as close as Tara imagined one could get with secular clothes. The woman, who introduced herself as Sister Mary Paul, appeared to be more than a decade older than Nanor, so likely in her mid-eighties, with thick gray and white hair and fair, heavily-lined skin.

The second woman, who was pregnant and looked to be in her late twenties, was black, with tightly braided medium length hair, and a warm smile. She wore khakis, a fuchsia maternity blouse and, despite the season, roped sandals. She also wore a plain gold wedding band on her left hand.

"We apologize for the alarm." Mary Paul waved her cane toward the seating areas. "This is our home and also serves as a retreat for those from outside, and we don't allow guests to bring in weapons."

"I'm Zavia," the younger woman said. "After the evanglist St. Francis Xavier. I chose it when I joined the community here."

"Zavia," Tara said. "That's familiar." Tara searched her mind, and it clicked. She realized Pir Ferit had mentioned not only Zavia but Alma. Who had to be the same Alma who'd approached Kelly. Tara had no idea what that meant.

"And you are?" Zavia said.

"Tara Spencer."

Zavia and Mary Paul exchanged glances.

"Let us sit," Sister Mary Paul said. "And you can tell us why you've come here."

As they talked, another woman brought out food, wine and sparkling water. As the scent suggested, all the bread in the basket had been baked fresh. Some loaves were long and narrow, others twisted, others took the shape of baguettes. Despite the thoughts racing through her mind, Tara focused on eating, dipping pieces of bread in turn in three different-flavored types of olive oil. Sophia reached for the tray of antipasto as Mary Paul opened a bottle of Syrah wine.

Zavia readily admitted to meeting with Pir Ferit.

Sophia raised her eyebrows. "Do you claim your pregnancy has any supernatural or unusual origin?"

Zavia laughed and twisted the cap off a bottle of sparkling water. "Oh, no. My husband is the lucky man, no question there."

"But you told Pir Ferit something else?" Tara said.

"I didn't out and out lie, but I let Pir Ferit believe I thought something mysterious was happening because I hoped to find out information from him."

"And did you?" Tara said. "Find out any information?"

"No. Did you?"

"I did. In a very, very roundabout way, it led us here. But tell me, first, did you meet anyone named Alma, another pregnant woman? Young, white?"

Zavia shook her head.

The food had disappeared rapidly, and after hearing they hadn't eaten since early in the day, Zavia left them talking with Mary Paul while she put together something more.

Tara took the opportunity to look more closely at the vase. Though no face had been carved into it, at least to her untrained eye it looked like it could be over a thousand years old. She made a note to ask about it later, not wanting to interrupt Sophia, who was explaining the trail that had led them to the cloister. Tara chimed in now and then, but for the most part let the conversation flow around her, enjoying the tart, layered taste of the red wine, and relaxing for the first time she could remember since leaving for Istanbul.

Alma wanted Kelly, who she still believed was Tara, to bring Fimi with them to meet Sophia in Pennsylvania.

"Absolutely not," Kelly said. "I'm not dragging my baby across the country. We barely know where we're going."

Pretending to be Tara was easier than Kelly would have guessed. She'd often tagged after Tara, and though she'd accused Tara of neglecting her to watch over Bailey, Tara had actually spent a lot more time with Kelly than her parents had been able to. Plus, Alma had never met the real Tara. What little Alma knew came from articles and posts about her. Lynette had carefully put away the family photos and screensavers before Alma arrived. There was a nearly five year age difference between Kelly and Tara, but people often mistook Kelly for older than she was. She didn't think it had to do with her looks, but with having spent more time with her older siblings as she grew up than with kids her own age, and with needing to behave like an adult once Megan had been diagnosed. Megan's first surgery had been the day before Kelly's twelfth birthday. Only Tara and Nate had remembered, sneaking a cupcake, candle, and matches into the intensive care waiting room and singing Happy Birthday at five minutes after midnight.

"But Professor Gaddini told you where to meet her." Alma bit into another of the coconut chocolate chip cookies Lynette had set in the center of the kitchen table. Lynette had been baking since learning Pete was in the hospital, and the kitchen smelled of melted butter and dark chocolate. "Mrs. Spencer, these are wonderful." Alma turned back to Kelly. "Do you change your hair a lot? In the photo I saw of you on-line, you had medium length dark hair."

"I do change it," Kelly said. "I don't like people to recognize me." At least whatever Alma had seen hadn't been a recent enough picture, or close enough, to notice the differences in Kelly's and Tara's facial structure or skin tone.

*Or she's playing along with us and knows I'm not Tara.*

"Where'd you see it?" Nate said. He sat at the end of the kitchen table, cradling Fimi against his chest.

Alma took another bite of cookie. "Oh, Facebook I think."

"Because I took all Tara's social media down," Nate said.

"Huh. Well, then it must have been a news article. I still think we should bring Fimi with us. Because maybe the nuns will want to see the baby. You're not afraid the nuns will do anything, are you?"

"We don't know who we might meet along the way," Kelly said. "And we don't know that they're nuns." She'd received a short message from Tara of where to meet without much detail. She hoped to get a longer explanation before heading for the airport.

"We're just getting answers," Alma said. "That's what this man Raphael told me. He said there's no danger, we just need to reunite the pieces of the document and we'll get answers. And I bet your professor has part of the document, and the nuns have the rest. So we just bring them this piece."

"When a person makes a point to tell you there's no danger, it's about as reliable as when someone says how honest he is," Nate said. His eyes flicked toward Alma and then to Kelly, and Kelly knew what Nate thought. It confirmed her own assessment, and Kelly trusted her brother's judgment of people more than anyone else's.

"But what could be dangerous about putting a document together?" Alma asked.

"I don't know," Kelly said. "But we don't need Fimi for it."

~

"So it was Pir Ferit's mention of two beliefs about Mary – Collyridianism and Antidicomarianitism – that led us here." Tara still struggled with the pronunciations, but she thought she was getting better.

Zavia returned with trays of fruit and cheese to go with the fresh bread, and she said a chicken was baking in the community's oven. Sophia poured herself a glass of sparkling water, and she sliced a lemon from the fruit tray and squeezed a section into her glass. Zavia put two slices and a lime section into hers.

"I've got to do something to spice it up," she said. "Ever since I got pregnant water's the only thing I can drink that doesn't make my stomach turn somersaults." She took a long drink and turned to Tara. "Here at the cloister, we've studied both the doctrines you mentioned. It's part of what drew me here, and led me to leave the Catholic Church, though I did at one time consider becoming a nun. I stopped before the novitiate stage. I couldn't get past the idea that, solely because I'm female, I could never lead a church. I could've gone to another Christian religion. I was exposed to several – my parents were unusual in our community in being Catholic. There were plenty of churches where I could have remained Christian, worshipped, and become a pastor. But as I pursued a divinity degree, I focused on the role of women throughout history in connection with religion. My studies led me to Mary Paul, and she helped obtain funding for me to be a visiting professor here."

"Professor?" Sophia said.

"Yes." Mary Paul nodded. She'd taken off her blazer. Her long-sleeved white blouse looked crisp, as if she'd ironed it only moments before, and its brightness made the gray in her hair look sharper and more silvery. "We are not a religious cloister but an educational one. As close as it remains to my heart, I left the Church some time ago. The 'Sister' title is an honorary one here. I hesitate to say our cloister is academic, as my goal is to be more practical than most of academia. We train women to be future spiritual leaders and teachers. How they use the skills they learn is their choice. It could be within a spiritual or religious community or in the larger world."

Tara spread goat cheese over a chunk of warm bread and bit into it. Both tasted fresh and almost sweet. "Nearly everyone we spoke to referred to this as a chapel."

"It was once," Mary Paul said. "And we prefer the outside world to believe it still is. In many ways, our program is controversial, so we publicize it very little. Those who come here say they are coming for a spiritual retreat. The word 'cloister' implies hidden. And we are hidden in the midst of the religious practices in the area. We simply don't stand out."

"Do the people who live here have a spiritual or religious practice?" Sophia said.

"It varies." Zavia pushed away from the table and rested her hands on the mound of her belly. Tara remembered sitting that way often during her pregnancy, feeling Fmi kicking. She hoped Fimi was truly safe at home in Missouri. "Mine is to meditate," Zavia continued. "Many would say I don't believe in God."

"Do you?" Tara said.

"I'm with Frank Lloyd Wright," Zavia said. "I believe in God if you spell it N-A-T-U-R-E."

"A pantheist then?" Sophia asked.

"I'm not a fan of labels," Zavia said. "But the study of the natural and the possible supernatural intrigues me, as does living a life of contemplation. My husband prefers being out in the world a bit more, so I live here. He visits."

"And the others here?" Tara poured herself a second glass of Syrah. It had a slightly spicy scent and taste she liked. She probably ought to keep her wits sharp, but it felt good to take a break from vigilance. And Sophia had stopped at half a glass, so she decided to let her mentor stay alert for both of them.

"A variety of practices," Mary Paul said. The older nun stood for a moment, one hand on the small of her back, stretched, and sat again. "I study writings about Mary and about other female spiritual leaders or goddesses. We have original writings about what the Catholic Church called the heresies about Mary, including the two you mentioned. As a tribute to our spiritual ancestors, we sometimes leave bread on a chair for Mary. That was part of the Collyridians' practices. But it is more in memory of them than worship, though that depends which sister you ask."

"And do any live like nuns?" Tara said.

"Are they celibate you mean?" Zavia motioned toward her rounded midsection. "Obviously I'm not. Some choose to be so they can focus exclusively on spiritual pursuits. Many women find the greater caretaking responsibilities for them in most heterosexual relationships make it hard to find enough time for a contemplative or studious life. But other women are sexually active. Celibacy is a personal choice."

Sophia took a bunch of grapes from the platter. "And what about Pir Ferit?" she said. "How did you learn of him?"

"You brought him to our attention," Zavia said, nodding toward Tara. "Inadvertently. You mentioned the Brotherhood of Andrew to someone who knew someone who knew someone else who gave the information to us. Sister Mary Paul believed the Koca Mustafa Pasha Mosque might be related to it."

Sophia turned to Mary Paul, her eyes sharp. "What caused you to focus on the mosque?"

"Instinct more than anything," Mary Paul said. "I studied Andrew of Crete decades ago. I never came across any evidence that his work related in any way to Chapter 12 of Revelation, the passage I understand was quoted to Tara to justify the Brotherhood interfering in her life."

"But you went to Istanbul anyway," Sophia said to Zavia.

Tara wondered if Sophia felt as suspicious as she sounded. Tara felt comfortable with both women, but she'd had two glasses of wine already, which was one-and-a-half more than she normally drank.

"I did," Zavia said. "We both thought it would make an interesting article regardless of any connection to Chapter 12. When I went to visit the mosque, I met Pir Ferit. Neither of us had heard of him before. I also met a very intense man who worked with him, Ismail."

They talked about the test with the chain, which had, in Zavia's case, swung and hit Ismail. Both Mary Paul and Zavia answered more questions from Sophia about the cloister and their studies.

"So you believe none of what's happened to me is related to Chapter 12 in Revelation?" Tara said. "The woman with the crown with six stars?"

It was the part of Chapter 12 in the Book of Revelation that Cyril had first quoted to Tara to convince her that her pregnancy matched a prophecy about a messiah.

Sister Mary Paul shook her head. "We don't know of any connection between that passage and Andrew of Crete. Or between the passage and you, though we can't rule it out."

"And no one sent you to Pir Ferit?" Tara asked.

"Other than Mary Paul encouraging me to visit the mosque?" Zavia said. "No, no one."

The evening outside had grown completely dark, and the recessed lights above the wooden table glowed on, illuminating the varied shades in the wood grain. Mary Paul's face looked paler but less lined, and the fuschia in Zavia's blouse shone brightly, warming her dark skin. Sophia had settled back into her chair, her shoulders less rigid, her hands relaxed.

"Hm." Tara wondered if Holmes had heard about Pir Ferit somehow because of Zavia's visit or if he'd simply, as he'd claimed when she'd asked, made the same connections Zavia had. The one time they'd spoken about his upbringing, Holmes had told Tara he'd become fascinated by religion at a very young age, in part due to his father's deep religious beliefs, but had become increasingly disillusioned with it the more he learned. He'd hinted at the same types of conflicts she had with her dad, though Holmes' had been on a much grander scale, if he'd been telling the truth. His father had been obsesssed with the idea of the end times. Holmes had begun his studies as a way to prove his father wrong, but had become more and more immersed in the subject himself, something his brother Henrik disdained.

"Have you ever heard of Rick Gettleman?" Sophia asked.

Both Mary Paul and Zavia shook their heads.

"So," Mary Paul said. "Back to you. Is there a specific reason you've come here?"

Sophia gestured to Tara.

"We're trying to piece together a document," Tara said. "We believe you have part of it."

"We may," Mary Paul said.

# 27

Using one hand, as moving the fingers of his other sparked pain in his wounded shoulder, Pete sent a message to Tara just before take off. He told her he was all right, and that he and Cyril would meet where she'd requested. After Cyril had returned the document section to Pete, Pete had inspected it carefully. Encased in the plastic folder, it appeared the same as when Paulina had given it to him, the pages yellowed, the edges torn, the language and its characters incomprehensible to him.

"But why?" he asked Cyil after the plane had taken off. "If the Brotherhood suspected a document existed and that you'd retrieved it, and they saw the two of us together, why try to stop us from returning to the U.S. with it?"

Cyril adjusted his seat back and frowned. "If it was the Brotherhood, my superiors probably didn't feel sure I'd bring it to them. I already told you they don't trust me. Do they have any reason to trust you?"

"No," Pete answered, thinking again of his promise to Father Saur. He hadn't told Cyril about that and didn't intend to. Before, he'd held back because he didn't trust Cyril and had meant to deliver the document to the pastor. Now it was because he didn't want Cyril to doubt him and perhaps pass that doubt on to Tara, in case Tara was inclined to listen to Cyril. Pete planned to tell her about it all himself, and about why he'd changed his mind, but he wanted to do it his own way. "No reason at all."

The plane dipped about twenty minutes after take off. Pete's paper cup shook, sloshing lukewarm coffee onto his fingers. Using his left hand, Pete wiped the coffee and stared out the window. Dense clouds surrounded the plane.

"Looks like we're in for a rough ride," Cyril said.

~

THEY TALKED UNTIL LATE EVENING, and Tara let Mary Paul and Zavia make a copy of the document section from Florence. After putting on black-framed reading glasses and studying it, Mary Paul confirmed that the chapel had what was likely the final piece of the document. She gave a copy of that to Sophia and said she'd begin translating the Florence section the next day.

"I'm too old to pull an all-nighter," Mary Paul said. "And I was never much good at it even when I was young."

Tara had trouble getting her cell phone to work, but she signed onto email through one of the chapel's computers. She found a message from her dad that he and Cyril would be landing in Philadelphia in thirteen hours. She sent as best she could how to get to the cloister, tearing up at the thought of seeing her dad. Despite their differences, he'd decided to come here and try to help. She felt a small surge of anticipation at seeing Cyril again, though she didn't know if she'd ever trust him. Much the way Sophia must feel about Rick/Holmes. Tara logged out of email and pushed thoughts of Cyril aside. She couldn't afford to get distracted.

Zavia took her and Sophia to adjoining narrow guest rooms with hardwood floors and off-white walls.

"So my dad decided to help me," Tara said to Sophia. Tara sat on her room's twin bed. It had a plain wood frame and was set the long way against the wall. Opposite it, a matching unfinished wood bookcase overflowed with hardback and paperback books, treatises, and pamphlets. A desk in the corner, in contrast, was neat, with nothing on its top. A small, clean bathroom joined the room to the identical one where Sophia would sleep.

From under the corner desk, Sophia drew the wood chair and turned it so she could sit facing Tara. Because of the size of the room, only two feet separated them. "It sounds that way."

Tara swallowed hard. "Though I suppose Dad could tell me that and not come here."

"It seems unlikely. There'd be no reason to send you any message at all."

"True."

"And Cyril?" Sophia said. "He's coming as well?"

"He is." Tara played with a loose thread from the white bedspread. The wine had worn off, and she felt both restless and tired. She wished she could go outside for a walk to clear her mind, but it was both too dark and too cold.

"How do you feel about it? Cyril coming here?"

Tara looked up. "Is it crazy if I say I hope it means he's really on my side?"

Sophia smiled. "Of course not. You've been through so much with him, I'm sure your hope is tempered with caution. But it's good to hope. Very few people are irredeemable."

"And you? I noticed you didn't tell Mary Paul and Zavia about Holmes' Rick Gettleman alias."

"I may yet tell them in case they need to be on guard, but I haven't decided."

Tara slept better that night than she'd expected. In the morning, there were fresh-baked orange cinnamon scones and blueberry muffins on the round wood table in the main room, along with orange juice, tea and coffee. Mary Paul, dressed in a dark skirt and blazer similar to what she'd worn the day before, but a pale blue blouse this time, said she'd already eaten. But she sat with them and drank weak black coffee, her reading glasses in her hand. She'd made some progress translating the document Tara and Sophia had brought but was having trouble understanding how it fit with the chapel's section.

"Part of it's missing," Tara said. "That's what we were told by Mareisa de la Vega, the woman we met at the synagogue near Florence."

"I unearthed Placida's story more than a decade ago and traveled to that synagogue," Mary Paul said. "Don't ask how – it's far too long a tale of combing through dusty manuscripts. But when I spoke with the caretaker there, I got nowhere. It was an older man then, and he claimed to know nothing about Placida."

"Maybe he didn't," Tara said. "Or maybe it's because you didn't have Pir Ferit's key."

Just as Mary Paul stood to leave for the chapel's library, Alma and Kelly arrived. They didn't look nearly as exhausted as Tara had felt on reaching the cloister, despite Alma's pregnancy. But they said they were tired. Their flight had gotten in late the night before, and they'd started the drive before dawn.

Alma sank into a chair next to Zavia. "I'm Alma," she said. "And this is Tara Spencer." She gestured to Kelly.

Mary Paul leaned forward on her cane, peered at Tara, then Alma, then back at Kelly. "Is it indeed?"

STRANYERO DROVE the winding mountain road, his mind flashing back to the other mountain he'd driven so many years ago in California to intercept Maya Kerkorian. Death was an inevitable part of life. But it had been such a miscalculation on his part. An overly simplistic solution that had solved nothing and led to the rise of Nanor Kerkorian and her community of women at Willow Springs. He wouldn't make that error again.

All the same, that didn't mean he shrank from killing in the proper circumstances. Which might be in place now. It would be a relief, after over a year of careful line walking between creating enough peril so that others hesitated to aid Tara and causing outright destruction. There were reasons a form of that word was last of the three Ds – *discredit, deny, destroy.* The Brotherhood, though not a corporation by any means, loved its corporate-style lingo. Stranyero had coined that phrase himself after the Kerkorian fiasco. The order of the words had been intentional. Destruction brought the most peril to both sides of the equation.

He glanced at the device on the passenger seat, a prototype more powerful than the most advanced computer available on the open market. The information from a bug Father Saur had planted on Pete's New Testament fed directly into it. Because Pete didn't always carry the book with him, and the listening device didn't function everywere, it had provided spotty information. Stranyero had no idea how Cyril and Pete had obtained the document section they carried with them. But combined with his other sources, Stranyero had heard enough to locate the Appalachian cloister. And he'd heard it soon enough to make his plans. He'd had to move heaven and earth, in the latter case, literally, but he felt confident. Cyril and Pete would bring the Armenian part of the document to the cloister. Stranyero himself possessed the Italian portion of the document stolen from Sophia and Tara. He didn't intend to share "his" document section with anyone if it wasn't necessary. Better only the Brotherhood learned the truth. But he suspected the copy from the synagogue would be enough for the former nun, despite the falsified version of the small missing section he'd planted with Alma. She'd been easy to manipulate. He'd used the Raphael moniker to further confuse the issue. If anyone else in the Brotherhood learned about the interaction with the girl, they'd assume it was the usual suspect, not Stranyero, who'd acted without authorization.

What a debacle the real Raphael had almost caused. Thank God Stranyero had sent Mullin to stop him from chopping off the infant's hand. Stranyero uttered a short blessing for Mullin's soul. The man had been the perfect cog in the Brotherhood's wheel – smart enough to get the job done, not smart enough to ask many questions or become troubled by morality's gray areas.

Stranyero eased off the accelerator on a curve. He didn't feel rushed. He'd ensured that, in the worst case scenario, Tara Spencer wouldn't be where she was expected to be, and the reading of the document, if it were reunited before he arrived, would be delayed. At best, Tara would no longer be an issue at all. Stranyero wondered if his chosen actor recognized the flaw in his logic, or the beauty of it, depending upon how one looked at it. It was like the test he'd read about in a ficitonalized account of the Salem witch trials. Tie their hands and feet and throw them in the river. If they floated, they were witches doomed to be burned at the stake. If they drowned, at least everyone knew no witches had been among them. And, true to Fenton MacNeil's credo, there would be no martyrs.

*No martyrs*, he thought. *Only young women so deluded they couldn't tell fantasy from reality.*

Tara winced. "I can explain." In the haze of exhaustion and relief the night before, she hadn't thought to mention Alma's belief regarding Kelly's identity. She turned to Alma. "We've misled you a little. I'm Tara. Kelly is my sister. She took Fimi home while I stayed overseas. We thought Fimi would be safer in the United States, and we wanted to create some confusion about where I was."

Neither Zavia nor Sister Mary Paul registered any expression, they merely watched the conversation. Tara tried to figure out if they seemed surprised or now harbored doubts about her, but both their faces stayed blank.

*Bet they could beat Nate in poker.*

Alma sat straighter and placed her hands flat on the round table. "So you're Tara?"

"Yes. Kelly let you think she was me because we wanted to hear what you had to say before telling you too much."

"And you wanted to get my document."

"I'm sorry," Tara said. "But we didn't know anything about you, and when you thought Kelly was me, it seemed safer at first to let you think so. And you still have your document. We'd just like you to share it so we can see if it fits with other pieces we're gathering and learn more about it. That's why you came, right? To learn more?"

Alma frowned. "That's awful. And I don't believe you anyway. You're just trying to get rid of me now that we're here and you think you can get my piece of the puzzle."

"Get rid of you how? You're here. No one's asked you to leave," Kelly said.

Alma pointed at Tara. "Show me some ID."

"I could," Tara said, "but it doesn't have my real name. I don't travel under my real name."

"I'll show you mine." Kelly took out her license and held it in a shaft of sunlight from the skylight above the table. "You'll see I'm Kelly Spencer."

"Well, if she can get fake IDs, so can you. I don't see any way to know who's telling the truth."

Tara's mind raced. She didn't need to prove anything to Alma, but she felt she ought to after having deceived her. And she wanted Mary Paul and Zavia to feel sure she was telling the truth.

"What difference does it make?" Sophia said to Alma. "You don't doubt that Kelly and Tara are sisters, do you, whichever you believe is which? You've only to look at them. And you don't doubt that they are both Spencers. You're the one who sought Tara/Kelly out. So why hesitate now about working together?"

Alma crossed her arms over her chest and sat back in her chair. "I just want to know who is who. And since there are no photos on line of Tara, how do I know?"

"Well, I'm older," Tara said. "You must know from the news stories that I was a junior in college when I got pregnant. Kelly's only just turned eighteen. Can't you tell?"

Alma eyed both of them. "I guess. But you two don't look that different."

"I don't know what else to say." Tara could feel herself clenching her teeth, and she stood and paced between the table and the closest bookcases, trying to relax her jaw and her neck muscles. Alma's section of the document was so small, it probably wouldn't matter that much if she didn't hand it over. But it was frustrating to come so close and face another roadblock.

Mary Paul motioned with her reading glasses toward Sophia. "I agree with Professor Gaddini. It hardly matters for your purposes which sister is which. And, regardless, I know from following the news that Dr. Gaddini is writing a book with Tara, so I'll take her word as to who is who."

Tara turned toward Mary Paul, struck by what the older nun had said. It was something that hadn't occurred to Tara the night before between the wine and all the questions she and Sophia had about the cloister itself. "If you knew about me, why didn't you seek me out?"

"My dear, we had no way to know if you truly experienced a supernatural phenomenon."

"Or if or how it related to our research," Zavia said.

"Also," Mary Paul said, "practically speaking, we believed if you truly had a virgin pregnancy and it did relate to us, you'd find us. That's the legend around the cloister coming into possession of the document. That the one for whom the message is meant will bring the pieces of the document together from the ends of the earth, and her role in the world will be revealed."

Alma tapped her foot on the floor. "I still don't know who is Tara, and I don't know anything about Dr. Gaddini, so that doesn't help."

"You're familiar with the Brotherhood, right?" Tara had finally thought of something that might persuade Alma.

"Yes," Alma said. "I told Tara – or Kelly or whoever she is – that I stayed with them for a while. At that facility with the archives."

"Did they mention a mark?"

Zavia set down her orange juice. "What kind of mark?"

"When the Brotherhood of Andrew sent people after me, one of them insisted I must have the mark of the Beast."

"The Beast?" Mary Paul said. "From the Book of Revelation?"

Alma jumped in. "Yes. I heard about that, but no one there really believes that there's a mark or that you're the Beast. Just that one guy."

"But you heard about my scar?" Tara asked. Alma nodded, and Tara unzipped her jeans. Despite everything, and how much she thought she'd discounted what anyone in the Brotherhood believed, she felt relieved learning that the religious order didn't actually think she was carrying the mark of the Beast. "Sorry, not trying to put on a show here, but I can't think of another way."

Tara revealed the side of her knee, and the S-shaped scar along it, to Alma. "This is the supposed mark of the Beast. Maya Kerkorian also had a scar in the same shape. Her grandmother, Nanor, told me a mark of a serpent isn't evil, and she doubts that it means anything at all. But there it is."

Mary Paul settled her glasses on her nose and held out her hand toward Alma. "Now," she said, "let us see your section of the document."

# 28

The whole group toured the three-story library. The rows of books in polished wood bookcases and original documents within glass display boxes made Sophia's eyes glow. She and Mary Paul settled at a long table lined with amber-shaded antique banker's lamps.

Kelly's eyes drooped, and Alma had one hand pressed against her low back, the other on the side of her stomach, as if supporting the baby inside her. They'd been awake since three that morning.

Zavia motioned to them. "Let's get you into dorm rooms so you can shower and rest. Fortunately, we have few students in the winter. If you'd come in the summertime, you'd all be relegated to sleeping bags in the main room."

Tara cleared the breakfast table. The chapel's communal kitchen was warmer than the main room. It had no windows, a white tiled floor, industrial-sized stainless steel appliances, a large double-basined sink, and a dishwasher that had broken the week before. Tara scraped plates and soaped a sponge, sending a eucalyptus and spearmint scent throughout the kitchen. She'd volunteered to do the washing, remembering how food scraps had nauseated her in the middle term of her pregnancy and thinking Zavia, who looked to be about five months along, might have the same issue.

After showing Alma and Kelly to their rooms, Zavia joined Tara at the sink. "Feel free to take a walk when we're done," she said. Today, Zavia wore jeans, turquoise tennis shoes, and a turquoise maternity blouse that stood out against the kitchen's black and white decor. Her long, thin braids were pulled back in a jeweled cloisonne clip. "It's not that cold today, and the garden and courtyard out back are beautiful. You may want to enjoy them in peace before more visitors arrive."

"More visitors?" Tara said. "You mean my dad and Cyril?"

Zavia took a washed plate from Tara and rinsed it in the second basin. "Them too. But I meant men from the Brotherhood. No matter how careful you were, they'll have followed you here. In fact, it wouldn't at all surprise me to find your friend texting them right now with directions. If she can get a signal."

"My friend?" Tara's pulse elevated and her muscles tensed, all the calm from the night before gone in an instant. "You mean Alma?"

"Yes, Alma. You disagree?"

"Not necessarily." A glass slipped through Tara's fingers, but she cushioned its fall with the sponge in her other hand so it didn't break when it hit the counter. "And I'm sorry. We didn't know any other way to get Alma's part of the document here."

"It's all right. With the way the document was split, I think it was inevitable that many people would be present when it was made whole."

"What if those people include the man who attacked Kelly and me in Istanbul? Or someone else like him."

"We'll know if anyone tries to enter with a weapon. Just like we knew about your knife." Zavia dried her hands, reached into her pocket, and set Tara's switchblade on the edge of the sink. "Which reminds me. In case you want it back."

"You're okay with me having it?"

"I talked to Sister Mary Paul. We're not concerned about you being a danger, and you've traveled with it this long, we figured you might feel uneasy without it."

"It wouldn't be much help against a sword."

"No," Zavia said. "But I think you'll find we have good security here. And not just for a cloister."

Tara scrubbed the pan that had been used for scrambled eggs. "Do you think Alma's document section matches what we found in the synagogue? We've only her word that it came from the Brotherhood. And, if it did, no way to know if it relates to our document sections."

"Mary Paul tells me it's ancient Armenian. Beyond that, only she'll be able to say for sure."

"Any idea what the cloister's part of the document says?" Tara asked.

"As I understand it, it's difficult to determine that without the entire writing, and it hasn't been in one piece for hundreds of years. You saw how interior sections are missing, so Mary Paul couldn't figure out much beyond what you already know. That it's part of a letter that the aunt of a pregnant woman in Armenia wrote after a spiritual journey. The pieces you brought, the piece we have, the piece that you expect your father to bring, all combined, hopefully will reveal everything."

Tara's stomach flipped from a mix of excitement and anxiety. Finally, she would get some answers. "And how did your section come to be here?"

The drying rack was filled. Zavia took another one from a cabinet, then pulled a stainless steel counter stool to the sink and perched on it before she took the next plate.

"During the early centuries after Christ died, the people who believed in

Collyridianism and Antidicomarianitism joined together to study and worship in secret. Few written records were kept. Few men and almost no women could read, and secrecy was paramount, so much of what we know about the spiritual order they founded was passed down orally. It's believed the author of the Armenian letter met members of the order during her travels, and she entrusted a handwritten copy of the letter to them. It's said that scribes created two or three other copies from that one. It became the order's mission to deliver a copy of the letter to each spiritual successor of the Armenian pregnant woman. But eventually the copies fragmented, and pieces became lost. Only one section, the one preserved here, survived within the order. If Placida, the woman who tried to emigrate to Florence, truly received an intact document, she was an exception. But as you learned, she wasn't able to survive or keep the letter whole."

Tara paused in her washing, letting the water run. "If there were handwritten copies, how do we know my dad and Cyril aren't bringing a version of what we already have?"

"We don't." One of Zavia's braids had come loose, and she refastened it into the jeweled clip. "We'll need to see when it arrives. However, it was always said the original pieces were in Armenia, here, and with the family of one of the other virgins."

"How long has the cloister been here?"

Zavia shook her head. "The 'cloister' refers to the hidden nature of the order, not a place. But the document has been in this building over a hundred years. It was brought here from Turkey, another reason that when I heard about the possible connection to the Koca Mustafa Pasha Mosque, I rushed there. That I was pregnant at the time was a happy accident, though it turns out it didn't help me learn more."

"And Pir Ferit?" Tara asked as she returned to the dishes. "If he was a messenger or guardian, does that mean he was part of the Collyridian/Antidicomarianite tradition?"

"I don't know. There's no reference to a 'messenger' or 'guardian' in the stories passed down to us, but certainly we don't know everything. His insistence on meeting only with a woman traveling with women suggests whatever tradition he comes from at least expected to complement those beliefs. There were men who shared them, but, as you can imagine, more women were drawn to it. And the more time passed, the more the tradition appealed only to women."

Tara thought of asking about the "one who will live forever" designation. But Mary Paul and Zavia hadn't mentioned that, nor had Alma, and she decided she'd keep it to herself. As much as she'd instantly liked and felt comfortable at the cloister despite the shrieking alarm at its entrance, it could be dangerous to share everything.

She finished the last pot and handed it to Zavia, then wiped her forehad. The steam from the dishwasher had made her sweat. "Do you feel sure I'm the one who should receive this message?"

"I do. As does Mary Paul. You're the one who put yourself at risk and pursued every lead. You're the one who found us. Alma merely latched onto you. But does it bother you? That it could be Alma? Or someone else?"

Tara turned to face Zavia, one hand resting on the sink's edge. "Not in the way you mean. It's not a competition. But I came here for answers and to not get them after all we've been though, I don't know if I could handle that."

"I hope you get your answers. Though I can't promise you'll like them."

Tara felt a jolt. It reminded her of Pir Ferit's comment about the story of Adam and Eve being cast out of the Garden of Eden for seeking knowledge. "Why do you say that?"

"That's the way answers are." Zavia hopped off the counter stool, moving with more grace than Tara had ever felt while pregnant. "But we try to find the truth here, no matter what. And make it available to all, not just a select few."

"That doesn't seem to fit with thousands of years of secrecy," Tara said.

"Secrecy was necessary along the way so the truth could ultimately be told. If we hadn't stayed hidden, our portion of the document would have been stolen, and the others hunted down and destroyed. That may happen yet. But I hope not."

When she heard a knock, Tara immediately set down her journal. She'd kept one on and off from when she was ten years old, and she'd tried to be diligent about it since Fimi's birth so her daughter would have a record of everything. But this morning she couldn't focus. She felt restless, and her thoughts raced.

She hurried to the door, hoping her dad and Cyril had arrived. But it was Alma. She wore her parka, hood down, lower portion tight over her swelling abdomen. She looked pale. "Tara, I screwed up. I think I really screwed up."

"What do you mean?" Tara gestured for her to come in.

"Can we walk outside? I could use some air."

"Yeah, that sounds great." Tara grabbed her coat, gloves, and phone, though she wasn't sure if the reception would be better outside or not. She got no signal inside. "Let me see if Kelly wants to come."

"She's sleeping," Alma said. "She might be mad if you wake her."

"Are you kidding?" They walked to Kelly's room. "She's my little sister, of course she'll be mad, but that's never stopped me. But seriously, I at least need to tell her where I'll be."

Alma nodded, looking a little shaky. Tara put her hand on Alma's arm. "Whatever it is, it'll be fine. We'll figure it out." Tara didn't have a good sense of who Alma was as a person yet or what the young woman's motives were, but she knew exactly how it felt to be pregnant, alone, and scared and couldn't help but have some sympathy for the young woman.

Kelly's eyes were half-closed when she answered the door, and she leaned against the door jamb. Tara told her what they were doing.

"I'll stay here," Kelly said. "I was napping, I'm kind of groggy."

"Sure, go back to sleep – sorry I woke you," Tara said.

Kelly blinked and straightened. "Nah, now that I'm up, I might find something to eat. I didn't have much breakfast."

"Would you tell Sophia we're taking a walk, then? We'll be back in twenty minutes or so." Tara turned to Alma. "I don't want to be gone any longer than that in case my dad gets here."

Stone paths wound through the garden behind the chapel. Bare low-hanging branches of Hawthorn trees formed a loose canopy overhead that filtered the faint winter sunlight. As Tara and Alma walked through and beyond the courtyard area, the trees became denser and blocked the wind that swept down the mountain. Though Tara hadn't worn a hat, she didn't feel cold. The brisk air felt good on her face.

"So what is it you're so upset about?" she asked Alma.

Alma rubbed her mittened hands together. "I told you a man from the Brotherhood contacted me and gave me the missing strip of the document."

"Yes."

"He's convinced that I, not you, am the real mother of the next messiah."

"Because?" Tara wasn't too surprised. There had to be some reason the man had contacted Alma.

"One thing is my child will be a boy," Alma said, "but that's not the main reason. He says you're a non-believer. I don't know if that's true, but if it is, I can see why he thinks I'm the One. I've been Christian all my life. Lutheran. I followed my church's teachings. We're a liberal church, we have women pastors, so I don't really believe it matters if the next messiah is a male or female. But I know I'm a virgin. I didn't have a boyfriend. And I know I'm religious, so what he said made sense."

Twigs crunched under their feet as they reached the edge of the courtyard. Tara motioned toward a trampled path through the woods that looked fairly easy to navigate.

"Okay." Tara wasn't sure why Alma was so disturbed. She didn't know what to think of how Alma had gotten pregnant, but she figured it wasn't up to her to decide that. They'd have some answers soon enough, at least Tara hoped so.

"Are you a non-believer?" Alma said.

"If you're asking if I believe everything in the Bible, or even everything in the New Testament, really happened, I don't."

"But in God. Do you not believe in God?"

"The Christian God?" Tara said. "Any god? I don't know. I mean, there's some reason this happened to me, some reason my baby was born and something special she means. So I guess I'm thinking there is some kind of divine being or at least power after all. But I don't know if it means there's a god like the God I was raised to believe in. I don't know if it really is divine. Maybe there's still some scientific reason."

Tara thought about the idea of Fimi being a clone. She didn't want to believe her daughter was the result of some science experiment, but that was no more far fetched than seeking answers from a cloister filled with non-nuns piecing together a document Tara had never heard of a month ago.

"I don't understand how you can still have questions given what's happened to you," Alma said.

"I don't understand how anyone who thinks could not have questions," Tara said.

The trees thinned, and the grade became steeper. Using extra calf muscles felt good to Tara after all the time in the car the last couple days. She glanced around, noting particular plants and the direction of the sun, so they'd be sure to find their way back.

"So you don't believe," Alma said.

"I don't know yet. Maybe I'm an unbeliever – I'm still trying to figure things out. That's why I'm going through all this."

Alma shook her head. "So the man's right about you."

"If he says I don't know what I believe, he's right. But I don't get what this is about. You said you screwed up. How?"

"I've communicated with this man," Alma said. "Raphael. He told me he was coming here, that he knew how to find the cloister. So not to worry when cell phone reception disappeared, that he'd be on his way."

"Zavia expected that the Brotherhood might send people here, if that's what you're worried about," Tara said. "I can't say I'm not nervous about that, given the things they've done, but Zavia also told me the cloister is ready. At least one of the residents came from law enforcement, if you can believe it."

Tara glanced at the time on her phone. They'd been gone about ten minutes, so they ought to turn back. She wanted to be at the chapel when her dad arrived.

"It's not him being here that worries me, though I'm sorry I didn't tell you sooner." Alma winced, and her face turned a shade whiter. She pressed one hand to the small of her back and pointed to a large boulder. "Can we rest a few minutes?"

"Are you okay?" Tara said.

"Yeah, my low back's been bothering me. I just need to get off my feet."

"Of course." The longer Alma took to get to the point, the more uneasy Tara felt being away from the cloister, but she didn't want to exhaust Alma or make her feel worse physically. "But then we should go back."

"Definitely."

The boulder was wide and flat enough for them both to sit on. The rock felt cold through Tara's jeans, but the sun shone straight down on her, warming her face and hair.

"So what's worrying you?" Tara said.

"It's a message I got from this other man."

"What other man?"

"I don't know his name. He was copied on some messages from Raphael. It seems like he was some type of mentor to you. He wrote back, probably not realizing it was coming to me, too. He said he's on his way, and he'll make sure you're eliminated."

Tara's heart dropped. *Cyril?* Had he betrayed her once more? She felt shocked, both that he might have and that it surprised her. She'd actually started to think he'd finally figured out what he believed, and that he supported her.

*Well, it's half of what I wanted*, she thought. *He finally figured something out.*

Then it occurred to Tara it could be Holmes. The word "mentor" seemed to apply more to someone much older than she was, and though the age difference between her and Holmes was about a dozen years, it seemed larger. Especially given that he'd dated Sophia, who she thought of as much wiser and who actually was Tara's mentor. But it couldn't be Sophia.

"What exactly did the messages say?" Tara asked.

"I'll show you." Alma turned on her phone and unlocked it. "It sounded almost like, I hate to say it, almost like he might have somehow kidnapped your baby."

Tara jumped to her feet. "What? What are you talking about?"

"Shit – no signal." Alma's fingers flew over her screen. "I'm probably wrong, I'm really probably wrong, it's just the way it sounded."

"You should've said that right away." Tara said. "We've got to get in touch with my mom, and the police."

Alma eased herself part-way off the rock until she was half-sitting, half-standing, her face still pale. "Your mom would have let you know if the baby were gone, wouldn't she?"

"There's bad reception here. She might have tried and not gotten through or not been able to leave a message." Tara took out her phone. Her call home initially connected, but cut off before the first ring.

"Don't panic," Alma said. "I'm not sure I'm reading these messages right. Here." She held out her phone, but the sun's glare made it impossible to read the screen. She waved toward a copse of trees in the direction of the chapel. "Let's try under there, then we can head back."

Tara nodded. Snow showered off the branches as they reached the trees. Whatever the messages said, Tara was heading back if she had to carry Alma.

"Look." Alma grabbed Tara's hand as if to pull her close to show her the phone. Instead, she yanked and pivoted, sending Tara off-balance and stumbling. Before Tara could right herself, Alma shoved her toward a mound of snow-covered branches on the ground.

Tara put her foot down, aiming for one of the heavier branches to steady herself, and extended her arms for balance. The branches snapped, and her ankle twisted. Pain seared through her foot and leg as she plummeted down through pine needles, sticks, and snow.

# 29

Raphael took a different route from Stranyero's, a slightly longer one that had fewer inclines and curves, allowing him to drive faster. He counted on his sense of urgency to get him there before Stranyero, but if he arrived after, it wouldn't matter. He and Stranyero had different objectives and different methods. He patted the shotgun next to him, feeling a sense of pride. Some in the Brotherhood, like Special Investigators Woods and Mullin, excelled in field operations. Others, like Stranyero, excelled in scholarship. Raphael, despite his single failure in Istanbul, excelled in both. Which ought to have made him the leader, especially given his pedigree. But, were that the case, he'd be preoccupied with leading the organization, not carrying out this mission. His mission. He no longer thought of it as the Brotherhood's mission. The Brotherhood might once have had resolve, but under its current hierarchy, it acted too seldom and hesitated too often. Each human life deserved reverence, yes, but not at the expense of divine purpose.

The signs were all there, regardless whether the Brotherhood officially recognized them. The sudden death of the last pope, the increasing number of disasters that once would have been recognized as acts of God but now were termed climate change by those without faith, the performing of what appeared to be miracles. Raphael didn't believe in coincidence.

Or, rather, he did, but he saw it as the hand of God.

The same hand that had guided him from the moment he'd learned from his father about the Brotherhood of Andrew's mission, and his place in the organization.

~

Ice and snow spattered over Tara as she fell. She landed on her right hip on the frozen slope beneath her, and the pain it caused blotted her ankle's throbbing for an instant. She slid half a dozen yards, then slammed into a shallow embankment, smacking her ankle again. The pain jolted to her head and she vomited. Something hurtled after her, but she couldn't process quickly enough to move out of the way. It hit her shoulder and rolled a few feet. In the faint light from the hole above her, Tara saw the item was cylindrical.

"It's a flashlight," Alma said.

Her voice sounded far away, as if she were at the other end of a long tunnel. Tara rested her head against the cold ground, no room in her mind for any thought or feeling beyond pain. When it retreated from ice picks to hammers, she registered scraping sounds above her and the fact that the cave was becoming darker. Alma was sliding a large rock over much of the opening through which Tara had fallen. Tara's lungs felt like they were closing along with the light.

"Alma?" Tara pushed herself to yell, but her voice barely came out at a normal level. "Alma?" Since Alma had pushed her, an answer didn't seem likely, but she needed to try.

Alma answered. "You'll be fine. If you're the One, you'll be fine."

"I'm pretty sure I broke my ankle."

"You'll be fine," Alma said again.

Tara twisted her torso so she could inspect the incline she'd slid down. It was less steep than she'd thought, and the ice shone in patches, with hard-packed dirt and some rocks and brush in between. If she weren't injured, she might have been able to climb back to Alma. Another rock covered more of the opening. The acidic smell of her own vomit assailed Tara's nostrils, and she switched to breathing through her mouth. She'd lost her cell phone during the fall. She felt around her, but couldn't find it.

"Alma, wait."

"'And these signs shall attend those who believe: in my name they shall cast out devils; they shall speak in new tongues; they shall take up serpents; and if they drink any deadly thing, it shall not hurt them; they shall lay hands upon the sick and they shall get well.' Mark 3:17-18."

Tara forced herself to breathe deeply rather than pant in panic. She dug her fingers into the frozen earth, breaking through a thin ice layer in the hope of hauling herself upward, but got only handfuls of dirt. Branches were being piled next to and around the rocks above her until only a sliver of light remained.

"There's another way out. Use the flashlight and you'll see it." Alma's voice sounded muted. "Past the snakes."

"What?" Tara fumbled for the flashlight, squeezing her eyes shut as she inched toward it, sending flares of pain radiating throughout her leg and foot.

"He said if you're the One, you can handle the snakes without getting hurt. So you'll be fine."

"You can't be serious. Alma, please."

Scraping and shuffling sounds, as if Alma were piling more rocks and sticks over the ones she'd already placed. Tara took another deep breath, her mind whirling, and fought back nausea.

"Alma, you think you're the One. So why do you think I can get out?"

"I know I'm not." Alma's voice sounded more muffled now, and it trailed off at the end of the sentence. "But I can pretend a little longer. He said there'll be cameras, you know? Broadcasting to the TARA2 game if not a news feed somewhere. I'll be on all over the world."

Tara bit her lip, focusing through sheer will power on the conversation rather than the jackhammer jolts of pain in her ankle and the throbbing of her hip. "Who said? Who convinced you to do this, and why do you believe him?"

"They'll be here soon – you'll be fine." The last hint of light disappeared.

*At least Fimi's probably safe,* Tara thought, *not kidnapped. That was a ruse to distract me. Stupid, stupid.*

In a sitting position, Tara inched herself back and sideways, attempting to slide toward where she thought the flashlight had landed. She should have grabbed it when there was still some light in this part of the cavern. She froze at what sounded like hissing, not sure if snakes really slithered below, or if she had imagined the hiss because Alma had said there were snakes. Or both.

6:17 HOLMES couldn't believe he'd lost them. The last location of the phone Tara had used in Istanbul was Sophia's home in Chicago, though Holmes felt certain she wouldn't have gone there. The last location for Sophia's phone was Nashville, making him suspect she'd put it on a UPS or Fed Ex truck, as he doubted she'd abandon Tara. Though they could both be in Tennessee. Still, more likely they'd diverted their phones and had separate, disposable ones available that he wasn't aware of. Their airline tickets provided no help, as the routes criss-crossed the country.

He could bring more of Holmes LLC's resources to bear, but then he'd need to justify it to Henrik. That was one of the many difficult parts of a closely held corporation – he and his brother knew one another's every move. Henrik indulged what he viewed as Holmes' hobby to an extent, but, surprisingly for someone otherwise so irresponsible, called a halt if Holmes engaged too many employees. Holmes couldn't understand how his brother failed to grasp the vital nature of Holmes' work. Along with working day and night to ensure Henrik's children's, grandchildren's, and great-grandchildren's futures as far as finances went, Holmes was caring for their souls.

THE HOUSE HAD FALLEN SO quiet, Lynette heard the ticking of the miniature grandfather clock from Pete's study on the other side of the first floor. Pete had called to say he'd landed and was on his way to Tara, but that had been hours ago. Lynette had tried his cell phone and gotten an out-of-service area warning.

She'd gotten the same for Tara's, Kelly's, and Sophia's phones. Nate was playing chess with Bailey in the basement family room, accompanied by Diedre from Willow Springs Security. Tara's best friend Kali had sent an email volunteering Diedre's services if needed, and Lynette felt better having the tough-looking woman there along with the rented security guard. But it didn't ease her mind as much as she'd imagined it would. Perhaps nothing could. The rented security guard sat in the recliner in the corner, reading. Lynette perched in the living room rocking Fimi, remembering how she'd held Tara so many years ago, and how anxious and determined she'd felt about finding a way to support herself and create a good home for her child despite the obstacles.

Now she felt anxious for other reasons.

The doorbell rang.

THE CAVERN SMELLED OF MUD, snow, and earth. Legs stretched in front of her, Tara shone the flashlight beam around. The incline bottomed out about twenty feet below her. She probably could slide down on her seat. But dozens, perhaps a hundred, snakes waited below, most coiled in place, their triangular heads lowered, eyes unblinking. The closest swayed across the ground a few feet from the end of the incline, tongue flicking. Harmless snakes didn't frighten Tara, she didn't have an aversion to them the way many people did. But these had diamond-backs and rattles at the end. They covered the floor of the cavern. It'd be almost impossible to cross it without stepping on one even if she could walk on her injured ankle. If she had to crawl on her hands and knees or her belly, she didn't see any way to avoid them, and her face would be in striking distance.

She felt around for her phone without success, moving at a glacial pace so as not to alarm the snakes, who so far were ignoring her.

Past the snakes, at the far end of the cavern, Tara saw an opening that might be large enough to squeeze through.

Past the snakes.

WEARING LATEX GLOVES, Sophia turned the page of a manuscript, a handwritten copy of a Collyridian document long thought lost. She started to ask Sister Mary Paul how the cloister had come to possess it, then wrote a note on the legal pad she'd found in the library table drawer instead. She saw no reason to disturb Mary Paul, who was laboring over the pieces of the letter collected so far, noise cancelling headphones over her ears. She'd been polite about Sophia's initial offer to aid in translation, but made it clear that Sophia likely would hinder more than help given her lack of fluency with ancient Armenian, Mary Paul's greater familiarity with her part of the document, and the still-missing section they all hoped Pete and Cyril possessed.

Accepting that her assistance wasn't needed, Sophia turned to the chapel's small but broad collection of writings on Mary, goddesses, and heresies. It included original works she'd never heard of. Ordinarily, she would have been fascinated and lost herself in them for days. But she found it hard to suppress her excitement at, and curiosity about, what the reunited document might mean for Tara or for Sophia's own view of the world. She didn't believe Tara's baby proved the existence of any god one way or another, but it certainly suggested a supernatural force. And suggested that Mary, too, really had been a virgin mother. Sophia had such mixed feelings about the Church's doctrine on that account that she didn't know what to hope for. She'd just need to see. Mixed with all her musings was a sense of guilt over her intellectual excitement given the terrible things that had happened the year before as a result of Tara's pregnancy.

So when someone pushed open the library's heavy oak door, Sophia felt relieved at the distraction. Light from the windows beyond the library flooded the room, silhouetting the slim figure in the doorway.

Sophia blinked and squinted. "Tara?"

The young woman stepped away from the light, and Sophia saw it was Kelly, hair a little tousled, her jeans and turtleneck wrinkled.

"Sorry," Sophia said. "Kelly. Everything all right?"

"I got a text from my dad – looks like he sent it hours ago. He and Cyril were on the way, so they should be here soon. Tara and Alma went out for a walk. I'm going to see if I can find them."

"I'll get my coat and join you. I hope they didn't go far."

Absorbed in her work, Sister Mary Paul never glanced up.

Sophia and Kelly exited the building. Wrought iron benches sat beneath heat lamps on a brick patio area just outside the doors, but the benches were empty. Sophia scanned the Hawthorn grove and the more densely wooded area beyond it.

No sign of the young women.

TARA STARED AT THE SNAKES. If she stayed where she was and didn't move, there was a good chance they wouldn't bother her. While she hadn't taken any animal behavior classes, most of her family's vacations had involved camping outdoors, and she knew rattlesnakes typically weren't aggressive.

If her dad and Cyril had arrived, one of them would surely come looking for her. She yelled, though it seemed like a long shot that anyone would hear her. All she succeeded in doing was setting a few more snakes slithering.

*But I can't wait here. What if someone did kidnap Fimi? And who knows what Alma's planning to do, and Kelly and Sophia have no idea.*

If Fimi were here, perhaps the baby could heal Tara the way she, or the two of them together, had healed Hamed. But Fimi wasn't. Tara rolled up the leg of her jeans, shaking as the damp, icy air sank into her exposed skin. The swelling around her ankle showed in the tightness of the sides of her boot. She thought back to the moments after Fimi's birth, to what had happened under the Arch, or might have happened. Could she heal herself? It was possible she didn't need Fimi.

*Time to find out.*

Tara shut her eyes, focused on the earthy smell of the air, the biting cold, the feel of the ground beneath her, the pain radiating from ankle to hip and back. She let herself be in the pain, become part of it. She breathed into it. Her heart rate slowed. She heard the snakes' whispering movements and flicking tongues and, eventually, sounds from beyond the cave's opening. Water streaming below a thin layer of ice, a flock of Dark-eyed Juncos trilling as they foraged for food in the nearby fir trees.

Uncertain how much time had passed, Tara opened her eyes. The pain had dissipated. She rotated her ankle. Not even tight. She slid off her boot and couldn't see any swelling. Shivering, she yanked her wool sock up, put her boot back on, and rolled down her jeans leg over it. The cold had sunk into her bones while she'd sat.

Breathing slowly to try to stay calm, Tara eased into a crouch, then stood. Her legs shook as if she'd just run a long distance, and her pulse fluttered in her throat, but the pain had disappeared, and her ankle felt stable.

If she didn't alarm the snakes, they might let her pass. It was just that there were so many, it would be hard to avoid stepping on them. And she felt so tired. At least she wore jeans and boots, so if one struck low it might not go through. Higher, though, and she'd be out of luck. She didn't know if she could heal herself again.

Tara inched forward.

# 30

Stranyero arrived in the clearing nearest to the cloister and parked next to a Jeep with rental plates. Twenty minutes later, the reporter from the *Pittsburgh Chronicle* pulled her own Jeep in. A videographer rode with her, though that mattered little to Stanyero. He planned to set his own recording for the Brotherhood.

After introducing himself, Stranyero checked the signal from the device Father Saur had placed in Pete's New Testament and smiled.

Assuming Pete had reached the cloister, Stranyero was less than than three miles from it.

TEN FEET from the cavern's exit, Tara lost her footing. She stepped on a rattler. It struck her knee, fangs piercing the denim and her skin. A stinging sensation spread through her lower leg, then it turned numb, though Tara didn't know if it was from the bite or panic.

*Keep moving.*

She might be able to heal herself again, but it didn't make sense to try in the middle of snakes, with one of them incensed. If she could get outside, perhaps they'd leave her alone.

She ran.

One more bite later, Tara gasped for breath at the edge of a tree. The snakes hadn't followed her. No longer a perceived threat, they'd lost interest in her.

She heard a wailing sound, muted by distance and the trees around her. It had to be the alarm from the chapel. She hadn't seen any other buildings in the area.

*Not Fimi, it's nothing to do with Fimi, she's not here.*

But Kelly, Sophia, her dad, Cyril – any of them could be in danger.

Whole body trembling, she examined the bites on her leg. The second was about three inches above the first. The area around both had swollen. She rolled her jeans leg tightly to try to block the spread of the venom to her heart, but not so tightly it would cut off circulation. She fingered her knife. She vaguely recalled seeing a Western where a man cut open a rattlesnake bite and sucked out the venom. But her dad had told her that didn't work.

What she needed was anti-venom. The cloister might have it, since Sophia had mentioned snake handlers in the region, but it was more likely Tara would need to get to a hospital. Still, most people didn't die from snakebites, even rattlesnake bites. Through a fog of exhaustion, she attempted to retrace her steps. She felt disoriented, uncertain from which way she and Alma had come. Using a long branch as a walking stick, Tara made her way forward, but her whole body cried out for rest. She leaned against a tree, then sank to the ground.

If she couldn't move further, she'd never get the anti-venom. She had to try healing the bites despite being drained from the previous time and the ankle break itself. At least the alarm had quieted. Maybe it had been her dad and Cyril arriving and setting off the metal detector.

Tara shut her eyes, resting her hands over the bites. Despite how tired she felt, rapid-fire images shot through her mind – Megan lying in her coffin, Kali bruised and battered in the hospital bed, Bailey, his face white, pitching to the ground. Cold wind seeped into Tara's body. She blinked, breathed the damp, chilled air, and tried again. Her mind wouldn't clear. Questions about Cyril's motives and memories of awful things he'd done intruded each time she tried to calm herself, along with questions. Was he trying to help her dad or using him to find out more about the document? Did he care about her? Had he changed from Brotherhood soldier to an independent man? Did anyone really change?

Clouds shifted to block the sun. The smell of pine became overwhelming, more like chalky floor cleaner than crisp winter foliage. Tara slumped sideways. She ached to lie in the snow. She'd never summon the energy to heal herself again, let alone hike through the woods afterward. She felt far from the cloister, far from home, far from her child.

Alone and away, with no prospect of returning.

CYRIL EXITED THE CHAPEL, Pete close behind him. They'd arrived fifteen minutes before, met by the black pregnant woman named Zavia that Tara had emailed them about. In the garden, Cyril saw Sophia and Tara standing in a grove of Hawthorn trees, their backs to him. They seemed to be scanning the courtyard, their bodies tense. A young white pregnant woman emerged from the woods and started toward the grove with its interwoven ceiling of tree branches. Cyril shivered. One of the many myths about the Hawthorn tree was that its thorns had been the ones in the crown of Christ. He hurried toward Tara. It had taken too long to convince Zavia of his good intentions, and he'd had to surrender the small handgun he'd obtained to replace the Glock he'd been unable to get through customs. The new gun had set off the metal detector, and Zavia had insisted it be locked away in a safe. There, it could harm no one. It also couldn't help.

Pete nodded at Cyril, which Cyril took to mean Pete still had the original portion of the document against his chest in a plastic sleeve. Pete had made a photocopy for the cloister while Zavia had locked Cyril's gun away, but had refused to give the original to anyone other than Tara. Cyril felt a moment of gratitude. He and Pete might still doubt each other, and Pete might still have questions about why Tara's baby had been born, but they'd come together and brought the document. Cyril hoped that would make Tara happy even if she'd never consider being with him again. The young woman with Sophia turned and hurried toward them. Only then did Cyril realize she wasn't Tara, but Kelly. She and Pete hugged.

Cyril scanned the courtyard, the trees, and what he could see of the surrounding woods and mountainside beyond it.

"Where's Tara?" he asked Sophia.

Sophia frowned. "We can't find her. We hiked part of the woods to the east," she gestured, "and nothing. We're going to try the south woods now. She went for a walk with Alma."

Cyril pointed toward the young pregnant woman near the treeline. "Is that Alma?"

When they reached her, Alma said, "I got tired, but Tara wanted to keep hiking for a while. She said she'll circle back soon. She needs some time on her own."

"But she knew my dad and Cyril were on the way," Kelly said.

Alma shrugged. "She figured it'd take them longer to get here. And that Mary Paul would need a while with the document anyway."

"That's not like Tara," Kelly said. "She'd want to know my dad's okay."

Cyril's heart fell. "She may not want to see me."

Sophia glanced at Pete. "Let's look again."

"I'll wait here," Kelly said. "Cyril can fill me in on what you've been doing."

"Gladly," Cyril said. "Your dad and I have been working together." Mentally, Cyril kicked himself. He sounded like an idiot.

"Which path did she take?" Sophia asked Alma.

THE VESTIBULE SMELLED of hot paraffin when Raphael burst into it. Beyond it, the chapel – if it could be called that – was deserted. But the breadbasket on the table told him he'd found the heretics. They must be elsewhere in the building. An alarm shrieked as he raced through the doorway, sending red pulses across the chapel.

*Metal detector.*

It didn't make him pause, it was only light and sound. But his senses sharpened. Where there were alarms, there might be guards, though the very firepower that had set the alarm off should be sufficient to deal with them. He ran across the chapel and through the door under the exit sign, into a wide hall with a stone tile floor. A heavy door on the right led to a library. He glanced in. A woman hunched over a table. Thin and old. *Not Tara.*

He raced through the dormitory, shoving open doors, finding most rooms empty, except for a small office, where he startled a black pregnant woman wearing khakis and a bright-colored blouse – *not Tara.*

Raphael burst out the rear of the building. Red light flashed off the interwoven Hawthorn branches and woods beyond them. Brush-covered hills rose into mountains in the distance where evergreens, firs, and spruces towered.

A young white woman sat on an iron bench to his left. Pregnant. *Not Tara.* Beyond the courtyard, a trim late fiftyish man with a crew cut and a tall woman with long straight dark hair moved toward the trees. *Not Tara.*

In the courtyard, next to Cyril Woods, stood a shorter blond-haired girl with a wiry build. *Tara?*

Raphael lifted the rifle to his shoulder.

~

THE ALARM WAILED. Red lights flashed, bathing the thorny tree branches in crimson. Nothing in the grounds or courtyard appeared out of the ordinary. Cyril swung to face the chapel, conscious of Kelly next to him, and Sophia shouting something from a few yards away. His hand dropped to his waist before he remembered.

His weapon was gone.

A stocky man in camouflage stood ten feet beyond the chapel, lifting a rifle to his shoulder. Cyril felt as if he were back before the Arch. Or back in the nightmares he had about that afternoon. Unlike in his nightmares, he didn't hesitate.

~

SOPHIA SPUN TOWARD THE CHAPEL. The alarm had wailed and flashed when Cyril and Pete had arrived, but it had shut off within a few seconds, and Zavia had sent another young woman out to tell them who had arrived.

Sophia registered the man, the rifle. Thankfully, Tara was still nowhere to be seen. The woods were most dense to the east, where Alma had emerged, and might provide some cover.

Sophia ignored Pete's cry when she grabbed his arm, jerking his wounded shoulder. She yelled to Kelly and Cyril, who stood several paces away, to look out, and pulled Pete toward the trees.

Cyril had spun toward the stranger, reaching for his waist. From the corner of her eye, Sophia saw the gunman raise his rifle. Cyril stepped in front of Kelly and charged toward the gunman.

Shots rang out.

# 31

The alarm's renewed shriek startled Tara into consciousness. She lay on the ground, numb from the cold, heart racing. Though she feared what it signaled, Tara felt grateful for the piercing sound.

She struggled first to sit and then to keep her spine straight. Remembering Nanor's advice on meditation, she let the wailing alarm wash over her and tried to think of a calming image to focus on.

"The Community Center." Tara spoke the words aloud to help her mind stay on track over the noise. She loved the social room at Willow Springs, with its glass wall providing a view of the garden. At night, uplights made the plants and walking paths glow. Inside had the scent of cinnamon or mint or wild cherries, depending what the women behind the concession counter made for dessert that day. She imagined sitting on couches and overstuffed chairs before the windows with Fimi, Sophia, Nanor, her mother and dad, sipping spiced tea and relaxing. When her anxiety threatened and disturbing thoughts arose, Tara imagined another friend or family member at the table, imagined that person smiling and hugging her.

After what felt like half an hour but was likely a few minutes, as the alarm still wailed, Tara opened her eyes. The swelling had disappeared and the wounds closed, leaving faint dots where the snake bite marks had been. Her teeth chattered, and she felt more exhausted, if that were possible. But, propelled by anxiety, she jogged toward the sound of the alarm, muscling through fatigue. "Just five more steps," she told herself over and over, "then you can rest."

She breathed heavily through her mouth, tasting the pine-and-snow-scented air. At the southeast edge of the woods, a dense patch of trees kept her partially hidden as she approached the courtyard.

A gunshot rang out. Tara froze, then inched sideways to get a view of the garden area, adrenalin sharpening her senses. A heavyset man in camouflage stood between the chapel and the Hawthorn trees that wove together in the courtyard, a rifle on this shoulder. Tara was to his right and behind him, about twenty feet away, still partially concealed but visible if he looked right at her.

Cyril lay facedown on the ground at the center of the courtyard. Sophia and Kelly were running into the trees opposite Tara, but her dad split away from them, as if he aimed to circle back toward the gunman. His gait was off, he favored one side, but he wasn't limping. Alma was nowhere to be seen.

Counting on the alarm to mask any noise she made, Tara found a rock the size of a bowling ball on the ground. Summoning all her strength, she darted from the trees, heart pounding. When she was within three feet of the man with the rifle she halted, spun, and flung the rock with two hands, pushing from her chest as if she were throwing a basketball. She aimed for the back of his head. He'd started toward Kelly, but must have heard her behind him at the last moment. He began to turn. The rock caught him in the side of the face. He screamed and stumbled sideways, then fell to the ground. He landed on his right side but kept his grip on the rifle. Tara had already dropped her hand to her jeans pocket and retrieved her knife. Ignoring the burning muscles in her arms and legs, she dove to the ground and drove the knife into the man's left armpit from behind.

Howling, he writhed on the ground. He managed to twist toward Tara, his whole body curled around the rifle. The man's face looked familiar, but she didn't have time to register why.

Pete reached them as Zavia appeared from the chapel, gripping a handgun, and ran toward them. A silver-haired man followed a few feet behind Zavia. He wore a dark blue cashmere coat and held a large handgun. Whether he meant to help Zavia or the rifleman, Tara didn't know.

THE GPS DIRECTED Holmes through Southern Illinois and across the border into Missouri. He'd been to St. Louis before for a trade conference, but had always flown in, so his knowledge of the outlying area wasn't great. After losing track of Sophia and Tara, he'd decided to work with what he knew, and he knew where Tara's family lived. On the passenger seat sat a screen that fed in posts and images from the TARA2 game. It showed the inside of a building, though he wasn't sure where the broadcast originated. Whoever had the camera walked outside toward a courtyard filled with Hawthorn trees.

The camera panned the courtyard. It was hard to be sure, but a young woman who looked like Tara struggled on the ground with a man in camouflage. Nausea started in Holmes' belly before his mind registered the man's familiar body shape. The BMW swerved as the camera focused on the man's face. At first, Holmes' mind simply refused to take in the features. He screeched the car to the side of the road, horns blaring behind him. Oblivious, Holmes peered at the small screen.

*Henrik?*

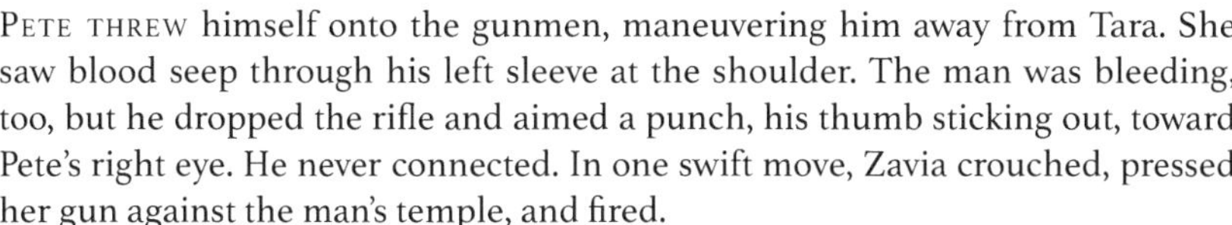

PETE THREW himself onto the gunmen, maneuvering him away from Tara. She saw blood seep through his left sleeve at the shoulder. The man was bleeding, too, but he dropped the rifle and aimed a punch, his thumb sticking out, toward Pete's right eye. He never connected. In one swift move, Zavia crouched, pressed her gun against the man's temple, and fired.

Blood and brains flew, splattering Pete's down jacket. Tara's ears rang from the boom of the gun. Cyril still lay about twenty feet away at the courtyard's center, but he'd rolled onto his side. The silver-haired man in the dark cashmere coat stepped between Cyril and Tara, blocking her sightline.

Zavia spun and pointed her gun, which she held with both hands, at the man. He dropped his weapon and raised his hands.

Pete helped Tara to her feet and kept one arm around her. Meeting the eyes of the man she guessed was Cyril's supervisor and father figure, Tara said, "Stranyero."

He inclined his head. "Ms. Spencer."

Kelly appeared behind Stranyero. Tara hadn't seen her approach, and she let out a sigh that her sister was unharmed. Before she could say anything, Zavia nodded to Kelly and said, "Call 911." Kelly ran for the chapel. Zavia pulled handcuffs from her back pocket and motioned to Pete. "Help me cuff this guy."

Pete squeezed Tara's shoulders before he stepped over to help Zavia. "This it?" he asked. "No one else got in the chapel?"

"No one," Zavia said.

Stranyero stayed silent. He didn't resist as Zavia led him away.

Pete returned to Tara's side. "You all right?"

"You're bleeding." Tara leaned on her dad, finding it hard to stay standing.

"I'll be fine." Pete reached inside his jacket and shirt and took out a plastic sleeve holding a piece of papyrus to show Tara. "I already gave Sister Mary Paul a copy. Tara, I'm sorry. I let you down in so many ways."

Tara took the plastic sleeve. "Dad, it's okay."

"No, it's not. You're my daughter, and Fimi's my granddaughter, and I haven't been there for you. But I am now. And I will be."

He hugged Tara. Tara hugged him back, careful not to squeeze his injured shoulder, warm tears trickling down her face.

Thirty feet away, beneath the web of Hawthorn tree branches, Sophia bent over Cyril. She glanced at Tara and nodded that Cyril was alive.

"He saved Kelly's life," Pete said.

Despite the spots that swam before her eyes as soon as she tried to move, Tara walked toward Cyril with Pete's help. Cyril's face was white and contorted with pain, but his eyes were open. Sophia pressed a folded green scarf above his knee. Blood had soaked through his jeans and into the scarf, but Sophia said it had started clotting.

Tara sank to the ground next to him.

"Don't touch me," Cyril said. "Tara, don't think of touching me."

WATCHING the text feed on her handheld device with the sound off, the Puppet Master nodded in satisfaction. The many hours spent enticing gamers with connections to news outlets had paid off. A freelancer had finagled a way onto the crew from the *Pittsburgh Chronicle*, the struggling but still surviving local paper Thomas Stranyero had contacted. Its reporters were willing to follow seemingly preposterous leads in the hope of uncovering anything unusual. The game hadn't run perfectly, but it had been sufficient to keep tabs on Tara and nearly all those who aided or opposed her, exactly what it had been designed to do. Now all of those people, other than Erik Holmes, had gathered at a chapel in the Appalachian mountains in Pennsylvania.

The Puppet Master would have liked to know where Holmes was, but none of the gamers had found a way to track him without his knowledge, unless he was with Tara. Not that anyone had likely tried very hard. The gamers thought Tara was the main point of the game.

The Puppet Master decided she'd better act. Holmes knew nothing about her, but that might not prevent him from interfering with her plan.

SISTER MARY PAUL barely heard the alarm, and she never noticed the gunman who peered into the library, then disappeared. Her attention stayed on her work. The small document section Alma had brought had made the task harder. After copying yet again and carefully cutting around the text of photocopies of the pages from Pete, Alma, and Sophia, Mary Paul had laid them out on the top of the glass sandwich that preserved the cloister's original papyrus section. Eventually, she concluded the piece from Alma came from a different document. Either that, or it had been created specifically to mislead any translator as to both the missing text and the shape of the gap in the document portion that had been stored for so long in the synagogue near Florence.

Once satisfied that she'd correctly arranged the separate pieces into a nearly-whole letter, Mary Paul had turned to the text itself. Some characters were clear. Others fell into the legible but doubtful category. Mary Paul placed a dot under those in the English translation on her yellow legal pad. Still other characters in the copies and papyrus had been lost due to damage. She noted those with elipses inside brackets. The gaps and flaws made for an uncertain reading of the letter, which frustrated her but wasn't unexpected. The cloister's section was in the best shape, so she focused on it, hoping it would give her context for the rest.

If Mary Paul had thought about the alarm, she would have concluded she could do little to aid anyone regardless. Her arthritic fingers struggled to hold her pen, and her eighty-eight year old neck and back muscles cried out at the many hours bending over the polished wood table. But she didn't think about it.

Before her at last was the bulk of the letter she'd heard about since she'd joined the cloister fifty years before. Like Professor Gaddini, Mary Paul had started in an order that encouraged academic and intellectual inquiry, but unlike Professor Gaddini, she'd sought out a new faith community rather than academia when her studies challenged her beliefs. Here at the cloister, everyone believed. In whatever way they chose, in whatever they chose, so long as it impacted human beings in a positive way, but they believed.

Like Nanor Kerkorian in Willow Springs, a community Mary Paul had studied but never chose to join, Mary Paul believed in balance. For thousands of years, since the time before Moses and Abraham, if those men had ever existed, the pendulum had swung toward men, aggression, and violence. Not that she believed men intrinsically violent. But when a culture glorified any group and imagined its god looked like them, it created imbalance within each person and the world. Now, in some small way, and after far too long, the pendulum could swing. That was what she expected this letter to confirm, though, as a scholar, she strove to set her expectations aside.

Having completed the letter's closing and a portion of its body, Mary Paul turned to the next most legible part – the beginning. She translated the first paragraph. Her knuckles turned white.

*This cannot be.*

~

"What? Why?" Tara knelt next to Cyril, shaky but feeling somewhat steadier now that her center of gravity was closer to the ground. She touched Cyril's cheek.

"Don't. Don't try to heal me. Sophia told me how much it takes from you."

Sophia nodded. "It doesn't look like he lost that much blood. He's more alert than at first, and he's stayed conscious."

"But it'll take time." Tara's eyes ached, and she shifted from kneeling to sitting and pulled her coat more tightly around her. "For the ambulance to get here. We're so far out of the way."

"I believe he'll be fine. Truly, Tara, if you could see yourself now, you'd agree with Cyril."

"Promise me," Cyril said. "I can't cause you any more harm. Promise me."

"All right."

Zavia appeared with a first aid kit and cleaned and bandaged Cyril's wounds. Kelly brought blankets. No one felt right about moving Cyril, though the temperature dropped as clouds gathered and wind swept down the mountain. As they waited, Cyril told Tara, with long pauses in between for both of them to rest, about the travels in Armenia. Tara held his hand as they waited for the ambulance and police to arrive, eventually lying on the ground next to him when her energy ran out. Pete stayed with them both the whole time.

# 32

Alma was found in her guest room, curled on the bed, staring at the wall. She'd run inside and called the police after Raphael started shooting. The detective who arrived on the scene first took her into custody after hearing how she'd forced Tara into the cavern. The gunman's body was carted off. Stranyero and Cyril claimed not to know him. Tara believed Cyril, but not Stranyero, who also was taken into custody. After saying he didn't know the gunman, Stranyero refused to say why he'd come to the chapel or brought a gun with him and instead invoked his right to remain silent. The paramedics, without out-and-out promising anything, assured Tara that Cyril would recover. The bullets had grazed him, and he'd lost a lot of blood, but the wounds hadn't gone deep. They carried him away on a stretcher, using a team of four so they could take shifts moving him to the clearing down the mountain where an ambulance waited.

After the police and paramedics left along with the two people from the *Pittsburgh Chronicle*, Pete called Lynette on the chapel's landline to update her and let her know he, Tara, and Kelly were fine. Lynette put Fimi on the phone for a few minutes, and she blew raspberries and said "ah-goo" when Tara spoke to her. Tara pressed the phone closer to her ear, wishing she could hear in person each new sound Fimi made and hold and rock her baby. At the same time, despite Zavia having apprehended the gunman and Stranyero, Tara felt grateful Fimi was over seven hundred miles away where it was safer.

"I'll be home soon, sweetie," she said, though she knew Fimi couldn't understand the words.

An hour later, Tara, Sister Mary Paul, Kelly, Pete, Sophia, and Zavia sat at the round table in the chapel's main room. It smelled of sandalwood incense. Sunlight shone through the skylight and the stained glass windows, casting colored designs on the table. Tara sipped a glass of water, her mouth and lips dry. Her dad had insisted she eat and then rest for forty-five minutes before the reading of the document. To her surprise, despite her pounding heart, she'd dropped into a deep, dreamless sleep. She still felt exhausted, but excitement – and anxiety – over what the message might be kept her alert. She spun a pen between her fingers. She wasn't planning to take any notes, but it gave her something to do. Pete put his arm around Tara's shoulders.

Sister Mary Paul's hands trembled as she resettled her reading glasses and lifted her legal pad.

"It's a letter to Rima Petrosyan, the young Armenian woman who, legend has it, became pregnant despite being a virgin. It's from her aunt." Sister Mary Paul cleared her throat and began to read. "'My dearest niece.'" Mary Paul's soft voice carried throughout the chapel and over the sound of the wind rattling the windows. "'I write to share what I've learned through my travels and studies. It has been difficult. As you know, many avenues of religious inquiry remain closed to a woman, though part of what I discovered is that this has not always been so. But more on that later. First, I must tell you what you are and what your role will be, and do my best to prepare you. For the burdens of – and dangers to – you, the Antichrist, are great."

# 33

Lynette and Father Saur sat at the kitchen table. Lynette had raised the temperature setting on the thermostat after seeing the priest shivering, but it hadn't helped much. He seemed unable to get warm. Diedre and the security guard had stayed in the living room with Fimi at Lynette's request. Father Saur didn't know Diedre was from Willow Springs, and Diedre didn't know Father Saur was the family's pastor, and Lynette decided to keep it that way. The less any one person knew about her family, the better.

"I'm afraid I've put your family in great danger," Father Saur said. "I believed the Brotherhood served the Lord's purpose, but now I'm unsure."

"What are you saying?" Lynette's hand shook as she poured the coffee, and some of it spilled.

Father Saur helped wipe the table, then stirred cream into his coffee so vigorously the liquid spiraled. "I'm concerned Pete and Tara may not make it back home."

"But I told you what Pete said. They're fine."

Lynette threw away the dampened napkins and tried to slow her racing heart. Despite reassuring Father Saur, and Pete trying to minimize the scene with the gunman, she didn't feel he, Tara, and Kelly were safe. And she worried about what the document might say.

A thud and a groan came from the living room. It took Lynette a moment to process the sounds, her thoughts had been so focused on imagining what might be happening in Pennsylvania. Fimi began to cry. Father Saur jumped to his feet.

A figure wearing a black ski mask burst into the kitchen and stiff-armed Father Saur out of the way. His head cracked against the refrigerator. Lynette was shoved into the pantry. Her upper back smacked into the shelves behind her. She threw herself forward and collided with the door as it slammed shut. Pain shot through her head. She pressed her palms against the door. Something heavy screeched across the kitchen floor.

More noises. The baby crying. Nate's voice. Shattering glass. Another voice, mid-range – low enough to be male but high enough to be female. Diedre's? Lynette flung herself against the door again. More thuds, like a body dropping. Fimi wailing.

Then the worst thing of all.

Silence.

# 34

The baby finally quieted, sucking on a small bottle of sugar water. Probably something her mother never gave her, given how conscientious Tara seemed to be when not carting the child off to Istanbul. The treat brought peace, a moment to catch the breath, pull over, and reprogram the GPS. No one left at the house was conscious other than Lynette, who would never break out of the pantry with the cabinet slid in front of the door. So it'd be some time before the police were called.

A chime came from her handheld device, the one she'd used to monitor TARA2 while traveling. The information the gamers had gathered and shared, combined with Tara's responses to the fake emails Diedre Hartman had sent as Kali, had been invaluable in tracking Tara, monitoring developments, and learning enough to get past Lynette's defenses. Diedre smiled. Everyone had thought that, as the aging head of Security at Willow Springs, she could barely understand technology, that it all had to be left to the next generation. While it had been a challenge running the game without Sagun discovering her role in it, Diedre had been more than equal to it. She was, after all, the Puppet Master.

Two miles later, Diedre changed lanes, exited the expressway, and pulled into a rest area. As she'd guessed, the message was from her mother. Diedre responded with her estimated arrival time. If she'd calculated correctly, before night fell, she'd be at the hospice.

She glanced at Fimi. "Rest up – you have work to do."

# THE CONFLAGRATION

---

THE AWAKENING BOOK 3

# 1

My dearest niece,

I write to share what I've learned through my travels and studies. It has been difficult. As you know, many avenues of religious inquiry remain closed to a woman [...] though part of what I discovered is that this has not always been so. But more on that later. First, I must tell you what you are and what your role will be, and do my best to prepare you, for the burdens on and dangers to you, <the> Antichrist [...] are great.

It is, I feel certain, a shock that I use [...] especially given how troubled you have been about being with child. Scripture says, "I am honored, and I am scorned. The holy person and the whore. [....] Peace I am, and because of me, war comes; [....]" I have reason to believe you will bear a daughter, and she will bear a daughter, that is [....] You must understand your power, which is great, but hide it from those who will deny [....] You must play your full part in guiding the world and be an example for your daughter as you both fight [....]

[.........................................................................]

[...] the Church, and destruction will be caused by you (pl.) and perhaps your child and (her? their?) offspring. You must not let that happen. Without you [...] will take over the minds and hearts of the world. <I have> foreseen others like you over the centuries [....] [...] in the name of evil, great [....]

Tara screeched her chair back across the hardwood floor. She felt confined, the cloister's vaulted ceiling suddenly too low. Everyone around the table turned to stare at her.

Sophia Gaddini reached out her hand, her tiny garnet ring flashing in the fading sunlight. "Tara, the word 'Antichrist' may not have meant then what it does today."

"I can't." Tara spun and ran from the main room, through narrow halls, and past the library. At last she shoved through the back door.

Outside, hawthorn trees wound their bare branches together above the courtyard to block the last rays of late afternoon sun. Near the center, the snow was still stained from the blood of the man who'd come to kill Tara only hours before. Ten feet beyond that, smaller droplets had sprayed from the man who'd stopped a bullet to save her sister's life. Tara breathed deep, the icy air hurting her lungs. Once everyone who'd tried to protect her knew the truth, or what the ancient letter that had just been read suggested was the truth, she doubted they'd be so eager to stand by her side. Perhaps they shouldn't be.

"Tara."

Tara looked over her shoulder. Sophia, face paler than usual against her long dark hair, held the heavy door ajar. As always, she stood perfectly straight, yet somehow with ease.

Tara stepped back. "I can't talk. I need to—need to—I've got to get away."

To where, she didn't know. The only hope for reassuring answers as to how or why she'd become pregnant a little over a year ago had ended today. All Tara's efforts, rather than revealing anything good about her and her child, had only proved the point of those who'd threatened and harmed her and her family.

"We don't need to talk." Sophia's warm voice, reassuring in its steadiness, underscored every way Tara didn't feel, could never feel again. "But much as the police combed the grounds, they can't check this entire area." Sophia gestured toward the mountainside, dotted with pine trees, their green branches looking black against the snow.

"Right." Tara had escaped two attackers already today. She didn't need to chance a third. But being indoors, sitting still, felt impossible.

Her friend knew her. "The workout room is down the north hall."

So instead of through the trees, along icy paths, up the mountainside, Tara ran on a treadmill. The one farthest from the windows. She doubted the former nuns who lived and worked at the cloister had installed bulletproof glass. On the other hand, given that one of them had appeared with a handgun earlier that day and saved her dad's life, maybe they had.

Tara kicked the treadmill setting up a notch, though already she felt breathless. Sweat trickled down her forehead. She had not looked at her dad once while they'd listened to the oldest nun read her translation of the pieced-together letter. Over the last five years, her dad had struggled with Tara's growing atheism and, later, with what he saw as her "claims" about her pregnancy contradicting the Church's teachings. He couldn't possibly handle this new revelation.

What frightened Tara more was whether she could handle it, not just for herself but for Fimi. Her baby, who'd never done anything wrong, who'd never asked to be born, who already was a target.

Her knees ached, her teeth clenched, and the treadmill whined.

"Tara."

Her dad, Pete Spencer, stepped in front of her, blocking her view of the dark tree trunks and branches straggling up the side of the mountain amidst a thin layer of snow. Technically, Pete was her stepfather, but he was the first, and in her mind only, dad she'd ever had. His hair had gone completely silver in the last few years, but despite that and the lines around his eyes, he looked younger than most men in their early fifties. He'd lost the small paunch around his middle during his travels in Armenia, and his slender frame looked tougher and stronger.

He waved her to stop. He wasn't smiling, but he didn't look afraid. That was something.

Tara turned the speed to half.

"Walk it out," Pete said. "I'll wait."

"Right." Once she'd cooled down, Tara stepped off the machine.

"You all right?" Pete said.

"I don't think that's remotely possible," Tara said. "Are you?" Her heart still pounded in her chest and throat.

"Yes." Pete spoke clearly and without hesitation.

Tara thought she must have heard wrong. She and her dad and others had traveled all over the world during the last month to find and reunite lost parts of an ancient Armenian letter to a young pregnant woman many thought was Tara's spiritual ancestor. And the first paragraph, the only part Tara had really listened to, referred to that woman as the Antichrist.

"How can you be?" Tara asked. "All right?"

Pete handed Tara a mug of tea. She hadn't noticed he'd been holding it. She breathed in the scents of lemongrass and eucalyptus, and her shoulders lowered the slightest amount.

"Thanks, Dad."

He squeezed her shoulder. They walked into the next room, a wide-open area with yoga mats on one side, free weights on the other, and mirrors all around. Recessed lights along the edges provided some illumination, but the main overheads remained off.

"I don't feel evil," Tara said. "But maybe I wouldn't. If I was born that way, it's how I'd always feel."

"You're not evil." Pete gestured for Tara to sit next to him on the stack of mats. "And surely you'd never believe Fimi's evil."

"No, I don't." Tara thought about what DNA testing had revealed about her own ancestry. "But I don't know where I come from, not completely, let alone Fimi's origin. And the letter was written to someone who might have been just like me."

"I don't care about the letter," Pete said. "I don't care what it says, means to say, or doesn't say."

"After what you went through to try to find part of it? After what we all went through?" Tara sipped the hot tea, and it burned the top of her tongue. She set the mug on the wooden floor. "And look at all the people who've tried to harm me or kill me since I got pregnant. That suggests I'm evil."

"That suggests they're evil, not you."

"Are you so sure? You of all people?" Her dad had apologized earlier that day for how badly he'd reacted to her pregnancy, but it didn't change what his beliefs had been at first and maybe still were.

Pete took her hand. "It took me time to accept what happened. I thought you were misguided or mistaken, yes. But it never, ever crossed my mind there was anything evil about you or Fimi."

"But the Antichrist—no one can think that's good."

"If the Pope himself walked in and swore on a stack of Bibles that you're evil and dangerous, or Fimi is, I'd tell him he's wrong."

Tears filled Tara's eyes. From someone else, the statement might be a rhetorical flourish or be meaningless, as the Pope's words didn't dictate what most people thought, or even what most Catholics thought. But the troubling thing about her pregnancy for her dad always had been the Church's insistence that she was a fraud. For as long as she could remember, Catholicism had been one of the most important parts of Pete's life.

"And the letter?" Tara said.

"You didn't have a problem disregarding Church teachings based on the gospels," Pete said. "We know far less about this document's origins or context. So why would you believe it's relevant or that you understand it after one hearing?"

"I—right." A few months before, her dad would have made his comment about the gospels with rancor. Now he sounded more matter-of-fact. And he had a point. She no longer took any writing at face value, so why take this one that way? "Maybe it's completely off base. Not connected to me at all." She felt her jaw unclench.

"It must mean something," Pete said. "People went to a lot of trouble to preserve it over the years, and others to try to keep you from getting it. But don't let one word in it determine what you believe."

Pete put his arm around her. She breathed in the scent of his aftershave. Before she'd become pregnant, before they'd been at odds, she'd always turned to him for grounding and connection. It was good to know she could again, no matter how wrong the rest of life seemed.

"You still seem pretty tense." Pete smiled. "Though I can't imagine why."

"Yeah, seriously."

"How about meditating?"

That, too, felt familiar and comforting. Though a devout Catholic, Pete had always said his most important spiritual practice was meditation. Tara had some success with practicing yoga for peace and calm, but she usually found sitting too difficult.

"It's not going to work."

"It's not supposed to 'work,'" Pete said.

"I know, I know." It was what he'd always said when he'd struggled to convince his five kids to quiet down and try mindfulness. "How about this? When I come home to get Fimi, I'll try sitting in your hemitation room."

Tara's youngest brother had learned the word "hematite" when someone brought one of the black crystals to school for show and tell, and from then until he was about eight, he'd confused that word with "meditate."

Pete laughed. "Deal."

Tara felt her muscles begin to unknot. In no way could everything be fixed, but at least her dad was with her.

The door to the exercise room flew open and the overhead fluorescent lights blinked on, hurting Tara's eyes.

Sophia held out the phone. "Tara, it's your mother. Something awful has happened."

# 2

The speakerphone sat in the middle of the long library table, books and manuscripts stacked around it. Tara's mother, Lynette Spencer, was on the other end of the line at the family's home in Rock Hill, Missouri, talking so fast her words were barely intelligible. Pete's face had gone white, and Tara's sister Kelly clutched the edge of the table.

Tara leaned toward the phone. "Mom, slow down. Father Saur came to visit, you were in the kitchen, and then what? What happened?"

"It was just the two of us in the kitchen. I thought Fimi was safe, Tara, it never occurred to me she wasn't safe. She was in the living room with Diedre and the other security guard."

Diedre Hartman, a tall, muscular former bodybuilder and police officer, was the head of security from Willow Springs, a women's community Tara had lived in briefly after Fimi's birth. Diedre had volunteered to stay at the Spencers' home to help watch over Fimi while Tara traveled overseas.

Tara's heart rate spiked. "And where is she now? Where's Fimi?" She stared at the glowing buttons on the phone. Everything else in the room had become hazy. Only the phone seemed real.

"She's been taken. She's gone," Lynette said. "Someone wearing a ski mask, wearing all black, burst in and knocked Father Saur to the floor and shoved me into the pantry. I banged on the door and walls for nearly an hour, Tara, and I couldn't get out. The cabinet had been slid across it. When Father Saur came to, he called the police and got me out, but that was over an hour later. He wrenched his back moving the cabinet. And Fimi was gone, she was already gone."

"Gone," Tara said.

"Your brothers and the security guard were all knocked out, maybe drugged the police said."

"What about Diedre Hartman?" Pete sat rigid, hands flat on the long wooden library table. "Was she drugged too?"

"No. She'd disappeared," Lynette said.

"So she took Fimi?" Pete said.

"Or someone took her and Fimi," Lynette said. "But her SUV is gone."

Tara paced in the small area between the table and the towering row of bookshelves behind it, scanning her memory for everything she remembered from the last time she'd spoken with Diedre. It had been at Willow Springs, and she'd encouraged Tara to move out of the community.

"Her mother was ill," Tara said. "Dying. I think from some type of cancer."

Twice since Fimi's birth, seriously injured people had spontaneously healed in the baby's presence. Diedre knew about at least one of the incidents. It had happened at Willow Springs. Tara let her breath out. If Diedre's mother was truly dying, she might have taken Fimi in a desperate attempt to save her. Which meant she'd have no reason to harm the baby, and Tara might get her back safely.

"Do you know that for certain? It's not just what she told people?" Sophia said. She'd been sitting quietly opposite Tara, the yellow legal pad she'd used while aiding in research earlier that day in front of her.

Tara's stomach turned over. "I don't know."

Sophia stood. "I'll contact Willow Springs and ask about that. And get Diedre's license plate number. They must have it on record."

Kelly twisted in her chair to look at Tara. "So that's good, right? If that's why Diedre took her, then she's not meaning to harm Fimi."

"Unless it doesn't work," Lynette said over the speaker. "Tara doesn't even know if Fimi really healed anyone."

"I think she did," Tara said. "We've got to get home." She hadn't lived at her parents' house in nearly two years, but it was still home, and it was the last place she knew her baby had been.

"We can't go yet," Pete said. "We're due at the police station in the morning about today's shootings. And the kidnapping might be related. We need to tell them about it, too."

"Related?" Tara said. "Everyone who was here today couldn't have been in St. Louis kidnapping Fimi. And the letter hadn't been translated yet when she was taken, so that can't be the reason."

"You don't know that," Lynette said. "Your dad's right, don't jump to conclusions."

Tara gripped the back of the wooden library chair in front of her. "We know the timing."

"But we don't know anything about motives," Lynette said.

"So? I want to talk to the police investigating the kidnapping in person. Staying here to answer questions about today's shootings, what's the point? The man who shot at Kelly is dead. The other people who might be involved were arrested."

Kelly reached over and grasped Tara's wrist. "Alma. What about her? She could've had something to do with this." Alma Duttenhaver was one of the people who'd tried to harm Tara earlier that day. She'd been arrested.

Tara looked at her sister. "You're right. She said something about a plot to kidnap Fimi. I thought she made it up to distract me from what she was really trying to do, but maybe it was true."

Kelly's shoulders slumped. "But she was here. Like you said. So she couldn't have actually taken Fimi."

"No, but it's a great idea." Tara sat and held both Kelly's hands in hers. "Maybe she knows something. It's worth seeing if she'd talk to me."

Pete shook his head. "I don't want you anywhere near Alma. Or anyone else who tried to kill you. We'll talk to the police here and then go home."

"But the police won't have the same context we do," Kelly said. "We can ask questions they'd never think of."

Tara put her arm around Kelly. Her sister was seventeen, five years younger than Tara, but they were the same height and shared facial features and a wiry build. That resemblance had almost cost Kelly her life earlier that day.

"There's no 'we.' You're heading home. Please," Tara said. "See what's happening there, and Dad and I will join you later."

~

THE RENTAL CAR'S headlights glinted off the guardrail along the curve. Tara clutched her phone, fighting the urge to tell her dad to head for the airport so they could take the next plane home. He was right. They needed to stay and talk to the Pennsylvania State Police tomorrow morning, and being where Fimi had last been would not bring her baby back. Plus she owed Cyril Woods—the man who'd taken a bullet meant for her—a visit. He'd saved Kelly's life, as the shooter had aimed at her, believing she was Tara.

"You don't owe him," Pete said. He kept his eyes on the road, for which Tara was grateful. The terrain in St. Louis included hills, but they were nothing compared to the winding Appalachian mountain roads. "Not after everything he did before Fimi was born."

"I thought you felt differently now," Tara said. When she'd sat with Cyril in the grounds of the cloister earlier that day, waiting for the paramedics, he'd told her all about his trip to Armenia with her dad to retrieve the part of the document hidden there. "He saved your life."

"That's true," Pete said. "And it's also true he could have taken that document section for himself. Or for the Brotherhood of Andrew."

The Brotherhood, a religious order, had interfered in Tara's life from the moment her pregnancy had become known. Cyril had once been a devoted member of it, and he'd told her he'd been instructed to bring the document section to his superior in the Order if he found it, not to Tara.

"But he didn't," Tara said. "And you still don't trust him?"

"I have a better opinion of him than I did before," Pete said. "But I can't forget that he endangered Bailey's life. Or ignore how he treated you. People only change so much so fast, if they change at all."

"I haven't forgotten any of it either," Tara said. Bailey was her youngest brother, and the one she felt most protective of. "But I might be able to forgive. Isn't that what we're supposed to do?"

"It is. But I never said I'm perfect. Forgiving can be dangerous."

By the time they reached Susquehanna Hospital, the sky had turned pitch dark. The patches of light cast by the scattered parking lot streetlights made the unlit areas seem forbidding. They found a spot near the main entrance. Cyril was only being kept at the small local hospital because the gunshot wound he'd sustained hadn't been deep. Otherwise, the paramedics had said he would have been taken to the Level I Trauma Center in Danville.

Tara's stomach tightened and her lips felt dry as they walked through the halls. If the Brotherhood had any involvement in Fimi's kidnapping, Cyril would be the best person to help. After he'd risked his life for her, she shouldn't have any question he'd do whatever he could. But he'd been taken away by the paramedics before the letter's translation had been read. Given his religiosity, the reference to the Antichrist might change everything.

The private room was barely large enough for a bed, a metal side table, medical monitors, and a visitor chair. Cyril was dozing, the head of his bed partly elevated, his thin, muscled arms sticking out of the paper hospital gown sleeves. Dark stubble covered the lower half of his face, becoming fainter beneath and across his high cheekbones. His crew cut gave him a military look, though he'd left the army four years before.

"Cyril?" Tara said.

He opened his eyes. He had light gray irises circled in charcoal, and black lashes that made the color more striking. But tonight his eyes were shot with red, and the skin under them looked bruised and slack.

He started to smile, but his lips froze. "What happened?"

"Fimi," Tara said. "She's been kidnapped."

Cyril fumbled for the bed control. "Who? What happened?"

"You remember Diedre Hartman? The head of Security at Willow Springs?"

The bed adjusted so Cyril could sit up and still be supported. His face was pale. "Tall? Bodybuilder type?"

"Yes. She came to my parents' house a few days back, after I'd sent Fimi there. I thought she'd be safer there than with me. Diedre claimed she'd been sent by Willow Springs to help guard Fimi. Which made sense to my mom. But while Mom was in the kitchen, someone broke in and locked my mom in the pantry. When she got out, Diedre and Fimi were gone."

"So Diedre might have taken her, or she might have been kidnapped herself," Cyril said.

"Right," Pete said. He stood at the foot of the bed, hands closed into fists at his sides. "But Sophia called Willow Springs, and no one there knew Diedre was coming to our house."

"They thought she took a leave of absence to be with her mother, who has breast cancer," Tara said.

"We'll find Fimi," Cyril said. "You'll get through this."

Tara rubbed her hands over her arms. "I have to."

"What can I do?" Cyril said.

"You used to belong to the Brotherhood," Tara said. "Do you think it—anyone from it—could be involved? Directing Diedre? Or taking her and Fimi for some reason?"

"Hard to say. I doubt anyone from the Order has told me the truth about anything for a long time. You think the kidnapping relates to the attacks on you today?"

"Do you?" Tara said. "I was hoping you might see something I haven't. I just keep hoping it's Diedre who took her, because that means I'll probably get her back."

"Both events could be related," Cyril said. "An attack on two fronts."

"Did you know the man who fired at us?" Tara said.

Cyril closed his eyes for a moment. "I've been struggling to picture his face. It happened so fast, and he was far from me. But I don't think I've ever met him."

"Is it something the Brotherhood would do?" Tara said. "Attack me again? Take Fimi?"

Cyril looked at the ceiling, as if the answers might be written on its white acoustic tiles. "I don't think the Brotherhood was behind either."

"But your former boss, Thomas Stranyero. He was there today," Pete said. "He had some reason for that."

A distinguished-looking man in his early sixties, Thomas Stranyero had been the second person to burst into the chapel's courtyard today with a gun, though he hadn't used it. When Cyril had belonged to the Brotherhood of Andrew, Stranyero had sent Cyril to Tara early in her pregnancy to protect her, or so Cyril had believed. But the Brotherhood's views about Tara had changed, as had Cyril's, more than once.

Cyril repositioned himself, wincing as if that slight movement made the wound in his upper leg hurt more. "Stranyero doesn't do his own dirty work. If he wanted to harm you, he'd send someone else."

"He didn't just appear," Pete said. "He pulled a gun."

"Even so," Cyril said.

To Tara's surprise, after a moment, Pete nodded.

"You're so sure you know him?" Tara said.

"Yes. No," Cyril said. "There was a lot he didn't tell me when he brought me into the Brotherhood, so I concede I don't know him as well as I thought I did. But I'm not basing my view on my personal relationship with him. I'm basing it on the decisions I've seen him make over the last eight years. The strategy he employs."

"So what was he doing there?" Tara tapped the fingers of her left hand on the bed rail.

"Probably hoping to gain information," Cyril said. "It's not like him to put himself personally at risk, to expose himself. If he'd known a gunman would be there, if he'd known the potential for bad publicity for him and the Brotherhood, he would have stayed a million miles away. Have the police made any progress on finding Diedre?"

"Not so far," Pete said.

"If she's been planning this a long time, I don't know if they will." Tara bounced on her heels, unable to stay still. "She's done security for over twenty years. I'm sure she knows how to evade police if she needs to."

Cyril grasped one of Tara's hands. His fingers felt warm over her icy skin. "Security at a small women's community," he said. "It's not like working for the FBI. They'll find her. And as soon as I'm released, I'll do whatever I can to help, you know that."

"There's something you should know. Before you commit to that." Tara withdrew her hand, not wanting to feel him pull away if that's what he was going to do.

Pete moved closer to Tara. "You're sure?" He turned to Cyril. "I'm not ungrateful to you for saving Kelly. And me in Armenia. But no one outside of the people in the room when the letter was read knows its contents. It's better—safer—to keep it that way."

"Then don't tell me," Cyril said. "I don't want you to wonder about me, if in some other way the letter's contents come out."

"You need to know at least one thing," Tara said. "So you can decide if you're still on my side—or not."

"I am," Cyril said.

"Listen." Tara wiped her sweaty palms on her jeans. Her nerves and the peroxide and disinfectant smells from the hallway made her feel queasy. "The letter was written by an Armenian woman in the sixth century whose niece was like me. She said she was pregnant and a virgin. And the letter to her sounds a lot like your Brotherhood's worst fears about me."

"It's not 'my' Brotherhood," Cyril said.

"You're ignoring the other part of what I said. You know what Stranyero believed when he told you to abandon me. And to do worse than that. And you listened."

"That's what the letter says?" Cyril tensed his whole body and gripped the bedrail.

"Suggests," Pete said. "May suggest."

Cyril took a deep breath. "It doesn't matter. The worst moments of my life came from following the Brotherhood's lies about you."

"But what if it were true?" Tara said. "What if you read this ancient document, the one you helped piece together, and there was something in there that said I'm the Antichrist?"

"Which it doesn't," Pete said.

"It can be read that way," Tara said.

"Tara, if you'd stayed and listened to all of it again, listened to the background—"

"It can be read that way," Tara said.

"Why are you jumping to the worst case scenario?" Pete said.

"Because the worst case happens. Or the most unlikely. When I missed my periods, I couldn't be pregnant, and yet I was. When Cyril said he'd help me, he abandoned me. Twice. When I finally found someone who seemed to know what was happening in Istanbul, he got killed. Bad things happen. Awful things. Horrible things."

Cyril reached for her hand again. Now his fingers felt cold. "I failed you before. So it won't mean much now, but I'm telling you, whatever that letter says doesn't matter. Words on a page are only that—no matter whose words they are. I don't believe in divinely inspired writings anymore. And I don't trust that men know how to interpret them."

Tara looked at him. "You need to be sure. I don't want you changing your mind mid-stream." She didn't think she needed to add "again."

Cyril glanced from her to Pete. "I'd like to talk to Tara alone for few minutes. If that's all right with both of you."

After Pete left for the cafeteria, Cyril said, "It's about the things I said to you in Armenia. After we slept together."

"You apologized," Tara said. "This morning." It seemed like it had been days ago when she'd sat with Cyril in the cold courtyard, afraid to move him, waiting for the paramedics, but it had been over eight hours. Now, despite her anxiety over Fimi, Tara's head felt heavy and she struggled to stand straight.

"I did?" Cyril said. "Everything's a blur after I hit the ground. It doesn't feel like I've apologized. And I know you've got more on your mind. Your priority is finding Fimi. So I'm not asking you to think about me, about us, if there is or could be an us."

"Good."

"But I am sorry. I was wrong to make love with you when I was so confused, and beyond wrong to blame you the next day. Nothing can excuse the terrible things I said to you, or my abandoning you. And Bailey....all I can say is I'll never do anything to endanger you or anyone you love again."

Tara's shoulders relaxed, and her jaw muscles loosened. "You did a lot to help my dad. And you saved his life and Kelly's."

"And I'd do it again. Not only to try to make up for the harm I've caused you and your family, but because it's right."

"Okay. Let's move on. Those were all terrible things, but we're past them."

Cyril inhaled, chest rising visibly, then let his breath out again. "One other thing. I thought about it a lot during my travels with your dad. I was wrong to say I loved you. Not because I don't have feelings for you. I do. But I raced into saying it to justify my change in direction. All those years I planned and studied to be a deacon, and then I was ready to throw it away. So I thought it must be love. Not any love, but *the* love. Of my life. And it might have been. Might be. But I wasn't ready yet. So it was wrong of me to say it."

"Cyril." Tara forced her worries about Fimi away for the moment. Things needed to be clear with Cyril. She looked straight into his gray eyes. "I knew you were in the midst of this huge change. So was I. We were in this moment, and we wanted to be together. Both of us. What you did and said after that was awful. But it's okay if you're not sure how you feel. I'm not sure. I don't need to know if you want to be with me forever. I'm twenty-two. And I have a baby, and no answers about how I became pregnant, or why, or what it means. I won't be thinking about who's the love of my life for a long, long time."

"Okay. Thank you. That makes sense."

"Okay." Tara smiled and squeezed his hand.

"So—what can I do to help?" Cyril said.

"Besides get better?" Tara said. "Think about anything you know about the Brotherhood that would help."

Pete knocked on the open doorway and handed a bottle of water to Cyril and one to Tara, along with a bag of peanuts. "You barely ate dinner," Pete said. "It's not going to help Fimi if you collapse."

After eating a few peanuts, Tara drank a third of her water in one gulp, then sank into the visitor chair. "We were just talking about what Cyril could do."

"I've been thinking about that," Pete said. "He could interview Stranyero."

"He wouldn't tell me anything," Cyril said. "He hasn't trusted me in a long time."

Tara leaned forward. "But Dad's right. If there's a chance he might know something that could help find Fimi, it's worth trying."

"He's more likely to be open with you than me," Cyril said. "I failed him, turned my back on him."

"But she's the enemy." Pete touched Tara's shoulder. "I didn't mean literally."

"I get that." Still, the comment made Tara shiver.

"I don't know the Brotherhood's true agenda," Cyril said. "But if Stranyero does view Tara as some sort of foe, that doesn't mean he won't be open with her. He likes a challenge. But just Tara, one-on-one." He glanced at Pete. "Don't put him on the defensive by double-teaming him."

# 3

Thomas Stranyero was being kept until his bond hearing in a holding cell at a police station barely the size of a two-bedroom ranch home. After passing through metal detectors, checking in at the guards' station, and being patted down, Tara was taken to an interior room with a window on one of its long walls and a flimsy looking conference table. She'd barely slept, and she'd awakened with her heart racing. The three cups of Chai tea she'd had that morning—one at the cloister, one while answering questions at the main Pennsylvania State Police headquarters in Mountoursville, and one during the drive to see Stranyero—hadn't calmed her.

She tapped her forefingers on the table, making it shake. An old-fashioned round clock hung on the wall opposite her. The rectangular window below it looked out on three small cubicles with low walls and, beyond them, an exterior window with a view of a snow-covered slope. The police had advised her that Stranyero could refuse to see her, but she hoped curiosity, or boredom, would make him agree to it.

Precisely at eleven a.m., when visiting hours began, Stranyero was escorted in. His charcoal gray suit looked not quite pressed but not as rumpled as Tara would have expected, given that he must have slept in it. Perhaps he'd simply sat up all night. He had silver hair and fine lines around his eyes, a nose with a straight bridge and narrow nostrils, and a defined jawline.

"Ms. Spencer." He rested his forearms on the table, wrists cuffed together. His knuckles had black and gray hair on them, and his hands looked callused, a contrast to his manicured nails. "How kind of you to visit."

"I need information."

"I assumed. You had quite an eventful day yesterday."

"Do you know where my baby is?"

She was careful not to say Fimi's name. Only family and close friends knew the baby was called by the nickname rather than by her full name, Sophia Fiona. It was a small point to protect, and perhaps too many people already knew the nickname, given Tara's large family Still, it gave her hope that when Fimi grew older, it would help her differentiate friend from foe.

*And she will grow older. I will find her and protect her and she will grow into an adult.*

"Your baby?" Stranyero's eyebrows raised and his pupils widened. If he wasn't surprised, he was a good actor. Which he might be. Based on what she'd learned from Cyril, at the very least, Stranyero knew how to manipulate people.

"She's been kidnapped. And I'm asking you by whom, and where she is."

He peered past her, as if looking at something in the distance, though he faced a blank wall. "I don't know."

Tara doubted that. She'd never figured out whether the Brotherhood was a vast organization with tentacles everywhere, a tiny fringe religious group, or something in between, but since her pregnancy, people from it had known tremendous amounts about her. "Why did you come to the cloister yesterday?"

Stranyero frowned and spread his hands as wide as he could, given the cuffs. "I can't tell you anything about yesterday. I've invoked my right to remain silent on my attorney's advice. If I could tell you, I would."

He seemed genuinely regretful, though Tara didn't know him well enough to judge. She tried questioning him anyway, but he wouldn't say whether he knew the man with the rifle, Alma Duttenhaver, or anyone named Raphael, which was the name of the man Alma had claimed she was corresponding with from the Brotherhood.

"What are the charges against you?" Tara said.

"Criminal trespass. A difficult charge to prove, I feel safe pointing out, given that the doors to that former chapel were unlocked and there are no signs forbidding entry. Open carrying a gun without a license, except that I have a license. Which my attorney will provide to the court. Assault. Attempted murder. Which are baseless charges."

The sheriff had told her Stranyero could be released today. Unbelievable.

"I expect I'll need to post a significant bond," Stranyero said, as if reading her mind.

"Which you'll be able to do."

"Oh, yes."

Tara pressed her palms flat on the table. "Did you instruct anyone to kidnap my baby?"

"I did not."

"What can you tell me about Diedre Hartman?"

Stranyero tilted his head to one side and took a moment to answer. "She's the head of Security at Willow Springs. Perhaps not the best at her job in light of certain events earlier this year, but I understand her specialty is old-fashioned law enforcement and brute force rather than technology."

That fit with what Diedre herself had told Tara. She'd said her failure to completely understand technology, and the slowness of Willow Springs in hiring someone who did, had led to breaches of the private community's security. One had happened while Tara was pregnant and visiting, the other when she'd lived there after Fimi's birth.

"You've never had dealings with Diedre?"

"I have not," Stranyero said.

"You didn't tell her to kidnap my baby?"

"I did not."

The light outside shifted, becoming grayer, and wind rattled the exterior windows. Chilled, Tara pulled the sleeves of her sweatshirt further down her wrists. "Could someone from the Brotherhood have taken my daughter without you knowing about it? By working with Diedre or separately?"

"Could they, if, hypothetically speaking, the Brotherhood did such things and if I were part of it?" Stranyero said. "It's physically possible, of course, for anyone to do anything without my knowledge. Would that happen? No." His tone was adamant, but a shadow flickered across his face.

"You don't look sure," Tara said. "People in your organization have gone off the rails before."

Stranyero's face reverted to faintly amused superiority. "You're referring to Cyril Woods and the things he's done out of his great love for you." His tone suggested how ridiculous he found the concept. "But he was at the chapel yesterday. He couldn't have kidnapped your child, and rest assured, no one with whom I'm familiar trusts him enough to enter into a plot with him."

At least Stranyero confirmed the unlikelihood of anyone plotting with Cyril. Tara wanted to trust Cyril completely, to feel sure he'd reached the end of the line with the Brotherhood. But the Order had once been the only thing that mattered to him, and Stranyero the only person he believed in.

"Why would anyone kidnap her?" Tara said. "You must have an idea, perhaps a better one than I do, about what she means for the world given your interest in her from Day One."

"The most logical deduction is that something about that letter of yours shows she is valuable. To someone."

Tara opened her mouth to say that the baby had been taken while the letter was still being translated, and that it seemed to say more about her than her daughter. But she stopped herself. Stranyero should have no way of knowing if the document had been made whole, or that it was a letter rather than some other type of document, and there was no reason to give him information he might not already have.

"Why do you say that?" Tara said.

Stranyero sighed. "Let us be candid with one another, Ms. Spencer, as candid as we can be under the circumstances. I know Cyril joined with your stepfather in trying to recover part of an ancient document. They then met you, Dr. Sophia Gaddini, and your sister at the cloister, a former chapel in Pennsylvania that, so far as I'm aware, none of you knew existed a month ago. So I conclude that Cyril obtained what he sought, and that other pieces of it were brought there by you, or perhaps hidden there, or both. Your child being kidnapped around the same time may be a coincidence, but certainly you must consider that it is not."

Tara's head ached as she struggled with what to tell Stranyero and what not. There was no way she was revealing the letter's contents, but he obviously knew it existed.

"I've considered it. But you just laid out the timing. A kidnapping requires planning. So nothing actually written in a document that was in separate parts of the world until yesterday could have triggered it."

"You're certain this was planned? It wasn't someone, such as Ms. Hartman, taking advantage of the situation?"

"What situation? The baby was at my parents' house in St. Louis. How could a document that hadn't yet been translated create a situation there?"

"That depends what it said. I can't help you if you don't give me that information," Stranyero said.

"I am so very far from convinced that you want to help me."

"I don't want to, not for your sake personally," Stranyero said. "But I do want to know who took your child to try to understand how she relates to my life's work, if she does."

"I could trust you more if you told me what your life's work is," Tara said.

"And I could trust you more if you told me whether you found all the sections of that document and what it said. Clearly there are some things we won't be sharing with one another. But let me ask you this. You were a college student."

"I still am." Despite the circumstances, Tara clung to her plan to finish college and eventually attend medical school, no matter how far down the road that had to be.

"Did you ever take a business course? An introduction to business at least?"

"No." Tara's major was molecular, cell, and developmental biology. It had allowed her to learn about cancer biology.

"I suggest you do so at some point. It will aid you in understanding the world."

Tara closed her hands into fists and looked at the clock over Stranyero's head. "If you have nothing to tell me, I'll go. I have another visit to make before my flight home."

Tara had been surprised to learn from the State Police that while Alma's visitors were restricted in the psychiatric ward where she was being held, Tara was the only person Alma had placed on her approved visitor's list.

Stranyero leaned forward. "This is my point: the first and most crucial goal of any organization is to perpetuate itself. This is true of every organization, be it a non-profit dedicated to feeding the poor, the Roman Catholic Church, or a pharmaceutical company. An organization can't do anything unless it continues to exist. So if I were instrumental in an organization, that would be my primary goal. Now that the birth of your baby is a *fait accompli*, an organization such as the one you imagine the Brotherhood to be would have nothing to gain by making you and she martyrs. Just the opposite, we'd be guaranteeing you widespread attention and perhaps devotees. But others may not feel that way. Your baby may affect whether many entities continue to exist, not only the one that you believe I'm involved in, or whether they are destroyed.

"Think of that when you think about who might have taken your child."

In the tiny waiting area beyond a set of locked double doors, Tara emptied her pockets and gave everything, including her wallet and phone, to Pete. "I'd feel better if I could come in with you," he said.

"There'll be guards," Tara said. "Alma won't be able to hurt me."

A month before, Alma had approached Tara's family in St. Louis claiming that she, like Tara, had found herself pregnant and hadn't known how it happened. She'd had a copy of a scrap of paper with writing in ancient Armenian, which she said she'd gotten from someone who belonged to the Brotherhood of Andrew. So Alma had been allowed to come to the cloister. Once there, she'd tried to harm Tara. Her plan had failed, and the police had arrested her for the attempt.

Tara walked quickly along the hallway. It had gray walls and industrial gray carpet and led to a second set of locked doors. She was buzzed into a windowless ward. At the back of the large main room, a man and woman in dark blue scrubs stood at a nurse's station. To their right, a uniformed guard was stationed at a standing desk.

Visitors in street clothes sat at small round tables with patients who wore gray sweatpants, green sweatshirts, and thick hospital socks with treads on the bottom. No shoes. A long-haired girl who looked to be about sixteen sat alone on a couch in a corner. She had bandages around her wrists. Despite looking less prison-like than Tara had expected, if people with depression came to this ward for treatment, she couldn't help thinking it wasn't much of an atmosphere for helping them feel better.

Tara wrapped her arms around herself, suppressing shivers. Her dad could be right. Engaging with Alma might only fan the flames of whatever resentment she had toward Tara, and the likelihood that she'd share anything was slight. Like Stranyero, she'd probably been advised by a lawyer to say nothing.

Alma entered through the interior door beyond the guard's desk, wearing the same types of clothes as the other patients, but hers were maternity. She was stick skinny other than her midsection, looking thinner than she had yesterday, though Tara couldn't imagine she'd lost weight in less than twenty-four hours. Maybe it was because she and Tara had both been bundled in winter clothing when they'd last seen each other. Alma's shoulder-length hair hung loose and wavy, and she looked younger than nineteen.

She grabbed Tara's hands. "You've got to get me out of here."

"I've got to get you out?" Tara stepped back, and Alma didn't let go. Tara took a deep breath and struggled to stay calm. Lashing out in anger wouldn't make Alma more likely to talk.

The guard shifted as if to intervene. Alma let Tara's hands drop. "I don't belong here. I'm not crazy," she said.

"I don't know that."

"You know why I'm here." Alma dropped into one of the padded vinyl chairs.

Its wooden legs shook. "I answered the police detectives' questions about why I did what I did and now they think I'm crazy. You can identify."

Tara's parents had believed she was mentally ill early in her pregnancy, when she'd kept insisting she didn't know how it had happened and then had started talking about the Brotherhood of Andrew. "Except I never tried to kill anyone."

"Neither did I," Alma said. "That was a test."

Tara sat, too, scooting her chair back to keep a few feet between them. "A test you had to figure I wouldn't survive." Alma had shoved Tara into an underground cave and blocked her in so the only exit was through a cavern full of rattlesnakes.

"But you did," Alma said. "Raphael told me you would if you were telling the truth about having had a miracle pregnancy. You insisted you were telling the truth. So there was no risk to you."

"That's not how I remember it." Tara suppressed the urge to argue about what Alma had believed and said when she'd put Tara in danger. All that mattered was Fimi. "But I'll try to help you if you'll answer my questions. Do you know where my baby is?"

After glancing at her phone a second time to be sure she hadn't missed any messages, Sophia Gaddini circled the bracketed ellipses on her handwritten copy of the translation and stared at each in turn, tapping her pen on the wooden table. The symbols indicated missing portions of the letter and could radically alter its meaning. She wished she had someone to verify the translation. Sister Mary Paul, the older former nun who'd done it, had been shaken by the words, and Sophia wondered if her emotions had influenced her choices. With a document this old and tattered, translation was as much art as science. Nuance and context mattered. But Sophia doubted Tara would feel comfortable putting the original in anyone else's hands, and her own grasp of ancient Armenian was limited.

She wrapped her overlong cashmere sweater more tightly around herself. The cloister's main room, with its hardwood floors, couches, and bookshelves, usually looked and felt warm and inviting. But today, gray morning light filtered down from the skylight, and the wind rattled the stained glass windows and seeped in through fissures in the building's aging concrete walls.

Sophia opened a tome on Armenian history she'd found in the cloister's library. She lacked the types of investigative skills that might help find the baby, but she knew how to research. She was halfway through the earliest Armenian version of the story of the serpent, Satan, tempting Eve in the Garden of Eden when a bell shrilled. She waited a moment, expecting one of the women who ran the cloister to appear. But Mary Paul had been worn out by the previous day's events and had gone back to bed after an early breakfast, and the other two women had driven Tara's sister Kelly to the airport.

A few key clicks on the computer hidden in the nearest cabinet gave Sophia a view of the ice-covered path outside that led to the cloister's double doors. A tall, broad-shouldered man stood there. He wore an expensively cut distressed leather jacket and driving gloves. His Stetson hat partially obscured his face, but his height, the set of his broad shoulders, and the squared chin made her think of Erik Holmes. Her pulse elevated. She'd known the billionaire businessman by another name during the two months they'd dated. But his distinctive way of carrying himself remained the same.

She flipped over her legal pad to hide the translation and laid the book on top of it. The bell shrilled again. Smoothing her hair and straightening the pearl clip that held it at the back of her head, Sophia hurried toward the vestibule. She didn't know how Holmes had found her. On Sophia's advice, which she'd tried to give objectively, not based on her feelings about his deceptive behavior, Tara hadn't told Holmes that the last part of the letter had been located here. Or that this former chapel existed at all.

But perhaps Holmes had seen the news footage of the shooting the day before, realized Sophia must be here, and come to offer his support. Eager to see him, she pushed open one of the heavy outer doors.

Holmes took off his hat. His eyes looked weary, with shadows under them, and his blond hair, threaded with silver, looked barely combed. Sophia had never before seen it anything but perfectly swept back from his face.

"Holmes," she said. "What is it? You look terrible."

He stepped inside. "Is Tara here? I must see her."

"LAST I KNEW she was at your parents' house," Alma said.

"But yesterday you said you saw messages. Between this person Raphael, who'd told you to test me, and someone else, messages that suggested my baby had been kidnapped," Tara said.

Alma shrugged. "I made it up. To get you to come close to me, to look at my phone. So I could do what I did."

"Did Raphael tell you to say that?"

"No. I just figured it was the best way to distract you."

"So there were no messages you saw about a kidnapping?"

"No."

"Could I see your phone?" Tara said.

"The police have it. I deleted the history anyway. So I wouldn't get Raphael in trouble."

"And you never met him in person? Raphael?" That was what Alma had told Tara's sister Kelly, but Tara wanted to be sure.

"I never did. He contacted me after I met with other men from the Brotherhood of Andrew. He wanted to help me. Unlike my family or anyone else."

"Help you how? With money?"

"Yes."

"And you didn't find that strange?" Tara said.

Alma sat straighter and put her hands on her hips. "You accepted money from Erik Holmes. Is that strange?"

Tara opened her mouth to say that was different, but she couldn't think of any reason why it was. Wealthy businessman Erik Holmes had come into Tara's life only months before, setting her on the trail of the ancient document. He'd wired her funds to travel and to hire security guards when she'd had to send Fimi home to her parents' house. She hadn't known much more about his motives than Alma did about the Brotherhood's when she accepted his help, and she still didn't.

"Could Raphael be the gunman?" Tara said. "The one who brought the rifle to the cloister?"

"There's no way," Alma said. "He'd never try to kill anyone."

"Are you sure? You hardly know him."

"You don't have to meet in person to know someone." Alma folded her arms and rested them on the swell of her stomach. "I answered your questions. Now you need to help me."

"I already told the police about my pregnancy." Tara jiggled her right leg under the table. "And all about what I know about the Brotherhood. That supports what you told them. I don't know what else I can do."

"Not testify against me," Alma said.

"What?" Tara said.

"No, you can testify to what I did. But promise you won't say you think I'm crazy."

"No one's going to ask my opinion. If they do, I can honestly say there's nothing you've said that I believe is delusional."

Tara asked whether Alma knew the man who'd brought the rifle to the chapel, or Stranyero, or Erik Holmes. She didn't. And she wasn't sure if Raphael had always contacted her from the same email or phone number.

A patient and visitor at the table beyond Alma were hugging. The clock over the door showed only a few minutes left.

Tara stood. "If Raphael contacts you again, will you let me know? If you can find a way to do that?"

"If he says it's okay."

The guard approached, motioning to the door.

"Please, Alma. I'm looking for anything that'll help me find my baby, and maybe he knows something. Something he didn't tell you."

Alma nodded, her hair swinging around her face. "I'll tell you if he contacts me, but not what he says, unless he says it's okay."

"Did he ever ask you to bring the baby to the chapel?"

Kelly had told Tara that Alma kept insisting they should take Fimi to the chapel, and Tara wanted to know why.

"I told you, he never said anything about her. Weren't you listening to me?"

"Then why did you want the baby to come to the chapel?" Tara said.

"Because I thought you should never let her out of your sight. Bad things would happen."

~

"She's not here," Sophia said. She kept her tone calm, but her heart had sunk at Holmes' question, and she felt foolish that she'd imagined he'd come to see her. When they'd last been together, they'd agreed to set aside their personal relationship, including whether they still had one, to concentrate on helping Tara. Apparently that was where Holmes intended to keep things.

He unwound his gray tartan scarf but made no move to enter the cloister's main room. "Is she nearby?"

"Before I tell you that, tell me why you've come," Sophia said.

"There's something important I need to tell the police, and I want to tell Tara first."

"The police? About the baby's kidnapping?"

The instant she said it, Sophia realized that was unlikely. If Holmes had information about the kidnapping, he'd more likely talk to the St. Louis police. But he had vast resources, and, aside from the Brotherhood's people, he was the only person she knew of connected with Tara who might be able to orchestrate removing both Fimi and Diedre. She didn't want her hurt feelings to influence her suspicions, but she couldn't ignore the possibility.

Holmes drew back. "No. Why would I know anything about that?"

"You are one of the people who appeared from nowhere, insinuated yourself into Tara's—and my—life, and learned a great deal about the baby," Sophia said.

"You know me better than that."

"I never even knew your real name when we were seeing each other."

Holmes shook his head. "I used a different name—pretended to be another person—but I never behaved like anyone other than who I am."

"How can I know that? How can Tara?"

He reached for her hands. He still wore his gloves, so she felt only the leather, still cold from outside.

"You're suspicious," Holmes said. "I would be as well if the situation were reversed. And I want to answer your questions. But my time is so limited. If Tara's not coming back soon—"

"Not for at least an hour. Probably more than that, given the travel times."

"I can't wait," Holmes said. "I need to see the police, then be in Delaware by late afternoon."

"Delaware?"

"An emergency board meeting. I had one of the corporate jets fly me in so I could stop at an airfield an hour from here. But it was foolish, and I've cut the schedule far too close."

Sophia let go of Holmes' hands. She'd known the man before her as an adjunct professor with a small income from a struggling antiques business. Not someone who had access to private corporate jets. Plural. Or who attended corporate board meetings. Nothing about their relationship had been based on reality.

Holmes opened the door. Gusts of frigid air swept in. "Before I go, will you at least tell me, did the document get pieced together?"

Sophia did her best to keep her expression blank. Instinct told her not to share anything with Holmes that he didn't already know. While that might have more to do with how he'd treated her personally than with any threat he posed, she'd learned the hard way there was no such thing as being too cautious. "I don't know what you mean."

Holmes sighed and let the door swing closed again. "Sophia, I'm the one who sent Tara to the mosque in Istanbul. I was with you in Florence. I know some type of ancient writing exists. Logic tells me that your efforts, and those of her father and that Cyril Woods character, and the women here at the chapel, all have to do with that."

"If you want to know what Tara and I were doing, or what anyone else did, you'll need to ask Tara."

Holmes drummed his fingers against the side of his thigh. "What if I tell you what I was going to tell her? Trade information for information."

Sophia crossed her arms over her chest. "I'm not bartering. It's up to Tara, not me, what of her affairs to tell you about. If you want to share with me, that's fine, but I won't reciprocate."

Holmes studied her for a moment, then said, "I have information about yesterday's shootings."

She put her free hand to her stomach. She hadn't seen the actual shootings from her vantage point among the trees, but she'd heard the shots and seen the aftermath. Cyril Woods bleeding and wounded, the gunman who'd invaded the chapel with the side of his head blown away. "It was horrible. I'm grateful Tara survived. And Kelly, thanks to Cyril. I'm grateful we all survived, but it was horrible."

Part of Sophia's ministry when she'd been a nun had been to counsel convicts and ex-convicts, so she'd known the dark side of humanity. But she hadn't experienced it firsthand until she'd begun helping Tara.

"I'm sorry," Holmes said. "You've suffered a lot of loss since becoming allied with Tara, seen a lot of carnage."

He stood with his hands at his sides. Two months ago, he would have put his arm around her, and she would have welcomed it. But two months ago, he'd been a different person. To her at least.

"Not nearly as much as Tara has," Sophia said. "So what do you know about yesterday?"

Holmes' face grew paler, and his eyes shifted downward.

Sophia touched his elbow. "Erik, what is it? What's wrong? You've turned white."

"It's my brother," he said. "Henrik. I had no idea he had any interest in Tara, in any of this."

"Henrik?" She'd read about Erik's brother, his fraternal twin, who'd taken over as the Holmes & Company CEO after Erik had stepped down. Henrik Holmes sought out the press as eagerly as Erik Holmes avoided it, and he was known as a bit of a ne'er do well. But she'd never heard anything worse about him. "What do you mean?"

"My brother is the man who came here yesterday to try to kill Tara," Holmes said. "And now he's dead."

# 4

As they got into the rental car in the hospital parking lot, Tara felt an almost physical need to get home to her parents' house. Her heart insisted if she could only walk through the door, she'd find her daughter there, though she knew in her head it wasn't so.

Her phone beeped with a text message from Sophia.

"Erik Holmes came to the cloister," Tara said. "To see me. But he couldn't wait for us."

Pete unlocked the car doors. "He flew here?"

"Sophia sent a link to a news story she said explains it."

They both got into the car. Tara held her phone between her and her dad and they watched, arms pressed together, transfixed as the scene from the day before played. Cyril dove in front of Kelly a second before the man with the rifle fired. Tara braced herself, not wanting to see again what happened next. But the screen froze on the gunman. He was dressed in camouflage, clutching his rifle. Intense eyes stood out in a pale face that looked paunchy around the jawline. A sense of familiarity nagged at Tara. Before she could search her memory, the news station superimposed a photo of what at first appeared to be a different man. He slouched at the edge of a roulette table, wearing an expensively tailored sport coat with a collared shirt, no tie, and jeans, diamond rings sparkling on his fingers. Stacks of gold and black chips lined the table in front of him. When the camera zoomed in on his face, Tara's mind clicked, perhaps because of Sophia's message. Absent the puffy jawline and shadowed eyes, subtracting what appeared to be an extra decade of aging, the man looked like Erik Holmes.

The sound had been turned off. Pete hit the volume button before replaying it. The news anchor said, "The alleged assailant at a small former chapel known as 'the cloister' in the Appalachian mountains in Pennsylvania has been identified as billionaire Henrik Holmes, CEO of H.E.R. Holmes & Company. His reasons for being at the cloister are unknown, as is why he allegedly shot at Kelly Spencer and Cyril Woods. Authorities declined to comment on whether they believe a connection exists between the events at the cloister and the kidnapping of Spencer's daughter, Sophia Fiona Spencer, which occurred late yesterday afternoon.

"Erik and Henrik Holmes are best known as the heirs of Stephen Holmes, who died over a decade ago. No one in the Holmes or Spencer families could be reached for comment."

"Henrik Holmes," Tara said. "What would he—play the beginning again. Just the first sentence."

After listening to the intro twice more, Tara said, "H.E.R. Holmes. Henrik, Erik, and—Raphael?"

"If that's true, no wonder Holmes needed to talk to you," Pete said.

AFTER STOPPING BRIEFLY at the cloister to gather their things, Pete and Tara drove to the airport. Traveling from Altoona, Pennsylvania, to St. Louis involved three plane changes, so it was after nine p.m. when they reached Tara's parents' house in Rock Hill, Missouri. The kitchen smelled of crisp bacon and butter. Her mom and siblings had made Tara's favorite dinner, which was breakfast: French toast, bacon, and scrambled eggs with Jack cheese. Tara drowned her French toast in pure maple syrup, something she loved but the family rarely bought because of its price. Her brother Nate had stopped and gotten it on his way from his apartment to the family home. The hugs from her siblings and mom helped Tara feel a little less frantic. After dinner, she spent half an hour in the living room talking with her family before closing herself into her dad's home office to call Holmes. She hadn't been able to reach him by telephone, but he'd texted her that he could talk on a video conference.

Normally clean-shaven, his face showed a shadow of stubble along his chin, and his eyes were bloodshot. But the light gray shirt under his charcoal suit jacket was starched, and his blond hair swept back from his face in perfect order.

"Sophia told you?" Holmes said.

"About Henrik? Yes. And I saw the news footage." Tara opened her mouth to ask Holmes why Henrik would come after her, and whether it was connected to the kidnapping, and what he'd known about his brother's activities. But she paused. Holmes' brother was dead, and that was terrible. She knew how it felt to lose a sibling. "I'm so sorry, Erik. For your loss."

"Thank you." He ran his hand over his hair. "I saw it happen in real time. Through the TARA2 game."

TARA2 was an alternate reality game based on Tara's life that had been started by an unknown game designer soon after Tara had given birth.

"Oh. Oh, no," Tara said. "That had to be awful."

"I shouldn't have been watching while driving, but I had it on in the background. I hoped it would help me learn if you and Sophia were somewhere safe. I pulled over when I realized one of the men fighting was my brother."

"And you saw him shot."

"Yes."

"I'm so sorry."

"I never knew he had an interest in you," Holmes said. "Never knew he held strong beliefs about anything. I don't understand it. Can't understand it."

"There's something I wondered based on the newscast. It'll seem like a weird question, but did Henrik ever use the name Raphael?"

Holmes blinked. "Raphael? No, not that I know of."

Tara sensed something more. "But?"

Holmes took a deep breath. "My father did. He was deeply religious. A fanatic, my mother called him."

"So why Raphael?"

"My father converted to Catholicism a few years after he and my mother married. My mother was Jewish, and my father pushed her to convert. To the extent of showing a complete lack of respect for her beliefs and heritage. He viewed her as a heathen. Called himself the 'Raphael' of our family, an angel opposing the 'demon' of disbelief. After they divorced, she was denied visitation because he fabricated charges that she'd abused us."

"That's—intense." Tara's mom had converted because she'd thought it would help her fit better with Pete's family, but he'd never pushed her to do so or shown a lack of respect for the religions of others. "And the 'R' in H.E.R. Holmes?"

"You're correct. It's for Raphael. But whether Henrik used the name—I don't know."

"You really had no idea he was coming after me?" Tara said.

"None. He knew I was interested in you, that I thought your pregnancy was an event that would change the world. But he expressed disdain for all things religious. That's how he reacted to our father's obsession—he walked away. From religion, from all but a figurehead position in the family businesses, from me."

Tara couldn't imagine any of her siblings walking away from her. Even when her parents had doubted her, her sibs never had.

"What about my baby?" Tara said. "Do you think Henrik was involved in her kidnapping?"

Holmes shook his head. "It doesn't seem logical. If his goal was to destroy you, why go through the trouble of kidnapping the baby? Far more likely Diedre Hartman acted on her own or for someone else."

"Someone else?"

"When I heard last night about the kidnapping, I engaged private security specialists," Holmes said. "Diedre Hartman's spending over the last three years appears out of proportion with her income. Not surprising, given her mother's worsening illness and need for care, but there's no apparent source of that income. She didn't remove funds from her retirement account, she didn't take a second job, she didn't have any freelance occupation that the team could find a record of."

"Three years ago," Tara said. "That's before I became pregnant."

"But not before the Brotherhood became interested in Willow Springs. The Order has followed the community from its inception decades ago."

"So Diedre was working with the Brotherhood of Andrew?"

"Possibly. Also, in the event you're concerned, I've given the police an account of my whereabouts at the relevant times with documentation. They contacted me."

"I had to tell them about everyone who might be involved," Tara said.

"I'd expect no less. I'm assuming you also told them about the Brotherhood."

"Yes. And I talked to Thomas Stranyero myself yesterday. He was no help."

Holmes' head reared back. "You talked to Stranyero? Whose idea was that?"

"My dad wanted Cyril to talk to him, but Cyril suggested me."

"You confided in Cyril Woods," Holmes said.

"I figured he'd have the inside track on the Brotherhood."

"Perhaps too inside." Holmes frowned. "I'd like to help you in any way I can. First, by visiting Willow Springs to see where Diedre Hartman lived and worked."

"Don't you have a lot to do with your companies with Henrik gone? Not to mention arrangements?"

"I can work anywhere. The larger question is, would the community allow me access?" Holmes said.

"I doubt it. Unless—maybe if I were there, and you came to see me."

"Are you willing to go there?"

"I—yeah, I can. Once the police are done with me here."

Some of the tension in Tara's midsection eased. With Holmes' resources, they'd have to be able to find Fimi soon, and traveling to Willow Springs would help her personally learn something about Diedre and why she'd taken Fimi, if she had. The last thing she wanted was to simply sit home hoping someone else located her child.

They talked a few more minutes until Holmes signed off to take another call. Tara sat in her dad's creaky office chair, arms wrapped around herself, longing for the warmth of holding Fimi. Between Holmes, herself, and the police, they'd find her. They'd have to find her.

THE BABY CHATTERING nonsense syllables woke Diedre Hartman. She unfolded from the couch in the sitting area of the small hotel suite she'd leased. It wasn't the Ritz, but it had French doors from the bedroom alcove to the sitting area, which featured the type of traditional-looking furniture her mother had once loved. If her mother was going to die—and Diedre was determined she would not—it wouldn't be in a nursing home surrounded by the stench of urine and disinfectant that prevailed no matter how expensive or well-staffed the facility.

Nor would it be in the rundown 450 square foot studio apartment Analise Hartman had rented when her house had been foreclosed upon. No longer able to work, Analise had been forced to go onto public aid, something she'd been too embarrassed to do until she lost everything. She'd refused money from Diedre for anything beyond necessities. Only when she'd been completely unable to manage had Diedre been able to step in. She'd never told her mother how she'd gotten the money to pay the exorbitant cost for experimental drugs or later for the hotel suite. Regardless how Diedre's views of the world had changed over the years, how she had changed, she wanted her mother to keep seeing her as the same young woman she'd so proudly sent to the police academy. Fortunately, her mother never asked, perhaps believing Diedre's ex had finally come up with all the money he owed her.

"Mom?"

No answer. Diedre rushed into the bedroom. Her mother lay asleep in the hospital bed, chest rising and falling. Diedre's own breath released in relief.

Analise Hartman looked smaller and thinner this morning than she had the night before. Her mother had never been large—all Diedre's bulk and height came from her dad. But her mother had been vibrant and unforgettable due to her determination and genuine love for others. Now she looked skeletal.

Diedre fed and changed the baby, then pulled a chair close to the bed, sat with the infant in her lap, and grasped her mother's hands. "Let's say a prayer, Mom."

It was the best way Diedre had come up with to explain what she was trying to do. And her mother's failing short-term memory offered one bright spot. Diedre could suggest a prayer every half hour and her mom, once so sharp and vital, wouldn't realize she'd done the same thing already multiple times.

"All right." Analise Hartman was only sixty-eight years old, but her breath had the dry, slightly sour smell Diedre associated with her grandmother before she'd died.

Diedre shut her eyes. In the video of the healing in Istanbul, the infant, though held upright between Tara's arms, had kept her eyes closed and stayed almost completely still, breathing evenly and deeply like a person meditating or in some sort of trance. Diedre hoped the relative quiet would help her reach a similar state. The suite was far from the elevators, so the only sounds were occasional doors slamming and voices. Diedre had called the hotel staff to tell them not to send housekeeping for the next two days, and she'd told the hospice workers she'd handle her mother's care from today on. If all went as she hoped, she and her mother would be gone soon, and the baby taken care of without anyone having seen her with it.

Diedre tried not to think about how thin a thread she'd hung her hopes on. Many believed this child had power. If she did, oh, if she did, Diedre could save the one person who mattered to her. After that, she didn't care what happened to her. Or the child.

~

Detective Willis, a tall African-American woman with grayish-white, short-cropped hair, strode into the small square room in the St. Louis County Police Department. Its Division of Criminal Investigation was handling the kidnapping investigation. Willis had a medium build and wore a navy blue pantsuit that looked almost like a uniform. Emerald-green-rimmed glasses framed her eyes. After introducing herself, she told them the police had found a last known residence for Diedre Hartman's mother, Analise Hartman, in Topeka, Kansas.

"Was she there?" Tara said.

"Neighbors said she moved out a month ago."

"Forwarding?" Pete said.

"It was a month-to-month sublet. Cash. So the lease was in another person's name." Willis sat across from both of them, laptop pushed to one side. She flipped to a police report in her paper file, ran a finger under a line, and looked at Tara. "I see here you refuse to identify your child's father."

"There is no father." Tara was used to skepticism from police, but her daughter's life was at stake. There wasn't time for the detective to get sidetracked. "I spent hours with the police in Pennsylvania on these questions yesterday."

"I'd like to hear it firsthand."

"I was involved with my high school boyfriend for years, well into my third year of college. We never had sex because I didn't want to risk pregnancy at least until I got my degree. Then I discovered somehow I was pregnant anyway. I've been tested psychologically, I've had medical tests done, I've seen specialists. And no one has ever explained how it happened or what it means."

"You understand why we keep asking?" Willis said. "In this type of situation, the most likely person to have taken the baby is the father."

"This type of situation?" Pete set his coffee down so hard it sloshed over the table. "There is no 'this type of situation.' You can't waste time grilling Tara about a father who doesn't exist. What about Erik Holmes? His brother tried to kill Tara. And the Brotherhood—those people have been after her ever since she became pregnant."

"We're following every lead." Detective Willis handed Pete a napkin to clean the coffee. "The best way you can help is to answer my questions."

After half an hour, the detective moved on from the subject of Tara's baby's paternity. She advised them that so far the alibi of Tara's biological father, or at least the man Tara had always believed was her biological father, checked out. She then asked questions about every other member of the family.

Tara found it almost impossible to stay seated and to answer politely, but she made herself do it. This woman was her best hope for finding her daughter.

"Let's move on to Willow Springs," Willis said. "I know next to nothing about the community other than that it's where Ms. Hartman worked and lived. It's a secretive place, apparently. A type of commune?"

"No." Tara wasn't sure what the exact definition of commune was, but she knew it implied some sort of joint ownership or pooling of resources. "The land is owned by its founder, Nanor Kerkorian. She's a pastor who started it as a haven for battered women. I don't know that it was secret exactly, but it certainly wasn't publicized. Now it's more of a general women's community. A place centered around women, where they can live peacefully."

"And exclude men."

"Yes. I mean, men can come into the community, just not live there, other than underaged children of women who are residents. Is it important, that it excludes men?"

"Hard to say what's important at this point. So when a boy turns eighteen, he's out?"

"I don't know. I guess. I only lived there for two months. And I was a little preoccupied, worried about taking care of my baby, keeping her safe." Making an effort to focus on the questions and answers, Tara struggled to ignore the tightness in her chest and stomach and to stop jiggling her leg under the table.

"So you don't know much about the community," Willis said.

"Just what I saw there. And what the founder—Nanor Kerkorian—and her granddaughter Kali told me. Nanor rents trailer homes to women who want to live there, or land to those who have their own trailers and want to move in. It makes it an affordable place to live. Nanor put a lot of her personal resources into a community center everyone can use. Women with all types of professions live there. Doctors, architects, horticulturists."

"And security personnel," Willis said.

"Yes. The community's pretty isolated. And because it started for battered women, Nanor didn't want to depend on outsiders. So she hired a security person."

"Diedre Hartman."

"I don't know if she was the first, but she's been the Security Head a long time."

The detective bounced her pen on the scarred conference table. "There can't be a whole lot of work for most of the women who live there. The nearest town, Blue Springs, Arkansas, is small."

"Some have jobs elsewhere and drive quite a ways. Some work from home. Some are semi-retired. Like the doctor. She was a surgeon, then became a general practitioner, then moved to Willow Springs to practice part time. She grows vegetables, too, and sells them in town."

"How did you learn of Willow Springs? Through Diedre Hartman?"

"No. I got a letter from Kali Kerkorian. She'd seen a news article about me. She wrote to me that her aunt had also said she was a pregnant virgin. In the 1960s. It caused family issues like the ones I had, and then she—the aunt—was killed in a car crash while she was still pregnant. Nanor founded the community in her honor."

Tara's throat tightened. Learning of Maya Kerkorian's death had been disturbing enough, but she'd later learned from Cyril Woods that three other women before Maya had claimed to be pregnant virgins. All had been killed before giving birth. One had been burned at the stake.

"So Nanor took you in," Detective Willis said.

"In a way," Tara said. "She believed my baby would be the reincarnation of her unborn granddaughter."

Willis raised her eyebrows. "You agreed with that?"

"No. But she wasn't scary about it or anything. She understood I could have a different interpretation of what was happening to me. She offered me a safe place to be no matter what I believed."

"Except it wasn't safe." Detective Willis scanned the papers in front of her. "Your baby was kidnapped the first time when you were living at Willow Springs."

"Yes, when she was two months old. It was the first time I went out without her at night. I got her back within days."

"And this Kali Kerkorian was babysitting her at the time."

"Yes." Tara felt uneasy about where the conversation seemed to be heading. "Kali was hurt very badly. She had nothing to do with the kidnapping. I felt awful about having left her in harm's way." Not only did it upset Tara that anyone would suspect Kali, it was a waste of time. The police needed to focus on people who really might have taken Fimi.

"And you also were attacked the first time you visited Willow Springs."

"Yes. No, not attacked. But two men broke in. Men from the Brotherhood."

"And Diedre Hartman was head of Security at Willow Springs when that happened?"

"Yes," Tara said.

"And you ended up dating one of the men from this Brotherhood who broke in. Cyril Woods."

"Dating isn't exactly the word I would use."

Detective Willis sipped coffee from a reusable Starbucks cup. Tara's and Pete's drinks had come from a vending machine that dispensed small paper cups with poker cards printed on them. "What word would you use?"

"It's complicated," Tara said. "But I didn't get involved with Cyril because he broke in. That's not how I met him. He contacted me first."

"Before breaking in?" Detective Willis said.

"Way before that. He came to me when I was pregnant and said my baby had a mission in the world. Might be a messiah."

"And you believed him."

*She thinks I'm a complete and total idiot*, Tara thought. *Or incredibly gullible. Or crazy. Or all of the above.*

"Not at first, no. But it meant something to me that he believed me. No one else did. About my not knowing how I'd become pregnant, and about not having had sex."

"How did he find out you were pregnant? Had you told a lot of people?"

"I'd told my family, my boyfriend, and my best friend. That was it. But Cyril was part of this organization, the Brotherhood of Andrew. They were tracking signs, looking for a new messiah and monitoring places where a virgin pregnancy was foretold to happen. Cyril was sent to check me out."

"So he was stalking you."

The detective's words sent a queasy, cold feeling through Tara's stomach. Sitting in this police station at a long table under bright lights and hearing the detective's questions, Cyril's past betrayals flooded her mind. But between literally taking a bullet for Kelly at the cloister and everything he'd done before that to help her dad track down the Armenian section of the document, she'd come to feel she could trust him. To believe he really was doing everything in his power to make up for how he'd acted in the past. It was the detective's job to be suspicious. That didn't mean Cyril was truly dangerous.

"Not in a threatening way," Tara said. "He was trying to protect me." She knew she sounded as if she'd deliberately gotten involved with a man who stalked and attacked her. But she couldn't help that.

"Except eventually he did threaten you, right? And worse. He's been arrested more than once for harm to your family."

"Yeah, that's true."

"Are you involved with him now?"

"No." Tara felt that was accurate. Her conversation with Cyril hadn't ruled out or defined any specific type of relationship.

Pete shifted in his chair. "Cyril himself clearly didn't kidnap Fimi yesterday. We were with him."

"There are a lot of moving parts," the detective said. "Where is he now?"

"I tried calling him on the way here, and he's not in the hospital anymore," Tara said.

"Did you try his cell phone?" Detective Willis asked.

Before Tara could answer, her phone buzzed. She half-expected a message from Cyril, as if talking about him could manifest it. Instead, she'd been sent a photo of Fimi in an infant seat, wearing her bright blue sleeper.

# 5

Her mother looked no different. Her graying hair still sparse, her skinny arms and elbows poking out over the sheets, her face emaciated. And now the infant was crying. After feeding and changing her, Diedre tried again. When nothing happened, she nearly shook the baby in frustration. "What's wrong with you?"

"What, honey?" Analise Hartman said.

"Nothing, Mom, just trying to compose my mind," Diedre said. She'd sent the photo of the baby hoping it would help her settle her qualms about stealing the child, but it had been a foolish thing to do.

"Just pray, sweetie. God always listens."

Sure. That was why Analise Hartman, who volunteered at the local homeless shelter and had served on two non-profit boards was dying while third-world dictators lived well and prospered. That was why Diedre's dad had been killed by a car thief he'd foolishly confronted on the street when Diedre was ten.

Diedre forced herself to sit still and breathe. Her heart rate slowed, her muscles relaxed. The sunlight filtering through the blinds warmed her shoulders and face. Peace settled on her, a feeling she associated with the time before her mother's diagnosis. Before she'd ever dreamed of taking money to spy on the people at Willow Springs, which was the only place she'd ever truly felt at home as an adult.

A beep and a click, like a latch releasing, sounded from the sitting room behind her, but Diedre, absorbed by the calm and buoyed by her hopes, never heard it.

~

Detective Willis returned to the conference room and handed Tara a printed copy of the photograph.

"Your phone is being passed on to the FBI, whose IT people will try to pinpoint where the photo was taken. It's likely the location feature on whatever phone was used was turned off, though."

Tara sat forward in her chair. "The FBI's involved?"

"Kidnapping is a federal crime. If they believe there's sufficient justification to expend their resources, they step in. They've done so here. Starting this afternoon."

"That's good, right?" Tara said.

"They have a lot of resources," Willis said.

Pete peered at the printout. Fimi sat in a baby carrier that rested on a mauve carpet with dark green edging. Behind her were what looked like curved chair legs with a mahogany finish. "It looks like a hotel room in the background."

"Quite possibly," Willis said. "Unfortunately, that doesn't tell us much."

"Some chains have distinctive color schemes." Pete studied the photo, tracing a finger across the carpeting. "I travel a lot for business. I've seen this pattern."

"In the U.S.?"

"Yes," Pete said. "It's not a Klimpton—they go for edgy, modern décor. This could be a Sheraton. Or Marriott or Hilton. Upscale enough for business travelers but not so much so that families can't afford it."

"I'll pass that on. It might help." Willis clicked a few keys on her laptop.

"The text offers some hope I'll get Fimi back soon, doesn't it?" Tara said. "The message says the baby will be returned when her work is done. That suggests it is Diedre who took her, and she plans to return her."

The detective folded her hands in front of her. "Could be. Or someone else might want us to think that. Keep us focused in the wrong direction."

Tara's heart sank. It had occurred to her that someone else might have sent the text, but she'd wanted to believe it came from Diedre.

"What's this 'work' referenced in the text?" Willis said.

Tara sipped her hot chocolate. It tasted too sweet and had turned lukewarm, but it gave her an extra moment to phrase her answer as best as she could. Detective Willis clearly hadn't believed her about her pregnancy, she was hardly going to believe Fimi had supernatural abilities. "Have you heard that my baby has—may have—the power to heal people?"

"The officer who spoke to you last night reported that you believe that."

"I don't know exactly what she does, or we do together, and I'm sure it will sound crazy to you."

Tara had already decided to leave out that she might be able to heal without Fimi. She'd had no idea that was possible until two days ago, when in desperation she'd tried to heal herself from rattlesnake bites and a broken ankle and had finally succeeded. She hadn't told the police in Pennsylvania because she knew they would never believe it. Now, having omitted it, she felt she couldn't tell anyone, not even Cyril or her dad, or they'd be in a position of knowing something the police didn't should the case against Alma go to trial. It couldn't relate to Fimi's kidnapping anyway because no one knew about it.

"But?" the detective said.

"But more than once when someone has been injured, I've sat with Fimi in my arms and put my hands on that person and there's this feeling. This peace, energy flow, I don't know how to describe it. And the person spontaneously recovers." Hearing it aloud, it sounded ludicrous to Tara, but she didn't know how else to describe it.

"So you told Diedre Hartman this?"

"No. But my best friend Kali—the one who lives at Willow Springs—is one of the people who was injured badly and was healed, and Diedre knew that. Also, a bystander recorded Fimi and me—mostly Fimi—during an earthquake two weeks ago where something similar happened and posted it. You can't see that much, but there are two paragraphs also posted describing what happened."

"That your baby healed a boy."

"That's what it says."

The detective asked for and noted the website where the video had been posted. "So an unlimited number of people could have seen that. Not just Ms. Hartman."

"True. But Diedre knew about the Willow Springs experience, so she'd have reason to believe the video was accurate, not some type of scam," Pete said.

Willis leaned back in her chair and looked at Tara over the rims of her eyeglasses. "Was it a scam?"

"Of course not. I didn't post that video, I didn't pass the hat after it happened. I knew what happened with Kali, so I tried to help a little boy. He recovered, and he and his mother were very grateful. I wish it hadn't been on video, but it was. And Diedre might have seen it, so what difference does it make if you believe I'm telling the truth or not?"

"But why would she take only the baby?" Detective Willis said. "Assuming Ms. Hartman believes these are real healings and not some sort of trick, both involved the two of you, not just the baby. If it were my mother, I'd hedge all my bets. She had to know she'd be found out anyway."

"Tara and the baby haven't been in the same place for some time," Pete said. "Men with swords came after her and her sister and the baby in Istanbul. After that, she sent the baby home to my wife, where guards could watch her."

"Why not go home with her yourself?" Detective Willis asked. "Why would you let her out of your sight when she'd been taken from you once already?"

Tara swallowed hard. "At the time, it seemed like the best thing to do. I had a lead on someone in Florence who could help me find out about what happened to me, why all this happened, what the baby's purpose is. And I thought that finding that out, in the long run, would make life safer for my daughter and me. Because I can't have her live her whole life in danger. And in the short run, with people coming after me, trying to kill us both, I felt sure she'd be safer at home with my mom."

Willis hit a few more keys on her laptop. "Two men with swords came after you in Istanbul?"

"Yes." Tara pressed her lips together, remembering the scene in the street.

Things had only gotten worse since then, and she was afraid to imagine what the future held for her child. When she'd been pregnant, she'd seen the *Pieta* in the Vatican and had felt a terrible kinship with the sculpture of the young-looking Virgin Mary holding the body of her dead son on her lap.

"And Erik Holmes stepped in. Drove in," the detective said.

Tara pulled her thoughts back to the present. "That's right."

"And ran one of the men down?"

"Yes."

"There's no official report of that incident that we were able to obtain."

"It happened," Tara said. "I don't know if Holmes filed a report. I don't know exactly what he did. I passed out. But he saved me and my sister and baby."

"So you sent the baby home?"

"Yes, with my sister. And I carried around this fake baby, a realistic looking doll, hoping if anyone was watching me from a distance, they'd think she was still with me. And we had private security guards at my parents' house, but Diedre must have fooled them."

Tara's hands shook, and her dad moved his chair close and put his arm around her. "You made the best choice you could at the time," he said. "You don't know what would have happened if you'd kept her with you. Or if you'd flown home, for that matter."

"Maybe," Tara said.

"Back to Diedre Hartman," Detective Willis said. "Why wouldn't she wait for a chance to take you as well?"

"If her mother was reaching the end," Pete said, "Diedre probably couldn't wait for an opportunity when the two of them were together."

"And she has good reason to believe I don't have any power to heal," Tara said. "My youngest sister died from cancer. If I had that power, Diedre had to know I would have healed her." It had been the worst thing that had happened in Tara's life until now.

"And you didn't have the baby then."

"No."

*But I was pregnant,* Tara thought, her mind spinning into a loop it had traveled many times before. The thought woke her regularly during the night, except that now her anxiety over Fimi had replaced it. What if she'd had the power to heal Megan and hadn't known it? But she couldn't do anything about that, and going over it again only drained energy she needed to get Fimi back.

"Also," Pete said, "the people who have been after Tara have always focused on the baby, not on her. It's like the Virgin Mary. There are no stories of miracles she performed while she lived, only Jesus."

"So we're talking about Christian scripture and beliefs?" Willis asked.

"Muslims believe Mary and Jesus existed, too," Tara said. "But not that either is divine. But I don't know if any of that has anything to do with me. Or with the kidnapping."

"So you don't believe you're like the Virgin Mary?"

"I don't," Tara said.

When Cyril and the Brotherhood had insisted her baby would be a new

Christian messiah, Tara had thought them delusional for more reasons than she could count, including that she wasn't religious. On learning her child would be a girl, the Order had reversed its position, but Tara still had found the whole situation almost impossible to comprehend. One day she'd been a college student holding off on sex so nothing interfered with her plans to apply to med school, the next she'd been pregnant and the target of religious fanatics. The only part of it all that had been good was Fimi. And now Fimi was gone, and there was a letter suggesting Tara had something to do with the Antichrist.

She did her best to answer the rest of the questions as quickly as she could so the detective could move on to whatever else she needed to do to track down Fimi.

At the detective's direction, Tara answered Diedre's text, saying, "Please don't hurt my baby. Please return her safely as soon as you can."

She got no response.

# 6

"Nothing here tells us anything about her." Tara stared at the neatly hung jeans, khakis, tank tops, and long and short sleeved T-shirts in Diedre's closet, then shut the folding doors. She'd asked to come to Diedre's trailer house on arrival at Willow Springs.

"It is spartan," Nanor Kerkorian said.

The seventy-six-year-old Willow Springs founder stood in the narrow doorway between the bedroom and main living area. She wore a deep orange and red wrap dress, and her salt-and-pepper hair lay in one long braid down her back.

"Diedre only lived in Willow Springs since her divorce five years ago," Kali Kerkorian said. Like her grandmother, she had long hair, but hers was black and thick. Her eyes had the same brightness as Nanor's. "Before that, she lived an hour away and drove in each day."

"Did the police take anything?" Tara said.

"No." Kali slipped past her grandmother and over to the kitchenette, where she started a kettle of water boiling. "They were more interested in cell phones, laptops, that type of thing, and she kept none of that here. We found photographs of her and her mother in her office. That's as personal as it got."

Tara looked through the cabinets and found boxes of cereal and pasta and canned food. The refrigerator contained orange juice, fruit, and two packages of wilted salad leaves. The freezer was stocked with meat and frozen vegetables.

"It doesn't look like she expected to be away permanently," Tara said. "Maybe the kidnapping was spur of the moment. A crime of opportunity." The idea made her feel better, made it seem more likely Diedre had seized Fimi in the hope that she could help her mother, but would return her no matter what happened.

Nanor settled into the rocking chair near the gas fireplace. The flame inside the iron grate burned blue and yellow. "I do not think so. She planned. She drugged your family. She had the means to do so with her. It is something I should have foreseen. The break ins, the security lapses. I believed the Brotherhood so clever to get into Willow Springs, to get around the measures Diedre and her new assistant put in place. It never occurred to me that it was she who was weak."

"Erik Holmes thinks she's been working with the Brotherhood," Tara said.

"That appears likely," Nanor said. "Perhaps she begins that way, she steps past propriety and law that way, for money, then it seems easier to her to take another step, one to more directly benefit herself."

Tara edged around the rectangular glass coffee table to sit on the couch. The Willow Springs trailer homes were built to be solid but small. When residents needed more space, they gathered in the open, comfortable areas of the Community Center or the cozier libraries and coffee rooms there, all of which were available to everyone for free. Tara liked the idea in theory, but after three hours of flight time and half again as long in Kali Kerkorian's car, she would have liked room to stretch.

A sweet, spicy caramel flavor filled the air as Kali handed around mugs of tea. Then she sat cross-legged on the sofa and linked her arm with Tara's.

"How would you feel about Erik Holmes meeting me here?" Tara said. "He's trying to help find Fimi, and he'd like to see where Diedre lived and worked."

Nanor's gray and black eyebrows raised. "He suspects the community is involved in the kidnapping?"

"Maybe. So I understand if you don't want him here. But I'd feel a lot more comfortable meeting him here than in a restaurant in Blue Springs."

The town was small, its largest diner having only ten tables. Nothing said in public would be confidential in any way.

"Invite him," Nanor said. "I am curious about Mr. Holmes. And it is possible he can help."

"You're sure you won't tell us what the letter said?" Kali asked. She'd inquired on the drive from the airport but had let the topic drop when Tara refused.

Tara shook her head. "I'm sorry." She glanced at Nanor, who was frowning. "Holmes asked about it, too, but I'm kind of overwhelmed. I don't know if I should share with anyone who didn't already hear the translation. I feel like I can't even think about it until Fimi's back."

Kali squeezed Tara's hand. "You'll get her back. You will."

Tara swallowed hard. "I hope so. I have to."

On the plane to Arkansas, she'd longed to reach the women's community, sure being with the people she loved there would help her stay calm and focused despite her anxiety over Fimi. But so far it had agitated her more. On her arrival, she'd been shocked to find every fourth or fifth trailer home empty. No children's scooters or toys on the lawns, no curtains on the windows. As recently as two years ago, there had been a waiting list to live at Willow Springs.

"And your young man?" Nanor said. "Where is he?"

"Cyril?" Tara sipped the tea. Its smooth taste made it easier to swallow past the lump that had been in her throat since hearing Fimi was missing. "He discharged himself from the hospital. Against medical advice, but he insists he's okay."

"And you trust him?" Nanor said. "Now that he helped bring together this letter that you will not share with us?"

"I do. At least, I trust him to tell me if he changes his mind about me, but I don't think he will." Tara took a deep breath. Nanor obviously wasn't happy about not being informed about the letter's contents. And now Tara had to ask another favor. "I know it's a lot to ask, given his history with the community. But I'd like to put him and Holmes together. Here."

Nanor rocked her chair a few times. "An interesting plan," she said. "You will tell them both in advance?"

"No," Tara said, "I don't think I will."

"Ah." Nanor nodded. "You do not trust your young man so much after all."

"With Fimi missing, I can't afford to trust anyone."

"Take care of it." Holmes cut the connection and pulled his rented BMW back onto the road to drive the last half mile. He disliked talking while driving, it distracted him, which was why he usually used a car service when he traveled on business. He sat in the back and worked while someone else drove. But he'd wanted a vehicle under his own control while at Willow Springs. He had no reason to fear for his safety in the women's community; he simply had no desire to stay once he'd accomplished his purpose. With Henrik gone, the Holmes & Company responsibilities shifted back to his shoulders. Though not quite as many as one might have expected. Despite all the ways he'd been in the dark about his brother, he'd been correct in one assessment. Henrik hadn't been spending his time on the business. The second and third in command at the company had been doing all the work. Fortunately, Holmes had chosen both of them, which made resuming his old duties less difficult.

As he came around a curve in the road, Holmes saw the brick wall that surrounded the motor vehicle parking lot for Willow Springs. He pulled directly in front of the security camera mounted above the gate. Tara had told him the wall and the barbed wire atop it had been added after the first break in by two Brotherhood members, one of them Cyril Woods.

Once he'd been admitted, Holmes parked at the spot a uniformed guard indicated, then followed her through another key-coded gate to an interior lot filled with golf carts. His plan for complete autonomy was stymied when she refused to allow him to take a golf cart on his own.

She drove him through the woods on dirt trails barely wide enough for passage. The trees thinned when they approached a creek that ran along the edge of the residential area. Ignoring his buzzing phone, Holmes once more ran through in his mind what he planned to share with Tara. He'd decided to be as open as possible, though it embarrassed him to admit how oblivious he'd been to his brother's activities. He'd been fooled by his own vanity. Always priding himself on how much smarter, more accomplished, more refined he was than his twin. Never considering that Henrik might be hiding under a careful disguise. Though perhaps someone else had manipulated Henrik, taken advantage of any one of his vices. But it seemed unlikely. Money did not buy everything, but it did buy insulation from many troubles the rest of the world faced. If Henrik had been manipulated it had been by someone subtle, someone who could reach him emotionally, not through threats or danger.

And then it might have been the other way around. Much as he didn't like to admit it to himself, let alone to Tara, perhaps Henrik had been the one pulling strings. Perhaps he'd kept tabs on Holmes and interfered deliberately. Henrik might have had no interest in the end-of-the-world scenarios the two of them had been raised upon but simply have acted based on sibling rivalry. Childish for a thirty-five-year-old man? Of course. But who was to say Henrik had ever outgrown childishness? And now he never would. For all that they had argued and vied with one another, Holmes had always hoped one day he and his brother would truly work together or connect. He'd sensed inside Henrik a stronger, wiser man waiting to emerge. Perhaps he'd been wrong about that, too.

All that he planned to share with Tara. And, more important, he hoped to use it to persuade her to trust him again, and to convince her the next steps he planned were the right ones.

The guard parked outside a sprawling one-story brick building. Holmes was ushered through an entrance hall, past a community notice board, and into a rectangular room with a honey-colored hardwood floor, a coffee bar, and floor-to-ceiling windows on two sides. Outside in the garden, tulips struggled through a layer of topsoil and bushes were just starting to green.

The room was deserted, other than three people gathered at its far end. Tara looked thinner than when Holmes had last seen her. Her jeans and gray cardigan hung on her. Across from her stood a short elderly woman wearing a flowing violet and mauve dress.

She must be Nanor Kerkorian, the community's founder. She had black and gray hair twisted into a bun on the back of her head. Next to Tara, but not touching her, stood a young man wearing black jeans and an ironed white T-shirt. His crew cut emphasized his sharp cheekbones, and despite favoring one leg, he stood with his back ramrod straight.

Holmes' jaw tightened. That last thing he'd expected was to find Cyril Woods here. Or anywhere with Tara. The former Brotherhood member or aspiring deacon or whatever the younger man presented himself as today was the biggest existing threat to Tara and her baby.

As he crossed the room and held out his hand to introduce himself, Holmes reevaluated everything he'd planned to reveal.

# 7

Tara, across from Nanor, kept her hands wrapped around a mug of Wild Sweet Orange tea. She'd felt cold since learning Fimi had been taken, and the hot drink helped with that and made her feel marginally less jittery, as did the scents of dark roasted coffee and powdered donuts in the air of the social room.

"What have you learned?" Holmes said. He and Cyril eyed each other across the round table. Even sitting, it was clear the CEO was taller than Cyril, and his sturdier build, expensive jeans, and tweed blazer made Cyril look wiry and scruffy despite his pressed T-shirt and jeans.

"Not much," Tara said. Her efforts during her two days at Willow Springs had left her feeling she was grasping at straws. "I talked with Diedre's coworkers and friends and neighbors."

"You alone? Or with Cyril?" Holmes said.

"Me alone. Cyril just got here an hour before you."

"And what did they tell you?" Holmes said.

"Diedre's mother was diagnosed three years ago with breast cancer, had a double mastectomy, and still the cancer came back. Nothing was helping. Her mom also had a series of small strokes."

Holmes sipped his seltzer water. "And does she have other family?"

Nanor shook her head. "Diedre's an only child."

"And she's divorced," Tara said, "and no one knows if she had cousins or aunts or uncles who might be helping her care for her mother. Or if she had friends outside the community."

"Her ex-husband hasn't heard from her in years," Cyril said. "I stopped to see him before coming here."

"So," Holmes said, "Diedre Hartman worked here twenty-plus years, and no one knew anything about her."

"We respect people's privacy here, Mr. Holmes," Nanor said. "Diedre preferred not to speak at length about herself. Still, I am not happy with myself for not seeing into her heart. I thought I had become wiser and less gullible with age. Now I find that is not so."

"There are people who fool everyone, Mrs. Kerkorian." Holmes' eyes flicked toward Cyril.

"What have *you* learned?" Cyril said.

Holmes shifted toward Nanor, his elbows resting on the table's edge. "I'm afraid I've invaded your privacy, Mrs. Kerkorian, but I hope you'll agree it was done for a good cause. I had my IT experts attempt to penetrate your security system, given the breach that occurred earlier this year. When he—" Holmes gestured toward Cyril— "and his colleagues broke in."

"Those weren't my colleagues," Cyril said. "I followed them to try to stop them."

"Regardless," Holmes said. "What's interesting is that we found no serious deficiencies in the system. In fact, my consultants tell me Willow Springs appears to have been well defended from a technology perspective for many years. The flaw, as is many times the case, was almost certainly human."

"Diedre," Tara said. Her stomach churned. If Diedre would leave a whole community of women, some who'd come to Willow Springs specifically for protection from battering partners, vulnerable, who knew what she might do to Fimi. Especially if the baby couldn't perform a miracle on command.

"I believe so," Holmes said. "It's also possible she was the one running TARA2, the alternate reality game, and using it to track you. Especially as the game is now shut down, which suggests its designer accomplished its purpose."

"But Diedre lacked advanced computer skills," Nanor said.

"So she told you. A perfect way to keep anyone from suspecting her," Holmes said.

"If she did run the game and track Tara," Cyril said, "then it's likely she also helped your brother find Tara."

Holmes shook his head. "I've found no evidence of ties between Diedre Hartman and my brother."

"But you said she might be working for the Brotherhood. If Henrik was a member, that's a connection," Tara said.

"If he was, he never told me. But perhaps Mr. Woods can tell us about that. Given that he met with his old mentor yesterday. That's the reason he checked himself out of the hospital early, whatever else he was doing. So he could catch Thomas Stranyero at the airport before he left the state."

"I know," Tara said. Cyril had told her about it on his arrival. In normal circumstances, she might find Holmes' ability to track people unnerving, but with her baby missing, she felt grateful for his resources. "Stranyero made him an offer. Us an offer. To allow us to research in the Brotherhood's archives."

"What good will that do?" Holmes said.

"We can look for information about any people or organizations that might be focused on the baby," Tara said. "The Brotherhood has materials not available anywhere else."

"You'll never be allowed to look at anything truly useful," Holmes said. "You're wasting your time."

Tara's stomach dropped. Holmes had hit on her one fear about the offer. She appreciated Cyril's attempt to use his connections, but success with it didn't seem likely. Still, there was nothing more for her to do at Willow Springs, and going home meant doing nothing but waiting and worrying.

Cyril squared his shoulders. "You seem to know a lot about the Brotherhood. What's your source?"

"Research," Homes said. "I was raised on end-of-the-world scenarios. My father believed the end times would come in Henrik's and my lifetimes, and we'd be faced with a choice. Join the Catholic Church and fight with it against the Antichrist, which he believed would rise this decade or next, or perish."

"Your father talked about the Antichrist?" Tara's whole body tensed. Cyril must have thought of the letter's words as well, for he shook his head slightly at her.

"Obsession with religion often, I find, goes hand in hand with obsession with evil," Holmes said. "I disagreed with my father, but outwardly I toed the line while striving to learn enough to prove him wrong. I read the same Andrew of Crete prophecies the Brotherhood claims to be devoted to. When Tara began getting so much publicity, I suspected her child might be the one to whom the prophecies refer."

"But not as a second Christ," Cyril said.

"No, and the Brotherhood never believed that of her either, no matter what you were told. It fears her child will be a messiah, but one that undermines Christianity."

"No one suggested that to me," Cyril said. "Ever."

"Of course not. You're too low in the Order," Holmes said. "And you were a true believer. No one tells true believers the truth. It tends to dim their zeal."

"Do you believe the Brotherhood still poses a danger to Tara and her daughter?" Nanor said.

"I do. Which is why I'd like Tara to move to one of the hotel complexes Holmes & Company owns." He turned to Tara. "I can guarantee your safety, and that of your child, once she's recovered."

"Go into hiding?" Tara said.

"Why not?" Holmes said. "Willow Springs isn't safe. The baby was stolen from your parents' home. And while I'd like to think Thomas Stranyero isn't planning to harm you if you go to the archives, do you want to bet your life on that?"

DETECTIVE SERGEANT LORETTA WILLIS exited the elevator of the Marriott Suites hotel in Oklahoma City at 5:15 p.m. The tip hotline had received a call that morning that a late model gold Jeep Compass—the type of compact SUV

Diedre Hartman had been driving—with a license plate covered in mud had been spotted about five miles away the night before, merging onto the John Kilpatrick Turnpike. Based on Pete Spencer's observation about the carpet, the FBI had narrowed the hotel chain in the photo to a Marriott. Coordinating with the Oklahoma state police, Willis had directed calls be made to hotels in the Marriott chain within a twenty-five mile radius of where the Jeep had been seen. The calls had led to this hotel, this crime scene. The result might mean bad news for Tara Spencer. Certainly it was bad news for someone. For Willis, it had at least provided her an excuse to step out of a deadly dull department meeting. She'd learned during her decades in law enforcement to appreciate what pluses there were.

A patrolman stood outside the door to Suite 604. No sounds came from inside. The evidence techs had finished hours ago.

"Anyone enter the room other than law enforcement?" Willis asked the patrolman.

"Only the manager who originally opened the door. She entered with a key card, turned on the lights, and backed out. No prints were found anywhere but the main light switch."

No one with the last name Hartman had registered at the hotel. But the detective who'd followed up on the phone calls had learned that two hotel guests checking out that morning had complained that a television had been playing day and night for two days in a sixth floor room. That had prompted the manager's actions.

*Tolerant guests*, Willis thought, wishing some of the people she dealt with were that easygoing. She nodded her thanks to the patrolman and stepped inside. A faint layer of dust from the fingerprinting covered the dinette table in the sitting room, which was deserted. The French doors to the bedroom stood half open, showing crumpled sheets on an empty hospital bed. Clear tubes still ran to the IV tree on the window side of the room.

Willis had seen photographs of Analise Hartman retrieved from Diedre Hartman's office at Willow Springs. She looked to be a happy, healthy woman in her mid-sixties. Her coworkers said the photos were at least three years old, so the elder Ms. Hartman had not yet been diagnosed with cancer.

The dead woman from the hotel crime scene photos had sunken cheeks and eye sockets, and she looked thirty pounds lighter and a decade older. All of which could certainly be the effects of the disease, the strokes she'd suffered, and her treatment. The woman lay on her back in the hospital bed, one arm resting on top of the blanket, palm open. Her long silver hair looked carefully brushed. Willis didn't see any obvious signs of violence, but only the medical examiner would be able to say how the woman had died.

Willis stood near the empty bed longer than she needed to. She saw far worse deaths in her profession. But her own mother was probably not more than ten years older than the woman who'd died here. It was far too easy to imagine herself at her mother's bedside. She was the one her mother counted on, the only daughter and the only one of her siblings who lived in the state.

At the desk, which also was covered with dust, Willis reviewed the reports submitted so far. No diapers, toys, or baby supplies had been found in the search of the suite. The bedroom closet had contained a carry on sized bag with a password-protected laptop inside. A puzzle for the IT people. Several clean nightgowns that likely belonged to the old woman hung there. A box with what looked like morphine drip bags sat on the floor.

The desk where Willis sat held no papers other than hotel information and instructions on the morphine pump.

Had the Spencer baby been here or not? Because no fingerprints had been recovered, even if DNA identified the dead woman as Analise Hartman, that question might never be answered.

TARA PRESSED her back against the door, heart racing. She'd stepped into the restroom to take a call from Detective Willis, leaving Holmes and Cyril to continue sparring with one another under Nanor's watchful eye. "There's no sign of my daughter in the room?"

"No. And no fingerprints at all, so it's impossible to say if Diedre Hartman was ever here, though housekeeping did receive a call from someone to say no service was needed, and someone put out the Do Not Disturb sign."

"What name was the hotel room reserved under?"

"That of a woman who died two years ago."

"Do you think Diedre was there? With my baby?"

"There's simply no evidence either way, unless or until testing shows DNA matching one or the other of them. We're searching for Diedre Hartman's SUV."

Tara cleared her throat. "It's good that you didn't find—I mean, since if the baby was there, she obviously wasn't able to heal Diedre's mother—at least I'm relieved that if she was there—" Tara stopped, unable to say the words.

"I understand, Miss Spencer. Yes, that your baby isn't here leaves open the possibility that she is still alive and well and with Diedre Hartman."

"Yes," Tara said, relieved Detective Willis, too, avoided saying "dead," as if somehow speaking the word could make it reality. Her hands shook, and the phone nearly slipped from her grasp. She felt a wave of sadness for Diedre's mother, at the same time worrying about how Diedre might react since the baby hadn't done her "work" of healing. Perhaps Diedre would abandon her somewhere where she could be easily found.

"I'll call you as soon as we learn anything more," Detective Willis said. "For now, don't tell anyone about this. We're attempting to keep it—one moment, I've another call."

The line went silent. Unable to stand still, Tara set the phone to speaker and rested it on the sink counter. She took a few breaths to calm herself, checking in the mirror to see that she didn't look too distraught, as that would prompt too many questions when she returned to the social room. Her eyes appeared too big, and her cheeks too hollow. She avoided looking at her hair, which had reddish-brown highlights now and was pulled into a ponytail. She'd changed it before leaving home, one of many versions meant to keep people from recognizing her. She never felt she looked like herself anymore, despite that she had no strong sense of how she ought to look. It had been so long since she hadn't been worried about being recognized.

"Miss Spencer?"

Tara grabbed the phone. "Yes, yes, I'm here."

"A patrolman found Diedre Hartman's vehicle."

"Vehicle? But not my daughter?"

"No, not the baby. But Diedre Hartman is inside."

"What did she say?"

"She's dead, Miss Spencer. Diedre Hartman is dead."

The room whirled around her. Tara lurched to the wall and pressed one hand against it. Whether Diedre had taken the baby in the first place or not, Fimi was gone, the best hope of finding her vanished. And Diedre Hartman, the tall, muscular redhead who'd seemed so strong and sure of herself, was dead.

"Miss Spencer?"

"I'm here. What—what happened?" Tara said.

"A gunshot wound to her left temple. A revolver was found near her. It may be a suicide. It may be a murder staged to look like a suicide."

"I see."

"Miss Spencer, I apologize, but again I need to instruct you to say nothing to anyone about this. We can't keep it quiet for very long, but I would like whoever has the baby to believe we're still searching for Diedre Hartman."

"Yes. Yes. Okay. No sign at all of the baby?"

"Nothing the officers who found the vehicle could see. We're having the evidence techs go over it. I'll let you know once they're finished."

"All right. Yes. Thank you."

Tara made her way back into the social room. Nanor stood leaning forward, her hands on the round table, saying something to both men. Tara couldn't hear the words past the rushing sound in her ears, though her vision seemed hyper acute. Cyril and Holmes both stood as she approached.

Tara gripped Cyril's arm. "Call Stranyero. Tell him we'll be at the archives as soon as we can."

# 8

"I love a payday." Yongnian Fjord, who sat in the front passenger seat of the rented BMW, counted the bills in the brown envelope. "But this is a little light."

Marie Glaston kept her eyes on the expressway. She and Yongnian both wore jeans and polo shirts. To all outward appearances, and per their IDs, they were a young professional couple on a much-needed vacation from high pressure jobs. "It's what we agreed upon."

Marie preferred to work alone, but one person to handle a woman as strong and smart as Diedre Hartman as well as a baby wasn't enough. Yongnian had been in the trade a year less than Marie, and he exhibited far more confidence than she had. She couldn't decide if he was arrogant or stupid. Their career was a challenging one. He'd survived this long without a single arrest, as had she, so perhaps his arrogance was well placed, but it worried her. Stealing a baby from a kidnapper didn't trouble her morally, but the legal implications were greater than in any matter she'd ever handled. She usually dealt in property.

"But now that we know the deal on why this baby is in demand," Yongnian said, "we could get more at the end of the line."

Yongnian had a reputation of angling for more at every step, one of many reasons Marie planned to arrive in Rome without him. Being around the man for two cross-country drives had been enough. He was attractive, his mixed Asian and Swedish heritage giving him a beautiful complexion and compelling eyes, but within fifteen minutes of meeting him his personality had overridden his appeal. Plus he'd shunted the paperwork onto her, despite that she was the one who'd hired him. Rather than pushing back, she'd decided to create an insurance policy.

"I'm not renegotiating," Marie said. "I agreed to interrogate Diedre Hartman because knowledge makes us more prepared for any obstacles we might encounter, not to rachet up the fee. Besides, my clients are good payers. I don't change terms in the middle."

Not only that, she'd paid Yongnian thirty times the usual fee, an acknowledgement that this was a riskier assignment than most. Over the past five years, Marie had gradually shifted to operating inside the law, but now and then she still skated the edge. This time across paper-thin ice. But she'd dotted every I and crossed every T, and it would be worth it. The completion bonus was large enough that she'd be able to pursue her dream of becoming a legitimate antiques dealer. Something she hadn't even known was a profession when she'd fled home at the age of fifteen.

She signaled and eased into the right lane. She had a few miles yet before the exit to LAX, but she believed in acting ahead. She didn't want to draw attention by any last minute lane changes. Her speed stayed at a steady five miles over the limit to blend with the slower lane of traffic. Most criminals were caught on minor traffic violations. Why someone with contraband in a car drove with a broken taillight, she'd never understand. But as a defense attorney she consulted on occasion often said, most criminals weren't rocket scientists.

The baby started fussing in the back seat, and Yongnian turned and waved a shiny rattle at her. The infant smiled. She seemed to like him. But that baby seemed to like everyone. She was far too trusting for her own good. Still, Yongnian was good with kids. Marie felt tempted to rethink bringing him with her.

~

THE BROTHERHOOD'S archives smelled of musty paper and old wood, mixed with recently burned incense. Tara perched on a cracked leather couch in the only corner of the main room not crammed with bookshelves and library tables. Cyril sat next to her, and Stranyero across from them in a wingback chair with stuffing showing at one of the seams. Above him hung a more-than-life-sized painting of a river and woods that Tara felt as if she could walk right into. It reminded her of how she'd imagined the kingdom of Narnia, the magical land in the C.S. Lewis books. For a year after reading the Narnia chronicles, she'd checked the back of the closet in every one of her relatives' homes hoping to find a secret passageway to another land.

Now returning to a normal life seemed as impossible as a journey to Narnia. The last information from Detective Willis had been that no trace of Fimi had been found in the vehicle. No verdict yet on whether Diedre had been killed or had killed herself. Tara clung to the hope that Diedre had dropped Fimi off at a hospital or police station or rest stop and the baby had not yet been found or identified.

"I'm sure you've guessed the Brotherhood has its reasons for allowing you to come here," Stranyero said.

"You want something from us in return," Tara said.

She wondered if Stranyero knew about Diedre Hartman's death. It hadn't been on the news, and Tara had told no one. As angry and worried as she felt, her heart ached. If Diedre had been trying to save her mother, she'd used illegal methods, and she should have been punished. But she hadn't deserved to die.

"There are no strings on your use of the libraries." Stranyero crossed one leg over the opposite knee and leaned back. "Whatever your answer today, you are still free to research here as long as you like."

"But?" Tara said.

"I have other ideas about where the baby may be." Tara's heart rate elevated. Stranyero lifted his hand. "No, I won't tell them to you. They may lead nowhere, and if I pass them on, I've no bargaining chip. Even my compatriots here know nothing of them. But the two of you can't be everywhere, and the police, as I'm sure you'll agree, have a limited perspective. So I propose we collaborate. I will follow my leads, and you follow yours. If you find your baby, well and good, and we are done. I'll still have achieved one objective, which is that your baby is found and any suspicion around the Brotherhood, at least as to her kidnapping, ceases. And the publicity surrounding her and you ceases, at least for now."

Tara found Stranyero's candor a relief. When she'd first met Cyril, he'd seemed cryptic and out of touch with the world outside his own narrow one, and Holmes struck her that way as well. Stranyero seemed to find laying his cards on the table, at least to the extent he was willing to share, more efficient, which she appreciated. The less dancing, the more quickly she could figure out if anything here would lead to Fimi.

"And if you find her?" Tara said.

"First, our agreement must be confidential. I will tell no one, not even those in the Brotherhood. You will tell no one. Not the police, not your family, not the esteemed Dr. Gaddini. Or Mr. Holmes, for that matter."

"And?" Tara said.

"I will return her to you, in exchange for one thing."

Tara's pulse pounded in her temples. "Which is?"

Stranyero's mouth tightened and his nostrils flared almost imperceptibly. "A copy of that Armenian letter."

"He might have Fimi already," Cyril said. "He could have taken her from Diedre Hartman. Or paid Diedre Hartman to take her in the first place, and all of this is a ruse." They walked outdoors in a shopping area about five miles from the archives. It was mid-afternoon, so it wasn't crowded, but a few shoppers strolled into and out of the stores.

"If he did, he'd offer to exchange right now." Tara's knees shook, but she didn't want to stop to sit on one of the wrought iron benches. She worried too much about being overheard should the Brotherhood or anyone else have people following them, and moving kept anyone from being too close to them.

"He has to know I'd be more likely to agree if he could give her back to me today."

"True." Cyril frowned. "He'll make the document public as soon as you give it to him."

"It doesn't matter. Not if it gets me Fimi back. Besides, my dad'll find something, I know he will."

Immediately after meeting with Stranyero, Tara had called her dad to ask him to work with Sophia to try to find out what the letter truly meant. Or, if she were being honest with herself, to find something that showed it didn't mean what it seemed to. The word "Antichrist" frightened her, and she could only imagine how the public would react to it, but she couldn't let herself be sidetracked. Not now.

"He will. And you're right, you have to make the deal," Cyril said.

They veered around a turned-off fountain, its basin filled with dried leaves that must have been under the snow in the winter.

"If Stranyero found her," Tara said, "is there any chance he'd turn her over to the police regardless? Would the Brotherhood really keep a baby?"

"I doubt they'd keep her. But she's not that old, and infants aren't that distinctive looking. They could find a home for her where no one would ask questions."

"Right." Tara fought a wave of dizziness and nausea.

Cyril put his arm around her. "You could agree with Stranyero and renege once you get the baby back."

Tara shook her head. "I thought of that. But one way or another, someday what's in that document is going to come out. Too many people know about it already. And I plan for Fimi and I to live a very long time. This won't be the last time I deal with the Brotherhood or Stranyero. We might need to make deals in the future. So it's better to be straight with him, and I'm hoping that keeps him straight with me."

Cyril sighed. "You're right. But I don't feel good about what he might do with that translation."

"I don't either," Tara said. "We need to find her first."

Pete Spencer paused in the hall outside Dr. Sophia Gaddini's office. It smelled like plaster dust and old carpeting. He hadn't told her he was coming. He didn't want her to refuse his request, and it would be harder to do that after he'd driven five hours from St. Louis to see her. On the phone the day before, Tara hadn't said why the letter had become more important to her, but the quickness of her speech and intensity of her tone told him something had changed.

A student conference seemed to be winding to a close inside the office, so Pete held off on knocking.

"This looks like a new idea." Sophia's voice, alto and warm, but a little hoarse. It was five p.m. Maybe she'd been holding conferences all day. "The point of the conclusion is to summarize what you've already said, to synthesize it for your reader. Not to introduce something new. Save that for the next paper."

Pete leaned against the wall. Construction had slowed traffic on I-55 near the southwest suburbs, which meant what should have been the last twenty minutes of his drive had taken an hour and a half.

A thin young woman carrying an overstuffed backpack exited the office. Pete knocked on the doorframe, then poked his head in. The office was interior, with no windows, but the sunrise apricot walls gave it warmth.

Sophia saw him and stood, brushing her long black hair away from her face. Her eyes seemed a bit weary. "Pete. Is there news?"

He shook his head. "No, nothing. But I need your help."

"I've only about fifteen minutes before the next conference," Sophia said, but she gestured toward a silver Italian coffee maker in the corner. "Espresso?"

Pete nodded. The caffeine might make him jittery, but he could use help staying alert.

"Tara's gone off to research in the Brotherhood's archives," he said.

After handing him a small china cup of espresso, Sophia moved back behind her desk, and he took the visitor chair in front of it. Its seat was still warm from the student.

"She told me," Sophia said. "She wants us to focus on the letter."

"Yes," Pete said.

What he couldn't say to Sophia, couldn't say aloud to anyone, was that he worried nearly as much about the Armenian document he'd helped piece together as he did about finding Fimi. He'd stay in Tara's corner regardless, but what the words on the page might mean for her and his granddaughter haunted what little sleep he got. He'd been afraid to ask his pastor what he knew about the term "Antichrist" for fear the man might be connected to the Brotherhood. Starting at the other end of the spectrum seemed the most logical alternate route.

"I've been doing all that I can." Sophia gestured to a stack of books and reams of printed pages.

"Anything useful?"

"One phrase in the letter—'Peace I am, and because of me, war comes'—struck me as familiar. I found it in *Thunder: Perfect Mind*, a text considered by some to be one of the gnostic gospels. Which is of particular interest because the letter refers to the quoted lines as scripture, suggesting some believers in the seventh century not only were aware of that text but saw it as sacred."

Pete leaned forward. "That's good, right? It undercuts this idea of Tara or the baby as the Antichrist?"

"I don't know. *Thunder: Perfect Mind* is full of paradoxes, or what were meant to be paradoxes at the time. War and peace; the honored one and the scorned one; the whore and the holy one."

Pete suppressed a shudder. The words were far too close to insults that had been hurled at Tara when she'd gone public on a television talk show with her claims that her pregnancy was supernatural. And, on a more personal level, to what she'd told him Cyril Woods had said to her after the one and only time they'd slept together. While he believed Cyril regretted that now and had changed, Pete still hoped the romantic relationship between Cyril and Tara didn't rekindle. Tara needed someone stable, someone strong enough to stay the course if anything revealed about Tara and Fimi threatened his beliefs. And no father was ever going to warm to a man who'd slept with his daughter, then called her a whore.

"Who wrote it?" he said.

"Unknown. The author is thought to be a woman based on the text itself. If *Thunder* is meant to be her name, that suggests great power. In Greek myth and the Hebrew bible, the highest god makes its presence known on earth through thunder."

The idea of the highest god wasn't reassuring to Pete. He believed in only one God.

"Does it mention Satan? Or the Antichrist?" Pete said.

"The translations I've found do not. There are missing sections, but I've not seen any interpretation suggesting those concepts might have once been part of it."

"The Brotherhood archives might have something about that text," he said. "If you could join Tara, you might be able to help."

"Even if the Brotherhood would let me, which I doubt, I can't leave until the semester is over." The reminder beep on Sophia's laptop sounded, and she glanced at it. "I wish you'd called. I would have reserved time for you. Or at least tried."

"There's no one who can cover for you?" Pete said.

He hoped she wasn't so scheduled that she couldn't take time for his main purpose in coming here. He might be able to manage without her, but he badly wanted support in confronting the personage he most wanted to see in Chicago. It smacked of superstition to be so unnerved, but Catholicism, the religion he'd practiced all his life, wasn't that far from superstition in many ways. Its most devoted followers still believe in miracles, novenas, and patron saints.

"I've stretched the limit of covering," Sophia said. "When I flew to Florence to help Tara search for the letter section reputed to be there, people covered for me. When I stayed at the cloister in Pennsylvania with her, people covered for me. There's a point where the students need my input, and where the University expects me to do what I've been hired to do."

"I'm sorry. You've put so much aside for Tara, and you've suffered personal loss, and now I'm asking you to do more. But I'm deeply disturbed. About Fimi. About this letter. About everything."

"I'd put all my work aside if I could," Sophia said. "But I've been getting pushback from my provost about my absences, as well as the controversy surrounding Tara. Long term, I can be far more support for her as a full professor of religious studies at a respected university than as an unemployed former nun. But I'll keep researching. And I'll do whatever else I can from here in Chicago."

Pete took a deep breath. "There is something you can do. Here in Chicago, if you're willing."

The next student appeared at Sophia's door. "Give me a minute," Sophia said, then turned to Pete. "If you return in an hour and a half, I'll be free for the evening."

"I can tell you right now." Pete didn't want to wait. He was afraid he'd lose his nerve. "I want to visit a church. The Apostolic Church of Satan."

# 9

They'd agreed beforehand that if somehow they were separated, society being what it was, a woman alone with a baby would be less noticeable than a man in the same situation. Also, Marie, with her heart-shaped face, lightly freckled nose, and long light brown hair, had those all-American looks that breezed her through security lines. Yongnian was half-Chinese, not a target for the TSA by any means, but not as apple pie as Marie. She'd never been chosen for a security search except during the post-911 days when the TSA had been both extremely vigilant and extremely concerned about not appearing to do ethnic profiling.

Yongnian thought those had all been his insights.

Marie punched in answers to the standard travel questions at the kiosk and scanned her passport. Yongnian was at a kiosk down the line, brow furrowed as he tried a second time. He wouldn't think anything of it. The machines here were outdated and notoriously bad-tempered. At least three other customers cursed in various languages at the screens while Marie proceeded to the customs agent.

Papers stamped, she turned back to catch Yongnian's eye and made a move-it-along gesture as if irritated at him for his ineptitude with the machine. It wasn't hard to summon the expression. She only had to remember the way he'd ordered her about throughout the operation, as if he had planned it and hired her, not the other way around. She longed to dash for the gate, but better to make it appear she was trying to keep him in the loop.

He jabbed a finger toward the machine, then gave up and headed for the podium where a live agent was stationed to deal with computer issues.

Marie pinched the baby to get her squawling, though not hard enough to hurt her. She inched close to Yongnian's lane and raised her voice. "Honey, I need to change her. I'll meet you at the gate."

Yongnian nodded. He no doubt didn't like being separated, but he would understand the need to draw less attention rather than more.

Marie hurried through the terminal. The error on Yongnian's passport was one that would keep him from boarding this plane, but not one that would get him into trouble or prevent him from traveling at all. If he were the legitimate traveler the passport said he was, he'd get on the next plane and meet his wife at their hotel. But he wasn't, and he'd know Marie would never wait for him overseas. Snafus happened when dealing with airlines, these days more than ever. That's why a half payment was always made up front. Because his mind wouldn't let him believe he'd been duped, Yongnian likely would never consider that Marie had done this deliberately.

She stopped at a Starbucks. A pumpkin spice latte was her favorite reward for a job well done. She inhaled the rich coffee bean fragrance that permeated the air as she paged through the news on her phone, one eye on the baby in the carrier. An article about Analise Hartman's death and Diedre's apparent suicide appeared as the barista handed her the latte. Marie nearly dropped it.

Dead? Both Diedre and her mother? Marie sank into the closest chair. She read through the article, then through three others she found, mentally cross checking the times with everything she and Yongnian had done. It was Yongnian who'd checked the feeding and nutrition tubes before they'd left, Yongnian who'd secured Diedre Hartman to the chair, Yongnian who'd been last to leave the hotel room. She'd told him to knock Diedre out again and tie her more loosely so she could eventually get free but couldn't alert anyone too soon of what had happened even if she wanted to do that, which seemed unlikely. He was then to take the hotel's shuttle to the beautiful landscaped park in downtown Oklahoma City where Marie would pick him up. She'd left him to it while she settled the baby in their rental car, then driven to a shopping center, cruised through it, and circled back to get him. He'd been where he was supposed to be when she'd fetched him, but Marie didn't know if Yongnian had done any of what she'd instructed him to do.

Her hands shook and her head spun. She sipped her latte, hoping the sugar and warmth would calm her. Perhaps Yongnian had gotten separate instructions from the client. But no. Acid rising in her throat, Marie traced every contact she'd had with her client and with Yongnian. She didn't see any way the two could have connected. And she didn't see how Yongnian could have gotten an unconscious Diedre out of the hotel without anyone noticing. Diedre's mother must have died of her illness and Diedre, in her despair, killed herself. She could have had a gun in the hotel suite. Neither Marie nor Yongnian had searched it. There had been no reason to.

Marie sat straighter, fighting to keep down the sandwich she'd eaten during the last leg of the drive. Sweat slicked her whole body. She hadn't signed on for this. She'd never intentionally push someone to suicide or kill anyone. But if her role in the baby's kidnapping became known, a prosecutor would certainly argue that no matter who pulled the trigger, the death arose from the kidnapping, which was a felony. Which made Marie a murderer.

All her defenses and rationalizations regarding her life's work, and the kidnapping, were meaningless now.

Tara dropped her pen and rubbed her forehead. She and Cyril assumed they were being watched, despite that Stranyero had arranged for Cyril to pick up the keys and necessary codes for the archives at a mailbox center and never appeared personally. For once, Tara's bad college habits of cramming before exams helped her. She channeled her anxiety over Fimi into focusing on the stacks of books and pages around her, and she was able to read numerous documents and keep most of the information in her head with minimal notes. Those she did take used the types of abbreviations and acronyms she'd relied upon for her biology and chemistry exams. If there were video monitors, the series of abbreviations ought to mean nothing to anyone but her.

So far she'd found nothing suggesting the Brotherhood had taken Fimi, or that the Order would want her for anything. All the writings fit with what Cyril had told her when he'd first come to her and when he'd first abandoned her. They were looking for the birth of the next messiah, but that child was to be a boy, not a girl.

Across from her, Cyril's pen scratched across his notepad. He'd told her he found it difficult to recall without taking extensive notes. It was his habit to learn by handwriting, despite that few people he'd gone to school with had done things that way. So he combed the texts he'd figured were better known to the Brotherhood already for minor details that might give them some information, while leaving to Tara the more obscure texts. She tried to take her cryptic notes on numerous topics, including ones that didn't matter to her, hoping to further obscure what was striking her as important.

Except much of the time she had no idea what might be important and what might not, and with every minute that went by, she feared Fimi was farther and farther away. She checked her phone regularly to be sure she hadn't somehow missed a text. She saw when the articles about the Hartmans' deaths came out, and she couldn't help stopping to read the on-line comments, hoping someone would say something that would offer a clue. No one did.

"The police are doing that," Cyril said. "You don't have to."

"I know," Tara said.

"There's no reason to upset yourself more."

"I can't get more upset than I already am. People have been saying what a terrible mother I am since before I gave birth. Sometimes I agree." Tara stood and walked away from the table. "What if all of it has nothing to do with the Brotherhood, or anyone's views about how she came to be or what she means for the world, and we're wasting our time? Someone might have taken her for a completely unrelated reason. Someone who wanted a baby, any baby, and saw the chance to steal her from Diedre."

Cyril walked behind her and put his hand on her shoulder. "The police know how to track down those kinds of leads. This they don't know. So it's not a waste. We're covering all the bases. All right?"

Tara nodded.

The next morning they started in the back room with the tall black metal cabinets that held materials on the Middle Ages. In the first hour, Tara found something that turned her insides to ice. She forced her face to remain blank. She needed more modern information on the same topic, but she didn't want to make it obvious in case she and Cyril were being observed. So she turned to another file, one on a completely different subject. Her eyes scanned the words without seeing them, and she scribbled abbreviated, nonsensical notes in her spiral notebook.

"I WISH YOU'D RECONSIDER," Sophia said as she and Pete stopped at a *Don't Walk* sign. It was before eight a.m., but already women and men in suits and business casual clothes hurried toward their offices. "What Evekial Adame thinks of the term 'Antichrist' means nothing, nor does the view of any present-day believer regardless of creed. Not that I credit him with being a believer in anything, including Satan."

"What about you?" Pete said. He'd awakened that morning to the news of Diedre Hartman's death. He couldn't imagine any way in which that could be a good thing for the baby, and it made him more determined to follow any path that might lead to information about the letter, his daughter, or his granddaughter. "Tara told me through your studies you gradually evolved into an atheist. So what, or who, do you think caused her pregnancy?" He held his breath for her response. Underneath all his other worries, he struggled with doubt over whether Tara's pregnancy proved or disproved the existence of God.

"I don't know," Sophia said. "It doesn't fit any established scenario, given that Tara's not religious. Yet something caused it, and if I believe her that it wasn't natural, then it must be supernatural."

"And so?"

The light changed, and they crossed Jackson Boulevard.

"And so I don't know," Sophia said. "If it is supernatural, that doesn't say anything about one god or any god. There could be a force more amorphous than that."

"But not the Catholic God?" Pete said.

"I don't think so."

Pete sidestepped a puddle. He'd come to Chicago before for work and had found it to be one of the cleaner large cities in the world. But the temperature had spiked into the fifties during the last week, melting the snow that had piled throughout downtown since February. Its disappearance had revealed crushed beer cans, cigarette butts, and grimy fast food wrappers, giving the sidewalks a soggy, dingy look. Pete glanced at the bank buildings on his right, searching for a street number without success. "Did we pass it?"

"No," Sophia said. "It's twenty north on the grid. Madison Street is zero, and we haven't reached that yet." They paused for a car turning left and cutting off the crosswalk. "You're sure you want to visit this church? In my view, Evekial Adame is a charlatan, interested only in sensationalism and money."

"But he's specifically said his Church is waiting for the Antichrist, who will arise in Evekial's lifetime," Pete said.

"That proves my point. Most Satanists don't believe in God or the devil. They're atheists."

"But not all of them."

"No, not all," Sophia said. "But even many of the theists view Satan as a deity more concerned with benefits to humanity than is the god of Christianity, Judaism, and Islam. Whether you see those religions as worshipping three different gods or the same one, all demand obedience above all. Satan allegedly does not. Also, Satanists seek knowledge. God warned Adam and Eve away from the Tree of Knowledge; Satan urged them toward it."

"There are extremist groups in every religion, every philosophy," Pete said. "Calling someone the Antichrist is extreme. So Evekial Adame is exactly who I ought to talk to, not the Satanists you're describing. Especially since now it looks like Diedre Hartman may not be the one who took Fimi."

In the middle of the next block, they reached what appeared to be an alley but had a green street sign designating it Calhoun Place.

"No wonder you didn't remember it," Pete said.

Calhoun Place was barely wide enough to fit a single vehicle. On both sides of it, tall brick buildings with black metal fire escapes zigzagging up and down them blocked the sunlight. The street ended in a loading dock.

"Apparently Evekial doesn't want to attract attention to the actual physical location of the church," Sophia said.

They turned and walked into the gloom. Sophia shone the flashlight from her phone on three plain dark gray doors in succession. The third had the street number they sought stenciled on it. She pressed the buzzer.

Pete shifted from one foot to the other. He agreed with Sophia's assessment of Adame's showmanship and of Satanism generally, but anyone who believed he had malevolent powers because of an evil supernatural being could be dangerous regardless of whether or not that being existed. A nationwide church that held such a belief was more disturbing.

Sophia had started to dial the church's number when the door opened.

Reverend Evekial Adame, one of twelve self-proclaimed "true" representatives of Satan, stood before them.

# 10

Pete recognized Evekial Adame from his website photo. He had jet black hair, a narrow jaw, and a slanting nose, and his eyes were a too-pale gray emphasized with the thinnest line of kohl-black eyeliner. Over six feet tall, he was thin enough that Pete wondered if he were ill. According to the information available about The Apostolic Church of Satan, Adame had founded its Chicago branch thirty-seven years ago. It had branches in eleven other major cities, including Portland, Oregon and New York City.

Adame gestured them in. "Professor Gaddini, what a pleasure to see you again."

Pete glanced at Sophia.

"We were on a panel together," she said.

The interior of the building contrasted sharply with the entryway. Wide corridors of buffed faux marble, at least Pete assumed it was faux, swept past high-end retail outlets and a café styled like a French bistro.

"Back when Dr. Gaddini was a nun," Evekial said. "And once more after she'd left her Order. As I recall, her views of me did not change drastically."

They'd reached a plain wood door with no number over it. Evekial waved his wallet over a square pad next to the door and it swung open. They stood at the back of a church. The altar looked similar to the Roman Catholic churches Pete had attended all over the world during his childhood. Against the backdrop of his father's frequent transfers within the military, the Mass had provided comfort and stability. Pete didn't need to know the language to know when to sit, stand, or kneel in a Catholic church, and he could recite the Lord's Prayer in eight languages by the time he was thirteen.

The mix of familiar and unfamiliar here jarred him. The altar held multiple gold chalices rather than one, and a plate of communion wafers sat in the open air rather than locked in a Tabernacle. A crucifix hung upside down behind the altar, so the thorns on the head of the man on it pointed downward.

The area for the congregation, if that's what it was called in this place, looked different, too. Rather than pews, semi-circles of wood folding chairs widened out in front of the altar. Along the sides of the chapel were hooks upon which hung robes of varying shades of red, with every thirteenth robe a black one.

"Everyone in the church wears a robe, not only those on the altar," Evekial said. "Black for leaders, red for congregation."

Sophia touched Pete's shoulder and motioned to the inverted crucifix. "It's not a symbol of Satan. Not traditionally."

"I disagree," Evekial said.

"Tradition has it," Sophia said, "that St. Peter, when he learned he was to be crucified, requested that he be crucified upside down because he didn't feel worthy of dying in the same manner Christ did. So some churches of St. Peter hang the crucifix just this way, inverted, in keeping with the story about St. Peter."

Though answering Evekial, Sophia had looked at Pete. He understood. This symbol came more from pop culture than religion and was meant to startle. But Pete wasn't sure that mattered. The rituals of the Catholic Church looked over-dramatic and at times cartoony to his wife, who had been raised Protestant, but that didn't make them less powerful.

"Christianity chooses its symbols, we choose ours," Evekial said. "The upside down crucifix shows we are contrary to the Church." He led them past the altar into an area with a baptismal font that also held a stainless steel sink and an industrial-sized refrigerator, freezer, and stove. "That's where we keep the slaughtered pigs."

"Pigs?" Pete said.

"For shock value," Sophia said.

"For communion." Evekial didn't seem disturbed by Sophia's comment, and Pete had the feeling it was an old argument between them. "The pig is the animal closest to a human in terms of anatomy. So rather than use bread and wine, we use pig's blood and flesh for communion. We name each pig for an enemy, and we believe by eating and drinking our enemies we rob them of their power."

"Sounds like shock value to me," Pete said.

Beyond the baptismal room and kitchen was a large office. An antique desk with carvings of what Pete guessed to be the Green Man, sometimes known as Satan, upon its front and sides dominated the room.

Evekial settled into the leather armchair behind the desk. "And transubstantiation doesn't? Your church believes through a miracle at every mass, the host and wine literally become the body and blood of Christ. Then you all eat and drink, making you actual cannibals. We only symbolize ingesting humans. Which religion is more shocking?"

A bench upholstered in red velvet with short legs sat in front of the desk. When Sophia and Pete sat on it, they were a few inches below Evekial.

"I didn't come to debate theology," Pete said, then felt disturbed that he'd referred to this discussion as theological.

"No?"

"We understand the First Apostolic Church of Satan believes the Antichrist will be born this century. Or has already been born," Pete said.

"And you're concerned it might be your missing grandchild?"

Pete drew in his breath. So much for subtlety. The man obviously kept on top of current events. But if Evekial was focused on Fimi, that meant he knew nothing of the letter's contents, which was a relief.

"Of course not," Pete said. "Why would you say that?"

"Why else would you be here?"

"Do you know of an organization called the Brotherhood of Andrew of Crete?" Sophia said. Tara had avoided mentioning the Brotherhood to the press, both out of fear of sounding crazy and out of concern for Cyril's privacy, but Pete and Sophia had agreed in advance that they didn't need to protect the Order if talking about it might help. It provided a perfect excuse for talking to Evekial.

"I don't." The answer came quickly, and Evekial leaned forward as if intrigued. Something about his demeanor, though, made Pete think he was well aware of the organization.

"It's a religious order that sent someone to approach Tara during her pregnancy," Sophia said. "Initially asserting her child might be a new messiah, then changing course entirely and suggesting her baby might be the Antichrist."

"I don't see what that has to do with Andrew of Crete," Evekial said. "Or with my church."

"The latter view might present a connection between your church and the Brotherhood," Sophia said. "Either type of organization might be highly interested in the baby and have kidnapped her."

"I resent your grouping my church with a Christian religious order. And I can't answer for what a Christian order, if that's what this Brotherhood is, might or would do or why."

"What about another church like yours?" Pete said. "One that worships the Antichrist or Satan or would celebrate the coming of either. Would a church like that seek out my granddaughter?"

"To what end would we kidnap such a child?" Evekial said. "If she did fulfill a prophecy, we'd need to do nothing, merely wait for her to grow and recognize who she is."

"How long would that take?" Pete said. "If that were true, when would you expect her to recognize that?"

Sophia shot him a warning look, probably afraid he was revealing that his real concern was about Tara. But Pete doubted anyone would assume that. The Western world was too steeped in the idea that the baby Jesus mattered, not his mother. So far as he knew, of the Christian denominations, the Catholic Church was the one that focused most on Mary, ascribing special status to her. But she wasn't considered divine, nor did the gospels show her as having any great influence on her son while he lived or on the movement.

"Hard to say," Evekial said. "A thousand years ago, one might expect as soon as she reached adulthood, considered to be early teens. Now, perhaps, the age of voting, or drinking, or any other landmark age. Perhaps later, given how many of the new generation of college students seem to need so much guidance and have such difficulty with independence."

Pete placed his hands on his knees, steadying his shaking legs. Tara had been twenty-one when she'd become pregnant. He'd meant it when he'd told Tara he could never for a moment imagine her being evil. But many of the Catholic Churches he'd attended throughout his childhood were Old World and deeply traditional, and he retained enough fear of evil to worry that it could seep in and take over in unexpected ways.

"What exactly do you expect the Antichrist to do?" Pete said.

"You misunderstand how this works. My church worships Satan, and Satan is always and ever existing, just as those who believe in Yahweh claim he has always existed and always will. Satan will take human form, or perhaps already has done so, but that does not mean Satan will be or has been born of a human woman or born at all. He may simply appear as a fully formed adult."

The muscles in Pete's neck loosened. "Is your use of 'he' intentional?"

Evekial shrugged. "Satan's ways are mysterious, and I wouldn't presume to predict. But gods take the form that humans need. God is still predominantly envisioned as male in Christianity, Judaism, and Islam. To successfully defeat such an opponent, to present a sufficient opposing force, I expect Satan would also need to be male."

"Or perhaps you're saying that to make us believe you have no interest in Tara's child," Pete said. He had no reason to believe this man had taken the baby, but he preferred to let him think that was the focus of their inquiry.

"Federal agents already questioned me and several members of my Church. If that's why you're here, you're wasting your time." He tapped his phone. "I have a breakfast meeting with donors in twenty minutes."

Pete glanced at Sophia. She spread her hands wide, which he took to mean that was news to her as well. He felt relieved that the FBI had become involved and was actually following every lead.

"We weren't aware of that," Sophia said. "I'd appreciate it if you could tell us, then, whether you believe any other churches might have such a motive."

"I've already given the police a list. Ask them for it."

Another surprise.

"One more question, out of curiosity," Pete said. "In your view, if a child were destined to be the Antichrist, would that child naturally grow to do the things the Antichrist would do, whatever those things are?"

"Are you mocking me?" Evekial said. "Are you mocking our religion?"

"We are not," Sophia said. "We're truly trying to understand the views of churches like yours."

"I can't answer questions about other churches. I only know mine."

"How many members does your church have nationwide?" Pete said.

"That's confidential. As you can imagine, there is a great deal of discrimination against Satanists, so most prefer everything about our membership be kept silent."

"And is Satan, in your mind, the same as the Antichrist?" Pete said.

"Of course," Evekial said. "And I expect he's already walking this earth and will manifest sometime this decade."

Pete cleared his throat, which had gone dry. "Manifest how?"

"To create peace. Though because of him, war will come."

FEELING both too paranoid and not paranoid enough, Tara drove their rented Toyota Corolla to a coffee shop fifteen miles away where she told Cyril what she'd found.

"Auction?" Cyril said, once they'd ordered. He spoke quietly, though they sat in a booth far from other diners.

"I'm not sure if it's an auction, like with a caller, or an open market. But supposedly they're held on certain significant dates, and very wealthy people looking for items with mystical or religious powers go there."

"People have always gone places to find objects reputed to have powers. There are shrines all over the world that sell those types of things."

"No," Tara said. "I don't mean medals blessed by saints or holy water. I mean hearts of saints that supposedly convey protection from physical harm, eyes of saints that allow one to see and alter the future. It's gross, and bizarre, but what if people really believe these things? And one of them took Fimi?"

Cyril covered her hand with his. "I know how disturbing it sounds. But those are old texts you looked at, correct? In cathedrals and churches throughout Rome, you'll find vaults that have saints' organs preserved. The Church in the Middle Ages held strong beliefs about the power of relics. At least, it led the people to hold those beliefs. Whether the Church leaders believed or not is hard to say."

The waitress brought Cyril's soup and Tara's grilled cheese and tomato sandwich with fries. After she'd left, Tara said, "So people did buy and sell these types of—items." The sick feeling in her stomach deepened. She pushed her plate away.

"People still buy and sell relics, though Vatican law forbids it. As far as I know, people don't buy because they believe the items have powers. They simply want to own them. And there are a lot of questions about authenticity. There are enough splinters being sold as parts of the cross on which Jesus was crucified to build a nice-sized log cabin."

"So you think it's all superstition? The idea of saints' organs having powers, I mean." Tara felt hopeful, but couldn't put aside the drawings she'd seen in the texts.

"Superstition is a kind of belief. But its current form is people praying to St. Anthony to help find their keys, or burying a statue of St. Joseph upside down to help sell their home. Or, in a less trivial way, praying a Novena to St. Jude for healing."

Tara's grandmother believed in novenas—repeating a certain prayer several times over the course of a week at the same time each day, then publishing in the paper or elsewhere. She had said many for Tara's little sister Megan and believed it had helped Megan live the years she had beyond her initial diagnosis with a brain tumor. Another relative had given Megan water from a shrine where the Virgin Mary had supposedly appeared.

"What I saw wasn't all in old texts," Tara said. "A current occult book seemed to suggest there are markets now, hidden away. Where people pay a lot of money, hundreds of thousands of dollars or more, for relics with power. Body part relics."

"No one sane would do that."

Tara slid the sugar dispenser back and forth between her hands. "It's not sane people I'm worried about."

"This could be something the Brotherhood left available for us to find to throw us off track. If one of their operatives took her, they'd love for us to run all over the country looking for a market that doesn't exist."

"But what if someone thinks Fimi's hands or her eyes or something have power? Are they going to try to chop her to pieces?" Tara's breathing became shorter and her chest tightened.

Cyril took the sugar dispenser out of her hands. "Tara. Stop."

"The illustrations in these books and binders were so vivid."

"All right. Suppose there are markets like this, and someone stole Fimi to sell her. I've combed through all the news coverage of what happened in Istanbul, I've watched the video. Nothing suggests there's something about Fimi's hands or legs or eyes or any limb or organ that heals. If anyone believes she has power, it's clear she had to be breathing and present. And calm. And possibly with you. So no one would pay money and dismember her. I'm sorry to be so graphic."

"No, I get it." The fluttering in Tara's stomach lessened. "If people took her for a power they believe she has, then they'll also believe she has to be alive. And calm."

"Yes," Cyril said. "So there's no reason for anyone to do anything terrible to her if that's the motive."

"Okay. But we need to check into the auction idea, try to figure out if there are sites like that now. Or markets that serve a similar function. Figure out who goes to them, where they're located."

"I agree, we'll look into that," Cyril said. "But right now, let's try to eat."

Tara took a bite of her sandwich. At least they had a plan, and she needed to force herself to eat. She'd lost six pounds in the last week, over five percent of her body weight, and Cyril was looking rail thin.

A new thought chilled Tara. "What if Diedre was angry that Fimi couldn't help and hurt her? Or killed her?"

"If that had happened, the police would have found Fimi's body. You don't think Diedre killed Fimi, disposed of her body well enough that no one's come across her yet, then got attacked and murdered herself?"

"No. But we haven't heard yet. She could have hurt Fimi, then killed herself in remorse."

"Nothing is gained by going down that road. It's far more likely someone took her from Diedre."

Tara barely slept that night, and when she did, scenes of Fimi's hands being chopped off filled her nightmares. She awoke in her room in the Motel 6 gasping. At three a.m., Cyril's logic didn't sound nearly as compelling to her exhausted mind as it had in the bright glare of the coffee shop. She called his room. He came over, pulled the ugly orange armchair next to her bed, and talked to her quietly, recounting plots of movies he'd watched as a kid until she fell asleep. In the morning, she found him curled up on the floor beside her bed. Separately they showered, dressed, and returned to the archives.

When she reached the airport in Rome, Marie checked her phone and found no additional news about the Hartmans or baby Spencer. She resisted the urge to call or text Yongnian to ask if he'd followed all her instructions to the letter. Creating any trail between them was a bad idea. She'd sweated enough when her outgoing flight had been delayed five hours, giving him time to catch up with her. He hadn't. For all she knew, he'd cleared Customs but seen the news and bailed. As far as the supposed snafu, if he suspected it had been her fault, he might never work with her again. That was fine with her. She felt confident he wouldn't spread the story around. It didn't put him in a good light. A solid operative always personally checked his own papers, just as skydivers packed their own chutes.

Fortunately, not a single law enforcement, security, or customs person had looked at her twice. No one ever had, but there was always a first time. Unlike Yongnian, she did her best to guard against getting cocky.

Marie stowed the large suitcase she'd brought with her in a locker. The suitcase contained numerous clothing items she didn't expect to need. She'd brought it for show, not wanting to attract attention by failing to check a bag on an overseas flight, but there was no reason to lug it around. She felt better now that she'd made it here, but she still had to get through the next eight hours.

After the baby was settled into the carrier and the carrier snapped into the cheap foldout stroller she'd brought with, Marie slipped into a restroom and changed into her suit. The infant stayed mercifully quiet. If Marie ever had one, she hoped the child would be this easy to manage.

She was still an hour ahead of schedule. She'd built in a long window for just the type of flight delay that had occurred. It was pouring outside. Marie didn't like lingering in the airport in case the authorities had figured out the baby had been taken overseas, but that was unlikely, and she'd blend better here than in the tiny shop that was her next stop. She wheeled the child through the airport stores, sipping an Italian espresso and browsing the bookstores. There were far more of them here than in any U.S. airport.

When enough time had passed, she followed the signs to the taxi stand. Deliberately speaking less-than-perfect Italian, she told the driver to take her to the Trevi Fountain. It was such a common destination it would be unmemorable, and it was only half an hour's walk to the Vatican from there. The rain had stopped, and strolling through Rome would be a perfect way to use the time before her first appointment.

"Are you all right, Signorina?" the driver asked in English.

Marie checked in the mirror. She looked pale and drawn. "Rough flight," she said. "New pilot."

The driver nodded. "You here on business or vacation?" he said.

"Both," Marie said.

She rested one hand on the baby, the other on her briefcase. It contained a sought-after fifteenth century amulet meant to ward off Lilith, a mythic woman sometimes described as Adam's first wife and other times as a demon. Marie had obtained it mainly as a legitimate reason to be in the area should anyone remember her, but it wasn't bad to collect two payments in one day.

"Modern times," the driver said. "Women taking their babies on business trips."

"It happens more often than you might think," she said.

# 11

Tara and Cyril perched on ornate chairs in the elevated portion of the vast marble lobby of the Midtown Manhattan Four Seasons hotel. Another time, Tara might have felt out of place in her worn jeans and long-sleeved T-shirt, her beat up duffle bag at her feet. But worries about Fimi overrode everything, along with a tiny hope that the information they'd found might help them.

"I don't see why we had to come in person." Cyril's posture was more rigid than usual, if that were possible, his back straight, shoulders squared.

"We had to fly through New York anyway," Tara said. It was one in the afternoon, and the lobby was fairly empty. "Stopping to see him is the least I can do after how much he's helped me."

A man in a tailored suit and tie left the gleaming concierge counter at the far end of the lobby and approached their armchairs. "Excuse me, miss. You're waiting for Mr. Holmes?"

"Yes," Tara said.

"He's been detained, but he asked me to inform you he expects to be here in a quarter hour. In the meantime, he'd like to offer you refreshment. What may I have sent for you?"

"Hot cocoa?" Tara said. She'd switched to that from tea when she wanted a hot drink. It provided easy calories, and she was still having trouble eating full meals.

"Water," Cyril said.

"Still or sparkling, sir?"

"Still." After the concierge left, Cyril said, "I don't like Holmes knowing what we're doing. Or where we'll be."

"Well, I do."

"You do? Why?"

"You're seriously asking me that? After what happened last time I traveled overseas with you?"

Cyril flushed. "I know I behaved terribly. But you said we're past that."

"We are. On a personal relationship level we are. But I remember how panicked I was being left in Armenia with barely enough money to get through that week, and no information about the church we'd gone there to visit. So if I don't have to, I'm not taking another trip on a shoestring with you without someone else knowing exactly where I am at all times."

Cyril met her eyes. "I don't expect you to forget. But whatever your feelings about me, I don't know if your back up should be Holmes."

When Holmes arrived, he spotted Tara and Cyril Woods immediately. They sat in a corner of the raised seating area on the lobby's east side, Tara looking even thinner than the last time he'd seen her, Cyril talking intently with her, leaning toward her, his knees not quite touching hers. Holmes suppressed a frown. He had wanted to talk to Tara by phone or video conference, but she'd insisted on coming in person. With Cyril. Holmes would happily have paid her dad's plane fare instead. Pete Spencer was a man he trusted, a man he knew wanted what was best for Tara and her child.

Holmes turned a third armchair around and positioned it so the three of them sat facing each other. "What did you find in the archives?" He waved to the waiter, who nodded and brought him a gin and tonic a few minutes later.

"References to auction or market sites where people trade in religious relics, ones they believe have powers. Saints' hearts, bits of hair or organs," Tara said.

"I'm familiar with relics," Holmes said. "On the high end of that trade are collectors. On the low end, novelty shops. Neither fits your child. Even if someone believes she has some type of power, she wouldn't be considered a relic."

"No, but people interested in powerful religious items might be interested in a baby who can heal, who was the result of a virgin pregnancy," Tara said.

"Did Thomas Stranyero tell you that?" Holmes said, as his mind flipped through reasons the Brotherhood might have steered Tara in that direction.

"No," Tara said. "I found information on it, put the pieces together."

She described how she'd honed her research and why she'd pursued the topics she had in enough detail that Holmes felt reasonably sure Stranyero hadn't left a trail of breadcrumbs for her for purposes of his own, and that Cyril Woods hadn't guided her. From the corner of his eye, he'd watched Woods' face as Tara spoke. But he couldn't get a read on the younger man. He had no doubt Woods was still involved with the Brotherhood, but he hadn't been able to prove it, or to prove the Brotherhood instigated Diedre Hartman's kidnapping of the baby.

Holmes settled back, knees spread wide and arms draped over the chair arms. "It's not completely outside the realm of possibility that there are people who, if convinced your baby has healing powers, would try to capture her and sell her. In the Middle Ages, there were rumors the church kidnapped children believed to have second sight. And later, in the mid-1850s, police in Italy seized Edgardo Mortara, a six-year-old Jewish boy who'd been secretly baptized Christian by his family's maid. The Vatican justified kidnapping and keeping the child because Jews were not legally allowed to raise Christian children. Still, today anyone who does such things would be considered an extreme or fringe member of any religion. Or would be someone simply seeking to profit from those who do hold extreme beliefs."

Tara's face turned pale.

Holmes touched the back of her wrist. He hadn't meant to alarm her. "Those types of people have every reason to take care of the baby or they won't collect. And if someone bought her, that person has the same incentive."

"Except if she can't do her job," Tara said.

"Babies are in great demand all over the world, Tara. Many people want children, ordinary children, and cannot have them. Having made an investment, whoever bought her would never harm or discard her. He or she would sell her as a baby for adoption."

"And I'd never see her again," Tara said.

"Yes, you would. Because I'm doing everything in my power to be sure she's returned to you. What did Stranyero want in exchange?"

"He didn't ask for anything in exchange," Tara said.

"Then your trip is a waste of time," Holmes said. "Stranyero wouldn't have left any valuable information for you to find in the archives if he got nothing out of it."

"It's the only lead we have," Tara said. "And we're not only planning to visit cities and towns mentioned in the materials. We're relying on Sophia and Nanor and Andrea Gutzman—the former professor who helped us find the part of the letter in Florence—to suggest what types of shops and markets and people to visit."

"Visit?"

"Yes," Tara said. "We plan to track down dealers in relics and the marketplaces that sell them."

Holmes gripped the arms of his chair. The baby, not Tara, was the target of those focused on what her child might mean for the world, but Tara mattered, too. Which meant she was in danger.

"I need to talk to you alone," Holmes said.

Woods frowned, but after Tara nodded, he stood. Holmes mentally marshalled his arguments during the moments it took Woods to reach the other side of the lobby and station himself near the revolving doors to 58th Street.

"You said 'we.' Cyril plans to join you on this trip?" Holmes said.

"I asked him to," Tara said.

"Neither of you are professionals. It would be better to leave the search to the police and my investigators."

"And what would I do? Stay at one of your condos?"

"Yes," Holmes said. "I have them all over the world. The ones near Breckenridge, Colorado, have excellent security. Plus skiing and pools and hot tubs. You can do whatever you like, contact whomever you like, and I'll keep in touch constantly and let you know if I've made progress."

"I'm not taking a vacation while Fimi is missing," Tara said.

"You're missing the point. It's not a vacation. It's a safe place." Holmes frowned. "I can find you a studio with no amenities if that'll make you more likely to accept."

"If there's the slightest chance of a lead to find my baby, I have to follow it up," Tara said. "You'd do the same if you were in my position."

"I would. And I do understand." He folded his arms across his chest. Things would be so much better for all of them if she'd only agree to let him protect her. "So let me follow up on it for you. Or accompany you. Or you and Cyril if you insist."

"I don't think that would be good," Tara said. "You're a powerful, wealthy man. Some of the people we'll be talking to are in the opposite position. They might open up to me as a young mom desperate to find her child, but they'd completely close off to you."

"I can pose as someone else. You know that."

Tara shook her head. "I asked Sophia about that, about what she thought when she believed you were Rick. She said she always wondered if you were from money. You seemed too well off for an adjunct professor with a struggling antique shop."

Holmes' teeth clenched. His biggest mistake in all of this had been pretending to be someone else with Sophia Gaddini. He'd not only lost a chance at a woman he might have had a real connection with, he'd undermined his credibility with Tara. "Sophia might not be the most objective person."

"No, she's not. But your dad had built multiple businesses before you were born. You don't know what it's like to be a normal person with a normal income. Or to not have the world fall at your feet. That's not a bad thing, but it's not the attitude I want to approach these people with. And could you abandon your CEO post for weeks at a time? Didn't you have to take over for Henrik?"

Holmes sighed. "I did." She was right, it wasn't feasible for him to go with Tara personally. His eyes scanned the room, pausing on a group of women carrying designer bags who came through the revolving door, shedding coats and scarves and laughing. Woods, too, watched them. At least the man knew how to stay alert to potential threats, which could come disguised in the most unlikely ways. "Why not call people? Video conference?"

Tara smiled. "There's a great example—do you think the whole world has access to the Internet and video capabilities? Anyway, I need to see people in person, and they'll want to see me, to know if they can trust me."

"It's not safe," Holmes said.

"Cyril will be with me."

"Excuse me if I don't find his track record impressive." Holmes struggled to keep his tone even. Hitting too hard on his suspicions about Woods might only make Tara more likely to align herself with him in the way that teenagers often dated exactly whom their parents despised. Not that he wanted to take the role of parent with Tara, but it sometimes felt as if he were doing exactly that.

"I get it. You don't trust him. He doesn't trust you. He didn't want me to tell you about going to the archives at all. Or about this trip. But I told him you can help more if you know what's going on. The flip of that is true, too. And remember, he's the one who found the document section with my dad," Tara said.

"Yes, and they'd both been shot by the end of it all. Tara, let the police do their job. Let me hunt for Fimi."

"I'm not stopping either of you. I won't be in your way. Or theirs."

"It's not as if you're going to see people who will want to help you. Think about it. The most likely thing that happened to Diedre is she tried to sell Fimi to the highest bidder and ended up dead."

Tara swallowed hard. "I got a call from Detective Willis yesterday. It's been ruled a suicide."

"Medical examiners can be bought."

"But why would anyone do that? Anyway, I'm looking for information, not trying to make deals. I'll be sure you, and the police, and my family know where I am at all times. I'll meet out in the open. If I have the slightest bad feeling, I'll stay away."

"It's not enough."

"It'll have to be."

Holmes sighed. Clearly, he couldn't separate Tara from Woods or convince her to stay in the U.S. So he'd change tactics, as he did in business. "How are you paying for this?"

"I have some funds left from what you sent me to travel to Istanbul."

"That can't be much. Are you planning to stay in hostels?"

"Yes. And inexpensive hotels."

"I'll wire you further funds." At least he could be sure she'd stay in safer places. Not that he'd leave her safety to that precaution alone.

"Are you sure? Even though you don't want me to go?"

"I obviously can't change your mind. At least I can help keep you safe. And if you'll agree, I'll have my people arrange some of the hotels for you along the way. A type of check in, so if you and Cyril don't arrive by a certain date, I'll raise an alarm."

"I—thank you, that's very kind."

"Repay me by being overcautious. Do not trust anyone. Including Cyril Woods."

Sophia Gaddini took off her faux fur lined gloves as she moved through the revolving door entrance of Smith & Wollensky. She'd chosen the famous steakhouse for her dinner with Thomas Stranyero because, while the chain had originated in New York, this location to her felt quintessentially Chicago. She loved its view of the Chicago River, the dark wood half wall in the restaurant's center, and the red leather booths that gave it a traditional steakhouse feel.

She'd wanted to arrive first so she could observe Stranyero when he entered and get a sense of how he felt about the meeting. But a silver-haired man at the far end of the polished wood bar stood as she reached the host stand. He dropped bills on the bar, picked up the navy blue cashmere coat draped over the bar stool next to him, and moved toward her, holding out his hand.

"Professor Gaddini." His grip was strong but not crushing. "Lovely to see you." He smiled as if he meant it.

"I'm surprised you agreed to meet me," Sophia said.

He was trim and looked strong in a scrappy way, neither too thin nor too muscular. His nose, angled and too long, gave character to a face that otherwise might have looked common. Though Holmes was by far more attractive in the classical sense, with his perfectly symmetrical face, high cheekbones, and broad shoulders, and must be at least twenty years younger, Sophia liked Stranyero's looks better.

"And I'm surprised you chose this restaurant," Stranyero said. "I assumed you were a vegetarian."

The host ushered them to a leather-backed booth far from the outside wall with its series of glass doors and windows. The glass allowed diners a clear view of the river below, but chilled the seats near it during winter and early spring. Sophia felt just as glad to be seated along the interior wall.

"On a more serious note," Stranyero said, "I'm surprised you contacted me at all."

"I enjoy talking with people whose perspectives differ from my own," Sophia said.

She hadn't told him on the phone that Tara had advised her he was looking for Fimi. She wanted to question him about why he was doing that, but she'd decided it was better to ask in person. That he'd tell her anything helpful struck Sophia as unlikely, but she'd been filled with nervous energy since Tara had flown overseas four days before. She needed to do more than read through ancient, nearly indecipherable tomes.

They spoke about the unusually cold weather and Stranyero's flight until they'd been been served wine and their salads—Sophia's mixed greens with vinaigrette, Stranyero's a traditional steakhouse salad drowned in bleu cheese dressing.

"What is the Brotherhood's interest in Tara?" Sophia asked.

Stranyero didn't look surprised at the question. "I can't share the Order's aims or its plans," he said. "But if you ask me something more specific, I may be able to respond."

"Why open the archives to her?" Sophia said.

"I'd like to see her child found. A kidnapped baby means news stories, attention, and people becoming more interested in, sympathetic to, and enamored of Tara Spencer."

"And that's bad?" Sophia sipped her Fiji water with lemon, ignoring her glass of Shiraz for the moment. She wanted a clear head.

"We don't believe her child is some type of messiah, but the more attention she gets, the more other people might believe that. They might begin to listen to her rather than the Church," Stranyero said.

"The Church meaning the Catholic Church?"

Sophia noticed Stranyero, too, was being conservative with his wine consumption. He'd ordered a glass of Cabernet but had barely touched it.

"The Christian church as a whole, so catholic in the literal sense," he said. "We support the Christian values that unite all Christian churches."

"That still doesn't explain allowing Cyril and Tara into the archives. If you believe information there will help find the baby, why wouldn't the Brotherhood do its own research?"

"I believed Ms. Spencer more likely than I to pinpoint what was relevant, and also to persuade others to aid her."

"But are you looking for the baby yourself?"

"What makes you think I am?" Stranyero speared a chunk of iceberg lettuce with his fork and raised it to his lips, seemingly unphased by her question.

"Tara said you told her you were doing so. And I'm wondering why."

"What was Ms. Spencer's opinion on that?"

"She had none. She's more concerned with finding her child than with your motives."

"Ah, but you are suspicious."

"I can't help but wonder if you or someone else in the Brotherhood has the baby already," Sophia said.

"I do not, though of course I don't expect you to believe me."

"And what about someone else in the Brotherhood?"

"Not that I know of or have been able to discover," Stranyero said.

"So you've considered the possibility."

Stranyero smiled. "I neither confirm nor deny, Professor."

They finished their salads as Sophia asked further questions about the Brotherhood and the archives. Though he told her little, Sophia enjoyed the back and forth. As Tara had said, he seemed straightforward when he did answer, and if he didn't want to answer, he told her so. In the middle of the conversation, she at last tasted her Shiraz. It was dark and fruit forward, but not overly sweet, just as she liked it.

When the waiter arrived with the next course, Sophia cut into her bone-in filet and found it a perfect medium rare.

"I assume you've considered that Erik Holmes may have taken the child?" Stranyero said.

"I considered that. I considered everyone. But I can't see a motive for Holmes, and he had opportunities to take the baby before when it would have been much easier to do so." She and Tara had traveled with Holmes for a short time in Florence. And, before that, he'd intervened to stop an attack on Tara and her sister in Istanbul. That time, particularly, Tara and Fimi had been vulnerable.

"But perhaps those other times it would have been obvious he was the culprit."

"That could be," Sophia said. "But what's his motive?"

"I admit I can't answer that. But motives are not always obvious, even to oneself."

"True. I don't think I can be objective about Erik Holmes in any event," Sophia said. "But tell me about Henrik Holmes. How long did he belong to the Brotherhood?" She didn't know if he had, but she saw nothing to be lost in posing the question.

"Ah, Henrik. Very sad. Who knew the man was such a fanatic."

"Is that what you believe he was?"

He sliced into his rib eye. "What else? To track Ms. Spencer, invade the cloister, fire at her—or her sister, believing it was she—with a rifle."

"You were there with a gun, too. You tracked Tara, too."

Stranyero glanced out at the river. "I, too, am something of a fanatic."

"It seems to me membership in the Brotherhood requires that to an extent."

"One might say entering a convent does as well."

"Nothing in my becoming a nun caused me to threaten people with physical harm or death."

"Yet priests and nuns believe in a Church that consigns people to eternal torment after death if they engage in certain conduct or hold certain beliefs. If the Church is correct, isn't that worse than physical death?"

"Is that how you justify your actions?" Sophia said. "Or the Brotherhood's actions? The Order might cause people's deaths but it's saving them from hell?"

"It's what I've believed for many years. Whether it justifies anything, I'm uncertain."

"Your people most likely caused my neighbor's death. Can you justify that?"

"In the explosion last year at your townhome. I heard about that. If the bomb was planted by someone in the Brotherhood, I'm unaware of it. But if it was, I recognize the futility in saying I'm sorry."

"Because you'd order it again."

"I didn't order it in the first place. But if such an action were required now? I can't say what I would do." He took a swallow of wine. "You ought to ask Erik Holmes about his upbringing. It might give you insight into what fueled Henrik."

She hadn't spoken with Holmes at any length since they'd met at the chapel. He'd been too busy, or so he'd said. But she didn't see any reason to tell Stranyero that. "I assumed there was some reason Erik felt so strongly against the Church, so whatever it was apparently affected Henrik in the opposite direction."

"That's accurate," Stranyero said. "To a point."

"Did Henrik ever use the name Raphael to describe himself?"

"He may well have." Stranyero placed a large stack of grilled asparagus on his plate.

"Did anyone else?"

"I'm certain at least one other person in the Brotherhood has used it, but that's all I can say."

"Do you know if Henrik ever contacted Alma Duttenhaver?" Sophia said.

"I've no idea."

"But you know who she is?"

"Of course. One of the copygirls, as the press calls them. The young women who, like Ms. Spencer, claim to have become pregnant without intercourse," Stranyero said.

"You don't believe Tara's claim is true?"

"I've no way of knowing."

Sophia finished the last of her garlic whipped potatoes, one of her favorite dishes at the steakhouse. "It still troubles me that you allowed Tara into the archives."

"So I take it you have advised Ms. Spencer not to have any dealings with the Brotherhood?"

It was an odd way to put the question. "Do you mean did I advise her against accepting your offer to visit the archives? She didn't ask me."

"I see."

They ordered dessert, a shared large slice of chocolate cake, one of Smith and Wollensky's signature dishes. Their conversation shifted, ranging from religion to the presidential race to relations in the Mid East. Stranyero expressed his views thoughtfully and avoided extreme rhetoric, the opposite of what Sophia expected from a man who belonged to a fringe religious order.

"I researched you," Sophia said as the waiter returned with their bill and four pink and lime green macaroons.

"I expected you would."

"You and Evekial Adame graduated Princeton the same year," Sophia said.

"Yes. We had a few classes together early on, but our majors were different."

"Do you know him well?"

"We've kept in touch."

"And what do you think of his Church?"

Stranyero shrugged. "Evekial always was a good showman, and a good businessman. He's found an excellent way to combine the two."

"You don't believe he's sincere?"

"In truth, Professor Gaddini, I'm beginning to wonder if anyone is."

Sophia discovered Stranyero had somehow paid the bill without her noticing it. They walked outside together, and he tipped the valet, who hailed a cab.

"You take the first one," Stranyero said, waving the valet away and opening the taxi's back door for her himself. "Thank you for the evening. Perhaps you'll agree to see me again next time I'm in town. I do like a woman who enjoys a good steak."

"Perhaps."

To her surprise, Sophia felt she would accept if Stranyero invited her to meet again. She was curious about the man. Her thoughts racing, she had to be reminded by the driver to give him her address.

# 12

Tara and Cyril reached Paris by train at about eight p.m. local time. It was the fourth country and sixth city they'd visited in seven days. They'd chosen their destinations with the help of Sophia, Nanor, and Andrea Gutzman. Holmes, too, had made suggestions, but no one had felt confident about where or how any auction sites might be found. During their travels, Tara and Cyril had talked to people who curated private art collections, caretakers of cathedrals and chapels, owners of occult and religious bookstores. On faint hopes and tentative suggestions, they'd traipsed through catacombs in Rome, single-artist museums in Venice, and lesser-known shrines and religious gift stores in Croatia, Spain, and Greece and found nothing. After Paris, they had only three more sites to visit, in Southern France, Poland, and Germany. Tara felt exhausted, but her anxiety over Fimi kept her moving forward.

The clerk at the hotel check in counter viewed them with skepticism as Cyril shrugged off his green army jacket and the fleece underneath, and Tara unlayered her sweatshirts. *Le Meurice* was the most stunning hotel of those Holmes had arranged. Until now, they'd mainly stayed in middle-of-the road hotels, usually sharing one room with two twin beds and a miniscule bathroom. Tara found she liked the comfort of Cyril being there when she woke at night, though usually he continued to sleep, which she envied. But Holmes had insisted to Tara that they stay in at least one fine establishment. Too tired to argue, she'd agreed, though it rankled her that he thought she cared about accommodations when her child was missing.

*Le Meurice* stood in the first *arrondissement*, steps from the *Tuileries* Garden. The black-and-white marble tiled bathroom adjoining her room was larger than the last apartment Tara had lived in. The claw foot tub along its far wall was long enough to lie down in. Which she did, grateful to Holmes after all. The hot water, scented bath salts, and quiet helped calm her for the half hour that she soaked. All the same, she slept as badly as she had every other night since Fimi's kidnapping, nightmares alternating with wakefulness. She liked the large Queen bed, but she missed Cyril's presence in the room. He slept in a smaller room at the other end of the suite. She finally fell asleep around four in the morning. Cyril knocked on her door at ten a.m.

Tara wound her hair, now black and long, into a bun on the top of her head, wore baggy clothes with an extra layer underneath to make her look heavier, colored in darker eyebrows, and applied heavy base and contouring to try to make herself look older. Overall, she thought she'd obscured her looks in case anyone was tracking them. And, at any rate, no one would expect her to stay at such an exclusive hotel.

They had croissants and the richest hot chocolate Tara had ever tasted in a room off the lobby. Thirty minutes later, they were inching their way through a security line at the *Palais du Justice*. The ceilings soared, and artwork graced the walls. Far grander and more beautiful than the few courthouses in the United States that she'd visited, Tara had been surprised to learn it was primarily a criminal court. In the days of the French Revolution, prisoners had waited in a jail below it to be transferred to the Bastille.

Once through the line, she and Cyril looked for a board that listed items to be auctioned off. The owner of an occult bookstore in Rome had told them about it. The items posted had belonged to criminals or debtors, seized by the government or banks. But some listings supposedly were not what they appeared to be. The owner had given them the example of a collector looking for a sliver of the finger of St. Francis. The listing would indicate a St. Francis medal with one hand raised, but the price would be far too high for a medal. If they could get past the person who answered the phone for the listing, they might learn the location of an auction where the illicit item would be offered.

The *Palais du Justice* tourist map didn't refer to the auction board.

Tara saw a woman wearing a robe, but not a wig, exit a courtroom. Guessing she might be a lawyer, Tara approached her. So far, they'd found most educated people in Paris spoke English very well. The woman did, but she waved them away, saying she had no time to talk to tourists.

A robed, round-shouldered man with dark curly hair overheard. "That is a judge. And one not known for being amicable." He took his robe off. Underneath he wore a short-sleeved dress shirt and dark dress pants. "I am happy to try to assist you."

His name was Sebastian, and he was a lawyer. He took them to the auction board in the center of a large, nearly empty hall with steep curved marble staircases at the end.

"You are collectors?" Sebastian looked them over, with their blue jeans and casual clothes.

"Sort of," Tara said. "I'm looking for antique dolls or children's portraits. Anything relating to infants or little girls, really." It had been the best cover she could think of.

Sebastian frowned. "You will not find many items like that listed here."

"It's a long shot," Tara said. "But a dealer in Italy told us she had good luck here."

Tara scanned the board, looking for anything that said *enfant, petit fille, jeune fille*, or *bébé*, words Andrea Gutzman had suggested she try. Her breath caught in her throat when she spotted a small rectangular posting in fine print at the bottom right corner of the board. "What about this one?"

Sebastian looked surprised as he translated the listing, which was for a statue of a female infant saint that was said to bring good fortune to its owner. The lowest bid accepted was ten times that listed for any other item.

Tara held her breath as Sebastian dialed his phone. This could be the lead they'd been traveling Europe in search of.

Sebastian spoke for a few minutes in French. Tara listened intently, as if sheer concentration could make up for her lack of French language skills. At last he hung up. "The owner is out today. But I obtained a number for him, and he speaks English."

Tara had to restrain herself from tearing the phone from Sebastian's hands as he dialed the owner's number. Finally, he handed her the phone.

"I'm calling about the posting at *Palais du Justice*," she said when the owner answered. "The statue of the infant saint. Would I be able to see it?"

"See it?" the owner said.

"To know if it's what I'm looking for."

"We can speak about it. I am away from the store today, but I can meet you at a café in *Ile St. Louis*."

The man's hedging gave Tara hope. If it were a normal item for sale, she assumed he'd tell her to come to his shop. She wrote down the meeting place.

"Odd," Sebastian said after Tara had hung up. "*Ile St. Louis* is a very expensive, exclusive area that includes antique shops. If that is where the shop is located, I find it stranger still that anyone from it would post on the auction board."

Cyril and Tara exchanged glances. The exhaustion had disappeared from his face, and his eyes looked bright. Her own heart pounded so hard it hurt her breastbone.

"Thank you," Tara said. "It was so kind of you to help."

"*De rien*," Sebastian said. "But *soyez prudent, s'il vous plait*. I suspect these are not good people you will be dealing with."

THE *PALAIS DU JUSTICE* stood in *Ile de la Cité*, the island next to *Ile St. Louis*. Beneath the pedestrian bridge between the two, the sun glinted off the *Seine*. As she and Cyril crossed the bridge, Tara glanced behind her. At different points throughout the trip she'd felt as if someone were following them, and the feeling dogged her now, but she didn't spot anyone out of the ordinary.

*Ile St. Louis* was quiet compared to the rest of Paris. Classic seventeenth and eighteenth century buildings converted to apartments and townhomes lined its narrow brick streets. A plaque on one building proclaimed that Marie Curie had lived in it. Two years ago, Tara would have felt overjoyed to see this historic area, to visit any of the places she'd been, but she'd had neither the time nor the money to do that. Back then, she'd been working and writing papers and cramming for exams, determined to keep her 4.0 GPA so she could maintain her scholarships and later go to medical school. Now that girl who worried about test scores and medical school seemed like another person entirely. One Tara could barely remember.

The café the antique store owner had directed them to had large windows overlooking the river. It was too early for dinner, but there was tea service, which included coffee for Cyril and rich hot chocolate for Tara, tiny sandwiches, more croissants, and crème fraiche. The sound of French music drifted over, and Tara was surprised to see someone actually playing an accordion at the back of the café. She'd assumed the music was piped in. Following the instructions the store owner had given, Tara placed the folder that had contained their train tickets right in the center of the table.

A man with a round belly wearing maroon pants and a yellow shirt entered about ten minutes later. He appeared not much taller than Tara, about 5'6", and carried a newspaper. Tara felt surprised when he joined them, as she'd expected the owner to wear a suit, as many French businessmen seemed to do. But perhaps he wanted to appear relaxed.

"*Bonjour, mademoiselle,*" he said. "You are the American who telephoned?"

"Yes, I am." Tara introduced herself and Cyril, using only their first names.

"And what is your interest in this piece?" he said.

Cyril answered. "A religious order I belong to has heard reports that this item has certain healing powers. We wish to prove that is not so and are willing to pay significantly to do so." It was the cover they'd decided upon in advance, as it seemed close enough to be the truth if anyone looked into Cyril.

"Difficult to prove a negative," the man said.

"True," Cyril said. "But we believe it a worthwhile endeavor. I'm afraid I'm not familiar with procedures here. May we see it?"

"I do not have it here, but I expect it to arrive before next week's auction. Give me a way to reach you, and I will let you know when it arrives."

Tara pressed her palms together under the table. The man's words didn't sound much like he was talking about a baby, but if he were, she might see her child soon.

"We'll be out of the country by then," Cyril said. "Could you tell us a bit more about the item so we know if it's the one we seek?"

"It is as described in the post."

"Perhaps its size?" Tara said. "Is it a large statue, say, the size of an infant of six or seven months?"

The man looked disappointed, and Tara's heart sank. "Oh, no, *mademoiselle*, this statue is very small. Three inches tall. We speak of different things. But if you tell me more about what you seek, perhaps I can direct you."

Cyril hesitated, and Tara jumped in. "We seek an object that size, that people believe has some sort of psychic power, that was stolen a short time ago. It's more like a relic than an antique."

The man stood. "Ah, *mademoiselle*, I do not deal in such items. That type of traffic presents too much danger."

Tara stood, too. "Please. It's very important. It's my child we're looking for. She's been kidnapped, and we believe she may be for sale."

Cyril looked shocked, but Tara felt being open made it more likely the man would help them.

The antique store owner's expression was stricken, but he didn't look that surprised. "A human child? Your child? For sale? But that is unacceptable. Impossible."

"Is it impossible?" Tara said. "Some people believe she has mystical powers. Much like a saint's relic might."

"*C'est horrible, horrible.*" The man sat again. "I heard rumors of such a thing, but prayed they were merely that."

"What rumors?" Cyril said.

"That a baby with powers might exist."

"How could we find her?" Tara said.

"This is not an item I ever would be involved with."

"But if you wanted to find it, what would you do?" Tara said.

He stared at her. "You give me your word you are the child's mother?"

"Yes. There are articles about me all over the Internet. I'll show you."

Tara and Cyril searched their phones and found news articles with Tara's picture. The man had to look closely because she'd changed her hair and make up, but eventually he was convinced.

"I believe you." He shook his head. "I will do what I can to guide you. You are following the correct trail in a way. Items that are, shall we say, delicate, they will not be in an open market to be seen, but their symbols might be."

"Symbols?" Tara said.

"Yes. Much as you thought the description of my statue might refer to your daughter, but this time it does not. But that is the idea. So go to the Paris Flea Market at its busiest time of day. Find the stalls with religious items. Look through everything until, perhaps, you see a symbol of your child. Then you can negotiate. You are in plain sight, but you are covered by the crowds."

"But I don't know what the symbol would be."

"The right symbol, it is one that makes sense to those who believe in the power of the item. It will not be valuable in itself, but it is always designed so that it draws the correct buyers and sellers, not just at the market, but everywhere."

They pushed him but he either didn't know any more or wouldn't say.

Before leaving, Tara asked, "Has anyone else asked you about my daughter, or about any infant or child?"

Tara held her breath. On the one hand, if someone had, it might suggest they were on the right track. But if it were Stranyero, he was ahead of them.

"No, *mademoiselle,* no one."

# 13

Marie smiled as she entered the lobby at Claridge's with its classic black-and-white checkered tile floor and sweeping marble staircase. She would have liked to stay at the famous hotel during her two days in London, but she'd reserved her bonus for the purchase of a small antique store in Galena, Illinois. It was an ongoing business, owned by a man whose children had no interest in taking over for him. Most of his income came from sales of kitschy tourist items and bric-a-brac, but he carried some genuine antiques, and that aspect of the store would be enough to satisfy Marie. She was borrowing a bit more than she'd meant to from the owner himself, and she knew antique stores were always a long shot, but she'd reviewed his books, and it was a good bet.

So far, no one had found her to question her about Diedre's or Analise Hartman's deaths, and she'd delivered the baby without incident to the *Del Sol* antique store a kilometer from Vatican City. The bonus had appeared as promised in her private account. The news media said Diedre Hartman's death had been ruled a suicide, and her mother had died of her illness, so Marie wasn't responsible for either. She felt as if she'd won handily at the roulette wheel, and now it was time to step away. She'd stayed with friends in Tuscany for a week and now was finishing her holiday at a modest hotel in London.

And if she couldn't afford to sleep at Claridge's, she could at least have afternoon tea there. The maître d' seated her on a cushioned chair near the fountain in the outer room. She could see the lobby, which made her happy. At her feet sat a box from Selfridge's with a beautiful rose-patterned Bristol china tea cup. Just one for the desk at her new store, though she longed for the entire set. A bit of irony to buy a new teacup for an antique store, but she wanted one beautiful new thing. A symbol of her independence.

"Ms. Vaccarezza?" a voice behind her said. She forced herself not to turn around, but couldn't stop her heart from pounding. She hadn't heard her real name, her birth name, in at least five years. She hadn't thought anyone knew it. "Mary Vaccarezza?"

She stared resolutely forward, though the classic lobby blurred in her vision.

A man walked around from behind her. He sat opposite her. "Perhaps you prefer Marie Glaston."

He had a plain oval face with a heavy forehead, making him look both ordinary and forbidding. He sat straight but with his shoulders relaxed, his hands resting on the marble table in front of him. She guessed him older than she was, but not by much. Probably early thirties.

"We have a mutual acquaintance. Yongnian Fjord."

Of course it would be Yongnian who would cause problems. She didn't think this man was law enforcement, or he would have shown credentials already. But he must have great resources, or he couldn't have found out her real identity. This had to be about the baby. She hadn't worked with Yongnian on anything else.

"Mr. Fjord profited quite handsomely from my interaction with him," the man said.

*I bet he did*, Marie thought.

"Perhaps you'd like to do the same."

"I have no idea what you're talking about," Marie said. "Please leave."

"Hear me out. I won't ask you to disclose anything about yourself. Or your client, for that matter. I simply work for someone who would like to nail down a timeline for certain events."

Marie said nothing, remembering the advice of her defense attorney friend. Silence was the best option. Silence could not hurt her.

The man leaned back in his chair. "You don't need to tell me dates. I have compiled them already, through train and plane manifests and from other sources. Nothing will appear to have come from you."

If that was truly what the man wanted, if someone would pay for that information, it must connect to her own guilt or to her client's, whoever that client might be. She never knew the end source of her work, but someone in the chain of intermediaries did, and she had no intention of jeopardizing any link. Part of the deal she'd made involved complete confidentiality, and she didn't intend to go back on that regardless of any sum offered.

"Let me show you my timeline." The man placed a page in front of her. It included her flights, car rentals, and train trips throughout the U.S. and Europe, those she'd taken, and those for which she'd bought tickets as alternates or red herrings for anyone attempting to do what this man had done. "And this is what we're willing to pay for confirmation of the arrival times and destinations. In U.S. dollars."

He pointed to a figure. Marie didn't glance at it. She guessed it must be astronomical, as even Yongnian, who always looked for a way to earn more, wouldn't have lightly given out information that could lead to a client's identity.

"Ms. Vaccarezza, please understand. The payment is a courtesy. We do not need to pay. At this point, we already have enough evidence to put you in serious jeopardy with the law. My client prefers not to involve law enforcement, to handle this as a private matter. But if forced, we will turn over what we know to law enforcement, and then you'll be placed under pressure to do far more than confirm dates and trips to avoid prison. Your silence now endangers not only your liberty but that of many people, including your client."

Marie stared at the man. He appeared completely calm. No fidgeting, no shifting, no hint of perspiration. She didn't know him well enough to know if he was bluffing.

"You already purchased these tickets," the man said, "and we've already traced the routes and put this timeline together. We can finish without you. But your input will save time. And will make us more certain of our conclusions. If you're worried about a link from you to us, the only link is the here and now. You and I, sitting together. And that's already happening, whether you show me which trips you actually took or not."

Marie stared at the timeline and lists of trips. She did not see how the information could lead to her client, but the man was right. If she were arrested, she'd be pushed to do far more. If she were convicted of felony murder, she'd be in prison the rest of her life. Slowly, using her finger only, she traced a circle around each city she'd visited. Then she stood.

"We'd still like to pay you, Ms. Vaccarezza. As a show of appreciation."

She gathered her shopping bag and gloves. "Pay for the tea," she said, and left.

~

Cyril and Tara hurried through the displays of knock-off designer purses and gym shoes at the edges of the market.

"He knew a lot for someone who claimed not to trade in stolen icons," Cyril said. "I hope he isn't sending us on a wild goose chase. Or setting us up."

"We talked about this," Tara said. They'd spent the evening before eating at a bistro in the Latin Quarter and rehashing everything the store owner had said. "Setting us up for what? He didn't tell us anyplace particular to go."

Still, Tara shared Cyril's unease. The man had seemed to both know too much and too little. At least there were people everywhere today, and other than keeping her bag close to her to avoid it getting stolen, she didn't sense any danger.

Cyril grasped her hand as they plunged into the mazelike area of stalls. "So we don't get separated."

She tried to stay close, but they were pushed about by people on all sides. Many languages were spoken, but primarily French. They found a number of religious stalls, scanning tables of Virgin Mary statues, gift boxes, St. Christopher medals, and baby Jesus pictures.

Tara glanced at the narrow path behind her and the twisting open rows between the stalls ahead. "Are you keeping track of how to get back out of here?"

"Yes. And see there." Cyril pointed out two Exit signs, though Tara couldn't imagine how they led out of the market, as they seemed to lead to openings that would only plunge shoppers deeper into the stalls. After that, though, she tried to keep track of where the signs were in relation to her.

They passed a booth with antique chests of drawers and armoires. Tucked in a corner behind the furniture stood a table that displayed a small painting of a tree, its branches bare, a dove sitting on the edge of every twig. Feeling a tingle of anticipation, though she couldn't quite say why, Tara pulled Cyril towards it.

"It's not religious," he said.

"It makes me think of the Tree of Life," she said.

In the center of the table lay a silver bookmark about five inches long and one wide. Tara ran her fingers over the engraving on it. It showed a naked woman kneeling on the bank of a stream, pouring water out of a bowl in each hand. Statues of saints, including the Virgin Mary, stood around it, but the bookmark lay flat, gleaming in the sunlight that filtered between the tent flaps.

She flipped it over. Nothing on the back.

"What?" Cyril said.

"It's familiar, but I'm not sure why," Tara said. "I feel like I've seen this before."

"The bookmark?"

"No, the design. After I got pregnant, I'm pretty sure."

A man appeared behind the table. "Bonjour, *madame*, *m'sieur*. Can I help you?"

"This bookmark, where did you get it?" Tara said.

"It is of interest to you?"

Cyril cut in. "We're looking for an item that might relate to this."

"What sort of item?"

"A sort of icon," Tara said. "Reputed to have healing properties."

The man was eyeing her, studying her face. "Many items may fit that description."

A dark complected woman about thirty years old walked over from the antique furniture section. She had a round, friendly face. She paused at the edge of the table to stare at Tara.

"This one is special," Tara said. Cyril's hand tightened on hers, and she knew he was warning her, but she felt on the verge of a breakthrough and couldn't bring herself to stop. "It's very important to me. I would pay a great deal for it."

"Tara Spencer?" the woman said. "You're Tara Spencer?"

The man swiped the bookmark from the table and ran.

Tara yanked Cyril's hand and they raced after the man with the bookmark, stumbling at corners, pushing past people who shouted insults after them. Tara couldn't tell if anyone pursued them or not. She ran as fast as she ever had. This was the closest she'd gotten to her daughter.

They darted underneath a row of scarves, nearly tripping on a wire beyond them that held neckties. Tara kept the man in her line of sight. As they turned a corner, Cyril knocked over a bin of old postcards tied together, and they scattered on the ground. He slid, dragging Tara down with him.

By the time they'd scrambled to their feet, the man had disappeared around a turn, but a second, and larger, man charged toward them, bellowing with rage. Cyril and Tara ran, racing through aisles and around corners. They reached the exit, gasping, and fell into an outdoor eating area. They both doubled over, eyes on the exit. No one came out after them.

"It had to be connected," Tara said. "I can't believe we lost him. We have to go back in."

Cyril shook his head. "Those people will be long gone."

"We have to try."

The woman who'd identified Tara at the table dashed from the market toward them just as Tara's phone rang, a staccato wail that she'd assigned to Stranyero. Cyril stepped between her and the woman, arms out to stop her.

"*Voilà, voilà*," the woman said, and thrust the bookmark into Cyril's hands.

Tara answered the phone, heart pounding.

"Ms. Spencer?" Stranyero said. "I've found your child."

# 14

"I don't like this," Sophia said. She sat in her study in her Dearborn Park townhome. Tara paced between Sophia's desk and the window that overlooked the parking area. Cyril sat on the edge of the small leather couch, hands on his knees. "You're positive you want to share the letter?"

"'Want' isn't the word I'd use," Tara said. She and Cyril had come here straight from O'Hare Airport. The woman had disappeared back into the flea market after giving Cyril the silver bookmark. They'd given up looking for her after an hour of scouring the market. It had been more important to get a flight back to the U.S.

"And the police?" Sophia said.

"Someone will provide an anonymous tip to the FBI as soon as I confirm I saw you create digital copies." Tara clutched her phone. Stranyero had insisted upon copies of both the pieced-together Armenian document and its translation. She didn't need to send them now, only have Sophia create them and open the secure portal, ready to forward once Tara gave the word that she had Fimi in her arms.

"We could give him an altered translation," Cyril said.

"He'll know," Tara said. "He'll have someone who can translate it."

"Then alter the original Armenian, too," Cyril said.

"I don't have the necessary expertise," Sophia said, "and there are few people who do, given the age of the document."

"Mary Paul?" Cyril said. "Or someone else at the cloister?"

Tara squeezed her hands into fists to stop herself from screaming. She and Cyril had half discussed, half argued all the angles in hushed voices on the flight from Paris to Chicago, and Tara still felt too afraid of losing this chance to consider his suggestions. But Sophia would be more objective, and Tara needed to get her input, hard as it was to move at what felt like a glacial pace.

"I called her to ask earlier today." Sophia held up her hand, probably correctly reading Tara's fear that she'd revealed too much. "I didn't tell her what's happening. I asked about the hypothetical possibility of creating an alternate version of the letter. She said any believable alteration would be difficult and time-consuming because the Brotherhood has a copy of one of three major parts of the original document. Plus we don't know for certain if that scrap Alma Duttenhaver provided is authentic. Mary Paul also stated she would not do such a thing regardless, as she has no wish to create forgeries." Sophia frowned. "Tara, I admire you for keeping your word. But I didn't give mine. I could call the police now, have someone arrest Stranyero."

"And then we'd never find Fimi. I'm sure he doesn't have her personally," Tara said. "Wherever she is, he's the one who knows about it. He's not going to tell if we have him arrested."

"We can do it after he has the tip called in, after the police have recovered the baby," Sophia said.

"No," Tara said. "I feel superstitious about it, like it would somehow jeopardize Fimi in the future. And it wouldn't be right. The letter will get out eventually, one way or another. This way I will have Fimi back. I need to get her back."

"All right." Sophia logged into the system.

Tara sent the message to Stranyero.

"What now?" Sophia said.

"Now we wait," said Tara.

THE FLIGHT to Miami felt interminable. They arrived in early evening. Tara would have felt exhausted from all the flight time that day if she hadn't been wired at the thought of finding her child. She'd called Detective Willis on the way to Midway Airport to tell her about the "tip" she'd received. The detective refused to say whether the FBI had received the same information and forbade Tara from going to the address herself. Tara hung up on her.

The rental car's GPS led them to an area with scraggly palm trees on either side and sun-faded adobe houses set almost against one another. The density and adobe made Tara think the area was low income, but Cyril researched on his phone while Tara drove and found it was fairly pricey. Land was scarcer in Miami than in St. Louis or Chicago. And adobe, which the sun damaged less than brick, was the preferred building material.

Tara pulled over across from two black SUVs with tinted windows that hid their interiors. "They're already here."

"You want to go in? We might disrupt the operation," Cyril said. "If these are kidnappers, they might take off."

Tara peered out her window. "The black SUVs will have them on alert already. Anyway, Stranyero said we'd find her here, not that these people took her. And I can't wait any longer."

Stranyero had refused to tell her who the kidnapper or kidnappers were. He'd said it wasn't part of their deal.

They knocked on the windows of the SUVs first and got no response. When they rang the doorbell, a woman in a dark pinstriped pantsuit answered, positioning herself so she blocked the doorway and any view of the inside of the house.

Tara explained who they were and said, "Is she here? My baby?"

The woman stepped outside, pulling the door closed behind her. "You can't be here. We will advise you once we've evaluated the situation."

"Please. She's been missing for weeks. If it's her, if it's not her, I need to know."

"Ms. Spencer, I don't know at this point in time. There is a baby here, and she looks similar to the photos of Sophia Fiona Spencer. But the couple caring for her says she is only five-and-a-half months old, and that she's their foster child, along with two other foster children."

"Just let me see her. I can tell if it's her."

The agent shook her head. "That won't be good enough. She's not old enough to speak or otherwise indicate you're her mother. We need to verify through fingerprints or DNA."

"How fast can that happen? And what happens to the baby in the meantime?" Cyril asked.

"You're not going to leave her here, are you?" Tara said. "Because she could be taken away again."

"It depends," the woman answered. "If it appears the foster parents got the baby through legitimate channels, most likely a judge will allow her to stay with them until her identity is established. We'll have your DNA compared to the baby's DNA to see if there is a match."

"How long will that take?" Cyril said.

"We'll try for a day or two."

It felt impossible to Tara wait that long, and it felt worse not knowing for sure if this was her daughter. She gripped the woman's upper arm. "Please let me see her before that. I get that it won't count as identification for legal purposes, but it would ease my mind if I knew for sure, in my own mind, that it's her."

The woman removed Tara's hand from her arm, but her touch was light. "I'm very sorry, Ms. Spencer, that's simply not allowed. But I promise you, we'll move as quickly as we can. I suggest staying at a hotel nearby, and I'll contact you tomorrow with an update."

Tara took the woman's card, which said she was an FBI agent, back to the car and called Detective Willis, who confirmed the agent's credentials, after reaming Tara out for going to the house in Florida.

"If it was your daughter, could you stay away?" Tara said.

"That is beside the point," Detective Willis said. "As soon as you return, you come into the station to answer questions about this 'anonymous' tip. Most tipsters don't call the victim as well as the police."

Tara wasn't sure how she was going to handle that, but it didn't matter. None of it mattered, so long as Fimi was returned to her.

It took her a long time to fall asleep that night, and she awoke at three in the morning sweating, her heart fluttering. She called Cyril. He answered before the first ring completed.

"What if it's all a ruse?" she said.

"The tip from Stranyero? Why?"

"Maybe we were onto something in Paris, and he found out and wanted to distract us."

"He couldn't have known we'd found that stall. Or that bookmark."

"He might have had someone following us. Thought we were getting too close and called me."

"But if this isn't Fimi, you'll never trust him again," Cyril said. "And you'll never share the document."

"True." Tara tried to slow her breathing, but her heart kept galloping. She pressed her hand to her chest.

"Tara?"

"Yeah. Yeah. I'm okay."

"Want me to come over? Neither of us is sleeping."

Tara met him in the vending area. They bought a paper cup of black tea for her since the machine had no cocoa and coffee for him and sat in Cyril's room, on the bedspread, alternating between playing Go Fish and Hearts. Tara curled up next to Cyril at last around five-thirty in the morning, her head on his arm.

It was another day and a half before they heard from the FBI.

# 15

"She's what?" Fenton MacNeil, a large man with meaty fists and a resonant, radio-announcer voice, paced in front of the fireplace in his private library. No fire burned there. Outside the temperature was mid-thirties, not particularly cold for Vermont in late March.

"The Antichrist." Stranyero held the translation in his hands. The lack of the original posed some problems for the expert whose services he'd sought, but he'd been assured this was a reasonably close translation. And it for the most part tracked the one Sophia Gaddini had provided, though he hadn't passed that on. He'd wanted an independent confirmation. The expert had added notes on potential meanings and interpretations.

"Give me that." MacNeil snatched the page from Stranyero. He sat at his roll top desk and read and reread it, running his finger under each line.

"Your translator says this could mean an enemy of Christianity, not the Antichrist," MacNeil said.

"What else is the Antichrist?" Stranyero said.

"My point is that this is not the stuff of *Damien, Omen II*, or *Rosemary's Baby*," MacNeil said.

"That's not how the public will see it."

The leaded glass windows beyond MacNeil looked out on a man-made lake bordered by denuded shrubs and evergreens. The water reflected the silver-gray sheen of the late winter sky above. The view reminded Stranyero of his recent stay in jail where his cell had overlooked a mountain slope. There, he'd thought without interruption or demands, something he'd rarely found time for in his decades-long quest to support the Brotherhood's mission and achieve personal success. He'd been disturbed by the insights the forced quiet brought.

"The public will never see it," MacNeil said. "Should never see it. Which is why you should never have made this deal. Until you persuaded Sophia Gaddini to upload it, the original remained secured in that cloister, and Gaddini no doubt locked away any translations."

Stranyero suppressed growing anger. From Day One, MacNeil had insisted the full document must be found. MacNeil had a habit of taking a position one day, then vehemently opposing it the next, but this was a serious matter, not a theological discussion.

"So you didn't want to know what it says."

MacNeil's eyes scanned the letter again. "Of course I did. The Brotherhood needed to know." He leaned back in his chair and eyed Stranyero. "You didn't find out who the kidnapper was?"

Stranyero shook his head. He'd stated that up front, and he didn't intend to elaborate. He knew MacNeil didn't believe him, and that felt fine. Let the man wonder what Stranyero knew. He wasn't Stranyero's superior in the Brotherhood.

"What methods did you use?"

Stranyero folded his arms across his chest and smiled. "We all have our secrets."

"Nonsense. I'm an open book."

Stranyero had once believed that. MacNeil appeared to say whatever was on his mind at the moment, resulting in his wild swings of opinion and occasionally offensive statements. But, like everyone, MacNeil had his hidden side.

"Better we focus on the letter," Stranyero said. "Control the release, but not be seen as the instigator of it."

MacNeil's brow creased for a moment before he spoke. "We'll make it appear to have come from the cloister. Someone there will be vulnerable enough to have done it, or for us to make it appear she's done it. Though not before we decide exactly what our spin on it is."

"It's clearly not gospel," Stranyero said.

"That goes without saying," MacNeil said. "What about planting the seed that it's a forgery? Something Spencer herself concocted?"

"No one's going to buy that the girl herself wants to be known as the Antichrist."

"Why not? Look at our friend Adame and his congregation. And all the alternate religiosos out there parading around in robes, lighting candles, casting 'spells.' The American public may have moved away from traditional religion, but it loves ritual. People need to believe they control the world around them. And Tara Spencer's a publicity hound. If she ever finishes that book she's writing with Gaddini, it'll drive sales through the roof."

"She shelved that project. After the *Janet!* fiasco," Stranyero said. "You don't believe the child is significant?"

MacNeil waved his hand. "We've established she's not the One we're watching for. She's some strange science experiment, but she's no harm to us."

Stranyero studied MacNeil's expression. "But whose science experiment?"

"What do we care?" MacNeil said. "The government's probably. It's of no matter to us. Whoever created that child will dispose of her eventually."

"Perhaps she does have some power to heal," Stranyero said. "Did you watch the video of what happened in Istanbul?"

MacNeil snorted. "I suppose you believe in the Easter Bunny as well. And that Christ actually walked on water. Does the term fable mean nothing to you?"

Stranyero cursed himself inwardly for raising the topic. It didn't matter what MacNeil, ever a pragmatist, believed. What Stranyero wanted to know was the Brotherhood's true position on all things mystic. With the passing of the leader who'd recruited him three and a half decades ago, the Order had shifted away from what Stranyero considered to be genuine religious devotion. What had taken its place wasn't yet clear.

"Fine," Stranyero said. "But the letter. Publishing it, we'll be creating a cult. Practically handing Tara Spencer a following."

"Of crackpots."

"But a following nonetheless. Is that what you want?"

"Why not?" MacNeil said. "If everyone's looking at her, no one's looking at us."

"A following gives her power."

MacNeil walked to the window, resting his hands on the sill. "So we prove she has no power. That she's a fraud."

"How?"

MacNeil turned around and smiled. "I have a plan. One that will have the advantage of killing another bird that's been a thorn in our side, if you'll pardon the mixed metaphor."

It took a second for Stranyero to connect the dots. "Willow Springs," he said.

"Yes. And to do it, I believe it's time to resurrect an old friend."

For many will come in my name saying, "I am the Christ," and they will lead many astray.

— Matthew 24:5

The thief [Satan] does not come except so that he may steal and slaughter and destroy.

— John 10:10

## 16

Tara sat with Fimi on her lap, trying not to clutch her, and waited for Sister Mary Paul—she thought of the older woman who ran the cloister in Pennsylvania as "Sister" though she was no longer a nun—to sit in front of the screen. She'd gotten on-line to call the cloister only after she'd held and played with Fimi for the entire afternoon. The baby seemed healthy and happy, and she'd come to Tara easily.

Sophia had sent off the documents hours ago. Tara needed to let Mary Paul know the letter might become public. She'd translated it, and she'd seemed the most troubled of anyone at the cloister by its contents. Tara also hoped Mary Paul could tell her more about the document's history and what it might mean, as well as what Tara should be doing about it now that she'd gotten Fimi back and could focus on it. Fimi was safe just now, but she faced a lifetime of danger and scrutiny, and anything Tara could do to alleviate that, she would.

It was Zavia, though, who slid into a chair in the cloister's office for the videoconference. The younger African-American woman was the first person Tara had met when she'd gone to the cloister. She'd been pregnant then, but was not now.

"You had the baby," Tara said, "I'm so sorry I didn't call you to check in. Everything went well?"

Zavia's long braids swung when she nodded. "A lovely little boy. And I understand you've been preoccupied. Congratulations on the return of your baby."

Zavia waved into the camera at Fimi but didn't smile, and her cheeks looked sunken.

"What is it?" Tara said. "What's wrong?"

"Sister Mary Paul," Zavia said. "She had a heart attack."

"No. Oh no. When? Is she okay?"

"I'm afraid not. It happened yesterday evening. She had emergency bypass surgery during the night. She made it through, but an hour after began bleeding internally and had to be taken back in. She died on the operating table."

"I'm so sorry. So very sorry." Tara's throat tightened. She wished more than anything Fimi had been back with her soon enough to have helped Mary Paul.

"It is very hard to lose her, though she had a good long life." Zavia's image wavered as she adjusted the screen at her end. "And seeing the letter reconstructed meant a great deal to her."

They talked about how Zavia and the others at the cloister were feeling, and Zavia's memories of Mary Paul, and the donations that were requested to the cloister's educational fund in lieu of flowers.

"I imagine her death will change a lot there," Tara said.

"That and the publicity. People find us every other day or so, asking to see the courtyard or hike the mountain."

Tara's heart sank. The cloister, a word for "hidden," had once been a chapel, and had evolved into a spiritual and philosophical retreat and educational center. While it had been over a century since it had truly been secret, it had remained the type of place that people only found through word of mouth.

"Is that a huge problem? I mean, of course it is, but is it going to cause you to move or change the programs?" Tara said.

"The change could be good in some ways. It's made it harder to be a retreat center. But we've been teaching leadership skills for small groups of girls and women for a long time. Perhaps it's time to expand that aspect of our work. If we do that, the publicity could help."

Tara drew a deep breath. "Unfortunately, there's likely to be more of it, and less favorable."

Zavia frowned. "Less favorable than attempted murder and a death on our grounds?"

"I had to turn over a copy of the letter to someone. It may become public."

"The letter? You gave it to the press? Without consulting us?"

Fimi started to fuss, and Tara bounced the baby on her lap. "No, no, not the press. But to someone else. Someone who helped me and demanded that in payment."

"Helped you—oh. Ransom."

"In an indirect way. That's all I can tell you. Please believe me, I never would have passed on the letter otherwise."

Zavia nodded, her mouth a thin line. "I imagine the cloister's role in holding a piece of the document for so many years, and Mary Paul's role in translating it, will become known as well."

"I don't know. I didn't say anything about that. And the letter might not become public. I don't know what this—person—wanted it for."

"And the kidnapper?" Zavia said.

"We still don't know who it was."

Zavia fingered the end of one of her thin, tightly wound braids. "I don't see what else you could have done. But the reference to the Antichrist—if people know we held the document safe for so many centuries, they might believe the cloister is some sort of haven for evil. It's ludicrous late-night movie material, but that's what the media loves. It could undermine our entire purpose. Is that what you wanted to talk to Mary Paul about?"

"Yes. And the content of the letter itself." Tara's heart rate quickened. She passed Fimi to Cyril and held up the bookmark. "And this. Does it or the design on it mean anything to you?"

Zavia leaned in to the screen, squinting. "I'm sorry, it doesn't."

Tara slumped in her chair. "I was hoping it connected to the women who kept passing the letter sections down through the generations."

"It might and I don't know it," Zavia said. "If you send a photo of it, I'll ask the others here at the cloister."

"Thank you. As for the meaning of the letter, did Mary Paul say anything after I left?" Tara asked.

"Very little. She often closeted herself in the library for hours at a time reading source materials."

"Materials? What materials?"

"She never told me. She only said what the letter wasn't. She'd hoped it would reveal that the virgin mother in Armenia, and the women like her later in time, including you, were reincarnations of the Virgin Mary. And that the revelation would take the Christian religion in a new, positive direction. Renew it. Bring in more young people. Provide a greater role for, and place more value upon, women because your child is a girl child. But based on the letter's text, she didn't think that was possible."

"But she didn't necessarily think 'Antichrist' meant an enemy of Christ."

"It doesn't need to be one or the other," Zavia said.

"That's what Mary Paul said?" Tara felt a surge of hope. She hadn't believed in God, or Jesus as divine, before this had happened to her. Now she simply wasn't sure, but she felt there must be something, some type of power. Something had caused her pregnancy.

"It's what I say. Remember, Sister Mary Paul is five decades older than me. She's a bit more traditional."

Tara's throat and lips felt parched, and she sipped some water. "So what do you think?"

"Pieces of the letter were preserved in a church, a synagogue, and by a Sufi. Then our portion of it was here, where information on Collyridianism and other doctrines the Church rejected about Mary are preserved. Our work focuses on uplifting women, and preserving the balance from the early days of Christianity where women and men were equal and had equal roles in the development of religion. Where everyone decided individually what the truth was, and no gender, person, or group had a lock on that. There's nothing else at the cloister that's about Satan, or devil worship, or evil doing. Everything here is positive. So why would this letter be the exception?"

"That makes sense to me," Tara said. "Did it to Mary Paul?"

Even before Zavia answered, Tara knew the response would be no. Zavia's words had the ring of a long-practiced argument, one she'd run through many times with someone who felt equally strongly the other way.

Zavia sighed. "She granted that my argument is logical. But she feared that the letter being the only document of that nature was significant for the opposite reason. That unlike other materials, it warned of a great and real danger."

# 17

"You gave the Brotherhood that document?" Holmes said. Even through the tinny speakerphone on the hotel landline, his voice hummed with anger. Cyril picked up Fimi and walked to the far corner of the room with her.

"To get my child back," Tara said.

"I was on the verge of finding her."

"But you hadn't found her," Tara said. "And now I have her back, and that's what matters. It's all that matters. I'm sorry I didn't tell you beforehand, but that was part of the deal. Not telling anyone."

There was a long silence.

"Holmes? Are you still there?"

"Yes, I'm here. At least tell me what the letter says. As it's likely to be public soon."

Tara glanced at Cyril. They'd talked about this earlier in the day. If she was sharing the letter with Stranyero, there was no reason to keep the contents secret from Holmes, though Cyril hadn't been happy about the idea.

Tara retrieved her copy of the translation. She read it aloud, complete with blank spaces and elipses. Her voice shook when she read the word, but Holmes didn't exclaim or audibly draw in his breath at "Antichrist." Not that she'd expected him to. He believed the Roman Catholic Church was the Antichrist, so he no doubt disagreed with the letter's message, but the use of the word would not shock him.

"Nothing is clear without context," Holmes said. "Without knowing what else was happening when the letter was written, without the missing sections."

Tara took the baby back from Cyril now that Holmes sounded calm. She found Fimi's warmth against her chest reassuring. "'Antichrist' sounds pretty definitive."

"The word is only used three times in the gospels," Holmes said.

"I told her that, too," Cyril said.

"And it meant adversary," Holmes said. "Not Satan. Not Lucifer. Not someone inherently evil unless you believe that you must be inherently evil to oppose Christ."

"But don't you believe that?" Tara said. "You call the Catholic Church the Antichrist because you believe it opposes Christ."

"Yes. And I see it as evil because of the way it does that. But that isn't necessarily what your letter writer meant. She may have been referring to an opponent of the establishment of Christianity. Much as I consider myself to be now."

"I hope you're right. Most people, most Christians anyway, see the Antichrist as the ultimate evil," Tara said.

"My only real worry about the letter is that the women at the cloister kept their part of it hidden for centuries," Holmes said, "as did the women in Florence and Armenia. Centuries. There must have been a reason for that. Which is another reason I hate seeing it in the hands of the Brotherhood."

Tara's throat constricted. "So do I. But I'd do it all over to get Fimi back."

"If I'd known, I at least could have helped you negotiate with Stranyero."

"I wasn't negotiating about my daughter's life."

"I can't believe Sophia didn't talk you out of the deal," Holmes said.

"She tried."

"Not hard enough," Holmes said.

Tara stood. "I gave my word."

"To Stranyero," Holmes said. "Why not go back on it? No one would fault you for that."

"I would fault me for that." Tara walked to the hotel room window, cradling Fimi in her arms. "I don't want to become like him. Become one of those people who believe it's okay to do anything to anyone if it achieves the 'right' end. And I may need Stranyero someday. I don't know what the future holds for Fimi. Or for me."

"There is nothing you could need him for," Holmes said. "Nothing."

**NEW YORK: Newly Discovered Document Suggests The Antichrist Walks Among Us**

The website ExtranaturalRevelations.com published this morning what it claims is a recently-discovered document. Written in ancient Armenian, the document appears to be a letter from a sixth century Armenian woman to her pregnant niece. It refers to the niece as the Antichrist.

Pieces of the letter supposedly were lost for nearly fifteen centuries, but were uncovered in Italy, Armenia, and the United States by friends of Tara Spencer, a young woman who claimed a year and a half ago that she'd become pregnant by supernatural means. The website authors, who remain anonymous, speculate that Miss Spencer is the spiritual heir of the pregnant Armenian woman and so is a modern-day manifestation of the Antichrist.

In a podcast released within an hour of the letter's publication, Reverend Frank McCoffell of the Brookings Christian University asserted that the letter is a fraud, as is Miss Spencer herself. Reverend Evekial Adame, leader of the Chicago, Illinois, chapter of the First Apostolic Church of Satan, issued a written statement this afternoon. In it, he argued that none of Miss Spencer's known actions show the type of evil conduct in which the Antichrist would engage. Expressing yet another theory, Nanor Kerkorian, minister and founder of the Willow Springs Community in Blue Springs, Arkansas, suggested that the letter shows a new branch of Christianity began in the sixth century in Armenia. Mrs. Kerkorian believes the movement was stifled because it rejected the established Christian Church and focused instead on female deities.

Tara Spencer could not be reached for comment.

"Our lawyer said I shouldn't talk to you." Eleanor Endicutt shifted position in the weathered wooden rocker, sliding a small purple pillow behind her back. She sat across from Tara and Cyril on the veranda of a beach restaurant overlooking the ocean. Her face had the gaunt, loose-skinned look of someone who'd lost a lot of weight in middle age. "My husband warned me against it, too. We don't want to be mixed up with whatever you're into."

"Whatever you've read in the press, I'm not 'into' anything," Tara said.

Stranyero had wasted no time leaking the letter. The last article Tara had looked at before leaving the motel referred to a source close to the cloister in Pennsylvania. Tara figured next she'd see the types of stories Zavia had worried about, suggesting the former chapel was a haven for devil worshippers or a coven.

"I know you can't help what the press writes about you," Eleanor said. "But with all the controversy surrounding you, it makes sense to me that your child was put into the foster care system."

Tara held Fimi more tightly in her lap.

Cyril leaned toward Eleanor. "You understand, Mrs. Endicutt, that she wasn't put there legitimately. Someone kidnapped her."

"So we've been told." Eleanor pointed at Tara. "I hope you're ready to take your parenting responsibilities seriously now. That's the reason I agreed to meet with you. I wanted to see what type of person we were forced to hand Amanda over to."

Tara pressed her lips together. The FBI had told her there was no evidence the foster parents were involved, and she reminded herself that, to this woman, she was a stranger taking a beloved infant away. "Whatever your reason, I'm glad you agreed to meet with us. We're hoping you can tell us something, anything, that might help us figure out who kidnapped my child."

Eleanor stiffened. "Everything was on the up and up as far as my husband and I knew. As far as we still know."

"I'm not sure what you mean by that," Tara said.

Two seagulls screeched and swooped past them toward a spot on the beach where a child had just dropped a bag of popcorn. Tara started at the noise, but Fimi giggled.

"I mean I understand you have powerful friends. You say the child didn't belong in foster care. Well, maybe she did, maybe she didn't. But you obviously know people who can pull strings to get her out."

Tara couldn't imagine what Eleanor Endicutt meant until she remembered one of the news sound bites had linked her name with Erik Holmes.

Cyril put his hand on Tara's. "Mrs. Endicutt, it must be distressing to have the baby taken from you, especially if no one spent much time explaining the situation, and given how law enforcement operates, I'm sure they didn't. At the same time, the news stories you've read made it clear Tara's baby was kidnapped some time ago, correct?"

"Yes, that's true."

"So regardless what you believe happened after that, you seem to me like someone who would think it very important that anyone who kidnaps a child be caught?"

Eleanor bit her lower lip, then nodded. "Yes. Of course that's important."

"That's what I'm hoping you can help us with," Cyril said. "If there's anything at all you can tell us, we'd appreciate it, because even if it seems unimportant it might help us figure out who took the baby in the first place."

"The police should be handling that."

"Yes, they should, and they are," Cyril said. "They're doing everything they can. But you know how it is in this country. Far more criminals than there are law enforcement personnel to apprehend them."

"That's true."

Tara felt grateful for Cyril's crew cut and his ramrod posture. The very aspects of his looks that made her wary when she'd first met him seemed to reassure Mrs. Endicutt. It irritated her that his approach was necessary, but it was no different from what she'd said to Holmes about the travels in Paris. Most people there had responded better to her as the baby's mother than they would have to him, and now it was her turn to sit back.

"I have a background in private security, and before that I was in the military. Knowing how overtaxed the police are, and knowing that now that the baby is found, they might need to focus more on other matters, I persuaded Tara we should speak to you to see if anything might have jumped out at you that the police might have overlooked."

"That's good of you," Eleanor said.

"I'm an old friend of Tara's. If you could walk me through the foster placement, I'd appreciate it very much."

"It was a social service placement like any other." Eleanor brushed her brownish-gray hair behind one ear. "We've fostered over eight children through that same agency, including four infants. We had no reason to think there was any issue with this one."

"Were you hoping to adopt?" Cyril asked.

Tara and Cyril had used the downtime at the hotel to research the foster care placement system. They'd learned that many couples who fostered babies wanted to adopt. It had made Tara wonder if the kidnapper's long-term plan had simply been to leave Fimi forever in the care of another couple, suggesting the main goal was to keep her away from Tara rather than anything more nefarious.

"Not really," Eleanor said. "There was a time when we wanted that. But we're in our late forties now. To be honest, we plan to stop fostering and do a lot of traveling in a decade or so."

"You said 'not really,'" Cyril said. "So perhaps if that had happened, if the baby could have become available for adoption, you would have been comfortable with it?"

Eleanor glanced at a group of young people running along the sand, swallowed hard, then looked back at Cyril. "We'd been told that was very unlikely."

"But not impossible?" Tara said.

"It's never impossible." Eleanor's voice cracked. "But it rarely happens. We knew that."

"It must have been a shock, though," Cyril said, "to have her taken so abruptly."

Tara kept a close hold on Fimi, still afraid to let go of her.

"We were taken completely by surprise."

"I'm really, really sorry about that," Tara said, and she meant it. She didn't need to imagine how Eleanor Endicutt felt losing a baby she loved. For all the woman's hostility, Tara couldn't help feeling for her. "You couldn't have known there was anything unusual about her."

"We didn't," Eleanor said.

"Now that you know the circumstances," Cyril said, "the things you had no way of knowing at the time, does anything seem odd to you? Anything that seemed perfectly right at the time, but in retrospect, only because you now know about the kidnapping, you realize was different from other children placed with you?"

Eleanor rubbed her forefingers along the bridge of her nose. "We got a call a week ago. The social worker said the natural mother was staying longer in rehab, that the clinic had decided she could benefit from an extended treatment program and that after it, the state would probably recommend a transition period where the mother would stay in a halfway house. So we would keep the baby during that time, with liberal visits from the mother."

"And that's unusual?" Tara said.

"Most young women or girls who have an infant and need drug rehab don't have funds for treatment, they're in some sort of state program. If they're lucky. So just on common sense, it seemed odd to me. With the Florida budget crises this year, how likely is it the state could pay for an extension?"

"But I'm sure you didn't question it," Cyril said, "given that someone official gave you the information."

"Why would we? We assumed the social worker knew what she was doing. And we were happy to have Amanda longer. She's an angel."

"Anything else that seems unusual in retrospect?" Cyril said.

"Well, even at the time, when we first met Amanda, we were surprised how healthy and well-nourished she is."

Tara smiled. "Are you saying my baby is fat?" Fimi had always been a little roly-poly, but no more so than most babies.

Eleanor gazed at Fimi. "No, she's perfect."

Tara felt sad again. She knew people, including an aunt and uncle, who were happy without having children, but this woman did not seem to be among them.

"So what surprised you?" Cyril said.

"The other babies who came to us through foster care," Eleanor said, "had been neglected or, worse, abused. They were usually undernourished and we had to take steps to try to help them catch up to their peers in weight."

They talked a while longer, but nothing came out that the police hadn't relayed to Tara. The FBI had already told Tara the name of the natural mother in the papers was an invention, as were her social security number and other background data, but so far no one had been able to tell how any of that information had gotten into the system. She'd been delivered to the local agency through the usual channels, but the intake files had disappeared without a trace.

"One last thing," Cyril said, as they all stood up to leave. "Does the name Thomas Stranyero mean anything to you?"

"No," Eleanor said.

"Or Erik Holmes?" Cyril said.

"Yes, he's one of the Holmes family. Brother or father or cousin of the one who got shot recently." She shifted her gaze to Tara again. "You had something to do with that, too."

"It was Erik's brother, Henrik," Tara said. "He attacked someone in my family, and a security person shot him."

"You really shouldn't have custody," Eleanor said.

Tara bit back an angry retort. The woman had just lost Fimi, and she was lashing out, but she had protected and loved Fimi. "I'm sorry you feel that way. But thank you. Not just for today, but for taking such good care of my baby."

"I did my best. I hope you'll start doing your best, too. Start behaving like a mother should."

PETE AROSE at 5:10 a.m. two days after the letter's publication. His eyes burned and his back and shoulders ached. He'd woken multiple times during the night, and each time his mind returned to the news stories about the letter, as well as the comments people had made about it on-line. All the same, he whistled Beethoven's "Ode to Joy," his favorite hymn when he played piano at church, as he made a quick cup of coffee and grabbed a muffin for the drive to the airport. Nothing could dim his joy at the recovery of Fimi and the thought of seeing his daughter and granddaughter again. Tara, Fimi, and Cyril were arriving at Lambert St. Louis at six-thirty a.m.

His Volvo was parked in the sloping driveway on the east side of the house. He loved the car, a second vehicle to the series of minivans he'd driven for the dozen years when all his kids had needed to be carted around in one vehicle. He'd bought the Volvo two years before Megan had been diagnosed, when there had been disposable income in the Spencer household. It reminded Pete of happier, more stable times. Normally, he parked it in the garage at night, but his son Nate had used the garage to change the oil in the family's Saturn the night before. Pete had thought nothing of leaving the Volvo on the driveway. The cul de sac where they lived was out of the way, and no one turned into it unless they lived there or were visiting someone who did.

The motion detector lamp above the garage turned on as Pete exited the house. It illuminated what looked like ice crystals sparkling across the asphalt. But it wasn't cold enough for ice. Pete stepped closer, crunching a few crystals under his feet, and saw the passenger window, which was on the opposite side of the car from him, had been knocked out. There were dark streaks across the windshield. Pete hit his key fob, and the car's interior light snapped on. Through the driver's side window, which was intact, he saw a small figure in the baby seat he'd placed in the car the night before. The figure was smeared with a sticky-looking brownish substance.

*Fimi, oh my God, Fimi.*

Pete's heart leapt into his throat. He ran for the car, telling himself it couldn't be the baby, that Tara's plane hadn't landed yet. At the last moment, he stopped himself from grabbing the driver door handle, though it was unlikely anyone had touched it, given the broken passenger side. He used the edge of his jacket over his fingers to open the door. The smell of blood and feces slammed into him and Pete stepped back, hand over his mouth and nose.

The dead piglet in the baby carrier was about the size of a seven-month-old baby, stuffed into a seat a bit too small for it, throat and stomach slashed, tubular, gummy intestines falling out.

Still holding his nose and struggling not to vomit, Pete read the words written in blood and shit on the inside of the windshield: "Death to Spencer's spawn."

# 18

"He didn't see who did it?" Cyril said.

"No." Tara shifted Fimi in her baby sling and grabbed her backpack. She'd whispered what her dad had found that morning to Cyril as they gathered up their three carry-on bags. Her hands shook. The plan had been to get out of the airport as quickly as possible, with her dad waiting in the departure area. They'd taken an early flight for that very reason, thinking the less traffic the better. But the incident suggested news of their arrival had leaked, and she had no idea who or what might be waiting for them. At least they didn't need to go to the baggage claim area. She'd been ambushed there before by reporters, so she had crammed everything into carry ons.

"It might not be connected to us arriving," Cyril said.

"Maybe not," Tara said. "But I probably should have asked Holmes if he could arrange a charter flight for us." It had occurred to her, but he'd been so unhappy about her decision to share the letter that she hadn't wanted to ask him for a favor.

The plane was small and had been only three-quarters full, making it difficult for Tara and Cyril to stay within a crowd as they exited the jetway. They'd dressed as out of character as possible. Cyril wore slouchy sweats and a backwards Cardinals cap. Tara had on wooly leggings under a heavy, long brown sweater, her hair pulled straight back in a pony tail, a bandana around her forehead. Fimi was in a sort of disguise as well. Tara had dressed her in dark blue pants and a light blue T-shirt with a fire truck on it and the words "Future Firefighter of America." Tara thought that was a fine outfit for a girl, but she knew most people would assume a boy baby wore it.

The corridor that led from the gate to the baggage claim was dead silent other than their fellow passengers. While Lambert St. Louis had become busier in recent years, there were few flights between midnight and seven a.m., and the only store they passed that was open was a Cinnabon. The sugar and cinnamon smell helped Tara relax a little. She'd often taken her brothers and sister Kelly for Cinnabons to cheer them up or at least occupy them when her parents were spending long hours with her sister Megan at the hospital.

She started hearing crowd noises—excited but indistinct chatter, shuffling feet—about a quarter mile before they reached the hall that provided egress from the gate area to the terminal. Her grip on Fimi tightened and the baby gave a little cry of protest.

"Give her to me," Cyril said.

"What?"

"Give her to me, and we'll separate. People will be looking for a young woman with a baby, right? Nothing in the news stories mentioned me."

That was another thing to thank Eleanor Endicutt for, despite how unpleasant the foster mother had been. She hadn't spoken to the press, and neither had law enforcement, so no one knew Tara had been in Florida at all or that Cyril was traveling with her. Tara hugged Fimi to herself, breathing in the baby's clean soap and baby oil sent. Letting go of her seemed like the worst idea in the world, but so did walking her through a crowd of strangers intent on who knows what. She transferred the baby to Cyril.

"Let's make sure what it's about before we part ways," she said.

"By the time we see them, they'll see us," Cyril said. "I'll stay here. You go ahead through and check it out. Then call me and tell me where to meet you."

Tara's chest tightened further with every step away from Fimi and Cyril.

She exited the gate area. A group of people surged toward all the passengers, calling Tara's name. She forced herself to ignore them and keep walking. Cyril had been right. The crowd ignored Tara and converged on a couple with a toddler, despite that she was too big to be Fimi, who was only seven months old. From the corner of her eye, Tara saw a young skinny guy with a shaved head holding a sign that said HEAL ME in large blue block letters. At least these people weren't coming to attack her, but she'd been in crowds demanding healing before, and it could be nearly as scary.

Her dad had told her to look for Nate's van rather than the Volvo or Saturn, as the police hadn't finished processing the car or driveway yet. Outside, though, Tara didn't see the van. After glancing around to be sure no one stood nearby, she called Nate and told him about the scene at the airport.

"We've got to get you away from those people," Nate said. "I'm about five minutes away. Where exactly are you?"

After she told him, he suggested she take the Metrolink to the next stop, leaving Nate to pick up Cyril and Fimi. She called Cyril and relayed the plan, then went back inside the terminal. But her steps slowed as she neared the light rail station entrance, and the muffin she'd eaten before boarding the plane flipped over in her stomach at the thought of leaving the airport and her baby. She veered to a coffee stand instead. It was open, perhaps using longer hours to try to unseat Starbucks.

She ordered a Tall hot chocolate—the smallest size, in imitation of Starbucks—and turned to watch the terminal. The crowd was smaller than she'd thought when zipping past—about nineteen or twenty teenagers. They didn't look frightening, but people seeking help often felt desperate and acted accordingly.

"Crazy, huh?" the barista said as she handed over Tara's hot cocoa.

"Yeah. Who are they?"

The barista shrugged. "No idea. They've been here since I opened. None of them bought anything. Don't want to leave their spot I guess. Or they're not into caffeine."

"That I don't get," Tara said, trying to sound casual. The terminal was far too deserted, and she ought not to hang around. But she slid into a metal chair at one of the two round tables near the stand and opened her shoulder bag to look for a book.

When she looked up, she saw one of the younger girls was pointing at her.

Switching gears, Tara pulled out her wallet, stood, and headed directly for the girl. Better to take the offense.

"Hey," Tara said. "Do you know where I catch the subway to downtown?" The MetroLink ran underground in spots, but no one local called it the subway, so she hoped that would make the girl less likely to think she was Tara Spencer from St. Louis.

The girl paused. "Uh, you mean the Metrolink? I'm not sure."

"Oh, I see the sign," Tara said. "Thanks. I hope I don't need exact change."

She walked away, resisting the urge to look back.

Pennsylvania – Title 50 Mental Health – 7402 – Competency to Stand Trial

§ 7402. Incompetence to proceed on criminal charges and lack of criminal responsibility as defense

(a) Definition of Incompetency to stand trial. Whenever a person who has been charged with a crime is found to be substantially unable to understand the nature or object of the proceedings against him or to participate and assist in his defense, he shall be deemed incompetent to be tried, convicted or sentenced so long as such incapacity continues.

Except for three people, the courtroom was empty. The prosecutor sat at one of two polished rectangular tables in front of the judge's bench. Alma Duttenhaver sat at the other. The lawyer next to her wore a navy blue skirt suit and looked not much older than Alma. Alma's mother's live in boyfriend had hired the woman. Where he'd gotten the money, Alma had no idea. He called himself an entrepreneur but never seemed to stay in any one business more than seven or eight months. He was always, as her mother put it, "looking for the right opportunity." Alma suspected the lawyer actually was part of TARA2, the alternate reality game based on Tara Spencer's life. Alma had started playing the game in the early days, right before Tara had given birth, soon after Alma had confirmed she herself was pregnant. Raphael, the man from the Brotherhood who'd contacted her about playing a real life role, had said he'd found Alma that way. Alma wished she had access to a computer or to her phone in the hospital so she could keep playing the on-line part of the game. If it was still running.

The woman in the skirt suit might or might not be an attorney in real life, but attorney was the part she had to play. She explained the rules of today's engagement. Alma needed to sit quietly until she was asked a direct question. Then she was to listen carefully and respond with "Yes," "No," or "I don't know," whenever possible. When asked about whether she understood the charges against her and the possible consequences, Alma was to say yes and not say anything about a virgin pregnancy or visions about angels. This was not the time to defend herself, and she absolutely should not argue with the judge or the prosecutor. If Alma could do all that, she'd be allowed to go home with her mother, because the entrepreneur was also paying a significant amount of money for a bond.

Alma didn't want to live with her mother again, but the ward where she'd been staying had made her depressed, with its lack of windows and no outside air or light. At least the other residents had been helpful. One explained that for this part of the game, the important thing was to do what people expected of you until they got bored, then you could go your own way and take care of what you needed to. That made sense to Alma, and she did have things to do. She'd heard about the Armenian letter. It had to mean that Raphael's darkest fears about Tara were correct. She felt certain now that TARA2 was a serious alternate reality game, one with a real life purpose. She needed to get her phone back to see if Raphael had sent her more instructions. And to exchange messages with Tara so she could determine if Tara was good or bad. As a pregnant woman about Tara's age who'd played the game for over six months, Alma felt certain she was the right person to make that call.

The lawyer didn't want to hear about any of that. She said Alma should stay far from Tara Spencer, and that she couldn't leave her home state without permission if she was released to her mother's custody. Alma would comply with that if the rules of the game didn't require otherwise, and she was determined to do her best in court. About five times the lawyer had told her that if she were found unfit for trial, she could be held indefinitely in a mental ward until she was found fit, and then she'd still have to have a trial. So she could get locked up for a long time. Alma didn't want to stay locked up.

She sat quietly at the long table, waiting to see if the judge would ask her anything when he arrived.

TARA JERKED AWAKE, heart pounding, and sat up. In the light from the bathroom soffit, she could make out the outline of the crib, and Fimi sleeping inside it, next to her bed. Cyril slept in the Queen-sized bed on the opposite side of the crib, the one closer to the door.

She didn't know what had awakened her. She listened hard, but heard nothing other than Fimi and Cyril breathing and a faint hum from a clock on the nightstand.

"Cyril?"

"Yes." He sounded alert.

They were staying in a hotel in Clayton, Missouri, a quiet, somewhat trendy town about twenty minutes from the Spencer home in Rock Hill. Nate had picked up Cyril and Fimi from the airport without incident, then retrieved Tara from a Metrolink stop several miles away. Their mom had reserved the hotel room under the name of the law firm where she worked as a legal secretary. It was a place one of the partners often had his out of town clients or experts stay.

Pete Spencer had come to see them after he'd finished with the police. He brought pizza for lunch and sandwiches for later so they wouldn't need to go outside that night. Tara had hoped to see her sister and brothers, too, but everyone agreed that it would be far too noticeable to have the whole Spencer family troop into one hotel.

"Did you hear something?" Tara said. "From the hall?"

"Something woke me, but it might have been you moving around. Not that I was sleeping well." Cyril got out of bed, walked to the door, and put his ear against it. Then he unlocked it and looked into the hall. "Nothing."

Tara pulled her knees to her chest under the blanket. "You think my dad's right? About some member of the First Apostolic Church of Satan leaving the pig?"

"They're not the only ones who know the anatomy of pigs is similar to that of humans," Cyril said.

"But it seems weird that when my dad met him, Evekial Adame made a big deal about the group drinking pig's blood and eating pig's flesh, and then there's this pig."

"But why would a member of that group say 'Death to Spencer's Spawn'? Evekial said he thought you weren't the Antichrist, so you'd think his church would ignore you," Cyril said.

"Sophia said his followers like the outrageous."

"Yeah, sounds like he's quite a showman."

"Yeah." Tara pulled the blanket tighter around herself. "I keep telling myself that. Then at three in the morning, all those years of Catholic school training kick in, and I think about a Church of Satan and it freaks me out."

"My school wasn't like that," Cyril said. "Or my church."

"Our parish is pretty conservative. My first-grade nun told us that anyone who said aloud or silently to themselves, 'I give my soul to Satan,' could never take it back and would be doomed to hell forever. After that, those words kept trying to form in my head."

"Like being told not to think about a white elephant."

"Yeah. So when I imagine that slaughtered baby pig my dad described, and the words, it makes me think of all of that."

"I doubt it was a Satanist. There are a lot of unbalanced people out there."

Tara shifted onto her side to look at Cyril, though she could only see his outline in the dark room. "Not making me feel better. Maybe I ought to take Holmes up on his offer of staying at one of his condo complexes. Just for a while."

"And then what?" Cyril said. "You can't live with him forever."

"It wouldn't be living with him. I don't think he lives at any of them."

"But you'd be under his control."

"I could always leave if it didn't work out. It's only control if he's telling me what to do."

"You already take money from him," Cyril said. "And you went to Istanbul based on what he told you."

"And it led me to information. And two of three pieces of the letter. How is that different from following up on the research Sophia and Nanor did?"

"I worry about you living under one of his roofs. About one person having that much influence with you. Especially someone who already has so much influence in the world as a whole. And whose brother wanted to kill you."

"Yeah, well, if you want to use logic."

"Why don't we talk about it tomorrow," Cyril said. "You should sleep."

But neither of them could sleep, so they turned on the lamp in the kitchenette and played cards at the table near the window and talked about books. Tara discovered Cyril liked mysteries and suspense novels as much as she did. They'd also read many of the same non-fiction books on religion and spirituality, though what they found there had led them in different directions.

In the morning, Cyril went out alone and brought back muffins and juice. No one accosted him. Nate had no college classes that morning, so he drove to the airport to see if anything was happening. He reported that the group of teenagers still stood near the gates, and they'd been there on and off throughout the previous day according to a magazine vendor. A reporter with a camerawoman had been talking to them when Nate passed through the terminal. It seemed no one realized Tara had already flown into St. Louis and left the airport.

Her sister Kelly was monitoring the news on-line, texting Tara whatever she thought might be important but leaving out the purely sensational aspects of the reports. Tara and Cyril spent the morning alternately entertaining Fimi by singing songs and making faces and playing with her toys, the TV tuned to cartoons in the background. Tara knew she needed to figure out next steps, but by tacit agreement she and Cyril simply enjoyed the day and having Fimi back. Tara was surprised how comfortably he interacted with the baby. It was a side of him she hadn't expected.

"Lots of babysitting," he said. "Our neighbors had twins when I was about twelve. They knew how bad things were at our house with my dad, so I think they asked me to babysit to give me a productive way to stay out of his way."

"I'm sure they needed a sitter with two babies."

"They did. But they had relatives nearby."

Restless by lunchtime, they ventured out to a local restaurant. No one looked twice at them, and Tara felt some of her tension ease. It helped that Clayton was too pricey for her to have ever spent any time there or frequented any of its restaurants. The expense was also why she and Cyril couldn't stay at the hotel very long. Her mom and dad had insisted on paying for the room, but Tara knew how tight their finances were. At the same time, she wished she didn't need to use more of Holmes' money. She didn't completely disagree with Cyril's concerns about the man.

"Maybe Sophia can arrange an apartment for me again," Tara said as they walked through a park that evening. Through her non-profit work, Sophia had gotten Tara and Fimi a studio apartment in a suburb near Chicago months before. "No one at the one in Brookfield figured out who I was."

"You were only there a month." Cyril unzipped his jacket. The sun was just starting to sink toward the horizon, but the weather was warm for late March.

"I could ask her if she could find a building with two apartments," Tara said. "If you wanted to live nearby. I mean, I know you want to get back to your own life at some point. At least I assume you do. So I understand if you have somewhere else you want to go."

He was staring forward, squinting in the sun, and barely listening to her.

"Cyril?"

As Tara turned to follow his gaze, a figure, silhouetted by the sun, dashed across the grass toward them. Cyril leapt in front of her and Fimi. Tara crossed one arm over the baby, who was snug against her chest in a baby sling, and yanked her switchblade from her jacket pocket. She held the knife out straight despite knowing she probably couldn't use it without endangering the baby. It might at least deter the attacker. She shifted to her right, trying to get the sun out of her eyes so she could see what was happening.

"For you," the figure called. It sounded like a young man's voice, medium pitched and filled with emotion.

Cyril rushed forward, but the person swerved to Tara's right. Trees behind him blocked the sun. Tara backpedaled, eyes on the young man she could finally see. He had long blond hair pulled back into a ponytail and Pentagrams painted or tattoed up and down his cheeks and neck. He jumped onto a picnic table twenty feet from Tara.

"It's all for you." He raised one arm, his jacket sleeve sliding toward his elbow, and lifted the other hand, in which he held a knife.

"No," Tara shouted as the man sliced the knife the long way across the inside of his wrist.

# 19

"I understand why you made a deal with the devil, so to speak. But I still wish you had spoken with me first." Nanor Kerkorian paced beside the round brick fire pit. She'd arrived an hour before, picked up by Holmes' car service at the airport and brought to his condominium complex. It was near the border of Texas and Arkansas, four hours by car and one by helicopter from Willow Springs. Nanor had taken a discount airline, requiring intermediary stops, so she'd remained standing since she'd arrived, saying she was restless from the flights.

Tara and Cyril sat on a stone half wall on one side of the outdoor patio. Tara held Fimi, ensconced in a quilted onesy, on her lap. The temperature was in the mid-fifties, so the night was nearly warm enough for sitting outside without a fire, but Tara liked having one. It reminded her of camping trips her family had taken together. And it allowed her to be comfortable outdoors in jeans and a T-shirt.

"I know," Tara said. "I'm sorry I couldn't tell you. But it got me the baby back."

"I suspect Thomas Stranyero is not done with you," Nanor said.

"I couldn't agree more, Mrs. Kerkorian," Holmes said. He, too, stood, though he stayed in one place by the fire, feet spread about a foot apart, staring at the red sun sinking into the wooded horizon. "Which is why I want Tara and the baby to stay here for the foreseeable future, not tell anyone where they are, and stay out of the limelight."

The older woman stopped and studied Holmes. "Out of the limelight, yes, until there is a better plan. But here? With you?"

Holmes raised his eyebrows. "There's somewhere you consider safer?"

Nanor sank onto a metal chair. "No. I can think of nowhere else. More people leave Willow Springs every week. Over half the residents have now moved away. Permanently."

"I'm so sorry." Tara's heart ached for the older woman. She walked over to her, thinking Fimi might cheer Nanor. "Would you like to hold the baby?"

Nanor held out her arms and smiled when Fimi settled into them.

Half an hour later, when they'd all gone back inside and Fimi had been put to bed, Nanor asked to see the translation Sister Mary Paul had done, as well as a photocopy of the original document. The group fell silent while Nanor reviewed both under the kitchen's bright overhead light. Only Holmes remained in the living room, reviewing phone messages.

"I still have a small amount of familiarity with the language of my ancestors," Nanor said. "And while I do not say this translation is wrong, translation is an art. It especially is challenging where pieces of a document are missing or illegible. That's what these symbols mean."

"Sophia explained that," Tara said. "Though it's not making me feel a lot better about the word "Antichrist'."

"Christ is not the same as Christianity. Christianity, the Catholic Church, these are institutions. Organizations," Nanor said. "If you oppose an organization, that is not evil."

Tara turned away from the table and began unloading the dishwasher. The scents of lemon and soap filled the air. "The boy who slit his wrists believing I'm the Antichrist didn't make that distinction."

"You do not know why he did what he did," Nanor said. "Many factors drive people."

"He told the police he worshipped the Antichrist and wanted to prove his loyalty." It had been the main reason she'd agreed to go into hiding when Holmes had called once again to offer a place for her, and for Cyril, in one of his complexes. She couldn't live with any other suicide attempts in her honor or put Fimi in more danger by being in the public eye.

Holmes looked up from flipping through screens on his phone. "If he hadn't read the word 'Antichrist' in the letter, something else would have set him off."

"Mr. Holmes is right," Nanor said. "This document merely supports what I thought from the beginning. Christianity, Islam, Judaism, all bow to a singular male god, and that is *not* how the world should be. Tara, you and Fimi oppose that. You offer the world the chance to remember when deities were feminine."

Tara wiped all the plates with a dishtowel though they were already dry.

"Fimi's gender isn't significant." Holmes approached the counter between the kitchen and living room. "There's no need to limit the conception of God, which is what happens as soon as God is assigned gender, be it male, female, or in between."

Cyril joined Tara, helping her put the plates in the cabinets. "But the women before Tara—the Armenian woman, the Jewish immigrant to Florence, and Nanor's daughter Maya—were also having female babies."

"So we've been told," Holmes said. "The woman who wrote the Armenian letter believed her niece would bear a daughter, but she didn't know. The Jewish woman was killed while pregnant, so no one knows her child's gender for certain. It's lore. Fables."

"My daughter was far enough along when she died that the fetus' gender was known," Nanor said. "And Tara's baby is a girl."

Holmes shrugged. "If you flip a coin two times in a row and it comes up heads, it doesn't mean anything magical occurred. But I do agree that the baby's purpose is to oppose the current religious paradigm. First and foremost, the Roman Catholic Church."

Tara placed the last dish in the cabinet, trying to keep her hand steady. "I'm relieved neither of you thinks 'Antichrist' means the devil. But I told you both before, I'm not on a mission to destroy established religions."

"How can you not oppose the Church when you have the power to do so?" Holmes said. "It instigates and perpetuates evil. The Inquisition, the Crusades, the burning of heretics, the forced conversions of Indians and Africans. More recently, the cover up of mass sexual abuse of children, the prohibition of birth control, and active work discouraging condom use. Over twenty-four million people in Sub-Saharan Africa have HIV, including babies whose mothers were infected by their husbands. I've compiled evidence of all these crimes."

Tara sank into a seat at the table near Nanor, her heart racing. "I'm not saying those aren't terrible actions that the Church took. But the things you say, and even some things Nanor says, sound so extreme it scares me."

Nanor and Holmes both began to speak, but Cyril held up his hands to stop them. "The letter is like scripture in that it can be read many ways. Tara only got Fimi back six days ago. She doesn't need to figure everything out right now. And she doesn't need us telling her what to think."

Nanor nodded and squeezed Tara's hand. "I am sorry. I become carried away. Your young man is right. You will find your own answers. You do not need us to tell you about yourself."

"To be clear," Holmes said, "I'm not proposing Tara do or not do, or think or not think, anything. The baby will bring down the Church simply by existing."

Tara shivered.

"If that were true," Cyril said, "if that happened, and I don't agree it will or it should, what then?"

"I'm uncertain," Holmes said. "To be honest, I never truly believed it would occur in my lifetime."

"You must have a plan," Cyril said. "And somehow I doubt that it's that you'll work with Mrs. Kerkorian to help the world find a new and better path."

"Perhaps I will," Holmes said. "Who knows?"

~

THREE ARTICLES about the Spencer baby appeared in Alma's newsfeed. She scrolled through each one in turn, forgetting the cup of coffee she'd made. She stiffened as she heard her mother's footsteps on the indoor stairs from the main house to the in-law apartment. This was the first time in the three days she'd been home that Alma had been allowed to use any electronic device. So of course her mother was checking on her.

Her mother paused in the narrow kitchen doorway. "You're not playing that game?" She spoke in the hesitant tone of one afraid to upset a skittish horse. She'd prevailed upon the entrepreneur/boyfriend to let Alma stay here despite his strong views about girls who got pregnant and weren't married. Never mind that he was living with her mother and they weren't married.

"No," Alma said. Which was true. She'd gotten a text from Raphael explaining that he'd engineered her release and she should wait to hear further from him. She'd also tried signing onto TARA2, but it wasn't running on-line anymore. She'd found the articles on her own. She clicked over to the local news organization's classifieds to hide them. "I'm looking for a job."

"Are you sure that's a good idea?" Her mom walked behind Alma, getting a full view of the laptop screen. "Who's going to hire you two months from your due date?"

Alma suppressed her irritation. Her mother didn't understand the TARA2 game—which Alma had no doubt was continuing to run, though now mainly off line—or Alma's purpose within it. All she knew was what she'd heard the prosecutor say at the hearing, that Alma had been manipulated by someone else in the game who'd taken advantage of Alma's distress and gullibility.

"A temp job."

"Well, that might work. I just don't want you to wear yourself out. Get too stressed."

"I'm not sick, Mom. I'm just pregnant."

After her mother finally left for work, Alma read the last article again. She couldn't decide if Tara had been playing the game and the baby's supposed kidnapping from her parents' home was part of it, or if Tara had really misplaced her baby, then been lucky enough to recover her again. She checked her phone, hoping Raphael would get in touch soon. Then Alma realized that he might be communicating in other ways, such as through messages embedded in social media platforms or webpages.

She clicked to a new page and saw it. A *St. Louis Post-Dispatch* report about the Pope. That was the main newspaper in the area where Tara lived, so it had to be important. He urged those who listened to his homily during his visit to that city to pray to the Archangels Michael, Raphael, and Gabriel for help fighting the devil. The angels, the Pope said, helped the faithful see through Satan, who presented as if he were good, but was actually evil.

Alma highlighted the passages. Now she needed to figure out what she was supposed to do. She clicked on the first link embedded in the article.

"WATER WITH LEMON FOR THE LADY," Holmes told the server. "And a bottle of the Belle Glos Pinot Noir with two glasses." He turned to Tara. "You can taste it, and if you don't like it, don't drink it. They'll cork whatever is left for me."

"Okay," Tara said.

She held Fimi in her lap, ready to leave if the baby fussed. So far, she seemed content to peer at the candle flickering on the low, square table in front of them and the tiny white lights strung around the archway between the restaurant's main dining room and the private alcove where Tara and Holmes sat. Cyril and Nanor had declined the offer to dine with them, opting to walk into the nearby town instead. It was Tara's third day at the complex.

After the server left, Tara handed Holmes the silver bookmark.

"This is what the woman at the Paris Flea Market gave you?" Holmes said.

"Yes."

"Did you recognize her?" Holmes said.

"No. All I can tell you is she had a dark complexion, a round face, and was about my height."

"Age?"

"I'd guess somewhere between Cyril's and yours, so thirty-ish."

"If you had a name, perhaps I could trace her. But otherwise—"

"What, that extremely general description doesn't narrow it down for you?" Tara said.

Holmes laughed. It made his face kinder and less intense, and Tara realized she'd never seen him this relaxed. Or wearing anything other than a suit. He had on jeans and a dark gray collared shirt unbuttoned at the top. No suit jacket. "You were thinking I could do magic perhaps?" he said.

"It'd be nice."

"Sorry."

The server reappeared with a wine bottle, which he showed Holmes, then opened.

"A toast." Holmes clinked his glass with Tara's. "To the safety of you and your child. And to your restarting school."

Tara had registered for three remote accelerated classes from St. Louis University. Her plan to go to medical school had been shelved indefinitely, but if she kept her high GPA, she might be able to revive it a few years down the road, when Fimi was older and things were settled, if that could ever happen. And if it never did, at least she'd have her Bachelor's Degree.

"To all of that," she said. "And thank you for letting me stay here."

The wine tasted of dark berries with a hint of black licorice. After a couple sips, Tara set the glass down, wary of drinking too much too fast despite that the complex overall seemed safe.

"What about a vendor list?" she said. "For the Paris Flea Market?"

"I checked," Holmes said. "The market runs continuously, and there are over 2,500 vendors that sell there. They don't register item by item what they'll be selling, so to find the woman, you'd at the very least need to know the shop name associated with the table where you found the bookmark."

"I didn't see the name."

Fimi had started dozing against her, so Tara settled her into the infant seat between her and Holmes.

Holmes held the bookmark close to the candle, then shone the flashlight from his phone on it. ".925" was stamped in small letters at the bottom. "This indicates sterling, 92.5 percent pure silver." He took a clean white linen square from his pocket and rubbed it across the center of the bookmark. The cloth came away with a black mark. "And it is silver, not just plated. True silver oxidizes in the air." He smelled it. "Also, no copper smell. But none of that narrows down its origin."

"What about the design?"

"It's beautifully rendered," Holmes said, "but I've never seen it before."

"That woman went to a lot of trouble to give it to me. I wish I knew why." Tara stared at the woman depicted on the bookmark. She looked serene. "If I could find whoever created this, that might tell me something, too."

"Or it might not." Holmes slid the bookmark under a napkin as the waiter approached with the appetizers.

Tara tried the shrimp cocktail first, which she liked though the sauce had a little too much of a cayenne pepper, Tex-Mex flavor for her. She bit into a mushroom cap. She didn't expect to, but she liked the buttery taste and the crunchy texture. It was wonderful to enjoy food again, rather than feeling so anxious it was like chomping on cardboard.

"Why wouldn't it help?" she said. "Finding whoever made the bookmark?"

"It might have been made by an artist whose inspiration had nothing to do with you. More significant is who linked this design to your child. Assuming the design is what's significant about the bookmark."

"Which brings us back to the unknown woman. Or the man at the booth."

"Did Sophia have any ideas?" Holmes said.

Tara shook her head. "No. Nanor said the figure of a woman pouring out water looked familiar to her. It does to me, too, but neither of us can place why."

"Maybe you should take a break," Holmes said.

"What?"

"You've been under so much stress since you got pregnant. Why not take a break? You're signed up for classes. Concentrate on them. Take advantage of the amenities here. Come back to all these questions fresh in a week or two, and you might see something you've been missing."

"You mean relax? That's a novel concept. It kind of makes me nervous."

"I understand that with all you've been through," Holmes said. "But operating in a perpetual state of stress won't help your daughter. It's all right to let down your guard for a while. You're safe here. You both are."

# 20

The sky had the faint grayish-pink tinge of early April twilight as Pete drove home from *Trattoria Aleata*, an Italian restaurant a few miles from the Spencers' home. He and his boss had met for an early dinner with the aim of getting Pete back up to speed for the return from the sabbatical he'd been given after Megan's death. Pete turned down Manchester, taking the long way to help him relax. He rode with the heat on low and the windows cracked open to feel the cool air rushing past. A waste of fuel, he knew, but one of his few indulgences. He enjoyed the illusion that his favorite vehicle—now repaired and repainted—gave him control over his world for the brief time he stayed within it.

When he turned the corner into the cul de sac, he heard chanting. A dozen or so people marched in a circle below his driveway, shouting and waving poster-sized signs on sticks. Diffused light from the faux gas streetlamps along the sidewalk silhouetted the figures. Inside the house, his younger son, Bailey, stood, hands pressed against the picture window of the upstairs family room, looking down at the protestors.

Deep voices every ten seconds shouted "Reject Satan!" while voices in a higher register intoned words Pete couldn't decipher.

He honked his horn, then laid onto it and inched forward until the circle broke and the four people directly in his path skittered out of the way. The crowd converged again as he drove up the driveway. Someone pounded on the Volvo's trunk.

Pete reached for the garage door opener but thought better of using it. The garage was attached, so he'd be giving these people access to his house. He fumbled for his house keys. Once upon a time, before Tara's pregnancy, they'd kept their doors unlocked. The older kids often forgot their keys, and a few of their friends had liked to come over to visit with Megan when she was home sick. Others dropped in when they didn't feel welcome at their own houses. The Spencer home had been a comfortable gathering place.

Keys in hand, Pete flung open his driver door, and headed for the house.

A short, squat woman wearing a long white jacket raced across the lawn toward him.

"Control your daughter," the woman said. "Set her on the right path." She had one hand at her side, almost behind her. She pointed the index finger of the other at him. "It's your job to control her."

Pete's daughter Kelly opened the front door for him. He turned to face the woman and the group.

"Get off my property." Though he'd shouted, Pete's voice got lost in the chanting. "All of you."

One of them flashed a spotlight onto a large poster board. It showed a magic marker drawing of a woman in a shining gold bikini stomping on a temple, bright red blood dripping from her hands. An arrow pierced her heart, and blood spurted from it. The caption read DEATH TO TARA A.K.A JEZEBEL.

"Reject Satan. Reject Satan," the crowd chanted, and the woman joined them.

"Get out. All of you. You call yourself Christians, you think you're good people, get out, get out."

Kelly grabbed his arm and pulled him backwards. "Come on, Dad."

The woman flung something at him. It clipped Pete's forehead, and he reeled back. More stones flew, and above him, the picture window shattered.

~

Cars, some double parked, lined both sides of the narrow Soho street. Alma couldn't imagine where she'd be able to sandwich in her Honda, despite its relatively small size. She didn't want to risk being towed, and she had no idea how diligent the traffic police were in New York.

A horn blared behind her. She put her foot on the gas.

"Raphael, help me. All saints and angels, help me. I'm here to do your work, so help me."

She repeated the words over and over as she piloted the car through the streets, ignoring her buzzing cell phone. Her mom had likely figured out that Alma had gone for more than a job interview, but that didn't matter now. Her mother wasn't part of Alma's mission. Her boyfriend had been, but only to play his part in getting Alma freed. Which he'd done very well, she had to give him credit for that, though it had only taken writing a check.

On her third try, she saw a spot a block from the apartment Raphael had told her about and eased into it. She'd known something would open when she called upon him.

There were five flights to hike up. Alma stopped to rest after the second and the fourth. She unlocked the door using a key she'd picked up at a mail drop ten miles away. The scent of incense with a sickly sweet undertone of fermenting plants hit her as she stepped inside. The source of the latter smell was a small square table that held three houseplants under the studio's only window. They hadn't all died yet, but brown leaves had dropped on the marred hardwood floor, and few of the vines remained green. So Raphael had been here often enough to keep them alive, or to believe he'd be able to do so, but not recently enough to have watered them.

A slim white double door refrigerator hummed along the back wall next to a stove top, a microwave, and a single-basin sink. In the refrigerator and cabinets Alma found bottled water, juice, and canned soup and rice. She opened a tomato juice and guzzled it, then explored the rest of the place, what there was of it. The floor's finish had worn almost completely away at the entryway and in front of the bathroom.

A cot stood against one wall in the main room. Corkboard covered the entire wall opposite it. Newspaper articles, printed pages, and clippings from the Bible were tacked all over it.

The articles included reports of weather disasters and verses from the gospels of Mark and Luke predicting that in the end times there would be earthquakes and "great signs from heaven" and that the sun would be darkened. Nothing about the attack on the cloister or the translation of the Armenian letter. Once Alma had read the letter's translated text, she'd understood why Tara hadn't released its contents herself. Whether the reference to the Antichrist was true or a clue in the game or both, Alma didn't know. Raphael hadn't answered her when she'd texted him that question.

After setting her backpack in the corner by the plants, Alma unpinned the printouts about various weather catastrophes. She flipped through them, unsure what Raphael was trying to tell her or how long she was allowed to stay in this apartment. Tara had asked her about Raphael, so maybe she knew about this place. But surely he'd have warned Alma if she ought not to linger here.

Underneath one of the articles was an index card bearing a hand-lettered question: "Is Baby Spencer human?"

"No," Alma said. She'd researched. Some insects and other arthropods could reproduce naturally through parthenogenesis; humans could not. So if that was how Fimi had been conceived, neither Tara nor Fimi was human, not in any real sense.

Alma texted Raphael. "I'm here. What should I do?"

> I saw the new heaven and the new earth; for the first heaven and the first earth passed away, and the sea is no more.
>
> — Revelation 21:1

> Then the day of the Lord shall arrive like a thief. On that day, the heavens shall pass away with great violence and truly the elements shall be dissolved with heat; the earth, and the works that are within it, shall be completely burned up.

— 2 PETER 3:10

~

TARA AND CYRIL emerged from the hiking trails to find Nanor pacing near the brick fire pit behind the condominium complex, Fimi in her arms. For the last seven days, the Willow Springs founder and Cyril had helped care for the baby while Tara worked on her courses nine hours a day, taking breaks occasionally to take Fimi swimming and to hike.

Burning torches added to the firelight, making the patio bright enough to see the deep lines in Nanor's forehead. "Your father has been trying to reach you. Did you not have your phone?"

"I shut it off," Tara said. "I've been getting hundreds of texts with Bible verses from someone. I think maybe Alma." The quiet walk had been a wonderful way to end what had overall been a peaceful, refreshing week. Now, irrational as she knew it was, Tara felt as if dropping her guard had caused whatever disaster Nanor was about to relate. "Did my Dad say why he needed to talk to me?"

"He is fine, but he called from the hospital. He needed stitches, as did your little brother. It sounds as if they will all be well, but your father was quite shaken. He did not want you to hear about this on the news."

Tara took Fimi from Nanor , trying to keep her breathing steady as she listened to Nanor tell her about the stone throwing and demonstration at her parents' house.

"What would set this off?" Cyril said.

"The Reverend Frank McCoffell gave a sermon on his cable show yesterday morning," Nanor said. "Without naming Tara, he denounced false prophets and warned about the Antichrist. Some of the protestors' signs read 'McCoffell's army.' The police arrested all of them. Already the spouse of one has gone on social media to complain about the persecution of Christians."

Cyril kicked a rock across the patio. "Unbelievable."

"All too believable, I am afraid," Nanor said. "This man, this reverend, is reputed to have spoken passionately. I doubt he meant to inspire violence, but he did." Nanor put her arm around Tara's shoulders. "But your family will be well. The house is damaged, but the doctors say they will be fine."

"For now," Tara said. "But I'm hiding out here on vacation, and my family's being attacked."

"You are hardly on vacation," Nanor said. "You are pursuing your studies, and keeping your daughter safe."

"It's not enough," Tara said.

~

TARA CLICKED OFF HER PHONE. "The man claims he never spoke to us." She sat on the couch and rubbed her forehead. She hadn't really believed the Paris antique dealer would know anything about the bookmark, and she'd half expected him to deny meeting them because they'd discussed contraband merchandise. But still she felt disappointed. The bookmark must mean something, and she hadn't been able to figure out what. She had no guarantee that if she did learn more, it would help her protect Fimi or the rest of her family, but it was the only lead she had other than the letter itself, and Sophia and her dad were focusing on that. Also without much success.

Holmes, wearing jeans and a polo shirt, appeared in the doorway to the sitting area off of the complex's game room. He had ordered the entire wing of the building closed off to anyone not connected with Tara. It allowed all of them to speak without fear of being overheard. "No success?"

Tara shook her head.

Cyril emerged from the corner by the pinball machines where he'd been pacing while making other calls.

"Anything?" Tara said.

"It's as if Pauline never existed," he said.

Holmes raised his eyebrows.

"The woman in Armenia who gave my dad a section of the letter," Tara said. "The part he and Cyril brought to the cloister."

Fimi started to cry, and Tara picked her up and paced between two stuffed armchairs.

"Did you learn anything about her?" Holmes said.

"Nothing," Cyril said. "You're welcome to try if you think you can do better."

"My people have had no luck," Holmes said.

"So we're at a dead end," Tara said. "Unless we can find those people from the Paris Flea Market. But there's no way I'm risking going there in person."

The words of Eleanor Endicutt, the foster mother, weighed on Tara. She wasn't traveling again, not with Fimi, and not without her. Fimi, who'd quieted for a moment, started to cry again, and Cyril walked over and took her, lifting her high in the air and bringing her down again to make her laugh.

Holmes sat in one of the armchairs, crossing one leg over the opposite knee. "Cyril could go back to Paris. He was there with you, he knows what those people look like."

"The odds that any of them returned to the flea market are slight," Cyril said.

"On what are you basing that?" Holmes said.

"We looked everywhere for them," Cyril said. "They clearly packed up shop right after we encountered them."

"But they may have returned," Holmes said. "After all, it's unlikely you and Tara visited on the one and only day they shopped their wares at the market."

"If they were there only because of the bookmark, they probably did leave for good," Tara said. "Especially the woman who gave it to me. It's like she was waiting and hoping I'd find it, or she'd been following us all along." Tara watched Cyril swinging Fimi in the air. The baby loved him, and she herself didn't want him to leave. Which might be influencing her view that his traveling to Paris would be fruitless. She needed to be objective for Fimi's sake. "But maybe we should think about that, if we can't figure out any other way to find that woman."

# 21

Alma scooted her chair away from the man with the fetid breath. Public library computer areas definitely served as a haven for unpleasant smelling people. But she'd been directed here. She kept an eye on the specific computer she'd been told to access. It had the browser she'd need pre-loaded. One advantage of a large city facility was that, unlike in small towns such as the one where her mother now lived, Alma did not stand out. She'd worn her too-big parka despite that the weather was in the mid-fifties. She left the coat on inside, making it much less likely her pregnancy would be noticed. She'd considered changing her hair color to further hide her identity, but that was too much like something Tara Spencer did. Alma was genuine, a real person, not merely a game player. And no one really cared what she did anyway, so she didn't need to worry that much about being recognized.

As soon as the computer she needed was free, she scooted into the open chair. She accessed a browser with an onion logo and navigated first to a site on the Deep Web. There, as usual, she found a series of phone numbers along with cites for Bible verses and the time and dates to send them, along with other messages. But this time when she clicked the link below the verses, she found a detailed map that she did her best to memorize. She didn't know if she'd have a chance to see it again before the time came.

She felt better than she ever had. It was more than the passing of her morning sickness. It was a sense of place in the world. Raphael had a plan for her. Which meant God had a plan. She didn't know what would happen once she'd carried it out, but she felt content. God was watching out for her.

~

Tara looked up from her Spanish 303 practice quiz. Nanor had emerged from the second bedroom clutching her phone. Her gauzy grey and violet dress hung on her and her whole body sagged. "Kali called. She asks me to return to Willow Springs. Those residents who still remain are now receiving more than Bible verses. Someone is sending threats, telling them the end is near, and that to avoid it they must leave Willow Springs and never return."

"I'm so sorry," Tara said. She typed in her last two answers, hit submit, and pushed her tablet aside, then picked up the spoon in Fimi's applesauce dish.

"You still think Alma is sending them?" Cyril said. He'd stopped in a few minutes before from the studio condo Holmes had provided for him across the hall.

"I don't know." Tara spooned applesauce into Fimi's mouth. The baby pounded her hands on her tray in delight. "I gave her my number when I visited her, but I didn't get the Bible verses until a few days ago, and my dad said she was released over two weeks ago to her mother's care pending trial. Plus I can't imagine why she'd threaten Willow Springs residents. She's never even been there."

"I do not think Alma sent the texts to Willow Springs," Nanor said. "How would she obtain the cell phone numbers of the women there?"

"The Brotherhood could get the numbers," Cyril said. "Especially if Diedre worked for them. She probably had a list and passed it on. Or if Fimi's kidnapper had her phone, that person would have a lot of Willow Springs numbers."

The FBI still hadn't determined who had taken Fimi from Diedre Hartman, though they had found traces of the baby's DNA in the hotel suite where Analise Hartman had died.

"Did Kali tell the police about the threats?" Tara said.

"Yes, for all the good it did," Nanor said. "They came to talk to our security people, and they asked that I visit the station in Blue Springs. They also went through the entire community trailer to trailer again. Looking for what, I am at a loss to imagine."

Cyril wiped applesauce off Fimi's mouth. "If there's danger to people at Willow Springs, Mrs. Kerkorian, perhaps you should remain here."

"I do not believe there is danger, but there is fear, and fear is powerful. I must go there to help calm these women."

"You want to persuade them not to leave?" Cyril said.

"I want for them whatever they want for themselves. I wish to help them, if I am able, to leave in the best way possible if that is their choice." Nanor sighed and sat in the armchair closest to the fireplace. "Perhaps the time for my community has passed. Perhaps it did what it was meant to do."

Tara reached for Nanor's hand. "Don't say that. It's a wonderful place. I'm sorry my coming there led the Brotherhood to break in and for the way it all snowballed."

"It was a wonderful place, but not so much in recent years. I should have sensed something was wrong with Diedre, should have realized she was the source of the security issues. At least now there are a few more options that did not exist for women when the community began. And women have more economic power than when it began, though there is a long way to go. It may be time for me to do something new to help bring the world into a new time in a different way."

Tara sipped her Chai tea, which had gone cold while she'd been taking her quiz and feeding the baby. "I'm glad you're still thinking about new adventures and undertakings."

"You mean at my age?" Nanor smiled. "One becomes truly old when one stops thinking of new undertakings. I hope I never shall."

"What if someone is trying to draw you back to the community?" Cyril said.

"I am an old woman. One advantage to being old in the United States is I am invisible. This robs me of power and gives me great power. It makes most people likely to see me as non-threatening."

"The Brotherhood isn't most people," Tara said.

"No," said Nanor, "it is not. But my faith has never been grounded in fear or bowed to fear. I must be at my Community if it is ending, as I was there at the beginning. Then, perhaps, you and I will meet again and I will help you move forward. I must go pack."

"You're leaving today?" Tara said.

Nanor nodded and pushed herself out of the chair. "I will say good-bye before I go."

"I don't like it," Cyril said.

~

> And no wonder, for even Satan presents himself as if he were an Angel of light.
>
> — 2 CORINTHIANS 11:14

> You are of your father the devil. And you will carry out the desires of your father. He was a murderer from the beginning. And he did not stand in the truth, because the truth is not in him. When he speaks a lie, he speaks it from his own self. For he is a liar, and the father of lies.
>
> — JOHN 8:44

~

THE OVEN CHIMED. Sophia finished tossing the fresh spinach leaves and romaine in red wine vinegar and olive oil and slid her pan of garlic bread out of the oven. The aunt who'd provided the only permanent home Sophia had known as a child would frown at her eating only this for dinner, but her peripatetic musician parents would understand. Sometimes she wanted to skip a full meal and eat only what she loved. She took a half full bottle of Pinot Noir from its spot on the kitchen windowsill, where the cold air coming through the glass kept it just chilled enough so that it lasted a week.

The phone rang, showing a now-familiar number. She slid onto a counter stool and answered.

"The father of lies," Thomas Stranyero said without any preamble. Sophia had called him after learning of his deal with Tara and they'd argued vehemently. When they'd spoken again, it had been to debate points of religion. Since then, he'd taken to calling her out of the blue. This was the first time he'd started with a Bible phrase. "Do you think that's an accurate description of Satan, Professor Gaddini?"

"I don't believe in Satan," she said.

"I used to," Stranyero said. "I'm not certain anymore."

"Why is that?"

"I do not find good and evil as black and white as I did when I was young. Or as I did a few years ago, for that matter."

Sophia poured half a glass of wine. Though she always stayed on guard and listened carefully for anything Stranyero said that might help or hurt Tara, she'd come to enjoy these odd exchanges. "Is a black-and-white view necessary to believe in the Devil?"

"It makes it easier," Stranyero said.

"So what's changed? For you?"

"I've discovered—no, I've acknowledged to myself at last—that some of my idols have feet of clay."

"Are you talking about the Brotherhood?" she said.

"I don't know that it's something I can share with you."

"Can't or shouldn't?" she said.

"Shouldn't. But I've been reading Bible versus about Satan, and they seem to speak to me."

"In what way?"

"My cohort here would say in the same way any divination tool does. Runes, I-Ching, horoscopes."

Sophia sipped her wine, enjoying its dark berry flavor and scent. "I'd say the same. Humans find patterns whether they exist or not. The daily, vaguely-written horoscope, the randomly drawn Tarot card, the impression on a piece of cloth, means something to each person who interacts with it, and each believes it reflects her or his personal circumstances or faith." Sophia took a bite of crisp garlic bread and spoke again after she'd finished. "But that doesn't make the insights gained unimportant. I've used cards with evocative images when sorting through a problem or struggling with a thorny theological issue."

"But isn't it empty?" Stranyero said. "Without God, doesn't it all become empty?"

"I suppose that depends what role your god has been playing."

"What if it's my own role I'm questioning?"

"I felt adrift at first when I left the Church," Sophia said. "For two years before I left, I focused on how and whether to move away from my old belief system, but I wasn't ready emotionally for the loss. Later, I found the freedom and beauty of not contorting my reason and emotions to fit a paradigm that made no sense to either."

"But what about purpose? Didn't that leave when your vocation left you?"

"Initially, yes. But my life feels more purposeful now. Every day, I must choose to what to devote my energy. I must decide what matters. When I was a devout believer, any purpose of my own was subsumed within that."

"That's a good way to describe it," Stranyero said.

"Are you having a crisis of faith, Thomas?"

"I've always thought most people believe in the god they need."

"And you no longer think that?" Sophia said.

"No, I do. I simply realized that I am one of those people."

# 22

Kali Kerkorian dropped a diffuser filled with Golden Monkey tealeaves into a small cast iron teapot and set the timer over the stove. Her dark hair hung down her back, freshly brushed, and she wore a long, colorful dress not unlike those her grandmother favored. She looked both young and energetic and older than her seventeen years. She'd flown to the condo complex the day after Nanor had safely reached Willow Springs. She planned to stay with Tara for a long weekend.

"I've been meaning to send you a photo of this." Tara handed the bookmark across the breakfast counter. Cyril was curled up on the couch behind her with Fimi, both of them napping.

Kali ran her finger over the Star design, eyes wide. "You don't recognize the design?"

Tara felt a surge of hope. She hadn't expected Kali to have any knowledge of the bookmark. "It's familiar, but I can't place why."

"It's from a Tarot deck, the Star card," Kali said. "See the water the woman's pouring into the pots? It means nurturing the earth but also, and primarily, healing. That must be why it's linked to Fimi."

"Oh." Tara dropped onto one of the counter stools. "So anyone who heard about Fimi healing that boy could have chosen this as a symbol."

Cyril sat up, rearranged the pillows so Fimi wouldn't tumble off the couch, and joined them.

Kali's hair swung as she shook her head. "No, no, do you not remember, Tara? I wish you had sent me the photo, I would have reminded you. It's what convinced you to trust me."

"Trust you?" Tara's mind flew back to the later months of her pregnancy when Kali had first written to her. "Oh. That's right." She turned toward Cyril.

"In the letter Kali sent me to introduce herself. She doodled an image on it, and now I remember. It was of the Star card."

"And that convinced you to trust her?"

"Not exactly," Tara said. "But it intrigued me. I'd played around with Tarot decks when I was traveling and trying to find a place to stay after the bomb was set off at Sophia's. One deck I found in a secondhand store had beautiful images. Upbeat. Nothing scary, like some Tarot cards have. And what Kali drew was so similar to what I'd seen that it felt almost like a sign. That plus the tone of her letter—it was so kind and thoughtful—made me decide to respond to her. A lot of people wrote to me, but I felt drawn to her letter."

"So why did you draw it?" Cyril moved behind Kali and retrieved a package of coffee beans from the cabinet.

"I used to doodle it all the time. It was inspired by a painting my Aunt Maya did for a community art class. Maya was killed before I was born, but I heard so many stories about her I felt I knew her. I liked her painting so much my mother gave it to me when I was about three, and it hung in my bedroom at my mom's for years. But then it got damaged in a flood—my room was on the ground floor—and I cried and cried."

The coffeemaker hissed and gurgled, and the smell of roasting coffee filled the air.

"I'm surprised Nanor didn't remember that," Cyril said.

"Grandmother probably did not see the painting more than once or twice. Maya did it only six months before she died, and my mother took it with her when she moved out. Grandmother did not visit us often. I was close with her, but my mother was not."

Tara turned to Cyril. "Kali's mother, Rose, and Maya were twins. Rose blamed Nanor for Maya's death."

"She wasn't the only one. Grandmother felt great guilt over her last words with Maya having been angry ones," Kali said. The timer dinged, and she took out the diffuser, set it on a saucer, and poured her tea.

"Did your mother ever say why Maya chose that image?" Tara said.

"She had a tarot reading when she was a little girl. The Star card was her signifier—the card used to represent oneself or one's question in a reading."

Pete Spencer stood in the narrow strip of gravel between a garage and a swingset. He'd moved his family, other than Nate, who had his own apartment, to live temporarily in Edwardsville with a friend of a friend of his brother's. A good friend, as she'd opened her home to all of them despite having three children herself and only three bedrooms. So far, there had been protests every morning and night at the Spencers' house, which now stood empty, but no further damage to it, and no one had figured out where the Spencers were staying.

Pete's finger hovered over the icon for Tara's number on his phone. Delaying would not make it easier to say what he had to say, but it would give her another few seconds of peace. Unless she learned of the news another way before she heard it from him. He hit the button.

"Hey, Dad," Tara said. Her voice sounded lighter than he'd heard it in ages. "I just got my results from my Spanish mid-term. A-. Such a relief."

Her words took him back to a time when his daughter's biggest concern had been keeping her GPA high enough to get into med school. He cleared his throat. "That's fantastic, honey. I'm really happy you're getting so close to your degree." He cleared his throat. "Our family's fine, but I'm calling with bad news."

"What is it?"

The wind kicked up, making the garage's eaves creak. It was a warm April wind, but still made Pete shiver. "That young man, the one who tried to slit his wrists in the park, was released from the hospital to his parents' house yesterday." Pete shut his eyes against the vision that had been in his mind since he'd heard the news, of a policeman appearing at the door of the young man's parents. After Megan's death, he'd attended a grief group briefly, but he'd had to stop. The stories of the moment the police knocked, the moment life changed forever, had been too hard to hear, too mountainous atop his own pain. "This morning, he got up early and snuck out of the house. He hitchhiked to an expressway bridge and jumped off it into traffic. The driver of the truck that hit him slammed on his brakes, but he couldn't stop in time."

"Oh, God. He died?"

"Yes." Pete stared at the white gravel under his feet, glaring in the late afternoon sun.

"I should have gone to see him," Tara said. "Explained that I'm not what he thought I was. That I don't want anyone to hurt anyone else or themselves because of me."

"He was unwell, Tara. You're not a therapist, or a doctor. Talking to him risked making him worse."

"Worse than dead?"

Pete's mind flew back to all the times Tara had tried to intervene and mediate her siblings' fights with one another or with Pete and Lynette. Lynette had always snapped at her oldest daughter, telling her to stay out of it. Pete thought it spoke well of Tara that she wanted to help everyone get along, but Lynette had insisted Tara needed to realize there were some things she couldn't fix.

"You aren't responsible for what other people do," he said. "You do your best to do what's right, and to be considerate of others, but you can't control them."

"What if there was something wrong with that boy that could have been healed?"

"Tara, you have no idea if Fimi can heal mental trauma and trying truly would have been dangerous. Not only for the young man, but for you and Fimi. There's a reason we're all hiding away. You can't risk bringing her into public until we figure out how to keep her safe."

Silence.

"Tara?"

"I ought to be able to do something good for other people. There must be some reason all this happened."

"We'll figure it out," Pete said, though his own efforts hadn't gotten him far. He'd been working with Sophia and with Andrea Gutzman, the professor in Florence who'd made a lifelong study of the different sects excommunicated from the Church for worshipping the Virgin Mary. He'd hoped that Gutzman's work could shed insight on the letter, hoped there was some connection, but so far nothing she'd unearthed had been helpful.

~

"Your dad's right," Cyril said. "You can't help everyone."

"I'm not helping anyone. I'm too afraid to bring Fimi out in public." The humid air in the lounge adjacent to the indoor pool felt stifling. Feeling queasy, Tara pressed her head against the cold glass door to the outdoor pool. It ought to be filled with kids bobbing around on yellow and orange noodles, but Holmes had reserved the entire indoor/outdoor area, complete with sauna, hot tubs, and cushy chairs alongside overflowing bookcases for them. She, Cyril, and Kali had come down with Fimi after dinner.

"With good reason," Kali said. She held Fimi in her arms.

Cyril put his hands on Tara's shoulders and gently turned her to face him. "It's terrible what happened. But no matter what powers Fimi has, or you have, neither of you controls everything. You're not God. You're not omnipotent. And you'll never survive if you try to take on everything."

Tara let her breath out and moved to the couch to sit. "That's true." But she shut her eyes and pictured the young man from the park running toward her, saw his jeans and dark jacket and his blond ponytail, and she couldn't remember his face. Everything had happened so fast.

Cyril sat next to her. "Much as I don't like staying here, you're right to stay out of the public eye. If you took Fimi out to heal people, she'd be a target again. And you might only encourage more people to become obsessed with her."

"I could try," Tara said. "Without Fimi."

"By yourself?" Kali sat on the ottoman across from them, still holding the baby.

"I healed myself after Alma's attack on me," Tara said.

"Perhaps that is what the Star card means," Kali said. "Maybe it represents you, not Fimi. Or perhaps healing is the power the Armenian letter speaks of."

"That could be. If so, I need to find out," Tara said.

"How?" Cyril said. "You can't go around this complex randomly trying to heal people. It defeats the purpose of staying out of sight. Better to focus on searching for that Tarot reader."

Kali's mother had remembered Nanor taking her and her sister Maya to an Earth Day festival in Pasadena where they'd gotten a Tarot reading when Maya was five or six.

"We can do both," Tara said.

"Tara could try healing you," Kali said to Cyril. "Your wound from getting shot at the cloister is not fully healed, is it?"

"It's not," Cyril said. "I can get around because there wasn't any nerve or muscle damage. But it hurts, and it's still ugly." He looked at Tara. "You think you could heal something that happened a month and a half ago?"

"I don't know," Tara said. Now that they were talking about it, she felt nervous she'd somehow make things worse for Cyril.

"I'd been in a coma four days when you and Fimi helped me," Kali said.

Tara nodded. "What do you think?" she said to Cyril. "Will you let me try?"

The Honda had disappeared from the parking spot, either towed by the city or tracked down by Alma's mother and her boyfriend. The latter of which would mean they knew she was here, so she didn't go into the apartment, but instead doubled back to the subway. She'd taken a large cash advance on her mother's credit card before she'd ditched it, so she had a lot of money, which she'd split between her pockets, a fanny pack, and her right sock. Before leaving to buy the last supplies Raphael had instructed her to get, she'd put all her other belongings in her backpack, so she had what she needed.

As people rushed past her to catch trains, Alma leaned against a grimy pillar and texted Raphael. When she received no response after fifteen minutes, she grew nervous staying in one place so close to the apartment. She took a train to the stop near the main library branch in Manhattan. It had a large park with ping pong tables and booths with free books and chairs. The weather was chilly and damp and felt more like mid-winter than early spring, but it wasn't frigid. The park was as good a place as any to sit and wait if she still hadn't heard from Raphael by the time the library closed.

Inside, she sat at a table with a pretty brass lamp near a window. She tried to focus on the book she'd chosen, a mystery novel by an author she'd never heard of that she'd chosen from a shelf of recent fiction, but she kept glancing out the window at the darkening sky. Closing time was in an hour. She didn't really want to sit or wander in the park alone, but she didn't know where else to go if Raphael didn't answer soon.

Tara pulled a blanket over Fimi, who slept on her stomach in the playpen. They'd decided to use Cyril's studio condo. It was far smaller than Tara's two bedroom, but Holmes was less likely to knock on Cyril's door, and Cyril insisted they not tell Holmes what they were doing. A long, narrow kitchen connected the living area to the sleeping nook where Fimi's playpen now stood next to the bed.

Kali backed away from the fireplace, where a fire crackled.

"There," she said. "You can concentrate on that the way people focus on candles when they meditate." She perched on one of the tall upholstered chairs at the breakfast bar.

The fire made the room a bit too warm, but Kali had suggested the smoky scent and the crackling sounds might help put Tara in the right frame of mind, given her experiences when she'd healed before.

Cyril wore a long sleeved sweatshirt and a pair of running shorts. The scar on his upper thigh stood out white and bumpy. The hair on the patch the hospital had shaved had regrown, but it looked coarser than the thick hair on the rest of his leg.

"I don't know if I'm more concerned I can do this or I can't," Tara said.

The link to Maya, the Star card, and healing had seemed plausible when they'd all talked about it, and Tara had agreed in theory it made sense to test her abilities, but now her arms and hands shook.

"It'll be fine," Cyril said. "No one outside this room needs to know what happens."

Tara nodded.

"I won't tell even Grandmother," Kali said, "if you don't want me to."

"If there's anything to tell," Tara said. She shifted so she sat cross-legged on the sofa, facing Cyril, who positioned himself on the ottoman in front of her. "It's only ever worked when I'm almost in a trance, and I don't know how to go into that on command."

"Yes, you do. You've done it." Kali walked to the fireplace. "Focus on the sounds of the fire. And its warmth, and the smell of it."

"Okay." Tara placed both palms on Cyril's legs, just above his knees. She shut her eyes. The last time she'd felt Cyril's skin this way had been in Armenia. Her body tensed as she remembered awakening the next morning to him yelling at her.

*Not now*, she thought, and imagined literally pushing the memory away, though she kept her hands on him. A picture of the pieced-together Armenian letter appeared in her mind instead, lying on the round polished wood table at the cloister. Tara tried to will her muscles to relax. She'd become less stressed and anxious after Fimi's return, but her dad's call about the suicide had underscored all her fears.

She breathed in, held her breath, then let it out. The warmth of the fire, its sound and smell, ought to have helped her relax. But another image popped into her mind, this one from a Catholic grade school trip to an art museum. The teacher had stopped them all before an artist's depiction of hell. The painting had shown a gleeful, pig-like Satan breathing sulfurous fumes as an invisible god flung human bodies at him. To Satan's right, people of all ages howled as flames consumed them, while to his left, others had been chained together and lowered into a grayish-blue sea, their eyes bulging and faces blackening as they struggled to breathe. The painting had given Tara nightmares for months.

Tara let air out through her mouth, trying to focus on the fire, hoping its crackling sounds would block out everything else the way the street noises in Istanbul and the birdsongs in the Pennsylvania mountains had done. Kindling snapped. Damp wood sizzled. A burning sensation flowed along Tara's arms.

Cyril yelped and shoved her hands off his knees.

# 23

Pete closeted himself in the upstairs bathroom down the hall from the bedroom in which his family had temporarily taken up residence. On his phone, he navigated to the Reverend Frank McCoffell's website. He'd been watching the man's sermons and other video clips regularly since the night of the attack. He hadn't told his family. He didn't want to worry them, but he didn't intend to be taken by surprise again.

A new video of an interview had been posted by a student at the university where McCoffell taught. The student's voice could be heard, but only McCoffell appeared on screen. He wore a gray suit and maroon tie and sat before a navy blue backdrop.

After some general questions, the student asked for his thoughts about the suicide two days before.

"It was a tragedy," McCoffell said. "A terrible tragedy, and I have no doubt Miss Spencer never intended anyone to kill himself because of her. But this is the result of devotion to the fantastic, to the spectacle, rather than to the word of Jesus Christ."

Pete's grip on the phone tightened.

"But Jesus performed miracles. He healed people," the student said.

"He did. Through the faith of the one who needed healing. He did not draw attention to himself. Indeed, he raised Lazarus from the dead without fanfare or hoopla."

"Are you suggesting Tara Spencer staged healings to get attention?" The student sounded to Pete as if she truly were at odds with McCoffell on this. Despite his anger at the man, Pete felt a kernel of respect for the Reverend for nonetheless posting the video.

"I do not know what she did or did not do," McCoffell said. "What we must keep in mind is that to be Christian is to support life and nurture it in all its forms. In contrast, Satan, the Antichrist, Lucifer, however we name him, brings only death. Physical death and a permanent death of the soul in the fires of hell to all who believe in him."

"When you say 'he,' does that mean you believe the Antichrist or Satan is male?"

McCoffell crossed his arms over his chest. "No, I do not. 'He' is a generic pronoun meant to refer to male or female."

"Is Tara Spencer the Antichrist?"

"Only God—and the Devil—know the answer to that question."

Pete flung the phone to the floor. All the frustration he'd felt in the last year and a half, all his anger at every religious leader who'd failed him, at every person who'd taken part in the attacks on his family, and at the police who seemed no closer to finding Fimi's kidnapper, coalesced around McCoffell. Pete couldn't do much for his daughter, but he intended to do something about that man.

KALI PUT on a pair of sunglasses and turned to Tara. "Are you feeling better?"

"You should be asking Cyril that," Tara said. After she'd fed Fimi and studied that morning, Kali had insisted she wanted to window shop at the high-end boutiques in the hotel complex. Tara knew her friend was only doing it to distract her from the failed attempt to heal Cyril the day before, but she went along.

"He is fine," Kali said.

Cyril had shown Tara after jerking away from her that he hadn't been injured. She'd squeezed his thighs above the knees so hard it had startled him, and it had sent a shot of pain through the gunshot wound, but that was all. All the same, Tara had refused to try again that day.

As they exited the shop, a sneezing fit seized Kali.

Tara handed her friend a tissue. "Allergic to the prices?" The sunglasses Kali had tried on cost as much as half a month's rent on the last apartment Tara had lived in.

"I am afraid I have not felt very well all morning. I think I will nap with Fimi today."

Back at Cyril's condo, Kali lay down with Fimi in the sleeping alcove. Tara watched the two of them sleep for a while, matching her breathing to the baby's rhythm to help herself relax. Then she walked into the living room.

"I want to try again," she told Cyril. "No fire this time."

"I'm willing," he said. "I told you I wasn't hurt."

"If anything feels strange to you, anything at all, you'll pull away again, right?" Tara said.

"I promise."

They sat on the floor this time, Tara cross-legged with her back against the wall, Cyril in front of her with his back to her. She rested both hands on his shoulders from behind so that if she squeezed too hard again, it wouldn't be anywhere near the still healing area on his leg.

"This might help." Cyril flipped the switch on a small table fan next to him. Gooseflesh stippled his bare legs. "The feel of a breeze. Very different from fire."

"But you're cold."

He smiled. "I've lived through worse."

The cool air felt soothing across her face, and Tara liked the fan's quiet whir. She drew in her breath. "Okay."

She shut her eyes. She concentrated on the air moving across her face and listened to the fan. In her mind, she counted.

*In, two, three four. Hold, two, three, four. Out, two, three, four.*

Each time the lingering scent of smoke from the day before filtered into her consciousness, she imagined the smell exhaling out her mouth with her breath and refocused on the moving air, the fan's white noise, the count. She heard Fimi hiccup, heard Kali repositioning the baby on the bed. The sounds blended into the fan's whirring, then into her count. Beneath and beyond the smoke, she detected a hint of lemon and eucalyptus, the scent of the bath products here at the condominium hotel. Footsteps sounded in the hall outside the condo. A man's and a boy's she thought, one gym shoes, one flip flops. An "Ode to Joy" ringtone that she guessed was from Kali's phone, but she let that thought go, too. It all blended into her count.

*In, two, three, four.*

"Tara."

She opened her eyes. "What? I almost got there." She felt relaxed but extremely tired and wished Cyril hadn't interrupted her.

Cyril twisted around to face her. "Look."

The skin on his thigh was healed. The wound had disappeared without any scar left, and the hair over the area had grown longer and silkier.

PETE SPENCER STRODE across the Brookings Christian Institute campus, ignoring the beautiful landscaping he passed—beds of yellow and pink tulips, stepping stones circling a placid man-made pond, carefully pruned pear and apple trees. His stomach burned. Unlike his wife, he did not love confrontation or any type of conflict. While Lynette chafed at times at being the one who always had to confront inept school administrators or shady car mechanics, in peaceful moments they'd agreed their partnership worked. They did their own version of good cop, bad cop. After Lynnette's aggressive approach, Pete spoke quietly and reasonably, suggesting a compromise that the other side usually accepted.

But this time he raced toward confrontation. He'd seen his daughter Kelly frightened and his son Bailey injured by McCoffell's supporters. His own forehead still ached where a stone had hit it, causing a concussion that had left him with migraines. He hadn't mentioned that part to Tara. He didn't want to worry her more.

He'd considered and discarded the idea of calling the Reverend Frank

McCoffell. Too many gatekeepers blocked access to him by phone. And had Pete gotten through, it would have been too easy for McCoffell to give a quick answer, or no answer, and hang up. Through contacts of friends in his Christian men's group, Pete had learned McCoffell's lecture schedule at the university and chosen what he hoped was the best time to approach: right after the morning's first class, when McCoffell had a half-hour break.

He found McCoffell in his office, which was almost modest—a surprise in light of what Pete knew of McCoffell's fleet of classic cars and three mansions. The desk and visitor chairs were Danish modern, blond wood with clean lines, the couch and armchairs equally plain. A gray area rug covered most of the hardwood floor.

Pete knocked on the door frame.

McCoffell looked up from his desk. He had an ex-boxer's physique—at least thirty pounds more muscle than Pete. "May I help you, sir?"

Pete had dressed as he would if meeting clients at the accounting firm where he worked, in a navy blue suit, crisp buttoned down shirt, and muted purple tie. He'd apparently chosen well, for his clothes almost matched McCoffell's, and though the Reverend appeared surprised at the intrusion, his pleasant, almost deferential tone suggested he might believe Pete a potential donor or colleague.

"I'm Pete Spencer. I need to speak with you."

McCoffell's eyebrows arched slightly, but he nodded. "I need more caffeine. Will you join me?"

"Black," Pete said, though it wouldn't help his acid indigestion.

McCoffell disappeared to fetch the coffee himself rather than calling an assistant, another surprise. Though perhaps the school did not spend its money on assistants any more than most corporations did these days.

The sturdy blue mugs McCoffell returned with had the school's name emblazoned on them. McCoffell sat in an armchair at an angle to Pete's, almost as if they were on a talk show. Which reminded Pete of the man's attitude toward Tara on the *Janet!* show. He felt heat rise through his body up into his ears.

"Now," McCoffell said. "Why have you come?"

Pete shifted his chair to face McCoffell directly, irritated with the man's attempt to take the offense. Pete had learned to stand his ground with his father, a military man, despite Pete never quite fitting the alpha male military ideal himself. He focused on the facts and on his outrage.

"Your followers," Pete said, "gathered outside my home and attacked my family. With stones. My younger son needed stitches. My house and car were damaged. More people arrive every day. They've stopped throwing stones, but they chant Bible verses and wave signs calling Tara a fraud, and the whore of Babylon, and Jezebel. They surround anyone who enters or leaves the house, including my children. You may consider that Christian behavior, but I do not."

"Nor do I," McCoffell said. "I did not instruct anyone to harass your family."

"Several of the signs said 'McCoffell's Army.'"

"People are so literal." McCoffell held up a hand as if to forestall a response. "I don't mean you. I mean those who listen to my sermons. I've referred to being part of an army for Christ. But I meant in a spiritual sense."

"Why an army at all?" Pete said.

"An army is necessary to defeat the Antichrist."

"No," Cyril said. "We absolutely do not tell him."

"I'm not necessarily saying we should." Tara slumped in an armchair in the small conversation area in the back of the complex's game room. She'd slept for four hours after healing Cyril and had awakened feeling exhausted and as if the walls were closing in on her. What her success meant, how it fit with the letter, whether people like the Reverend McCoffell would call her a false prophet or charlatan or worse all made her insides churn and her teeth chatter. Kali had wrapped her in blankets and suggested the three of them come here to talk so Tara would feel less confined.

Kali handed Tara a large plastic bottle of vitamin-fortified water from the vending machine. "It will help you regain your energy."

Cyril sat on a loveseat across from Tara, Fimi next to him in her infant carrier. "The less Holmes knows about Tara the better."

"You still don't trust him," Kali said.

"I don't. For one thing, he's still pushing me to go to Paris again. He wants me out of the way."

Tara took a long drink of vitamin water. "You don't think Fimi and I are safe here?" She fought to keep her eyes open. Her whole body felt weighted.

"The security is top notch," Cyril said. With his army and private security background, Cyril possessed the experience to make that assessment, but Tara heard the hesitation in his voice.

"But?" Kali said.

"It's Holmes' complex," Cyril said, "and I still don't understand why he's helping Tara so much. And her family as well."

"He explained it," Tara said. To her own ears, her words sounded slow. She struggled to remember all that Holmes had said during their dinner the week before. She could picture the seared salmon and asparagus, and almost taste the flourless chocolate cake he'd ordered for them to split for dessert, but his exact words about his vision for the future escaped her. But she knew she'd relayed them to Cyril almost word-for-word the next day.

"There's something he's not telling you," Cyril said. "Fimi simply existing, simply growing into whoever she'll be, will help bring down the Roman Catholic Church? There must be more to it. I understand his personal issues with the Church, even his philosophical ones, though I disagree with him. But he's putting a great deal of personal time and money toward keeping you and Fimi here. Why?"

Tara shared Cyril's concerns over what Holmes might expect from Fimi. He'd insisted once too often that he didn't feel Tara or Fimi owed him anything. But she believed that he didn't intend to push Fimi into anything.

"It's a lot of money to you," Kali said, "or to me or Tara. But I asked our security person—the one who is left whom I trust—to research Mr. Holmes. Everything he told Tara about his family history is true. Also, his net worth is so high that if you put together all the money he advanced Tara for travel and living expenses during the last three months and quadrupled it, it is equivalent to you buying me a medium-sized latte. I am grateful for the financial help he has provided Tara. But for him, the money spent is not out of proportion to what he claims are his goals."

Tara felt as if her chair were rocking. Not in a frightening way. More like the soothing back and forth she remembered from being a little girl and drifting to sleep on long trips in the back of the family's minivan.

"The expense might be inconsequential to him," Cyril said. "But he's not buying her a coffee. He's involved in her entire life."

Her friends' voices now came from far away. Tara forced one eyelid open to see Fimi, now in Kali's lap, clapping her hands together. The baby was happy, her friends were here, she longed to let herself drift into sleep. But she did her best to follow the conversation.

"His aims aren't that different from Grandmother's," Kali said. "Yes, he is more focused on the Catholic Church, but since she started Willow Springs, Grandmother advocated the overthrow of all three major monotheistic religions. And you do not worry about her."

"Your grandmother told us exactly how she believes Tara and Fimi will accomplish their purpose—by being an alternate option for people," Cyril said. "A female archetype or messiah. Holmes has never been clear on what exactly his plan is or how Fimi fits it."

A grinding sound from behind her startled Tara. She bolted upright, her eyes darting to Fimi, who was fine.

"It was only the vending machine," Kali said.

Awake now, Tara drank more water, then said, "Holmes hopes to dismantle the Church's power structure and begin again."

"Begin again how?" Cyril said. Fimi fussed, either at the noisy machine or the volume of Cyril's voice, and he stood and paced the room, rocking her. When he spoke again, his voice was calmer. "He can start a new type of Christianity if he wants to, but he can't start a new Roman Catholic Church."

"I doubt he wants to start a new Roman Catholic Church." Tara reached for the stack of snacks Kali had set out on the table, choosing a small box of chocolate chip cookies.

"Then what? His own church?" Cyril said.

"I don't know. He doesn't know," Tara said. "Yet. But he's never harmed me, and we can leave any time."

Despite her words, Tara felt uneasy. She wanted to trust Holmes because she felt safer here than she had anywhere. But she could be wrong.

"Then let's leave," Cyril said. "You mentioned before Sophia finding you an apartment."

"I doubt Professor Gaddini has access to anywhere with this level of security," Kali said.

"I'd bring my whole family here if I could," Tara said. She had asked her dad about doing exactly that, but her parents and siblings couldn't abandon their entire lives to hide with her. Bad enough they were in Edwardsville, Illinois, adding thirty minutes each way to her parents' and Kelly's commutes. She ran her hand through her hair. Her forehead felt oily and her hair damp, as if she'd been sweating. "I know you don't like feeling under Holmes' thumb. But I don't see a good alternative."

Cyril stopped near Tara's chair, bouncing Fimi, who'd quieted. "It's not being under his thumb. All right, it is. Partly. And it's how he feels about you."

"What do you mean?" Kali said.

Cyril leaned against the arm of the chair behind him. "Tara and I may never be together romantically. I understand that. But that doesn't mean I want to see her with Holmes."

"With Holmes?" Tara relaxed, relieved that Cyril's fears were grounded in jealousy, not facts. Having finished the cookies, she opened a package of peanut butter and carrots. "He's not interested in me."

"No? He's spent two weeks here with you when normally he's flying all over the world managing his corporations. The hotels we stayed at courtesy of him were the most upscale in Europe. Your condo here has two fireplaces and a whirlpool tub. You can't tell me he's not trying to impress you."

"This complex is near Willow Springs. That's why I chose it. As for the rest, that's just his lifestyle."

"A lifestyle he may want to show you he can provide," Kali said. "Though I cannot say I have personally spent enough time with him to evaluate how he sees you."

"He's too old for me. And he's still interested in Sophia."

"I'm the last to argue with you," Cyril said. "But a thirteen-year age gap isn't one most people find insurmountable. I doubt that Holmes sees it as large. And if he is interested in Dr. Gaddini, why hasn't he contacted her?"

Tara reached over and touched Cyril's knee. "If that's what you're worried about, seriously, don't. You're right, I don't know about you and me. But I don't see Holmes in a romantic way. And if he does have some feelings for me, doesn't that at least suggest he isn't trying to hurt me or work against me?"

Cyril frowned. "That didn't stop me."

# 24

"The Antichrist." Pete's lips stuck to his teeth as he said the words. From the standpoint of sheer reason, he shared Sophia's view that the Armenian woman who'd written the letter had not meant Satan or the actual Antichrist as that term was understood today. But he feared hearing that any religious leader, particularly one with an advanced theology degree, saw Tara that way.

McCoffell waved a hand. "I'm speaking metaphorically."

"And is the Antichrist, metaphorically, Tara?"

"Not necessarily," McCoffell said. "I don't know what that letter she pieced together means or if it's authentic. Or if it was correctly translated. None of that matters. With or without the letter, your daughter—or, rather, your stepdaughter—represents a force opposed to established religion."

"Tara's never claimed that."

"No, but her parlor tricks suggest it."

"Parlor tricks."

"Her child's supposed healings of others."

Pete's pulse pounded in his head. "There is evidence she and her child were able to heal a boy of serious injuries after an earthquake. That's not a parlor trick."

"So you believe they have that power?" McCoffell said. "Or at least that the child does?"

"I don't know. I don't know exactly what happened in Istanbul, and Tara isn't certain either. But she is not staging parlor tricks."

"It doesn't reflect on you." McCoffell leaned forward, elbows on his knees, fixing his eyes on Pete. "She's not even truly your daughter. Not biologically."

"So many aspects of that statement are wrong," Pete said. "Including that you think what matters most between parent and child is biology."

McCoffell straightened his sport jacket. "Most Christian churches, especially your own, think it is. Otherwise why insist Joseph was not Jesus's father, that God Himself was?"

"To show Jesus' dual nature as God and man. Not because Joseph was any less Jesus' father."

"But he's not much of a character in any of the stories, is he? He's hardly mentioned."

"You're dodging the issue," Pete said.

"Fine." McCoffell spread his arms wide. "For argument's sake, let's say these are not parlor tricks, that a young woman has a baby with the power to heal. From where does that power come? If God meant for us to heal the ill and maimed, the churches would be filled with people seeking a cure, and they all would be cured. But that is not the reality of our world."

"Jesus healed," Pete said.

"Through faith. Your daughter has not professed faith. She's not bothered to have her child baptized, has she?"

"None of that warrants calling her the Antichrist."

"I did not call her that. If you listened carefully, at most, I suggested she is a fraud."

"And we should be grateful for that," Pete said.

"Not at all. But I'm suggesting that, given what the signs they created say, my 'followers'—as you call them—are not taking orders from me."

"But you are spurring this behavior," Pete said.

"Surely you realize religious leaders can't control everything their followers do. Otherwise your daughter would bear a great responsibility for that young man who killed himself."

Pete gripped the arms of his chair hard enough to make his knuckles turn white. "Tara didn't tell that man to do that. She didn't tell anyone to do anything, she didn't suggest anyone do anything. I did listen to what you said. While calling her a fraud in one breath, in the next you implied she leads people astray, that she's a false prophet, when she's never attempted to lead anyone."

"What is she attempting to do?" McCoffell said.

Pete fell silent for a moment. "Her life's been too chaotic since she learned she was pregnant to have a focus."

"But what does she want?"

"To live her life. Keep her child safe. Stay out of harm's way."

"Yet she conducted an apparent healing by her infant of a boy in full view of cameras. As of last week, that video had garnered over a million views."

Pete's hands closed into fists. "What was she supposed to do? Not try to help the boy because someone might record it? She can't help what other people do with videos they make without her consent."

"Just as I cannot help what my followers do."

"No, you don't have complete control. But you can tell them to stop this campaign against her."

"I can't promise they'll listen."

"You can promise you'll tell them." Pete had learned to be a broken record with people like McCoffell, or his own father. It was the only way to keep them on point rather than letting them take the reigns of the debate.

McCoffell sat back in his chair. "All right. I give you my word."

"When will you tell them?"

"When would you like?"

Pete took a moment to get past his surprise that McCoffell had agreed. "This Sunday. On your show. And today on your website."

"Fine. I'll do both."

"And then stop speaking of her at all," Pete said.

"I can't agree to that. But I will say this, I will be mindful of how I speak and what I say, and I am willing to talk with you again. Here's my direct line." McCoffell handed Pete a small square card with his photo in color and a number. "It truly was not my intent to have anyone harass you or your family."

When Pete reached the door, he paused and looked back. "What was your intent? In your sermon. What was your intent?"

"To protect people."

"From my daughter?"

"From miracles."

~

HOLMES PACED the private conference room in the complex's business center, ear buds in. He spun around when someone knocked on the door. Seeing Tara through the glass panel, he told his caller, "Update me again tomorrow. I've something else to attend to."

"Everything all right?" he said when he opened the door. Since she'd arrived, Tara had never initiated contact with him, though he'd told her more than once he was happy to talk with her any time.

"Fine," she said. But she looked tired, with circles under her eyes. Still, he was happy to see she'd continued to gain weight. The main reason he'd taken her to dinner the other night had been to ensure she was eating enough.

"But?" he said.

Tara sat directly across from him at the small round conference table. "Here's the thing. Cyril told me he thinks you've helped me partly because you're interested in me. Romantically. I don't think so, but in case that's an issue, I want to clear the air."

Holmes raised his eyebrows. No surprise Cyril Woods, smitten with Tara despite plotting against her, would be jealous, but he was impressed that Tara had decided to address the issue directly despite any risk she might perceive in doing so. "All right."

"I'm not interested in you that way," Tara said. "I appreciate all you've done for me and for my family. But I don't see it leading to a sexual or romantic relationship."

"Nor do I," Holmes said.

"Also in the 'just in case' category, I don't agree with your view that the Catholic Church needs to be overthrown, which I'm pretty sure you know. I'm not ruling out changing my mind someday, but right now I disagree with you. And as Fimi grows up, I won't push her to go along with your agenda."

"I understand," Holmes said. He wasn't worried. Larger forces were at work, and so long as the baby was kept safe from those allied against her, she would serve the purpose she was meant to serve.

Tara let out her breath. "Good. I figured we were on the same page, but I wanted to be sure."

Holmes smiled. "We're on the same page. But I appreciate your wanting to clarify everything."

Tara started to stand, then settled into the chair again. "If you have another few minutes, can I ask you something?"

"Of course."

"Were you ever really interested in Sophia?"

Holmes blinked. He hadn't expected this line of inquiry.

"I was thinking about relationships," Tara said. "And I got to wondering."

"From the moment I met her," Holmes said, "despite having had an ulterior motive in seeking her out."

"Then why haven't you tried to see her? I mean, I know you're busy, but you must be able to make some time if you really care about her."

Holmes folded his hands in front of him on the table. "My assessment is that she doesn't want to see me again, other than in connection with our efforts to aid you."

"Did she tell you that?" Tara said.

"Not in so many words."

"Sophia's someone who says what she means and means what she says. In a thoughtful, kind way, but she's very clear. If she didn't want to hear from you again, she would have told you."

Holmes' initial reaction was that he read people well, and he'd correctly evaluated Sophia's state of mind. But Tara knew Sophia better than he did. He'd always had so many other issues in his mind when he was with her. "Perhaps I leapt to a conclusion."

Tara smiled. "Perhaps."

"My turn," Holmes said. Tara asking about his personal life had opened the door for him to ask about hers without raising flags. "What place do you expect Cyril Woods to have in your life and that of your child?"

"He's a good friend," Tara said. "I've come to trust him. I find him attractive."

"So a possible boyfriend?"

"Maybe. But each time I think about that, something inside me freezes. I flash to things he said and did in the past, and my feelings flatline."

Holmes nodded. Tara's instincts had improved. In his experience, leopards might very well change their spots, but they remained leopards. "You've obviously thought about it."

"I have," Tara said. "I don't want to hurt anyone's feelings. I don't want to mislead him."

"Do you think how you feel about him might change?" Holmes said.

"I don't know."

"You know that I don't trust him. But he's welcome to stay here as long as you do. Which I hope will be a long time. And if you do decide to leave, please tell me. So I won't worry something's happened to you."

"I'll tell you," she said.

Holmes decided to leave it at that. She wasn't ready to consider how duplicitous Woods might be. But so long as she stayed under his care, he'd consider it for her.

PETE DROPPED his hand from the doorknob. "From miracles?"

"These days," McCoffell said, "people obtain entertainment, handle banking, share their views with thousands, instantaneously. At the click of a button. There is no need to wait for anything, to thoughtfully consider one's beliefs. To work. God does not deliver material goods or miracles or happiness at the click of a button. God does not deliver signs when we need them most. Sometimes, God does not deliver."

"I don't disagree." Pete's hands dropped to his sides. When his daughter Megan had been diagnosed, people in the parish had urged him to pray novenas or travel to shrines or make donations to have rosaries said, insisting Megan would "get a miracle" that way. As if God were a power-drunk despot demanding the right words be said or the correct hoops be jumped through before He'd deign to heal a dying child. "But what does this have to with Tara?"

"Drama surrounds her. A supposedly spontaneous pregnancy. A public birth seconds after an attempt on her brother's life. A mysterious ancient letter pieced together from all corners of the world. Her story is mesmerizing whether people believe her about the origin of her pregnancy or not. How can a sober, down-to-earth message to live a good life day after day, week after week, without excitement, without miracles, compete?"

"There's plenty of drama in your preaching," Pete said, thinking of McCoffell's thunderous public persona. But underneath that, something nagged at him about a previous part of the conversation, something that flitted through his mind that he couldn't quite grasp.

"Yes, there is. But people are coming to see your daughter as magic, one way or another. Some will throw stones, but others will beseech her for help. Prayers. Cures."

A scene from the rock musical *Jesus Christ Superstar* that his daughter Kelly had worked on flashed through Pete's mind. The lepers converging on Jesus, overwhelming him.

"They'll want to touch her baby," McCoffell said, "they'll ask for tokens. Look at all the people who buy water from that shrine at Lourdes, all those who flock there every day. It's a well-organized tourist destination, but how would one young woman handle such an influx? She won't. People will be disappointed. They will blame her. They will turn on her."

"That's it," Pete said, barely conscious of speaking aloud. His mother had sent him a video of her and his father's visit to the Lourdes shrine along with a vial of holy water she'd purchased there for Megan. She'd taped nearly the entire village, the grotto, the nighttime Procession for Mary, the underground mass. She'd insisted Pete sprinkle the water on Megan while she watched the video, hoping that it would heal her. Urged by the desperation in his mother's voice, Pete had done it, but without hope. But what about that video could matter now?

McCoffell was still talking. "Not that I believe in saints or healings by them," he said. "Those are pagan Catholic rituals."

"Pagan," Pete said. That was it. "Yes. Reverend McCoffell, thank you for seeing me. And for your promise."

He practically ran through the campus to the car, eager to watch the video to see if what he remembered was correct.

After her talk with Holmes, Tara lay in the sauna, soothed by the feel of hot wood under her back. Her limbs felt heavy. Despite sleeping fourteen hours straight the night before, thanks to Kali getting up with Fimi, she still felt tired. She'd tried healing Kali's cold, and it hadn't worked, but it had worn her out.

Cyril had disappeared in the late morning to do research outside the complex's walls. He was convinced Holmes monitored all the communications and traffic through the Internet connection there. He planned to look for information about Earth Day festivals in Pasadena in the hope of tracking down the Tarot card reader.

Tara awoke when the sauna timer went off. She dived into the pool. The cool water revived her, and she emerged feeling more alert.

"She likes to be read to," Kali said. She had Fimi on her lap. "She'll be a smart girl." Kali closed *Hand, Hand, Fingers, Thumb* and picked up *Green Eggs and Ham*.

Tara smiled. "I hope so." She reached for her laptop, and her smile faded. "She'll need to be." Her new knowledge that she could heal without her baby had only added a layer of complication to their lives. It was an amazing power to have, but she had no idea how to decide when to use it. The letter had said she should hide her power, and there must be a reason for that. Yet it couldn't exist only so she would hide it. It must have been given to her for a reason.

Tara made herself concentrate on her studies, and by dinner time she felt almost ready for her next exam. Cyril strode into Tara's condo, wearing a pressed gray T-shirt and jeans and carrying a folder full of documents.

"Look." He fished out a color copy of a photo of a woman and placed it on the kitchen counter.

Tara peered at it. "Is that the woman who gave us the bookmark?" She seized the magnifying glass Cyril offered.

"It's not, but I thought so too at first."

Tara nodded. "You're right. She's too young. But this really looks like her. I remember this wide face and rounded chin. It all made her look nice somehow. Friendly. Couldn't this just be an older photograph?"

"I thought you were looking for information on Earth Day," Kali said. "Trying to find the psychic who did Maya's reading."

"I was. I believe the reading was done by this woman's mother, who is now deceased," Cyril said. "I traced every psychic at the Pasadena Earth Day celebrations during the years when Maya was five, six, or seven."

"That sort of information wasn't easily available back then," Kali said. "Did you use Brotherhood sources?"

"No. I still have access to databases from when I worked at the private security firm. And contacts. There was definitely some luck as well, but that's as far as it took me, because this can't be the woman Tara and I met in Paris." He tapped the photo. "This woman, Lena Perez, was killed two years ago in a car crash, run into by an intoxicated driver."

"So there's no connection to me." Tara's body sagged on the chaise lounge, her exhaustion returned. The only quasi-lead they'd had into the meaning of the bookmark was gone. A tiny sliver of her felt relieved and wished she could use this as an excuse to focus on nothing but her schoolwork for a while longer. Give the press more time to forget about her. But her family was still outside and exposed, and she needed to find answers for her daughter for the long term. The vision of her child as a second Christ, meeting the same end as the first had, haunted her.

"I wouldn't say that." Cyril took another printed out article from his folder. "Look at the intoxicated driver's name. And his photo."

Tara slid the page closer to her. The driver's hair color stood out in the photograph. The camera had given it a brighter shade than she remembered. The caption read: "Patrick Mullin had a blood alcohol level .01 below the legal limit."

"Mullin," Tara said. "Why would the same Brotherhood member who came after me kill the daughter of the psychic who read for Maya Kerkorian thirty years ago?"

# 25

Alma rode the subway to the Greyhound bus station. Through various connections, she could get from New York to Little Rock, Arkansas. Then she could catch the Magic Bus to a gas station in Blue Springs. After that, she'd need to hitchhike or, if she had money left, see if the station could call a cab that would take her there.

After she bought her ticket in cash, she spotted a young man in the waiting area whose leather coat was open, revealing a T-shirt that said, "Walk with the angels."

Alma ran to him, grateful she might not need to make the entire journey alone. "Raphael? Are you Raphael?"

Forty-five minutes later, Alma sat with her parka scrunched against the inside of the bus so she could use it as a pillow. She needed to sleep and conserve her energy, and she felt safe with Raphael sitting next to her. He'd pretended not to know her at first, and she'd realized she ought not to have used his real name in public. So she played along, introducing herself by the fake name he'd created for her and asking if he'd sit with her to the first stop. He agreed after she bought him a soda and sandwich in the station. It made sense to her that he didn't have money of his own, because where would an angel get cash?

In this incarnation, Raphael had dark, almost black hair, and stood about a foot taller than she did. He walked as if he were bouncing a little with each step, and his teeth, though a little yellow, looked perfectly straight.

*Funny,* Alma thought, *bet he had braces when he was little.* But then she reminded herself that this was just a form Raphael chose to take, not a real person. She still felt happy he'd decided to be young and attractive looking. For the first time since she'd been arrested, she didn't feel lonely. That had been the hardest part about finding out Tara might be an enemy. She'd wanted to have Tara and Tara's family on her side. She'd wanted to know what that felt like.

"You'll stay with me the whole way, won't you?" Alma said to Raphael. "It's hard only hearing from you by text."

"Shhh." He stroked her hair and kissed the top of her head. A feeling of peace swept through her, and she let herself drift into sleep.

~

"I'M SO sorry to hear that." Through her picture window, Sophia saw a black car pull up in front of her townhome, shiny in the late afternoon sun. She smoothed her hair and took her short black wool coat out of the closet, phone pressed to her ear. "I'd been hoping you'd find some connection between the design on the bookmark and the Collyridians or other worshippers of Mary."

"I'd hoped so, too," Andrea Gutzman said. "But the history of Tarot doesn't date that far back. And as to the meaning of cards, the earliest decks weren't created as divination tools. People played a card game a bit like bridge with them. That's why you see four suits in the deck, as well as cards that look like kings and queens."

The doorbell rang. Sophia opened the door and waved Holmes in. He wore a double-breasted beige trench coat cinched at the waist and expensive-looking driving gloves.

"But the design itself could have predated Tarot," Sophia said, trying to focus on Andrea and Holmes simultaneously. She'd agreed to have dinner with Holmes when he'd called her earlier today, telling herself it would help her get a better sense of why he'd entered Tara's life and, by extension, hers, not because she hoped he'd finally try to set things right between them. But she'd spent nearly half an hour on her hair and make-up compared to her usual ten minutes.

"It could have," Andrea said. "But so far I've not found a reference to it. I'll keep checking. And I'll let you go, as I heard your doorbell, and it's almost midnight here in Florence."

Holmes glanced around at Sophia's living room and dining area as if he hadn't been here before, though he had as his Rick Gettleman persona. Sophia squeezed her phone into her small vintage evening bag. "Where are we headed?"

"That depends," Holmes said, "on whether you'll reconsider New York. My jet's at Midway."

Sophia picked up her keys from the mosaic side table near the door. "Thank you, but no." As exciting as it would be to start a date being flown to Manhattan in Holmes' private jet if they had established that they were, in fact, dating again, Sophia wanted to focus on understanding what was happening between them, if anything, and his answers to her questions about Tara. Not be dazzled by a nighttime flight and whatever over-the-top restaurant he might take her to.

"Tara's still comfortable living at the complex?" Sophia asked as Holmes opened the back door of the black car and slid across the seat. April was cold this year in Chicago, and the car had the heat blasting.

"Yes. As is Cyril Woods."

Sophia couldn't see Holmes' face very well, but his tone told her everything. "Not fond of him, are you?"

The driver made a U-turn where Sophia's street dead ended, then drove north out of Dearborn Park.

"It astounds me that Tara's forgiven him," Holmes said. "He and the Brotherhood caused so much trauma, not just to her but to her entire family. If my viewing of the news video is correct, Bailey died that day at the Arch."

Sophia raised her eyebrows. She hadn't been in a position to see exactly what had happened in the moments after Tara had given birth, and Tara's account had been jumbled. Her little brother didn't remember anything. The doctors said it was a form of traumatic amnesia. "You believe the sniper hit Bailey?"

"No, the sniper hit Woods, and the moment it happened, Woods' hand jerked, and the needle plunged into Bailey's neck. I've watched it a hundred times. Bailey staggered toward Tara and fell. Dead. She reached him, touched him, and brought him back to life."

"I don't know how you can tell that from a video."

"I can't. But I'm fairly certain I know what was in that needle. From my research on the Brotherhood. No one lives through it."

"You believe Tara has the power to bring people back from the dead?" Sophia shivered despite the car's warm interior.

"It was the child. The moment after Tara gave birth, the moment after the eclipse, her power must have been with Tara. Allowing Tara to perform miracles."

"And now?" Sophia thought uneasily of the admonition to the Armenian letter writer's niece that she must understand her power and hide it. "Do you believe Tara has that power now?"

"The baby does. That's why she must be protected at all costs."

"She should be protected because she's a human child."

Holmes waved his hand. "Of course. For that reason as well. Which is why I don't like someone as unstable as Cyril Woods around her."

"It's Tara's choice."

"Yes. Which is why I haven't asked Woods to leave the complex. Also, I can keep an eye on him there."

The car crossed the DuSable Bridge over the Chicago River. Sophia gazed out the window at the lights reflecting off the water, reminded of her dinner with Stranyero. Despite his later actions, which were reprehensible, she couldn't help thinking his motives were easier to comprehend than Holmes'.

Holmes had taken off his gloves, and he took her hand, his fingers warm around hers. "I should have said this on arrival. I'm so sorry I ever misrepresented myself to you. I should have been up front about why I came to your home last Christmas Eve."

"Yes, you should have. At the very least, you should have told me after our first date. I understand not meeting me initially under your own name, but once you began to know me, you ought to have told me."

"I'm slow to place confidence in anyone. It took me time to feel you'd be candid with me regardless who I was. And once I knew you well enough, it seemed too late to backtrack and admit I'd lied. That doesn't excuse my behavior, but I hope it helps explain it."

Sophia glanced out the window. The car was passing the beautifully lit sandstone Water Tower, which looked like a slender ancient castle, a second time. The driver must be killing time to allow them to finish their conversation. She didn't know if she could trust Holmes' words. Telling him how much she still missed the man she'd known as Rick Gettleman might be merely asking to be hurt again.

"But you never told me the truth. I found out because Tara brought us together. I'm not sure if you ever would have."

"I would have."

"Because it was the right thing to do? Or because you knew I'd put it together eventually, given your involvement in Tara's life?"

"Because it was the right thing to do. I wanted a real relationship with you. I still want it. I hope you do, too."

~

"Mullin is the man from the Brotherhood who attacked you in Istanbul?" Kali said.

"There and elsewhere," Tara said.

Cyril pointed to the photo of the woman who resembled the bearer of the bookmark. "He ran over this woman. She died at the scene."

"Ironic, considering how he eventually was killed," Tara said.

Kali peered at the article. "All he got was probation?"

"He was below the legal limit," Cyril said, "and it was his first offense. He expressed remorse. He stopped and tried to help her."

"And no one dreamed he might have done it on purpose," Kali said.

"Yet he must have. It can't be coincidence." Tara's eyes shifted between the two photos.

"No, it can't," Cyril said. "Kali's Aunt Maya, a pregnant virgin, killed in a hit and run decades ago. Perhaps by the Brotherhood, given that Nanor found Thomas Stranyero's card in Maya's room. Then this woman, daughter of a Tarot reader who might be able to explain a symbol that connects to Maya and you, killed by Mullin soon after you became pregnant."

"Did you know Mullin had a crash and killed someone?" Kali said.

"No," Cyril said.

Kali frowned. "How could you not? You worked together."

"Yes and no," Cyril said. "Mullin and I had the same role, which meant we were usually sent different places on different investigations. And the Brotherhood isn't much for sharing information, as you might have guessed."

Kali flipped through the different pages. "There are so many articles here about Mullin. You never saw any of them? Or a news report on TV or on-line?"

"These are all local papers. But if I had seen one, I would have thought Mullin made a terrible mistake. That it was a tragedy. There's nothing here that would raise a flag for me."

Tara studied the clearest picture of the victim's face. "She really looks like the woman who approached us in Paris."

"I agree," Cyril said. "I checked, and she has a sister with a last known address in London. But that was fifteen years ago, and it's no longer good. The library closed before I could get further. I'll go back tomorrow."

When Cyril stepped away to the restroom a few minutes later, Tara asked Kali, "Do you not trust Cyril?"

"I am uncertain," Kali said. "I know he did much for you over the last few months. But less than a year ago, on the Brotherhood's orders, he committed crimes."

"People can change. Especially when they reexamine their beliefs."

"Yes, they can," Kali said. "But it is wise to be cautious. With your heart as well as your child."

# 26

Holmes ordered two types of caviar, the first at $125 an ounce, the second at $150. He showed Sophia how he liked it best, spread on the small round blinis atop a thick layer of crème fraiche and nothing else.

"And the rest of this?" She gestured toward the small bowls of finely chopped egg yolks and whites, capers, and onions.

"I don't like to adulterate the taste," Holmes said.

They sat in the cocktail area off the lobby of the Four Seasons Hotel in the 900 North Michigan building in Chicago. The glass wall on the lobby side allowed Holmes to watch people entering and exiting, and he did so periodically while still focusing on Sophia.

Sophia experimented with the accompaniments. "I like it with the minced onions and egg whites, though overall I'd say it's an acquired taste."

"Wait a few days," Holmes said. "See if you're craving it. Then you'll know if you like it."

Sophia laughed and looked around at the marble floors, the crystal chandeliers, and the grand piano where a man in a tuxedo played classical pieces. "Then I'll know I'm in trouble. This is not in my budget. It's amazing how many people seem to be able to afford this level of luxury."

Holmes shrugged, wondering if he'd made a mistake in not choosing a less high-end setting. "It's expensive, yes, but not so much as you might think. For double the price of a Hyatt or Sheraton, the room size and service level are quadrupled, if not more so. Depending upon the type of travel you need, it's a bargain."

"Assuming one can afford to pay double in the first place. Or go away and stay in a hotel in Chicago at all."

"True."

Sophia took another blini, spreading the fish eggs carefully with the small silver spoon so none of them fell onto the plate. "Do you have any idea who took Tara's daughter?"

Holmes suppressed surprise. It was the question he'd planned to ask her. She might have accepted the date for one of the same reasons he'd made it. Sadness rolled over him. Until she'd said that, he hadn't realized how much he longed to be the man who took this smart, engaging woman out to enjoy her company, and he wanted her to want the same from him. They ought to be increasingly drawn to one another to the point where it took effort to slow down and behave as sensibly and warily as their circumstances required, not be sharing a date to assess what information the other had. Otherwise, he didn't differ much from the aspects of his father he admired least.

"Erik?" Sophia said.

*Tell her*, a voice in his head urged. Oddly, the voice was Henrik's. Having Henrik serve as his conscience amounted to true irony. Henrik had acted in accord with his values, yes, but in the most dangerous of ways. Holmes, on the other hand, cared about Sophia as a person, as he did about Tara and the baby. He didn't see them only as pawns in a quest for the greater good. That made him different from his father and Henrik. But perhaps not different enough, as he couldn't ignore the greater good.

"I suspect the Brotherhood," he said. "Perhaps Thomas Stranyero himself."

Sophia shook her head. "I don't think so. I had dinner with him, and my strong impression was that he was sincere when he said he no longer believed Tara or the baby should be targeted by the organization."

Holmes set down his spoon. Tiny black eggs flew. "You had dinner with him." The revelation swept away all temptation to confide in her everything he'd kept from Tara. That Sophia and Stranyero would meet or speak was something he'd never contemplated.

"I was curious about why he was searching for the baby and why he'd allowed Cyril and Tara into the Brotherhood's archives. I called and asked if he'd be in town anytime soon and asked if he'd like to have dinner. He told me when he'd be here on business and so we met."

"What business?"

"I didn't ask. I guessed he'd be no more forthright than you."

Holmes barely noticed the barb. "You met with him knowing this deal he'd forced Tara into?"

Sophia set down her glass. "I didn't know there was a deal at the time."

"But you knew he'd harmed Tara and her family in the past."

"I knew the Brotherhood had, yes."

"Stranyero is the Brotherhood," Holmes said.

"You seem to know him very well."

"I met him years ago when I began exploring the Brotherhood. He tried to recruit me." Holmes hadn't expected this line of conversation, so he wasn't sure how much was safe to reveal. He'd assumed all Sophia's contacts with Stranyero or the Brotherhood had been through Tara.

"And failed?" Sophia said.

"Yes, and failed. You think I secretly belong?"

"Apparently your brother did."

"Stranyero confirmed that?"

"In the most roundabout of ways. He asked a lot of questions about you. Your relationship to Tara. How you'd come to know her. And, by extension, me."

"And you answered." Suspicions coalesced in Holmes' mind. Sophia might be telling the truth about her conversation with Stranyero, or she might be editing or embellishing what she shared to gauge Holmes' reaction. He'd never thought her manipulative, and he still didn't think she was, but he needed to be wary. Too much was at stake to rely only upon his instincts about her.

"Only things I saw no risk in revealing," Sophia said.

"There's risk in simply meeting a man like that."

"In public? We ate at Smith & Wollensky. I took a cab home. There was no risk, and the chance to get information from him was too good to resist."

He studied her face when she spoke. "You bought into it," he said. "You fell for his charm."

"I perceived that he was trying to charm me. I've learned from history. I knew he wasn't calling merely for the pleasure of my company."

"Of course he wasn't."

She raised her eyebrows at him.

"You know what I mean," Holmes said.

"I do. At any rate, I was playing the same game. I aimed to impress him in the hope that he'd speak more candidly."

Holmes sipped the vodka that had come with the caviar. His hand remained steady.

"And did he?" he asked.

"How can I know without any way to check that what he said was true?"

"And what did he say?" Holmes asked.

"That his and Tara's goals overlap to some extent. And that he's beginning to question his devotion to the cause."

"A perfect way to appeal to a former nun." Holmes almost admired Stranyero's cunning. "Why you ever let Tara share that Armenian letter with him is beyond me."

Sophia straightened her back. "Let her? Perhaps you haven't noticed. Tara is an intelligent, competent young woman. She chose to do what she did."

"She depends upon you for guidance."

"She seeks my advice, but decisions about her life are hers to make. Her child was at risk. Her life was the one to be impacted. And I don't see what other choice she had. I'd never advise her to gamble that the police would locate the baby in time to save her."

"But for Stranyero to force her to reveal that letter is appalling."

"It's beneath contempt to use a child's life as leverage. But he did find her. The one who 'forced' Tara was the kidnapper."

"And again I say, Stranyero is the most likely suspect. He collected the ransom."

"Logic says you are correct."

"But you don't believe it?"
"I don't."

THE BUS SHUDDERED TO A STOP. Alma jerked awake. The brownish-green fields stretching along the two-lane roads out the window told her they were far from the city. She checked the display over the driver's head. 7:40 a.m.

She felt clear-headed and rested. The seat next to her was empty. She'd sat close to the tiny restroom in the back of the bus to accommodate her need for frequent bathroom visits at this stage of pregnancy. She glanced at the lit Occupied sign. Funny to think Raphael needed to pee like anyone else. But in his human incarnation, Alma guessed that was how it worked.

She stretched. Her body twisted and her arms moved too easily. She reached for her waist. Her fanny pack had fallen off. She searched next to her and under the seat, then in the aisle.

"You lose something, honey?" a woman across the aisle said. Alma didn't recognize her. She must have gotten on during one of the stops Alma had slept through.

"My fanny pack." The woman helped her look around the seat, both of them gripping the seat backs when the bus lurched.

A teenager, a girl, exited the restroom.

"You're not Raphael," Alma said.

"Not last time I checked," the girl said, and squeezed past them.

Alma felt in her back pocket. Her main cash stash was gone, too. All she had left was what she'd hidden in her sock. She stumbled forward to the bus driver. She described Raphael. The driver squinted at her. "That guy got off one or two stops back."

"Was he carrying a black fanny pack?"

The man shrugged. "No idea. He got his luggage and left like everyone else."

Alma made her way back to her seat, eyes burning with tears.

"I'm sorry," the lady across from her said.

"It's all right," Alma said.

"Was he your boyfriend?" the lady asked.

Part of the TARA2 alternate reality game required keeping the narrative going no matter what happened. Alma realized this woman must be part of the game. She was pushing Alma to improvise.

"Yes. We had a fight."

"Maybe he'll call you," the woman said.

Alma reached into her parka pocket. Relief flooded her when she felt the familiar rectangle form. At least she had her phone. She texted Raphael to ask why he'd left her alone on the bus.

It took over an hour, and many miles, for the answer to come. "I don't understand your question. I wasn't on a bus. Stay on track."

Fields had given way to hardwood forests. Alma stared out the window at the full-leafed elms and maples the bus rolled past, determined not to cry. She moved her feet closer together, wedging the backpack more tightly between them. At least she still had it, and it held a little bit of cash. And her knife, the one she'd finally used to fend off her mom's previous boyfriend. At least the entrepreneur was not a lech. A low bar, but one most men couldn't meet, so she'd give him points for that.

Raphael understood what men were like. This must be his way of forcing her to learn to get by on her own. She'd gotten too dependent on him. He'd helped her part of the way, and it was up to her to do the rest. She'd be fine. She already knew what she needed to do at Willow Springs to prove herself to Raphael forever.

By the time he finished the fourth flight, Holmes felt short of breath, but he didn't pause until he stood in front of the door to the Soho condominium. The tenant listed on its lease had insisted on a substantial fee for providing the keys, supposedly in case Holmes damaged the place. He'd admitted he'd been paid two years of rent in advance in cash, and Holmes' security team had traced a path from the tenant to Henrik as the final sublessee, so as executor of his brother's estate, Holmes was entitled to entry. But dragging the owner and tenant into court was the only way to prove the chain and allow Holmes inside lawfully, and he didn't want a record of his brother subleasing the condo in any event until he knew what it contained.

It spanned only 300 square feet, half the size of the suite Holmes was staying in at the Four Seasons in Manhattan, and smelled of dead plants. One hand towel and one bath towel, both dry, hung in the bathroom, which boasted a tiny corner shower, an old-fashioned sink with separate faucets for hot and cold, and worn but clean tiny hexagonal black-and-white floor tiles. The refrigerator held bottles of water. The small aluminum garbage can under the sink contained orange peels and the remains of three Lean Cuisine frozen entrees, tomato sauce dried on the plastic trays. So far as Holmes knew, Henrik never ate frozen dinners, let alone ones designed to be low calorie. But he knew so little about his brother, he couldn't be sure the remains weren't from Henrik.

Articles and notes tacked to one wall, which had been covered in cork, dominated the room. Henrik had pinned verses from the gospels of Mark and Luke about the end times and "great signs from heaven" next to reports of weather disasters and notable events, including the eclipse that had started two minutes earlier than predicted when Tara's baby had been born.

Another article dealt with methods of testing for the Antichrist, including one where a finger or limb of the suspect was cut off. If it regrew, that person was the Antichrist. Holmes had known about that supposed test for a long time, and he assumed Henrik had as well. Henrik must have cut it out to build the case in his own mind against the baby or against Tara, not because it was new information. Which suggested Henrik had been one of the swordsmen who had come after Tara in Istanbul when Holmes had intervened. He ran his fingers over the article. He had almost killed his own brother.

He turned to the small square table in the corner. At first he didn't notice the drawer, as it opened on the side of the table pressed against the wall, and the browning plant branches hanging over the tabletop obscured its depth. Inside it, he found a spiral notebook filled with Henrik's neat printing. He was left handed, and he'd struggled throughout Catholic school to please the nuns, who disliked the backwards slant of his cursive. Holmes sat on the cot near the window.

He expected disconnected emotional ravings. Instead, Henrik had laid out, step by step, the reasoning behind his plan to test both Tara and the baby. When he didn't succeed in the test or in capturing Fimi, he'd assembled other evidence, all of which led him to conclude Tara was the Antichrist. He'd also documented a disagreement with the Brotherhood's approach to her. The Brotherhood, according to Henrik, had tried to stop him, probably believing his pursuit of Tara only brought her more attention. Henrik had forged ahead, accepting that he might be given the death penalty, imprisoned for life, or murdered if he tracked Tara down and killed her. He felt it was worth the risk to save the world. And he hoped if he were killed before he could end Tara's life, his death as a martyr would inspire someone likeminded to go after the baby.

Three hours later, having read the journal twice, Holmes set it aside and stared out the window. Henrik's reasons for trying to kill Tara didn't surprise him, but what Henrik had written about the inner workings of the Brotherhood did. If his brother had accurately recorded the dealings between the Order and Cyril Woods, it undermined Holmes' rationale for every action he'd taken since Diedre Hartman had kidnapped Tara's baby.

# 27

Alma's feet and back ached from the three-mile walk. The only cab that served the town of Blue Springs had been seventy miles away, so she'd decided she might as well hike to the community as stand in the service station and wait. Her swollen feet made each step of the last mile agony, and she longed to yank off her hiking boots, but then she'd be standing in socks on cold gravel. She pressed the button near the wrought iron gate again. The camera above her head glared down at her.

"Yes?" The voice over the intercom sounded clipped and confident.

"I'm Alma Duttenhaver. I'd like to see Nanor Kerkorian."

"I don't see an appointment for you."

"I don't have one. But I've traveled over a thousand miles to get here. I'm pregnant, and scared, and I need her help."

Alma had paid close attention during the brief time she'd lived at Tara's house, and she figured that was the best way to appeal to anyone at Willow Springs. It was a women's community, a haven, and it was supposed to help women in trouble.

"Please wait."

Alma gave in to exhaustion and sat on the ground as the minutes ticked by. The gravel felt cold through her jeans. The clouds above darkened. Rain would make waiting more unpleasant, but it would make her more of a pathetic figure, so it wouldn't be all bad. She did her best to ignore the voice in her head, which sounded a lot like her mother's, that said she *was* pathetic. And gullible. She'd texted Raphael from Blue Springs to tell him she was still on track, that she'd understood his message. He hadn't answered yet. What if someone was taking advantage of her belief in Raphael and pretending to be him? That was what had probably happened with the young man on the bus. She'd given her cell phone number to a few people who'd been locked in the psych ward with her. One of them could have found it funny to send her around the country chasing phantoms. She'd also given the number to Tara, who might be getting back at her. But Tara wouldn't send her to do anything that might potentially harm anyone at Willow Springs, and the people at the psych ward didn't know anything about the community, so far as Alma was aware. So it must be Raphael. It had to be. Which could still make her pathetic, as while she felt Raphael was with her in spirit, she didn't know if he understood day-to-day life for a pregnant girl. For any girl. She had no confidence he'd come get her if things went wrong.

The intercom crackled. "What do you want with my grandmother?" It was a new voice.

"Kali Kerkorian?" Alma said. She'd read about Kali's supposedly miraculous recovery from a brain injury.

"Yes. What do you want from Grandmother?"

"Shelter," Alma said, "and advice. I've done some things wrong, really wrong. After I see Nanor, I plan to go back home and wait for my trial the way I'm supposed to. But I don't understand what's been happening to me, why these things happened. I want to talk to her about it."

Cold rain droplets spattered Alma, and she pulled her hood over her hair. She half-wished she had come for Nanor's advice. The woman sounded like she'd been almost like a parent or grandparent to Tara. But that was the problem Raphael needed her to fix. Nanor Kerkorian stood staunchly in Tara's corner.

"We'll have to tell the police you're here," Kali said. "You violated your bond."

"I know," Alma said. "Please let me talk to her first. That's all I want."

"Take off your backpack and set it inside when the gate opens," Kali said. "But you stay out there."

"Okay."

Alma stood, knees popping, and pushed the backpack inside the gate as instructed. Her jeans were soaked now. After a few minutes, the gate buzzed open again, and Kali instructed her to walk inside, hands in the air. She proceeded that way through the automobile parking area and into a second gated interior lot filled with golf carts.

A security guard in a khaki jacket and pants stood there. She held up Alma's knife. "What were you planning to do with this?"

Alma claimed she was exhausted, which she was, to put off the meeting with Nanor until morning. Kali scheduled it for eight a.m. After Alma settled into a guest trailer, she meandered the grounds, matching the community to the map of it that she'd memorized. It was a challenge with all the winding, narrow dirt roads, but as best she could tell, the map was accurate. The number of dark, deserted trailers surprised her, though Raphael had told her many residents had moved out. She carried her backpack with her. It contained all her belongings, minus the knife. The guard had accepted Alma's claim that she was a scared pregnant woman who of course traveled with a weapon to protect herself. And, as Alma had hoped, the seriousness of the weapon and its confiscation meant that other than advising her that smoking was prohibited outside of designated areas, the guard said nothing about Alma's cigarettes and matches.

The chapel stood about two miles from Alma's trailer. It was a plain, quiet place, no soaring steeples, no stained glass, no holy books. Just a lot of wood benches, stone, and green and yellow paint, except for the back of the chapel. There, a wall-sized painting of the Mayan ruins hung. A plaque below it said it was in memory of Maya Kerkorian, daughter of Willow Springs' founder Nanor Kerkorian and the inspiration for the whole community. Though not part of her instructions, Alma lit a row of candles in front of the painting. She felt she ought to honor Maya before she did what she'd come here to do. Something like the way the American Indians had prayed to animals before they killed and ate them.

Raphael had told her there were no services held in this chapel. The women had some type of service every Friday night at the Community Center, and the chapel was reserved for visiting speakers and individual, contemplative prayer, which included lighting candles. After inspecting the chapel for hidden cameras, Alma stuffed as many of the long tapers and thick pillar candles into her backpack as she could. It would save her a trip later.

The soft cricket sound of her phone alarm woke Alma at three a.m. She'd slept dressed in her navy blue sweats and a long-sleeved dark T-shirt, so she needed only to put on shoes.

She started near the Community Center, not far from Nanor Kerkorian's home, then worked her way out toward the main path in the woods that led to the golf cart lot. The many empty trailers made her job easy. There were no security alarms set to keep intruders out. She had only to pull down the shades or blinds, place a circle of candles in each bedroom, paper shavings beneath each one, light the wicks, and whisper the Lord's Prayer. She used the widest, sturdiest candles, the ones she thought would take the longest to burn down to the shavings, in the trailers closest to occupied homes. Raphael had promised her everyone would have plenty of time to get out before the Conflagration, but she figured it didn't hurt to use some insurance. At her last stop, she texted him she was about to leave. Then, as instructed, she smashed her phone with a hammer she'd found in the Community tool shed and left it in the center of the last circle. She didn't like doing it, as it was her only link to him. But she'd promised.

Her heart raced as she hurried through three miles of woods, stumbling occasionally on a thick root or rock, but always righting herself. Raphael had assured her that the security system had been designed to keep people out of Willow Springs, not pen them in, so she had no need to worry about being able to escape. And he was right. She made it out of the woods, through the golf cart lot, and into the automobile parking area without incident. She felt tempted to wait there until a siren went off to be sure everyone got out. But that made it more likely someone would notice her. She pushed through the outer gate with no resistance. As Raphael had promised, there was no password to exit. She hiked across the dark, deserted road, through the field beyond it, and toward the trees. She'd been hoping Raphael would send someone to keep her company, but Archangels no doubt had many more important things to do. The sky was still dark when she found a clear spot of grass between some bushes. She could hide here and watch for the explosions. She didn't understand how her candles would trigger them, but Raphael had told her not to worry about that. She had only to set everything in place, say the prayers, leave the community, then turn herself in when the time was right.

Alma didn't know what would happen to her after that, but everything Raphael had told her about Willow Springs and how the plan would work had been accurate, so she felt more certain he'd keep his promise to take care of her. She shut her eyes. She was so tired. She meant to sleep only a few minutes, but it was light out when she awoke.

Ten minutes later, the first explosion sounded.

# 28

Tara turned onto her back in the pool, enjoying floating. She'd woken up today with energy again. Fimi sat in her infant seat four feet away from the pool, accompanied by Holmes and a sitter from the hotel's service. Kali had gone home two days before to Willow Springs. Tara kept an eye on Fimi, but she wasn't worried. Holmes had security guards at the entrances and exits to the pool area. Tara was celebrating acing the final in one of her accelerated classes and being three credits closer to her degree. She had another class to start studying for soon, but it was an easy one—a Humanities 101 level she'd missed along the way.

Holmes had cleared his schedule this morning as well, taking a hike with her around seven a.m. in the wooded area beyond the resort. Tara dove to the bottom of the pool and swam underwater, loving the brief feeling of weightlessness and of being cocooned. Holmes had suggested Tara and Fimi stay for a year, saying it would give her a chance to rest after finishing her college credits, and figure out how to handle the public's reaction to the contents of the letter. Tara felt tempted. Her dad had told her McCoffell had promised to try to stop the protests. If Tara stayed out of the public eye, she'd be less likely to inspire further demonstrations or violence. So far, no one in the press or otherwise had figured out where she and Fimi were living.

Tara swam to the edge of the pool and lifted herself out, ignoring the ladder. She needed to change. Cyril had left for a meeting with Stranyero, who claimed to have something important to discuss with him. Cyril was hoping to get information about the bookmark or the woman from the Paris Flea Market whom he'd had no further luck in finding. As soon as Cyril returned, Holmes was flying Tara, Cyril, and Fimi in his helicopter to Willow Springs to spend one last afternoon there with Kali and Nanor before the community closed.

As she was drying off, Tara's cell phone rang. Seeing Kali's number, she answered immediately.

"Hey, can't wait to see you," she said, expecting a similar response.

She heard sobbing and sirens.

THOMAS STRANYERO SET his briefcase on the bar. It didn't contain enough evidence to stand up in court, but it would change Cyril's life. And possibly Stranyero's if anyone learned he'd provided it, but no one would. MacNeil might guess, but he'd never be certain.

"I apologize for the delay," Stranyero said. "I had to answer a call right after exiting the plane."

He took the bar stool next to his former protégé. He'd deliberately arrived half an hour late. Fenton MacNeil had asked him to keep Cyril occupied and away from the condominium complex for at least three hours. It was part of MacNeil's plan to discredit Willow Springs and Tara Spencer. He wouldn't share details, though he'd assured Stranyero neither Spencer nor her baby would be seriously harmed. Stranyero had couched his questions in terms of concern about the Brotherhood's culpability if anything happened to either. He didn't feel certain he could trust MacNeil's answers, but he'd agreed to the request because he'd been looking for a reason to talk with Cyril that wouldn't raise his colleagues' suspicions.

"It's fine," Cyril said. "What did you want to talk about?"

It was nine in the morning central time. Cyril sipped what looked like Perrier. Stranyero waved the bartender over and ordered a screwdriver and a glass of ice water.

"I'm wondering what it's like," Stranyero said, "outside the Brotherhood."

"Why?" Cyril said.

Stranyero shrugged. "I was your mentor. I recruited you. I still feel some responsibility for you."

"I'm fine."

"Your belief in God remains unchanged?"

"I don't need the Brotherhood to believe in God," Cyril said.

"I never suggested you did." Stranyero stirred his drink but held off on tasting it. He had no intention of drinking more than one. No sense dehydrating before getting back on a plane. "You had a mission from the Brotherhood to carry out God's plan. Now what do you have?"

Stranyero recognized the defiant jerk of the chin and set of the shoulders. "I still feel I'm fulfilling my real mission," Cyril said.

"Guarding Tara Spencer?"

"I'm not her guard."

Stranyero nodded. "True. Erik Holmes does that quite well."

Cyril's mouth turned down. "Holmes isn't her guard."

"Then what is he? Her keeper?"

"He's offered her a safe place to stay. She accepted."

"And you are staying there as well, correct? So what's your 'real' mission?"

Cyril folded and unfolded a corner of his cocktail napkin. "Living a decent life following the tenets of Christ."

"That sounds pompous. And vague," Stranyero said. "Too vague to provide a sense of purpose."

Cyril flipped screens on his cell phone, then held it out. "Does this mean anything to you?"

Stranyero looked at the phone, which showed what looked like a newspaper photo of Lena Perez, the Argentinian woman Special Investigator Mullin had run over. If Cyril had found it, he must know of the connection to Maya Kerkorian. But he doubted Cyril understood Perez belonged to forces that had opposed the Brotherhood almost since the time of Andrew of Crete. "The unfortunate victim of Investigator Mullin's DUI. How did you come across it?"

"You knew he'd killed someone?" Cyril said.

"A tragic accident." Stranyero sipped his drink. It had too much orange juice and not enough vodka, but that was all right. He needed to stay clearheaded.

"An accident is when you slip and fall on the ice," Cyril said. "This looks like a deliberate action."

"Why do you say that?"

"Because this woman is connected to Maya Kerkorian. And to Tara."

With effort, Stranyero kept his face expressionless. He hadn't been aware of any overlap between Lena Perez and Tara Spencer. "That's not possible. This woman died before Ms. Spencer became pregnant."

Cyril started to speak, then took the phone back and put it in the front pocket of his T-shirt.

"If you're imagining I know more about the woman," Stranyero said, "you're correct, I do. But as you're no longer a member of the Brotherhood, I can't share it with you."

Cyril swiveled on the stool and met Stranyero's eyes. "Are you trying to get me to come back?"

"No one wants you back."

He expected Cyril to recoil, but the younger man merely nodded. "Good. Because I feel right inside now. I'm no longer running from myself. It's hard. But it's real."

"And the Brotherhood wasn't?" Stranyero asked.

"It was real for you. For Mullin. But I wasn't sincere. I thought I was, but it had more to do with what the Brotherhood saved me from being, from thinking about. The Order, the mission, was never an end in itself."

"It was for me." Stranyero cleared his throat. "It is."

"I used it to escape who I was rather than build a life for myself."

"And that's what you're doing now? Building a life?" Stranyero said.

"Trying."

The bartender came by, but both men waved him away. Stranyero stirred the orange-tinged ice in the bottom of his glass. "A life with Ms. Spencer? You've been at her side since the day at the cloister."

"I don't know if that means anything for the future," Cyril said.

"It can't be easy to imagine a future when you're living under Erik Holmes' wing," Stranyero said.

"He makes Tara feel safe."

"In a way that you can't." Stranyero glanced at his briefcase. He still felt unsure. It was one thing to tell Cyril about the trail of evidence had it led to the Vatican, as Stranyero had expected it would. But instead it had led to the son of the man who'd recruited Stranyero into the Brotherhood. Despite his growing doubts, Stranyero still felt loyal to that man, and so to his entire family. But Cyril had been his protégé and was still his responsibility.

"That's true." Cyril stared at his half-finished glass of carbonated water. "I wish it weren't, but it is."

"You can find a new purpose. You're young."

Cyril studied his mentor's face. "You're not old."

"I didn't used to think so." Sixty had not seemed old to Stranyero until recently. His parents' generation had been old, most of them, at that age. The women shifted to stretchy pants and wore outdated styles, the men practiced groaning when they stood from a chair, dreamed of retirement, then died within a year or two of their sixty-fifth birthdays. Now the professionals he knew worked well into their seventies. Not because they had to, but because they enjoyed it. Or, if they retired, they traveled, they volunteered, they started new business ventures. He had nothing new he wanted to start. He'd never contemplated a change in direction. Never contemplated a change. "The Brotherhood is my life."

"What about your wife?" Cyril said.

"We divorced a year after our youngest child moved out."

"And your career—is it bound to the Brotherhood?" Cyril said.

Three men in suits entered where the bar opened to the airport terminal. Stranyero waited to answer Cyril until after the men settled in seats on the other side of the lounge. "I could separate my business from the Order. Not that I have plans to do that. To do anything. But if I did, going forward that would not trouble me."

"Then what would?"

"You've rejected the Brotherhood. How do you justify the extreme actions you took because of it? The crimes?" Stranyero said.

"I can't. What I did, so much of what I did, was wrong, but I can't change it. I can only do better now and in the future."

"That works for a twenty-eight-year-old," Stranyero said.

"So it's better for someone older not to change?" Cyril said.

"Perhaps. But then, I'm not a fan of change." Stranyero slid his briefcase closer to him. It contained a paper trail for the foster placement, links to the org charts of companies related to the placement, corporate filings, copies of car rentals and tickets paid for by Mary Vaccarezza/Marie Glaston. He signaled the bartender for another drink. "What if Ms. Spencer falls in love with someone else? The esteemed Erik Holmes for instance?"

Cyril's chin lifted, his jaw squared. "It won't change what I believe or don't. I haven't shifted from worshipping God or Christ or the Brotherhood to worshipping Tara. I've stopped worshipping."

"All the same, perhaps you'd like some ammunition against Mr. Holmes?"

THE HELICOPTER ROTOR beat the air. The sitter, Holmes, and Tara, who carried Fimi, ducked under it. Holmes jumped into the pilot seat. Once in the air, Tara planned to text Cyril to fly to Arkansas ASAP. She hadn't been able to bring herself to leave the baby at the complex with only the sitter despite all the security. It had to be someone she trusted entirely. Nor had she been willing to wait for a helicopter pilot to arrive other than Holmes. Kali had said the firefighters were still trying to control the flames, and Nanor had not yet been located. She'd gone for a run at eight a.m. Kali hoped that meant she'd been well away from the trailers when the fire had started, but it had spread throughout the woods. The recent light rain lessened the spread, but flames still raged in some spots and sputtered in others.

Holmes swiveled in the pilot's chair and shouted to be heard. "One last time, Tara. Reconsider. Stay here with the baby. I'll fly there and see what's going on. I'll bring Kali back if that's what you want."

"No, I have to go, I might be able to help."

"You can't bring the baby to the fire."

"I won't," she shouted back. "Just go."

Tara's teeth clenched, and she made herself relax her arms so she wouldn't grip Fimi too hard. Whoever had set off the explosions might have done it solely to destroy Willow Springs, but it might also have been to bring her and Fimi there. But she had to go. If Nanor or others were hurt, she might be able to heal them.

The flight time was less than an hour, but the jolting and airsickness kept Tara from using her phone. As they neared the area, she forced herself to look down. She saw spots of yellow and orange flames across an area that must be Willow Springs. They landed in a field about a mile away, and a car Holmes had arranged waited for them.

Tara felt panicked at whether to tell Holmes, the sitter, and Fimi to stay in the helicopter or come with her in the car. If she and Fimi had been lured here, danger might await them at Willow Springs.

"It doesn't matter," Holmes said. "I've got a weapon, I'll protect her."

Tara shook her head. "We can't risk anyone grabbing her, or shooting you."

"I'll take off again if I need to," Holmes said. "I have enough fuel."

Tara nodded, and the driver sped her toward Willow Springs. As they approached, Tara saw Kali standing outside the outer parking lot in the midst of police cars, ambulances, and fire trucks. Tara ran to her and they hugged. Kali's face was grime and tear-streaked, her hair singed, and she had burns across one arm. But she'd gotten out of her and Nanor's home.

"The empty trailers," Kali said. "They think it started there, one explosion after another."

Smoke choked the air. Black billows of it spewed from the community. Rain continued to sprinkle. Tara hoped it would turn into a downpour.

A cameraman stood on a flatbed truck against the wall, filming over it into the parking area and beyond. A news helicopter hovered above. A newscaster interviewed a survivor and, for the moment at least, didn't seem to notice Tara.

"Grandmother has not been found," Kali said. "She may be lying somewhere unconscious, she may be dead. You must help her if she's found."

"I will. I'll try."

"With Fimi too?"

Tara felt torn. She couldn't bear seeing Kali's anguish, and she couldn't stand to lose Nanor herself. But to bring Fimi here amidst the smoke and all the people posed too much risk.

"I can't."

"She's my family," Kali said. Kali had never been very close with her mother, and it was Nanor she lived with and loved.

"I'll do everything I can," Tara said.

"If you can't heal her here, perhaps if they get her to a hospital," Kali said. "You could bring Fimi there."

"Yes, yes, I can do that."

Ambulance lights flashed, smoke billowed, and people were brought out and whisked into ambulances. But no Nanor.

Tara started to try to help some of those brought out, but Kali grabbed her arm.

"Please don't," Kali said. "I know it is selfish, but the paramedic said so far they will survive. No one is badly burned. If they bring Grandmother out, she will need you more. She is old, and she has been amidst the smoke so long. We will go to the hospital later for everyone."

"How many more are in there?" Tara said. Her heart pounded as she considered whether she could take Fimi to the hospital later and try to help everyone else. Maybe with Holmes standing guard so no one snatched Fimi away, she'd feel it was safe.

"It can't be many," Kali said. "Another large group left yesterday, so only twenty of us remained, for which I am grateful. Sagun was taken earlier to the hospital with smoke inhalation. Her trailer is near the perimeter, so she was able to raise the alarm and escape through the access road at the back without injury. She got several others out as well."

"So, what, three might be in there, including Nanor?"

Kali nodded.

Tears filled Tara's eyes. All this was due to her. It couldn't be a coincidence. Even before the fire, the fallout from her pregnancy and notoriety had emptied Willow Springs. All she and Fimi seemed to bring was destruction and danger. Which was what the letter had said: "Destruction will be caused by you."

She looked up and saw two helicopters.

Kali followed her gaze. She pointed to the dark blue one. "That was here earlier, it's a news copter."

Tara didn't know if the other belonged to Holmes. It was gray like the one she'd ridden in with him. Her throat, already raw from the smoke, tightened. She hoped it wasn't him, as that meant there'd been some threat on the ground to Fimi.

She glanced over her shoulder and couldn't see the car that had brought her here. It was blocked by emergency vehicles and local police cars.

She pulled out her phone to text Cyril, though he'd probably already reached the complex and gotten the message she'd left there. As she did so, the slate-gray copter flew out of sight.

## 29

The whole shrine was built around two women—Saint Bernadette Soubirious and the Lady in White, an apparition Saint Bernadette had claimed to see in the grotto at Lourdes. Yet it was robed men who crossed the altar of the underground church, one after the other, kissing each other on the cheek as they passed. Pete sped up the video so they moved more quickly, grateful that he'd been able to unearth the old VCR from beneath the boxes of used car and motorcycle parts in the garage.

His wife sat on the double bed behind him, taking out her earrings. "You braved the protestors to find this why?" Lynette said. The Spencers were still living crammed in one room in Edwardsville, Illinois, minus Kelly, who'd gone to stay with Nate at his apartment.

"For this. And the protestors were gone." It was twilight now on the screen, and the camera panned past a row of stone buildings. Pete froze the video on a store, then held a magnifying glass over it so Lynette could see the small square stained glass windows on either side of its entrance. The interior lights shone through them, illuminating the designs. One had what was likely meant to be the Lady in White. Pete pointed to the other image. "Here. In the window."

Lynette peered at it. "A woman pouring two jugs of water into the spring at Lourdes."

"But why do you think it depicts the spring at Lourdes?" Pete said.

"Because that's where this store is."

"Right. And if it were somewhere else, you wouldn't assume that."

"Okay, a woman pouring water into an anonymous spring," Lynette said.

Pete unlocked his phone and opened the photo Tara had sent of the silver bookmark from Paris. He held it next to the image.

"Oh," Lynette said.

"Yes."

The sounds of their hosts' daughters' voices came from down the hall. They were trying to convince their parents to let them sleep in the tent in the yard that night, rather than on the floor in the living room.

"But how does this help?" Lynette said. "So the bookmark has a design that also appears at Lourdes."

"A design from a Tarot card. At a Catholic shrine. That's why it nagged at me."

"If this were in the church I grew up in, I'd be shocked. But Catholicism has always had pagan leanings."

"Tarot's not pagan. And the Church is against all types of divination—runes, Tarot, palm reading. That I meditate makes Father Saur nervous," Pete said.

"All right, so something at Lourdes might relate to the bookmark."

"Must relate to it. I want to go there to find out how."

"You're due at work Monday," Lynette said. "Your firm's not about to give you more time off."

"I can be back by then if I leave tomorrow morning."

"Or you could research on the Internet."

"I did. So did Nate. There's nothing at all on-line about it, other than Nate found one photo of the window. It was on a site of someone who took the same tour Mom and Dad did, but a year earlier. I talked to Mom, and she doesn't remember it. Not the store, not the window."

"So call someone at Lourdes. They must have a tourist division. A directory. Something," Lynette said.

"I tried. No one could pinpoint the store. One person thought she might have seen it, but she wasn't about to go wandering around searching for me."

"We can't afford another overseas trip. We couldn't afford the first one."

"I know," Pete said.

"No. Not Erik Holmes."

"I don't like accepting his money any more than you do. But I called him yesterday, and he agrees with me that this must mean something."

Lynette put her hands on her hips. "He also wants to take down the Catholic Church. Is that where you're headed?"

"Of course not. But this is a last chance to help Tara before I return to work. Certainly she's not going to take Fimi overseas again, or leave Fimi with anyone to go there herself."

"Let Cyril go. Or Holmes. He's wealthy, he flies all over the place in his private jet."

"No one is going to tell Erik Holmes anything. Or Cyril."

"And they'll tell you."

"Yes. Because I'm Tara's dad. Like the woman in Armenia did."

"Tara doesn't need you to be her hero, Pete," Lynette said. "She needs you to help her find some semblance of a normal life."

~

A FIREFIGHTER and a paramedic came through the gate carrying a stretcher with a body on it.

Tara's phone vibrated insistently. She glanced down as Kali ran toward the stretcher.

The text came from Cyril.

*Get Fimi back. Holmes took her from Diedre Hartman.*

"What?" Tara said aloud. That couldn't be right.

*How U know?* she wrote back.

"Tara." Kali's voice drew her back to the scene. Kali stood with the paramedic a few feet from the stretcher. The firefighter had disappeared.

Tara ran toward her friend.

"I'm sorry," the paramedic said. She had a hand on Kali's arm. "I believe we found your friend's grandmother. Everyone else has been accounted for. We tried everything to revive her."

"I can't look," Kali said.

"I will," Tara said, but she glanced up. Was that Holmes' helicopter hovering, or another news copter?

Her phone buzzed and she squinted at the message: *Stranyero said.*

She looked back at Kali, whose eyes were fixed on Tara's cell phone, either to avoid looking at her grandmother or because she couldn't believe Tara was texting someone at this moment.

Tara knelt at the stretcher, adrenalin churning through her. She felt as if she were hovering somewhere outside her own body as she stared down at Nanor. At the same time, her mind raced, trying to figure out how she could get Fimi back from Holmes without tipping him off.

The older woman's face was contorted, as if she'd died gasping for breath. She had no burn marks. She wore a dark green running suit, and grass stains of the same color streaked her palms and the insides of her wrists, as if the color had bled in lines onto her skin.

Grass stains, Tara thought. She must have put her hands out to stop her fall.

She stood and nodded to Kali. "It's her. I'm so sorry."

Her cell phone buzzed again. "It's Fimi," she told Kali. She didn't want to add worry to her friend's mind, but Kali needed to know why Tara's full attention wasn't with her. "Cyril says Holmes is the one who kidnapped Fimi."

"Oh, no." Kali's eyes flew to the stretcher, back to Tara, then to the paramedic. "We need a few minutes."

The paramedic nodded and walked away.

"Tara, I'm sorry to ask, but please." Kali knelt on the other side of the stretcher, her tears gone, her face solemn and frightened. She met Tara's eyes. "Before it's too late and they take her away."

ALMA COULDN'T STOP SHIVERING, despite waves of heat from the fire washing over her. Her whole body ached, and the baby pressed against her bladder. She'd already relieved herself once in the woods, but she felt too exhausted to go through the process again. Earlier, she'd wished for binoculars so she could see the scene play out, now she only whispered prayers, alternating between God and Raphael. She'd done everything she'd been told to do, so why was no one coming to help?

Then she remembered. She was supposed to turn herself in. She struggled to her feet. It took tremendous effort to tramp through the bushes and trees and into the field, but she managed. Police cars lined the road half a mile away. Perspiration poured down her face and body. The air looked wavy. She pushed herself forward a few more steps, then one more, then collapsed.

~

TARA PEERED AT THE SKY, searching for helicopters, eyes burning. She fumbled with her phone, hitting Holmes' number, but got no answer. If he were flying, though, he might not answer. In the rush, she hadn't put the number for the sitter into her phone.

"Tara."

Her fingers flew over the keys. *Meet me in the field. 5 min.*

Holmes might not see the text. And if he didn't plan on bringing Fimi back, a text wouldn't prompt him to do so. But he hadn't hurt Fimi before and hadn't tried to take her away from Tara since her return. She held onto those thoughts and turned her attention to Nanor. She needed to help the older woman if she could. She swallowed hard and sat on the ground cross-legged, feeling the hot earth beneath her. She rested one hand on Nanor's upper arm, the other over her heart. Nanor felt warm to the touch. She could not have been gone long, or perhaps it was the heat from the fire.

Around her, people shouted and ran. The helicopter rotors beat above them. Tara pushed worries about Fimi away, resisting the urge to run from the area, to run to a police officer, to run to someone, anyone. Her child would be fine. She would be safe. Holmes would bring her back. The sooner she focused, the sooner she could make sure of that.

She breathed in, struggling to relax, but the smell of smoke assaulted her, speeding her heart further until she felt it would burst from her chest.

*Fraud. Fire and brimstone*, she thought. The Reverend McCoffell's words rang in her ears. She couldn't do this, she'd never be able to do this. And if she could, what did it mean? The Antichrist brought only death in the fires of hell. Was that why these things kept happening? Why Fimi kept being in peril? Perhaps she didn't belong with Tara, perhaps the Universe was taking her away for a reason. Perhaps Holmes was the good guy, and Tara was not.

"I am not evil," she said, not realizing she spoke aloud, but aware of the question in her voice.

"Tara," Kali said. In her friend's voice, Tara heard everything. Loss, anger, fear. Desperation. And a need for Tara to focus, to put aside her own anxieties, to put aside what the events might mean to her, about her. What Holmes might do, what McCoffell might say, what the world might believe.

"Yes," Tara said.

She breathed in through her nose. Rather than fighting the smoke smell, she let it fill her, imagined it as black smoke. She let her fear fill her, and her anger, and then imagined it flowing out the top of her head. Something Nanor had taught her to do with her anxiety and panic. She opened her mouth to exhale and pictured the smoke's color lightening to gray. She breathed that back in, and this time saw it turning white. Then she imagined clear, fresh air, so real she could taste it. She smelled Nanor's jasmine perfume, and the lilies that bloomed at Easter in her parents' yard, and the lilac scent from her own grandmother's garden. She saw the colors swirled together in a long flowing dress worn by Nanor, and Nanor spinning to let it furl out. She heard Kali's voice exclaiming, felt Nanor's chest rise and fall, not dramatically, not with a gasp, but as if she'd been breathing all along. Though Tara's eyes were shut, she saw the older woman shift on the stretcher, smile, sit.

And still Tara breathed, caught in a whirl of life and beauty.

She felt the ground beneath her legs cool and imagined that coolness sweeping through the field and beyond, along the road and into the residential area, around the winding paths, through the woods, past the chapel, into the golf cart lot and the automobile parking area beyond it. As if transported back in time, she heard singing from the Friday evening services at the Community Center, remembered the twinkling lights, the long-haired fiddle player dancing through them, the women's voices at the first service she'd attended there. The beauty and freedom and stillness she'd felt then swept through her now. She felt rain, warm and cool at the same time, on her face and arms. She imagined the plants at the Community Center garden growing outside its windows, how beautiful they looked through the floor-to-ceiling glass in the social room, and how the floodlights beneath them illuminated their beauty at night.

"Tara, oh my God, Tara."

Kali's voice brought her back, and Tara opened her eyes. She gripped the stretcher to keep from losing her balance, but faltered because Nanor no longer lay upon it.

Nanor and Kali stood, embracing. The air had cleared, no tinge of smoke remained in it. The ground had not only cooled, but the grass and plants had greened. In a daze, with Kali supporting her, Tara moved toward the gate, looked through it at the lot. The grass that had been trampled stood tall. The half-burned trees along the lot's edge now stood revived, full-leafed and green. Though the cars and trucks parked there showed scorch marks, the earth appeared as if it had never burned.

"Beautiful," Tara said.

The trees began to waver, the ground felt uneven beneath Tara's feet, and everything went black.

# 30

The camera zoomed in on a reporter standing in front of the Blue Springs village hall next to a fire truck. She'd just finished interviewing the paramedics who'd brought Nanor Kerkorian out of Willow Springs on the stretcher.

"Despite the claims of emergency personnel and Mrs. Kerkorian's granddaughter, questions remain regarding the alleged death of the founder of Willow Springs. Nanor Kerkorian, known to many in Willow Springs as 'Grandmother,' studied, practiced, and taught meditation for nearly five decades. Just as some monks are able to put themselves into suspended animation, stopping their vital signs, a former Willow Springs resident speculated that Kerkorian put herself in just such a state to avoid smoke inhalation. If that's true, Tara Spencer's touch merely brought her back to a full waking state. Skeptics cannot deny, however, the footage showing the fire, the widespread damage to the flora and fauna, and its utter and total reversal.

"Spencer fainted at the scene and has yet to regain consciousness," the newscaster continued. "She was medevacked to a trauma center in Texas. Exactly which hospital has not been made public, and her family members could not be reached for comment.

"Alma Duttenhaver, a nineteen-year-old woman wanted in Pennsylvania for violating bond conditions after assaulting Tara Spencer, was also found unconscious near the scene. Witnesses saw her emerge from a wooded area half a mile from the fire. Residents of Willow Springs say the young woman, who is seven months pregnant, arrived at the community the night before asking to speak with its founder. She regained consciousness and is being held by the Arkansas state police."

The screen showed the flames, the smoke, the damaged land, then its rebirth and regrowth as if on a fast-motion camera, then footage of Tara Spencer being loaded into a helicopter on a stretcher.

Stranyero had entered through the back door of Fenton MacNeil's library a few seconds after the report had begun. MacNeil sat in an armchair with a tall back, feet flat on the ground, spine straight, eyes fixed on the television.

"Not quite what you expected?" Stranyero said.

"Not quite," MacNeil said. His voice was low, without its usual power or sarcasm. He didn't turn to look at Stranyero, but he did press the mute button.

Stranyero took the wingback chair opposite MacNeil. "How did you manipulate the girl? Alma."

"The same way you did," MacNeil said. "Texted her as Raphael. Henrik Holmes ought to be pleased that we made so much use of his moniker."

"There's no evidence I ever posed as Raphael."

"Nor that I did. Her cell phone went up in flames."

"How did she get so many explosives into Willow Springs?"

"Use your head." Some animation returned to MacNeil's face as he waved his hand. "She brought nothing but matches and cigarettes."

"Ah, of course. The explosives were put in place long before she arrived."

"Yes," MacNeil said.

"And then remotely activated by someone else. Someone wholly unconnected with whoever placed the explosives."

"Of course," MacNeil said.

"So Alma Duttenhaver only believes she set off the fires." Stranyero felt mildly nauseated. Over the decades, he'd wholeheartedly taken part in plots with MacNeil that differed from this one only in degree, not in kind. But he'd lost his relish for it. Which might be the key to the real power Tara Spencer had. And which was perhaps why MacNeil had cut him out of this one, other than giving him the tangential role of keeping Cyril out of the way.

"All those years of cultivating the local police force paid off," MacNeil said. "I doubt Nanor Kerkorian trusted them, but she could hardly refuse them access to her community." Color had returned to MacNeil's face as he described his triumph, but he paled again on speaking about the Willow Springs founder.

"And you fed the press the story about Kerkorian being a devoted meditation practitioner," Stranyero said.

"She is a devoted practitioner."

"Not such that she can put herself in suspended animation."

"No. But it's easy enough to fool people who want to believe."

Stranyero stared at the television, where photos of Nanor Kerkorian throughout her life were flashing. "Which means Tara Spencer raised someone from the dead. And rejuvenated the earth."

"Or made it appear that way," MacNeil said. But he, too, kept staring at the screen.

Tara smelled rubbing alcohol and antiseptic. No smoke. No fragrances from the trees and shrubs around Willow Springs, though she felt sure that's where she was. She could picture the small field across the street from the community, outside the gated lots. Holmes had flown her to a larger field about a mile away, and she'd left Fimi with him. Her heart rate elevated. She tried to open her eyes, but they felt too heavy.

*Fimi.*

The air was wrong. Too clear, too flat. She heard muted voices. Not people, she didn't think. A television or radio.

There should be wind. And heat. And smoke.

*Where there's smoke there's fire.*

The burnt land, the smoke. Nanor dead on the stretcher. Kali and Nanor embracing. The trees regrown. But Fimi—something about Holmes and Fimi.

Tara struggled to sit, but her limbs felt like gelatin. "No." She'd meant to shout, but her voice sounded shaky and small.

The effort to move and speak exhausted her.

VOICES AGAIN. She recognized Cyril's, but not what he was saying. Her mom asked for a diet soda. She didn't hear Fimi.

She wiggled her fingers.

"Look," Cyril said. "There."

His hand gripped hers, just the right amount of pressure.

"She smiled," her mom said.

"Squeeze my hand, Tara, can you squeeze my hand?"

She did.

"Nothing," Cyril said.

THE BED HAD BEEN RAISED a bit so she was almost sitting. The air still had that antiseptic feel, but it was stale, too, with an undertone of ammonia.

*A hospital? Like a hospital....*

Yes, because she'd done something. Something amazing. Healed someone, and it had knocked her out.

Tara fluttered her eyes. Bright lights, metal side table, IV tree. A curtain along the left side of her bed.

"Tara?" Cyril said.

She opened her eyes. Cyril stood at her side. Kali joined him an instant later.

"We thought you were waking up, they said you were, but we didn't know if we should believe it," Kali said.

"Fimi?" Tara said. Her throat felt dry and raspy.

"Yes," Cyril said. "She's good. She's fine. Perfectly fine."

The word "perfectly" worried Tara.

Kali touched her upper arm. "It's true, she's fine, she's with your parents. I'll call them. And a nurse, I will get a nurse."

Kali disappeared and Tara drifted away again. When she opened her eyes, a woman in scrubs was checking her blood pressure. "The resident will be here soon," she said. "And we've called a neurologist."

It seemed odd that the doctor hadn't come yet. And that Kali hadn't returned, and her parents hadn't arrived. But Cyril remained, stepping in when the nurse disappeared, holding her hand.

"Cyril?"

"Yes."

"Fimi's really okay?"

"Yes."

"Then why do you have such a strange look?" Tara said.

"She's perfect, I promise."

"But?"

He sighed. "Tara, you've been out a long time."

"But Fimi's all right? And Nanor?"

"Yes. They're well, as are your parents, and siblings, and everyone. But...you remember the fire?"

"Yes. At Willow Springs."

"It's been a long time since the fire. Probably much longer than it seems to you."

"How long?" Tara said.

"No one can believe you've awakened so alert and healthy."

"How long, Cyril?"

Kali entered the room. She bent down, out of Tara's sightline. When she straightened, she held a blond toddler in her arms.

"Thirteen months," Cyril said.

# AUTHOR'S NOTE

A lot has changed since I started Book 1 of 4 of *The Awakening* series. Back then, *The Awakening* featured six different pregnant virgins, and their story was meant to be finished in a single book. I submitted the first three chapters—all I had written at the time—and an outline as part of my application for the thriller writers' section of the 2005 *Maui Writer's Retreat*. Being accepted is probably the best thing that ever happened to my writing. The retreat included an optional session where the participant wrote her or his twenty-five-word "What If" novel tag line on a white board in front of a conference room full of people. Then author John Saul and his writing partner Mike Sack critiqued it, which was known as being "Sauled and Sacked." Saul and Sack did not pull punches. That made the session both extremely valuable and a bit nerve-wracking.

I felt nervous, but at least I wasn't bringing my What If in *after* writing and revising an entire suspense novel, something I'd done a few years before. Seeking feedback at the very beginning turned out to be a wise choice. Saul, Sack, and my retreat instructor, thriller writer Gary Braver (now my favorite thriller author—check out *Gray Matter* in particular) all agreed that six pregnant women was five too many. Gary helped me narrow down to one protagonist and yet keep my theme of women banding together to combat forces that threatened their lives.

Obviously, I chose Tara Spencer as the protagonist. A few of the other women characters—including Sophia Gaddini and Nanor Kerkorian—morphed into (non-pregnant) allies and friends of Tara.

It took me nearly three years to finish drafting and revising the manuscript, as I was practicing law 55-65 hours a week at a large law firm at the time. Mostly I fell down on the job when it came to marketing. My only free hours were on Friday nights and Sunday mornings, and I nearly always chose to write fiction rather than try to sell it. I did get a few short stories published, and I received encouragement and thoughtful comments on *The Awakening*, but no publishing contract. One editor at a well-known publisher liked it a lot and thought it had potential, but didn't have room on his plate to work with a new writer. Even so, he very kindly took time to suggest revisions, for which I will always be grateful.

Then, in early 2007, my parents were hit by an intoxicated driver. Both eventually died from their injuries. That year was very difficult for everyone close to my parents. Most of the writing I did was in various personal journals, and most of it was angry, sad, and depressed.

I also reevaluated my life. From Day One of law school, I'd had in the back of my mind that I'd like to run my own law practice. I wanted to be my own boss. And I wanted to work at a slower pace so I could devote more hours to writing and still have time for friends, family, and things like reading books and seeing movies. So, in 2008, I started my own law firm.

It turns out being your own boss is fantastic. And demanding. And time consuming. The good news is that by the time I returned to *The Awakening* around 2010, I could see how to fix the issues the editor who'd written to me had pointed out. I revised, revised, revised. Just as I'd begun thinking about sending out queries and perhaps tracking down that editor, I came across more than one article in the *Wall Street Journal* about authors independently publishing their own work. Once again, that desire to be my own boss took over. I opted to publish *The Awakening* myself.

Other than finding a professional graphic designer to create the cover, I did almost everything wrong from a marketing standpoint. I had no marketing plan, I didn't have Book 2 in progress, and I hadn't made enough time to learn about the business side of publishing. Despite my stumbles, *The Awakening* gradually gained a readership. A few years later, I faced another crossroads. My law practice remained extremely busy. It was the dream of most solo lawyers—working far more and earning far more than I'd envisioned. I realized that if I ever wanted a quieter life and more time to write, I needed either to move to a larger space, expand, and hire a full-time assistant and at least one other lawyer, or stop taking so much work. Having devoted so much of my life to law already, I decided it was time to focus on flipping my work life to three-quarters writing and one-quarter law rather than the other way around.

My publishing and writing moved forward faster after that. I'd worked on *The Awakening* on and off over a span of six years. In late 2014, a little over three years after publishing *The Awakening*, I released *The Unbelievers*, Book 2 in the series. Book 3, *The Conflagration,* was published a year and half after that, and the fourth and final book, *The Illumination*, is being released a year later.

As with my previous books, I could not have finished *The Conflagration* without help from many people. These include Alastair Stephens from Storywonk, who did an initial and extremely helpful story edit; beta readers Dan, Jennifer, Chris, and Steve; and final readers/proofers Shiromi, Betsy, and Steve. (Yes, Steve gets a double bill and should get a quadruple one or more for all the times he's read *The Awakening* and its sequels.) I also owe a debt to Carly Neigh, who designed the original covers for *The Unbelievers* and *The Conflagration.*

Most of all, thank you for continuing to follow Tara. *The Illumination*, which will finish Tara's story, is now available. I used a list of the questions that appear throughout the first three books and worked hard on answering them.

To receive bonus materials from *The Awakening* series, you can visit my website, www.lisalilly.com, and sign up for my email list.

If you've enjoyed *The Awakening* series so far, please post a review wherever you purchased the book or on your favorite book review site. That will make it easier for new readers to find the series.

# THE ILLUMINATION

---

THE AWAKENING SERIES, BOOK 4

# 1

Peering over her shoulder, Tara Spencer looked out the City Museum's front plate-glass window a second time. The rust-colored panel van still cruised the parking lot. She saw no sign of the protestors who'd surged into the hospital lobby the day before, though, shouting and demanding to see her.

An elbow to her right rib sent her stumbling sideways. Pulse racing, she regained her balance and scanned the entrance area. Her attacker had been a balding middle-aged man shoving past to the ticket window, trailed by three little kids. Tara breathed deep and let the air out to a count of five. The doctors had warned her against discharging herself. Once they'd gotten past their astonishment at how she'd been able to speak and walk and talk after being in a coma for so long, they'd cautioned her that not only physical deficits but mental and emotional ones would make her life challenging for some time. She was determined not to let that stop her from meeting the person she'd come here to meet, a person who claimed to have the key to protecting Tara and her daughter from the mobs and the worst factions of the Brotherhood of Andrew.

Tara plunged into the crowd, showing her ticket to a young girl in camouflage shorts and a tank top.

*Really? Young girl?*

The young woman's tank top bore the logo of SLU, the university where Tara had been a junior when she'd learned she was pregnant. Like Tara, the ticket taker was about average height, but her exposed arms and legs looked muscular, not too-thin like Tara's had become. The girl's tanned complexion held up well in the unflattering fluorescent lighting that turned Tara's olive-toned skin green. And she was dressed to look cute and draw attention as she did her job, while Tara wore clothes designed to blend. Tara's blond hair was tucked under a baseball cap—Cardinals, like half the people here—and she wore a large gray T-shirt, jeans on the baggy side that made her look bigger, and gym shoes.

The lighting and clothes weren't the only reasons Tara felt a decade older than the other girl and probably looked it. She limped on her left side, and the fingers of that hand wouldn't close all the way. Dark circles under her eyes made her look more tired than she felt. And being away from her baby—no, from her daughter, who was a toddler now—made it feel hard to put one foot in front of the other. But she couldn't risk taking Fimi with her. The world had changed in the last thirteen months, and not for the better.

The picketers that had surrounded the hospital meant Tara couldn't ask anyone who needed to stay anonymous to visit her there. For her own safety, though, Tara hadn't wanted to meet in a private, secluded place. But she did want to stay hidden.

The City Museum presented the perfect solution. It was less museum and more jungle gym/playground/hazardous junk yard. On the ground floor, kids climbed rope ladders and swung between trees that grew out of openings in the concrete. Adults with kneepads crawled through clear plastic tunnels. Tara had held her high school graduation party here, playing tag with her friends and siblings in the sprawling artificial caves. She planned to repeat that event for her college graduation, however delayed that might be. Despite the doctor's cautions, she'd already registered to finish the on-line courses she'd begun before the coma.

As she headed for the caves, her eyes flitted from person to person, alert for possible threats, but her arms dangled at her sides, feeling awkward and useless. For the last four days, she'd held Fimi whenever the child would let her, which wasn't often. Unlike the happy baby Tara remembered, the one who'd opened her arms to everyone and loved to be cradled, Tara had awakened to a toddler who preferred to walk on her own and play by herself. And who didn't talk, despite having chattered nonsense syllables that sounded almost like words when she'd been seven months old. The doctors said Fimi's brain was normal, that some children simply learned to speak late. Tara had begun to talk at nine months. She couldn't help worrying that the same type of trauma that had put her in a coma had affected her daughter's brain development.

Tara pinched a cloth-coated blue rubber band she wore around her wrist. It sprang back with a quick, light sting that interrupted her spiraling thoughts. She'd learned the trick in her first occupational therapy session to help her brain refocus when she drifted off task. It was a side effect from the coma that her doctors said would improve in time. They couldn't say how much time.

Twisting sideways, Tara slipped through a narrow oval opening about a foot off the floor in the faux rock face. She'd come out of the coma thinner than ever, so she had no doubt she'd fit. Inside the caverns, she maneuvered to a secluded area, stepping carefully on the uneven ground. Pre-coma, she could have run.

A tall guy ducked in with her for a moment, then out again. He probably thought nothing of Tara standing so still. Lots of people used these caves for hide and seek. It made it a good place to go unnoticed, but also to ambush people. She watched the path through a crack between two rocks, alert for anyone who might have followed her.

A slim, muscular woman with a smooth, dark complexion and black hair pulled into a ponytail strode past. She moved at a measured pace but held her shoulders back, head lifted as if a string were pulling it up from above. Her backpack's logo, a giant wheel, stood out purplish-white in the dim caverns, as if it were under black light. She glanced neither right nor left.

Tara slipped onto the path behind her, her feet steadier this time. When they entered a cul-de-sac, the woman turned around.

"Excuse me," Tara said, "are you a star?"

Saying the prearranged line made her feel as if she were in a bad spy movie, but that pretty much described her life since she'd learned she was pregnant two and a half years ago. Two people she trusted, her dad and Cyril Woods, had worked together to find this woman, but she'd refused to speak in person with anyone but Tara.

The woman gave the right answer. "Who do you think I am?" Her voice sounded like the one Tara had heard on the phone. It was pitched not quite as high as Tara's and the accent sounded like a mix of British, Spanish, and another dialect Tara couldn't identify.

"A cousin," Tara said.

She believed this person to be the cousin of a woman Tara and Cyril had met in Paris. That woman had risked her life to give Tara a silver bookmark that bore an intricate design, but she had disappeared into a maze of antique stalls and vendors before Tara could ask what it meant.

"I am Oni Perez." Oni held out her hand to shake. Her grip was firm but not overbearing.

"You have proof?" Tara said.

"Because the woman you met in Paris looked white and I look black?" Oni said.

"Partly," Tara said. "Also, I'm a tiny bit wary of people who say they want to help me."

Oni eased her hand into her back pocket. "Just getting that proof." She handed over her phone, which cast a bluish light in the dim cavern, after swiping through a few images. Tara recognized Oni at different ages in photos of a multi-racial family. She often had her arms around a girl who in later shots looked like the young woman Tara had met at the Paris Flea Market. The two were shown together getting into a gondola, walking under the Eiffel Tower, and on outdoor camping trips.

"Our fathers were brothers, both from Argentina. My cousin's mother was a pale Swede. Mine was a Nigerian black woman. Now you," Oni said. "Because you don't look anything like your photos, and I know your sister posed as you more than once."

"Which almost got her killed. I'll never let her do it again." Tara maneuvered the ripped hole in her jeans above her right knee so Oni could see the scar. Shaped like an oblong S, it appeared to slither up her leg when she flexed the muscle. She'd used it to prove her identity more than once, and she guessed Oni knew of it.

"And?" Oni said.

Tara slid the silver bookmark from her front jeans pocket. She kept a tight grip on it, but held it out so Oni could see the female figure etched into it, pouring water out of two vases, one in each hand.

"And the back?"

Tara flipped it. Oni used the flashlight on her phone to examine the 92.5 marking indicating it was pure silver.

"Satisfied?" Tara said.

Oni nodded, her ponytail swinging. "Yes. This is the bookmark my cousin gave you."

Though no one had entered the cul-de-sac, groups of people had crossed the path to it while Oni and Tara had been talking.

"Okay," Tara said. "Let's get somewhere more secluded."

Tara led the way to the lower levels along winding paths that looked like dead ends unless you knew them well. She made sure to stay to the left of Oni, keeping an eye out for the unmarked path that eventually exited the caves. She had no intention of being blocked in. She kept her phone in her hand in case she needed to text for help.

They stopped in a small cavern they had to crouch to enter. It smelled damp. An artificial waterfall ran one level above, and a trickle of water leaked through an overhead crack. Lichen shimmered in puddles of water-filled depressions in the rock floor.

Tara straightened, the top of her head grazing the rocky roof, and turned to face Oni. "We won't be disturbed here. No one likes this cave."

"No kidding. Nice slime," Oni said.

"So?" Tara said.

"I have something that can help protect you and your child. But you need to promise to work with me, to keep me involved, because my life is on the line here, too."

"You didn't tell my dad that part."

Oni shrugged. "I'm telling you."

"You think the Brotherhood will come after you?"

"If they find out who and where I am. My sister—the one who first told me of my mission in life—is dead. My aunt, the tarot reader who tried to guide Nanor Kerkorian's daughter—dead. My cousin, whom you met in Paris—dead."

Tara's body sagged against the damp wall. She'd known about the first two women. Cyril had discovered their deaths when trying to learn more about the bookmark and its origins. But she hadn't known the woman who'd given her the bookmark also had died.

"What happened?" Tara had lost her youngest sister, whom she still thought of every day. She couldn't imagine an aunt, a sister, and a cousin all gone. "And when?"

"After she crossed paths with you, I heard from her less and less. She was sure she was being followed. The last time she emailed me was ten weeks after your coma began. I reported her missing to police in France and Spain, but it took another two months before anyone had anything to tell me. And then it was that she'd died eight weeks before. Supposedly she slipped on a wet rock on the *Promenade Plantee*, hit her head at a freak angle against a stone fountain, and died instantly."

"I'm so sorry." Tara stood straighter. Her upper arm felt cold and slimy. She'd been leaning to one side without realizing it and had pressed against the cave wall. "Why didn't they tell you right away?"

"A bureaucratic snafu, supposedly. And her passport was missing. It took all that time to put together my report with her unidentified body."

"That's awful."

"So you see why I'm afraid. When she told me her fears, I felt sure you were part of it all, a shill sent to the Paris Flea Market to draw her out. But once I saw you heal the earth, and heal the old woman, I knew you were real."

Thirteen months ago, a fire had started in Willow Springs, a community founded by Nanor Kerkorian, a woman who'd been like a mother or grandmother to Tara. Tara had placed her hands on Nanor, shut her eyes, and cleared her mind. Nanor not only had come back, but so had the earth, the grass, and the trees. In the instant before she'd collapsed, Tara had felt awed and powerful. When she'd awakened, her mind and body were damaged, her infant daughter was thirteen months older, and fear had replaced the peace she'd so briefly felt.

"I healed people before Nanor," Tara said.

"Not on live television with reporters right there. Not that couldn't have been staged."

Muffled voices and shouts came from elsewhere in the museum, and Tara heard the rumbling of the children's train from the second floor. For an instant, she thought she heard Fimi's distinctive laugh, but it faded. She hadn't heard her daughter laugh since before the coma.

Tara snapped the rubber band to force her mind back to Oni.

"So what can you tell me? What's the key to protecting my daughter?"

Tara held back on Fimi's name, which was actually a nickname. Her hope, probably pointless now, was that keeping the nickname known only to those she considered family would help keep her from being lured away by a stranger.

Oni crossed her arms over her chest and widened her stance, nearly filling the cramped cavern. Her arms had small but well-defined muscles. "You need to promise first. Promise you'll work with me, keep me informed and involved."

Tara's stomach tightened. She needed whatever information Oni had, but she didn't know how much to trust her. The doctors had warned that she might not make the best decisions until her brain fully healed.

"I could lie and say I promise and not mean it, but I don't want to do that," Tara said. "I get that you're scared. I'm scared too. I can't decide now whether I'll trust you and keep you involved forevermore."

"No one's saying forever. For now. I want to be part of whatever you decide to do with what I have to give you," Oni said.

"How can I say that when I don't know what it is? I'll work with you as much as I can so long as that seems safe. I'll do my absolute best not to do anything that puts you in more danger. That'll need to be good enough."

Oni pursed her lips and nodded. "That's fair. But keep in mind, your enemies are my enemies. We're better fighting them together than separately."

Tara rubbed her upper arms with her hands, shivering as much from Oni's words as the damp air. She still wasn't used to the idea of having enemies, and despite being an agnostic now, her years of Catholic grade school training made her feel she must have done something terribly wrong for so many of them to be religious people. Because of the Brotherhood of Andrew and other fanatics, it had been years since she'd been out in public without fear, and she'd had to abandon college a year short of her degree. Her dad had told her that at least once a week during her coma demonstrators had converged to yell and throw rocks at the Spencers' home, forcing them to vacate it. Now the house did nothing but drain her parents' finances.

"What do you have for me?" Tara said.

"The bookmark is the key, and it goes with this." From her backpack, Oni retrieved a thick folded document. She unfolded it to expose a color photocopy of a creased, frayed world map with red dots across it. "My cousin left this with me for safekeeping when she went to Paris. This is the only copy. The original's in a safe deposit box in London."

Tara shone the flashlight from her phone on it. "What are the red dots?"

"My best guess is each—"

Tara pushed away from the wall, squared her shoulders, and faced Oni head on. "Guess?" The doctors had warned that her temper might flare easily, especially if she got frustrated. She knew she could be reacting out of proportion, but she couldn't stop herself. "Your best guess? I go through all this to arrange a safe meeting place, somewhere you won't be recognized, away from my daughter, and what you have for me is a guess?"

"Shh." Oni poked her head outside the cave. "Someone might hear you. Pull yourself together."

"I'm six days out of a coma, and I got here, so I'm pretty damn together."

Oni blew air out of her mouth. "It's an educated guess."

Tara breathed deep and exhaled to a count of ten, another exercise the occupational therapist had taught her. "All right. Tell me."

"I suspect each dot is where a woman like you, one who discovered she was pregnant though she'd never had sex, supposedly lived. See, here's one in California around where Nanor Kerkorian's daughter lived."

"But there's hundreds of dots. There've supposedly been at most six pregnant virgins. If I'm the sixth."

"The Brotherhood told you that, right? Why believe them?"

"There's no dot in St. Louis for me," Tara said.

"It's an old map."

"It can't be that old. It includes the United States."

Oni frowned. "Just listen, all right? My cousin told me a woman like you, who survived to give birth, poses a unique threat to the Brotherhood of Andrew. Maybe can take it down for good. Which makes you dangerous, and puts you in danger. I belong to a line of people called guardians, meant to protect and aid those women. You know of the guardians, right?"

"Yes."

"The bookmark and map were passed down through generations of guardians."

"But how do they work? How do they help?"

Oni refolded the map, her movements jerky. "Do I look like an oracle? That's what you and I need to figure out."

Tara took off her cap, ran her hand through her hair, and replaced the cap. "Look, I appreciate your coming here. I really do. But you said you could help protect my child, and I'm not hearing anything about that."

"The Brotherhood's your biggest foe. Taking it down will protect her."

"But I thought you had something that would help right now. That would help us live a normal life."

"That's never going to happen for you," Oni said.

Tara's head began to ache, the pain starting in back and surging forward behind her eyes. "It is. Somehow. I'll protect my daughter, and I'll finish college, go to medical school, make a good life for both of us."

"Fine, but first you have to survive. People all over the world saw live footage of you healing the earth and bringing Mrs. Kerkorian back from what looked like death, right? The Brotherhood's been trying like hell to deny that happened, but a lot of people believe it. Believe in you. So now they need to destroy you."

The noises from the crowds beyond the cave area were growing louder. Tara rubbed her forehead. "You're full of good news."

Oni inched closer to Tara and pushed the map into her hands. "That's why we need to figure out how to use the bookmark and map to defeat them."

"But if I don't threaten the Brotherhood, if I don't go after them—"

"They'll come after you. And it's not only the Order. It's the world. All the earthquakes, the blizzards, the tornadoes, since your child was born. It's all connected. You can't walk away."

"That sounds like something the Brotherhood—"

Tara's phone buzzed. She pulled it from her side pocket and stared at the message from Cyril Woods.

*get out now*

# 2

*Protestors know you're in there*

Tara shoved the map into her pocket, grabbed Oni's hand, and half-ran, half-stumbled up ramps of faux rock to the metal staircase along one side of the caverns. On the first step, her weight came down too hard on the outside of her left foot. Ignoring the pain that shot through her ankle when it twisted, she gripped the railing and kept climbing.

"It's her." The acoustics made it impossible to tell from which direction the voice came, but the next words made it clear it was Tara who'd been spotted. "She's awake."

Her family had refused to confirm or deny for the press the reports that Tara that had come out of the coma. Now everyone would know.

*One more flight.*

Feeling lightheaded, Tara pushed herself. Another level up, she pulled Oni into a dark side corridor that led to the mid-level entrance of a giant tornado slide that ran through the museum's center. She didn't turn on her flashlight because that would make it harder to see anything outside its beam, plus pinpoint their location for anyone around them.

"Switch," Tara said. She held out her baseball cap, letting her blond hair fall around her shoulders. When she'd last been in the public eye, she'd been a redhead, so she wasn't worried about her natural color giving her away. She pulled off her gray T-shirt. She had a tank top underneath.

Oni shrugged off her backpack and maneuvered its flap to cover the logo, donned Tara's T-shirt, and put on the baseball cap. She twisted her own hair under it.

"I'll call you tonight," Tara said.

Oni nodded and ran farther up the metal stairs, clicking on the light on her phone to draw attention. Tara half-walked, half-ran across the metal walkway and shoved herself into the slide. Her dizziness increased as she hurtled down.

She landed flat on her back on the mat at the bottom. Her left shoulder felt bruised, and her tailbone was sore, but she felt no sharp pain. A freckled man with an eagle tattoo on the side of his neck leaned over her.

"Are you all right, miss? Did you hit your head?"

"No." From outdoors, Tara heard multiple voices chanting and shouting, but no one in the museum appeared particularly interested in her. The people pursuing her must have followed Oni. Or were in the slide. Taking the man's hand, she stood.

"Easy," he said.

"There she is." The voice came from above her. A bearded face peered through a net in the trees across from her.

Tara didn't wait to see if the person was talking about her. She hurried to the wide staircase near the entrance. She hoped her awkward gait would lead people to believe she'd simply had too much to drink. The museum had a bar attached to it. Since she'd been old enough to think about it, she'd wondered why the museum's founder had thought that a good idea given all the exhibits to climb and jump off. But right now, she was grateful that it helped her look like just another inebriated college kid.

Near the entrance, a series of rolling pins arranged into another slide whirled and clanked as people slid down rather than descending the main stairs. Tara climbed up, the rolling pins' clatter drowning out shouts of twenty or thirty people waving signs in the parking lot outside. On the second floor, the child-size train whistled. Tara limped past it into a neon-lit coffeehouse and bar area. She paused in an alcove, half hidden by musty-smelling bookshelves filled with magazines and paperbacks.

*Exit, exit, exit. Near here but where?*

She knew the City Museum inside and out, but the circuits in her brain felt sluggish. Knees shaking, she leaned against the wall and took five slow breaths. The therapist had said the key to retrieving memories when stuck was to go at them a different way. Tara thought of her favorite visit to the museum. She'd taken her youngest brother, Bailey. He'd spent hours running around the skateboard park, ducking around the older kids, but what he'd loved best were the funhouse mirrors.

*The mirrors.*

Tara poked her head out of the alcove. No one was looking in her direction. Beyond the coffee bar, she wound her way through the mirror maze, past dead butterflies pinned into display cases, and into the architectural section. There, stone gargoyles gazed down at her as she navigated half-walls with scrollwork rescued from to-be-demolished buildings. In the rear corridor were the stairs to the fire exit.

She burst out the double doors to the back parking lot. An alarm blared. Beyond the chain link fence that enclosed the rear parking area, clumps of people shouted at one another, their voices a low rumble. Some waved signs Tara couldn't read. She heard the word "Satan" and thought she heard the word

"Peace," but that might have been wishful thinking. No one seemed to have noticed the alarm, so focused were the protestors on screaming at one another. Heart banging in her chest, Tara scanned the area. The alley looked like the best escape route.

Two grungy-looking men in jeans spotted her. They broke from the crowd and raced toward the fence. A dozen onlookers followed.

The fence rattled as one of the guys jumped onto it. He yelled something she couldn't decipher, his voice deep and gravely. The other leapt onto the fence as well, shouting, "Tara, save us!"

The memory of a young tattooed man slashing his wrist while shouting at her in a park flashed through Tara's mind.

The rust-colored panel van roared around the corner of the building, tires squealing. It braked in front of Tara, and the side door slid open.

THOMAS STRANYERO SLID out of bed, careful not to disturb the woman sleeping next to him. He descended the stairs quickly and silently. Though he'd stayed overnight less than a dozen times, he knew which of the townhome's floorboards squeaked, which doors needed oil, and how to disengage the back deadbolt without a sound. In the narrow kitchen, he pulled on jeans, socks, a turtleneck, and gloves, all black. He added a black cap in case his silver hair glinted in any of the streetlights.

He'd noticed the green Infiniti following him three days ago. It hadn't completely surprised him. He'd kept a low profile since Tara Spencer's apparent raising of the dead and healing of the earth. Life had been simpler with her in a coma. The Brotherhood of Andrew had been in a watchful waiting mode.

But now his new love Sophia Gaddini was slipping away for quiet conversations, no doubt on a phone other than her own. She hadn't told him yet that her friend had awakened. He admired her restraint. He wished he could tell her it was unnecessary. But the man who'd been lurking in the Dearborn Park neighborhood for days like a jealous lover on a stake out indicated otherwise.

Outside, the air felt like a sluice of hot water against his face. After midnight, and it was still over ninety degrees. Stranyero retrieved a tire iron from Sophia's Toyota, which was parked in the townhome association's private lot, then glided through the shadowed walkway between the homes on one side of the block and the other. He jimmied the half-hearted deadbolt of the eighth rear fence gate south of Sophia's. The residence itself had a strong security system, but that didn't worry him. He didn't need to break in, merely to pause between this townhome and the next. Neither one had a dog or outdoor floodlights, so it was the perfect place to view the Infiniti while making his call.

With the white noise of all the air conditioning units running around him, he couldn't hear whether a phone rang inside the vehicle. The man he suspected lingered in it wasn't foolish enough to turn on a light. But he'd recognize Stranyero's number.

The call went to voicemail. Stranyero didn't identify himself. He never did by phone, but they all knew one another's voices. "I'm standing on the sidewalk near a townhome on Dearborn holding a tire iron. I'm either about to vandalize a late model green Infiniti and disappear into the night or to have a civilized conversation with you. You've got five minutes to decide which it will be."

Three minutes later, the Infiniti's driver door opened.

# 3

Fenton MacNeil was a large man, over six feet tall with a sloping stomach and wide shoulders. At sixty-nine, he was nine years older than Stranyero. His breathing became heavier as they neared the spot a mile south of Sophia's townhome where Dearborn Street dead ended. The park beyond it had a circular walking path surrounding a wide expanse of open lawn.

The two men moved into the shadows. The perfect amount of streetlamp light reached them so they could see one another's faces but could easily fade into the night should one of Chicago's finest appear. The park had closed at eleven. At the moment, its only other inhabitants were a man sleeping on a bench out of hearing distance, scores of gnats, and the unseen locusts emitting high-pitched humming from the trees. The humid air clung to Stranyero's skin.

"You may as well admit it," MacNeil said.

Stranyero spread his hands. "I admit. I'm in love." He usually opted for as much of the truth as possible. It made later discussions less complex.

MacNeil stepped back. Clearly he hadn't expected an outright admission. "With Sophia Gaddini."

"Yes."

"A woman half your age."

"A bit more than half," Stranyero said. "Though I'd never disclose a lady's age without her permission."

MacNeil slammed his fist into his opposite palm. "This is not a joke."

"Of course not. But neither is it a great mystery."

Stranyero suspected his calm baffled MacNeil, despite that his ability to keep his composure was one of the reasons MacNeil liked working with him. The larger, older man raised his voice, waved his arms, and pounded the table. Stranyero spoke evenly. Were MacNeil caught sleeping with a woman so firmly in the opposite camp, he would have gone on the attack over anyone daring to follow him. His opinions were always strongly held and more strongly expressed, though they could vary from hour to hour. Stranyero, on the other hand, collected a mountain of information before deciding anything, and rarely changed his views. Which was part of what had made the last year so hard.

"I'm surprised it took you this long to figure out," Stranyero said. "My tenure with the Brotherhood truly honed my stealth skills."

"How long have you been seeing her?"

"Seven or eight months, give or take. We became quite good friends initially through little more than email and telephone calls."

MacNeil slapped an insect that had landed on his forearm. "I take it, then, that you'll be resigning."

"I'll be doing nothing of the sort," Stranyero said. "I've been a greater aid to the Brotherhood than ever. Who do you think advised the council the instant Tara Spencer awoke?"

MacNeil pressed his lips together. "I assumed someone was conducting surveillance. I didn't know it was you. You're playing both sides of the fence."

"It appears that way," Stranyero said. "But if you insist on my withdrawing, I'll do so, assuming it's what the Cardinal wishes."

The Cardinal was one of three men on the Brotherhood's leadership council, the only one whose identity was known to Stranyero or anyone other than the council itself. He wasn't actually affiliated with the Roman Catholic Church so far as Stranyero knew. He seemed to simply enjoy using the title and possibly confusing others with it.

"That's what he'll wish," MacNeil said.

"You're always certain," Stranyero said. "I envy you that. No matter what course you take, no matter if it is the opposite of the one you advocated yesterday, you're certain."

MacNeil's quick changes were something anyone who worked with the man knew well and abhorred, but by unspoken agreement no one commented upon it given his high rank. Stranyero found himself enjoying the freedom that his reckless involvement with Sophia Gaddini afforded him. If his relationship with her ended in his being exiled, he might as well enjoy eating a few sacred cows along the way.

"That's ridiculous," MacNeil said.

"Ah, and you're certain of that as well. So predictable."

"I'll speak to the Cardinal tomorrow."

"Please do. One thing you may wish to keep in mind. Dr. Gaddini is quite close to—is a mentor to—Tara Spencer. How valuable might it be to have someone so close to her remain in the Brotherhood?"

"It's of no value," MacNeil said. "And yes, I'm certain of that as well. The moment Tara Spencer learns of the relationship, your source of information will dry up. No doubt Sophia maintains her guard with you already. She may be more than half your age, but she's no spring chicken."

"No, but she is vulnerable when she falls in love. You may recall Erik Holmes having quite the effect on her," Stranyero said.

He kept his tone light, but his neck muscles tightened at the thought of his rival. A thirty-something billionaire CEO who'd been raised by a fanatic, Holmes was a genius at running the conglomeration of corporations his family controlled. But the man made one appalling choice after another in every other aspect of his life. What galled Stranyero most was not the choices, but that Holmes never seemed to learn from them. Though he was better than his now-dead brother.

"That she shows poor taste in men is without question," MacNeil said. "That she's putty in your hands because of it, I doubt."

Stranyero shrugged. "Doubt all you like."

"And Sophia? How much does she know about you?"

"Dr. Gaddini knows that technically I'm still married if that's what you're alluding to."

"Being 'technically' married is like being a little bit pregnant." MacNeil waved his hand. "But I'm referring to nothing so plebian as that. I'm wondering if you've told her about Maya Kerkorian."

Stranyero stiffened for an instant as the image of the young woman's face, white in the glare of his headlights so long ago flashed through his mind. Then his shoulders dropped again. "I will. If I need to."

"That may dim her ardor."

"She has a great capacity for forgiveness. Many women do, I find, especially those who ought not."

~

It took Tara a week to recover her energy after the excursion to meet Oni. She stayed with her dad in Edwardsville, Illinois, where he lived on the third floor of a rambling Victorian with Tara's sister Kelly. With Tara's mom and brothers living in downtown St. Louis, there was just enough room for Tara and Fimi in the spare bedroom and Cyril on the living room couch. The rental was informal, through a friend of Pete Spencer's, so no paperwork existed. So far, no reporters or protestors had found her, but Tara had been afraid to draw attention by returning to St. Louis for more therapy.

She'd spoken to Oni a couple times by phone, and they'd made a plan to meet in Chicago. Tara wanted to seek assistance from her friend and mentor Sophia Gaddini, and from Nanor Kerkorian, who'd settled about ten miles from Sophia so her granddaughter could attend a nearby university. A university that had a program that might allow Tara to finish her degree and apply to medical school at last.

Before all of that, though, Tara had another visit to make.

"The odds are against learning anything useful," Cyril said. His hair had grown into a longer crew cut during Tara's coma, but he still sat with the same rigid military posture. His gray eyes scanned the street and rear and side view mirrors as he drove.

Tara sat in the back seat of the rental car. Her free hand rested on her daughter's arm. Fimi, fastened in a car seat, was placing plastic keys into a shoebox, shaking it, and taking them out again. She made no sounds. She'd lost much of her baby fat while Tara had been in the coma, and she looked like a slightly thinner and taller version of Tara at that age. When she shut her eyes at night, Tara imagined the stages of that year of transition from infant to toddler. Her family had been wonderful at taking video for her, but it wasn't the same. She hadn't been there to feel the change in her daughter's weight when she picked her up, to see her blond hair grow thicker and longer. That she might still hear her daughter's first words was no comfort. She'd rather have missed Fimi starting to talk than have her be twenty-one-and-a-half months old without ever uttering a word.

She took a swig of water. "I need to try."

Cyril met her eyes in the rear view mirror. "You're under enough stress already. Talking to your ex-boyfriend won't help."

"He won't be there," Tara said. "Just Roger."

Cyril put on his signal and changed lanes. "Bad enough."

One of many things Tara had been shocked to learn on awakening was that her ex-boyfriend had gone into business with a former college classmate of hers to start a mind-body-spirit healing center a few weeks after her coma had begun. Supposedly, it was called the Church of Tara because Tara's story had inspired the classmate, Roger, to change his ways. When she'd known him, those ways had included concocting lies about Tara to get onto a talk show.

"I'll live." Tara shifted position to ease her aching left leg. She wished they could have kept using her brother's van, but it was too recognizable. They'd rented this compact car because it was the cheapest one available.

"Roger should've emailed you the information he's collected," Cyril said. "If he really wants to help, not just lure you into visiting his center."

As part of creating the center, Roger had researched prophets, psychics, and other people, including children, who were rumored to have healing abilities. Tara wanted to learn everything she could about how using those abilities affected people and what might be done to speed recovery from any side effects. She hoped it would tell her if Fimi's muteness related to the times she'd helped Tara heal people. She also needed to learn about controlling the ability. She could choose to heal someone or not, but she didn't know if the same was true for Fimi. The first time it had happened had been spontaneous. Tara had to be sure Fimi didn't do that again and end up in a coma, brain damaged, or worse.

"He says it's too much to copy," Tara said.

The drive to Violet Island, a small manmade island near Choteau Island in Madison County, Illinois, took about thirty minutes. The tiny landmass where the Church of Tara stood could be reached only by a pedestrian bridge from Missouri. They left the car in a gravel parking area. Cyril carried Fimi as they crossed the bridge, which was filled with cracks. The island itself lacked side-walks, so Tara didn't bring the stroller. She had more trouble than her daughter with the uneven terrain. Fimi hopped over rocks and ran around the trees and shrubs. Tara rested twice during the two-mile walk, but only for a few minutes both times. A big improvement over where she'd been even two days before.

The only building on the tiny land mass was the Church of Tara, an actual former church built in the 1900s. Scaffolding had been set up on one side of it, and tuck pointing of the crumbling bricks was underway. The front façade appeared completed, making it look slightly sturdier and less worn than Tara had expected. A bell tower stretched toward the sky, which today was gray and layered with clouds.

Roger Mitchell met them on the front steps. He wore beige cotton drawstring pants, a soft white T-shirt, and rope sandals. "Welcome, welcome." He took Tara's hands in both of his in the manner of a politician or a pastor. "Wonderful to see you again."

When he'd been her lab partner, he'd had a thin, reedy voice. Now, he spoke in warm tones and his voice resonated. She guessed he'd taken voice coaching.

Despite hoping he might be able to help her, Tara couldn't bring herself to be friendly with Roger. She pulled her hands away. "I can't really say the same."

When she'd been pregnant, Roger had blindsided her with false claims that he'd slept with her and that she'd been sexually active with multiple partners. Now his heavy cologne and silk shirt had been replaced by patchouli oil and cotton, neither of which made Tara believe he'd changed. At least, as promised, Jeremy was absent. The way her emotions had been ping ponging, she didn't feel like she could handle seeing the man she'd once expected to marry.

Roger opened the double doors to let them in. "I understand. You've probably seen the public apology I made and recorded, but I want to say in person how much I regret that I lied about our past to get onto that show. Your example, the way you've persevered, showed me the error of my ways."

"That and flunking out of school," Cyril said. He'd researched Roger when word had gotten around about the center, compiling all the information he found for the lawyers Tara's mom worked for.

Roger looked at his feet. "It's true. But Tara's example caused me to commit to healing myself and others spiritually. My switch to a more honest, open life cured my stomach ulcers, improved my relationships, and brought me success, which is why I opened this place. I want to share that message of hope and healing."

He gestured to the far end of the center where thirty or so men and women on yoga mats practiced Cat pose under a colorful print of a goddess. To their right was a glassed-in area with sitting pillows and candles, and to their left were bookshelves interspersed with wooden benches. A room nearer the entrance had long tables with monitors and rows of laptop connections.

Cyril frowned. "And use Tara to get free publicity."

Roger turned away from Cyril to focus on Tara. "As I explained to your mother's lawyer friend, the 'Tara' is a reference to the earth mother goddess, not to you, though of course I appreciate your inspiration. And our lawyers assure me that our trademark application is the first one for the name 'Church of Tara'."

"Whose idea was all this?" Tara said. "Yours or Jeremy's?"

Roger's eyes shifted upward and to the right. "We came up with it together."

Tara's ex-boyfriend had been close to finishing his MBA when he'd broken up with her, believing her pregnancy meant she'd slept with someone else while refusing him. Jeremy had been frustrated with the family restaurant business and had felt hamstrung by the way his parents blocked every innovation he suggested. Tara guessed working with Roger, who had never so much as held a job, allowed him to finally call the shots. Why he'd done it in a way he must have known would hurt Tara, she couldn't understand. They'd known one another since grade school, and by this time he must realize she'd told the truth about not knowing how she'd become pregnant. Not only that, she'd later learned from his sister that he'd been cheating on her.

"Can we talk privately?" Cyril said.

"In back." Roger pointed to wicker shelves. "You can leave your electronic devices there. Most people prefer everything here natural and peaceful. Nothing works very well on the island anyway."

Tara started across the hardwood floor without dropping off her phone. She wasn't about to be any more disconnected than she had to be. Cyril kept his as well.

In the back office, Roger stationed himself behind a polished mahogany desk, and Tara and Cyril sat on padded chairs in front of it, stacks of cardboard boxes behind them. Tara held Fimi on her knees. The toddler kept her back stiff, as if she were merely tolerating being held, rather than settling into Tara as she'd once done.

"I put what I could onto a portable drive," Roger said. "And I'm loaning you five books that had too much helpful information to excerpt. Two are on ancient mystics with healing power. The other three are more contemporary, but please be careful with all of them. They're rare volumes." Roger gestured to a giant cardboard briefcase that had wheels and a handle. "You can keep the case. It might be a little hard to wheel over the island terrain, but it's better than lugging it."

"Thank you," Tara said, surprised Roger had gone to that much trouble. "I appreciate that."

And she did, though her shoulders tightened and her head started throbbing at the idea of going through that many books and who knew how much data. She hoped her friends in Chicago could help her.

"The drive is organized in folders by topic," Roger said.

"Thank you for that, too."

"After you've reviewed it, perhaps you'll consider coming here and giving a talk about your ability to our members," Roger said.

Tara shook her head. "I appreciate what you did. But I'm not looking for attention. And I'm not okay with you using my name or pretending to be affiliated with me, no matter how many lawyers say it's legal."

Cyril shot her a glance, maybe thinking she shouldn't be difficult with someone who was actually being helpful. A good rule, but one Tara felt incapable of following at the moment.

*Should've waited 'til I felt better.*

She'd expected Roger to bristle, but he didn't. "I understand you see it that way." He leaned forward, hands flat on the desk in front of him. "But I'm not pretending. I haven't claimed to be affiliated with you. All our literature makes clear the name is because I was inspired by your example to become a better person, not that you started this place or endorse it." He said the words as if reciting from a brochure.

"But the name must make people think that," Tara said.

"I can't help what people think. You saw there are no pictures of you here, and if you've been to the website, you know there are no photos there."

"You don't think 'earth goddess' invokes the image of me healing the earth?" Tara said.

Roger shrugged. "For some, perhaps."

"What about that room with the sign that says All About Tara," Cyril said. "I'm guessing that's not about the goddess."

"What?" Tara hadn't noticed the sign. It bothered her that her powers of observation were slipping. The doctors said she couldn't expect her mind to be in top form right away, if ever, but she wasn't ready to accept that. She needed to be sharp to shield Fimi and to get into and through medical school.

"It's in that room with the laptops and tables," Cyril said.

The overly sweet patchouli scent of Roger's incense was making Tara feel nauseous, and Fimi pressing against her stomach made it worse. She shifted the child over to Cyril, much as she hated letting go of her.

"You're right, that room's about Tara," Roger said. "For years, Tara, you've been struggling to understand the origins of your pregnancy, your power, why your baby was born. I've collected every publicly-available article, video, blog post, and social media comment about you that I could find. It's all available in digital format. As is additional information on healing—all the articles, ebooks, and reference materials I could find. Normally, you need to be a member to access all of it, but I've made you an honorary member."

"You put together information about Tara and healing and you're selling it?" Cyril said. His voice rose. Fimi frowned and thrust her head forward, the precursor to crying.

Tara reached over and tickled Fimi's stomach, something she'd loved as a baby, but that now made her scrunch her whole face together. Cyril lifted her and bounced her on his legs, and her face relaxed. Tara looked away.

"Not selling it," Roger said. "It's one part of a package we offer members, along with classes, gong baths, chakra dancing, and other mind-body-spirit techniques." He slid a card encased in plastic across the desk to Tara, along with a key fob. "You can set up your account from home—or wherever you're staying. To show how much I trust you and want to help, you can come here any time day or night using this fob, and here's keys for this room, and the clock tower, and the storage room. Members don't get that. Only Jeremy, me, and now you."

That Roger could on the one hand say he wasn't using her life as the basis for his center and on the other sell people access to information about her made her want to throw everything in his face, cartload of documents or not. But her mom's lawyer had said Jeremy and Roger had dotted the I's and crossed the T's, and Tara didn't have a trademark on her name, so there was nothing to be done. Tara swept the keys, fob, and card into her cupped hand and struggled to fit them into her pocket. It took forever. Her finger dexterity wasn't good on her left hand, though she'd been trying to do as much as possible with it.

Perspiration broke out on Tara's forehead, and she took another swallow from her bottle of water. The room had started to feel small.

"Why don't we go," Cyril said. "The doctors said you need a lot of rest."

"I've rested enough," Tara said. "What about the demonstrations? There was one at the hospital, and two people had Church of Tara signs."

"I saw a video of it. I assure you, none of those people are members of the Church of Tara," Roger said. "I don't know who's making it appear my center is involved. We preach peace and tolerance, and no one wants to draw attention to you. You saw how none of the class members so much as paused when you entered. No one asked for your autograph or tried to talk to you even though I told them you'd be touring the facility today."

"You told them I'd be here?" Tara stood, and she felt as if the floor under her feet was rolling like the deck of a sailboat in high winds. "There are people out there who want to kill me and my child, and you tell them where I am to fill a yoga class?"

"I let a select group of members know. Would you rather I not and you get mobbed the moment you set foot in the door? But you see—no demonstrations out front, no one followed you here. I made it clear you were not to be disturbed." Roger stood as well. "Tara, truly, I mean you no harm. Come to our gong baths and you'll see. The shaman sessions might also help you heal. I've given you a free lifetime membership."

It would have been so easy for one of those people to tell someone who told someone who hid in the foliage at the edge of the bridge. Someone with a rifle or machine gun. Or a knife to run out and attack as soon as they stepped foot on the island.

*I'm such an idiot.*

Tara vomited on Roger's desk.

# 4

Thomas Stranyero hated running. He'd tried jogging in his early forties and hated that, too, so he'd turned to a combination of weight lifting and a rowing machine to stay in shape. It had kept him fit and trim ever since, though as he'd approached sixty, he'd realized he had to work out quite a bit more and eat a great deal less to stay that way. Having Sophia in his life added incentive to both live long and look his best.

Now his loathing for running served as the perfect disguise. Dressed in running shorts, a Chicago Bears T-shirt, and expensive track shoes, a sweatband around his head and dark sunglasses obscuring his eyes, he doubted Sophia would recognize him no matter how close he got to her. To be safe, though, he kept more than one group of people meandering along Navy Pier between him and her.

She was easy to track. She wore the same dark A-line wrap skirt and rose-colored blouse she'd had on when they'd said good-bye that morning. Her long black hair fell in waves down her back. Plus she had a distinctive way of moving, a grace and a faint but decipherable sway, exaggerated now that she was hurrying. She'd told him she had faculty meetings in the morning and student meetings in the afternoon, and no doubt she did. But a hesitancy in her manner told him there was something she was omitting. Such as this sojourn to Navy Pier.

The sun beat down and reflected off the water, making the back of his neck sweat. Even the breeze felt hot. He wished Sophia would duck a second time into the shops inside the Pier. She'd gone in once. He'd hung far back for fear of being spotted, and she'd exited a few minutes later carrying a plastic shopping bag. Now she continued outside, passing Margaritaville and the Chicago Shakespeare Theater. He increased the distance between them as the crowd grew thinner.

When she reached the east end of the pier, Stranyero posted himself at the railing, looking out at the lake while watching Sophia from the corner of his eyes. Spray that smelled slightly fishy hit his face. Tourists mainly visited the south side of the pier. All the restaurants and stores faced onto it, and that side had a view of the expanse of Lake Michigan. The north side overlooked a water treatment plant. Sophia rounded the corner to that side anyway.

She moved into shadows cast by the building and, surprising Stranyero, pulled off the wrap skirt. Underneath, she wore bike shorts. She took off the blouse, revealing a black tank top underneath. She rolled the clothing together and pulled her long hair into a ponytail. She, too, now looked like a runner, especially after she switched her sandals for tennis shoes from her bag. The outfit made her look different enough that a stranger would have difficulty picking her out. As would an acquaintance. Like him, Sophia stayed in good shape, but she abhorred strenuous aerobic exercise. She walked a treadmill or strolled the lakefront instead.

Ironic that they'd used the same type of disguise. Yet another way they were compatible. He'd never been with a woman like her. The way she focused on him when he spoke, as if nothing were more important than his words, and the calm, thoughtful response to his doubts about his most deeply-held beliefs steadied him. She gave him room to explore, without hurrying him, without judgment. He had no question that until now, she'd offered the same sort of kindness to Tara Spencer. She'd probably been the only one to set the young woman's mind at ease since she'd learned of her pregnancy. This meeting between her and Tara Spencer couldn't possibly go that way, though. Stranyero had taken that away.

A year ago, he would have called that progress.

As Sophia exited Navy Pier and passed the bus stop, Stranyero jogged after her despite his protesting knees, less worried now about being seen. If she looked back, the buses would block her view. Sophia entered a gate to a narrow island that jutted into the lake. He didn't follow. He'd be far too noticeable. The metal sign on the gate said the park was named for a Medal of Honor recipient from Vietnam. Stranyero hadn't known this park existed, and he'd bet most Chicagoans were unaware of it. One mantra he'd heard about directions in Chicago overrode all others: "The Lake is always east." Yet to anyone who stood on this outcropping, Lake Michigan would be both east and west.

Sophia paced next to a wide concrete bench. Another observer, someone who hadn't followed her, might think she was cooling down from a run. To Stranyero's eyes, she appeared nervous. He forced himself to back away, hoping she was waiting for Tara, whom Sophia hadn't seen since she'd awakened. Stranyero could think of no one and nothing else that would cause Sophia upset. Sophia loved Tara like the younger sister she'd never had. Her family relationships were few and distant, other than her oldest aunt, who'd passed away in January.

He glanced toward the strip of beach where a group of kids dragged half-deflated air mattresses across the sand. No matter how Tara took the news, it would put a barrier between the two women.

Lost in thought, Stranyero almost missed seeing the couple with the stroller and what looked like a large briefcase on wheels. It was always hard to identify Tara. She constantly changed her hair, clothes, and mannerisms, including the way she walked, to avoid being recognized. Now she had a limp—probably not an affectation but a residual from whatever had caused her coma—and looked bony rather than slim.

Stranyero's former protégé, Cyril Woods, appeared unlike himself as well, moving with a former jock waddle rather than his usual ramrod ex-military posture and wearing a backwards baseball cap. That fashion trend always made Stranyero mentally subtract ten points from the estimated IQ of any young man wearing it. Sophia had once admitted with some embarrassment that she held the same stereotype and had to actively push against it when dealing with her students. But for disguise purposes, for Cyril, it was perfect.

TARA PUSHED THE STROLLER, and Cyril wheeled the briefcase behind him. Inside it were two of Roger's books about ancient mystics. Tara figured as a professor and former nun, Sophia was the one to review those. She'd left the medical materials in the car, figuring reading that fit better with her science background. The fifth book on mind-body healing she planned to give to Nanor.

She had a copy of Oni's map inside a waterproof pouch in the purse strapped around her body. Sophia had been the first person to believe Tara about her virgin pregnancy. She'd helped Tara find an ancient letter written to the first woman they knew of who'd been in Tara's position. She'd also spent the months of Tara's coma learning as much as she could about the people the Church had branded heretics for their views on the Virgin Mary. Those groups might have led to the guardians, individuals like Oni meant to protect women like Tara over the last two thousand plus years. If anyone could figure out what the markings on the map meant, it was Sophia.

A woman in running gear near a concrete bench waved. It took Tara a moment to realize it was Sophia. Her movements a bit uneven, she hurried forward and wrapped her arms around her friend.

"I'm so glad to see you. So glad," Sophia said. "I can hardly believe it."

"I know." Tara laughed, and to her own ears, she sounded like her old self, though she knew from the expression on Sophia's face she didn't look like it. "All those months of watching me sleep, right? It had to be a thrill a minute."

"I was happy to visit you," Sophia said. "Not happy, of course, that you were in that state, but I wanted to spend the time with you."

"Mom said you read aloud to me. I appreciate it. I don't remember it, but I appreciate it. I'm sure it helped my brain stay active," Tara said.

Sophia hugged Fimi and Cyril as well, and they walked to a concrete outcropping with two wrought iron benches in the shade. Tara put one leg up and then the other to stretch her hamstrings as she told Sophia about her health and the old-fashioned ice cream parlor they'd stopped in on the drive from St. Louis. Sophia paged through Roger's two books.

"But that's not the most important thing that happened." Tara reached into her purse for the map. "I met someone who knows about the bookmark."

Sophia held up her hand. "First, I need to tell you something."

Tara sank onto the bench across from her friend. "What's wrong?"

"Nothing." Sophia brushed a stray hair from her ponytail behind her ear. "Not from my perspective. But it may be from yours. I've been seeing Thomas Stranyero."

"Seeing him. Like dating him?"

"Yes, dating him. For several months."

"Huh." Tara stared at the expanse of blue water reflecting the cloudless sky. When she'd met Thomas Stranyero, after having heard about him from Cyril, she'd been surprised to find she liked him in a way. He'd spoken to her as if he respected her intelligence. As if he respected her. But that was beside the point.

"He started calling me after—well, after Fimi was returned to you," Sophia said.

Tara met her friend's eyes. "But he blackmailed me. The letter he made me turn over caused those demonstrations. And worse." Tara would never forget the young man who'd killed himself out of what he said was devotion to her. "And it's why my family can't live in the house I grew up in anymore. It's why they've split apart so it's easier to hide."

Tara disliked the whining note that had crept into her voice. She'd never been a whiner, but she'd spent the five-hour drive from St. Louis looking forward to getting Sophia's advice. Looking forward to Sophia's quiet words helping her feel calmer and more able to grope her way toward some sort of normalcy. The doctors told her it was a miracle she was functioning at all, that she hadn't needed weeks or months of rehab. But all Tara felt was how much she'd lost. And now even Sophia couldn't be counted on.

Sophia, whose hands were normally still, twisted a small ring on her right hand so the garnet caught the light, disappeared, and caught the light again. "I haven't forgotten."

"It kind of seems like you have," Tara said.

With the help of a Sufi elder in Istanbul, the first person Tara had met who claimed to be a guardian, Tara had discovered the ancient letter that Stranyero later forced her to reveal. It had referred to an Armenian woman like Tara as the Antichrist and had escalated the backlash against Tara. She knew it wasn't the only factor, but one among many, so she couldn't lay the chaos that followed entirely at Thomas Stranyero's door. But that didn't absolve him.

"His actions were foremost in my mind when he started calling me," Sophia said. "I had no intention of getting involved with him. I offered him support through a spiritual crises, as I would offer to anyone who came to me."

"He claimed to have a spiritual crisis?" Tara said.

"He never said that. But his initial calls to me were about his struggles with his faith." She paused and glanced toward Cyril, then looked at Tara again. "His choices. Not just the recent ones, those since your pregnancy, but his whole life. It seems meeting you and talking with you influenced him significantly."

"I've been hearing that a lot lately," Tara said.

Sophia's hands had stilled, and her gaze steadied, her eyes fastening on Tara's face. "We talked theology for months. I had dinner with him another time when he was in town. I found him surprisingly candid. And intelligent. And, ultimately, attractive."

"You don't think that was his plan?" Tara said.

"I don't believe he intended to romance me when he began calling. He doesn't strike me as the manipulative type."

"But neither did Erik Holmes when you met him," Tara said.

In other circumstances, she would have felt bad bringing up Sophia's brief relationship with the man who'd tricked her into believing he was someone else, then betrayed all of them. But since she'd awakened, the ground under her had shifted constantly. She didn't know how to deal with this new revelation.

"You're right. I didn't see that at first about Holmes. Which is why I've examined Thomas' every move, word, and thought carefully."

Tara raised her eyebrows. "Not to question your observational skills, but it's kind of a stretch to think he isn't plotting something. To do with me."

She glanced sideways at Cyril. His expression was too carefully blank, as if he'd already known about Sophia's relationship with Stranyero. She felt her face flush. How could he not have told her? She took a deep breath and let it go, counting to five in her mind. She needed to make decisions in a rational way, not based on the roller coaster her emotions had become.

"That's what I would have thought if he'd started out romancing me," Sophia said. "But he didn't. Though I realize he could have been playing a very long game."

"Could still be playing it," Tara said.

"I don't believe that. Thomas gradually told me his fears. The doubts he couldn't share with anyone in the Brotherhood for fear of being forced out before he was ready. He said he shared some of them with Cyril when he brought him the information about Erik Holmes' involvement in Fimi's kidnapping."

"He did," Cyril said.

"What's there to be ready about?" Tara said. "He's got another career. He doesn't need the Brotherhood to survive."

"No, he doesn't. His finance career is separate." Now Sophia looked out over the water. The wind had picked up, and waves rolled away from them and toward the opposite shore. "It's an issue that will determine where we'll go from here, if anywhere. But I understand the challenge for a person with a religious vocation. It's not only a career. It's a family. A home. It's hard to leave even when you know it's not the right place to be, when your heart is no longer there."

"You see him as having a vocation?" Tara said. "Like yours when you were a nun?"

"It's how he sees it." Cyril leaned forward, elbows on his knees. "It's how he trained me to see it. Other people in the Brotherhood of Andrew may be there for other reasons—for the power it might get them. Stranyero likes the power, too, he wants to advance. But he believes. Or he did."

"But saying he's struggling with his faith—it's the perfect way to draw in an ex-nun," Tara said.

"I know that." Sophia stood and paced in the small space between the two benches. "But whatever he ultimately decides, I'm certain that's not what he was doing. He couldn't share his fears with anyone outside because no one knew of that part of his life. And he listened to and respected my responses, including the ones he found it hard to hear. And he drew me out, listened to my thoughts, asked about my feelings in a way few people ever have."

Tara felt a moment of guilt. She counted on Sophia to be there for her. She'd most likely been taking her friend for granted, assuming Sophia had no need for someone to listen to and support her. But Tara couldn't bring herself to do it now. It was too dangerous.

Sophia rested her hand on Tara's shoulder. "Tara, I'm aware I could be badly mistaken about him. That's why I never tell him anything about you. Not a word. Your being in the coma allowed him to avoid deciding what to do about still being a Brotherhood member and allowed me to avoid what I'll do if he stays in it. But while he may still choose the Brotherhood, my instincts tell me he'll let me know if that's the case. He won't hide it."

"But the things he's done—"

"I'm no longer a nun, no longer a Catholic. No longer a believer in God. But I believe in forgiveness. As do you. You forgave Cyril, who did equally terrible things. Worse things."

"I did," Cyril said.

"I forgave Cyril," Tara said, "but I'm not getting involved with him again. There's a difference between a friendship, or engaging in theological discussion, and a romance."

"I'm not asking you to trust Thomas. I'll never share anything with him that you don't want me to."

"You won't need to," Cyril said. "The Brotherhood could bug your car, your condo, your classroom."

"No doubt they could," Sophia said. "But that only supports my point. They can do that whether I'm involved with Thomas or not. If anything, him being around makes me more cautious. I use disposable phones for anything to do with Tara, I don't keep anything at home, my studying is done at my office, and I lock rare books and manuscripts in my safe. I take notes only in code and keep the most vital items only in my mind. There's nothing Thomas can gain from me. Nothing he's tried to gain."

"That you know of," Cyril said.

"That I know of."

"But what kind of relationship is that? You can't share so much of who you are." As she spoke, Tara fingered the small purse still strapped around her, conscious of the map inside it. She still wanted Sophia's opinion, but not if it meant Stranyero would learn of it.

Sophia sat next to Tara. "I can share everything of who I am. And for whatever reason, I'm able to, when that's been hard for me in the past. Maybe because he's been so vulnerable with me. It's your secrets I can't share, and I wouldn't share them no matter whom I was seeing."

Tara flexed and stretched the fingers of her left hand. Her left shoulder and leg ached, and sweat dripped down her back and chest under her T-shirt. At least Sophia was keeping her guard up, but that couldn't possibly be enough.

"Is this why you wanted to meet outside?" Tara said. "To tell me this where we couldn't be overheard?"

"Yes. And so he wouldn't know I'd seen you or that you're in Chicago."

"I don't want him to know anything about me. Not through you."

Sophia touched Tara's arm. "Then he won't. I know my relationship with Thomas is a shock to you. I won't tell him anything about you that's not public knowledge unless you say it's all right."

"Can you do that? Really?" Tara said.

"It's no different from when I was a nun," Sophia said. "I kept the confidences of anyone who sought my help. And I'll keep yours. If it worries you too much, though, if you need me to stop seeing Thomas, I will."

# 5

A saxophone player at the far end of the concrete tunnel below Lake Shore Drive played the Turtles' *Happy Together*. The notes came at a slow pace, each drawn out an extra beat. With the tunnel's echo, the cheerful song sounded more like a funeral dirge.

"Why didn't you tell me about Sophia and Stranyero?" Tara glanced down at Fimi, who'd refused her hand and grabbed Cyril's instead, sending a pang through Tara's heart. The child toddled along, apparently unbothered by the tunnel's uneven pavement and urine stench. Tara pushed the empty stroller. "It obviously didn't surprise you."

"Sophia asked me—and your parents—not to say anything to you until she could speak to you in person."

"My family knew?" Tara suppressed a further angry retort. Since she'd awakened, she felt angry all the time. It made it hard to tell a genuine response to what was happening from an exaggerated one due to brain trauma.

Near the stairs, a gray-haired man in ripped work pants sat on the pavement beneath a chalk drawing of the Ferris Wheel on Navy Pier. His cardboard sign said he was homeless and asked for money. Thinking of her family's vacant home and how long it had been since she'd had a permanent place to live, Tara fumbled for change in her jeans pocket. She dropped it into the man's Styrofoam cup, keeping a close eye on Fimi the whole time.

"Sophia felt she ought to tell your parents and me. So we could decide if we still wanted her help," Cyril said.

"Which you did."

"Her research with Professor Gutzman is how your dad and I found Oni. We'd never have tracked her down otherwise." Cyril folded the stroller and wedged it under one arm, picking up Fimi with the other for the climb up the steps to Ohio Street. "Sophia may have gotten involved with Stranyero, but that didn't turn her into someone else."

"I know." Tara grabbed the railing to keep herself steady. In the past, she'd always taken steps at a run.

"But you're worried," Cyril said.

"Aren't you? She's right that Stranyero's been honest with me, at least he seems to have been. But he always has an agenda. You know that. You know the types of things he's ordered people to do. Ordered you to do. Doesn't it scare you that she's involved with him?"

"Yes and no. He was more than my guide to the Brotherhood. He was like a father, a much better father than mine ever was. I still believe he's a good person. He took a wrong path, that's all."

Sunlight hit Tara's eyes as they reached the corner of Ohio and inner Lake Shore Drive. Roaring from a string of motorcycles weaving amongst other vehicles assaulted her ears. "For his whole life."

"His whole life until now. He believed the end justified the means. So did I."

Tara bent to unfold Fimi's stroller and settled her into it. She felt winded from the stairs, something that never would have happened to her before, not from one flight. In college, she'd played intramural basketball, and while she hadn't been the best player, she'd been able to stay on the court longer than anyone else without a break.

"He's sixty years old," Tara said. "It's not like you, not like he was drawn in when he was young and struggling and had a difficult family situation."

"How do you know? He might have been just like me."

Fimi kicked her feet, but Tara managed to maneuver the harness around her. "But he stayed in for decades. When you realized you were wrong, you changed."

"Regardless of your view of Stranyero, you trust Sophia, don't you? Trust that she won't share anything you don't want her to?"

Tara straightened. "Yeah, I do. I'm not going to ask her to stop seeing him. It wouldn't be right, not if he makes her happy. But I really wanted her insights. I don't know what to do with the map. Or Oni. Who we should call I guess."

Cyril called Oni. She'd driven separately and was still a hundred miles outside Chicago. When he finished talking with her, he turned to Tara, who'd just given Fimi the last of the water in her water bottle. "You said I've changed. But is it enough?"

"What?"

"You told Sophia you'd never become involved with me again."

"Oh." The words had slipped out without thought. Tara gripped the stroller handles with sweaty hands. "I didn't realize I'd said that."

"Did you mean it?"

Tara studied Cyril. His gray eyes that matched the sky behind him, his military bearing and short hair, his sharp cheekbones. He'd been friend, enemy, her only lover, and an ally. He'd abandoned her and returned more than once, but for the last year that she could remember, that she'd been awake, he'd been there for her.

The idea of him not being in her life made Tara feel like a hole was being drilled in her heart. But the memory of the things he'd said after the one and only time they'd made love flashed in her mind each time she looked at him. It was as if her brain had been rewired by the coma, editing out the good times they'd had when they'd lived in the same condo complex, keeping Fimi safe from the outside world.

"When we last talked you hadn't made up your mind about us." Tara licked her lips, which felt dry. The hot sun seared into her forehead. "You said you didn't know if you'd been right to say you loved me. Has that changed?"

She hoped it hadn't. She needed more time to adjust to who he was, and who she was, post-coma.

"It was too soon then," Cyril said. "I didn't know you well enough yet. But now I do."

An ambulance raced past, sirens blaring. After it turned a corner, Tara said, "My parents told me everything you did while I was in the coma to help keep me safe. Taking the job in St. Louis, sharing shifts watching over me at the nursing home, being on hand to care for Fimi. It means a lot to me. I want you to know that whatever else happens."

"But?"

"But—" A wave of dizziness hit Tara. She pressed one hand against Cyril's chest.

"Let's get in the shade." He guided her into the shadow of a tall glass building. She leaned against a concrete planter while he consulted his phone. "Can you make it a couple blocks? I saw a Starbucks on our way."

Ten minutes later they sat on a shaded patio adjacent to a medical building. Tara sipped orange juice after pouring some into Fimi's sippy cup. Cyril drank ice water.

"I haven't exactly been able to focus on my personal life since I woke up," Tara said after she'd finished half the juice. "Or since...forever." She'd started to say since she'd become pregnant, but she didn't want to utter those words in front of Fimi, whether or not her daughter could understand them. None of the awfulness that was Tara's life was Fimi's fault.

"We don't have to talk about this now." Cyril drained the last of his water. "I shouldn't have asked. You've got enough to deal with, recovering from the coma, missing thirteen months of your life."

Tara rested the cold juice bottle against her neck. "There's this pressure in my head all the time. And I feel weird. Wrong. So all I can tell you is at this moment, right now, I care about you, but I can't see a future for us. I don't know if it's the things you said after we slept together, the way you turned on me, leaving me in Armenia, so that I won't ever feel safe opening up to you. Or if it's just stuck in my head for some reason to do with the coma."

"It's too soon. I shouldn't have asked you." Cyril jiggled the ice in his cup. "So what now?"

"About us?" Tara said.

"About Sophia. Show her the map? Tell her about Oni? Or keep her out of the loop?"

Tara slumped in the chair. She wished someone else would make the decisions, except she didn't trust anyone else to do that. "If it was just me, if my decisions affected only me, I'd take the chance. But it's Fimi's life, too."

"And a lot of other people's, if Oni's right that you can somehow end the Brotherhood."

"No pressure." Tara finished the last of the orange juice, grateful for its chill as it slid down her throat. The plastic bottle felt slippery against her fingers. "I hope Nanor will have some advice."

THOMAS STRANYERO STOOD at the security counter in the gleaming lobby of FOUR40, the skyscraper that housed the Chicago Stock Exchange. He wore a new charcoal pinstriped suit, and his silver hair glinted in the light. He'd skipped a tie and unbuttoned the top button of his crisp white shirt so as not to feel as if he were still at the office.

Sophia crossed the marble floor, her green cocktail dress hugging her. The ruby pendant and bracelet she wore had been bequests from her aunt. Stranyero felt pleased she'd worn the favorite pieces to this dinner. It suggested she saw this, as he'd hoped, as a romantic outing, not a meeting of representatives of opposing sides. Her lipstick matched the hue of the pendant, setting off her cream-colored complexion.

He held out his arm. She took it. Her fingers felt cold through his suit jacket.

"You may proceed, sir," the uniformed desk clerk said. The electronic gate to the elevator banks swung open.

"And we're going where?" Sophia said. "And celebrating what?"

"Coming out as a couple," Thomas said. The idea had come to him that afternoon as the perfect setting for his proposal. Happily, Everest had a table for him, one at the windows, though they'd had to arrive at 5:30 for the early seating. "The Brotherhood is aware of us now, so we may as well stop hiding when we see each other. As to where, you'll see."

At the thirty-ninth floor, they switched to a different elevator with a single button.

The maître d' led them across an elevated section of interior tables beneath a large crystal chandelier and down two shining black marble steps to a square table near the floor-to-ceiling windows. The dozen or so tables in this seating area were two deep. A one-foot bronze sculpture stood at the center of each.

A woman in a navy blue suit brought a tiny table where Sophia could set her vintage evening bag. An equally well-dressed man brought champagne flutes and explained the menu.

Night had just fallen. Sophia gazed at the lights sparkling west toward the horizon. "It's beautiful."

"Most definitely," Stranyero said, looking at her.

"How was work?" she said.

He smiled, but felt a pang at her question, one a normal couple might ask and answer as a matter of course. "I held a video conference. Annoyed my staff."

"By wearing that?" She gestured at his suit.

"Among other things." The brokerage firm where Thomas was a partner had a subsidiary with downtown Chicago offices. Since he'd started seeing Sophia, he'd worked from there more often than anywhere else. His love for formal attire forced the rest of his Chicago team to the less casual side of business casual. Which he thought was a plus despite their objections. Clients in his firm's league wanted their advisers to look conservative. "And you? Was your day a good one?"

"Not entirely. But that's nothing I can share."

Stranyero set down his glass and reached across the table for her hand. "I wish you could. You're my friend, my lover, my confidante, and I want us to be open with one another."

She withdrew her hand. "You tell me next to nothing."

"I tell you everything that matters most."

And he did. She was the only one to whom he confided his doubts about the Brotherhood's mission. Any thinking man had doubts, so he'd harbored a few over the decades he'd devoted to the Order. He'd often been saddened by his role, but he'd believed he'd acted for the greater good. Tara Spencer's pregnancy and how the Brotherhood approached her had made him wonder about that greater good. Only Sophia knew how much. He was determined, whatever course he took, to be as honest with her as possible. And to see she was hurt as little as possible.

A gray-haired man brought over a decanter of *Chateau L'Eglise*. It had a medium body with a darker flavor than he knew Sophia preferred, but he hoped that, as with many other wines he'd introduced her to, after a few sips it would grow on her.

"The Brotherhood must be a part of your life that matters most," Sophia said.

Thomas' jaw tightened. He wished he could delay this conversation until he felt sure of where he stood with both her and the Order, but Tara Spencer's emergence from her coma meant he couldn't. "I tell you everything I can."

"As I said, next to nothing," Sophia said.

Another suited woman set down small rectangular plates with three spoonful-sized *amuse bouche* on each. The flavor of the first one—tomato sorbet topped with crème fraiche, half a grape, and osetra caviar—momentarily drove other thoughts from his mind.

Everest never disappointed.

"I know she's been discharged from the nursing home," he said after Sophia finished the second tiny appetizer, a cold cucumber and rhubarb gazpacho in a spoon made to look like a tiny long-handled pot.

"I'm sorry?" Sophia said.

He suspected she'd followed the switch in topic, but didn't want to reveal it in case he was fishing for information.

"She was discharged over a week ago with strict orders for follow up care which she has not, in fact, been following." Stranyero paused to drink his gazpacho. "If you have any influence, I suggest you try to convince her to listen to her doctors. Her parents' home remains unoccupied. She was spotted at a museum in St. Louis but hasn't been seen since despite surveillance on the condominium where her mother lives, her older brother's apartment, and on the house where her father lives. Cyril Woods recently took a leave of absence from his private security job, so my guess is he is with her. He rented a compact car from Enterprise that he indicated would be driven out of state, so it's likely she's come here. To see her old friends Nanor and Kali Kerkorian. And you."

"Are you telling me this to show the breadth of the Brotherhood's information network?"

"I'm telling you so you won't worry I'm trying to get information from you. I already have it. You must realize the Brotherhood monitored her the entire time she was in the coma."

The tables were spaced far enough apart that Stranyero wasn't worried about being overheard by other diners, but he spoke quietly and avoided Tara's name due to the staff hovering.

"Of course," Sophia said.

At her clipped tone, the third *amuse bouche*, which had a peanut butter and fennel flavor, fell to dry fragments in his mouth. It didn't bode well for what he planned to suggest to her.

A server approached, and Sophia nodded when Stranyero suggested they forgo the nine-course tasting and order from the menu. Perhaps she, too, was thinking nine courses would make for a very long meal if this discussion went where he feared it would.

"The surveillance doubled down once she became conscious," Stranyero said. "Her family did a good job protecting her privacy, as did Cyril, but a nursing home can't be completely secure."

"Exactly how many people have been watching her?" Sophia said.

"I don't know."

Everything in the Brotherhood was on a need-to-know basis for the very reason that people were not perfect. They talked in their sleep, they had crises of faith. They fell in love with others who didn't understand the Order's aims. What he'd avoided making clear to Sophia was how much he needed to know.

"A guess?" she said.

"Probably a well-placed person at each medical facility she was at, and at least one other person in the St. Louis area. Plus someone here, since you and Nanor Kerkorian are here. A roving investigator overseas. But these are only guesses."

"Are you the someone here?"

"No." They fell silent as their wine glasses were refilled. A lobster cocktail was set in front of Sophia, and salmon fumé in front of Stranyero. The salmon tasted as fresh and rich as if it had been caught that morning. "If you're upset because you've talked to her," Stranyero said, "you don't need to hide it. You don't need to tell me about it, but you don't need to hide it."

Sophia swirled the wine in her glass, watching the dark red liquid spiral. "I told her about us. She took it better than I had any right to expect, but not well."

He sighed. "You have a right to be happy, Sophia. And a right to a personal life. I realize I'm presuming you're happy with me, and that my statements are self-serving. But all the same. Every decision you make doesn't need to be based on your desire to protect others."

"It does need to be based on my conscience."

"Yes." Stranyero, though not typically one to fidget, flipped his appetizer fork over and back. "I've a suggestion that may help you with that."

Sophia leaned forward. "You're leaving the Brotherhood?" She'd never asked him to do that. He knew she was afraid, correctly, that he'd say no. No doubt seeing Tara Spencer limping toward her with sunken cheeks, dark under-eye circles, and a prominent collarbone, had pushed her over the edge.

"No," he said.

Her shoulders sagged.

"But the reason I won't do so is different from what you might believe. Making a clean break now will do nothing but cut me off from information. I can better help her—and you—from the inside."

"I doubt she'll want help from you given what happened last time."

"The total result wasn't ideal for her, I agree," Stranyero said. "But I did find her child for her. And pinpoint the kidnapper, despite that he was never brought to justice."

"I don't know that she'll see it that way," Sophia said. "But what are you proposing?"

"For over three years, I've had access to certain Brotherhood materials only available to those at the highest levels. They reside in the library of a colleague who reached that level before me. I never thought it necessary to examine them until I began exploring the doubts I've told you about."

"And?"

"The Brotherhood of Andrew is governed by three men. I know the identity of only one. I can't tell you his name, but he serves as a representative in his home state's Congress. While he has no affiliation with the Roman Catholic Church, he's known as 'the Cardinal,' and often wears bright red Cardinal's robes. When I asked him why, he said it was so if people found his face familiar, they'd assume he was a Church dignitary and not connect him with his true identity. I suspect he has a bit of a flair for the dramatic, but be that as it may."

"This is what you learned from the materials?"

"No, I learned of him in the course of my work. What I discovered recently is that once Tara awoke from her coma, this man declared war on her."

Sophia pulled her evening wrap around her shoulders. "*Peace I am, and because of me, war comes.*"

"Yes," Stranger said.

He'd memorized the ancient Armenian letter that purported to be about a young woman similar to Tara who'd lived—and died along with her infant daughter—in the seventh century. When he'd seen the word "war" in the Cardinal's communication, he'd thought of the letter immediately, and of the line Sophia had just quoted. It came from an ancient gnostic gospel. He didn't know what it meant, but it couldn't bode well for Tara Spencer or her child.

Sophia sipped her water as the appetizer plates were cleared. "Upsetting, but not exactly news given the approach the Brotherhood has taken to Tara's pregnancy. Aiding at first, then stalking, threatening, and attacking."

"But before now it was all designed to force Ms. Spencer to recant her supposedly false statement that she'd become pregnant but had never had sex. Now my understanding is that the Brotherhood has long suspected her story is genuine. And because she can't be convinced otherwise or frightened into silence, and she has revealed an ability to perform what many would call miracles, the strategy of discredit and deny has shifted to destroy."

Sophia swallowed. "Literally destroy? But is this truly new? Brotherhood members came after Tara before."

"Those attacks were not sanctioned by the Order. The men who performed them were outliers. But their philosophy has now become the Brotherhood's."

"Why?"

Stranyero frowned. "I don't know. I once believed Ms. Spencer must be evil if her story was true, or at least that her child must be evil or her existence would result in great danger to the world."

"Which would make killing Tara acceptable to you?"

"Under a certain moral code it would. It's the same as the ethical question of whether you would kill Hitler if you could go back in time and save countless lives by doing so."

"So you're fine, then. You believe what your Order tells you about Tara, and you believe it warrants murder."

Stranyero folded his hand around Sophia's chilled fingers. "I don't. That's what I'm telling you. Over the last year and a half, I've found it more and more difficult to believe she is or will cause evil. What's as significant is that I'm no longer convinced the leadership of the Brotherhood believes that. But they mean to destroy her all the same."

They fell silent as their entries were set on the table. Sophia ignored her Beef Wellington. Stranyero ate one of the small round potatoes next to the New York Strip.

"And your proposal?" Sophia said once they were alone again.

"For now, that if there is any question Ms. Spencer has, or you have for that matter, I'll do my utmost to find the answer from the materials now available to me or, if I can do so without revealing my intent, by asking questions."

"You'll be her spy?" Sophia said.

"Yes."

"And in the process, you'll be the first to learn what her concerns and questions are."

"That's true."

Sophia's hands wrapped around the chair arms. "How can Tara trust that you're truly on her side? You're no doubt telling the men in the Brotherhood the same things you're telling me."

"I am," he said. "But I promise you I will not share anything I learn from you or Ms. Spencer with them."

"We'll have no way of knowing if you're keeping that promise," Sophia said.

Stranyero cut into his steak. Blood ran along the white china plate. "That's true," he said. "You won't."

# 6

"What do your instincts tell you?" Nanor said.

The older woman sat on a sleek, narrow couch, her long violet and rose skirt flowing around her. The windows behind her overlooked the Berwyn Metra railroad station. Nanor had rented the furnished walk up apartment after her community in Arkansas had been destroyed by fire, choosing the location so her granddaughter, Kali, could commute without a car to the University of Illinois Chicago. The modern furnishings clashed with the worn hardwood floors and sagging doorjambs. More than that, the stark and spare L-shaped living and dining area jarred Tara, and the clanging train bells from the station set her on edge. She sat stiffly on a foam-cushioned chair with a hardwood frame. It all felt so different from Nanor's and Kali's home in Willow Springs. That had been crowded, with an overstuffed couch, a grated fireplace, and bright throw pillows everywhere.

Nanor at least looked the same, with her black and gray hair pulled into a knot on the back of her head and her eyes sunk in wrinkles. Copies of articles and book chapters on psychics, miracle workers, and healing were spread out around her, some on the square cube that served as a coffee table, some on the marred hardwood floor, and some on the couch.

"I don't know," Tara said. "I've never felt so cut off from my instincts in my life."

Cyril leaned in the open doorway between the living room and the small entryway that led to the common area landing and stairs. "He did identify Fimi's kidnapper, and there was no real benefit to him for doing that. He already had what he wanted from Tara."

"But he didn't give enough evidence to put Holmes in jail," Kali Kerkorian said. She sat cross-legged on an armless chair holding Fimi on her lap. The toddler had spent a lot of time with Kali while Tara had been unconscious. And before that as well, when Tara and Fimi had lived briefly in Willow Springs. Fimi wrapped Kali's long black hair around her fingers, holding it but not tugging on it.

"I'm not sure that would have been possible," Cyril said. "Holmes worked hard to cover his tracks. Which doesn't help you decide anything, but I don't know what else to tell you."

The old Cyril, the one Tara remembered, would have insisted on his position, whatever it was, eyebrows lowered, shoulders back. While she'd forgiven him for all he'd done, she could never have seen any future with that man. It was good he'd learned there were gray areas, that he'd learned some flexibility.

"He may have been involved in kidnapping Fimi, and that's why he knew of Erik Holmes' role," Nanor said.

Tara shifted on the seat, unable to get comfortable on the firm cushion. "Holmes never said anything like that to the police."

"How could Mr. Holmes say such a thing to any authority?" Nanor said. "That would have required admitting he'd been involved."

"True." Tara stood to stretch her legs, unable to sit still. At least she had energy today. They'd arrived at Nanor's in the late afternoon yesterday after the visit with Sophia. Tara had barely made the introductions between Nanor, Kali, and Oni before she'd dropped off to sleep on the couch. She'd awakened later in the twin bed in the guest bedroom, Fimi sleeping in the crib beside her.

"And do not forget whose card was found among my daughter Maya's possessions after her death," Nanor said.

"So you don't think I should trust him," Tara said.

Nanor frowned, deepening the wrinkles that ran from either side of her nose around her mouth and down to her chin. "Make use of him perhaps, but trust him? He is the one to worry about more than these unnamed Brotherhood members he speaks of. I find it impossible to comprehend that Dr. Gaddini is involved with him. But of course I cannot be objective."

"I don't think she planned it." After sleeping on it, Tara didn't feel quite as angry as she had yesterday at Sophia. It wasn't as if she hadn't made her own very bad decisions when it came to love. "And I was out for over a year. I couldn't expect her to put her life on hold."

"I would expect it," Nanor said. "But I am old and not flexible."

"You never seem old to me." Tara walked to the wall in the dining area, studying the photo array. It included ones of Nanor when her two daughters had been infants through the present. When the girls reached their twenties, the photos of Maya disappeared, and gray began to streak Nanor's jet black hair. But regardless of wrinkles and gray, once Tara had gotten to know Nanor, she'd discovered her view of anyone in their mid-seventies as elderly made no sense. Nanor jogged every day, read five or six books a week, and until recently had run the entire Willow Springs community. None of that fit Tara's view of old.

Nanor rubbed the back of her neck. "Ah, but I begin to feel it. Perhaps because I discovered I dislike change. But let us not get derailed. What reason does Stranyero give for you being more of a target now than before?"

"Sophia said healing you and the earth convinced some Brotherhood members that I need to be eliminated because I'm—what that letter said."

Tara didn't want to speak the word "Antichrist," despite that Nanor and Sophia had both assured her that the ancient Armenian letter that used the term had most likely meant an opponent of the established Christian church, not the Satan of horror films.

Kali unwound her hair from Fimi's fingers and handed the child a tiny teddy bear to hold instead. "But that happened before you fell into the coma. And no one attacked the hospital or nursing home."

"According to Oni, the Brotherhood and all my enemies were hoping I'd die a natural death, and they wouldn't need to risk exposing themselves by going after me. But it's not like I know her well. She could be wrong or feeding me misinformation."

For now, Oni remained at the apartment she'd be temporarily sharing with Cyril while they stayed in the Chicago area. Tara had introduced her to Nanor and Kali, but hadn't invited her today because she wasn't sure yet how much she wanted to share.

"You struggle with whom to trust," Nanor said, "which is natural and important. My answer, though, is the one I have given you before. You must look within yourself, within your heart. Your heart told you to trust me and to trust Kali."

"I had doubts about both of you until I knew you better."

"That was sensible." Kali started brushing Fimi's hair in long, slow strokes.

Tara had tried to do that earlier and Fimi had fought her. She knew it would take time for her daughter to get used to her again, and if only she knew for certain it would happen, or that Fimi would start talking, she'd find it easier to wait. Tara had started reading some medical case studies this morning on people with psychic abilities and had found nothing useful connecting healing powers and brain function. Nothing worrisome, but nothing useful.

She snapped the rubber band she still wore around her wrist, stopping the spiral into fears about what might be wrong with Fimi and forcing her mind back to Thomas Stranyero.

"So is it just that I need to get to know Stranyero better?" Tara said. "And Oni for that matter? But how? If people from the Brotherhood mean to kill me, I can't exactly sit around playing checkers with everyone until I figure them out."

"No, but sitting by yourself could help," Nanor said. "You need to reach a clear, calm place beyond the emotions of the moment."

Tara's stomach rolled and she paced around the glass dining table as she spoke. Her limp, at least, was becoming less pronounced. "You mean meditating? Look what happened when I did it the last time to trigger my healing power."

*Again the whining.*

Tara stopped moving and took a deep breath. While she knew in her mind it had almost certainly been the effort to heal Nanor and the earth that had sent her into the coma, not the act of meditating, it was hard not to associate the two. But she had to get a grip, had to push past her fears and find a way to protect Fimi once and for all. So her daughter could grow up safely, and they could both live as close to normal lives as possible, however improbable Oni or anyone else thought that was.

"I am not suggesting you try to enter a meditative state to heal anyone," Nanor said. Rather let your mind and soul become empty. Clear. So you have what is known as a beginner's mind. Do nothing. Think nothing. Then decide whom to trust and what to do."

"It's hard to sit still," Tara said. "Since I woke up, I either want to move or to sleep. Not sit."

Nanor spread her hands wide. "You asked my advice."

"THE SITUATION IS UNPRECEDENTED," Stranyero said.

His chest and armpits damp under his dress shirt, he shifted into the shadow cast by the single tree that grew in the rooftop garden. He was unclear why the Cardinal had come to Chicago. The Order didn't have a base of operations here so far as he knew. But the longest-serving member of the Brotherhood's leadership council didn't need to explain himself to Thomas Stranyero, nor explain the choice to meet under the glaring sun at three in the afternoon. The eighty-seven-degree heat no doubt kept the masses of people who worked in this building from stepping out for a rooftop break, so perhaps it was privacy the Cardinal craved. But an air-conditioned conference room would have been so much more pleasant.

"True," the Cardinal said. His breath smelled of garlic, marinara, and onions, and Stranyero had to resist the urge to step back. "But that's no reason to forego action. What's MacNeil thinking?"

The band of tension around Stranyero's chest tightened. He didn't know if the Cardinal was looking for an answer or testing Stranyero's loyalty to a long-time colleague.

"Acting rashly would benefit no one," Stranyero said, which he believed. In no way would Stranyero call Fenton MacNeil a man hesitant to act. His real problem was acting quickly and without enough planning, as the fiasco of the Willow Springs fire had shown.

"Rashly?" the Cardinal said. "The girl remained in a coma for thirteen months. He had ample time to prepare."

"I didn't say he's unprepared. That any of us are. We merely haven't decided on a course of action. That's why I came to Chicago, to nail down a last detail, then choose the right course, which is paramount."

The Cardinal's eyes narrowed. "What detail?"

"A source who knows Tara Spencer's physical condition in depth."

Stranyero didn't expect the Cardinal to ask the source's name, as the upper echelon operated from a standpoint of plausible denial. But he was ready to supply it. If MacNeil knew of his relationship with Sophia, the Cardinal knew as well, so there was no harm in sharing her name.

"So you feel MacNeil remains in top form?" the Cardinal said.

"I do."

"That's your personal view?"

"Is there some reason it shouldn't be?"

"I sense tension between the two of you. He's asked many questions about your personal life."

"How kind of him to be concerned," Stranyero said.

The Cardinal laughed, a deep bass chuckle. "You'd be wise to keep an eye on the competition. But, as I told Fenton, don't let your desire to move up blind you to the benefits of working with those you fear being elevated above you."

Stranyero felt a thrill in the pit of his stomach. So the rumors of a vacancy on the Council were true, and far from doubting Stranyero, the Cardinal saw him as a contender. Despite his advancement over the last few years, he'd thought there were more layers between him and the Cardinal, and he'd feared MacNeil might have the advantage. He filed this information away in his mind to consider later. It might affect his strategy regarding Tara Spencer. And, necessarily, Sophia.

"Of course," Stranyero said. "But I assure you MacNeil is prepared for multiple courses of action. He simply considers choosing the right one paramount."

The Cardinal waved his hand in irritation, the sleeve of his crimson robe swaying. "That goes without saying, and that MacNeil wasted time saying it to me yesterday suggested he has nothing to report beyond vague generalities. Hoping the girl dies a natural death is no longer an acceptable strategy."

"Now that she's awake, none of our strategies rests upon that." Sweat trickled down from Stranyero's hairline. He resisted wiping his forehead, not wanting to appear nervous. He couldn't imagine how the Cardinal could not perspire wearing those robes. The man must have had his sweat glands sealed. "But we must act in a way that presents the least risk of ending the cycle forever. Or exposing us."

The Cardinal shrugged. "Perhaps. But we're all forty years older than when this chapter began. Too many men become slower to act as decades pass."

"Perhaps that's the result of wisdom."

"Not this time. I'm authorizing others to act as well as MacNeil. If you see a path to end this sooner than tradition prescribes, you need not obtain agreement from him so long as you're confident. Merely see to it that you don't work at cross-purposes."

The Brotherhood of Andrew's unspoken mantra had always been one of asking forgiveness rather than permission, at least for those who were truly valued. But it surprised Stranyero to hear it stated, particularly after MacNeil's debacle and the previous attempt on Tara Spencer's life by a rogue Brotherhood member. Welcome as the vote of confidence from the Cardinal was, it put him in a difficult position. Delay had been his friend.

"Of course," Stranyero said, keeping his voice steady.

The man in red nodded in dismissal, then strode across the rooftop garden to the glassed-in escalator that would take him back down into the world.

# 7

His golf umbrella and trench coat kept Stranyero's upper body dry. His black dress pants were soaked from ankles to knees. Rain had pelted the entire St. Louis area and beyond all morning, and the island lacked sidewalks, so he'd been forced to tramp across mud and grass. He hadn't done his own fieldwork in years, but he couldn't trust his subordinates—or his peers, for that matter—not to report his every move before he made it to the Cardinal. Or to MacNeil.

Thunder clapped, and a few seconds later lightning streaked the sky. The center was closed Monday evenings, and Stranyero was twenty minutes late for his appointment. All the same, a young man clad in loose pants, a woven shirt, and sandals opened the massive double doors with a smile and offered hot towels and slippers.

Roger Mitchell led him to a side room with photographs on the walls and long tables with multiple small viewing screens.

"Where would you like to start?" Roger entered a password to open a hidden bare bones menu. "We have footage from Tara's childhood, her college years, her appearance on *Live with Janet* while still pregnant. And then there's what I call the miracle footage and the news reports while she was in the coma and after she awoke."

Stranyero had his own agenda and a separate set of directives from MacNeil, neither of which required viewing the pre-pregnancy videos, though he might do that down the road. "Let's start with *Janet!*"

"I'm a bit embarrassed by my behavior on the show," Roger said. "I hope you'll excuse it."

"So you're confirming you lied on the program?" Stranyero said. "You never slept with Tara Spencer?"

Roger hung his head and slumped his shoulders in an exaggerated manner that set Stranyero's teeth on edge. "I'm ashamed to say it, but I did lie."

"And you don't know of her having sex with anyone else?" This late in the process, Stranyero didn't doubt Tara's claims that she'd never had sex before her child had been conceived, but as he always told his special investigators, every assertion must be reexamined at every step.

"I don't," Roger said.

Stranyero clicked on the video, which began running in fits and starts.

"The wireless service here isn't ideal," Roger said. "I'll go remove any other devices. That should help."

Stranyero spent over three hours, mainly because the Internet dropped in and out. Access to the center's private materials was smoother, but also took time, as it required sorting through portable storage devices.

He stopped in Roger's office before leaving. "I'll be back early tomorrow if that's acceptable."

Roger closed the book he'd been reading. It looked like a self-improvement manual, complete with a front cover photo of a smiling guru with large white teeth. "You're welcome any time. As a member, you have full access to the private catalogue during business hours, but I'm happy to allow you early entry. And if you'd like a premium membership, you'll also get unlimited classes—"

"No." Stranyero had paid this huckster the basic membership and added fees for materials he could get from his own people solely so he could work under the Brotherhood's radar. He didn't need to pay extra for chakra balancing or shaman training or whatever other snake oil the man was selling. "I would, however, like to make a significant one-time donation if you personally would do something for me."

"Absolutely," Roger said.

"Tell me everything you know about Tara Spencer."

SITTING cross-legged between the twin bed and crib, Tara tried a meditation where she counted her breaths. Her heart pounded so hard she feared a heart attack as she kept flashing back to the flames searing across Willow Springs. After three attempts, she gave up, lifted Fimi from the crib where she'd been silently playing with the teddy bear, and spoke aloud about other options. Tara hoped her voice would stimulate her daughter's own speech. And draw the two of them closer. Fimi didn't respond verbally, but she tilted her head to one side and watched Tara's face.

Kali appeared in the doorway. "Is your daughter giving you good counsel?"

Tara laughed. "Yes, she's very wise. A great listener." Her smile disappeared. "If only she'd talk."

Kali brushed Fimi's hair away from her forehead. "She will eventually, I am sure of it. And to listen is wise indeed. I hope you don't mind, but I couldn't help overhearing and have a suggestion. It seems to me one person can tell you for certain whether Stranyero took part in the kidnapping."

Tara sighed, resting her chin on the top of her daughter's head. "Erik Holmes. But it makes me sick just to think of him."

"It is likely the only way you'll get the truth. We've heard only secondhand what he said when the police questioned him. As Grandmother points out, he'd hardly implicate himself by identifying Stranyero as his partner."

"So why would he tell me the truth?"

"I doubt he'll tell you the whole truth and risk prosecution, but he may tell you enough. My guess is he would like a chance to try to explain and to justify himself—not that I believe justification is possible."

Two days later, Tara and Sophia stood in the basement level of an aging combined office and condominium building that had once been a postcard printing factory. While Tara didn't feel ready to share the map with Sophia or tell her about Oni, she valued her friend's insights into Holmes. Holmes also trusted Sophia more than any of Tara's other friends, so the logistics of the meeting had been arranged through her.

"Do you need this back?" Tara held a keycard out to the red-haired young woman assistant who'd met them.

The card, which had been messengered to Sophia's office, allowed entry into an underground walkway that connected this building and others like it to Dearborn Station. The late 1800s former railroad station housed retail and office space on multiple levels, which made it an ideal place to enter and disappear. It also was an underused space, so Tara could easily have spotted anyone following them.

"Keep it," the assistant said. "You'll need it if you want to take the Pedway on your way out."

She patted Tara down thoroughly. Tara had half-expected this and tried to stay still and relaxed, but it was an effort not to push the woman's hands away.

"Is this necessary?" Sophia said when the assistant turned to her.

The assistant shrugged. "If you want to stay."

Sophia submitted to the search. The assistant directed her toward the sagging, carpeted stairs leading to a ground floor law office.

"If I can't accompany Tara, why did I need to be searched?" Sophia said.

"Not my rules," the woman said.

"Is this acceptable to you?" Sophia asked Tara.

Tara straightened her clothes and felt the edges of her wig to be sure it had stayed in place. One of five wigs her younger sister had found for her, this one was brunette and cut in a business-like bob. "It's okay. Holmes told me no one could be in the conference room with me." It was one reason she'd left Fimi at Nanor's under the guard of Cyril and Oni.

"You're sure?" Sophia said.

"If he planned to hurt me, this wouldn't be a very good way to go about it. You, Cyril, and the Kerkorians know where I am. And so do the police. I left word with the detective who handled the kidnapping case, and I told Holmes I was doing that."

The assistant guided Tara down a corridor with a scuffed tiled floor and faded gray walls. Tara guessed the law office must belong to some acquaintance of a colleague of Holmes', as none of it looked upscale enough for the billionaire or any of his close business associates.

Before knocking on the conference room door, out of habit Tara reached into her front jeans pocket for her phone but found nothing, as the assistant had confiscated it.

Holmes opened the door. He wore a designer suit, a tailored buttoned-down shirt with monogrammed cuffs, and polished Italian loafers. While he was dressed as impeccably as Tara remembered, he looked far more than a year older. Though in his mid-thirties, when Tara had last seen him, Holmes had already had a few silver threads in his perfectly waved hair. Now they threatened to outnumber the blond. The sculpted features of his face had slackened, and lines had formed around the corners of his mouth. His grief over the death of his brother had taken a toll.

He waved her in. "Tara. I'm so pleased you wanted to see me."

He sat at the head of the long conference table. A scratch in its finish revealed particleboard beneath the wood veneer. The room's only other furnishings were stacks of cardboard storage boxes sagging against the flat green walls. All of it added to Tara's view that this wasn't a place Holmes frequented.

She sat on the long side of the table, a few chairs from Holmes.

"If you hadn't called soon, I'd planned to reach out to you," Holmes said. "I have information you might find helpful."

"The only thing I want to know is whether Thomas Stranyero told me the truth about my daughter's kidnapping."

Holmes settled back in the vinyl chair. "What did he tell you?"

"That you kidnapped her."

"If you believe I did, you couldn't possibly expect me to answer that. The statute of limitations on kidnapping is long, and I've no desire to go to prison."

"I also want to know why you did it," Tara said.

"If you think that I'm the culprit, you must already have a guess about motive."

"You might have had some warped idea that you were protecting her."

In the hours when she'd been unable to sleep the night before, Tara had considered why Holmes might have taken Fimi. He hadn't harmed her. He hadn't asked for anything, unless he really had been working with Stranyero. But after the baby's return, he'd succeeded in convincing Tara and Fimi to live in a condo complex he controlled. So she'd guessed at the reason.

"She was protected," Holmes said.

"The people who had her had no idea who she was. Or that she'd been kidnapped. You call that being protected?"

"I can't speak for the kidnapper, whoever that might be. But in my opinion, that was the safest place imaginable for her. An anonymous family who knew nothing, so they could say nothing that would tip anyone else off to her real identity. Nor could you."

"And you were the one to decide that," Tara said.

"I never said I decided anything. I'm speculating on motives. And I will observe that you weren't making decisions in her best interests."

Tara frowned. "What does that mean?"

"You insisted on keeping Cyril Woods, whom you knew was a member of the Brotherhood of Andrew, intertwined not only in your life but in your daughter's. I was convinced he presented a danger to both of you."

"Cyril left the Brotherhood—"

"So he claimed."

"You have evidence otherwise?"

Holmes rested his hands on the table. "Evidence? No. But the Brotherhood, while not connected with the Roman Catholic Church, is much like it in that no one really leaves. It stays in the psyche, doing damage. Tremendous damage."

"If you're so sure he's a danger, I'm surprised you didn't eliminate Cyril yourself."

Holmes shook his head. "That's the Brotherhood's way, and it was my brother's way, but it's not mine."

"But taking a child from her mother—that's okay."

"Again, I never said I did that. But there were—and still are—larger issues than whether you got to spend time with your daughter or always knew her location. The fate of the world rests on her shoulders. And yours. I'll never apologize for doing everything and anything to be sure no harm comes to either of you."

Tara pushed back from the table and stood. This was the closest she'd get to an admission given that he couldn't very well risk her calling the police and telling them he'd admitted to kidnapping her daughter. His audacity made her regret coming to see him. "Having all the money in the world doesn't make you qualified to reach in and rearrange other people's lives."

She headed for the door. She'd find answers another way.

"Tara, wait. I don't randomly interfere with other people's lives. But I was certain your child's fate was to save the world from the most powerful, pervasive, and corrupt organization that ever existed, that still exists. You couldn't expect someone who believed that to leave her survival to chance."

Tara snapped the rubber band around her wrist and stared at the plain wood door to the hallway. She breathed deep to the count of five. She needed to calm down. She needed to get as much information from Holmes as possible for Fimi's sake, regardless of Holmes' past actions or that she didn't share his obsession with bringing down the Roman Catholic Church or his view that her child was the one who would do that. She turned around. "What about Thomas Stranyero? Will you confirm he had no role in the kidnapping?"

"You should be asking him," Holmes said.

# 8

Thomas Stranyero pulled his rental car into the Galena courthouse parking lot. A lawyer from what he thought of as the real world had told him it was the best place to park on weekends when tourists flocked to the small town. Wanting to blend, he forced himself to meander down the hill and along the main street with its boutique shops and quaint restaurants. One store window displayed more pairs of novelty socks—of any socks—than he'd seen in one place in his life.

A block later, the scent of dark chocolate from a gourmet candy and coffee bar filled the air. Stranyero paused. He suspected Sophia would love every item inside. But she might recognize the store name and ask why he'd been to Galena. He could invent a legitimate business reason for being here, but he preferred to avoid occasions that required falsehoods. A gesture that wouldn't save his relationship with her in the long run, but he made it anyway. His trip to St. Louis had been easier. His day-to-day business affairs took him there often enough.

*Affair de Coeur* stood two blocks farther northeast than he'd expected based on the street numbering. Inside, as he'd hoped, a young woman with a heart-shaped freckled face and a wide smile presided at the counter. Had he not known better from his research, he would have guessed her a former Miss Bloomington or Miss Belleville, pretty enough to win the local pageant in a small city or large village, but not sophisticated or striking enough to bring home a Miss Illinois or Miss USA crown.

"Ms. Glaston," he said.

She looked up from the local newspaper on the counter. "Can I help you, sir?"

"A former client of yours referred me. After a fashion."

Her face grew still. She'd been open for business for less than a year, and so far as Stranyero knew, she didn't offer interior design or consulting or any other service that might involve clients. So she was already on alert, as he'd intended.

She closed her newspaper. "I've changed careers, so I doubt I can help you."

Changing careers was an interesting way to put it. On another day in another life, Stranyero might have been seeking her advice rather than her services.

"I suspect you can," he said. "I need someone to procure an item that I believe falls within your area of expertise from a church in Armenia. The item relates to a previous project of yours."

The Church of Tara research had yielded little Stranyero didn't know. The section on Tara's dad, Pete Spencer, being shot in Armenia, though, had caused him to re-listen to his own recordings from the trip Spencer had taken with Cyril Woods.

"I specialize in French décor and furnishings," Marie said, "past and present. If it's not an item that would normally appear in my collection here, and I doubt it is given its origin, I cannot help you."

"You'll be well compensated," he said.

"Pay is irrelevant. I'm a sole proprietor. I've no one to run my shop when I'm away."

"Any lost profit will be more than covered."

Stranyero wondered how much profit there could be. On entering, he'd spotted five patrons. An older woman sorting through table linens, two teenagers exclaiming over the framed prints on the side wall, and a middle-aged couple browsing the antique dining sets.

"It's not merely lost profits." Marie's index finger tapped the counter, but she held the rest of her body completely still and kept her face blank. "This is my first summer. I'm building a reputation. People need to learn about my store, remember that it's here."

"Of course. But there's more than money at stake. Once you understand who referred me and have seen my paperwork, I'm certain you'll agree."

"Paperwork?" Her eyes scanned the room, resting on each customer. The teenagers were in earshot.

Stranyero lowered his voice. "Copies of train and plane tickets, for example, from various trips you took a year and a half ago."

Her lips pulled back and her pupils dilated, making Stranyero regret his errand. After all these years and all the decisions he'd made, he'd never been able to block the short-term pain of others the way MacNeil could. MacNeil pursued the mission with no sympathy for the other side. Stranyero felt it all but moved forward anyway. He thought that showed greater dedication.

"I'm not here to cause you trouble." Stranyero prided himself on telling the truth whenever possible, and he felt that statement qualified. Not because it was literally true, but because anyone who heard it would understand he meant precisely the opposite, much like a new manager at the first meeting after a takeover saying no staff changes were contemplated or an Internet comment beginning with, "Not to sound racist, but...."

Marie's fingers gripped the glass display counter. "You're looking for a similar type of work?"

"No, I'm offering you a way to atone for that previous work. This transaction is entirely legal. It's simply a difficult item to persuade the current custodian to part with."

The last part was an understatement. Stranyero had personally tried to obtain the ancient Armenian journal, or at least a copy of it, for decades. The Brotherhood had tried for centuries. The document was reputed to include the story of a young woman who'd claimed to be pregnant and a virgin in 642 C.E. No emissary from the Brotherhood other than Cyril Woods had so much as been able to confirm the journal's existence. Cyril had been granted a glimpse only because he'd been traveling with Pete Spencer.

"Why do you think I'd be effective?" Marie said.

"Your reputation for locating difficult-to-find items. As well as for persuading rather than demanding or stealing. Your last acquisition notwithstanding."

~

"I'm asking you," Tara said.

"What's your interest in Stranyero?" Holmes said.

"Not your business. If you don't want to answer, I'll go." She put her hand on the doorknob behind her.

Holmes folded his hands on the table in front of him. "Here's what I'm willing to tell you. I never worked in conjunction with Thomas Stranyero on anything. And I've no reason to believe he was involved in kidnapping your daughter."

Tara thought for a moment. Her mind had begun to feel clearer over the last twenty-four hours, but she wanted to be sure she was applying solid logic. Holmes had every reason to point a finger at Stranyero in retaliation for Stranyero accusing him of kidnapping, and he hadn't. She could hardly expect Holmes to outright admit to committing a felony. This was the clearest confirmation she'd get that he alone had kidnapped Fimi and that Stranyero hadn't been involved.

"All right," Tara said. "But before we get to whatever else you want to talk about, what assurances can you give me that you won't try to take my child again?"

Tara's second major reason for leaving Fimi at Nanor's had been her fear that Holmes would try to do just that.

"Even if I were inclined to try that," Holmes said, "Stranyero's dossier on me would prevent it. As the prosecutor or state police must have told your parents, while there's insufficient evidence for the government to indict me for so much as a parking ticket, it obviously would raise serious questions if your daughter disappeared again. I can't fight the Church if I'm in jail. Nor would anyone take my message seriously."

She nodded and resumed her seat, this time at the opposite end of the table from Holmes.

*At least I can thank Stranyero for something.*

"So what information do you have for me? Not that I'll believe whatever you tell me or trust your intentions."

"Your daughter remained safe when you were in the coma, as did you," Holmes said.

"You're taking credit for that?"

Holmes shook his head. "Not sole credit. The Brotherhood was strangely dormant. But I counteracted certain other threats."

"From whom?"

"From some of the people you've seen in these demonstrations and protests —the ones insisting your actions at Willow Springs show you're the Antichrist, or your daughter is."

Tara ran her hand through the bangs on the brunette wig. "I guess I'm an idiot to think saving Nanor and renewing the earth, which are good things, ought to have reassured people I'm not dangerous."

"You didn't just save the woman, Tara. You brought her back from the dead. Even for those people who think she hadn't truly passed on, was in some sort of low level state of consciousness, it's an inexplicable feat, along with healing the earth itself from fire damage. I interviewed the people who saw it personally, including the emergency personnel, who confirmed that Nanor Kerkorian was dead. You have restorative powers, so it's clear to me that you and Fimi both must be pivotal to the struggle between good and evil."

"I've no idea why I can heal people. And I had no idea about the plants or the earth. I wasn't trying. It just happened."

"Perhaps your pregnancy or giving birth triggered your latent abilities. I wish I could tell you what that means. But for those who want an enemy, who love drama, it's a perfect signal of Biblical end times."

"I don't get why that automatically makes me an enemy."

Holmes shrugged. "People resist change. For over two thousand years, Christians have spoken about God in a certain way, professed a belief in one God, the *Father* Almighty and in Jesus *the son*. Not God in the form of a young woman."

"No one said I'm God. No one."

"But the Armenian letter at the very least suggests you are meant to oppose Christ. I read that as meaning organized Christian religion and the Roman Catholic Church. Others see it as being opposed to Jesus himself. And what are the demonstrations and riots but holy wars in the microcosm of St. Louis?"

"That's an extreme way to see it."

Tara shivered. Since her late teens, she hadn't believed a supreme evil being existed any more than she'd believed a supreme good one did, but so much had happened during the last two years that anything seemed possible. Worse, in Istanbul, she'd had a vision of war, with her baby as a bomb that ignited it. Holmes might be certain Fimi had been born to set Christianity back on the "right" path—in his mind, away from the Roman Catholic Church—but Tara had yet to find proof of that. And if it were true, it wasn't as if that ensured a safe or happy life for Fimi.

"You don't need to claim you're a god—or a goddess, I suppose the correct term is," Holmes said. "There's never a shortage of people who create religion where none exists. Look at the historical figure of Jesus. He was a Jew whose people believed in the coming of a messiah that would overthrow the Romans and re-establish the throne of David. Now people the world over insist he and his apostles founded the Roman Catholic Church."

Tara's head ached. She and Holmes had argued before about his views of the Church. "There's no point in debating about the Church."

"No, there's not. But regardless whether you agree with me, my belief that your daughter will bring down the Church coincides with your desire to protect her. So while you were in the coma, I did my best to learn everything about the silver bookmark you showed me. It took a long time. My free time is scarce, and all the efforts were my own, as I didn't want anyone else to find out about it." He pulled a densely-printed sheet of paper from the leather briefcase at his feet.

Tara leaned forward in spite of herself. She didn't want to ally herself with Holmes, but Oni had said the bookmark was the key to protecting Fimi. "And?"

"I learned nothing about the bookmark itself. There's no reference to it anywhere. But a design similar to the one that appears on it also appears in hundreds of places in the world." He slid the page across the table to her.

Tara slumped in her chair. "That's not that surprising. The design's not unusual—it's a rendering of the Star card in the Tarot deck."

"It is surprising," Holmes said, "because it appears most often near churches, synagogues, and mosques, and in outdoor shrines relating to the Virgin Mary. Not places one would expect to see a Tarot card."

Tara studied the list. It included Lourdes, a Roman Catholic tourist destination centered on a supposed apparition of a Lady in White believed to be the Virgin Mary. Her dad had been there and had seen the bookmark's design rendered in stained glass in a bookstore window, but he hadn't been able to learn any more about it. She didn't recognize the other locations. She'd need to see how these sites corresponded with the marks on Oni's map. Maybe these were the red dots.

"I would have begun visiting these sites myself," Holmes said, "but it would have drawn attention to them, and I've no way of knowing if that's a good idea. If I can help you explore further, though, I'll be happy to."

Tara folded the page and put it in her jeans pocket. She couldn't forgive Holmes for having kidnapped Fimi, but he didn't strike her as an enemy at the moment. "That's it?"

"That's it. Despite my research, I didn't learn anything more about the origin of the design or the bookmark itself."

They both stood.

Holmes opened the door for her. "I'll walk you up. I'd like to say hello to Sophia."

"If you wanted to see her, why the secret meeting?"

"I'd happily have met her in public after you and I cleared the air. I knew what your first questions would be about, and I couldn't risk witnesses. Or being recorded. Electronic surveillance devices are ineffective in that conference room."

The office upstairs was wide and open, with interior brick walls and a row of large windows across the front. Sophia paced near the entrance. She looked relieved to see them both emerge from the staircase.

Her phone returned, Tara checked her messages, standing at the far end behind an empty desk to give Holmes and Sophia some privacy. Sun shone through the windows above the desk, hitting Tara in the face. She shifted position, but it was still impossible to read her screen. She stepped sideways again, into the shadow of a bookcase.

An old-fashioned bell rang as the door to the street flew open. A small, oblong object hurtled into the office.

# 9

A layer of snow coated the ground, last season's yellowed grass poking through it in random spots. Shivering, Sophia crouched to place a bouquet of orchids, her aunt's favorite flowers, next to the headstone. Pain seared through her right ankle, and she lurched forward. She pitched onto her hands, overextending her wrists. Her fingers burned with the cold. Snow and ice crunched under her body as she fell sideways. She couldn't move. Her foot throbbed. Needles shot from her ankle to her pelvis. The air smelled of rotten eggs or spent firecrackers.

"Sophia? Wake up. Sophia!"

She blinked. It had been a mistake, a dream. The pain would cease when she opened her eyes and saw her aunt alive and calling her name.

But Tara leaned over her. The burning in Sophia's leg lessened, but live wires still sparked around her knee and ankle. Above her, exposed metal ductwork crossed the ceiling. To one side, a brick wall. To the other, a desk.

The attorney's office.

She remembered Erik Holmes shoving her toward Tara, remembered flipping over a desk and landing hard on the floor, then hearing an explosion.

"Lie still," Tara said.

"Not moving." The effort to speak caused bright spots in Sophia's vision.

Tara moved her hands along Sophia's leg. Strands of dark brown hair sprang out around her face, which was covered in sweat. Circles as dark as bruises shadowed the area beneath her eyes. She must have already healed Sophia part of the way, depleting herself.

"No," Sophia said.

"I'm being careful." Tara kept her hands on Sophia's lower leg, sending a faint vibration through the skin and muscles.

Sophia shifted away, despite arrows of pain radiating down her shin. "Stop." She swallowed, fighting nausea. "I can speak. Wiggle my toes. It's enough."

"But—"

"You'll make Fimi an orphan."

Tara's hands fell away. The vibration stopped, and the pain increased.

"I'll live," Sophia said.

"Holmes won't," Tara said. "I called 911, and I tried. But there's nothing—I couldn't—he must have thrown himself on the bomb or whatever it was. I couldn't—"

Sophia grasped Tara's wrist. "You can't save everyone. You can't."

CHICAGO – A concussion grenade hurled into a ground floor law office yesterday afternoon killed Erik Holmes, CEO of H.E.R. Holmes & Company. Also injured was Sophia Gaddini, a former nun and professor of religious studies at DePaul University.

The attack took place in the Printers Row neighborhood of Chicago. Witnesses describe the assailant as a Caucasian male, tall with a medium build and dark hair. No arrests have been made.

# 10

Dear Tara:

If you are reading this, it means you finally awakened from the coma, which pleases me to no end. But it also means I died, negating my need to be circumspect about my actions.

It has been nearly nine months since you healed the earth at Willow Springs and raised Nanor Kekorian from the dead. Each day I feel less sure that you'll awaken, so at last I'm setting down the things I feel I must tell you, including the mistakes I made.

My first one was misjudging Cyril Woods. When I arranged for your daughter to be taken from Diedre Hartman, my plan was to rescue Fimi and return her to you. Your determination to keep Woods involved in her life, however, changed my plan. I believed him to be still involved in the Brotherhood. I thought he had traveled to Armenia with your stepfather to obtain the missing part of the letter for the Brotherhood, not for you. Only Stranyero blackmailing you to obtain the complete letter convinced me that Woods had not already passed it on to his superiors.

By then, obviously, you had recovered Fimi, and there was no benefit to telling you the truth. I knew if I did you would no longer trust me enough to accept my help, and I felt certain that living in one of my secure complexes was the safest place for both you and your child. More important, I still believed Woods was an inside person for the Brotherhood. I assumed he'd failed in his mission to convey the letter to Stranyero, blocked somehow by you, your stepfather, or Sophia. Only after I read my brother's diary did I realize that Woods is what he seems. A young man with deep conflicts about his faith, but who has in fact abandoned the Brotherhood of Andrew.

That does not mean I trust him. He's done so much harm to you—and I speak knowing the same can be said of me—that he can't be relied upon to act in your best interests. To my mind, it's worse that his actions were rarely designed to hurt you. Nothing is more dangerous than a person who believes his actions are necessary for the greater good and who cares not for the consequences to individuals. Again, I speak from experience.

Due to the reservations expressed above about Woods, I've included caveats in the trust I've set up for you and your daughter. None of the money can be used to pay any expense of Cyril Woods or to benefit him in any way. Beyond that, the funds that the assets in the trust generate are yours to use. While the amount that funded the trust will seem large to you, I assure you it represents far less than 1% of my estate, so do not concern yourself about whether this will cause any difficulty for my nieces and nephews, who are my main heirs.

While I doubt the normal life for which you long is possible, I want to do all I can to help you achieve it. If you hesitate to accept funds from someone you view as a kidnapper, see it as my poor attempt to recompense you and your daughter for any harm you suffered. You can travel freely, you can finish college and pay for medical school, and you can fund your daughter's education. First, though, I hope you'll pay for guards for your and Fimi's safety—so long as you do everything possible to ensure those guards are trustworthy.

On the subject of possible harm I may have caused, the woman I hired to retrieve Fimi from Diedre Hartman was carefully and personally chosen by me, though she never knew I was her ultimate employer. Her area of expertise was procuring rare antiquities, including ones of religious significance. (She has now retired from that trade.) At times she procured them in somewhat questionable ways, but always without incident or harm to anyone. She has no history of violence. In her personal life, she is known for being good with people, including children. That is why I chose her. Your daughter was safe and protected while with her. I similarly vetted every intermediary, as well as the foster parents.

None of this will, I'm sure, change your view of me. But it should assure you that your baby experienced as little trauma as possible.

My mistake there was failing to anticipate Diedre Hartman's actions after the baby was taken from her. Had I known how unstable she was, I would have arranged for a watch to be kept upon her. Not because I believe she deserved to be saved from herself, but because I'm sure you felt for her despite her actions. If I could have spared you that pain, I would have.

I also erred in my lack of understanding of my brother, Henrik. I foolishly believed his pretense of being a playboy and ne'er do well, the lazy counterpart to my drive and determination. It fit with my view of him generally, and with my exalted view of myself.

My father is another area of blindness for me. I had no idea he'd become a Brotherhood leader. I suspected he was a member but was oblivious to the depth of his involvement. He recruited for the Order. His successes include Thomas Stranyero and, decades later, Henrik. He never approached me, no doubt correctly realizing I rejected all his views. Is it odd that I feel hurt all the same? That's a feeling I'd never confide in anyone, and I say it here because I know you'll read it only if I'm gone.

In addition to learning from Henrik's diary that Woods had, in fact, been opposing the Brotherhood, I learned more about the Order itself. Henrik's information appears to have come from a series of conversations with my father. Those discussions sparked a decade of intense though surreptitious investigation by Henrik.

If his conclusions are to be believed, the Brotherhood of Andrew existed long before Andrew of Crete, and long before Christ, though under different names. The story Woods fed to you, which he may have believed, that the Brotherhood was watching for a "new" messiah based on Andrew's visions, appears to have been an evolution of the Order's mission or perhaps simply a myth created to woo Christian followers. If Andrew's visions occurred at all, the story of him foreseeing six pregnant virgins after the Virgin Mary at most refined rather than began the Brotherhood's mission. How Jesus Christ—historical or mythical—fits with the Brotherhood remains unknown to me.

None of this information changes my view that you and Fimi are meant to destroy the Roman Catholic Church, the true enemy of Christ. It merely suggests that this struggle began much earlier than I realized. Jesus Christ was, in my view, the latest incarnation of God. The Church that rose up allegedly in his name was only one in a line of powerful institutions that subvert and oppose Him.

The other information I learned from Henrik's diary confirmed much of what I suspected. It was he who killed the Sufi in Istanbul I initially directed you to, Pir Ferit. If Henrik learned of Pir Ferit from me, I regret that. Henrik also is the second man who attacked you and Fimi with a sword in Istanbul. His goal was to cut off a finger or toe of the baby to see if it regrew. If so, he would have been convinced the child was the Antichrist. This was an approach favored by a faction of the Brotherhood, though not necessarily an officially-sanctioned approach. He later decided the test was unnecessary. He found the eclipse when the baby was born and the later series of weather disasters proof enough. He may also have been instrumental in a plot to kill Pope Matthew I before he could publicly state anything favorable about you. This is questionable, though. The Brotherhood, so far as I've been able to determine, is not a part of the Church, nor does it run it.

Over the last nine months, I've redoubled my efforts to infiltrate the Brotherhood. It stretches throughout the world. Most of its members, perhaps all of them other than the three council members, know little of the true mission. Like Cyril Woods (and, for a long time, my brother) they believe their goal is to find the next messiah after Jesus Christ and to eliminate agents of the Antichrist. They will do anything to this end, at times defying their superiors, as Henrik did when he attempted to kill you in Pennsylvania.

I suspect the real mission is darker and more ancient, but I've hit roadblock after roadblock in attempting to discern it. If I do, you will be the first to know. In the meantime, I intend to turn my focus to the silver bookmark you showed me.

As I doubt I will do it in person given the risk to myself, let me close by telling you how sorry I am for the pain I caused you by keeping from you the knowledge of your daughter's whereabouts. For the sake of my and my brother's legacies, I hope you will not make this information public. If you do, however, I understand.

Very truly yours,

Erik

P.S. My will leaves sums to Nanor and Kali Kerkorian to rebuild Willow Springs if they so choose. While you renewed all living things, many buildings were badly damaged. The community remains vacant. I hope Mrs. Kerkorian will use the funds to supplement her insurance payments and begin again at that site or elsewhere. Regardless of my disagreements with her, she has my respect and admiration for all she accomplished in the wake of her daughter Maya's death.

~

Tara sat on the foot of the twin bed in the guestroom, Holmes' letter in one hand and her phone in the other. She dialed while watching Fimi, who sat on the floor silently turning the pages of a picture book. The volumes Roger had given Tara, now stacked under the crib, didn't report any instance where people who supposedly performed mystical healings suffered language problems or permanent brain damage, though some, like Tara, had collapsed afterward, and one had fallen into a coma for a month.

The medical literature Tara had read also didn't suggest it was alarming that Fimi hadn't spoken yet. But her child's silence worried her. She also remained afraid to try to heal anyone again or enhance her own body's healing processes. She'd had a migraine for twenty hours after partially healing Sophia. At least she hadn't found anything suggesting meditation itself was a risk. Some people reported visions (or hallucinations, according to the medical texts) from meditation, but no one had been injured by it.

Tara clicked the volume on her cellphone when Sophia answered, but it was already at the highest setting. She could barely hear her friend. Sophia was in the hospital recovering from a second surgery to her ankle. She'd insisted Tara stay away, as demonstrators had already picketed the main hospital entrance and tried to learn her room number.

"I feel terrible that Holmes is dead," Tara said after telling Sophia about the letter. It had come that morning, two days after Holmes' death. It had been sent first to her parents' house and forwarded to the post office box her family now used. Tara's dad had Fed Exed it to Nanor under the name of the person Nanor had sublet the apartment from. "But I can't believe he's still insisting he did the right thing. So I'm angry, too. And grateful that he's still trying to help. Is that weird?"

"No," Sophia said.

Tara knew she ought to let her friend rest, but hearing the voice on the phone, faint as it was, helped her feel less unnerved about the grenade attack. She glanced at the time. She'd limit the call to five minutes.

"Why would the Order have been formed before Christ do you think? To watch for him? Were people watching for a messiah back then?" Tara said.

"Every culture has tales," Sophia said. "Of saviors. Prophets."

"Nanor says 'messiah' only means anointed one. That it doesn't need to be Christian."

Fimi finished the last page of the picture book and flipped to the front again.

"True." Sophia said. "This may explain why my research...into the Collyridians... stalled...I didn't look at writings before Christ."

Tara ran her hand through her hair. "Why would you? If they formed partly to deify Mary, Jesus' mother, why look for anything predating her?"

"I should have...." Sophia's voice trailed off. "She's connected to goddesses."

"Right." Tara remembered that from her first conversations with Sophia and from the research she'd done herself when she'd learned she was pregnant. It all seemed like a thousand years ago. "I should let you rest."

"Have you thought more....about Thomas? He mentioned materials...."

"Sophia? Are you still there? I should let you rest."

Sophia cleared her throat. "Brotherhood secrets. He's willing to let you look through materials with Brotherhood secrets."

"I thought he just wanted to be a sort of spy. Not do anything active."

"My brush with death... frightened him."

"I feel a little better since Holmes confirmed Stranyero had no role in kidnapping Fimi. But I still don't know if he really wants to help."

~

"But who ordered it?" MacNeil made a slicing gesture with his right hand, punctuating each word, though only Stranyero could see it. He'd traveled to MacNeil's Vermont mansion to meet with MacNeil and take the call from the Cardinal in the comfort of MacNeil's two-story library. The Cardinal had called them on an audio-only line. No one in the Brotherhood believed in appearing on any camera when discussing issues relating to the Order.

"You're telling me it wasn't either of you," the Cardinal said.

Stranyero sat in his favorite wingback chair to one side of the wrought iron spiral staircase that led to the second level. As soon as Sophia had been wheeled out of recovery from her second surgery, he'd left to catch an afternoon flight to Vermont. He worried she might not remember that he'd waited until she'd awakened and he'd been assured she was stable, as she'd been drifting in and out of consciousness. But he'd been with her and talked with her the entire first day after her initial operation.

"It wasn't me." MacNeil glanced at Stranyero. "I can't speak for my colleague."

Stranyero doubted MacNeil believed he'd ordered the attack, or he'd have arranged to speak to the Cardinal alone. Most likely, McNeil wanted to assess how Stranyero and the Cardinal reacted to one another.

"Nor I," Stranyero said.

"Yes, I suppose your doing so makes no sense," MacNeil said, "given that you spent every waking moment at the hospital since it occurred. I'm surprised you tore yourself away from the lovely Sophia's presence to come here."

Stranyero had expected MacNeil to be aware of his actions. What the man didn't know was that all of it had been discussed with the Cardinal in advance. He waited to see if the Cardinal would share that.

"Thomas acted exactly as he should have," the Cardinal said. "He needs these women to believe he's on their side."

"Fine," MacNeil said, though the flush rising from his neck to his face said otherwise. "Back to my original point. Whoever planned the attack should be excommunicated."

Stranyero studied his former mentor. MacNeil's obvious ire seemed to confirm that he hadn't orchestrated Holmes' death. So one of three things had happened: the Cardinal had given someone else orders to throw the grenade, the Brotherhood had another rogue member on its hands, or the attack had been carried out by someone outside the organization.

"The party must be dealt with, yes," the Cardinal said. "But in the end, there was no real harm."

*So the first option*, Stranyero thought. *Interesting.*

"He was overzealous, yes," the Cardinal continued, "and too dramatic, but drastic times—"

"Don't call for suicidal measures." MacNeil strode to the back window of his library. It overlooked a man-made lake. He'd once told Stranyero it lowered his blood pressure to look at, but judging from his jerky movements and rigid posture, it wasn't working. "We're still within the first 700 days of the child's life. If she or Tara Spencer had been killed, it would have ended any hope of a messiah. Our plan for consolidation would fail. If someone in our organization risked that, that person is a serious liability."

"Only if you assume Spencer was the target," the Cardinal said. "If the target was Spencer's allies, the direct hit on Holmes achieved its purpose."

Now Stranyero stared at the lake, too, counting the ducks drifting by to keep his expression relaxed. The birds appeared peaceful, but only because the glassy surface concealed the effort it took them to move.

MacNeil spun around to face the phone. "The plan should have gone through me if that was the approach."

The Cardinal's deep laugh boomed through the speaker. "You must learn to respect the initiative of others, Fenton. You have strong leadership skills, but advancing in this organization requires more than ordering people about. Worry more about the mote in your own eye."

"And what is that mote exactly?" MacNeil said.

"Your failure to discover Tara Spencer's plans."

MacNeil stood directly over the phone. "Tara Spencer has no plans. She's been out of the coma less than two weeks. She's spent time with her friends and family and accompanied Sophia Gaddini to meet Erik Holmes, who could have shared nothing she didn't already know. She's worried, but she's soothed by the fact that nothing happened to her or her child over the last fourteen months."

"What of the Mexican woman who contacted her? What have you learned about her?" the Cardinal said.

MacNeil's eyebrows rose, and he shot a look at Stranyero, who shrugged and stifled a smile. So Sophia had kept something from him. Or Tara had kept it from Sophia. Either way, he felt pleased the two women had withheld information. He'd always liked strong adversaries, especially when the stakes were high.

"We're working on it," MacNeil said. "We'll find out exactly who she is and what her role is."

"See that you do," the Cardinal said.

When the call was over, MacNeil turned to Stranyero. "You didn't know there was a new player?"

"I didn't. Ms. Spencer's clearly become more circumspect with Dr. Gaddini."

"It's just as I said. As soon as the girl knew of your relationship with Sophia, she clammed up."

"It won't stay that way," Stranyero said.

Oni, her dark hair pinned back, her hands in fists, paced around the glass table in Nanor's dining alcove. "More meditating isn't going to magically reveal answers. Holmes died after providing the list of shrines. That makes it and the map the most important leads we have. We at least need to visit the points where they overlap."

In the corner of the living room area, Tara rocked in Nanor's worn rocking chair, the one piece of furniture that had survived the fire. Behind her on the wide windowsill, a vanilla pillar candle burned, but its scent didn't calm her. The sight of Holmes' mangled body had imprinted onto her retinas. Each time she shut her eyes to start to meditate, she saw it again and heard the explosion. She didn't know how to turn that off, which she'd need to do to get into any sort of trance state. But Oni's plan didn't sound better. It was a shot in the dark, and it might expose her and Fimi to more people with grenades and guns.

"My dad visited Lourdes while I was in the coma," Tara said. "He saw the design in the bookstore's stained glass window. And what did that accomplish? No one at the store remembered why the design had been used or who ordered it, and they didn't have any records. So all that happened was he spent money on plane tickets and travel. For nothing."

"He must have missed something," Oni said.

"Or the designs all over the world were just meant to lead to the bookmark, which we already have," Tara said.

"Miss Oni, you scorn the thought of magic. Are not the pregnancies themselves magical?" Nanor's voice came from the galley kitchen.

"I call them curses," Oni said. "And sitting in one spot and breathing isn't going to change that."

"And flying about the world will?" Nanor said.

Tara glanced at Fimi. The toddler knocked over a four-block tower she'd built without uttering a sound and started a new one. Tara couldn't think of her pregnancy as a curse, and she didn't wish her daughter didn't exist. But she understood Oni's point. At twenty-one, Tara had been a year from finishing her degree and moving on to medical school, with plans for getting married to her then-boyfriend and having children after that. Now she was struggling to finish college on-line and constantly feared being unable to protect Fimi and ensure she reached adulthood.

"Yes," Oni said. "And Cyril agrees with me. We know where to look for answers. The shrines."

"Of course he does," Tara said. "He'd always rather do something than nothing, even if it's the wrong thing."

"It's not wrong," Oni said.

"Your plan is based on information a kidnapper provided." Nanor emerged from the kitchen with a pitcher of iced herbal tea and a stack of glasses. "That he has died does not make him trustworthy."

"Someone killed him right after he met with Tara. I'm guessing that means he's on our side, not the Brotherhood's," Oni said.

"The target may have been Tara." Nanor poured the tea into three glasses and one plastic sippy cup.

Tara shivered and pushed herself out of the chair. She joined them at the glass and chrome table, laying the page of shrine locations Holmes had given her on it. "Which is why I can't drag Fimi all over the world. And I'm not going anywhere without her." She looked at her phone, hoping for a message from Cyril. He'd gone to the hospital in disguise. She'd asked him to see for himself how Sophia was.

"You're also not getting any messages from on high telling you what to do," Oni said. "Right?"

"Not so far, but it doesn't mean I won't." Tara sipped the tea. She liked the faint raspberry flavor, but the reddish hue made her think of Holmes' severed index finger, which she'd stepped over to get to Sophia, covered in blood. She set down the glass, her stomach knotting.

"You try too hard," Nanor said. "When you had a vision of Protennoia in Armenia, it was after you had let go of trying. You had reached peace."

While visiting Armenia toward the end of her pregnancy, Tara had finally decided to let go of her quest for answers. That same night, she'd seen a large serpent with multi-colored scales that turned into a woman who called herself Protennoia. Later, she'd learned most of the words Protennoia spoke, and her name, came from a once-lost gnostic gospel. Tara's other vision, prompted by the Sufi elder, Pir Ferit, had been far more disturbing, including a troop transport vehicle, soldiers, and a bomb.

"The one in Istanbul came when I passed out," Tara said. She'd come to on a cold stone floor in Pir Ferit's study.

"Again, not trying," Nanor said.

Oni grimaced. "So should she knock herself unconscious?"

"Just because something isn't your way doesn't make it wrong," Tara said.

"But what good did those visions do you?" Oni took a long drink of tea, obviously untroubled by the color. "The one with the figure called Protennoia led you to start telling everyone about your pregnancy, which got you exactly nowhere. Worse than nowhere."

Nanor sat and moved the tea pitcher aside. "It got her an audience with the Pope."

"Yeah, and he died right after," Oni said.

"It also helped lead me to the Sufi elder and the Armenian letter," Tara said.

"Which did nothing but make you afraid," Oni said.

Nanor pointed a finger at Oni. "Your own mission in life is based on ancient prophecies. Yet you deride them."

"All they did for my family is get all the women killed," Oni said. "I want to make sure Tara and I don't end up just like them. If there's something those visions brought Tara, something that helps us, fine, keep trying. But otherwise, let's take action."

Tara gathered Fimi, who had wandered over, in her arms, grateful that the child had sought her out. "The first vision happened when I was relaxed, but it was also after I bonded with Nanor's Armenian relatives. And Protennoia—she had features of different people in my life, including Nanor. The second came after Pir Ferit touched my face. He said it was foretold that the One Who Would Live Forever—that's who he was looking for—would have a vision of a battle when he did that."

"So perhaps the trigger is a connection with others linked to those who have had mystical pregnancies," Nanor said. "Relationships are a powerful force. If we wait until Kali returns from class, and we all sit together—"

"Count me out," Oni said. "I'm not the sit and breathe type."

"But you are of the line of the guardians, like the Sufi was," Nanor said. "And Kali and I are related to Maya, another virgin who became pregnant. These connections must matter."

"I was never told about visions or meditating," Oni said. "Other than Brother Andrew's supposed visions, which Holmes' letter suggests were total fabrications."

"Just try the group meditation," Tara said. "If nothing happens, we'll try to narrow down the list of shrines, and Oni, you can visit some of them. But only after we see if Nanor can help trigger a vision."

Oni gripped the back of the dining chair. "It's a waste of time. But I'll try once."

"Several times," Nanor said. "Meditating under such pressure, it will require more time to relax."

Oni blew air out of her mouth. "Once. Then I'll see."

# 11

Tara held her daughter's tiny fingers in her right hand, and felt Nanor's warm grip around her left. She was amazed the older woman could still sit on the floor cross-legged without hurting her knees. Oni sat between Nanor and Kali, and Kali held Fimi's other hand to complete the circle.

The blinds had been drawn. At first when she shut her eyes, Tara was right back standing over Holmes' body. But Nanor squeezed her hand and began talking the group through breathing exercises. Tara did her best to focus her mind on inhaling and exhaling and on the people around her. Gradually she relaxed for the first time since the grenade attack. It helped that Cyril had returned from the hospital. He'd reported that Sophia was recovering well. Now he stood near a window, keeping watch on the street outside so that Tara felt free to let her mind drift.

Fimi shifted position on the floor, but didn't break the circle. All their breathing came in rhythm.

Scenes from the fire at Willow Springs flitted through Tara's mind, and each time, Tara sat a little straighter and breathed a little deeper. Finally, she saw nothing. No memories, no flashbacks. She was aware only of the faint light from the flickering candles around the room as it filtered through her closed eyelids.

"Tara," Nanor said. "You're sitting on a concrete bench in an outdoor stone kitchen like the one at the home of my relatives. It smells of dough. It's night. The wind is warm, and light from the full moon shines on you."

Tara felt the wind on her face and smelled the yeast of the lavash she'd helped make when she'd visited Nanor's family in Armenia. She tilted her head back. Stars sparkled against the sky. A serpent with scales that shifted colors in the moonlight glided toward her and rose on its tail. It morphed into a woman with long dark hair like Kali's, but with eyes set in wrinkles like Nanor's.

Unlike the way the vision had happened in Armenia, now Tara's siblings and mother appeared next to the woman. Her mother held Fimi.

"Once it begins, it must end," the woman said, and everyone disappeared. The outdoor kitchen became a different stone structure, larger and more solid, with a yawning opening. Inside were rows of burial crypts.

Tara gasped and opened her eyes.

~

"YOU SAW a tomb because we were just talking about Holmes' death," Oni said. "You saw your siblings and your mom because you miss them. It's all the power of suggestion."

"I miss my dad, too, but he wasn't there," Tara said.

Fimi had dozed off during the meditation. Tara had put her in the crib, then returned to the living room to tell them all what she'd seen.

Oni shrugged.

"What about what the woman said?" Cyril asked. He remained at his post by the side window.

"Probably something Tara's unconscious picked up somewhere," Oni said. "Or just her wish that this would all be over."

"Tara had a very specific vision," Nanor said. "It must have meaning."

"You don't know that," Oni said. "But we do know the bookmark is a symbol of the guardians. So while you all went on a vision quest, I thought about how to narrow Holmes' list. Tara doesn't want to travel all over, and I can't visit every shrine on my own. It would take too long and cost too much. But I can visit every one near where we know a virgin pregnancy occurred or was predicted to occur even if it never happened. Starting with the locations closest to St. Louis."

"That makes some sense," Cyril said to Tara. "No one knows Oni's connected to you. The Brotherhood doesn't know about her. Sophia doesn't, the press doesn't. So if someone sees her at a shrine, it won't matter."

"And you and I stay here with Fimi?" Tara said.

Cyril nodded. "With additional hired guards, if you want to start using Holmes' money."

"Let's send a guard with Oni," Tara said. "I don't want her out there alone."

"I'll be fine," Oni said. "The only problem is, my cousin never told me where all the pregnancies happened."

"There are three that I know of other than Tara," Cyril said. "In Armenia, Spain, and Syria."

"There's at least one more," Oni said. "In the early 1800s, but she was also in Missouri."

"How did she die?" Tara asked.

"Hit by debris during an earthquake. She was eight months pregnant. The earthquake—actually a series of them—caused a tsunami that made the Mississippi river run backwards."

"I knew there couldn't be a happy ending," Tara said. When she'd met Cyril, he'd told her three other women like her had died—one in a church fire set by an invading army, one in an earthquake, and one by being burned at the stake during the Inquisition.

"The map has dots in a lot more places than that," Oni said.

"Maybe they're predicted pregnancies. If that's what all the dots mean." Tara turned to Cyril. "Where else were there supposed to be pregnant virgins?"

"I only know about the St. Louis area, which is what led to you," Cyril said. "No one told me about any other predictions."

"The Brotherhood must know," Tara said.

Cyril raised his eyebrows. "You want to ask Stranyero?"

"No, not ask him. I don't want him to know we're interested. But it's worth finding out more about those 'secret' materials in the library he mentioned to Sophia."

# 12

"Is there something you forgot to tell us?" Fenton MacNeil stood in the same spot in his library, hands in his pockets, towering over the phone.

With a few well-placed phone calls, Stranyero had learned who had informed the Cardinal that a young woman named Oni Lopez—who was part Argentinian, not Mexican—had come to the United States to meet Tara Spencer. It was Evekial Adame, Brotherhood member and founder of The Apostolic Church of Satan.

Stranyero hadn't yet decided whether or how Oni affected his plans about Tara Spencer.

"About?" Evekial spoke in the deliberately deep voice he used on the phone or when preaching.

Stranyero could picture him, with his dyed jet black hair and emaciated frame. He was no doubt wearing one of his ostentatious red robes, which MacNeil had explained any number of times amounted to overkill of the worst sort, feet up on his antique desk with its Satanic carvings. Not that Evekial had anything to do with Satanism. It was the man's idea of camouflage. He had a group of Church members who either believed all of it or simply enjoyed the spectacle and donated handsomely to be part of it. He'd also drawn his share of detractors from those who claimed to be actually devoted to Satan. Evekial enjoyed jousting with them.

"There's more than one matter you've failed to report?" MacNeil said.

"If it's about the death of Erik Holmes, I was as shocked as you," Evekial said. "If you were shocked, that is."

Stranyero sighed and refilled his glass with two ice cubes and Ballantine's whiskey from MacNeil's wet bar. Evekial had never absorbed the idea of caution.

Despite the Brotherhood's technology, there was always an off chance someone was listening.

MacNeil clenched his large hands into fists. "The man had many enemies, but none of us on the phone were among them so far as I know."

"So why call me? I've been diligent." The bass tones were gone, and the faint whining notes that replaced them set Stranyero's teeth on edge.

"If you're diligent, as you put it, why did you fail to tell us about the new person in Tara Spencer's life?" Stranyero said.

"You mean the heretic?" Evekial said. "I'm very proud. Sixteen months you searched for her, and she appears out of the woodwork after I host one prayer circle."

"First, you didn't think it important to tell us that?" MacNeil said. "And second, she didn't appear because of your prayer circle, you idiot, she appeared because Tara Spencer regained consciousness."

"I told the Cardinal about it when he contacted me," Evekial said.

MacNeil's mouth dropped open, then closed with a snap. Stranyero felt almost as surprised. That the Cardinal had contacted Evekial Adame directly suggested the cut-rate showman might be under consideration for the council leadership position. Which suggested the man had hidden depths or the Brotherhood was far shorter on manpower than Stranyero had ever imagined.

"I'm your point of contact," MacNeil said. "You should have told me regardless."

"You never want me to bother you."

MacNeil's face grew redder. "With your ridiculous faux-Satanic rituals, don't bother me. If it has to do with Tara Spencer, bother me."

MacNeil banged the speaker button when he hung up.

"So Evekial is after an exalted position. And has a chance of getting it," Stranyero said, disturbed that a charlatan like Evekial might be considered competition for him.

"That can't be true. The man's a menace, with his loose lips and his parading around. The Cardinal merely wants to keep us on our toes."

Stranyero drowned the last of his whiskey, leaving the ice clinking in the bottom of the glass. "You're vulnerable after the debacle with Tara Spencer bringing a woman back from the dead—"

"Nanor Kerkorian was not dead. She'd put herself in suspended animation."

"No one inside buys that story," Stranyero said. "And there's no way to spin Ms. Spencer healing the earth. You're the one who got that reported by national and international news outlets."

MacNeil threw himself into his leather desk chair. "I had my instructions."

Stranyero had always suspected the Cardinal had ordered MacNeil to orchestrate the fire that had destroyed Willow Springs, Nanor Kerkorian's women's community. But people at the top often conveniently forgot the orders they'd given once plans went awry.

"As did I. But since when has that mattered?" he said.

~

The next morning, Stranyero set the stack of pages on the polished desk. "This is all of it?"

Marie Glaston sat opposite him. She nodded. She'd pulled her hair into a French knot and wore a designer suit and glasses with dark Burberry frames. She could easily pass for a business associate, not that anyone in the office-sharing suite had paid any attention to her or to Stranyero when he'd arrived this morning straight from O'Hare Airport. It was the beauty of the time-share model applied to workspace. He'd used this particular location roughly eight times a year for the last five years and had never seen the same people twice. The only aspect he didn't like was the heavy scent of lilies from the floral arrangement along the interior brick wall in the reception area. It gave him a headache.

"And the original?" he said.

"I couldn't get that. The priest's wife flat out refused."

Using the equipment on the credenza behind him, Stranyero scanned the pages and saved them on his portable drive, bypassing the shared network. "But she spoke to you. And showed you the original journal about Rima Petrosyan."

He returned each page to the stack after it scanned. He wasn't familiar with all the hand-printed characters, but he knew enough to recognize the language.

"Yes. Though I've only her word that it's the right one," Marie said. "I don't read ancient Armenian. Or modern Armenian, for that matter."

"How did you persuade her?"

"Told the truth."

Stranyero swiveled his chair to look at her. Honesty could be disarming, but in this case, he would have expected a counter-effect. "Including who asked you to obtain the journal?"

"Yes."

"I instructed you not to do that." He caught the last page before it fell to the floor, shut off the scanner, and typed in a sequence to ensure no trace existed on the shared memory.

Marie leaned back, her knees and ankles pressed together. "You also told me to come back with the journal no matter what. That's what I did."

"You're sure this isn't a substitute? Carefully created to mislead?"

"I can't be sure," Marie said. "But it seems unlikely the priest's wife would have two journals, a real one and a fake in case an enemy happened along."

"Our Lady of Sorrows kept this record secret for thousands of years, so it doesn't seem unlikely at all."

"But you said in the past the leaders there denied its existence. Why not simply do that now?" Marie said.

Stranyero leaned back in his chair and stared at the exposed ductwork above him. "To plant misinformation."

"I don't know what to say. There was no way I could have it authenticated," Marie said. "She wouldn't let me take it anywhere. But it appeared consistent with seventh century bound manuscripts from that region. The cloth binding, the thread, the papyrus."

"And you told her you'd learned of its existence from Cyril Woods and Pete Spencer?"

"Yes."

What he'd told Marie to say if necessary was true, after a fashion. He'd had an electronic bug placed on the Bible of Tara's stepfather, Pete Spencer, and had persuaded Pete's pastor to send him to Armenia to watch over Cyril Woods. Cyril had seen the journal and described it to Pete, which was how Stranyero had learned that it had not, as he'd once been told, been destroyed.

"Name dropping alone wouldn't convince her," Stranyero said. "She didn't give the journal to Woods, after all, only let him see it. Why provide it now?"

"She said the time had come for it to be released."

"Did she say how she reached that conclusion?"

Marie shook her head. The diamond chip earrings she wore caught the light. "She said Tara Spencer's healing of the earth was a sign."

"How certain are you that this photocopy is the actual journal you saw?"

"I copied the entire journal myself. Every page."

Stranyero studied Marie. The young woman appeared relaxed, her hands on her thighs, her forehead clear of lines. He couldn't imagine why she'd lie, and she could hardly have concocted these pages to satisfy him. She didn't have the expertise, and he hadn't allowed her enough time. He handed the pages back to her. "Keep these for now. I'll let you know where to deliver them, and I want you to be able to state honestly and definitively that they are the exact copies you made from the journal."

"Should I stay in town?" Marie said.

"Not necessarily. But don't return to your store yet. I want you ready to travel."

After Marie left, Stranyero drummed his fingers on the desk. That Tara Spencer had awakened and the first 700 days of her child's life were almost over might explain the priest's wife sharing the journal. But he couldn't grasp why she'd taken the chance on Marie.

He pivoted to look out the window. Across from him, the twin circular towers of the Hyatt O'Hare rose. He wished he had time to go downtown to see Sophia, but a call from Tara Spencer had come in while he'd been in the air. The message she'd left meant he needed to head back to Vermont this afternoon.

He took out his phone, but his finger hovered over the contact icon. He needed a translator, but he knew of only two who might have the necessary expertise. Sophia, who'd spent much of her free time during Tara's coma studying the ancient language, and the academic the Brotherhood usually consulted.

He wasn't ready to share his discovery with either one.

"We can't be certain how long we have," Nanor said.

"Okay." Tara blew a kiss at Fimi through the video feed on her phone. "Be good for Kali, sweetheart."

But Fimi had already turned away, her attention drawn to a popup book Kali held.

*At least she loves books. That must say something about her intelligence.*

Tara dropped the phone in her pocket, shoulders sagging, and ignored the hollow feeling in her chest.

They left the rental car on a residential street lined on either side with parked vehicles. Tara's limp was nearly gone, and she felt fairly rested, but her steps faltered when she and Nanor crossed a railroad track and entered a wooded area. Nanor showed no sign of flagging. If anything, she seemed to have more energy now than when Tara had lived at Willow Springs. It was Tara with her altered gait, not Nanor, who made the pace slow. Using GPS to navigate, it took twenty-five minutes to cover the remaining mile to the man-made lake Stranyero had told them about.

They stared at the towering mansion that, according to Stranyero, housed a library that included the most secret Brotherhood texts and documents.

"You think he really only recently learned of this library?" Tara said. "If not, when he let Cyril and me into the Brotherhood archives last year, he knew there wasn't much useful there."

"It is possible he was unaware of that," Nanor said.

"You're defending him?" Tara said, surprised. Nanor had long suspected Thomas Stranyero had driven a vehicle the police believed, based on tire tracks, had swerved into her daughter Maya's lane of traffic, resulting in Maya veering off the road to her death. But they'd never found the vehicle, and the only evidence was a card with Stranyero's name on it that Nanor had found in Maya's bedroom.

"Not defending," Nanor said. "Maintaining an open mind. Bias damages the one who holds it nearly as much as the one it is used against."

Stranyero had disarmed the outdoor perimeter security so they could enter through a rear service door. He'd also given them codes to access the library. As soon as they did, Tara texted him. He met them, wearing dress pants and a starched gray collared shirt, and collected their cell phones. He said he was unwilling to risk them taking photos of any documents. The library had no photocopiers, scanners, or printers that they could use to copy any of the materials. One of the Brotherhood's primary security measures was the use of paper, which was more easily preserved and less easily distributed than digital information, and the restriction of methods of duplication. He pointed to an intercom on the wall near an oversized painting.

"I'll be in the front music room," he said, "watching the circular drive and garage entrance there. I'll contact you through this if necessary."

Tara didn't like relying on Stranyero, but the worst he could be setting them up for was a trespassing charge, and given that he had permission to be here and had let them in, that didn't seem like a significant risk. The library itself overwhelmed her, with its stacks of aging books, spiral staircase, and leather couches and chairs. Before they'd arrived, he'd laid out on a long mahogany reading table a set of files, documents, and books that he said were the most protected, and therefore most likely to be relevant, of the Brotherhood's items. He'd also given her an overview of which sections of the library included what.

Nanor surveyed the materials Stranyero had segregated. After checking a variety of shelves and books to see that Stranyero had been accurate about the organization at least, Tara gravitated toward rows of wooden file cabinets with bronze handles. All were unlabeled, and if there was an order to them, Tara couldn't figure it out. But it was at least possible she could start at the beginning and rifle through all of them in a few hours.

Nanor examined several books on the table. "Many of these are in Latin or Greek."

"Is that a problem?"

"I studied both as part of my divinity degree. I am, however, fluent in neither."

Tara wished Sophia had been well enough to accompany them, as she read both languages. "It's not like we want to rely on what Stranyero chooses for us."

"No, but I am quite curious about his choices," Nanor said.

Tara opened a file drawer in the fifth cabinet from the left, the tenth from the right. She figured Stranyero would expect her to start at the beginning, end, or middle, so if he'd rearranged to make certain papers harder to find, an odd starting point was best.

After an hour and a half, Nanor said, "I found a handwritten document that includes passages with the phrase the Sufi guardian in Armenia used for you—The One Who Will Live Forever. It speaks of 700 days, but too many portions are missing for me to understand to what that refers."

Tara checked that the beeper she'd brought with her was on in case Kali needed to reach her. It communicated only numbers, not text, and couldn't be used for photos, so Stranyero had let her keep it. She figured the baby was safe with Kali, Cyril, and Oni, and she'd hired security guards, but she liked being reachable.

She handed Nanor a file folder. "Maps. The one on top shows the whole world. It's one of those based on a globe, where they cut out parts to make it lie flat. A lot of the countries don't exist anymore. The maps at the end look newer. I think the legends are in Greek."

Nanor paged through the file. "They are. The later maps show the development of various branches of Christianity. Nothing about shrines or virgin pregnancies."

Tara's heart sank, but she couldn't expect to have found the predicted locations of virgin pregnancies that easily. Cyril had found Tara in the first place because Stranyero had told him a virgin pregnancy would occur in the St. Louis area. He could no doubt explain how he'd known that, but she preferred not to ask him directly and reveal that it mattered to her. Trusting him felt too much like inching through a desert filled with land mines.

Half an hour later, Nanor showed Tara a sheaf of pages. "These describe a ritual that relates to the virgin pregnancies," Nanor said. "Or perhaps to birth or baptism. There also are references to finding the *pieta*, the virgin mother. That is all I can determine from this."

Tara found a file folder that included her birth certificate and her and Fimi's DNA test results. After her school records was a handwritten page noting five "contact dates," all within a year before the time Tara's mother would have learned she was pregnant with Tara. Tara rubbed her hands over her arms, wondering if someone from the Brotherhood had contacted her mom or Ray Tigue, her mother's college boyfriend. Tara had believed most of her life that Ray was her biological father, though she always thought of her stepdad, Pete Spencer, who'd married her mom when Tara was three, as her dad.

Her mom would have told her about anything unusual that might relate to Tara, and she noticed and questioned things. Everything. So if anyone strange had contacted her, she would remember. Ray, on the other hand, had been drinking and taking a lot of drugs at the time. He'd gone on to spend much of his adult life in prison for the crimes he'd committed to get drug money and for minor dealing offenses. He'd finally gotten sober and had stayed out of prison since.

Nanor held out a slim, worn volume with threads hanging from its spine. "This book is in English, and it has two chapters on Andrew of Crete."

Tara took it. Neither Nanor nor Sophia had ever located any historical records supporting that Andrew had visions, only that he'd been devoted to the Virgin Mary and had been killed for defending Christians who revered the cross and other icons.

This book also didn't identify any writing by Andrew or anyone else about his visions. It did have a section, unrelated to the parts about Andrew, about a prophecy based on Chapter 12 of the book of *Revelation*, the chapter Cyril had quoted to Tara when he'd first met her. According to the book, Chapter 12 indicated the first sign of the Apocalypse was a woman wearing a crown with twelve stars who gave birth to a male child—a messiah—destined to rule the earth. Each set of two stars represented the eyes of a child, meaning the world had six chances for the messiah to survive.

The Beast, or Antichrist, each time would try to devour the child and plunge the world into darkness unless the child was born on holy ground.

"This fits what Cyril told me when I met him," Tara said. "Except that there's nothing about Brother Andrew's visions. Which is weird, because that was key, according to Cyril."

"Key to the prediction that there would be six potential messiahs after Jesus Christ? Or that the child was a messiah?"

"Both." Tara flipped pages. "The timing is odd. This chapter says a prophecy about future virgin births was recorded by the bishop of Salamis around 375 C.E. He was working on his most important work refuting heresies. Including the ones about Mary that the Collyridians and later the guardians evolved from."

"375 C.E.," Nanor said. "Centuries before Andrew of Crete was born."

"Which definitely does not fit what Cyril was always told."

Nanor shook her head. "It seems there is no connection between Andrew of Crete and the virgin pregnancies. More likely the pregnancies—yours, Maya's, those of the women in Spain, Syria, and Armenia—related instead to the 'heretics' the bishop wrote about."

"That's a lot to read into it," Tara said.

From the beginning, Nanor had argued that her daughter Maya and Tara were meant to raise girl children who would bring down the three major religions—Judaism, Islam, and Christianity—that centered around a single male god. She couldn't help thinking that affected Nanor's interpretation.

"Not at all. The Bishop attacked heresies. We know of two major groups of heretics whose views on Mary were contrary to the evolving Christian Church. The Collyridians saw her as a deity, which the Church denounced, and the Antidicomarianites believed she'd had sex, which the Church also denounced. And the Bishop wrote about future virgin pregnancies. I see the dots connecting."

"Because you want to see that. I understand your view of Maya and her daughter's purpose, but the Bishop wrote about a lot of people who opposed the beliefs the Church adopted at the time on all kinds of topics, not just Mary."

"But you have changed your views from when we met, have you not? You believe you and your child have some function relating to the divine power of the Universe?"

"I got pregnant somehow, so I believe there are forces beyond our understanding, beyond human, that caused that," Tara said.

"And surely you don't still fear they are evil?" Nanor said.

"Fear it? Yeah, I fear it. I grew up Catholic. But I don't believe it." Tara put up her hand. "I also don't believe it's all about wiping out certain religions and replacing them with something else. That sounds too much like the people who vandalized my parents' house, or who start religious wars."

Nanor looked up from the ledger she was studying. "I never countenance violence. Or wars other than for defensive reasons."

"But look at how many supposedly religious people do. I don't want to be part of Onward Christian *or* Anti-Christian Soldiers. And if Fimi's a clone of me like my doctor said, I don't think she will either."

"Supplanting male religion need not mean violence. And it need not mean 'replacing' them." Nanor waved her hand in an encompassing gesture as she spoke, as if drawing all the books and papers in the library into her own orbit. "It can mean freeing the world from the dominance of a male god. Allowing people, all people, freedom to find another way. Their own way."

"Maybe," Tara said. "But we should focus on reviewing materials for now, not arguing."

Nanor sat at the table again. "Yes, you are right. I get carried away. I prefer not to make multiple treks here. Travel is wearing."

Tara couldn't see any evidence that Nanor was worn out, but she was happy for any reason to drop the long-running debate. Her fingers a little shaky, she turned the pages of the volume. From Day One, Nanor had held strong views about the purpose of Tara's pregnancy, and Tara had resisted the idea that she was part of a master plan to trounce the religion she'd been raised in and that her dad still so firmly believed in. For all the differences between Nanor and Erik Holmes, they were aligned on that point.

It made Tara's stomach churn. She didn't want to be a leader of a new religion, and she didn't want her daughter to be. She wanted them both to have lives where they could be out in the world and with other people without fear, and without stirring up hatred.

A few minutes later, Nanor jumped to her feet and pointed to a paragraph in a handwritten ledger. "This must be about you. About women like you. If I am translating correctly, there is a twenty-to-forty-year cycle for when the pregnancies can occur. The Brotherhood tracks this cycle."

Tara hurried to Nanor's side, thinking of the five dates she'd written down. All twenty-three years before she'd discovered she was pregnant.

"And here is a reference to where the pregnancies will or should occur," Nanor said. "With hundreds of locations."

Tara scanned the list. "A lot of these match Oni's map. She was right about that." She'd done her best to memorize the general locations of the red dots, afraid to bring her copy of the map for fear of it getting into Stranyero's hands. She felt good that she'd been able to do it, that the memorization skills she'd relied on throughout college were returning to her.

Tara started writing the locations in her spiral notebook. When she was halfway done, the intercom crackled. It was Stranyero. The owner of the home had returned.

She and Nanor closed the files and books they'd been looking at and replaced as many as they could before hurrying to the library's rear door.

"I don't know about you, but I could use a drink." A booming voice sounded as if it were just outside the door.

Tara tried to turn the knob, but it wouldn't open.

# 13

Tara's knee popped as she crouched behind two tall bookcases on the second level. Faint beeps echoed across the library. Someone typing in a security code, she guessed.

"Did you find what you were looking for?" It was the same voice she'd heard from the hallway, resonant and loud. "It's not like you to burn the midnight oil."

Heavy, sure footsteps sounded below her. She hoped Nanor was sufficiently hidden and not too uncomfortable.

"It is quite like me," Stranyero said. "I simply don't typically do so in your library."

Tara crept forward and inched two books apart so she could see the floor below. Thomas Stranyero stood at the bar, pouring whiskey. He handed one glass to the man next to him, who was half a head taller and at least forty pounds heavier. While Stranyero's hair shone silver, this man's was dull gray with a small bald spot in the center that caught the light. He drank his whiskey in two gulps and held out his glass for a refill.

"And to what do I owe this honor?" the larger man said.

"I'm working on a project of my own," Stranyero said. "Which I'll share if it bears fruit."

The books she'd moved had stirred up dust. Tara swallowed to try to alleviate the tickle that started in the back of her throat.

"Share now." The man examined the books on the table and flipped the one about Andrew of Crete open. "Perhaps I can help."

Stranyero moved out of Tara's sightline. She longed to reposition herself, but she didn't want to draw attention.

"Are you that threatened by me?" Stranyero said.

"Not at all." The large man paused behind the chair Nanor had vacated a few minutes before. "But I do like to keep abreast of developments. So tell me, what sort of development is this? Are you researching for your own purposes? Or aiding the lovely Sophia?"

"That amounts to the same thing, doesn't it?" Stranyero said. "The more I learn from her, the more I'm able to aid the Brotherhood's efforts to end the threat once and for all."

Tara's stomach tightened. Stranyero said it so offhandedly, so easily, that it had the ring of truth. She shifted to kneel on the hardwood floor.

The large man slammed the book shut. "Let's not get carried away. We can win this battle—must win this battle—but the war will continue."

"But whoever succeeds this time around will be particularly well rewarded," Stranyero said.

"And at a level commensurate with his experience, let us hope." The man strolled to the other end of the table and paged through a file there. The only one Tara had left out was the one with the maps in it. "You've certainly pulled some interesting materials. They ought to keep you occupied for some time."

Tara tried to read the man's voice. It seemed lighter, as if he were relieved. Which could mean what she and Nanor had found were the least relevant items. A wave of exhaustion swept through her. Perhaps the list of locations that seemed to match Oni's map meant little or nothing.

"Would you like to join me?" Stranyero said.

*What? Get him out of here.*

"I think not. There are no answers to be found in books and papers."

"If not in books and papers, then where?"

The irritation in Tara's throat returned, threatening to become a cough. She inhaled quietly through her nose, pressing her lips together and swallowing again. Her eyes watered. She wanted to hear the answer and would have been grateful to Stranyero for asking the question if she didn't so desperately need to cough.

"The Order's collective memory," the man said.

"Which you're part of?" Stranyero said.

"Yes, though I admit not as much as I'd like to be. But you and I need to be concerned with strategy. Which depends on the other side. Are heretics in close contact with Tara Spencer?"

While the man spoke, Tara had cleared her throat as quietly as possible. Now she leaned forward, intent on Stranyero's answer, as heretics must mean the guardians.

"Not that I know of. But Dr. Gaddini doesn't tell me everything."

Tara liked that he referred to Sophia as "Dr. Gaddini" when talking to this other man. It showed respect. Or it was carefully calculated to suggest to Tara that he respected Sophia. But if he didn't usually talk that way, the other man would know it.

"Find out. Every time we think we've eliminated that threat, another appears. In the meantime, enjoy your research. Whenever you're ready to tell me, I'll be all ears."

Tara gritted her teeth and swallowed again, suppressing a cough until the footsteps receded, a door slammed, and endless moments of silence ticked by.

Eventually Stranyero returned. "All right."

Tara eased down the spiral staircase, clutching the railing. "Did he know we were here?"

When she'd feared being caught, the rush of adrenalin had sent her scrambling up the stairs with no hesitation, her motor skills almost normal. Now that the man was gone, her bad leg shook. Nanor emerged from behind a row of shelves, gray hairs springing from the back of her bun.

"It's hard for me to say," Stranyero said. "He's usually forthright with his views, so my first thought is that if he'd realized you were here, he would have made it known. But as you may have guessed from our conversation, both of us have a chance to move up in the organization. Everyone's playing things a bit close to the vest."

"You seek to advance in the Brotherhood?" Nanor said.

"It's possible I could do so. So could the man who was just here."

"You won't tell us his name?" Tara said. Her brother Nate, who could normally find anything on the Internet, had attempted to determine the owner of the house through public and not-so-public records, but had fallen short. He'd found only corporations within corporations, all with numerous board members, none of which pointed to any particular person.

"If it becomes important to you, to your plans, I will. But I don't see how it could assist you now. While I've changed my views on the Brotherhood's mission, I'm not ready to reveal any more of its secrets than necessary to keep you from harm."

Nanor crossed her arms over her chest. Her frown deepened the lines of her forehead. "Of course you are not."

Stranyero smiled. "Likewise, I'm sure that while you're willing to accept my help, there are many things you are not sharing with me."

"If you've changed your views on its mission," Tara said, "why won't you leave the Order and tell people about it? You must know enough about some of its members to expose them."

"You don't stop an organization like this by exposing its individual members, even if it could be proven in a court of law that they've engaged in illegal activity. You stop it by making the organization irrelevant."

Tara's mind raced as she tried to sort out what she could safely ask Stranyero.

"What did that man mean—the Brotherhood's collective memory has the answers?"

"The Brotherhood, much like the old Catholic Church, doesn't encourage anyone to learn more than he needs to know. Each has a piece or pieces of knowledge. Those who know the whole have great power. The rest of us do not."

"I suspect you wield significant power," Nanor said.

"Not as much as you may believe, Mrs. Kerkorian." Stranyero turned back toward Tara. "While you were in the coma, the mandate—except at the very highest level, where I do not yet reside—was watch and wait. Now that you're awake, it's changed, but I've yet to understand exactly how much and in what way."

Tara swallowed, her throat tight. "Other than declaring war on me."

"Yes. War can mean many things, and it can be fought on many fronts. If you'd tell me what you're looking for, I could help more. But we've danced this dance before, and I doubt your steps have changed."

"They haven't," Tara said. "And since you blackmailed me last time, they're not likely to."

Stranyero punched in codes at the rear door. It sprung open. "A valid point. All the same, you can't walk the fence forever. I understand, perhaps more than anyone, why you're trying to. But without my help, you can't win against the Brotherhood. And when I say you can't win, I mean you can't survive, and neither can your child." He pointed to a path along the side of the house. "You have ten minutes before the floodlights come on again, so be sure you've cleared the trees by then."

~

STRANYERO PAGED through the folder that contained Tara Spencer's birth certificate. He'd seen most of the documents in it before, including the DNA test results showing Fimi Spencer was Tara's clone, and that Tara was a combination of her mother's DNA, Ray Tigue's, and that of a third—and unknown—source. He'd assumed that source was divine.

The list of contact dates, though, was new to him and suggested the Brotherhood had interacted with Ray Tigue or Tara's mother, Lynette Spencer, before Lynette had become pregnant. That possibility made him wonder. He'd been with the Brotherhood for twenty years by then, yet he'd heard nothing about anyone contacting Ray or Lynette. More important, he'd been unaware that the Brotherhood had any idea in advance what two people were likely to parent a young woman who would later claim to become pregnant without sexual intercourse.

MacNeil appeared twenty minutes after Nanor Kerkorian and Tara Spencer left, an abundance of caution from a man whose patience was extremely limited. "They're gone?"

Stranyero nodded. "They have been for some time."

"What did they focus on?"

"This." Stranyero slid a stack of pages, minus the information about the contact dates, across the table.

"It won't help them," MacNeil said.

"Unless it includes a way to stop the Spark," Stranyero said. The Spark was an aspect of the Brotherhood he'd learned about a year ago, partly by combing the Brotherhood archives and MacNeil's library, and partly by pretending to know more than he did, leading MacNeil to inadvertently reveal details. But the man was careful, so Stranyero had not learned much.

"There is no way to stop it. If there were, those heretics would have found it."

Stranyero thought of the Armenian journal Marie had brought, still safe on his personal drive and in Marie's hands. He'd at last found a translator he trusted, but the work progressed slowly. For decades, MacNeil had been trying to obtain the journal, so he must believe something in it would hurt the Brotherhood. To know what it was would give Stranyero great bargaining power. No—it would give him great power, period. Once he had it, he could decide how to use it. He pushed aside what Sophia might say about that chain of reasoning.

"You're certain?" Stranyero said.

He studied MacNeil's face but saw no trace of worry. He'd always thought MacNeil a poor liar, a man who showed his emotions plainly on his face, but these days he felt less sure. The man might have layers he'd hidden under bluster and outrage, using an outward appearance of emotional volatility to hide iron control.

"The guardians have subverted it time and again," MacNeil said, "but they've never been able to stop it. It's why I had no concern about your charade here. Did it have the desired effect? Does Tara trust you now?"

"I'll contact Dr. Gaddini later and try to find out," Stranyero said.

# 14

"Is it that you'd feel weird about seeing Ray again after all this time?" Tara asked her mom.

Tara and Cyril sat on a leather couch in front of floor-to-ceiling windows. Lynette Spencer appeared on the flat screen TV/monitor on the opposite wall. Her face looked less rounded than Tara was used to. She'd lost about twenty pounds during Tara's coma and was no longer plump. She shook her head. "There's nothing I feel 'weird' about, Tara."

"Because we don't have to talk to him in person. We can call him."

Tara sprinkled more cinnamon on the foam of her hot chocolate. She'd bought it in the lobby of the building where she was now staying along with a security guard. The trustee for the trust Holmes had set up had reserved a temporary three-bedroom rental in an anonymous high rise in downtown Chicago. He'd also arranged a recurring transfer of funds to Tara's account. She'd used it pay for Oni's travels to thirty-five locations they'd chosen by cross-referencing the map, the list of shrines, and the list of locations from the Brotherhood. Cyril was still living in the Berwyn apartment near Nanor so that none of the trust money directly benefited him per Holmes' instructions.

"I don't understand what you're trying to accomplish," Lynette said, "and I don't want you to get hurt."

Behind Lynette, Tara could see the exposed brick in the loft her mom was renting in a multi-unit building in downtown St. Louis. Tara's little brother Bailey sat at the kitchen island, blond head bent over a handheld video game. He sat too still, though, and Tara knew he was listening. Every day, Lynette drove him to junior high before returning downtown to the law office where she worked as a secretary. The commute was inconvenient, but safer than staying in the family home where protestors threw stones and supporters had once left lit candles in the grass, setting the lawn on fire. Tara felt relieved that at least she'd be able to use money from the trust to pay the mortgage and taxes on the vacant house. She'd already wired her dad funds to have a security system installed, complete with security guards making rounds at night.

But she worried about Bailey. He must miss the family home as much as Tara did, and the yard, and his friends in the neighborhood. Plus in the last few years, all his siblings had left. His little sister had died, Nate had moved out, Kelly was living with their dad in Edwardsville to be near her school once the term started, and Tara had been on the run or in medical institutions. The kid who'd grown up in a house crammed with people who loved him to pieces had become an only child.

Tara snapped the blue rubber band, forcing her thoughts back to the conversation. Her thoughts and emotions were more under control these days compared to when she'd first awakened, but she still struggled.

She'd missed whatever Cyril had asked her mom.

"He ducked out on me," Lynette said. "First he pushed me to have an abortion, then he ducked out."

"You expected a different reaction?" Cyril said.

"Neither of us was ready to be a parent, but I didn't think he'd be horrified. I thought he loved me. And I thought he'd adapt. He was an easy-come, easy-go kind of guy. He drifted in and out, didn't get uptight about anything."

Fimi, who'd been napping on a comforter on the floor, rolled onto her stomach and opened her eyes. Tara handed her a picture book with a St. Bernard puppy on the cover. She seized the book.

"So if he'd drifted away over time, that wouldn't have surprised you," Cyril said.

"I knew he wasn't the most responsible person in the world." Lynette tucked her blond hair behind her ear. "But for him to insist on an abortion and take off when I wouldn't have one, that surprised me. And to take no interest once I had Tara, that surprised me, too."

"He showed me photos of me he saved. And letters you sent," Tara said. "So he had some interest."

"I initiated all of that. I'm glad to hear he kept everything, but he rarely responded, and he never asked about you."

Tara felt her heart twist. She wished her mom were a little less forthright.

"Did anyone odd contact you or him in the nine months or so before you got pregnant?" Tara said. "Anyone who might have been connected to the Brotherhood?"

Lynette frowned and made a "hmpf" sound. "Tara, if that had happened, don't you think I would have told you by now?"

"We need to make sure," Cyril said. "That's why we'd like to talk to Ray. To see if anyone contacted him."

"You think way back then the Brotherhood interfered?" Lynette said. "Did something to Ray?"

"Maybe." Tara said.

"That's as logical as anything to do with you I guess," Lynette said. "It might explain your weird DNA results."

"Thanks, Mom. I love feeling like a freak of nature." Tara sipped more hot chocolate and returned the mug to a coaster. The marble-topped coffee table and soft leather furniture made her afraid to touch anything for fear of marring it.

"You're so sensitive. I'm not commenting on you as a person, just on your situation. You have to admit your life is bizarre."

"And again I say, thanks so much."

"Let's stick to the point," Cyril said. "We need to find Ray. As best as I can tell, he's disappeared."

"Why didn't you say that in the first place?"

"We did," Tara said. "I said we couldn't find him, and you started arguing with me."

Despite being irritated, Tara found it reassuring that her mom once again was arguing about everything. It must mean Tara was looking and acting healthier and more normal. During the first two weeks after she'd woken up, her mom had been super nice and polite, making Tara more afraid she was going to die.

"I wasn't arguing—"

"What we need," Cyril said, "is any information about him that might help us locate him. Anything at all. You said he came to see Tara a few times in the hospital and the nursing home?"

Tara squeezed Cyril's hand, grateful for him cutting her mom off and keeping the conversation on track.

"He did. He was traveling a lot with his band, but every time he passed through, he stopped in."

"How many times?" Tara said.

"Six or seven. He gave me his new cell number and address."

Lynette rattled them off.

Tara's shoulders sagged. She'd been hoping her mom knew something she didn't or could offer reassurance about why Ray might have moved. "We tried that number. And his old one. Both are out of service, someone else lives at that address now, someone who doesn't know Ray."

"When did he move?" Lynette said.

Cyril scrolled through notes on his phone. "A week after Tara woke up. No forwarding address. He hasn't answered Tara's emails. Did anyone call and tell him she was all right?"

"I called him the third day, when news had already started leaking that she was awake. I didn't want to say anything before because we were trying to keep it quiet. He said he'd get in touch."

"He never did," Tara said.

Lynette spread her hands wide. "That's Ray."

"But it's not, Mom. Not the way he's been to me since we reconnected. It's not like we talked every day, but he was happy to be part of my life again. He told me he'd always see himself as my father no matter what the DNA tests said."

"But what does Ray see as being a father? Sending a check once in a blue moon and seeing you three times in the twenty-two years of your life. I don't see anything ominous in him being MIA."

Tara opened her mouth, but Cyril spoke before she could. "No matter how you see it," Cyril said, "Do you have anything that would help us find him?"

Tara let her breath out, glad Cyril had stopped her. She would have kept arguing with her mother.

"He didn't say he was moving."

"What about his band?" Tara said. "Did he say anything about future plans?"

"No. Oh, wait. He did. I was only half-listening. I figured it was a lot of puffing, you know, trying to make it sound like they were going somewhere after all these years. He said they had a manager now. Someone trying to get them better gigs. Before bigger audiences, maybe overseas."

"Maybe that happened," Tara said. "He's on a long tour and that's why he let go of his apartment."

"I doubt it," Lynette said. "Have you ever heard his band?"

"SORRY, I haven't a clue where your dad might be," Ely Wells said. "Haven't seen him since our band split up decades ago. I'll ask around a bit for you if you like."

Tara paced the kitchen area, staring out at Chicago's skyline and the narrow patches of Lake Michigan's blue water visible between the tall buildings. With information her mom had provided, Cyril had finally located a bass player who'd known Ray in Oklahoma City. The bass player didn't know where Ray was, but he remembered a drummer named Ely Wells whom he thought had known Ray in college, and Tara had found Ely on social media and arranged a call.

It seemed strange to hear Ely refer to Ray as her dad. To her, "Dad" was Pete Spencer. But the reference also made her smile, as it suggested Ray had cared about her enough that a friend from long ago saw him as a father.

"Were you with him when he was seeing my mom?" Tara said.

"Oh, yeah, and for a few years after. He talked about you all the time."

"But he'd never met me."

"He lived for those letters your mom sent about you. Never answered them, but he saved every one."

"Did anything unusual happen around when my mom told Ray she was pregnant?"

"Besides leaving her behind?"

"Leaving her behind?"

Fimi rolled in on a toy giraffe and waved at Tara. Tara waved back, and Fimi scooted away again.

"You didn't know?" Ely said. "I always felt bad about it. After our last show—about fifty miles from the college—Ray insisted we pack up and take off while Lynette was passed out in the motel room. He left her a note and money to get back to the dorm, but it must've been awful for her. He only told us later she was pregnant. I wanted to punch him out. I almost did, but our lead singer stopped me. This was all before cell phones, so she didn't have a way to reach him. She left a few messages at places she knew we were playing over the next month. But he never called her back that I know of."

Tara sank into one of the padded dining chairs. "I—wow. I didn't know any of that."

"Your mom probably didn't want to poison your mind against him."

So her mom had shown a little restraint about bad-mouthing Ray.

"I tried to talk him out of handling it that way, out of abandoning Lynette, " Ely said, "but he kept claiming it was better. That he wasn't fit to be a father, would only mess up you and make your mom's life harder."

"Because of his drug use?"

"Drinking, drugs, all of it."

"Did he say anything about anyone contacting him, anyone unusual, the year before my mom got pregnant?"

"You mean the study?"

"Study?" Tara grabbed her spiral notebook from the granite counter.

"He had this bizarre story about a biology grad student who paid him to take some sort of herb or drug or something. As an experiment, and Ray had to sign what must have been a non-disclosure agreement. He got paid a lot, what seemed like a lot to him. He spent it on guitars and drugs."

Tara scribbled notes.

"Tara? Are you there?"

"Yes. Yeah. My mom told me he always had new guitars. She couldn't figure out how he got the money. He said his father won some lottery money, a small prize, and sent it to him."

"Yeah, well, according to Ray, it came from this study. He didn't say much about what the drug was supposed to do, but he was worried when he found out Lynette was pregnant, convinced it'd mess with the baby, that she'd have a child with all sorts of issues. And it was his fault, because he wasn't supposed to take other drugs or drink alcohol with it, he'd been warned, but he'd done it anyway."

Ray had been in A.A. and N.A. for years now, and he'd stayed sober. But his younger self had no use for any of that. Anyone who'd known him at all would have known he'd keep using no matter what.

"How many people were in this study? And was it run by the University?"

"No idea," Ely said.

Out the window, the sky clouded over, turning the lake from blue to flat gray.

"So Ray left because he didn't want to deal with the special needs child he thought he might get," Tara said. She felt disappointed in Ray all over again.

"I don't think that was it," Ely said. "More he didn't want your mom to have that heartbreak, so he pushed for an abortion. Then he felt so guilty, he couldn't face it. I also think he really believed you'd be better off if he stayed away. I was his best friend at the time though, so I'm not quite an unbiased observer."

~

As she waited for Oni to return from visiting the shrines, Tara combed through Roger's materials again for information that might help Fimi. She also met with an administrator at University of Illinois at Chicago, where Kali was majoring in urban planning, and made arrangements to enter early the following year to complete her degree. But otherwise, she felt stuck. Nate searched the Internet, Cyril made phone calls adopting various cover stories, and Sophia made inquiries through colleagues, but no one found anything about any studies that matched what Ely had described. Nor could they find any trace of Ray Tigue.

Her mom suggested the family visit Tara and follow up on the vision Tara had seen during the meditation with Nanor. Tara made the arrangements for their lodgings herself, so even the trustee wouldn't know they would be in town. She rented a two-room apartment in the Lincoln Park area of Chicago. Her mom, her sister Kelly, and her brother Nate drove in so there would be no record of airline tickets. Bailey traveled to Edwardsville to stay with their dad. Tara would have liked him to come, but she didn't want to put him at any risk. He'd nearly been killed the day she'd given birth, and she wasn't about to endanger him again.

Nanor sat in the armchair to one side in the living room. Nate had his feet up on the wood veneer coffee table, and Kali perched on a storage cube that doubled as seating, twisting her long black hair around her fingers. Lynette sat on the couch next to Tara.

"So where's Oni? I thought she'd be here. She's supposed to protect Fimi," Lynette said.

Tara lit a small incense cone. Vanilla and spice filled the air. "Oni's focusing on the bookmark, visiting some of the shrines where it appears. Anyway, in my vision, it was only people in our family and Nanor's who were there."

Lynette moved the incense cone to the center of the coffee table, away from Nate's feet. "Huh. This Oni's not very dedicated if you ask me. She's too all over the place."

"She's visited nearly all the shrines we decided on already," Tara said.

"She's extremely dedicated," Cyril said. He stood near the window, watching the street below. Every few minutes he shifted his gaze to his phone, which he'd tied into the apartment's security cameras. He had a view of the vestibule and the hallways in each floor just outside the elevators. "And skilled. She helped us find Ely Wells."

"You know what they say," Nate said. "It takes a fanatic to spot a fanatic."

Nanor moved an armchair so it filled out their circle. "Let us begin. If you're ready."

Tara nodded.

"Join hands," Nanor said.

"And, what, sing Kum-by-yah?" Lynette said.

"And be silent," Tara said.

"Focus on my voice and words," Nanor said. "Because all of us appeared in Tara's last vision, my hope is that all of us joining hands with her, supporting her, will bring her back to it and that she'll learn something new to guide her."

Nanor talked them through deep breathing and, after a few interruptions by Lynette, the room fell quiet. Fimi slumped against Tara, fast asleep.

Once again, Tara stood in the outdoor stone kitchen in Armenia. She felt the wind on her face as the serpent glided toward her. It stopped and its head rose in the air, as if it were ascending an unseen tree. It was exactly as it had been when she'd visited distant relatives of Nanor's on a farm in Armenia. Tara inhaled, almost tasting the lavash she'd helped the women there make.

Lightning streaked across the sky, thunder clapped, and the serpent's lower body split and formed legs. Another flash of lightning blinded Tara. When she could see again, the serpent had turned into Nanor, her eyes set behind layers of wrinkles. She held what looked like a vase made of stone. Nanor poured liquid from her free hand into the vase. The lines in her face disappeared, her hair became long and dark, and she turned into Kali. She, too, held a vase. Or a jar, Tara wasn't sure.

Kali took off its lid and poured liquid out of it onto her feet. More lightning, and now Kali, Nanor, and Tara's mother and siblings were all there, each putting something into the stone vessel. Fimi was at Tara's feet, and she lifted her arms to be picked up. Kali now became Protennoia, the goddess Tara had seen in her original vision. Protennoia bent down to let Fimi put something into her vessel. Behind her, Tara again saw the tomb, but this time it didn't worry her.

The vessel turned into a cloth-bound book in Protennoia's hands. "Once it begins, it must end," she said.

Tara reached for the book, her whole body trembling. She felt in the depths of her heart that at last she'd have answers. She'd know how to protect her child and herself. How to resume a normal life. How to ensure Fimi learned to speak.

Lightning struck. The book charred. Its ashes scattered in the wind.

# 15

Oni poured herself a glass of water from the faucet. Her bags sat inside the doorway of the high-rise apartment. It was five-thirty in the morning the day after the vision and already it was over ninety degrees outside, with ninety percent humidity.

"So you'd just been talking about the bookmark design and your family, and you'd seen old books in that library. No surprise that's all in your 'vision'."

"But we all had the same vision," Tara said. "We meditated together. My mom, Nanor, Kali, Nate. Afterward, I started telling them what I saw and heard, and everyone else had experienced it, too. Exactly the same. That must mean something."

The air conditioning kicked higher, sending cold air blasting over Tara's head. Cyril took Oni's bags into the third bedroom and returned to join them at the dining table. Fimi was still asleep in the room she and Tara were sharing.

"Nanor was probably talking to you all through it, so you all saw the same thing," Oni said.

"No, it was like last time," Tara said. "Nanor only started the meditation, she didn't dictate the vision."

"You probably didn't realize it," Oni said.

Tara ran her hand through her hair. She'd had it cut, and it hung shoulder length and straight, like she'd kept it through most of college. It made her feel more like herself. She'd put a wig on again if she went outside. "Why are you so skeptical?"

Raindrops spattered the windows, and thunder rumbled in the distance.

"Nanor likes to lead, to feel important," Oni said. "She's kind of irrelevant at this point in her life, at her age. Plus her whole community literally went up in smoke. You feel bad about that, so you're playing along, trying to make her feel important."

"She is important," Tara said.

"Because her daughter had a virgin pregnancy like you did? I'm sorry she had that loss, I am, but Maya Kerkorian didn't survive. So maybe you shouldn't be taking advice from her mother."

Lightning flashed. More thunder boomed, and the lights blinked off. Out the windows, the entire downtown area had gone dark. Cyril and Oni found and lit candles while Tara checked on Fimi. The toddler still slept soundly.

Tara returned to the kitchen. "So you think it's Nanor's fault Maya got killed?"

"Not her fault." Oni dropped into a dining chair near the window. "But all her mumbo-jumbo wasn't able to stop it. Or my cousin's death, or my aunt's."

Cyril set a wide pillar candle near the center of the round marble dining table. "That's the fault of whoever killed them, not Nanor Kerkorian."

"I'm only saying she might not have all the answers," Oni said.

"You're also not overflowing with answers," Tara said.

"But I did bring you the map. Which led us to these."

Oni set down a thick 9" by 12" envelope. She took out printed color photos from all the shrines she'd visited. "They're on my phone, too, but I thought it'd be easier to look at them printed. Except that now we have a power outage."

"Here." Cyril shone a flashlight on the first photo. "Let's not use anyone's phone battery if we don't have to."

"Did you find anything strange at the actual shrines?" Tara said.

"No," Oni said. "I hiked through each one that had a hiking trail. Some had a lot of people, some had no visitors. Some shrines had longer or shorter trails or larger or smaller areas for prayer. But I didn't see anything that seemed significant or that they had in common other than the designs. Which were usually somewhat hidden."

Cyril studied the first few photographs. "Hidden how?"

"For one thing, pretty small. These are close-ups. On one, there was a rock formation with a statue of the Virgin Mary on it. If you walked around the back, at the bottom of the rock was the design, maybe four inches by two inches."

"Did any of the people around you notice the designs?" Tara asked

"There was one. It was carved with a lot of other drawings on a stone wall along the path to a group of outdoor statues. A kid asked her mom about it, and she thought it was a zodiac sign."

"Close, I guess." Tara studied the next few photos. "The last vision, the one while you were traveling, involved two vases or vessels or jars. Each of these designs shows two as well."

"But you knew that," Oni said. "The bookmark has two, one in the woman's right hand and one in her left. So the vision didn't add anything."

"I'm just saying, maybe that's important that the vision featured two. You only knew about one vase, right?" Tara said to Cyril. "The one in the photo you gave me when we met?"

"What photo?" Oni said. "I never heard of that."

"It's a photo of a vase with a carving on the front," Cyril said. "It's supposed to be the pregnant virgin in Armenia from the seventh century."

"And you had it why?" Oni said.

Cyril shrugged. "I didn't ask. Stranyero gave it to me to show to Tara. Evidence of another woman like her in history."

Oni frowned. "Except how is that evidence? It was just a photo. It could have been anyone's face carved into an ancient vase."

"I know," Cyril said. "I'd ask plenty of questions about it now. But back then, I didn't question. I followed orders."

"Hm."

"We should go through all these photos with a magnifying glass," Tara said. "Or enlarge them more. See if any show a woman's face."

"Or try to find the real vase from Cyril's photo," Oni said. "If you're so hyped about your vision, well, there was a vase in it, right? More than one?"

"I saw a vase like it once," Tara said. She shut her eyes. "It was at the cloister I stayed at in Pennsylvania. With the attacks that happened afterwards, and Fimi going missing, I forgot about it. But it looked a lot like the one in Cyril's photo. No carving though."

"The cloister? You mean that former convent where you almost got killed?" Oni said.

"Yeah, that one," Tara said.

"So, that seems like a good place to check," Oni said.

"Having been almost killed there, I don't think Tara should go back," Cyril said.

"I'll go," Oni said. "I've got no interest in hanging out and studying books or waiting for divine revelations."

A call to the women at the cloister revealed there were three vases there similar to the one Tara had seen. None had carvings, but they all appeared to be from the same time period.

"I'll bring them all back," Oni said. "There are two vases in the design, so the one with the carving, even if it is important, isn't the only one that'll matter."

"Makes sense. If we had Internet, I'd book a ticket," Tara said.

"We can set up a hotspot with a phone," Cyril said. "If your laptop has enough battery power, you can use it."

Tara slid her phone and laptop across the table to Cyril. Sheets of rain plummeted to the street outside. Lightning flashed again.

Cyril started clicking keys, but his phone rang. "Don't know the number," he said. He answered, listened for a few minutes, then told the caller to hold and hit the mute button. "It's a woman who says she was sent to Armenia to retrieve a copy of the journal I saw in the Church there."

"How'd she get your number?" Tara said.

"Journal?" Oni said.

"It was kept by a chronicler of Our Lady of Sorrows," Cyril said. He got a little more information from the woman on the phone and told her he would call her back. "The church the Armenian woman in the seventh century attended, the one who said she was a pregnant virgin."

"Also the church she died in," Tara said. "In a fire."

Oni stared at Cyril. "You actually saw it? My cousin tried to track it down, and she said it was a myth, that it didn't really exist."

"I had it in my hands," Cyril said. "I read part of it, as best I could, but it disappeared while I fell asleep, waiting for Pete, Tara's dad, to return. Last year while Tara was in the coma we tried to reach someone at that church again. But no one admitted to meeting us or that there was a journal."

"But how did this woman today know how to reach you?" Tara said.

"I don't know. Besides your family, only Stranyero, Sophia, and the Kerkorians have this number. And Holmes had it from when we lived in his complex."

"So his estate people could know it," Tara said. "Is she from Holmes' estate? Is that who sent her to Armenia?"

"She wouldn't say."

"Did she describe the journal?" Tara said.

Cyril relayed what the woman had said. It sounded like the antique journal Cyril had seen and also like the clothbound book in Tara's vision. She wondered if it meant anything that lightning had struck the book in her vision and had struck in real life the moment the woman called.

*Next I'll be reading tea leaves.*

"Do you think the priest's wife, the one you met at the church, would really share the journal with a stranger?" Tara said.

"She wasn't someone easily persuaded," Cyril said. "So no. But I only spoke with her briefly. Perhaps this woman knew the right thing to say."

"Or it's a scam," Oni said.

"Right," Tara said. "But it's probably worth talking to her and seeing this journal. Unless she'll send it to us?"

"She won't. She has instructions to deliver it into your hands directly. She says she'll come to us," Cyril said. "But that means telling her where we are, which I don't like."

"What was in the journal you saw?" Oni asked Cyril.

"My Armenian's not good," he said. "But it talked about Rima Petrosyan, who became pregnant at nineteen and said she was still a virgin. There was something about a vision and Rima's aunt and the fire in 642 A.D., the year Armenia was invaded. An army set fire to Our Lady of Sorrows. Rima and her baby were trapped and died. The letter from the aunt arrived after that. A local artisan carved her image into a vase. The one in the photo I showed Tara."

"The Brotherhood must know that history. So this could be a scam," Oni said. "With fake documents."

"Or the priest's wife could be a guardian," Tara said.

Oni shook her head. "I never heard of a guardian in a church in Armenia."

"But most guardians don't know about one another," Tara said. "That's what Pir Ferit told me. It's one of the failsafes. Right?"

"I still find it suspicious," Oni said. "Why would Holmes take such a roundabout way to help you from beyond the grave?"

"Let's find out," Tara said.

# 16

They met in Springfield, Illinois, the woman's choice when Tara suggested they meet somewhere near St. Louis. She figured naming her home city wouldn't give anything about her real location away, as people would expect her to be there. The choice made her think the woman might be based in Illinois.

Though it was the capital of the state, the city looked to Tara more like a suburb or small town. The restaurant Cyril picked for the meeting after researching was a well-lit diner that smelled of crisp bacon, melted cheddar, and breakfast sausage. He and Oni and a security guard stayed in the car a few blocks away with Fimi, and Tara waited in a booth with cracked faux-leather seats and a wood grain table. It reminded her of the diner where she'd first met Kali Kerkorian. Another security guard sat at the other side of the room, dressed in jeans and a baggy T-shirt and sipping coffee at the counter.

A young woman slid into the booth across from Tara. She appeared to be in her late twenties or early thirties, with a heart-shaped face, freckles, and wide set eyes. She looked nothing like Protennoia. She held out her hand. "I'm Marie Glaston."

Tara wiped her hand on her jeans and shook Marie's hand. "Hello."

"This is for you." Marie handed over a sheaf of photocopied pages. "These come from the priest's wife at Our Lady of Sorrows in Armenia."

"I thought you were bringing a book."

"I saw the journal, but I wasn't allowed to take the original. This is the copy I made."

Tara recognized Armenian characters from the ancient letter she'd pieced together in the past. She didn't know whether her vision meant she should trust this woman or be suspicious of her or whether the lack of the actual journal was significant. After all, it had burst into flames in the vision.

"Is the original still there?"

Marie sipped ice water. "As far as I know."

"Why did you go looking for it?" Tara said.

"I was sent to obtain it. My specialty is antiquities."

"Antiquities," Tara said. "Including relics?"

Marie nodded. "Yes."

When Fimi had been kidnapped, Tara had found out there were markets where religious relics might be sold, and that discovery had led her to the bookmark. It had also made her think someone who collected relics might have stolen her daughter. That and Holmes' description of the person he'd hired to take Fimi from the first kidnapper, Diedre Hartman, added up to Marie being the one.

"Did Erik Holmes hire you? Or did his estate?"

"The person who hired me won't allow me to tell you."

Tara put the pages into her backpack. She couldn't read Armenian, so it would be no help to look through them now. "Doesn't that bother you?"

"When I'm researching and obtaining items, I'm often hired by people whose names I don't know. Or I should say, when I used to do that for a living. I don't any longer. I haven't for over a year. This is a special case."

"So you don't know if you ever worked for Erik Holmes, for instance?"

"I don't. He may have been in a chain of people who retained me at some point, or he may not have been."

They paused while the waitress took their order. As Marie ordered a decaf coffee and asked about the bacon and egg platter, Tara debated whether to press further. The news of the FBI's investigation of Holmes for Fimi's kidnapping had been well reported, so Marie must know that was why Tara was asking. It was unlikely she'd admit to being part of it.

"How did you find Cyril's number? Or know to call him?" Tara said after the waitress disappeared through the metal double doors behind the lunch counter.

"The person who hired me gave it to me," Marie said. "I was told it was the best way to reach you."

Tara glanced at the security guard, who peered at his phone, his back to her. Many people knew that Cyril was connected to her, but few had his number, so it could be Holmes. Or Stranyero. This might be his roundabout way of helping her or setting her up for something.

"What are you expecting to get from this?" Tara said.

"Nothing," Marie said. "I was paid by my client, and he told me to bring to you exactly what I obtained from the priest's wife at Our Lady of Sorrows. Do what you like with it."

"How do I know you gave me an accurate copy?"

Marie shrugged. "You've only my word for it. Though I understand Mr. Woods saw the journal before and read part of it. Perhaps he can verify at least that the words are familiar."

"The man who hired you told you that, too?"

"He did."

That left Tara more confused. Until they'd told Oni about it, only she, Cyril, and her dad knew that Cyril had seen a journal in Armenia.

"Here's a number where you can reach me." Marie slid a card across the table. "If I can help further, please let me know. I've followed your story in the news, and I'm very sorry for all the struggles you've had. Very sorry."

THE NURSE HANDED Sophia a small paper cup with a Vicodin. "You should be resting."

"I slept most of the night," Sophia said, though she hadn't. A fever had kept her hospitalized longer than the surgeon had anticipated, but the antibiotics were working, and she felt almost clear-headed.

The Vicodin took the edge off the pain, but didn't suppress it, and it left her feeling nauseated. She'd dozed fitfully until five a.m., then had given up and pulled out the document Cyril had Fed Exed to her. She'd had him send it to a close friend in her department rather than to her home. She didn't want Thomas to see it. Even if he were truly on her and Tara's side, if he learned of the journal about the Armenian pregnant virgin he'd need to tell the Brotherhood to maintain his cover.

*And if he's not on our side....no, I made my choice. I'll be cautious for Tara's sake, but I believe him.*

Her spinning thoughts added to her nausea. She pushed them from her mind and translated another phrase. Her ancient Armenian had improved over the last year. Still, she couldn't match the fluency of someone who spoke the modern version and had studied the language for decades, as Nanor had, so Nanor had assigned her the less complex passages. Despite that, she doubted she'd be able to translate more than three-quarters of a page a day. At least she could look for key phrases and names throughout the writing. It kept her mind off Thomas, who hadn't contacted her since late yesterday morning.

Three naps and another Vicodin later, Tara called.

"Nanor said she has enough to start discussing," Tara said. "How about you?"

"I'll add what I can. Who all is there?" The tinny sound of Tara's voice made Sophia certain it was a speakerphone discussion.

"Nanor. Cyril. A friend of Nanor's named Oni."

"Someone new?" Sophia said.

"Yes. But we trust her."

Sophia was about to argue, but it hit her that the woman must have been around for some time or Tara wouldn't include her in the discussion. Which meant Tara had been keeping things from Sophia. Her body sagged back against the bed, and her arm, holding the phone, felt weighted. She'd expected her relationship with Thomas would make Tara more reticent, but she felt terrible about it all the same. She was used to being someone people trusted and felt at ease with. Someone they confided in without anxiety.

*At least she still came to me for help.*

"Would you like to start, Dr. Gaddini?" Nanor said.

It seemed strange to hear Nanor say "Dr. Gaddini." It might be a further sign of distance. Or simply professional respect. She didn't know Nanor Kerkorian all that well, but she felt she did through hearing about her from Tara.

Sophia cleared her throat. "Yes, thank you. Though it will take some additional study to be sure of my analysis."

"That is so for me as well," Nanor said.

Outside, lightning flashed, brightening the hospital room for an instant. The weather had alternated between rain, clouds, and storms since Sophia's admission.

Sophia walked the group through the brief history the journal gave of Rima Petrosyan and her death, as well as her child's. That had been less difficult to translate, as she already knew the story.

"The passage I translated this morning claims the invading army focused on this church because of Rima, because of some report they had about her, or some sort of fear about her. She and the baby were trapped in the church during the fire. Rima was found curled around her baby, as if she were trying to protect the child from being burned. Rima had burns everywhere."

"What do you think of the passage directly below that, the last full sentence?" Nanor said. "It suggests to me that the author believed Rima deliberately suffocated her child."

Sophia shifted the lilies Thomas had sent her. She loved their fragrance, but combined with the alcohol smell of the hospital, it was giving her a headache despite the Vicodin. "I thought the author indicated Rima's baby's death was inadvertent. But either way, the baby did not die from the fire itself."

"How could they know that?" The voice on the other end of the phone was alto but sounded young, with an accent Sophia couldn't place. She guessed it must be Oni. "It's not like there were autopsies in those days."

"The author infers that from placement of the bodies and lack of burns on the infant's skin," Nanor said.

"I agree," Sophia said.

"Does it matter whether Rima suffocated the baby or she died of smoke inhalation? Dead is dead," Oni said.

"It may," Nanor said. "Some passages suggest Rima was trying to perform some type of prayer or ritual to protect her child. It had be done within 700 days of the infant's birth."

"700 days," Tara said. "There was a reference to that time period in the library materials."

"Yes," Nanor said.

Sophia flipped to the next page. "I saw that, too. But I thought it was a reference to baptism. The Church at the time taught that unbaptized babies could not enter heaven. And many children did not survive past their second or even first birthdays, so I took it as an urging to baptize all infants as soon as possible."

"If there's any way to protect Fimi, I need to know," Tara said. "And if 700 days matters, we don't have much time. She's twenty-two months old, so that's, what—"

"About 660 days," Sophia said.

"But whatever it was, it didn't work," Oni said. "The baby died. If whoever wrote this is telling the truth and your translation is right."

"Oni points out a major issue with these pages," Sophia said. "With the entire journal. We don't know when it was written, why, or how much is based in fact. The post-fire account could have been written immediately after the tragedy or years, decades, or centuries later. Though perhaps Mrs. Kerkorkian can tell from the word usage."

"I cannot," said Nanor. "Ancient Armenian continued to be used in writing even as Middle Armenian and more modern dialects developed. I am fairly certain, though, that there are at least two different authors. One wrote the portion that covers Rima Petrosyan's death and the aftermath, and another—or perhaps two others—wrote the parts about her life and the church's history."

"Is one author Rima?" Cyril said.

"It seems unlikely she would have known the history of the church in such detail." Sophia said.

"Perhaps," Nanor said. "There are mixed reports regarding gender roles in ancient Armenia. And we know Rima was unusual. She was nineteen, old at the time to be unmarried, and her aunt traveled extensively and alone, also atypical."

The mention of the aunt made Sophia think of her own aunt, the woman who'd raised her, whose death six months before had been part of what had brought her and Thomas beyond friendship. Sophia had many acquaintances, but few very close friends. If Stranyero was now gone, she'd lost two in the last six months.

*It's only been twenty-four hours. Don't jump to conclusions.*

"Anything we didn't already know about Rima?" Tara said. "Or what she was trying to do?"

"Not that I've seen so far." Sophia sipped water from the cup at her bedside table. She felt cooler than she had when she'd woken up that morning. She hoped that was a good sign.

"I have no more to report at this point about Rima Petrosyan," Nanor said. "But more significant is a passage I found about the Spark of Life."

"Spark of Life?" Sophia said. She began paging through the photocopies, looking for the word Life. "As in the painting?"

"There is a painting called that," Nanor said. "But here it is linked with the Brotherhood."

"I saw that painting," Tara said. "In the Sistine Chapel when the Pope invited me to visit. My guide said God's finger touching Adam's was referred to as God conferring the Spark of Life to Adam."

"Yes," Nanor said. "It may have another meaning here. It appears in the same section with a discussion of a ritual by the Brotherhood, but I have not been able to parse it out yet."

"I thought you said Rima was doing a ritual," Oni said. "Not the Brotherhood."

"Yes," Nanor said. "There are references to both. Though the Spark of Life may be a prayer or ceremony."

"Which is it?" Oni said.

"Translation is an art," Sophia said. "Not a science. I see, here, the Spark of Life. Intriguing."

"This is an ancient language neither Professor Gaddini nor I is expert in," Nanor said. "We are attempting to work too rapidly to be certain of much."

"I've seen the Spark of Life somewhere else," Tara said. "Not only at the Vatican."

"There are reproductions everywhere," Sophia said.

"No, not the whole painting. Just the hands with the fingers almost touching," Tara said.

Sophia pictured that part of the painting in her mind, focusing on God's finger and Adam's a breath apart. "I have, too. That part alone—the hands and fingers in a circle."

Sophia heard clicking keys in the background and assumed Tara was searching on a laptop.

"Have you ever heard anything about a Spark of Life ceremony, Cyril? Thomas never mentioned it to me," Sophia said.

"I've never heard of it," he said. "Other than the painting."

"Found it, "Tara said. "Where I saw the hands. Sophia, when are you being discharged?"

"Tomorrow morning, barring surprises. Of which I've had enough."

"Great. I'll talk to you then and we can figure out where to meet. In the meantime, I need you to do something, if you're well enough."

Sophia listened as Tara explained her plan. She, Nanor, and Cyril all argued against it, but Tara was determined, and Oni supported her.

After Sophia hung up, she dialed the number for the First Apostolic Church of Satan.

# 17

Thomas didn't answer her message about being discharged or any of her voicemails. Sophia asked her friend Jasmina Price from the University to meet her at the hospital so the doctor would release her.

"I'm surprised." Jasmina unlocked Sophia's front door and pushed it open. "He's never so much as been late for dinner, and he doesn't come get you from the hospital?"

"We had a serious conversation not long ago." Using her crutches, Sophia swung across the threshold. She'd been able to walk quite a ways in the hallway with them at the hospital, but now her knee ached and her ankle was screaming. "About our future. Or perhaps lack of future."

Though they hadn't directly talked about it, Sophia had felt the significance of the dinner at Everest. Thomas had said they were celebrating coming out in public, but despite the excellent food and wine, nothing about the evening had felt celebratory.

"Did you break up?"

"Not that I know of."

The townhome appeared as Sophia had left it, her wingback chair close to the fireplace, a book she'd been reading lying on the Chinese garden stool next to it. The counter between the kitchen and dining area gleamed, as did her appliances. She'd cleaned just before leaving to visit Erik Holmes with Tara. It felt as if the conversation with Holmes and the explosion had happened months ago rather than a week. She'd missed the funeral, making it unreal that Erik Holmes no longer lived.

"Coffee?" Jasmina said. "Or tea, given the hour?"

"Tea, thanks. There's some herbal in the cabinet over the microwave."

Through the pass through window, Sophia watched Jasmina fill the tea kettle. Thomas was a neat man. Neater than Sophia, who leaned toward order over chaos but didn't feel the need to empty the dishwasher the moment the cycle finished or fold laundry the instant the dryer stopped. Still, Thomas left traces. His reading glasses on the counter near the canister set when he wasn't using them, his briefcase between the altar cabinet just inside her door and the wall, a stack of change emptied from his pocket onto the coffee table.

All those things were gone.

Sophia opened the front closet door. Thomas' black dress shoes, brown dress shoes, and black gym shoes were missing. Though Jasmina protested her climbing the stairs, Sophia made her way to the third-floor master bedroom, leaning heavily on the railing and her friend's shoulder, and gritting her teeth at the pain. Thomas' half of the closet stood empty. The middle drawer in her chest of drawers, too, was bare.

Sophia sank onto the bed. Jasmina sat next to her and put her arm around her. "I'm sorry."

"So am I," Sophia said.

~

Sophia's crutches stood propped against the tiled wall. She and Tara sat in an underground café two levels below the Daley Center in Chicago.

"It's risky," Sophia said. "Very."

On the floors above them, people bustled in and out of courtrooms, but here only a few lawyers sat going over notes on their laptops. Two of Tara's security guards, wearing suits to better blend with the attorneys passing by, stood at various posts in the Pedway outside the café. The air smelled of a mix of frying hamburgers, coffee, and a urine stench from the Blue Line subway terminal a quarter mile away.

"Only a little," Tara said. "We need information. You said it yourself, a complete translation will take weeks if not months."

Sophia had agreed on the phone the day before to question Evekial Adame using a technique Stranyero favored. They'd pretend to know all but a few details about the Brotherhood and the Spark of Life and see if Evekial would fill in the rest.

Tara was counting on him being a Brotherhood member because he'd gone to Harvard with Stranyero and because his unusual church had a design on its website that seemed to be drawn from the Spark of Life painting. Sophia thought those weren't unreasonable ideas, but she felt less sure of the wisdom of trying to pry information from Evekial. She was hoping to convince Tara to table the idea until she and Nanor got further in the translation.

"To pretend we know more than we do," Sophia said, "we'll need to tell Evekial we're aware of the Spark of Life. If he is a Brotherhood member, that could make the Order more zealous in its efforts against you."

Sophia couldn't bring herself to call it a "war." All her training to become a nun went against that. Crusades, holy wars, those things were part of the Church's past. While the Brotherhood wasn't a subset of the Catholic Church, it was a Christian order, so far as she knew, and ought to be bound by the same moral code.

"Yeah, it's a risk. But it's already been 661 days since Fimi's birth. We've got to do something." Tara had calculated the exact figure the night before.

"Nanor didn't suggest the Spark of Life related to the 700 days," Sophia said. "That's whatever Rima was doing."

"Right, but it's all mentioned in the journal. Which other people may have, including people in the Brotherhood."

Sophia had studied the passages about what Rima had needed to do within 700 days of her child's birth, but neither she nor Nanor had yet been able to figure out the exact task or how it might protect the child, if it did. The references to the Spark of Life were no more detailed, though it appeared to be something the Brotherhood had done, possibly to "cause life." Which might mean a virgin pregnancy like Tara's, but Sophia couldn't be sure. She wished she had months to pore through the translation.

"That's why I agreed to do this. But acting on a fragment of an ancient text in a language I'm barely familiar with is contrary to all my theological and academic background."

"If Evekial can give us context, though, won't that make translating quicker and easier?"

"It might. But we don't know if we can trust anything he tells us," Sophia said.

"But it could help," Tara said. "We'll be careful what we say, get whatever we can from him, and get out."

Sophia sighed. "Very careful."

~

Carvings of the Green Man, sometimes viewed as the Devil, decorated the front and sides of Evekial Adame's antique desk. The guards split up to cover the entrance to his study and the church itself, which was deserted. Tara felt grateful again to Holmes. Without the extra security, she wouldn't have felt comfortable coming here, or leaving Fimi with Oni and Cyril.

"Professor Gaddini, I'm flattered you've come back to see me, and in search of an expert no less," Evekial said. His neck, shoulders, and arms looked spindly, but his height and intense gaze made him an imposing figure. Black eyeliner on his upper and lower lids intensified his eyes, which already stood out below his high forehead. His hair was jet black and thinning. "But as I told you before, I am not a member of the Brotherhood of Andrew. Why not ask your friend Thomas Stranyero? If anyone is a Brotherhood member, it is he."

"He's your friend, too. And he ended our relationship," Sophia said.

"I'm sorry to hear that," Evekial said, but the corners of his mouth twitched as if he were holding back a smile.

"You're the only person he mentioned as knowledgeable," Sophia said. "The only deist he respects."

"And you have the Spark of Life on your website," Tara said.

At the bottom right corner, under his Church's logo, she'd spotted the two fingers touching.

Evekial smiled. "Excellent eye. Few people recognize that small portion of the painting isolated from the rest. Which is fortunate, or I might have copyright difficulties."

"If you're not a member of the Brotherhood of Andrew," Sophia said, "why include a symbol of its most important effort?"

Tara relaxed her jaw and resisted the urge to clench her hands together. This was the first bluff. Sophia and Nanor had guessed that the Spark of Life related to the virgin pregnancies, including Tara's, and that the Brotherhood, rather than watching for them, might be causing them. But it was a leap based on little more than the mere fact that the phrase appeared in a journal about a seventh-century pregnant virgin.

Evekial leaned back in his chair, one knee crossed over the other in what, to Tara, appeared to be a deliberate attempt to show a lack of concern. "What effort?"

"With your intellect, your research skills, and your knowledge of ancient cultures," Sophia said, "despite being an outsider to the Order, I'm certain you figured it out, and no doubt before I did."

At the praise of his brain power and knowledge, Evekial's eyes brightened. "Figured what out?"

"The Brotherhood claims it is watching for a messiah," Sophia said, "but it's actually been attempting to create one. To use the Universe's power to trigger virgin pregnancies for thousands of years. What puzzles me is why you'd use that symbol, if you're not part of the Order."

Tara held her breath, hoping the bluff would work.

"You've accused me yourself of enjoying tweaking religious leaders. Subverting their symbols. You were correct. The upside down crucifix is particularly effective."

"But the Spark of Life—it's the opposite of what you stand for," Tara said, plunging in though she still felt unsure if Sophia had guessed correctly. "The Brotherhood wants to create a messiah, an incarnation of God on earth, and you're looking for the Antichrist."

Evekial laughed, his whole upper body curving forward as he crossed his arms over his stomach. "Oh my dear. You are refreshingly naïve." He glanced at Sophia. "You haven't explained how this works?"

Sophia opened her mouth, shut it again, then spoke. "I hoped not to disillusion her. But apparently it can't be avoided."

Evekial leaned toward Tara, elbows on his desk, smiling again. "The Brotherhood isn't trying to create a messiah in the way you mean. Not one like Jesus Christ, whether you are thinking of the historical man who existed and preached against the authorities of the day or the legend that arose after his death."

"It's not? What is it trying to do? " Tara said.

"Create a leader. One behind which it can consolidate first the three main monotheistic religions—Judaism, Islam, and Christianity—and then all religions."

"That's not possible. Even if that could be done, the beliefs are too different," Sophia said.

"There are differences, yes, " Evekial said. "But look at how Christianity spread, and that was before the age of mass communication."

"Spread, but also caused division," Sophia said.

"The Brotherhood of Andrew will learn from that example and improve upon it."

"And my role?" Tara said.

"None. If the Spark of Life was used on you, you're simply unlucky," Evekial said. "And a failure. The Brotherhood tried to Spark a leader and failed, getting your daughter instead. It must be a male child."

"That makes no sense," Sophia said. "If you're telling the truth about the plan, if it's not based on *Revelation*, there's no prophecy about a male child."

"I can't say if it's based on *Revelation* or not. But it is based on reality. The world won't unite under a woman. Too many would refuse, but women the world over already bow their heads to a male god."

"Fine, let's say the attempt on me was a failure. Why me in the first place? Is it random?"

She wanted to know why Ray and Lynette had been targeted. It might give a clue to how the process worked regardless what else Evekial would tell them. She didn't want to reveal, though, that they'd learned about the approach to Ray.

"No idea," Evekial said.

"There must be a reason," Tara said.

"To be honest," Evekial said, "I can't imagine what it was. Your close ties to your parents, brothers and sisters, and grandparents make you an unlikely mother of the type of leader the Brotherhood needs. The ideal mother of a child to mold is one with little familial support and without strong ties to others. One more vulnerable to needing the community and guidance the Brotherhood can offer."

Tara shut her eyes for a moment, all the stories her mom and Ray had told her about their short life together running through her mind. From outside, to the Brotherhood, it would have seemed the perfect set up. An addict who drifted in and out, likely to take off and leave his pregnant girlfriend. The girlfriend with a challenging family situation of her own and no financial support from anywhere. But Lynette was a lot stronger than anyone gave her credit for, and she'd built a stable, secure life for Tara. Tara had always taken that for granted. She'd thank her mom next time she saw her.

"Why tell us all of this?" Sophia said.

Tara opened her eyes again to see Evekial spread his hands wide. "To free her." He met Tara's eyes and nodded. "Go. Live your life. Your child isn't special or chosen, not inherently good or evil. She's a normal child. You can't stop the Brotherhood, and it's unlikely there will be another attempt to create a leader for many decades. So forget all these concerns."

Tara wondered how much Evekial was lying about and how much he simply didn't know. His stress of Fimi as normal suggested he wasn't aware that Fimi was actually a clone of Tara, and his discussion of the ideal type of family situation suggested he didn't know that the cycle began not with Tara but with her parents.

"If we can't stop them, there's no harm in telling us how the Spark of Life works, how it starts the virgin pregnancy." Sophia brushed her hair behind one ear, leaned back, and crossed her legs. "Unless you're not authorized to know that, which I would understand. Thomas told me there are levels of knowledge in the Brotherhood."

"No one person knows that," Evekial said. His eyes blazed. "If Thomas implied otherwise, he's lying. Boasting."

Sophia nodded and stood. "I'm sure that's true. I didn't really expect you'd know. Thank you for sharing what you could."

"Wait. Sit." Evekial rubbed his chin. "I've heard rumors. I hardly credit them, but if you tell me what you know, I'll see if I can fill in any blanks."

Of course, he wanted to test their knowledge. Or pick their brains for information that had been kept from him. Tara hoped Nanor and Sophia had guessed right.

Sophia sat again. "The Brotherhood caused at least five pregnancies over the centuries, including Tara's, using the Spark of Life. Each time so far the woman has died during pregnancy or she and the child have died soon after the birth. It's said that each child was female. The process starts long before the pregnancy, perhaps decades before. There is some act or ritual by the Brotherhood or its members that triggers the pregnancy," Sophia said.

"You'll never learn the details of the ritual," Evekial said.

"You've tried?" Tara said.

"I've inquired. I'm curious, as is Thomas. But it is forbidden to write down the steps of any Brotherhood ritual, not only that one. With the Spark of Life, one person in each generation knows the whole. Others take part, but only in pieces. It keeps it secret."

"And you're not the designated person," Sophia said.

"I have not been so honored." His face drooped from his eyebrows to the corners of his mouth.

"Why would the process begin so early?" Sophia said. "Decades before the pregnancy?"

Evekial shrugged. "I don't know that it does. What's your evidence of that?"

"I'll disclose my sources if you disclose yours," Sophia said.

"Well put." Evekial glanced at his monitor. "I've hit the limit of what I can tell you, and I've another appointment. I hope you'll both take my advice and stay out of this from now on."

"One more thing," Tara said, "because I'm not sure I understand. The Brotherhood's goal is that everyone believes in the same god?"

If that really was the goal, it would fit in a way with what Cyril had told her so long ago, it was simply a broader goal, not limited to Christianity. But it seemed like a wrong way to get there. If the Brotherhood believed there was only one God with a capital G, it shouldn't need to force the issue.

Sophia looked at Evekial and shook her head slowly, as if putting the pieces together.

"The concept of God is a means, not an end," Evekial said. "Religion, faith, those are the vehicles of the Order, not its goal."

"What's its goal?" Tara said.

"Power," Sophia said. "And control."

"Of course," Evekial said. "Of the masses, of the governments, of the institutions of learning. What else would it be? So you see, if that disturbs you, you are better off with your daughter taking no part in it. Count your blessings and go in peace."

TARA PACED in front of the floor-to-ceiling windows. She'd returned to the high rise after leaving Evekial, entering through a side door and taking the freight elevator. Sophia had walked here separately, coming in through the main lobby. Nanor and Kali had entered there, too, but via a coffee shop that connected the high rise and an adjacent office building rather than from the street.

Tara felt a mix of relief and anger at the idea that men, not some otherworldly force alone, had caused her pregnancy. It meant she could stop searching for and worrying about the meaning, about whether her pregnancy arose from good or evil. But it also meant that actual people had reached into her life and sent it in a direction she'd specifically chosen not to go. She'd avoided sex because she understood the responsibilities of parenthood. She'd planned to finish college before taking the smallest chance and to finish medical school before attempting to get pregnant.

But the Brotherhood members didn't care about her plan. Before she'd been born, before her mother had become pregnant, they'd set out a course. Her mother's life, Ray Tigue's, Tara's, Fimi's, none of them mattered. It was somehow worse than if the Brotherhood members had known her and deliberately altered her life. As it was, their actions showed no recognition of her, or of anyone involved, as a human being. They'd condemned her and Fimi and who knows how many women before them to lives of fear, danger, and horrible deaths.

"It's unbelievable," Tara said.

"You're certain that's what Evekial meant?" Kali sat on the leather couch, her expression grim, her hands closed into fists on her lap. "The Brotherhood wants to gain power by consolidating all these religions, so they cause all these women to become pregnant against their will?"

"And when it doesn't work out to their satisfaction, ensure the deaths of those women," Nanor said. "And with Rima, of her infant as well."

Nanor sat at the dining table continuing work on the journal, her mouth set in a firm, hard line. No doubt she was thinking of her daughter Maya dying on the side of a road. Tara glanced at Fimi, who leaned against Kali on the couch, watching a video with earphones on. She hoped that was enough to block out this talk of death.

Oni stood at the long end of the room. She folded her arms over her chest.

"You're surprised? There's a reason the guardians have opposed the Brotherhood forever."

"Not very successfully," Tara said. "The pregnancies keep happening. I'm not sorry I have Fimi now that she's here, but forcing pregnancies—it's a horrible thing to do. And worse that they arrange to kill the mothers and babies after."

Nanor reached for the stack of photocopied journal pages. "The guardians have been quite successful in one way, according to what was written here. After Rima's death, her aunt learned that the guardians, while unable to stop these forced pregnancies, were able to ensure each child was a replica of the mother, thwarting the goal of creating a male leader."

"A clone," Tara said. "Or later-born twin, as my doctor put it when she gave me the DNA results."

"Yes, though the word 'clone' would not have been known at the time," Nanor said. "Nor would 'twin' have made sense to anyone, as that concept is linked with two babies born together. The Armenian words literally translate to a child who would be the woman all over again."

"Disqualifying her from leadership," Kali said.

"But to see the woman as the Antichrist because rather than their desired boy child she is having a girl? That's extreme even for extremists," Tara said.

"So-called honor killings of women go on every day," Oni said.

"But even her aunt referred to Rima as the Antichrist in her letter," Tara said. The reading had frightened her when she'd heard it and had given her nightmares since.

"You struggle because you view the Antichrist as an evil figure," Nanor said. "The guardians likely arose from the joining of the Collyridians and Antidicomarianites. The early Christian church denounced both groups as heretics and saw them as Anti-Christian. The groups clearly rejected major aspects of Church doctrine, so perhaps they embraced the term. As for the Brotherhood seeing the women as evil and eliminating them, it is sadly not so difficult to view those with whom you disagree as evil."

"Particularly when you believe God is on your side," Sophia said. She'd sunk onto the chair opposite Nanor, her crutches resting against the floor-to-ceiling windows. "It's the very nature of religious wars."

"But can all religions consolidate?" Cyril said. "I was taught Christianity is unique, and the one way to God is through Christ."

"And don't forget, you have to be the right kind of Christian," Oni said. "My great-grandparents believed Protestants would end up in hell because they weren't Catholic, and I know born-agains sure the Catholics are going to hell. So, basically, if you're Christian, everyone who doesn't subscribe to your brand is going to hell."

The corners of Nanor's mouth twitched in a faint smile. "In some ways, true. Though there are similarities among the major monotheistic religions. Judaism, Christianity, and Islam all have a single, male God who requires obedience above all. They share the story of Abraham being willing and ready to kill his son, no questions asked, when a voice he believes is his God's tells him to do so. On the other hand, there are significant differences. In Islam, the problem for humanity is seen as pride and self-sufficiency; the solution is submission to God. In Judaism, the problem is exile, and the solution is the return to God. Christianity focuses on sin and salvation."

"And all of this is the view of Evekial," Sophia said. "The purported view. How accurately that portrays the Brotherhood of Andrew's actual aims or his own understanding of them, we don't know."

"If Evekial is telling the truth, though, and your reading of the journal is right, this will keep going forever," Tara said. "They'll keep trying to create male leaders and keep killing women because they'll keep conceiving girls."

"Seen that way," Oni said, "maybe you're right, the guardians haven't accomplished much. We stopped the leader but we might've made the cycle worse for the women."

Tara sank onto the large ottoman near Oni. "Yeah, I'm going with dead being worse than being forced to be the mother of a Brotherhood leader."

"The Brotherhood's first steps are denying and discrediting," Sophia said. "Thomas told me that. It was a change in the Brotherhood that he helped push through."

"If you stop kicking your dog, does that make you a nice person?" Oni said.

Nanor looked up from the pages she had spread across the dining table. "It need not go on forever. I've been cross-checking meanings, and I'm now satisfied that the guardians had more success than at first it appears. They found a way they believed not only would stop the Brotherhood's Spark of Life but would ensure a girl child could survive and that she and her mother, as I had always hoped, would eliminate the very three religions the Brotherhood sought first to consolidate."

"Eliminate? How?" Tara said. When Nanor had first raised her view that Fimi's purpose was exactly what she was now suggesting, Tara had balked. She didn't want to trounce anyone else's religion. She still felt uneasy about that. But if it was the only way to end women being terrorized and killed, and ensure she and Fimi had lives beyond hiding, fighting, and running, then that's what she'd do.

Nanor ran her finger down her notepad. "That part is not completely clear. But I was able to decipher more this morning. According to the last pages of the journal, the ritual Rima could perform needed to occur within 700 days of the child's birth. The Order believed that if the child was killed before she reached her 700th day, the Spark of Life ceremony would never work again. So the threat of the child would be ended, but the hope of a future leader would be gone as well. After the 700 days, however, the Order could freely kill the child."

"May I see?" Sophia said.

Nanor slid two highlighted and annotated journal pages over to Sophia.

Tara pressed her elbows against her sides. "Can we get to the part about how the child can *not* be killed?"

"That is the ritual," Nanor said. "If done before the 700 days, the child and mother will be forever protected from human forces seeking to harm them. Also, the Spark of Life ceremony will no longer work. There will be no future Brotherhood leader to expand its power over the world."

Heart racing, Tara calculated the days again, though she'd done it multiple times before. "So we have 39 days. What's the ritual?" Tara said.

Nanor frowned. "I have only begun that part of the translation. So far I see that whatever the woman needs will be within her reach, placed there, it appears, by the guardians. Not only the woman and child must take part but her family and those in the line of guardians."

"Which sounds a lot like my last vision," Tara said.

"Yes," Nanor said. "So your vision—the vision we all shared—perhaps provides more clues. We must each write down exactly what we recall, and Dr. Gaddini and I will continue to work on these pages and do our best to fit it all together."

"And if you can't do it in time? If the 700 days passes?" Cyril said.

"Not only are Tara and Fimi at great risk, it is likely that in another twenty to forty years, another woman will be subject to a virgin pregnancy, assuming the Brotherhood performs its rituals and tasks," Nanor said.

"And because of the guardians, there will be a girl child again," Oni said.

Nanor nodded and rubbed her forehead just above her eyebrows. "Correct. Which means the Brotherhood again follows its deny, discredit, destroy cycle, ultimately killing the mother and child if necessary."

Tara stood and gathered Fimi in her arms. "That's not going to happen. None of that is going to happen. If it takes everything I have, if I have to fight the Brotherhood one-on-one, Fimi will be protected, and no one will suffer through this ever again."

# 18

"She has what?" Fenton MacNeil's voice almost crackled.

Stranyero lowered the volume. He'd planted a listening device in Evekial Adame's study that afternoon when he'd stopped to visit the man on a pretext. Since then, he'd heard a dull discussion of fundraising and another about the ordering of cheaper black candles. Now his stealth was finally being rewarded. As he listened on earbuds from his firm's Chicago office, the voices came through so clearly that Stranyero felt sure MacNeil must be visiting Evekial Adame in person, not merely speaking to him on the phone. Which in itself was interesting. Evekial must be convinced he was indeed advancing in the Brotherhood for both Stranyero and MacNeil to visit him the same day.

"Recorded history preserved by the line of priest's wives at Our Lady of Sorrows," Evekial Adame said.

"That journal was destroyed," MacNeil said, "in the church fire that killed Rima Petrosyan and led to her offspring's death."

"Apparently not," Evekial said. "My source indicates that the journal was procured by Dr. Sophia Gaddini, who is reviewing it as we speak."

A scraping sound came through. Stranyero guessed it might be Evekial sliding his chair back from his desk so he could pop it into recline mode and enjoy MacNeil's frustration. Stranyero, on the other hand, hunched forward, his forehead perspiring. As usual, Evekial had his facts right and wrong. Stranyero hadn't wanted to be pinpointed as the source of the document, but he didn't want Sophia targeted. Whoever had killed Holmes—and he hadn't determined yet who that had been—might decide to pursue her as well.

"Use your head," MacNeil said. "Sophia Gaddini's only left the hospital this morning. Before her admission, she was in Chicago for the entire summer.

There's no point at which she could have traveled to Armenia to retrieve that journal."

Stranyero doodled names on the yellow legal pad in front of him. Each one was a person he thought might be spying on Sophia.

"She didn't go there," Evekial said. "She hired some other woman to do it."

"Hired her with what money?" MacNeil said.

"She's a professor. They rake in the dough. And her books sell well."

"Your premise is wrong, as are your assumptions. I've had Sophia Gaddini's finances looked into," MacNeil said. "She earns a decent salary as a full professor, but her books have barely earned back their advances, which are not large. She donates 10-15% of her income per year to various charities, so she's continued to tithe despite leaving her order and the Church. She pays a mortgage and property taxes on her Chicago townhome, and invests what she can in index funds for retirement. She has all of five thousand dollars liquid in a money market fund and two thousand in a checking account. So unless she has a fairy godmother, she could not afford the services of a specialist to fly to Armenia."

Stranyero nodded. He'd provided that information to MacNeil himself, and it was accurate. Sophia had been careful about anything to do with Tara Spencer, but she hadn't kept her financial information equally guarded. He'd accessed her account from the laptop on the desk in her home office, having watched her type in her banking password often enough. Too used to living alone, he guessed, or unconcerned whether he understood her finances. Her email and correspondence had much stronger protection.

"However Gaddini got the document, she's translating it as we speak," Evekial said.

"If she told you that, she was bluffing," MacNeil said. "There's no way she managed to extort a valuable ancient journal from the women protecting it without appearing in person. Women who, by the way, have managed to evade our efforts for centuries."

"Unless those women wanted to help her," Evekial said.

Stranyero raised his eyebrows. For the most part, he thought Evekial, who'd come into the Brotherhood as a legacy, was a bulb that burned only medium-bright, but now and then the man had a flash of insight.

"Help her why?" MacNeil said.

"Because she's helping Tara Spencer. If we think Spencer's the one who may defeat us, don't you think the guardians see her as that as well?"

"The Brotherhood's own investigators destroyed the journal in the tenth century."

"So they said," Evekial said. "You think times were different then? That no one fudged their reports and said what their superiors wanted to hear? Those investigators knew it'd be another twenty or thirty years before the cycle began again, and they knew the odds were against the woman giving birth regardless. So what did they care?"

"Not everyone is so cavalier as you," MacNeil said.

"I'm not saying that's what I'd do."

*It's exactly what you'd do.*

"Really?" MacNeil said.

"I'm saying that's what many people would do. And the severe penalties back then for failing a mission—well, who was likely to admit failure? Better to claim the documents were destroyed. The guardians certainly weren't going to contradict them."

"Fine. You may be right. But we're still back to how Sophia Gaddini got the money to hire an expert."

"Spencer gets donations through that website her friend set up," Evekial said. "That must have paid for it."

Stranyero had leaked that misinformation so no one would wonder where funds to pay Marie Glaston had come from and trace them back to him. The website, set up by Vicki Turano out of love for her former best friend, did solicit donations. But they were nowhere near enough to pay for Tara's outstanding doctor bills.

"And how did she find someone to make this trip for her?" MacNeil said. "We've had a watch out for Cyril Woods, Spencer's relatives, the Kerkorians, and that Argentinian woman, and none of them left the country."

"My guess?"

"I don't want more guesses," MacNeil said. "I want information. Do you have information?"

Stranyero strained, but didn't hear a response from Evekial. He must have made some response, though, because MacNeil said, "That's what I thought. When you do have information, let me know. I'm staying at the Peninsula until Thursday."

Stranyero waited half an hour before reaching for his phone to call Evekial Adame. MacNeil might not be interested in guesses, but Stranyero was.

Before the call commenced, though, his other line buzzed. It was Fenton MacNeil. He had a task for Stranyero that couldn't wait.

"700 DAYS?" Lynette said, her eyes wide. She was alone in her apartment, drinking a cup of coffee after work. She'd called on video to ask how the meeting with Evekial had gone but had launched into criticisms before the entire story could be explained. "If all of this in the journal is actually true, you've got less than six weeks to figure this out."

"You don't think it's true?" Cyril said.

Nanor and Kali had returned to their apartment, but Oni sat cross-legged on the ottoman holding a bottle of water. "It might not be. It's a photocopy of an ancient journal we know next to nothing about. Plus, who knows who this Marie Glaston is or if Erik Holmes really sent her. Or if he meant to help Tara if he did."

"I called the lawyer who represents Erik Holmes' estate," Sophia said. She sat at the dining table, reviewing Nanor's notes and additional journal passages about the ritual. "He couldn't disclose anything he'd done or hadn't done, but he was willing to say he'd never heard of Marie Glaston."

"So she used another name," Oni said. "She obviously was holding back quite a bit."

"Something you're familiar with," Lynette said. "It's impossible to believe your cousin didn't tell you about the 700 days."

Oni banged her water bottle on the coffee table. "She didn't. And if she had, how would it have helped? I wasn't convinced Tara was the One until after she brought Nanor back from the dead and healed the earth, and she went into the coma after that. You couldn't have done anything then."

"You could have told my family," Tara said. "Sophia could have researched, tried to figure out what we needed to do."

"It's forbidden," Oni said. "The guardians may reveal the truth only to the One Who Will Live Forever. I've broken with tradition too much already being so open with your family and your associates." Oni jerked her head first toward Sophia and then at Cyril, who sat in an armchair, laptop on his lap. He was researching the construction and modifications of the shrines, hoping to find more information on why and when the designs had been added to them.

"Fuck tradition," Tara said. "This is my life we're talking about. And my child's life. Every woman you or Cyril know of in my situation was killed, and the only other one who gave birth saw her child die, too."

"I didn't ask for this, either," Oni said. "Every woman in my line has been killed, too."

"Let's focus on what we know," Sophia said. Her shoulders slumped, the bridge of her nose shone with oil that had accumulated over the long day, and shadows underscored her eyes. "There's a ritual Tara can perform, with Fimi. Tara's visions suggest it may be best to include her family and Nanor's. Oni's been told the bookmark and the map are key. At each shrine, the rendering of the design shows a woman holding two vessels. When Cyril met Tara, he gave her a photo of a vase with a carving of what he believed to be an Armenian woman—whom we now believe was Rima Petrosyan—who was also a pregnant virgin."

"So what about the vessels?" Tara turned to Oni. "You ready to check them out? The ones at the cloister in Pennsylvania?"

"I've been ready," Oni said. "More than ready."

"That sounds like a wild goose chase," Lynette said. "If the women at the cloister had something that mattered, they would have given it to Tara last year."

"Then I'll chase." Oni stood and tossed her water bottle into the recycling bin. "They might not have known it was important, and there's no reason for me to stay here. If the journals are right, the Brotherhood's best bet is to wait Tara and Fimi out for 700 days. Block her from finding whatever she needs for the ritual, but not attack her. I can best protect her by finding the vessels."

"But not everyone connected with the Brotherhood believes that about not attacking Tara during the 700 days," Lynette said. "Right? Or the grenade attack wouldn't have happened. Or the attempts on her life at the cloister."

Sophia closed her yellow notepad. "I'm with Oni and Tara on this. The grenade was probably not meant for Tara. The one time he visited me, Thomas told me the leadership was angry at whoever threw the grenade, but that person was targeting Holmes, not Tara, on the basis that Holmes might be in a position to help her."

"And we believe everything Thomas Stranyero says," Lynette said.

"It's information," Sophia said. "Like the journal, we don't know how true it is or not. Tara also has hired security as well as Cyril here. And it appears no one has realized she's in Chicago."

"Except Evekial," Tara said.

"True. Which suggests it may be time for you to leave the city, much as I enjoy having you here."

"Either way, there's nothing for me to do here," Oni said. "I can't translate the journal. And while I can fight, if three hired security guards and Cyril can't keep Brotherhood fanatics and protestors at bay, I doubt I'd tip the scales. But so far when I traveled, no one's bothered me, and the Brotherhood doesn't seem to be following me. So why not have me check out the vases."

"She's right," Tara said. She understood her mom's worries, and she felt uneasy about Oni traveling, as she was less certain than Oni that the Brotherhood didn't know about her. But if the bookmark mattered, the vases did too, and they needed every piece of the puzzle they could find. "I'll call the cloister and tell them you're coming."

# 19

Thomas Stranyero nodded to the bartender as he entered The Palm steakhouse in Washington, D.C. The bartender nodded back and cut his eyes sideways toward the far end of the bar. Stranyero followed his gaze and slid onto a barstool next to a man in a tailored gray sport jacket, jeans, and a buttoned down white shirt with monogrammed cuffs.

Stranyero tapped the man's shoulder. "Hello, Senator."

The senator stiffened, but he swiveled toward Stranyero. "Thomas. What can I do for you?"

"You assume I'm seeking something."

"Aren't we all?" The senator waved to the bartender for another Scotch but didn't offer a drink to Stranyero.

It didn't matter. The bartender brought Stranyero a glass of his favorite Cote du Rhone. He'd gotten into the habit of drinking red wine rather than hard liquor from his evenings with Sophia.

"I'm curious how well you know Fenton MacNeil," Stranyero said.

The senator's eyebrows rose. "Isn't he retired?"

"From certain things, yes," Stranyero said. "But not from others."

"Is that so? I thought you might be taking his place."

"Where did you hear that?"

"A mutual acquaintance of ours stopped to see me a month or so ago."

Stranyero didn't need to ask if it had been the Cardinal. He was the only one the senator would refer to that way. Though he didn't understand the true nature of the Brotherhood, the man knew enough not to name anyone too high.

"What did he want?" Stranyero asked.

The senator downed half of his Scotch. "Interestingly, to ask how well I knew you. Perhaps the three of you ought to sit down and talk one of these days."

"MacNeil hasn't come to see you?" Stranyero said.

"He has not. I told the Cardinal you were the best man for any job, by the way. If that's what you've really come to ask about."

Stranyero took a swallow of his wine. The deep taste gave him an almost physical longing for Sophia's fireside. Their winter had been quiet, often reading the same books so they could discuss them. Occasionally she'd played piano for him, and he'd shut his eyes and imagined the whole world fit into her front room. He gripped the edge of the shiny mahogany bar. He'd made his choice, and he needed to see it through.

"It's not," Stranyero said. "But thank you for your support. I'm truly looking for your insights into MacNeil. I believe you worked with him when he sold his first company."

"Indeed," the senator said. "That was twenty-five years ago. How could that help you now?"

"It's the last time anyone got the better of him. I understand he severely undervalued his assets."

"A mistake he never made again," the senator said.

"And do you believe it was as a result of his inexperience?" Stranyero asked.

"In part." The senator finished his Scotch and slid the empty glass toward the bartender. "It was also due to his personal investment."

"Financially?"

"Again, in part. Mainly, he put his heart and soul into that business. It blinded him. That hurt him more than his inexperience."

"Hurt him in that he lacked confidence?"

"The opposite. He was overconfident. He ought to have considered my strengths and anticipated my moves, but he was certain he'd covered all his bases and further research was a waste of time. He knew best."

"In your opinion, has that changed over the years? He's clearly gained experience, but is he any better at staying objective when his heart and soul are involved?"

"I'm not sure I've known him to put his soul into any effort since," the senator said. "He hasn't in any business dealings we've had."

"But if he did," Stranyero said.

"If he did," the senator said, "I doubt he'd be anymore clear-headed than he was twenty-five years ago. There are some things about a man that never change."

THE NEXT MORNING, Cyril drove Oni to the rental car facility so she could obtain a different vehicle for the twelve-hour drive to Pennsylvania. Nanor and Kali had returned to the high rise. They sat across from one another at the round dining table, Nanor reading aloud from the journal, Kali taking careful notes.

The three of them contacted Sophia. She'd texted that she was too exhausted from the day before to meet in person, but she spoke to them via video call. She had her hair pulled back from her face and looked a little less worn than she had when she'd left the night before.

Tara told them all that she wanted to call Marie Glaston.

"Why?" Sophia said.

"I'd like her help," Tara said. "That is, if she'll tell us who hired her. Otherwise, it's too risky."

"How can she help?" Sophia said. "She's not a translator. Not as far as we know."

"No, but we're running out of time, and she knows artifacts. And art. Depending on what she tells us, if we feel we can trust her, we could show her the bookmark and the photos from the shrines. See if she spots something we missed."

"I don't know, Tara," Sophia said. "If she is willing to help, it'd most likely be to get a look at everything we have."

"Holmes already knew about the bookmark and the shrines, so if his estate hired her, she might already know that too. So what's the harm in her seeing them?"

"We do not know that Mr. Holmes hired her," Nanor said.

"So you're also concerned about this idea?" Sophia said.

"I am. I do not oppose it outright, but I am not sure what we ought to share with this Marie Glaston, if anything," Nanor said.

"There was also lightning in our vision when Protennoia gave me the journal," Tara said, "and lightning when Marie called."

"It's stormed frequently over the last couple weeks," Sophia said. "We can't read much into that."

"Also, the lightning struck, and it charred the journal," Nanor said. "That is worrisome."

"Charred—just a minute." Sophia disappeared from the screen, then appeared again with a stack of photos in front of her. "Tara, walk me through that vision again. All of you, as you all saw it. I want to listen while I look at the photos of the shrines."

Tara did, and Sophia listened intently. "So you all put something into a vase, and then Protennoia poured liquid out of it."

"Not out of the same vase, out of a different one," Kali said. She pulled the photos out and spread them on her half of the table. "She put something in one vase, and poured liquid from the other."

"As in the design," Sophia said. "The goddess holds two vases. She pours liquid from one into a lake in most of them, though sometimes into a river. From the second vase, she pours liquid onto the earth."

"Wasn't there something about a river in that Chapter 12 of Revelation that Cyril kept quoting to you when he met you?" Kali said.

"Yeah," Tara said. She did a quick search on her phone. "There's the part about the dragon or beast opposing the woman who will give birth to a male child who will rule the earth. Hm. This translation adds 'with a scepter'."

"Phallic issues," Kali said, making Tara smile before she returned to the Revelation verses.

"It says that the serpent 'spewed water like a river' from his mouth. The water streamed past the woman and swept her away. But the earth helped the woman. It opened its mouth and swallowed the river. After that, the dragon—now it's a dragon, not a serpent—gets angry and goes off to 'wage war against the rest of her offspring'."

"A river of serpent spit," Kali said. "Lovely."

"The body of water in all these photos appears fairly calm. Non-threatening," Sophia said. "The woman appears calm, not worried about a dragon or serpent or its offspring. So perhaps there's no connection."

Nanor, too, had started inspecting the photos. "Also, the goddess appears to be adding to the river or lake in most of them."

"There's something odd about the water, though." Sophia held up a photo of the design carved in rock. "The charring made me think of it, because it could be ashes. If you look closely, you'll see it's not clear liquid being poured into the river. There are specks in it." She pointed with her pen. "I thought they were flaws in the rock itself, but they appear in several of the designs."

Nanor flipped the pages from the journal, running her finger down one and then the other. "Here. A reference to anointing. One anoints not only with liquid, with oil, but often with herbs or spices. Perhaps there is some type of anointing that is important here. Perhaps that is part of the ritual Tara must orchestrate."

"But we don't know if the bookmark design relates to the ritual. Or why Protennoia said 'once it begins, it must end'." Tara sank onto one of the dining chairs.

"There must be a ritual, a way to stop the process, or the Brotherhood wouldn't be so concerned about you and Fimi," Sophia said. "They'd simply increase their efforts to discredit you or to intimidate you into going into hiding. But Thomas told me they declared war from the time you awoke."

"But how is it performed?" Kali said. "The journal seems sparse on details."

"Which is why I want to call Marie," Tara said. "If the bookmark and shrines are key, we need someone who can help interpret them."

Nanor sighed. "I do not like it, but I have no better suggestion to offer. Dr. Gaddini?"

Sophia frowned. "Nor do I. The only other person that comes to mind is Andrea Gutzman. But with Tara's permission, I already ran this past her, and she's also stymied."

Professor Gutzman, an expert in heresies involving the Virgin Mary, had helped Tara and Sophia find a missing fragment of a prophecy about Tara as well as the cloister in Pennsylvania itself, so Tara had felt safe sharing the bookmark with her. But she hadn't been able offer much help regarding it or the shrines, though she'd agreed to try to track down the origin of the vessels.

"So Marie is it," Tara said.

"I agree," Sophia said. "But that doesn't mean I like the idea."

A BLUE AUDI drove half a mile behind Stranyero. It had appeared when he'd driven through Blue Springs, the village a few miles west of Willow Springs, the community Nanor Kerkorian had founded. Stranyero was surprised not that he was being followed, but that whoever was tailing him was being so obvious. It couldn't be anyone he'd trained.

Two curves before the gated parking area, the Audi dropped from site. Using tools he'd brought, Stranyero broke open the chain around the gate. The electronic system of locks had shorted during the fire that had raged through the community. It had never been replaced. He parked in the outer lot.

He stowed the tools in the trunk and took out the soft-sided rifle case. He had no doubt that if he walked back, he'd see the blue Audi in plain sight on the side of the road. He'd heard the newest special investigators for the Brotherhood lacked any subtlety in field operations. Excellent at on-line stalking, they saw little use for doing anything in person. But Fenton MacNeil was smart. Electronic surveillance might tell him where Stranyero was if a monitoring device were properly placed, but it wouldn't show what Stranyero did. MacNeil could have simply sent a partner with him to be sure Stranyero stayed in line, but that would violate protocol. The Order had pursued its goals while remaining largely unknown for thousands of years by a combination of networking and isolation. Single-person acts were hard to prove in a court of law.

Pieces of scorched wood and metal were littered through the gravel. There had been a clean up effort, but not much of one. He broke into the inner lot, which had once housed golf carts. Those had been taken away, so he'd be hiking through the woods. He wore hiking boots, camouflage pants, and a matching long-sleeved shirt despite the heat. It would keep bugs off his skin and make him harder to spot.

He shouldered the bag and checked his water supply. He needed to traverse nearly twenty miles round trip, and it was over eighty degrees. He'd packed power bars as well, just in case.

Stranyero settled his cap on his head, hoping he looked like a hunter, and plunged into the woods.

IT WAS AN ELEVEN-BLOCK WALK, one Sophia would have done in twenty minutes before her injury, but now she took a cab. It let her off on the corner of Madison and LaSalle Street. She'd transitioned from crutches to a cane, and she leaned heavily on it as she ascended the steps of St. Peter's Church.

She'd come to the church not because she still believed in Catholicism but because of her aunt, the woman who'd practically raised her. When she'd died six months ago, Thomas had appeared at the funeral. They hadn't been dating yet, but they'd spoken many times on their disposable phones, and she'd told him about her aunt. The woman who'd provided the stable home while her parents traveled across the country and world playing music. The woman who'd introduced Sophia to religion, who'd encouraged her vocation, and yet who'd understood when she'd had a change of mind and heart. The one person who'd encouraged Sophia through every step of her life.

The wake, held in Boston where her aunt had lived, had been filled with others who loved her, but none of Sophia's small group of friends, all of whom lived in or near Chicago, had been able to come. Her parents had, yet Sophia had felt alone. The funeral mass left her empty and silent. While others expressed gratitude for her aunt's long life, which Sophia understood on an intellectual level, she'd felt a gaping hole in her life. At 37, she was losing the person most like a mother to her.

At the graveside, Sophia had looked up to see a figure striding across the road, his dark wool coat standing out against the snow. She'd recognized him though they'd only met in person three times. He hadn't told her he was coming, and he shouldn't have done so. Thomas Stranyero, high ranking member of the Brotherhood, at a funeral with Sophia Gaddini, friend and mentor to Tara Spencer. But he'd stood at her side. He'd taken her hand.

And now he, too, was gone.

Sophia stepped into the quiet vestibule. It was off hours, no masses or confessions were happening. In the pews, a handful of people sat or kneeled, as was usually the case at St. Peter's. The giant form of Jesus on the cross looked down at them. As always, Jesus the Son and God the Father took center stage. At first as that had begun to sink in, Sophia had felt that the men who ran the Church, who'd created these rituals, badly needed a father figure, that the way they imagined God must fill a deep and unmet need. Later, the more she read and studied, she saw it a different way. They didn't long for this male authority figure, they didn't need him to care for them, they identified with him. He was them and they were He. The scandals over priests abusing children shocked and saddened her, but the Church cover up did not surprise her. She didn't know why it had surprised anyone. A group of men with unchecked power, a group of men who believed they were sanctioned from on high. Where was the surprise that they had protected themselves and their own?

Sophia skirted the pews and slipped into one of the alcoves. The church was run by Franciscans, one of whom was a long time friend of hers. In the corner of a shrine to the Virgin Mary he'd allowed her to place her aunt's copy of the Bible. Thomas had suggested the idea. A beautiful book with red leather binding, embossed lettering, and her great-great-uncle's inscription. No one in the extended family had wanted it. She'd felt it right that it be somewhere her aunt had loved, somewhere that others might read it. Her aunt's grave was far away, and Sophia had never been one for visiting cemeteries. So when she needed to remember her aunt's thoughtful support, or when she needed peace, she came to this quiet place in the center of downtown Chicago.

She took the book into her hands now. From the choir balcony above, an organ began playing the notes of *Joyful Joyful*, a hymn Sophia would have liked for her aunt's funeral. The arrangements had been made by her aunt's son, though, Sophia's cousin, who was twenty years older than Sophia and barely spoke to his mother, but who had the closer blood connection. He'd chosen flat, somber hymns, ones that spoke to him and perhaps to the woman he'd known as mother, not the woman Sophia had known.

Her aunt had also loved the Psalms. Too many of the Old Testament stories were filled with murder, incest, and anger, she said, but the Psalms were filled with beauty. Sophia's favorite was Ecclesiastes 3, and the song *Turn, Turn, Turn* based on it was one of the few folk songs she enjoyed. She could almost hear Pete Seeger's warm tenor singing about a time for all seasons under heaven as she flipped pages to find it.

*A time to be born, a time to die.*

It offered the comfort Sophia sought. The bulk of the psalm didn't mention a divine force, didn't try to justify how a supposedly all-powerful, all-good god failed to answer the prayers of those caught in war-torn countries or of those who offered counsel to inmates or of children in cancer wards. It simply said that life brought happiness and pain, joy and sadness, that each phase must be lived through and taken as it was, rather than railed against.

Thomas had appreciated her love for the verse. And, despite that love, her hesitancy about even its words of comfort. She'd counseled people who never got the joy to balance the pain, whose circumstances rarely allowed a time for rejoicing. But most had at least some measure of each.

Many of the Bible pages contained her aunt's handwritten notes in the margins. She expressed thoughts about the meaning of the passages, sometimes disagreeing, sometimes approving. Despite having been raised in the Catholic Church at a time when it had been far more traditional and rigid than now, she'd rejected many of its teachings. Sophia paused to read a few of the thoughts. Next to one about the man being the head of the woman in marriage, her aunt had written, "Guess again." Sophia smiled.

Ecclesiastics 3 began mid-page near the center of the book. Sophia drew in her breath at the handwritten note next to it.

*Trust.*

Next to the word were 10 digits. All of it was in Thomas' handwriting.

# 20

It took longer to get through the woods than Stranyero had expected. When Tara Spencer had healed Nanor Kerkorian and then the earth, the plant-life seemed to have gotten a boost toward overgrowth. He could barely find the dirt paths that had once provided access for the community's golf carts. The tall grass hid them and shrubs stretched across them. Tree branches hung low, forcing him to duck beneath and around them. Twice he nearly lost his sense of direction. He wondered how his stalker would do. He hadn't heard the man so far, so he must be hanging back.

Nanor Kerkorian had meant her community to be a difficult one to reach for those who didn't know the way, as it had begun as a haven for battered women. Nature had taken up where she'd left off, adding to the barriers. His phone couldn't pick up a signal. The satellite dish that had once brought service to Willow Springs had been damaged in the fire, and his handheld compass didn't help much on the winding paths.

After forty minutes, he reached the clearing where the chapel stood. Its outer concrete walls remained, but the wooden doors had burned away, and moss and plants grew over the stone floor. The interior wall with its mural of Maya Kekorian was half-charred, her features obscured.

It was a shame Nanor Kerkorian had refused to sell the land for many reasons, including that the site itself could be lovely. He inspected the area to be sure his information was correct, then kept moving.

He passed the guest area where a lone trailer remained. Most had been taken away by their owners, if functional, or sold for scrap. This one appeared to be in fairly good shape. He wondered if it was the one Tara Spencer had lived in during her time here. It might have been left as a memorial. Or for Nanor Kerkorian's use if she ever decided to return, which seemed unlikely. She'd begun a new life with her granddaughter in Chicago near Sophia.

Staying among the trees, Stranyero edged nearer the trailer. No sign of movement. Its blinds had been pulled down, and its front door was shut. Stranyero weighed whether to check it out further or continue on. If he didn't reveal himself now, though, it was possible anyone in the trailer would never notice him.

The paths in the residential area were clearer than in the woods, but the intact trailer caused him to move more cautiously, staying amongst the trees whenever possible. He now felt grateful for the overgrowth Tara had spurred. He wished he'd been at the community in person when it had happened. Seeing it on video had been striking, but he doubted it matched experiencing it live. Firefighters claimed the shift in the air was amazing. First, the smoke had cleared, the charring scent fading. In the next instant, they were overtaken by earthy scents of moss, green leaves, dew, and fresh-mowed grass. As they inhaled, they'd felt a sense of exhilaration. Only then had they noticed leaves unfurling, trees standing taller, grass turning from burnt brown and black to green. Had Nanor Kerkorian wanted to rebuild, she could have, for the land now was lusher and richer and healthier than before.

*She ought to thank us for that.*

The instant the thought ran through his head, Stranyero pushed it away. MacNeil wouldn't laugh at such a comment, as he never laughed, but he'd appreciate it. Sophia, on the other hand, found no humor in destruction, nor in death. Tara had brought Mrs. Kerkorian back, but that didn't negate the death. Fenton MacNeil had not meant for that to happen, had claimed he had done his best to prevent anyone from dying, but he must have known it was possible. He'd judged it a risk worth taking. That he hadn't asked Stranyero to take part didn't alleviate his responsibility. These were the methods the Brotherhood had always used, and Stranyero had stayed with the Order for decades after he'd first come to understand that.

The stalker had resurfaced, blundering through the trees probably a mile or so behind Stranyero. The sound carried on the breeze across the empty area. Stranyero ignored it, wiping the sweat from his forehead and pushing on past a cluster of burnt-out trailers near the community center. That building had survived fairly well, being made of brick, and its once-tended gardens now grew wild, filling the air with the scents of lilacs. Lily pads covered the entire surface of the pond beyond it, tiny frogs perching on several of them, their hooded amphibian eyes watching Stranyero as he skirted the pond. He felt as if they knew where he was headed. Knew that beneath the rifle in his bag was something else.

He found what he hoped was the grave five miles beyond the residential area, marked by a translucent diamond-shaped white crystal embedded in the ground. The crystal probably had some sort of significance, and if Stranyero understood what, he might know whether it was a grave marker. But he didn't.

It glowed in the early evening sunlight. No outline in the grass showed where a burial plot might have been dug. But he knew Maya Kerkorian's body had been moved from a cemetery in Glendale, California, in the late 70s, when Nanor Kerkorian had moved to Arkansas and founded the community. She'd wanted the grave hard to find and unmarked. Despite her communal nature, the woman obviously felt some privacy was in order. Stranyero wasn't sure her closest family members knew where the body lay, as the plot in Glendale still bore a gravestone memorializing both Maya and the baby she'd been pregnant with when she'd been killed. Anyone visiting the grave would never know that plot was empty.

He unzipped his bag and lifted out the rifle. His body tensed. Until now, his cover story of being a hunter would have been accepted without question. He unzipped the pouch beneath, took the shovel, and began to dig. It took several hours, but eventually he unearthed a coffin. He dug a trough next to it, dropped his tools into it, and jumped in after. He paused to listen, making certain no one was approaching who might try to trap him there.

*That's ridiculous. I could climb out again if dirt were dumped on me.*

He reassured himself that he had enough climbing equipment with him. He could jump atop the coffin and scramble out.

He heard birds chirping from above him, and wind whooshing through the trees.

He forced the coffin open. To his relief, only bones lay inside, the rest of the body—or bodies—having decomposed. Ideally, he'd collect only the fetal bones, but his research told him those had likely disintegrated. He wasn't sure he would have been able to sort them out regardless. He took instead any bone that hadn't clearly, to his untrained eyes, belonged to an adult.

By the time he finished, his velvet bag was full.

Marie Glaston sat in the end chair at the conference table, her back straight, her hands folded in her lap. Tara sat on the other end. Nanor Kerkorian had joined them. Oni hadn't yet returned from the cloister, and Cyril remained in the high rise with Fimi and two security guards. Tara had reserved a small conference room in an office building on Clark Street. The view was of an alley and loading dock three floors below.

"Can you hear?" Tara said. The laptop to one side showed a screen with the background of Sophia's study at home, but not Sophia. She'd moved away from it to lie on her couch, exhausted, but had said she would listen. Tara wanted her opinion about Marie before deciding how much to tell her.

"Yes." Sophia's voice was faint, but clear.

"Go ahead," Tara said.

"I heard back from the person who hired me," Marie said. "Not by phone, but by text from the number I had. I was told I could write down a name for you, but not to speak it, in case anyone is listening."

"Okay," Tara said. She slid a pad of paper across the table and a pen. Cyril had always been paranoid about the Brotherhood eavesdropping, and though she didn't see how they could have learned of this meeting place, she wanted Marie to speak freely.

Marie wrote something and slid it back.

Tara looked at the name. "Really?"

She didn't know why she felt surprised. Thomas Stranyero had been the one to tell Cyril that Holmes was Fimi's kidnapper, and Holmes had confirmed it. Now he'd sent Marie to get a journal that might help Tara. Maybe Sophia had been right about his change of heart, though that didn't explain why he'd disappeared.

She showed the page to Nanor. The older woman put on her glasses to read, then took them off and nodded. She seemed less surprised than Tara.

Tara texted the name to Sophia. They were both using disposable phones, so she didn't think the name would be intercepted or traced to either of them.

"Oh," Sophia said. "What number did you have for this person?"

Tara tried to read the emotion in her friend's voice, but Sophia sounded so tired, it was hard to say.

Marie wrote it, and Tara sent it over.

*Same one I had*, Sophia texted back.

Tara wondered if that were better or worse. The phone was working, but Stranyero wasn't answering Sophia.

"That's all I know," Marie said. "Other than this person claims to have never hired me before. For anything."

Tara nodded. Stranyero's way of emphasizing he'd had no role in the kidnapping, which Holmes had confirmed, but that perhaps Marie had.

"So do you work for the highest bidder?" Tara said.

"No," Marie said. "I was honest when I told you I run an antique shop. Bringing you the journal was a special project from my previous career, but that's over."

"But before," Tara said. "Highest bidder?"

"Not always. Some jobs I didn't feel right about. Most were perfectly legal, simply challenging, like getting this journal. Others were questionable because the laws governing the places where the objects were located remained unclear or were in themselves unjust. Others, I admit, involved what some might call theft. But always of objects. Often from people who'd obtained them by questionable means themselves."

Tara started to ask more, but Nanor shook her head. Tara waited, thinking Nanor meant to speak, but she didn't.

After a few moments of silence, Marie shifted in her chair. "Except once. I was working toward changing my life. I was offered enough to achieve my dream of buying the store. I'd found one that I wanted. Antique stores, as a rule, are more a labor of love than income-generating. This had an antique section, but also enough gift items, cards, and tourist items to make it turn a modest—very modest—profit. I didn't have enough for a decent down payment. I was afraid the owner would sell to someone else. And like many others, this job involved stealing from a thief, so I told myself I could justify it."

Tara gripped the phone in her hand. It answered a question that had never been completely resolved. Marie had taken Fimi, but not from Tara's family. From the first person who'd kidnapped her.

"So you had completed that phase of what you call your career," Nanor said. "Why return to it?"

"I was threatened with exposure for that last project," Marie said. "Paid well, but still threatened with exposure. And also, when I learned it might help you, Tara, I thought it was a way of making up—of easing your life given all the troubles you've had."

The threat of exposure fit with Stranyero, too. No law enforcement person had ever traced the kidnapping to Erik Holmes or mentioned Marie. But Stranyero said he'd followed a chain, and Marie likely had been a link in it.

"When were you told to bring the copy of the journal to Tara?" Sophia asked. Her voice sounded a bit more energized than before.

"When?" Marie said.

"Yes. And were you told to bring it directly to her? Was it looked at by anyone first?"

"There was a delay, but I always kept my copy. I gave you the exact one I made. After a few days, I was told to contact Cyril so it could be delivered to Tara"

"When were you told you could reveal who hired you?" Sophia said.

"Yesterday."

Tara's phone buzzed in her hand.

*We need to talk. Without Marie in the room.*

# 21

It took Nanor and Tara twenty minutes to return to the high rise so they could talk without Marie and away from the conference room. Sophia, at home on the narrow couch in her study, struggled to sit so that she could see Tara's face. She owed it to her friend to give the best information and advice possible and to be as clear-headed as she could be.

"Okay," Tara said. "What should I know about Stranyero?"

"I'd hoped he would appear again and tell you this himself. I reached him late this morning. He shared information with me. You and Nanor guessed he'd been behind Maya's death, and he confirmed that is true in a way. He wasn't the mastermind, or the driver, but he was in the car. He agreed with the decision."

Tara nodded, her expression unchanged. "I figured that might be the case."

"It was a long time ago," Nanor said. "But it is no less painful to hear that aloud."

"I believe over the years, especially over the last two years, his beliefs changed," Sophia said. Her throat felt dry, and her lips parched. "But I realize that can't make up for your loss. And there's more. He manipulated that poor, sick pregnant girl into coming to Tara."

"Alma?" Tara said. "He got Alma to set fire to Willow Springs?"

"No. Not that. Before that. He contacted her, pretending to be someone on her side, and convinced her to visit your biological father—the man you thought was your biological father—to get information about you."

"Ray? What? When?"

"While you were in Istanbul meeting Pir Ferit. Alma didn't learn a whole lot from Ray, but she got a sense of you as a person, which made it easier for her to approach your family and claim she sought your help. She gained their sympathy, which led Kelly to bring her to the cloister and you into the literal snake pit."

"That was Stranyero?"

Sophia swallowed two Advil from the bottle she kept in her desk and returned to the couch. Her head had been pounding since she'd spoken with Thomas. He'd always warned her he'd done terrible things, but she'd chosen not to consider until now the exact nature of them.

"Yes. He orchestrated it. His view at the time—only two years ago—was that it was the best way to take you out of the way so he could arrive at the cloister and obtain the letter while others were panicked searching for you."

"And that I might die was just a bonus?" Tara said.

Sophia felt sick to her stomach at the thought. She breathed deeply. "He did not believe you'd die. The odds of dying of a snake bite in the U.S. are near zero, and the cloister had anti-venom on hand. But he knew it could happen. And had it, you and Alma both would appear to the world as deluded young women pretending to have virgin pregnancies and fighting over who was more important. He did not think you'd be killed. So no martyrdom."

"So he manipulated a pregnant teenager, possibly pushing her into a delusional state, and he was absolutely fine with the idea that I might die," Tara said.

"Perhaps not absolutely fine, but yes, he was willing to risk that."

Nanor appeared on screen next to Tara, leaning forward. "Distressing as this is regarding the past acts toward Tara, it also suggests the Brotherhood does not fear killing Tara during the first 700 days of her daughter's life."

"I thought of that," Sophia said. "I couldn't ask Thomas about it without revealing what we knew, though now if the journal truly came through him there's no reason not to inquire. But perhaps the prohibition is only against killing the child. Or perhaps indirect actions are acceptable. Had the snakes caused Tara's death, it would have been at Alma's hands, despite that she'd been manipulated into it."

Sophia didn't relish talking with Thomas again. He hadn't said a word about why he'd left her abruptly, and despite the terrible things he'd told her today, she still felt the loss.

"And the man who came after me with a gun?" Tara said. "Was that at Stranyero's order?"

"No. He said no. He had no control over that man, who'd gone rogue from the Brotherhood. But he did use the man's chosen name—Raphael—when he manipulated Alma."

"So he did send Alma to Willow Springs."

"No, he did not. He claims someone else in the Brotherhood did that, also using the name Raphael, and that was when Thomas's views began to change. Or perhaps not began, but that's what turned the tide for him such that his conversations with me deepened, turned into a true exploration of his doubts. He saw himself in this other man, and was revolted."

"So before that he was only trying to draw you in. To manipulate you."

Sophia sighed. "Again he says no. He freely admits he hoped to learn information from me when we met for dinner the first time, just as I hoped to gain information from him. But he says he started calling me because he felt he could explore philosophical and religious questions. Which is all we talked about for the first few months. I saw an increase in his doubts around the time that he would have learned about the use of Alma as a weapon, though he obviously told me nothing about it at the time. His questions grew. His belief that the ends the Brotherhood sought justified any means wavered. Also, after his conversations with you, he could not bring himself to see you as the Antichrist, however that is defined." Sophia shut her eyes, trying to recall what else Thomas had said in their hurried conversation. "Cyril played a role."

"Cyril and Stranyero talked?"

"Only the times you already know about. But when Cyril kept seeing you as a good person, even after it became questionable whether you returned his feelings for you, Stranyero started to think Cyril might be right."

Tara's face had gone pale. "But he stayed in. He's still part of an organization that routinely manipulates a sick girl and plans arson and murder."

"He still says he's working from the inside."

"Do you believe him?" Tara said.

"I don't know. I always felt I knew if he was telling me the truth, and now I don't," Sophia said.

"How did he contact you?"

"He left me a message of sorts with a phone number. I found it today."

"What do you think?" Tara said. "Given that Stranyero apparently sent Marie, how much should we tell her?"

Sophia shut her eyes again to keep back tears. She didn't want her feelings to interfere with Tara's decision. "I think my view is irrelevant. I can't be objective about Thomas. It would be wrong of me to try to influence you. I'm afraid I've no advice to give."

Tara lugged the laptop the five blocks back to the conference room, her stomach churning. Nothing Sophia had said had truly surprised her, but it sickened her all the same. She couldn't decide anything about Stranyero now, but time was running short to figure out the ritual.

Nanor remained silent as they walked, and Tara did her best to let go of any conscious thought. She stared at the buildings around her, some soaring and glass, others squat and worn, others stately, and listened to the sounds of brakes and car horns and far off sirens. The bustle felt oddly calming. The people rushing around her didn't know about Tara's troubles, and the buildings would stand for decades after Tara was gone.

As they ascended the elevator to the eleventh floor, Tara shut her eyes. She wanted Marie's insights, and her gut told her Marie would be honest with her.

After they'd all settled at the conference room table again and reconnected with Sophia, Tara said, "Can I share information with you without you telling Stranyero?"

"Yes," Marie said. "My obligation to him is over."

Tara withheld the bookmark, but she showed Marie the photos of the shrines where its design appeared around the world.

"I can't tell you why, but the design at all these shrines might be significant for me," Tara said.

Marie looked at the first few photos. "Strange. It's the Star card from the Tarot deck, which I wouldn't expect to see at any religious shrine. Tarot started as a card game, and later was used as a divination tool. At best, religious people view it as a party game; at worst, as a tool of the devil. This card has a positive message, though. Healing the earth." She glanced at Tara, probably remembering footage of when Tara had done exactly that. "Which fits, I suppose."

"We think the identical vases the woman holds are important," Tara said.

"They're not identical," Marie said.

Tara glanced at the nearest photo. "They look like it to me."

"They're not." Marie slid one of the larger photos to Tara. "First, see here, and in every photo, there's what looks like a vase in one hand. It's held low, near the water, but the opening faces up, toward the sky. The liquid could as easily be arcing up from the lake into the vase as down from the vase into the body of water."

Tara looked at the photo under the magnifying glass. "You mean these tiny lines here? We thought they might be specks in the water."

"I disagree. Those markings are an indication of motion, and I read it as up, not down, while the other is down."

Nanor studied the photos as well, borrowing the magnifying glass from Tara.

"So the vases are the same, but the water or liquid differs," Tara said.

"Not exactly. While the vessels she holds in her right and left hands match in each photo, the vessels differ from one photo to another." She passed across another photo. "Compare those two."

"At the neck of each, you mean?"

Now that it had been pointed out, Tara saw that in some photos, the necks of the vessels were narrower than in others. She thought of the bookmark in her pocket, trying to recall if the vessels in the woman's hand appeared identical.

"And body shapes. Some are squatter and wider," Marie said.

"So each artist rendered them a bit differently," Sophia said. "Is that significant?"

"Yes, because these aren't different renderings of the same pieces. Some artists drew vases," Marie said, "and others drew urns."

"Urns." Tara thought of the tomb in her vision and shuddered. "Burial urns?"

"Yes."

Tara pulled a few more photos over to peer at, and Nanor, across the table, did the same. The idea of urns matching the vision, a vision Marie couldn't know anything about, made her decide it was worth showing Marie the bookmark.

Tara slid it across the table. The silver gleamed. "What do you think about this? It's where we first saw this design."

Marie studied it for several minutes. "It combines elements from the designs. Or vice versa—the designs use partial elements. On the bookmark, the woman holds a vase in one hand and an urn in the other. Liquid pours from the urn to the woman's feet. Liquid flows up, though, from the river—I'm fairly sure it's a river, here, not a lake based on its narrowness—into the vase. You could read these differences as male and female. In much traditional symbolism, the female receives, so she would be a vase, receiving the water from the river. The male gives or disgorges, so that would be the urn disgorging onto the ground."

Nanor raised her eyebrows. "You see these as sexual images?"

"Perhaps sexual. After all, reproduction usually is sexual," Marie said. "And these are supposed to have a message for Tara."

"But my reproduction wasn't sexual. My body produced my baby without sex."

"It could have to do with gender," Marie said. "Rather than sexuality."

"Marie's use of the word 'vessel' reminds me of a Bible verse," Sophia said. "In the first letter of Peter, he refers to woman as the 'weaker vessel'. Here, we have two types of vessels. One that could be viewed as female, the other as male, yet both are controlled by the woman."

"A woman who appears strong and calm," Marie said.

"Also, it is the Star card," Sophia said. "The sun was traditionally linked with male gods, the moon with female gods. The Star is neither."

"It's closer to a sun," Marie said. "The sun is a star, merely the brightest to our eyes on Earth."

"Yes. But the rest of the imagery is feminine. So this suggests a blend of both," Sophia said.

"None of which helps me right now," Tara said.

"It comports with my view," Nanor said. "Tara and her baby are here to right the balance, to counteract thousands of years of male domination of religion in the West."

"That sounds better than eliminating the male-dominated religions," Tara said.

"I am not convinced I am wrong about that," Nanor said.

"I'm obviously not familiar with your previous discussions," Marie said, "but couldn't it be to combine the two? The design suggests harmony to me."

Nanor shook her head. "My fear is, if combined, the male will still dominate, and the female will disappear."

"Regardless what it means," Sophia said, "It suggests we ought to search not only for a vase but for an urn."

"That I can't help with," Marie said.

# 22

Cyril carried Fimi as he and Tara made their way through the crowd in St. Louis' Union Station mall. Now that both Evekial and Marie knew Tara was in Chicago, it had seemed like the right time for her to leave the city, and she'd longed to spend time with her family. Plus, her mom had some news to share, though she hadn't said about what. Two security guards trailed them, far enough away to be inconspicuous, but close enough to intervene if anything threatening happened.

While Tara had been unconscious, the city had completed renovations and added a lower level to Union Station with more stores, a food court, and a games and amusements area. There, people secured by bungee cords flew high in the air doing flips and figure eights off of a giant trampoline. A few years ago, Tara would have loved such an activity. Now it made her dizzy to look at. She wasn't sure if it was a lingering effect of the coma or that she'd had so much real peril in her life that she didn't crave the adrenalin rush.

Fimi reached for another child's popsicle, so Tara bought her one, pleased that her daughter was communicating what she wanted with actions if not with words. She stayed silent, though, when Tara asked her if she wanted grape or pineapple.

"At least I can spend without worrying," Tara said. She wanted to focus on the positive, and she was grateful to Holmes every day for the funds he'd left for her. But it hurt her heart that Fimi still preferred Kali or Cyril to Tara, and that she still wouldn't speak. Between them, she, Sophia, and Nanor had reviewed all the materials Roger had provided and found no help regarding Fimi's muteness. On the one hand, that suggested it might not be a side effect of Fimi healing people. On the other, it left Tara without a solution.

They headed for the new underground walkway that was similar to the

Pedway in Chicago. This one led to the apartment building where Lynette Spencer now lived. The rest of the family had gathered there.

Cyril glanced behind them. "No one following who shouldn't be."

They zipped through a side door, circled back to be sure the guards had come in after them, and took the long way to Lynette's building where the doorman let them in only after checking IDs and calling ahead.

Once inside her mom's apartment, Tara slid the deadbolt above the burglar bar.

Her little brother Bailey ran over and hugged her.

"Hey, squirt," she said, though he was now nearly as tall as she was. He'd turned thirteen while she'd been in the coma, and his face had lost all its little-kid roundness. Bailey and Fimi both made her more conscious of the time she'd lost.

"You're back," he said.

"Looks like it," Tara said.

Her brother Nate hugged her as well, then perched on a stool at the counter between the kitchen area and the main room. Tara squeezed in next to her sister Kelly on the love seat. Kelly put her arm around her sister.

"This place is small," Tara said.

"It has to be, Tara," her mother said. With her weight loss and the gray that had crept into her blond hair, Lynette Spencer didn't look quite like the mom Tara remembered. "We have two households now. This is what we can afford."

Her mother didn't say "because of you," but Tara felt it. While she'd been in the coma, everyone had agreed the family would be less findable, and less of a target, split apart. She'd offered to help pay for a larger place with the money from Holmes' estate, but both her parents had declined, though they'd agreed she could help pay for the family home.

"I wasn't criticizing," Tara said. "Just commenting. I like it. That's a cool sleeping loft."

"I've barely used it myself. Kelly slept in it during the summer."

"It's still cool," Tara said. "So you said you have something to tell me?"

"I heard from Ray."

"What?" Tara said. "Why didn't you text me?"

"I heard from him right after you said you were coming home, so I thought in person was better. But you can't tell your dad I spoke with him."

"What? Why not?" Tara said. Pete Spencer, Tara's stepfather, was the man she'd always thought of as her dad. He knew that, and she couldn't imagine he'd be upset about her contacting Ray.

Lynette drew a chair over from the dinette and sat across from Tara. "Your dad's having a rough time dealing with all the changes. Megan's death, the family being split apart, your coma. Doubts about the church. He'll never say it, but he feels he failed, that he should have been able to do more."

"He has to know that's not true," Tara said.

Kelly squeezed Tara's hand. "He's been depressed. He started seeing a therapist."

"Why didn't you guys tell me?"

"We figured you had enough on your plate," Nate said. "Miraculous baby, miraculous coma recovery, crazy religious cult stalking you. You know, the everyday stresses of an ordinary life."

"He'll work through it," Lynette said. "He didn't want to worry you, so he didn't say anything."

"I—are you guys okay?" Tara said, glancing from Nate to Kelly to Bailey. She still felt protective of all her siblings, though Nate and Kelly were grown now, from all the years she'd watched out for them when their youngest sister, Megan, had been so sick.

"We're good," Nate said. "It's been rough for everyone with Megan gone, and we were afraid we'd lose you too. But we've been coping. While you were in the coma, when the family moved apart, we made a point to call or meet at least once a week to check in, make sure all of us were hanging in there."

And there it was again. The year of her life missing. Her brother Nate had finished college, her sister Kelly had started, Bailey was in junior high. All living apart, all trying to keep the family together. All during a time that to her had seemed like a few days or weeks at most.

"Okay," Tara said. "I'm glad to know that. But why would Dad be upset if you heard from Ray?"

"I just don't want him to feel worse that you need Ray's help and not his," Lynette said.

"If you think it's an issue, I won't say anything to him," Tara said. "So where is Ray?"

Lynette sighed. "In Europe. He refused to say exactly where, but he called me yesterday. You must have made an impression on Ely because he found someone who knew someone who got word to Ray that you were asking about him. Ray didn't know your new number, so he contacted me. He says right after you woke up from the coma, the same day the protestors stormed the hospital, he came home to find his place ransacked. He knew our family couldn't live at our house anymore because of those types of incidents, and he got spooked and took off."

"Did you ask him about what happened when you were in college?" Tara said.

"He didn't remember anything beyond what Ely told you about. He didn't know why the man wanted him to try the herbs. He did say herbs, not a drug trial. When he tried to find out about side effects, the number he had for his contact was disconnected, and the storefront where they'd met had been rented to someone else. He actually thought he might have hallucinated all of it except for the extra cash."

"You think he was telling you the truth?" Nate said. "He really didn't know what the potential side effects were before he took the herbs?"

"I think he wants to believe that," Lynette said. "It's easier than believing he risked harm to me and to any baby that might be conceived."

"But he didn't expect to conceive, right?" Tara said. "You were using protection?"

"It failed, but we were. Who knows, maybe it failed because of the herbs."

"Has anyone threatened him? Now, I mean, or before he went overseas?" Tara said.

"No, not that he told me. He just got frightened, and he has a friend from his prison days who's in a band somewhere in Europe, so he went there. If you really need him, he promised he'll at least talk to you by phone. But do you? Need him? He's pretty stressed, and we've already learned everything we can about what happened."

~

CYRIL SET a large cardboard box on the small square kitchen table and took off his coat. He'd picked Oni up from the airport and driven her to the studio apartment in downtown St. Louis that Tara had found through an apartment-sharing site. The apartment was a large rectangle, with a galley kitchen at one end, two double beds, a crib, and a pull out sofa at the other, and a living/dining area in between with a fireplace on the long wall opposite the door. Tara could have rented a place with separate bedrooms, but she felt better being gathered in one room, especially at night. She'd secured another apartment on the floor for the two security guards.

To comply with the trust's terms, Cyril had rented a second studio apartment across the hall. Now that Oni was back from Pennsylvania, he and Oni planned to stay there, with him guarding Tara and Fimi during the day and Oni staying with them at night.

Oni slit open the box and lifted a stone vase from it. "This is the one that was displayed in the cloister's main room. There are no carvings on it, but it might be important since there were two vases in that vision."

"I thought you didn't think the vision mattered," Tara said.

"I don't. But you do, so why not bring it? And there are two vases in the bookmark design."

"Actually, now we think it's two different vessels we need. A vase and an urn," Tara said.

"How can you tell?"

"They have different shapes," Tara said.

Oni shrugged. "Each of these is different." She took out a second, slightly larger vase. It was wider than the first, but didn't look like an urn to Tara.

The postcard-sized photograph Cyril had given her what seemed like eons ago—when she'd just discovered she was pregnant—lay on the table. Tara compared the vase before her to the image. Its color was similar to that in the photo. Worn swirls had been carved into the front. She couldn't quite make out what the drawing had been, but it wasn't a face.

"This isn't it," Tara said.

Fimi, in a highchair near the table, waved her hands at the vase.

"Wait," Oni said.

The second box contained one vase packed in brown paper. As Oni began unwrapping it, the sun slid behind the clouds, leaving the large room shadowed, so Tara flipped on the overhead light.

"See?" Oni held out the vase.

One side was worn, but when she inspected it Tara saw faint indentations that might be a woman's eyebrows, with a nose and the lips beneath it. She held the postcard next to the vase. As with the first time she'd seen the young woman's face, she was stuck by the expression of loss.

"This might be it," she said. She reached for the vase, wanting a closer look. The instant her fingers touched it, lightning flashed, thunder cracked, and the interior lights blinked out.

Another flash of lightning was accompanied by a bang inside the room. A streak of electricity shot from the fireplace and hit the photocopy of the journal, which was sitting on the coffee table. The pages burst into flames.

Tara let go of the vase in her surprise, but Oni caught it. Fimi began to cry.

Cyril grabbed the fire extinguisher from under the sink. He sprayed the flames, which sputtered in the foam, leaving charred bits of paper, just as Tara had seen in the vision.

Tara lifted Fimi, rocking her to soothe her, and stared at the singed coffee table and destroyed copies, heart pounding. The research could continue, as Nanor and Sophia had their own copies, but the burnt pages must be significant.

"Once it begins, it must end," she said, remembering what Protennoia had said after the journal had charred.

"But what does that mean?" Oni said.

Cyril opened a window near the double beds. "The lightning seemed to be triggered by the vase. Maybe once you start assembling what you need for the ritual, you need to complete it."

"Or what?" Oni said. "Terrible things will happen?"

"I'm guessing at the least more weather disasters," Tara said. She turned on the news. A newscaster warned of flash flooding and reported that the St. Louis Arch had been struck by lightning.

Fimi quieted. Tara pulled a kitchen chair far from the window and sat with her daughter on her lap. She was relieved that Fimi had been nowhere near the fireplace, and that she seemed undisturbed and happy for Tara to hold her.

"So this vase must be the key, if this isn't all a massive coincidence," Tara said. "But what about an urn?"

"I brought everything that could qualify as a vessel from the cloister," Oni said. "The leader I spoke to there said the vases were passed down to them from the Collyridians who came before them, but they don't know where those women obtained them. The only one who might have known is the former nun who passed away last year."

Tara studied the face on the ancient vase as she breathed the smoke odors mixed with the humid outside air from the open window. She wished the woman in the carving could speak to her and provide answers. "When I last talked to Sophia, she said she's still gotten nowhere. She consulted Professor Gutzman in Florence again, but she has nothing for us yet."

"How many people are you talking to?" Oni said.

"As many as I need to," Tara said. "We don't have a lot of time."

"Less talking. More doing. Didn't that journal say whatever you need will be within your grasp?"

"Which could mean within the knowledge of people I know," Tara said.

"I DON'T KNOW how I can help," Ray said. "I told your mom everything I remember about those men who came to see me, and what I did before you were born. Before you were conceived."

Tara paced around the kitchen table. The photos of the Star card design lay spread across it. She kept away from the fireplace, though Cyril and Oni had blocked it with fireproof screens and closed its flue. "What did they say to convince you to take part in the study?"

"I don't remember," Ray said. "I was just thrilled to get money for doing nothing. All I needed to do was keep a journal of what I took and my sexual activity and mail it to them."

"Your sexual activity?" Tara winced. She didn't really think of Ray as her father, but it still made her a little uncomfortable to hear about his sex life.

"Yes. Your mom didn't tell you that part? The herbs were supposed to counteract sexual problems some men have as a result of drinking or drugs."

"So they were happy you did drugs?" Tara said.

"It's part of why they chose me. Or so they said. They found me because I had small time drug arrests. But I was supposed to stop while I took the herbs."

Tara didn't know if her mother had been the target, and they'd tailored the cover story to fit Ray's lifestyle, or if they'd started with him and whoever happened to be involved with him was the unlucky woman.

"And you didn't find anything a little bit weird about all of it?" Tara said.

"It was all weird. I've told you before, though. That's the danger of addiction. Nothing else matters. It's about getting the money to get the next fix."

"Were you that bad off at that point?"

"Maybe not that bad. But someone offers me money to take part in a research study that encourages me to have sex? What college guy is going to turn that down?"

"You didn't worry about side effects?"

"It crossed my mind. But they said it was the third stage of trials, and that the worst effects had been drowsiness and dizziness, nothing long-term."

Rain drummed against the windows and on the streets and sidewalks outside.

"You didn't want to maybe check it all out? Do a little research?"

"Tara, I was nineteen. Three years younger than you are now. I've no doubt you would have looked at all of it, but at twenty you were a pre-med student. I had a half year of junior college to my name, and all I cared about was playing my guitar and enjoying life. They gave me some glossy literature, I signed on the line, I took the herbs. Sure, I panicked when I found out your mom was pregnant, but I didn't really think there'd be a bad effect. I would have left anyway. It's what I do."

Tara stared at the rain streaking the window above the kitchen table. It was definitely what Ray did.

"So why this time?" Tara said. "Mom said your place was broken into, but why did that make you run?"

"It was so soon after you woke up, and everything I had relating to you was gone. Every photo, every newspaper clipping. My laptop. Anything that might connect me to you. Gone."

"Like they were looking for something."

"Yeah. So I figured better to get out of their path."

"Had you had any unusual visits? Anyone who seemed interested in me? Anything else that made you feel threatened?"

"Nothing recently. But yeah, the break in made me feel threatened. And that young pregnant woman, Alma. She'd joined my church group and gotten information about you from me, and I had no idea she was doing it, then she used it to go after you. So I left. I figured it was better for you, too, if no one could find me."

Her mom hadn't mentioned that part, that Ray had wanted to protect Tara by leaving. She'd always seen him in the worst light possible.

Lightning flashed, and thunder rumbled in the distance. Tara glanced toward Fimi, who sat on the floor near the couch playing with a toy tanker truck. Unlike most children, storms didn't scare her. She saw them as exciting light and sound displays despite the lightning bolt through the fireplace the other day. Lynette had said Tara had been exactly the same way.

"You said not recently," Tara said. "Something unusual happened earlier?"

"Yeah, but I don't see how it had to do with you. It was seven or eight weeks after you healed Nanor Kerkorian and the earth. Every day in the mail for maybe two weeks, I got an envelope with a Madrid postmark. Inside was a drawing of what looked like a red-breasted robin on it. And underneath it, it said 'cot'. In small letters."

"Like a cot you sleep on?"

"I guess. And there was red dripping down from the bird."

"That's just weird," Tara said. "What made you think it had to do with me?"

"Nothing, really, other than it's strange, and everything that's happened to you has been so strange."

*As good a description of my life as any.*

"Did you save any of those pages?" Tara said.

"I put them in the back of that album I keep about you. So they got stolen, too."

~

"I GOT IN," Oni said. Her voice came in a whisper.

Tara peered at the screen. Oni was transmitting video with the camera on her phone from a small archeological museum in Crete. The image jumped, as photography was prohibited. Oni had her phone in a pouch around her waist with an opening. Most of what Tara saw were pillars and pedestals, though one display case filled with statues covered an entire wall.

"In the first through fourth centuries now," Oni said.

She'd walked through the fifth through eighth and had seen nothing that looked like what Professor Andrea Gutzman had described. Based on the journal, Marie's thoughts, and the vase Oni had brought back, Andrea had pinpointed urns made in the second or third country in Crete as the most likely ones to match the bookmark's design. This was the third and last museum that had collections that might encompass the urn Tara needed.

Tara held her breath. If Andrea was right, Oni might come across the urn at any minute.

"Look at these," Oni said. The reddish brown urns looked similar to the ones in photos Andrea had sent as examples. The video screen flipped higher and focused on a printed sign in Greek and English. Tara saw a reference to the third century but couldn't make out the rest of the words. "Oh, here—oh. No."

"What?" Tara said.

The screen showed a worn tile floor as Oni bent forward to read. "It says this case holds items that by legend belonged to the priestesses at a temple to Athena."

"So?" Tara said. Sophia and Nanor were working on some way to get the museum to part with the urn if they found it, but knowing it was there was a first step. Tara leaned toward the screen. "Oni? Is there an urn?"

"Not anymore," Oni said.

# 23

Oni tracked down a docent, who advised that the curator was out but would return the next day. A few minutes before noon the following day, Oni found the man in his office.

"The pieces are on long-term loan," the curator said. Tara could hear the voices, but couldn't see anything but the man's knees. He wore what looked like linen dress pants and spoke English as the British spoke it.

"To where?" Oni asked. "And why doesn't the display case say that?"

Tara wished Oni would sound less combative. She understood Oni's impatience. It had taken a day and a half to get to meet the curator. Tara felt frustrated, too, but she had a sense from the man's voice that he didn't like being hurried. He also probably didn't like being bombarded with questions from a stranger any more than anyone else would.

"We are short staffed, and someone tore down the sign a few weeks ago," he said. "We'll be posting a new one soon."

There were four pieces missing from the display case.

"How long ago were they loaned out?"

"About a year ago. I'll need to check the records, but I believe they're due back in six months."

"And where are they?"

"Various places."

Tara clenched her hands. They had only fifteen days left of the 700.

"Can I get a list?" Oni said. "With photos?"

"What's your interest in them?"

Tara bit her lip. She herself wasn't very good at spinning stories. She tended to blurt out the truth. But Oni easily spouted the cover story that she was a graduate student researching items potentially relating to the transition from goddess worship to Christianity in certain cultures. She said it without hesitation, not seeming as if she needed to think about it before answering, or as if she'd rehearsed it in her hotel room a hundred times.

"I only found out about them recently, and my paper is due at the end of the month," Oni said.

"Hm," the man said. "I'll see if I can locate a list and mail it to you if you'll give me an address."

"Is there any chance you could find it now?" Oni said. "I hate to rely on the mail."

"As you can imagine, we're quite short staffed. Not much funding for museums these days."

Tara gritted her teeth. In the time the man had spent chatting with Oni, she bet he could have looked through his entire office. It had taken twenty minutes of pleasantries before he'd told her about the pieces. But most people in Europe didn't rush through things the way everyone in the U.S. did. In normal times, Tara would probably appreciate that, but not now.

"If there's a way I can help—" Oni said.

"No, no, if it's that urgent, I will stay late tonight and find it for you."

"That'd be wonderful. Thank you."

"Where are you staying? I can meet you somewhere nearby for dinner and give you the list then."

Tara's stomach tightened. It was too hard to read the man's tone, so she didn't know if he was hinting at some sort of quid pro quo or merely taking advantage of meeting an attractive woman and hoping she liked him, too.

"I'm about a mile from here. Why don't you call me when you have the list, and we can choose a meeting place. Drinks are on me," Oni said.

AT BAR HAVE *view of street he'll take if he walks from museum*

Oni had tried the phone in the pouch again, testing it as she waited at the bar, but the ambient restaurant noise had made it impossible for Tara to hear anything but clinking plates and glasses. So they'd given up on that approach, and Oni had switched to texting.

Tara sat on the sofa. It was nearly one a.m. in St. Louis, and Fimi slept in her crib in the corner. Cyril lay on the double bed against the wall. Rain drummed against the windows. It had barely stopped since Tara had touched the vase, though the electrical storm had died down. The Mississippi and Missouri Rivers were both rising.

Ten minutes later Oni texted again.

*Think I C him turning corner*

Cyril rolled over and sat up. "Did they meet yet?"

"Not yet."

He poured decaf coffee for himself and heated water for tea in the microwave while Tara stared at the phone. It buzzed again as Cyril set a chocolate chai on the coffee table in front of her. She found the spicy cocoa scent calming, and she needed the caffeine to stay awake.

*Someone behind him*

*Going outside*

Another ten minutes went by with no further messages. Tara checked the phone twice to be sure the sound was on.

"Where are you?" Tara said, as if Oni could hear her.

Cyril read the texts over Tara's shoulder. "Maybe she met him on the street and had to put the phone away."

"Why? Everyone texts. He wouldn't think anything was weird if she's texting her friend about meeting a guy."

Cyril frowned. "Maybe it's different in Crete."

"Doubt it."

A half hour later, Fimi cried in her crib. Tara tried to soothe her back to sleep, but she kept crying until Tara lifted her out and brought her to the couch. Cyril sat at the kitchen table reviewing the latest translation notes Nanor had sent. He kept glancing at the phone.

"You're worried about her, too," Tara said.

"She can handle herself," Cyril said, but stared out the window. Tara joined him. The streets were shiny with rain and deserted. St. Louis wasn't a late night city.

At last the phone started buzzing.

*Guy on street mugged curator*

*Ran after him but couldn't catch up*

*Young guy skinny dark hair very fast*

*Stole curator's wallet keys and shoulder bag that had the list in it*

*At police station*

Tara and Cyril waited, playing blocks with Fimi, who insisted on throwing most of them onto the couch rather than building with them.

Cyril retrieved a red block and placed it on a wall Fimi was building. "I should tell you something."

"What?" Tara said.

"Oni and I—we've gotten pretty close."

"Close? As in, seeing each other?"

"Not yet. But there's an attraction there. For both of us, and I wanted you to know before anything happened."

"Oh."

Cyril touched her shoulder. "It's not that I don't still care for you. I do. But I think if you felt the same way, even with all that's going on in your life, it wouldn't be so hard for you to sort that out. When you really want to be with someone, it's not that complicated."

"You're probably right," Tara said.

She felt a weight in her stomach, though. She hadn't given Cyril any encouragement, and it wasn't fair to try to hold him back from finding happiness with someone else. She knew he'd stay her friend. Still, it felt like another loss. She bent over the blocks, letting her hair swing forward to hide her face.

Forty-five minutes later, Fimi was back in her crib, and Tara texted a question mark to Oni. She got no response.

Tara paced the floor. "Should I call her?"

"She'd text if she could use the phone," Cyril said.

Another fifteen minutes passed. "What if something's wrong?" Tara said. "If she had the list, she'd have told me by now."

"Probably. But I don't think you should call in case she is hiding the phone for some reason."

The phone buzzed again.

*Gave police description told them what happened*

*Filling out police forms*

*Don't want to seem too anxious about list*

*Will ask when he's done about other copies*

An hour later, Oni was still at the station. Tara figured either a mugging wasn't a priority, or the forms took forever. Oni texted at last that she was loaning the curator some cash, as his ATM card had been taken and all the banks were closed.

"I hope this isn't some sort of scam," Tara said.

The rain had slowed to a spatter. Out the window, water from the street flowed over the curbs and toward the buildings.

"She's smart," Cyril said. "She wouldn't fall for that."

A few minutes later, Oni texted that she and curator were heading back to the museum so she could get another copy of the list.

Cyril took out a deck of cards and dealt a hand of gin rummy. They played until the texts began again.

*At museum*

*Back office looks neat but he can't find the list*

*Not sure where he left it*

*Think someone broke in but no signs*

*Can't tell him that b/c he might suspect there's more than my grad paper at stake*

Cyril shook his head. "It has to be the Brotherhood. Or someone connected."

"You think they followed Oni?" Tara said.

"Maybe. Or they've been watching that museum. Or followed the same chain of thought we did."

"Suggesting Stranyero gave them the journal too," Tara said.

"Or they're monitoring him without his knowledge," Cyril said.

The phone buzzed again.

*Has electronic files on the exhibit*

*He's signing onto computer now*

Tara's hand started to ache, and she realized she'd been clutching the phone. She loosened her grip.

*Trouble getting in*

*Trying again screen opened*

*No*
"What?" Tara said.
*System crashed*
*all records gone*

## 24

"What about at his home?" Tara said. Oni had returned to her hotel room and called from her laptop. On the screen behind her was a twin bed and a small chest of drawers.

"I thought about that, but I was afraid whoever it was broke into his flat, too," Oni said.

"Right," Cyril said. "And if that was the case, and you were so eager to get that document, he'd think you were involved. You might end up detained by the police."

"Exactly," Oni said.

"But if he gets home and that's the case, won't he still think that?" Tara said.

"Yes, but he doesn't know my real name or where I'm staying. Neither do the police."

"Except you gave them a statement," Tara said.

"I showed them false papers. I'm not an idiot," Oni said.

"You just walk around with false papers?" Tara said.

"After so many guardians getting killed? You bet I do."

"So we're nowhere," Tara said.

"Not quite," Oni said. "I watched him sign in. I memorized his user name, password, and the site address."

Tara set her tea on the coffee table. "But if it's down—"

"Doesn't matter," Cyril said. "The museum must have a restore program, and they'll probably run it tomorrow. So we have Nate sign in and see what he can find. Even if the list isn't there, there'll be shipping information."

"Why not have Oni do it?" Tara said. Tara's brother wasn't a hacker on a grand scale, but he was pretty good. All the same, she didn't like asking him to do anything that could get him in trouble.

"I don't want to expose her," Cyril said. "Just because the curator doesn't know who she is or where she's staying doesn't mean the Brotherhood is ignorant. She should come straight home. Also, Nate'll know how to hide his tracks, and he might be able to find the shipping data from one of the local Fed Ex or DHL locations to see what the museum has shipped out recently."

Six hours later, Nate emailed them a list of all items shipped by the museum over the last four months. It was the most he'd been able to narrow it down, but it still included over forty items identified only by numbers. Tara clenched her teeth. If the pieces were all over the world, that couldn't possibly be enough time to find them all.

"But get this," Nate said when Tara called him. "All the items were sent to museums, universities, and religious locations. I researched each one in case you needed to contact them, and I found information for all but one. The Charles Darwin University East. There's a Charles Darwin University, but not with East as part of the name. Yet East has a separate website, a good looking one. It would fool anyone not looking for a scam. But there is no actual university."

"You're sure?" Tara said.

"Yeah. I could tell you all the ways I verified that, but it'd take about an hour."

"It must be a cover," Tara said. "Whoever got the urn didn't want anyone to find out where it was sent or realize the urn was the important piece."

"What about the address for the University?" Cyril said.

"Bogus," Nate said. "It's in Australia, but the street address is a restaurant called Gillanbone. It's been there for six years. And before you ask, yeah, I called and the person who answered said they never heard of the Charles Darwin University East. I was the second person to call and ask today."

"Second," Tara said. "That answers one question. The mugger was after the list."

"Or the curator's trying to track down his items," Nate said.

"Maybe," Tara said. "But he must have a lot to do after the break in, and he didn't seem too concerned about the items that had been loaned out when he was talking to Oni."

"The University name or address must mean something," Cyril said. "And the items went somewhere."

"Other records in the museum's system show the pieces destined for Charles Darwin University East were picked up. So the curator had no way of knowing the address was bad," Nate said.

"I'm surprised you accessed so much," Tara said. "Could it be some sort of set up to lead anyone who looks down a wrong path?"

"I don't think so. Yeah, the museum doesn't seem too worried about hacking, but I don't see any reason why it should be. They don't have a lot of valuable items or cash. It's a very small scale museum."

"So the urn and the other items aren't valuable?" Tara said.

"Based on the records, not much there is, at least not compared to the more significant archeological museums. If I were the curator, I'd've wondered why a university wanted to borrow that urn and why a grad student also was interested in such a short time period."

"He might be wondering that," Tara said. "But hopefully Oni didn't say anything that'll lead back to us."

~

STRANYERO SET the velvet bag on the altar. The bones inside it clinked. Beneath the inverted crucifix, a coiled snake enclosed in a terrarium stirred from its slumber.

The tassels of Evekial Adame's loafers showed beneath his bright red robe as he inched further away from Stranyero and the terrarium. "If we're about to do what I think we are, I still say this is premature."

"It matters little to me what you say." MacNeil strode toward the altar from the baptismal area. "You are radically uninformed. The guardians interfere with our efforts, now we'll interfere with theirs."

"I don't know what that means," Evekial said.

"That doesn't surprise me." MacNeil lifted the snake and placed it across his own shoulders. It settled around his neck. Stranyero had to give him credit. His florid face didn't show a bead of sweat. He must have been practicing all these years, anticipating the possibility of a day like today.

Evekial edged further away.

"But Evekial has a point," Stranyero said. "Every text says a new cycle can't be started until the current virgin and her offspring are dead. And that we can't be the ones to kill them."

"I neither confirm nor deny your interpretation of my intent or this ceremony. Regardless, every text," MacNeil said, "is all of two texts. The rest have been destroyed or lost, so no one knows what the others said."

"There are three, if you include the journal located in Our Lady of Sorrows," Stranyero said. He'd held back on admitting he'd obtained the journal and knew its contents when he'd made his deal with MacNeil. If he revealed it now, it could undermine all his efforts. Before he decided whether to do that, he needed to know what ritual MacNeil was planning.

"And if we had a copy of that journal, I'm certain it would say the same thing," MacNeil said.

*Not exactly*, Stranyero thought.

"Does the Cardinal approve of this?" Evekial said, eyeing the snake. Its head glided down and around MacNeil's waist. "A premature ritual can unbalance the energies, creating bad karma for all of us."

"Cut the crap," MacNeil said.

"I've built my life on these tenets," Evekial said.

Stranyero inwardly shook his head. When Evekial had started the Church nearly forty years ago, he'd done it half-laughingly, saying what a good cover it was for their work, with the added bonus of donations from those who took it seriously. Over the decades, though, he'd begun to drink the pig's-blood, both literally and figuratively. Or he'd always bought into the beliefs he'd professed to ridicule and was having the last laugh on them by getting the Brotherhood to support them.

"No one buys your mix of New Age and Satanism with a side of insanity," MacNeil said. "If you're afraid to take part, you can leave. But if you leave, that's it. No more funds for your shiny altar, no more denunciations from the pulpits, keeping you in the news. This church will be converted into a useful outpost for one of our allies."

Stranyero put his hand on MacNeil's shoulder, avoiding touching the snake's body. He'd handled snakes before, it was a right of passage, but he didn't enjoy it. "Breathe. This can't be good for you. And you're disturbing your mascot there. Evekial annoys me as well, but he has a good heart."

MacNeil took a deep breath and let it out gradually. He'd confided in Stranyero that his blood pressure medication hadn't been working as well as his doctor had hoped. He was under strict orders to cut back on work and stress. Both of which were impossible, so he'd asked Stranyero to do the unthinkable—remind him to remain calm. Stranyero had taken the confidence as a sign that he'd won back MacNeil's trust, though given the man's mercurial nature, that might be temporary.

"The Cardinal instructed me to do whatever is necessary to deal with Tara Spencer," MacNeil said. "I deem this necessary."

Evekial inched farther from MacNeil and the rattlesnake and closer to the altar and the exit beyond it. "All right. I'm with you."

"Good. Find me the candles. And robes for Thomas and me, but not those ridiculous red and black ones."

"Those are all I have," Evekial said.

Stranyero waved toward Evekial's study. "Send your assistant out. One of the area churches must have a few they can lend."

The city of Chicago was rife with churches and temples, many of which had at least one clergy member who belonged to a prayer circle or Bible study group tangentially connected to the Brotherhood despite knowing nothing of the Order itself. It made accomplishing large tasks simple.

"It's still pouring rain," Evekial said.

"Does she not have boots?" Stranyero said.

"He, and he's afraid of lightning."

MacNeil sighed, shoulder heaving. "This city has skyscrapers everywhere. Lightning isn't going to bypass the Willis Tower and the John Hancock Center and a hundred other tall buildings to hit him. Tell him it's his job."

The snake bobbed its head from side to side.

Evekial swallowed hard and headed for the door that led to the baptismal font and his study.

MacNeil sighed. "Now that that's settled." He motioned toward a notebook that sat on the nearest pew.

~

ONI DROPPED her duffel bag next to the couch. "I think I know who took the urn. My cousin."

"Your cousin?" Tara said as she slid over to make room for Oni on the couch.

"My cousin gave you the bookmark in Paris, and she gave me the map a year before that. Sometime after she met you and before she died, she must have arranged for the urn to be retrieved so it could be available to you when you woke up."

Cyril walked over from the kitchen area holding Fimi. "If that were true, why wouldn't she send it to Tara?"

"Too easy for it to fall into the wrong hands while she was in the coma. Plus, the idea is to be sure different people have parts of the puzzle so the Brotherhood can't stop us by getting rid of one person."

"I still don't get why you think your cousin was involved," Tara said.

Oni tightened the ponytail holder at the back of her head and smoothed her jeans. "You will. First, it was picked up by someone from a fictional university, so we know it wasn't actually taken for an exhibit. Second, the fake university is in Australia. My cousin's favorite book was *The Thorn Birds*."

Cyril handed Fimi over to Tara, took out his phone, and started typing into it.

"And?" Tara said.

She'd never read the book. From her first year of college on, most of her reading had been non-fiction related to her class work. When she had read novels, they had been suspense. But she'd stopped that soon after she'd become pregnant. With her entire life rapidly becoming one threat after another, reading about other people, often women, facing danger and death didn't feel like entertainment.

"She was always saying she wanted to live on an Australian sheep station like Drogheda, the one in the book," Oni said. "She walked around speaking with an Australian accent, and she decided to become a Catholic because of Father Ralph. My mom tried to explain to her that the relationship between the main character and Father Ralph wasn't exactly an endorsement for joining the Church, but she didn't get that until she was a lot older."

Cyril looked up from his phone. "Gillanbone."

"Yes," Oni said. "Cyril texted me that the name of the restaurant at the fake university's address was Gillanbone."

Tara raised her eyebrows. "So?"

Cyril answered. "That's the name of the fictional town in Australia near the sheep station where the family lived."

"So your cousin left a clue you'd understand," Tara said. "And created a fake university website. Would she know how to do that?"

"Probably," Oni said. "She had her own business and created her own site for it. And all she needed was to fool the museum enough to let her retrieve items that weren't all that valuable on their own anyway."

"Nate said the website's designed to appear as if it's been around for decades, but it was started a month after she met me at the Paris Flea Market and gave me the bookmark," Tara said.

"Which still doesn't tell us what happened to the items," Cyril said.

"If she left a clue based on *The Thorn Birds*, would she have left something else in a copy of the book for you?" Tara said.

Oni shook her head. "She didn't read paper books. Anyway, her brother was the executor of her estate, not me. So if she meant to leave a message, she wouldn't have done it that way."

Oni walked to the window. Another storm had started, and lightning streaked down from a heavy layer of clouds. Three seconds later, thunder rumbled. Several of the older downtown office buildings and a lot of homes along the rivers had flooded over the last two days.

"Might she have told her brother something?" Tara said.

"I doubt it. But I'll ask him if she said anything strange, or anything about the book."

"Did he know she was a guardian?" Cyril said.

"No. Her mother told her and me, and we were the only ones in the family. We were told there were other guardians throughout the world, but most don't know anything specific about the others."

Tara nodded. She'd met one of them before Oni. Pir Ferit, the Sufi elder who had been killed soon after she'd visited him.

"And your cousin lived in Paris," Cyril said.

"Her home was in Madrid, actually, when she died, but she spent a lot of time in Paris."

"Madrid," Tara said. "Ray. He got envelopes from Madrid. A few weeks after I went into the coma, after I healed Nanor. No return address."

Oni nodded. "It makes sense she'd send something to someone else you knew. So there'd be multiple ways you might find what you need. What was in the envelopes?"

"Each one had a drawing of a robin red breast, what he thought was a robin. Dripping what looked like blood. What's a thorn bird look like? Is it a real bird?"

Cyril did a quick search on-line and found a photo of a red-breasted bird some people referred to as a thorn bird.

"That has to be why those were sent to Ray. The envelopes were from your cousin," Tara said.

"Which put them within your reach," Oni said. "And Ray's a good choice—someone she knew you'd talk to, but who was a little bit removed. Who wouldn't understand, but who would remember. What else was on the drawings? Anything?"

"The word cot."

"Cot," Oni said. "That I don't understand. What the hell?"

"It's your cousin," Tara said.

Tara called both, but Sophia and Nanor had no ideas based on the journal.

Cyril printed the word in large letters on a piece of paper and set it on the table between the three of them.

"It has to relate to the urn and the other items," Cyril said.

"But cot?" Oni paced. "What was she thinking?"

"A Google search of the word brings up camping equipment," Cyril said. "Second page has more of the same, plus Commissioned Officer Training for the

Air Force. A market report called the Commitments of Traders. Oh, and Columbia Time."

"Unless the urn is hidden at a stock exchange, air force base, or South American country, not helpful." Tara looked at the search results. "But those're all acronyms. If it's an acronym, the T could be for Tara."

"Something of Tara," Oni said.

Tara and Cyril spoke together. "The Church of Tara."

~

STRANYERO STARED at the Latin words on the lined yellow page. Beyond those phrases commonly used in the Latin mass, Stranyero recalled little of what he'd learned of the language in Catholic high school. He caught a reference to the second creation story in Genesis, the one where Eve came from the rib of Adam rather than being created by God simultaneously with Adam, and another to Abraham's wish for a son.

"We'll start without the robes," MacNeil said. "First hour, Thomas, you repeat your section aloud while I pray in silence. Evekial, while your assistant finds us robes, you personally track down our next two participants. Send one in after Thomas exits. Thomas will shred the pages he read. I'll give our second participant his instructions. When he leaves, send in the third. You, Evekial, will be the fourth, then we'll rotate through again. About forty minutes per session. That's it. Go."

Evekial scurried from the room, letting the heavy door between the chapel and the baptismal area bang shut.

"How many times are we rotating?" Stranyero said.

"As long as it takes. Why? Have you somewhere else to be? With the lovely Sophia for instance?"

"I made a clean break," Stranyero said. "I simply have business to attend to, which you interrupted."

"You can't leave. I need you to keep eyes on Evekial when the other two take their turns. I don't want him spying and trying to piece together the entire ceremony."

The secrecy suggested it might be the Spark of Life after all. The use of the second Genesis creation story and the fact that MacNeil had handwritten the Latin, which must have taken him hours, also supported that idea.

"You'll remain in the chapel throughout?" Stranyero said.

"I will." MacNeil smiled. "It'll be like a filibuster. I hope my bladder will hold out."

So if it was the Spark of Life, MacNeil was the one man in the Brotherhood who knew the entire ritual. Stranyero's heart felt heavy. He hadn't expected to feel disappointed at this late stage that MacNeil remained higher in the Order despite all Stranyero had done, but he was. On the upside, once Evekial took his turn Stranyero would have some freedom, as MacNeil needed to stay in the chapel.

He sat in the first pew, ready to begin.

"Standing," MacNeil said. "Always standing. But be sure our friend left before we begin."

Once Stranyero confirmed the study, baptismal area, and vestibule were empty, MacNeil motioned him to start chanting.

TARA REACHED ROGER THAT EVENING, calling as she sat at the kitchen table while Cyril read to Fimi on the couch and Oni read through the further translation notes Nanor had made while Oni had been in Greece.

Tara asked Roger if any items had been sent to the Church of Tara by donors. She didn't identify Oni's cousin, the imaginary university, or the museum, not wanting to share too much.

"We get donations all the time. Things people feel resonate with what we stand for or with what they know about you."

"How many?"

"Items? We've gotten hundreds. Maybe a thousand."

Tara's heart sank. That was a lot to go through. "What sorts of items?" she said.

"Why? Do you think we're doing something wrong?"

"No, no. I'm actually hoping to get some insight on a problem I'm trying to work out. Sorry, I know that's really vague, but I don't want to say more right now."

"You still don't trust me," Roger said.

*Can you blame me?*

But Tara couldn't antagonize Roger now. "We haven't had the best experiences together, and I really don't know you that well," she said. "But it's not that. It's more of a..." Tara's mind flew through everything Roger had said to her about his center. "...a personal spiritual issue. If I reach a point where I'm at peace with it, I'll share."

"Yeah, all right. I'd appreciate that. Knowing more about your journey will inspire our members in their own quest for awakening."

"Great. So any items you've gotten spontaneously from donors?"

"Spontaneously?"

"Yeah, where you didn't make a direct request?"

"Oh, sure. Most are like that. I've yet to go through all of them."

"But the ones you have gone through, what sort of things do people send?"

"Everything from crystals to gold jewelry to dishes to clocks. You never know what has meaning to a person."

Tara wanted to ask directly about urns or vases, but she didn't want to tip her hand. "How about larger items? Dishes, pottery, art?"

"Yeah, that too."

Tara shifted position to stretch her legs toward the galley kitchen. She flexed and released her foot as she spoke. Her motor skills had improved a lot over the last week, and she'd gotten lax about her physical therapy exercises. Doing them while talking to Roger helped ease her tension. "What do you do with it all?"

"We haven't completely decided. Jeremy wants to sell anything valuable, like the gold jewelry, to help fund the center. He says it's no different from someone sending us a check. But I feel like we ought to figure out why it matters to each person and see if we can put it to some use in our center. And if not that, maybe donate it somewhere that would be consistent with our mission."

Tara had to admit that it sounded like Roger was serious about trying to do good. And his description of Jeremy fit with what she remembered of her ex-boyfriend. He'd worked in his family's restaurant for years, including while pursuing his MBA, and had been the most practical of all the Turanos.

"So you still have everything that was donated?" Tara said.

"Yes."

Tara let out a sigh. "Is it all at the center?" She couldn't bring herself to call it a church.

"Yeah, pretty much."

"What's not?"

"Jeremy took some items to be appraised. The ones he thought might be worth something. He said we ought to know the value before we made a decision, which I guess is right. Good business anyway."

Tara had no idea whether Jeremy would see an old urn as potentially valuable. She didn't think he knew anything about antiques or archeology, but he'd probably wonder about it. "Which items?"

"I don't know. I left that to him. I'm not about money or profit. I concentrate on the messaging, emotion, and spirit."

Tara took a sip of water before speaking. She was back to wanting to shake Roger, but only because she needed answers so badly. He and Jeremy actually sounded like good partners. One to make sure the bills were paid, one to run events and classes and deal with people. If he was telling the truth. "Did he sell any of them?"

"Not that I know of," Roger said.

Tara wondered if Roger would know. She wanted to think Jeremy wouldn't cheat his business partner, but he hadn't exactly been forthright in his relationship with her. Her fingers tightened on the phone. The urn could have been sold for cash and be who knows where. She hoped Oni's cousin had considered that, that she'd only felt safe shipping the urn if it didn't look valuable. Maybe it was beat up and chipped and looked worthless.

"Do you know how many items he got appraised?"

"No idea."

"Do you think half of them?" Tara said.

"No, no, not half. Maybe ten percent. Because he was complaining that people send us junk, and now we're going to have to deal with it. Spend money disposing of it is what he said. So most of it we should still have."

Ten percent of a thousand was still one hundred. But better than if Jeremy had removed all of it.

"I'd like to look through it. What's there at the Center."

"Sure," Roger said. "You have a key. I told you, you can go in any time. Just try to leave things the way you found them. And it's better if you come outside of business hours if you don't want to get attention from the members. Our first classes start at 9:30."

"Okay."

Tara glanced at the clock. Already it was near ten at night, and with that schedule, she'd need to be at the center by 5:30 to have time to open very many boxes. If she had to extend into normal business hours, she would. It was more important to find the urn now than anything else.

"I can look for you if you tell me what you hope to find," Roger said.

"No. Thank you, but no. I'm not even quite sure what I'm looking for."

"So true for all of us," Roger said. The lofty tone in his voice edged her opinion back a notch. He sounded like he was playing a role.

"I'll probably go tomorrow," she said.

"Just leave everything as you found it, or Jeremy will have a heart attack."

"I'll do my best," Tara said. That her best might include needing to take one of the items with her was something she decided it wiser to omit. Time enough to tell him afterwards if what she needed was there.

Before ending the call, Tara confirmed with Roger that the pedestrian bridge to the island wasn't in danger of washing out with all the rain the St. Louis area had been getting. Like Choteau Island, though, the island where the Church stood had been built high above the water level. Roger said there were massive puddles forming, but at least a handful of members had made it there every day over the last week.

While she'd been talking, Cyril had checked different weather sites. Little additional rain was expected in the next few days.

"So we go first thing tomorrow morning," Tara said. "Before the Center opens and, I hope, before Roger thinks to tell Jeremy about my call." She turned to Oni. "Can you stay in the car on the Missouri side with a couple of the guards to let us know if anyone else crosses the bridge? You can join us if there's any sort of problem."

"You're expecting trouble?" Cyril said.

"Nothing specific," Tara said. "But I'm always expecting trouble."

"What about Fimi?" Cyril said.

"I'll bring her with. So far, when she's been with me, she's never come to harm or been taken away."

Cyril nodded. "I'd feel better if I stay outside the church with at least one guard to keep an eye out while you look inside. So you should bring someone else to help you search and keep watch on Fimi."

"I don't want a crowd," Tara said. "The more people, the more likely to draw attention."

"Not a crowd. Just one other person. Someone you know won't tell anyone else."

"I'll ask my mom."

"And the ten percent of the items Jeremy might have taken?" Oni said.

"That's my next call," Tara said.

## 25

Even to Vicki, Tara didn't want to say too much without knowing how likely her former best friend was to help. She started by asking if Jeremy had stored items from the Church of Tara at his home.

"There's nothing at his place unless it's really small," Vicki said. "He's got a house, but it's tiny. No basement, no attic. Just a kitchen, living room, and bedroom."

Tara wondered if Jeremy lived alone, but she didn't ask. The girl she'd been a few years ago would have wanted to know, despite how badly things had ended, despite that Jeremy wasn't the person she'd thought he was. But the Tara of today didn't have room for that girl's feelings.

"Does he have any sort of antiques or old items that could have come from the center?"

"Jeremy? His taste is early modern Ikea, all assembled himself despite his total lack of building skills. It's all on a slant."

"What about your mom and dad's? Could he have stored anything there?"

Vicki was living with her parents while she finished college. "We all have things here," she said. "You know the basement."

Tara had spent so much time when she was growing up at the Turanos they'd taken to referring to the second twin bed in Vicki's room as Tara's. "Yeah, I think there's a few things of mine there, too."

"I haven't noticed anything new downstairs."

"Would you? Notice if anything were different?"

"Maybe not. You want me to see what I can find?" Vicki said.

"Yeah. Please. Before your parents get up tomorrow."

Tara heard water running in the background. "Okay. I guess I can. Sorry to sound so unenthusiastic. I'm on this two-week cleanse and the no-caffeine part is making life hell. Getting up tomorrow morning—let's just say I'm not looking forward to it without coffee, even if I go to bed right now, which is what I was going to do."

"I wouldn't ask if it wasn't important," Tara said. "Really important."

"Really? Okay, what am I looking for?"

"Old vases, jars, urns, anything like that. Old as in first through tenth centuries."

"I'll just look for very old. I'm majoring in art history not archeology."

"You should probably come up with a reason in case your parents ask what you're doing. I don't want them to mention anything to Jeremy."

"I'll tell them it's related to school."

"Great. Text me if you find anything, okay?"

"Will do."

"And don't mention to anyone I'm going to the center."

"Got it."

THE SUN SHOWN down as they tramped across the island. Tara's limp was completely gone, and she felt fully recovered physically, but even so, the hike was a challenge. As predicted, the skies remained clear, and despite the early morning sun being no more than a faint yellow ball lifting from the horizon, it was hot. Humidity made the air feel thick to breathe. Tara and her mom were both soaked with sweat, as was Fimi, though the toddler didn't seem to mind. She peered around at the trees and flowers as she walked, and she wasn't fazed by being carried when the mud made the area impassable for someone so small.

Tara wiped her forehead and hit the bell on the center's door. Despite precautions, she half-expected Jeremy to be there. She let her breath out after a few seconds when no one answered. Feeling grateful to Roger, she waved her key fob over the electronic box. He might be a publicity hound who'd sold her out on national television, but at least he was being supportive now in exchange.

Oni had parked near the bridge in Missouri. They'd decided she'd draw less attention alone. Two guards sat in a car in a pull off area a mile away, ready to drive to Oni at her call or Tara's. Tara had seen no one else during their walk across the island, but it was only five-thirty a.m.

Cyril stationed himself, along with another security guard they'd brought, outside the doors of the Church of Tara.

Inside, Tara and Lynette took off their mud-caked boots and put on heavy slipper socks from the bin. They found the storage room, and Tara's heart sank at the stack of boxes. Vicki had texted at midnight that she'd finally found what she thought were Jeremy's boxes in the attic rather than the basement. Tara awoke to find two more texts with updates saying she'd seen nothing that matched Tara's descriptions so far, but she'd start again in the morning. Just in case they found the urn, Tara had called Nanor and asked if she and Kali could come to St. Louis. With only ten days left, if the urn provided the last key to the ritual, she wanted them all in the same place.

Fimi sat in the center of the storage room on a play mat Tara had brought with. Cyril came in briefly to help sort boxes by size and weight. After he returned to his post outside, Tara and Lynette used box cutters to open the first row. They took out each item and replaced it. They were on the third row when Tara's phone chimed.

*On my way found something*

Tara answered, asking for more information, but Vicki didn't respond.

"She's probably already driving," Lynette said.

"I should have told her to hide anything she found for us to look at later. I don't want her driving around with it. Or carrying it. What if it breaks?"

Her call went to voicemail. Tara glanced at the time stamp. Vicki had sent the text half an hour before.

"The reception here probably isn't the best," Lynette said.

"Yeah," Tara said, but she was already envisioning Brotherhood members blockading Vicki's car and stealing whatever she'd found the way they'd done to Tara and Sophia in Florence.

"Don't let your imagination run wild," Lynette said. "There's nothing you can do. At least if she brings the item here, if it's what we need, we can stop hunting through all this."

Twenty minutes and twenty boxes later, Tara heard Vicki's voice, "Hey."

Tara stood, her knees popping. "We're back here. Or I am."

Her mom had gone into the office to try to find something else to entertain Fimi.

Vicki bounced into the room. Her perfume scented the air with a mix of citrus and spice. She had a beaded purse over her shoulder, but it wasn't large enough to hold a vase or urn. Tara felt relieved that there was no chance what she needed had been broken, but disappointed that she still needed to search through all these boxes.

"There's good news and bad news," Vicki said. "Bad news is Roger babbled to Jeremy about you coming here, and now he's on his way. He doesn't want you 'rifling through' the storage area."

"What is his problem?"

It seemed ridiculous after all she'd been through and everything at stake, but Tara felt her stomach tighten at the thought of seeing Jeremy. He'd reacted so badly to the news that she was pregnant, especially considering he'd been cheating on her with a hostess at the Turanos' restaurant. She hadn't seen him since, and she'd never quite forgiven him. The bizarre part was that he seemingly hadn't forgiven her, though what she had done wrong in his book she couldn't imagine now that, to her mind, it must be clear to him that she had not, in fact, cheated on him. Unless he still didn't believe that.

"Sorry. Shared genes definitely doesn't mean I understand him," Vicki said. "The other thing is, I looked at every box. No vases or urns."

"I thought you said there was good news."

"I found this, which looks pretty old and shows a woman holding vases."

Tara took what looked like a worn medallion. It had the Tarot Star card design.

"She is holding vases, right?" Vicki said.

"Yeah, this is amazing. Was there anything on the box saying where it came from?"

"Yeah, but it's just a mailbox number from Australia. I took a photo of it. I also hid the box in my closet."

Where the fictional University stood. It must mean something.

Tara glanced at the time. They had only an hour before the center opened. Vicki took Lynette's abandoned box cutter and slit open more boxes, and Tara began looking at addresses, hoping for something that might have a clue in the return address.

Forty minutes later, she found five with Australian return addresses, two boxes from Madrid, and two from universities.

There were two urns among them. Tara examined one, repacked it, and set it to one side as a maybe. She noted the box number and content in a note on her phone. She meant to keep a log of anything she took to give Roger when it seemed safe to do so.

Vicki took out the other urn. Unlike the previous one, this had a lid, and it had tiny holes punched into it. The color matched that of the vase Tara had at home. Vicki pointed to a depressed circular area at the front. "The medallion?"

"Let's see."

Vicki handed Tara the urn. Unfamiliar lettering circled the opening, and more of it had been carved into the inside of the urn. Tara took the medallion with the bookmark design from her pocket and fitted it into the circle.

The back room lit as lightning flashed. At the same instant, the entire building seemed to shift, knocking Tara and Vicki to the ground.

# 26

A booming sound came from outside, and the whole building shook. It reminded Tara of when she'd heard the top of a large truck slam into an overpass near her job at a Laundromat during college. But no vehicles were allowed on the island.

"Something hit the building," Vicki said.

Tara jumped to her feet and headed for the office. "I don't think so."

Vicki followed.

Droves of rain had begun again, pounding the Church's roof. In the office, Lynette stood under a doorway, holding Fimi in her arms. The toddler didn't seem upset. She clapped her hands together when she saw Tara.

Splattering sounds filled the room as the rain hit harder.

"It felt like a small earthquake," Lynette said.

"Earthquakes and thunderstorms at the same time?" Vicki said.

"It's possible." Lynette reached around Fimi and took her phone from her pocket. "I'm surprised I didn't get an alert. Oh. No service."

Fimi pointed over Tara's shoulder. "Mommy. Snake."

Tara froze, transfixed by Fimi's first words. Tears filled her eyes. "Oh, sweetheart."

"Snake!" Fimi pointed.

Tara looked over her shoulder, expecting to see a tiny garden snake from the weeds outside. One could easily have entered with them without being noticed or found its way in here earlier and nested among the boxes. She was ready to kiss it, she was so happy Fimi had spoken.

Instead, she saw the multi-colored tail of wide serpent, similar to the one she'd seen in her visions. It slithered away from the office and toward the main room.

"Can you see that?" she said to her mom.

"What?" Lynette said.

Tara glanced at Vicki. "The snake."

Vicki shook her head.

"Stay with Fimi, stay under the doorway," Tara said.

"There could be aftershocks," Lynette said.

"I'll stay near doorways," Tara said.

She hurried after the serpent that only she and Fimi could see, her heart rate elevating. But she didn't feel frightened. In Armenia, when she'd seen a serpent it had been multi-colored and turned into the woman who called herself Protennoia and offered Tara advice and peace. And if the advice hadn't worked out perfectly, it hadn't been frightening.

Lightning flashed again, illuminating the railing on the stairs to the tower as Tara entered the main room. Roger had mentioned there was more storage upstairs, and Tara had planned to check it next, but she didn't intend to go into a tower in the aftermath of an earthquake. The serpent glided toward the stairs. Tara clicked off a photo, though she didn't expect the snake to appear.

She heard footsteps behind her and turned around. Lynette stood clutching Fimi under the doorway from the storage area.

"You still don't see it?" Tara said.

"No," Lynette said. "And you can't go into a tower right after an earthquake. Or in a lightning storm for that matter."

"I'm not."

Tara watched the serpent continue its assent. She needed to know what it meant, why it was there, but she couldn't risk her life. After what seemed like an eternity, it appeared again, head down, slithering to the church's floor. It inverted and rose toward the ceiling, morphing into a woman's figure as it did so. She looked different from the Protennoia Tara had seen before. She was young, with long blond hair, and she wore a white gown.

Thunder rumbled.

"I am Protennoia," the woman said. "The three in one."

Tara turned to see if Lynette had heard, but her mother was dropping toward the floor in a faint. Tara grabbed Fimi, who was fine. She ran to the storage area. Vicki, too, had passed out. Tara held Fimi tight against her and clicked the record function on her phone. The woman's voice sounded like Sophia's.

Beyond the woman was a large, open window with a view of the river. The wind blew in on Tara's face, and she breathed in, trying to stay centered. A few raindrops hit her cheek.

"What do you want?" Tara inched toward the woman.

"Look at the sky," the woman said.

In the distance, a funnel cloud formed as lightning flashed.

"This is only the beginning," the woman said. "Once it begins, it must end. You've begun it."

"*I've* begun it? I didn't ask for any of this."

"But it did begin."

"Do you mean finding the vase? And the urn? But I don't know what that all means, what it's for."

"You must end it," Protennoia said.

"End it? How?"

"And there will be a great rain from the heavens, and thunder, and lightning bolts. And the winds will battle the land, and people will battle one another. Until the earth shakes and opens and swallows the woman whole, and the whole world with her."

"Are you saying this is my fault? The weather?"

"The cycle has begun, and now it must end."

Tara took another step toward the woman. "You keep saying that, but what do you mean? I know there's a ritual I can perform. Tell me what it is."

It seemed too good to be true that a vision would appear and tell her the steps for the ritual.

"You must right the world. Return what was given to you, what was forced upon you, and that will end it."

"Return it? It? My child?"

Protennoia gestured at the river. "Cast her upon the waters."

"What? No. There's no way I'm killing my daughter."

"Genesis 22:2, 'And God said to Abraham, take your only child whom you love and sacrifice the child on a mountain where I show you.' Like Abraham, you must prove you fear the Lord."

Tara held Fimi more tightly against her. "No, that's not right. It's not right."

"Do not worry. Like Isaac, your child will not die."

Tara backed away. "Damn right she won't."

"Show your obedience, and she will be assumed into heaven, full in body, fully alive, as was the Virgin Mary. Do this and the world will return to its natural cycle. Your life will be what it ever was, what it ever should have been. That is the end of the cycle. That is the ritual you must perform to right the world."

"The assumption of the Virgin Mary isn't even in the Bible," Tara said.

"At the end of your life, you too will be assumed like Mary was. Allow your child this elevation now and you free her, yourself, and the world, and you will see her in the afterlife."

"That's crazy," Tara said.

The ground shifted, throwing Tara off balance. She tripped and instinctively cradled Fimi's head with her hand. After she righted herself, she sank onto the floor, thinking she was better with a lower center of gravity. Protennoia didn't react to any of it or pause her flow of words.

"Your daughter was never meant to exist. She is not a human. Not in her own right. She is merely a duplicate of you. Two of you in the world creates imbalance. That is the cause of the floods, the storms, and the earthquakes since her birth."

"If that's true, it's not her fault."

"Fault matters not. Only returning her, allowing her to return to heaven, will reset the world. She will be happy and safe. The destruction caused by you will end."

"If that's the only way to end this, take me. I've lived twenty-two years, she's not had two. Take me if having both of us here is wrong."

"Your daughter is the one who was wrongly created. You must set this right. If you don't, destruction will be caused by you."

Tara shivered. The words came directly from the ancient Armenian letter she'd traveled the world to piece together.

"This can't be the answer. Why should I listen to you?"

"If you don't do this now, your daughter will die rather than being assumed into heaven, as will you. And until that happens, the unrest, the fights, and the violence will continue. All manner of natural disasters—tornadoes, floods, earthquakes—will escalate. By refusing my order, you put your family, your city, country, and the world at risk. And when you are dead and your daughter is dead, the cycle will begin again. You can stop it, but only if you return what was given to you."

Tara's mind raced. Her daughter had finally spoken, had called her "mommy," and she'd done it to point out this serpent. Tara didn't know what that meant. That the serpent was to be feared? To be listened to? But killing couldn't be right. That was one thing Tara had always agreed with Nanor about from day one. Killing in the name of God was wrong.

Tinkling sounds filled the room from all the wind chimes swaying. A deep bell tolled, its vibration filing the air.

*It's a test. It has to be. To see if I'll protect Fimi.*

"I'll find another way," Tara said.

Protennoia extended her arms, reaching for Fimi. "Since you awakened, you've been searching for guidance, longing for someone to tell you what to do. How to end the turmoil in the world. Now you have it. Now I've told you. You must listen."

Holding Fimi tight, no longer sure it was a test, Tara shook her head. "Never."

The building shook again, and a crash came from the storage area. Dust rained down. A ceiling beam wiggled. Tara leapt backwards before it plummeted to the floor. Her back slammed against the wall. Fimi started to cry.

"It's the only way to stop the destruction," Protennoia said.

Tara shouted this time. "No."

"Is it done?" Vicki said. She, Lynette, Tara, and Fimi huddled together under the heavy oak conference table. Tara's knees ached, as she'd been cross-legged for the last half hour, bouncing Fimi in her lap to try to keep her calm. The child hadn't spoken again or made any sound once she'd stopped crying.

Pictures had fallen from the walls, and glass shards lay all around them. Ceiling beams had come down. Candles, all unlit, had toppled everywhere. The monitors in the computer area had flopped on their faces, and the wall-mounted television screen had tumbled off the wall face first onto the conference table.

"I think so," Tara said. The rain had stopped a few minutes before, and there hadn't been thunder or lightning for twenty minutes, nor any aftershocks.

Lynette crawled from under the table. Tara scooted out, watching for glass, keeping Fimi in her arms.

"I'll check the urn," Vicki said. She'd told Tara she'd put it back into the box and shoved the box under Roger's desk.

"Be careful." Tara stood and surveyed the destruction.

Vicki appeared in the doorway holding a box. "It's intact."

"You did the right thing, Tara," Lynette said. "I don't know what or who the woman in the vision was, but you couldn't do what she said."

Cyril and the guard, who'd sheltered in the entryway, joined them.

"No, I couldn't." Tara peered out the window. Tree limbs lay half-submerged in mud. "But I don't know how to stop this."

They swept and straightened, taking turns playing under the conference table with Fimi in case there were aftershocks. The small television in Roger's office turned on, but it had no reception, and the satellite channels were out. After an hour with nothing more than minor tremors, they all left, struggling through mud that covered their boots and sucked at their feet. Wind whipped at their faces, and Tara held Fimi pressed against her body to shield her. Tara stepped carefully along the muddy paths, careful to avoid branches and twigs across them.

They stopped once to transfer Fimi to Lynette, as Tara's arms ached.

The wind died down at last. Flashing red light filled the air as they approached the pedestrian bridge to Missouri, illuminating plastic bottles, fast food wrappers, papers, and other debris littering the riverbank.

Police tape and uniformed officers blocked access to the bridge. Oni stood at the opposite end. She waved to Tara. Tara assumed that meant Oni was all right, but Oni waved harder and gestured toward her ear. Tara retrieved her phone from the diaper bag. Several messages had come in as they'd been traversing the island. The wind had drowned out the alert sounds.

"What's happened?" Lynette said to the officer as Tara opened the messages, all from Oni.

*Jeremy heading your way*
*couldn't stop him*
*Told him too windy to cross*
*Too dark*
*He's kind of a*
*on ground*
*shaking*
*can't see dark*
*under car*
*something hit roof*
*better now will see if I can spot Jeremy*
*called 911*
*his briefcase on bridge*
*No Jeremy*

# 27

ST. LOUIS –An earthquake, funnel cloud, and a series of thunderstorms hit the St. Louis area within the same hour late this morning, leaving at least twenty people dead. Nineteen deaths occurred due to floods, downed power lines, flying debris, and lightning strikes. One person drowned after plunging from the pedestrian bridge between Violet Island and Missouri. Authorities are withholding the names of the victims pending notification of next of kin.

The epicenter of the earthquake was in Webster Groves, Missouri. It was rated 6 on the Richter scale. The last earthquake of this magnitude in the St. Louis area occurred twenty-four years ago.

St. Louis rests upon the New Madrid fault. The most severe earthquake along that fault occurred in 1812. That quake forced the water of the Mississippi River to rise into the air and the river to run backwards, and it was reported that church bells rang as far away as Boston. The 1812 quake caused fewer deaths than occurred today, however, mainly because industry and buildings were not so common along the riverbanks.

The funnel cloud that appeared above the Mississippi River moments before the earthquake this morning took meteorologists by surprise. An expert at the St. Louis office of the National Weather Service said the weather patterns could be attributed to *El Nino*. Noting that the weather conditions earlier in the day included a clear sky with no wind and 50% humidity, however, the NWS stated that the odds of high winds, particularly ones sufficient to cause a funnel cloud, were 1 in 10,000.

~

"Bless me, Father, for I have sinned," Stranyero said. He'd deliberately chosen a traditional church that he'd never attended before and that had the old-style blind confessionals. It smelled of incense. "It's been thirty years since my last confession."

"Thirty?" the priest behind the sliding door said.

"There are reasons." Stranyero folded his hands over one another. He would have forgone this, but the Brotherhood's plans put him at enough risk that he didn't want to chance being judged without seeking absolution. Whether it could be granted remained to be seen. "I've been doing the Lord's work. Outside the framework of the Catholic Church, but the Lord's work nonetheless."

"And are you still?"

Stranyero took a deep breath. "I believe so."

"Doing the Lord's work should not keep you from making your confession."

"It does if the Church disagrees on how the Lord's work should be conducted. I've done things that I believed were right, that I believed were necessary and justified."

"And that you now see were wrong?"

"Let me ask you something, Father. Were not the Crusades against the Church's teachings? Yet Popes found mass killings justified to spread the faith."

"Did you come here to confess or to argue?" the priest said.

Stranyero shifted on the kneeler. "Perhaps both."

"The Church is made up not only of God but of men," the priest said, "and so it is no more perfect than men are. Your example should be Christ, not the humans who run his Church."

"The Pope is said to be infallible."

"Only when he proclaims a doctrine of faith or morals. Regardless, while some of the Church's actions may raise questions, that's no excuse for one's own wrongdoing."

"No, but it does make our choices complicated."

"If you're hoping I'll tell you the acts were not sins, I doubt I'll be able to. Which I suspect you know. Though, obviously, I can't say without hearing your confession."

Stranyero nodded, despite that the priest couldn't see him. "It's why I've come."

"But if you believe the acts were not wrong, you've no need of absolution."

"That's not so under your reasoning," Stranyero said. "A mortal sin is a mortal sin regardless of the sinner's intent, is it not?"

"In some instances. So tell me, in good conscience, can you vow not to repeat these acts?"

Stranyero stared into the blackness. He hadn't come to argue theology with a priest. He and Sophia debated such ideas at length. And agreed on many of them, though he'd remained a Catholic and she had not.

"That's why I've been away for so long. I saw no point in confession if I weren't able to offer genuine remorse."

"Correct," the priest said. "To be forgiven, to be reconciled, does not mean license to sin again. It means a genuine change of heart. Are you capable of genuine change?"

"I come to you with genuine remorse." A door banged in the Church somewhere, and humid air from outside filtered in. Stranyero loosened his tie.

"That sidesteps the question. Are you able to change?"

"It would alter my entire life in ways you can't imagine," Stranyero said.

"I can imagine quite a bit. I've been in twenty parishes in five countries. I've heard confessions of acts I pray you couldn't fathom."

The thought comforted Stranyero. He wasn't alone. "And did those people take a new path afterwards?"

"Some did. Some did not. For many, I have no idea."

"Does that matter to you?"

"It matters for them. It matters to God. But I've no control over it. I can only do my best to do what I've been ordained to do. The rest is in God's hands."

Stranyero no longer felt sure he believed in any god in that way, a god concerned with each person's day-to-day actions and lives. The universe was vast, and he felt sure if there were a creator, that creator had more to do than listen to the petty entreaties and grievances of the human race. Yet vestiges of his old faith remained. A faith purer and less questioned. A faith that demanded he seek absolution.

"I realize how dramatic this sounds, Father, but I do not exaggerate. Many people I know, love, and respect would be lost to me if I took a new path. And the one person who matters most to me, after confessing to her, I suspect I've lost her already."

The flatness in Sophia's voice, the lack of her usual warmth and empathy when she'd said she needed to think about what he'd told her, made him fear the worst. He didn't blame her. Their relationship had been doomed from the start.

"You have come here today," the priest said. "The first time in thirty years. Take the first step at least."

"Telling you my sins?"

"Yes."

"How much time do you have?"

~

USING HER CANE, Sophia walked north on Dearborn Street. The leafy overhanging trees in her neighborhood gave way to converted warehouses and storefronts, then to aging stone and brick buildings interspersed with shiny glass buildings as she passed through downtown.

She slowed in the Theater District. Her physical therapist had raised her daily exercise goal to two miles a day, which fit perfectly with her destination. She checked her watch. She still had thirty minutes to reach the Dearborn entrance to the Riverwalk that ran east and west along the Chicago River. Plenty of time.

A block from her destination, Sophia's phone rang. Not wanting to juggle it with her cane, she waited until she reached Wacker Drive. There, she sat on one of the chairs that was fashioned as part of a concrete planter. Few people other than the occasional tourist sat in these spots. They provided a beautiful view of the river below as Sophia listened to a voicemail from Pete Spencer.

Voice breaking, Pete said he was calling with sad news about Tara's ex-boyfriend. Sophia still had a few minutes until her meeting. She called back. The honking and other traffic sounds behind her made it hard to hear Pete as he told her about Tara's vision and Jeremy's death. The noise probably had made her voice a bit garbled, too, as she tried to comfort him, but it also meant no one walking behind her could overhear.

After she hung up, she stared down at the sun gleaming off the river and the people walking, jogging, and biking along it. A fleet of bright green kayaks sped by. It seemed strange to Sophia that so many could be enjoying this lovely summer day when the news Pete had relayed was so tragic.

Her ankle didn't quite feel rested enough, but she was out of time. She made her way down the concrete steps, gripping the railing. At the café at the bottom, she ordered an iced cappuccino. She turned around, and Thomas Stranyero stood before her.

"How are you?" he said.

He looked more casual than she'd ever seen him, wearing black sweat pants and a plain white T-shirt with gym shoes. Large, dark sunglasses hid his eyes and part of his face. The café had been her and Thomas' favorite spot for late afternoon coffee when he'd been able to get away, so despite his different appearance it seemed almost normal to see him there.

"As well as can be expected," she said.

Sophia gripped her cappuccino, her other hand on her cane. Her thoughts raced with which topics to raise with Thomas first. The death of Jeremy Turano? The journal from Armenia? She couldn't ask him about the vision urging Tara to kill her daughter because he would have no way of knowing about that. Sophia trusted him, despite being uncertain about any relationship with him, but Nanor and Tara did not. She decided to let him begin the conversation. He had contacted her, after all.

Thomas took her elbow. "Let's get out of the way. I don't want to be seen."

As they'd done every other time they'd met here, they pivoted east and walked toward the Vietnam War Memorial Wall.

"I don't have much time," Thomas said. "Fenton MacNeil—the man I've worked most with at the Brotherhood—is headed for St. Louis. He believes Tara's on the verge of figuring out the ritual to end the Spark of Life ceremonies forever, and he intends to stop her."

"How?" Sophia gripped the head of her cane, keeping her voice low so others on the Riverwalk wouldn't hear.

They passed the kayak rentals and tour boats and veered from the path onto the riverbank. The grass beyond the boats had never really filled in. Today, as usual, all the high-backed wooden lounge chairs were open. The exposed dirt and rocks kept most people away, and the tall chairs hid anyone sitting in them from the view of people on the path or the street above. It made it the perfect meeting place.

"MacNeil won't tell me his exact plans," Thomas said after they'd settled into their usual chairs. "But if it were my operation, first I'd try to keep her from obtaining whatever she needs for her ritual to stop the Spark. But I suspect it's too late for that or he wouldn't be panicked."

Sophia willed herself to keep her eyes and body steady, not wanting to reveal anything, though her stillness no doubt told Thomas she was being careful to hide her feelings and thoughts. The two of them had never discussed the Spark of Life, the ritual, or the journal. She'd last spoken with him before she'd known he was the one who'd hired Marie Glaston. "And second?"

"I'd try to steal and destroy the sacred objects."

"Sacred?" Sophia found the word interesting. It suggested the Order didn't truly see Tara or her efforts as evil.

"It's a term of art. It doesn't mean good or evil. Just sacred in the sense of being used in a ritual."

"What would those objects be?" Sophia said.

"I know no more than what was in the journal," Thomas said. He met her eyes as he said it, but she wondered if he were holding back.

"So you, if you were MacNeil, would try to destroy any sacred objects Tara had or might be able to obtain," Sophia said.

"Yes. And third, if necessary, kill her or her child. Or both."

Sophia straightened her back. Her pulse pounded in her throat. "I thought the Brotherhood believed killing her or her child would have terrible consequences, at least before a certain time."

"There's no time to be coy," Thomas said. "You've had the journal translated, I'm sure, and that idiot Evekial no doubt spilled secrets in his futile quest to persuade Tara she's unimportant. So you must know there's a belief that until Tara's daughter reaches her 700th day, killing her will end the possibility of a messiah. Some in the Brotherhood, though, believe that's a legend. Some are inclined to let her live out her life, keep opposing her, and keep trying to restart the cycle. But others, including MacNeil, believe that her death can be caused indirectly. The cycle was restarted after the Spanish pregnant woman was burned at the stake by a mob, and after the Armenian woman and her child died in a fire set by invaders."

"You're saying the Brotherhood influenced the people who caused those tragedies?"

"I'm saying some in the Order either are convinced that's how it happened or are willing to risk it. Better to take a chance on ending the cycle forever if we must than to let Tara and her daughter undertake the ritual and end it for certain. And better no messiah ever than one opposed to us now. That MacNeil refers to as Armageddon."

"Does he mean that literally?"

The idea of Armageddon made Sophia's stomach flip and her fingers turn to ice. She struggled to ignore her body's visceral reaction, grounded in late night horror movies and decades of Catholicism, much of it passed down from an aunt with Old World beliefs. She needed to evaluate Thomas' information and his possible motives as objectively as possible.

"Yes." But Thomas shook his head as he said the word. "To the top brass at the Brotherhood, the end of the Order might well be the equivalent of the end of the world. On the other hand, many are pointing to the weather disasters, including the combination of the earthquake, funnel cloud, and storms as signs that the world is in fact ending."

"All this because a woman may have given birth to a female messiah. How weak and threatened the Brotherhood must be to react this way."

"It's not that simple," Thomas said.

His words fueled anger that helped Sophia set aside the horror movie scenarios. "I'm beginning to believe it is exactly that simple."

"Many of these men believed they were doing what was required by God. Including me."

"At some point, that's no longer an excuse. We all need to take responsibility for our own actions and choices."

"That's what I'm trying to do."

Sophia took a deep breath to calm herself. The air smelled of river, fried food from the restaurants farther west, and fresh earth. "So you're convinced MacNeil means to kill Tara."

"I don't know what MacNeil means to do. That's what worries me. He's been balancing the interests—the danger the ritual poses with the danger of killing Tara and her child. But there's long been a faction that sees the former as the most frightening outcome. I sense MacNeil's beginning to lean that way."

"Why not go to the police?"

Thomas spread his hands wide. "I've no evidence of any wrongdoing. Robed men chanting in the Church of Satan might strike them as an odd religious practice, but it won't get anyone arrested."

"I assume you want me to warn Tara?"

"Yes. I'm going to St. Louis to try to stop the faction and keep watch on MacNeil, but I may not be successful."

"I'll go with you," Sophia said. It was one way to be sure he was really trying to stop MacNeil rather than help him.

"No. You'll put yourself at risk. And you'll slow me down."

"I'll stay out of your way." Sophia gestured to her cane. "I realize I'm of little help in a physical confrontation. But I can help with strategy."

"It will spark MacNeil's suspicions again if he happens to see us together, and I've worked hard to allay them. Even meeting you here is a risk."

"We could have spoken on the phone instead."

"I know." Thomas took her hand and pressed it against his heart. "I didn't want to leave without seeing you again."

She felt moved despite her doubts. "You're acting like you might not survive this."

"I might not," Thomas said. "But I'm also aware that you may not want to see me again. So forgive me for intruding on you this one last time."

Sophia's throat tightened. She nodded.

Thomas stood. "Tell Tara to be careful."

"She knows to be careful."

"No. Truly careful. To hide as long as she can, unless she's forced to reveal herself to perform the ritual. It's all that might save her now."

"Might?"

"Yes. If she figures out and completes the ritual. There's no guarantee MacNeil himself won't kill her afterwards out of spite, but it's rumored that her ritual ensures she and her daughter can't be harmed after it. Ever."

"Rumored?"

"No one knows. The ritual's never been completed before. Never been started for that matter. Some don't believe there is a ritual."

"But what does she need to do? How does she perform it?"

"You know what I know, Sophia. The documents in the archives, the journal from Armenia. That's what I know."

Sophia nodded, still unsure whether to believe him, but convinced he wasn't about to reveal anything more. She moved to stand, and he helped her steady herself.

"I want to be part of what you're doing," she said. "There must be a way I can help."

He sighed and studied her face. "There is one. If you're willing to take some risk."

## 28

Tara dropped her keys onto the narrow shelf just inside the apartment door. She brushed her hair, still damp, away from her face. She felt numb.

Her mom and dad followed behind, her dad carrying Fimi, who'd fallen asleep on the way home from the Turanos' house. He put her in the crib at the far end of the room.

"She didn't mean it, Tara," Pete said.

"She did," Tara said.

They'd been silent the whole drive back. Lynette and Tara had gone with Vicki to tell her mother about Jeremy's death. Divers had retrieved his body from the river half an hour after Tara reached the bridge. On hearing what had happened, Mrs. Turano had screamed that Tara had killed her son, that he never would have been part of the Church of Tara had Tara stayed out of his life, and he never would have been on the bridge that day.

Tara had said nothing. There was nothing to say.

Pete had met them at the Turanos'. Rain had begun while they'd been inside the house, and it drove sideways into their faces despite their umbrellas as they walked to Pete's car. He drove them to Tara's apartment where Oni and Cyril waited with the urn.

Lynette began making coffee and heating water for tea. A rich roast scent filled the air as Tara sank onto a kitchen chair and fished her phone from her pocket. She'd had it on silent while at the Turanos' home.

There were three calls from Sophia, and a voicemail left after the third.

Oni saw the notifications. "You should check. It could be important."

Tara felt exhausted, as if hundred pound weights had been attached to her limbs. It took all her effort to hit the Play and Speaker buttons. As the message played, she hunched over the counter, her head sinking into her arms.

FORCING herself not to look around in a way that might make her appear worried, Sophia headed for LaSalle Street. Even without the heat, she'd be sweating, for she'd never broken in anywhere before. Though perhaps this plan wasn't quite breaking in.

When she paused at a stoplight, she hefted her cane in her right hand, imagining swinging it at anyone who accosted her. But while her balance was fine while standing, she still needed the cane to steady her when she walked. Which didn't truly matter. The reality was, if there were some sort of physical confrontation at the Church of Satan, she'd no doubt lose. At 5'7" and 120 pounds, she was slighter and less strong than almost any man. She'd need to rely on her wits if she were caught.

The main door was on Calhoun, a narrow street off LaSalle that looked like an alley. Two brick buildings bordered it, shrouding the street in shadow, and fire escapes criss-crossed up their sides. She hit the button alongside the heavy metal door and waited. After a minute—she checked the time on her phone so as not to appear too impatient—she tried again. And again two minutes and five minutes later.

Satisfied the Church was deserted, Sophia returned to LaSalle Street, her heart hammering against her breastbone. She walked a half block to Washington, barely avoiding colliding with a woman on the far side of a group of five spread across the sidewalk alternately chatting with one another and staring at their phones. At times Sophia despaired at how many people her age lacked basic social skills such as leaving room on the sidewalk for others or conversing without glancing at electronic devices.

The air felt cool inside the office building complex she entered, and the marble floors shone. Beyond the main elevators with their gold doors, she followed a corridor that led past a series of restaurants and shops many people walking outside had no idea existed. It was one of the things Sophia loved about Chicago. So many buildings had interior connections and plazas not visible from outside, just as some had entrances to the underground Pedway with its own stores, restaurants, and businesses. Before the attacks of September 11, 2001, these interior and underground mini-cities had been easier to traverse. Now many required key cards and codes to access.

Thomas had given her his.

Across from a cafeteria-style diner, she found an unmarked gray door with a square panel to the right. Swiping Thomas' keycard opened it. She stepped into an anteroom with two sets of vinyl seats, side tables with magazines, and a water cooler. She paused for a drink, using one of the paper funnel cups. It seemed like something she would do if she'd come here on a legitimate purpose, and she was parched. The humidity outside intensified the heat, and she was sure she'd dehydrated during the walk over.

A plain wood door to her left had a small round buzzer. She hit that, waited, and hit it again to be sure no one was inside. She wore a long, lace-edged tank top, and she used the fabric in front to cover her fingers before she typed the code into the keypad. She had lightweight gloves with her, but she felt too warm to put them on yet.

"Hello?" she said as she opened the door, raising her voice. She wasn't sure what story she'd have for being able to get this far into the Church, but calling out seemed wiser than risking someone attacking her.

The carpeted study appeared deserted. At one end stood Evekial Adame's large antique desk with its carvings of the Green Man. It occurred to her that she'd most often seen the figure on Tarot Decks. She wondered why Tarot kept appearing in Brotherhood locations, but that wasn't why she'd come. She slipped on the gloves.

Thomas had told her to place the bugs and get out. He'd put listening devices before in Evekial's office, but they'd been discovered when Evekial's assistant had decided to clean out and organize the space. Stranyero had persuaded Evekial that rival Satanic churches had planted them, looking for proof that Evekial was mocking Satanism, not practicing it. Now Stranyero wanted a replacement device in the office and in the church itself. Sophia quickly found the spot he'd described under the lip of the pot for a small bamboo plant.

She tiptoed to the far door and pressed her ear against it. She heard nothing. The place appeared abandoned. Which made sense. It was 6:30 on a Wednesday night, and Thomas had told her there were no services then. Apparently Evekial and his staff weren't ones to burn the midnight oil even in trying times. Thomas also was expecting Evekial to be on his way to St. Louis and to call in to speak to his assistant tomorrow, perhaps providing information about MacNeil's plans.

Sophia slipped through the door to a chilly interior room. It contained a marble baptismal font, and two industrial-sized freezers. She didn't look inside. From a previous visit with Pete Spencer, she knew they contained butchered pigs whose flesh and blood were used in a parody of communion. A giant oven for preparing the pork and a microwave for heating the blood stood in between the freezers. Beyond that room was the chapel. A small amount of ambient street-lamp light came through the narrow windows high on the outside wall. Sophia paused at the threshold to let her eyes adjust to the dark. More robes hung on the walls near the pews, and an inverted crucifix hung over the altar.

She stepped inside. And heard the rattle.

FIMI WOKE up while Sophia's voicemail played. Lynette and Pete were playing with her and Cyril and Oni were debating whether the apartment was a safe place to stay when Nanor and Kali arrived.

Both embraced Tara, but she barely registered their presence. It felt like she was in a fog. She kept going over the events of the last two days in her mind. Had she figured out sooner that the urn might be at the Church, or gone there without calling Roger first, or called Jeremy herself to convince him to let her search without his interference, Jeremy's death might have been averted. She hadn't loved him anymore, and she'd still been angry with him, but she'd never have wanted anything bad to happen to him.

Nanor laid her hand on Tara's shoulder. Her fingers felt warm and she smelled of jasmine. "This is a tragedy. I am sorry it happened. You must focus, though. Only ten days are left. I translated more of the journal while we traveled. What I learned may perhaps fit with this new object."

Tara nodded, but in her mind, all she heard were Mrs. Turano's accusations, and all she saw was Vicki's face twisted by grief. Jeremy's wake was the following night, but she knew she wouldn't be welcome even if Sophia hadn't urged that she stay in hiding.

Kali slid onto the chair next to Tara and handed her a mug. "Drink."

Like an automaton, Tara sipped the tea. It was hot and smelled and tasted of cinnamon laced with honey.

On the other side of the table, Nanor examined the urn. It looked old and worn on the granite countertop, its rim chipped, its lid barely affixed to the neck.

Oni handed her a flashlight. "It's got characters printed on the inside."

Nanor removed the lid, set it carefully on the table, and shone the light into the urn. "Aramaic. The language spoken in Judea."

She tilted the urn toward Tara, who looked at the lettering, but it meant nothing to her.

"What does it say?" Oni asked.

"'It must end where it began'."

Tara shuddered.

Lynette left Fimi with Pete and edged toward the kitchen area. "What is it?"

"Protennoia said something like that, and she said I need to end it by killing Fimi."

"That cannot be correct," Nanor said.

"That's crazy," Lynette said.

"It's what she said. I couldn't kill Fimi, I can't. But I did kill Jeremy."

Kali placed her hands on Tara's shoulders, turning her chair so they were face-to-face. "You did not kill Jeremy. The earthquake and tornado did. You did not set any of this in motion. Not the earthquake, not the tornado, not the storms."

"And not your pregnancy," Oni said. "It's looking like a bunch of old guys chanting Latin and handing out herbs to Ray did. Blame them, not yourself."

"Miss Oni is right," Nanor said.

"Protennoia warned me terrible things would happen, people would die, if I didn't do what she told me to do. And ever since I've woken up, the fights, the riots, the deaths—"

Lynette put her hands on her hips and spread her legs farther apart as if blocking a doorway. "Tara, you've got to stop."

"Remember our conversation when we met," Nanor said, "about the Akeedah?" The older woman thrust her head forward and peered at Tara, her dark eyes intense. "Tara?"

Tara forced her mind back to what she and Nanor had spoken about. She felt as if she were wading through the mud on the island again, her brain worked so slowly. It all seemed so long ago. "The story of Abraham and Isaac. Protennoia mentioned it, too. She told me Fimi, like Isaac, wouldn't die. I didn't believe her."

"Akeedah literally means the voice of God," Nanor said. "Abraham hears a voice he believes is his god, who tells him to sacrifice his son. Abraham ties his son to an altar and raises his knife, ready to kill Isaac. God intervenes to stop him, blessing him for his obedience and willingness to sacrifice what's most dear to him, his son."

Tara nodded. The story had troubled her the first time she'd heard it in mass as a child, and she and Nanor had talked about it during her first visit to Willow Springs.

"You told me when you were still pregnant that you believed Abraham was wrong," Nanor said "You said it was the wrong test. Why?"

Tara struggled to remember the rest of the conversation, though she didn't see why it mattered.

"Because...because the voice told Abraham to do something wrong. To kill a human being. And Abraham does it. He doesn't question, he doesn't say killing isn't right, he doesn't ask if this voice is really God's. Or if it is, whether that's a good god to follow. One that demands a willingness to commit murder for no reason other than being told to do it."

"Today you did what you said Abraham ought to have done," Nanor said. "You acted on your values and what you believe is right."

"It's true," Lynette said. "There was nothing else you could do, and second guessing will only make you depressed."

At the moment she'd refused the woman's demand, Tara had felt sure and certain. Her whole being had cried out against ending her daughter's life, no matter what the woman said about heaven. Now nothing seemed clear. "Maybe Protennoia wouldn't have let me hurt Fimi. If she *was* testing me, I failed. And Jeremy died."

Kali grasped Tara's hand. "It's awful your friend's brother died, but it is not a judgment on you, and it's not your fault. No good god operates that way."

Nanor nodded. "And if there were an all-knowing being, such a test would be unnecessary, for that being would see into your heart and know what you would do. A test would only be torture. So I say, if Protennoia is a god, she is not a god I would follow. And we do not know if that was Protennoia."

"She said destruction would come, and it did. So whether she's good or not, her predictions are accurate," Tara said.

Oni frowned. "Destruction had already come. Weather disasters have increased ever since Fimi's birth. A birth that happened during a lunar eclipse that came early, in itself a weird occurrence. So no big points to this Protennoia, if it was her, for predicting more bizarre events. I agree with Nanor for once. It's Jeremy's bad fortune that he got caught on the bridge, but that's all it is. You didn't push him onto it. You didn't ask him to meet you at the Church."

Tara's shoulders slumped. "I get what you're all saying, I do. But I look at everything, the letter from Rima Petrosyan's aunt saying Rima will cause destruction, the talk about the Antichrist, the people who died today, not only Jeremy but nineteen more people who didn't do anything wrong—maybe I couldn't do anything about any of it. Maybe it's not my fault, but it feels like it. It feels like it is. And nothing anyone says is going to make any of that better."

SOMEONE SHOOK HER. Tara rolled onto her back on the couch, her body still heavy, as if she were sinking into quicksand. Her brother Nate stood over her.

"We need to talk," he said. His voice was quiet.

Tara sat. Her parents, Nanor, Kali, and Oni were gathered around the kitchen table, heads bent over something, except for Pete, who stood a foot behind Lynette, holding Fimi in his arms and rocking her.

"Sorry about Jeremy." Nate hugged her. It didn't fix anything, but it made her feel better. She remembered little of her life before Nate. He'd been born when she was three, the colicky baby only she could make laugh and smile. As they got older, she'd taught him to tie his shoes and make paper airplanes, and he'd taught her how to sneak out the bedroom window when they got grounded and to space caffeine properly for optimal all-night study sessions. Now he pulled her out of the apartment into the common area hallway. They stood near the door to the emergency stairs, which were on one end of the building. The hallway curved at the opposite end, leading to the elevator bank. "Don't worry, Cyril's watching the elevators on the monitor. No one's going to surprise us."

Tara leaned against the wall. "Okay."

Nate leaned next to her, much as they'd stood as teenagers when they'd watched their younger siblings play on the swing set. "So this vision you had, the woman in it, did she look like the person who called herself Protennoia and talked to you in Armenia?"

"Not totally," Tara said.

"How about at all? Like, in some way other than that she was female?"

"Not much more than that," Tara said. "She was young. And white. And Protennoia was kind of all ages at once, and her skin was brown."

"And when you were on that talk show after your first vision, what did you say about how Protennoia looked?"

Tara shut her eyes and pictured herself sitting next to the talk show host before the live audience. "Nothing, I don't think. I said I had a vision where a snake morphed into a woman who told me to tell the world about my pregnancy."

"So anyone who saw that show knew you had a vision of a woman who talked to you, and who called herself Protennoia, and whom you listened to."

"I didn't say on the show that she called herself Protennoia. And I hadn't heard her say 'once it begins, it must end' yet."

"Sophia knew those things, right? So Thomas Stranyero probably knew, which means the Brotherhood knew. And anyone who did could have used all of it to try to manipulate you into doing something."

Tara stood straighter as she thought about that. "Yeah, but how could the Brotherhood—or anyone—make me have a vision?"

Nate shrugged. "How could anyone make you pregnant? Other than the usual way, I mean."

"You think the Brotherhood did it?" Tara said. "Sent a fake vision?"

"I don't know. Do you?"

Tara rubbed her forehead. "It's possible."

"Which would make whatever she said bullshit," Nate said.

"Yes."

"And if it was Protennoia and you could go back right now, would you be sure if you threw Fimi in the river the storms wouldn't happen or Jeremy wouldn't cross the bridge?"

Tara shook her head slowly. "No."

"And would you be sure if you pitched Fimi out the window, she wouldn't die, she'd go right to heaven?"

"No. I don't know if I even believe in heaven."

None of what had happened to Tara had convinced her that what she'd learned in grammar school and Sunday mass was true, that there was one god in heaven who had talked through a burning bush, handed down stone tablets, and sent his son to earth to die and be resurrected, or that there was a fallen angel presiding over hell, ironically ready to punish anyone who disagreed with God. Sometimes she wished her pregnancy had shown her all that because she would have known whom to trust and who could protect her.

"So if you could go back right now, you wouldn't do anything different?" Nate said.

"No."

"And if Dad told you the Pope told him to kill you and to take it on faith that it'd all be fine and it's the right thing to do and he refused, would you think he deserved to be punished?"

"I see where you're going."

Nate pushed away from the wall and faced her. "So that's a No? Because I want you to finish this."

"You're right. No."

"And you wouldn't think Mom or any of us or one of Dad's past girlfriends should die because Dad made that choice?"

"No."

"Okay then." He opened the apartment door.

Tara took a deep breath and followed him inside. "Okay."

# 29

Sophia froze and scanned the room. Something caught the light below the crucifix. Afraid to step closer, she inched back and fumbled for the flashlight function on her phone. She shone it slowly around the room and finally saw the giant terrarium below the altar. Inside it, the rattlesnake stretched into an S, its head raised but stopped by the glass terrarium lid.

Sophia let out her breath. Giving the snake a wide berth, she navigated the perimeter of the chapel. Despite her research showing the positive associations with serpents before the Garden of Eden story, she shared the common phobia of snakes. The being's flat eyes and scales made her uneasy. It shook its tail, causing its rattle to echo throughout the chapel.

Thomas might have mentioned Evekial being a snake handler. She'd thought that practice limited to rural areas, but apparently not. Or it might be connected to the ritual Thomas had taken part in here. Which could be fitting. If it related to creating life, it also might relate to Genesis, which gave a serpent an outsize role. But it seemed more significant that Tara also had reported seeing a serpent in her recent vision.

She placed the bug in the pocket of the third-to-last crimson robe in a row that hung on the east wall. Something crinkled under her foot as she turned back toward the baptismal font. She bent down and found a few scraps of paper with Latin on them. She put them in her purse and walked the floor. She took the additional scraps she found as well, forcing herself to ignore the snake's rattle.

In Evekial's office again, she eased both doors partially open so she'd hear anyone approaching. Whichever direction a sound came from, she hoped she'd have time to exit the opposite door. Sophia opened each desk drawer, uncertain what she hoped to find. There were real estate closing documents for the church and old personal credit card and bank statements for Evekial.

She found a full page of Latin prose in an unlabeled file. She flattened it on the desk to take a photo of it, as there was no photocopier. A scanner next to the laptop probably served that purpose, but if she scanned, the image would be saved, making it clear someone had been here. She emailed the photos to herself as a back up.

The laptop required a password. She stared at the screen. Thomas had told her most people's passwords were far too easy to guess. Most of hers now used a variation of her high school boyfriend's favorite author's name plus two numbers and characters she alternated between the letters. Before Tara, she'd actually used his first name, something easier for someone who knew her well to guess.

Being in a secret religious order, Evekial ought to be using a difficult password. But given how loose-lipped he'd been when she and Tara had talked with him, it was worth a try. She typed in Satan and got nothing. The same result with Beast and various combinations of his name. The screen warned her she had only two more chances. TheGreenMan worked.

Once in, she discovered why he had such weak security. Most of the documents were church financial records. Though Evekial carefully followed the rules on donations and reporting so as to keep the non-profit status, it appeared to be quite a profit center. Evekial's salary ten years ago had been higher than hers was now, and she was a full professor with tenure.

One file included *veritas*, the Latin word for truth, in its name. The password was the same as the laptop's. The document was written in Latin, but she had trouble making sense of it, as the words were interspersed with what appeared to be dates and other groups of numbers. She hit print, and the laser printer on the desk whirred into life.

A clanging sound came from the other room. She leapt from the chair, forgetting her injury. Her ankle twisted, and she clamped her lips shut to keep from crying out.

Light snapped on in the chapel and spilled through the crack in the door. Sophia exited the screen, stuffed her phone and the pages into her bag, grabbed her cane, and hobbled to the anteroom, pulling the door shut behind her.

Without looking back, she moved as quickly as she could across the marble floor to the nearest exit. On the street, she spotted a group of people and maneuvered behind them, ignoring the pain in her ankle. She was headed the opposite direction from home, but that didn't matter now.

"WHAT DID I MISS?" Tara said.

Kali and Lynette scooted their chairs apart to make room for Tara at the kitchen table.

"After 'it ends where it began," there is a citation inside the urn to Exodus 30:22-32," Nanor said.

"Wait," Tara said. "That's not what the woman said to me, and it's not what Protennoia said. Both said 'once it begins, it must end,' not 'it ends where it began.'"

"So this is new," Kali said.

"Definitely," Tara said.

"What do the Exodus verses say?" Nate asked as he took a gallon of chocolate ice cream from the freezer and started dishing it out. It was his and Tara's favorite snack, and she found herself hungry for the first time since early that morning.

"They provide ingredients for sacred anointing oil," Kali said.

Tara looked at a close up photo of a shrine. "So that could be what's being poured from the urn. And the word End in both phrases—the end of the cycle?"

Nanor nodded and tapped her notebook. "Very likely based on an additional passage I translated. I also spoke further with Sophia about her progress. We have learned more about how your pregnancy happened. Men of the past called on the Soul—sometimes also referred to as the Universe—to create new life in their image, but the women of the past called on the Soul to shift it into their image."

Oni, who stood leaning against the stove, pursed her lips. "We more or less knew that."

Nanor ignored her. "The next page stated that The One Who Will Live Forever—which I believe first would have been Rima, and now Tara because both reproduced themselves—can end both cycles. So no one else can ever use the Soul to force a woman to become pregnant against her will."

"Which we also knew," Oni said.

Nanor frowned, her forehead creasing. "We guessed. Based on the words of Evekial Adame and the designs on the bookmark and shrines. That is not the same as knowing."

Nate slid a bowl of ice cream and a spoon across the counter to Tara. "So that and the phrase 'it ends where it began'? Not exactly breaking news."

"I agree," Lynette said, shaking her head when Nate pointed to the ice cream. "For all the trouble you went to for the urn, it's not providing much of a clue." She turned toward Tara. "Not that I'm saying you shouldn't have tried to get it."

Tara spooned the ice cream into her mouth. It froze her teeth, but the familiar taste calmed her.

"I think it's a good clue." She felt almost grateful to her mom for stating what Tara had been feeling earlier. It made her see that it was wrong. "We've got an urn and a vase, the two objects the woman in the design holds. We've got a pretty good indication that sacred oil is involved in the ritual, and Marie said liquid was being drawn into the vase and out of the urn, so we probably need to put the oil in the urn. Sophia said Stranyero mentioned sacred objects, so that also seems to fit. And it's anointing oil, so someone needs to anoint someone. Or all of us anoint each other if everyone in our joint vision needs to be there."

Referring to a vision made Tara pause, but she pushed the words of the woman at the center away. Nate was right, she couldn't have done anything other than she had, and if the Brotherhood could call on a power to make her pregnant, it could probably send her a vision to try to make her kill her daughter. Who knows, a Brotherhood-created vision might have caused Rima to kill her child.

"And we know when," Nate said. "Within ten days."

Kali pushed her long, black hair behind her ear. "So the question is where. Where did It begin, whatever It is."

"I'm thinking it has to be my pregnancy," Tara said. "Although that's a problem, since I don't know what moment I actually became pregnant, so that leaves the where a mystery."

She finished the ice cream and slid the bowl across to Nate for a refill. Not the healthiest meal, but better to eat ice cream than nothing at all, and she didn't feel ready for more substantial food.

"When did you know you were pregnant?" Oni said.

"I missed a period, then I missed another. I went to Student Health, who told me I was pregnant and I didn't believe it. Then I saw my doctor and she told me."

"That doesn't really narrow it down," Oni said.

"It must mean the whole pregnancy cycle, not only your pregnancy," Lynette said. "This can't all be only about you."

"Also, even Tara's pregnancy began before her," Kali said.

"Meaning?" Oni said.

"These men who came to see Ray," Kali said. "Whatever they did affected him and the conception of Tara. It seems to me that's where it started."

"But then we could keep going back," Tara said. "To my mom's conception. To where the very first virgin pregnancy ever occurred. Meaning Rima."

Pete had been standing between the kitchen and living room areas holding Fimi and listening. Now he said, "Or the Virgin Mary."

Lynette shot him a look but didn't comment.

"None of the documents we've seen mentioned Mary or Jesus," Nanor said. "Not the Armenian letter, the journal, or the Brotherhood's records. So I believe we are safe not going back that far."

"But the urn has Aramaic writing," Pete said. "Doesn't that suggest it's from the time of Christ?"

"A form of Aramaic is still used today by some Eastern Christian churches," Nanor said. "Old Aramaic was used through the second century and middle Aramaic through the 1200s. So the language itself does not indicate the age of the urn."

"Or whose urn it was?" Nate said.

"Correct," Nanor said. "Also, Jews in the time of Jesus and Mary buried their dead. Cremation was considered a pagan rite and was frowned upon."

"So it's not the urn of the Virgin Mary," Pete said.

"It is not," Nanor said. "Nor could it be Rima's if it is from the third century."

"What about where Tara gave birth," Lynette said. "That's a beginning. It happened with the eclipse, and that was the first strange event in the skies linked to her."

Tara's labor had begun during a press conference the Brotherhood had forced her into. To protect her brother Bailey, she'd started to say her pregnancy had begun the usual way and that she'd been lying about not knowing how it had happened. A labor pain had doubled her over before she could finish her sentence. She'd given birth soon after, the gleaming sides of the St. Louis Arch above her. She saw the Arch in her mind's eye, and something about it seemed important. Something she had read and ought to remember.

"A good thought," Nanor said. "We also have a vase, often used as a symbol for the maternal, the female energy or deity, and fertility."

"And an urn," Oni said, "a symbol of death."

"What about Chapter 12 of Revelation, the one that's supposed to contain the prophecy," Nate said. "The river of spit. Tara gave birth under the St. Louis Arch, which is right on the Mississippi River."

"The Church of Tara is on that same river," Tara said. "And Jeremy died in it."

Nanor shook her head. "That is your sadness speaking. The start is either the start of the whole cycle, which we do not know, or the start of you and Fimi."

The idea of the Arch itself nagged at Tara. She took out her phone and searched for the exact words of Chapter 12 of Revelation.

"The start might be the Brotherhood Spark of Life ceremony," Kali said.

Chapter 12 didn't help. Tara set down her phone and reached for Nanor's notebook with her handwritten translation of the journal pages she'd covered so far. "I read something. Maybe in the letter from Rima's aunt. Or in her journal," Tara said. "Something that reminds me of the Arch."

She'd avoided studying the letter too carefully since she'd awakened. She didn't need the word Antichrist emblazoned on her brain.

"Neither mentioned an arch," Nanor said.

"Not that word specifically. Maybe an entrance. Or doorway."

Tara flipped through the pages, running her finger under the words. Nate took another section and did the same.

"Here," Tara said at last. "The journal says there are places where the mundane and the divine intersect. There are people who are good at bringing out the spirit aspect of humanity. Those people gravitate toward those places, those intersections. No, wait, all people do. People are drawn to those spots and build at them. For the ones who can particularly tap into the spirit that animates life, the intersections are especially significant."

Lynette peered over Tara's shoulder. "And that helps how?"

"It's here somewhere, something around this part. It's another word for intersection, a different translation." Tara kept reading, forcing herself to concentrate despite her mom literally breathing on her neck. "Here. It's also translated as a gateway. Rituals and prayers are especially powerful at a gateway."

"So?" Kali said.

"The St. Louis Arch," Nate said. "It's called the Gateway to the West."

# 30

"So it's used in some toothpaste," Nate said. His eyes flicked as he scanned an article on his laptop. Another earthquake had occurred that morning, not as high on the Richter scale, but causing power outages and fissures in older buildings all the same. "And in Ayurvedic medicine. And in a lot of churches, including the Roman Catholic Church, as part of the sacramental chrism—just a fancy way of saying anointing oil—used in services. Also there's myrrh gum."

"It says free-flowing myrrh, so I'm thinking not gum," Tara said.

It was the day after Jeremy's death. They were crammed together in a small Residence Inn hotel suite in Belleville, Illinois. Fimi sat in a highchair next to Nate, and Nanor and Kali sat on the loveseat. Nanor wore dark gray pants and a plain white blouse rather than one of her usual brightly-colored, flowing dresses, a concession to make her less easily recognizable.

Oni had paid cash for the suite and checked in using her false papers. Through a bug Sophia had placed, they'd learned that Evekial was headed to St. Louis to hunt for Tara, as was the man whose library Tara and Nanor had been in, Fenton MacNeil. Belleville was about twenty-five minutes from St. Louis, and it was a town none of them had spent time in before. Tara hoped it was close enough to the Arch to serve as a home base and far enough to make them harder to find.

"Oil," Nanor said. "You'll want myrrh oil. You could find it in a church, but the Brotherhood may have members in the churches."

Tara finished a blueberry muffin and fed Fimi more oatmeal. Her daughter hadn't talked again since pointing out the snake. If other people hadn't heard, Tara would have worried she'd hallucinated it. But she hadn't, and she held onto

Fimi's two words, one of them "Mommy," with her whole heart. She'd talked once, and she would again.

"So where else do we go?" Tara said.

"You don't go anywhere," Cyril said. "I'll go."

Nanor frowned. "They'll be watching for you."

"They'll be watching for all of us," Tara said.

"I will go," Nanor said. "There's an Ayurvedic center thirty miles from here where I've bought things before. No one will find it strange that I am there. I should also be able to get cassia. It's a type of cinnamon. Chinese. Nate, you go to a grocery store. Buy other items to obscure your purpose, but purchase olive oil. A store with organic sections also should have very fine cinnamon and pure cane."

"How much?" Nate said. "I'm not too familiar with shekels as a unit of measurement. Google says it's the current currency of Israel, which I'm guessing is not what the Book of Exodus was referring to, or a unit of weight of uncertain measure."

Tara gripped the spoon. "What if we don't get the amounts right?"

"This ritual will not rise or fall on technicalities," Nanor said. "The good in the Universe does not depend upon the precise words one says or the rigid adherence to measurements. It hinges on intentions and actions in the larger picture. The essence of a rule, not the letter of it."

"How can you know for sure?" The table shook for a few seconds, one of many aftershocks since the earthquake the day before. "Awful things happen, seemingly at random. Maybe there's no sense to any of it. No order. No purpose."

"Your pregnancy was not random. It was caused through men influencing the power of the Universe. My lifelong study of the Tao, Buddism, and all philosophies tells me the Universe follows rules. Many are not the rules we human beings would choose, but rules nonetheless. The force of mind and heart and soul needed to influence those rules is not about dotting i's and crossing t's. It is about intention and action. Choices and motives. Not checking boxes on forms."

"I hope you're right." Tara breathed deep and stared at the Exodus verse, reading it more carefully this time. "But it doesn't matter. We can make it proportionate. Twice as much myrrh by weight as cinnamon, same weight of cinnamon as cane. Match the cassia to the myrrh. If the proportions are right, the mixture will be right, we'll just have a little more or less of it than the verse calls for. We should err on the side of more."

Nate nodded. "I'll pick up a scale, too."

"Do we mix it here," Kali said, "before we go to the Arch?"

"Yes," Nanor said. "Do as much as possible here so you're exposed the least amount of time. The Brotherhood men no doubt will be watching any area they suspect is important. There are nine days left. They must expect we will try soon."

~

The morning after breaking into the Church of Satan, Sophia sat in a microfiche room at DePaul University's main library in Lincoln Park. She set the documents from Evekial's office on the desk next to her. She'd translated the handwritten Latin scraps, and the words suggested to her they'd come from a ritual involving the rattlesnake. It didn't appear to have anything to do with generating a new life, or fertility, or pregnancy. The wording instead seemed aimed at a sort of hypnosis.

As for the file she'd printed, Thomas had told her the numbers most likely corresponded to letters but would require a keyword to decipher. The Brotherhood typically used keywords from the Liturgical Digest. The date in each passage identified the volume, and she was to look at the third word in the third line of the third article. The Holy Trinity of codes, he'd said. So here she was, looking at the Liturgical Digest from March 26, 1918. The code word for the first paragraph was Spiritus. Every paragraph after that required retrieving another volume and locating the next keyword.

The microfiche room was empty, so she returned the coiled film to its plastic holder and shifted to the long table behind her to spread out. It was arduous, and her back began to ache as the hours passed, but it was the type of work Sophia loved. Paragraph by paragraph, line by line, and word by word, she deciphered the text. It appeared to be cut and pasted copies of communications between Evekial and the man known as the Cardinal.

For security reasons, Tara was the only one who kept a key to the Residence Inn suite. She stayed inside it with Fimi and a security guard while the others went out to collect ingredients.

Cyril found what he needed first. He texted Tara to tell her he was on his way back.

About twenty minutes later, there was a knock on the door. First the guard and then Tara peered through the keyhole. Tara saw Nanor's face close to the door. Gray hairs had sprung loose from her bun and fell around her face. She looked unhappy, and Tara figured the older woman had been unable to obtain an ingredient. Kali was visible a foot or so behind her.

Tara opened the door, and Nanor was shoved inside. Next, Kali inched in, her body rigid. A short, thin man stood behind her, nearly hidden by her. He'd wrapped his arm around her neck and held a knife pressed into her throat. He had curly blond hair and wore a burgundy suit and matching dress shirt.

"He threatened to kill her," Nanor said.

"I never saw him, Tara." Kali's eyes were huge and round and her lips trembled.

The man motioned to the security guard with his free hand. "Drop your weapon and stand against wall." He nodded at Tara. "You, too. With your spawn."

Kali shook her head. "Don't." Her voice trembled.

Tara scooped up Fimi and stepped backward until her shoulder blades hit the wall behind her. The guard drew his handgun and crouched, his movements slow.

"Now," the assailant said. The knife trembled, and he yanked Kali tighter against him.

"Do it," Tara said.

The guard set the gun on the floor. Nanor remained frozen next to her granddaughter a foot inside the doorway.

Fimi started to cry.

"Put your hand over its mouth," the man said.

"Let my child go," Tara said, "and let Kali go, and you can do whatever you want with me."

The man scowled. "That's not how it works. The spawn must die by your hand. If you don't kill it, I'll kill your friend and her grandmother, then I'll find and kill everyone in your family."

The man pressed the knife into Kali's skin. Kali shut her eyes. Her eyelids trembled, but her face looked calm. Tara glanced sideways at the guard. His eyes darted around the room, and one hand was easing behind his back. Tara hoped he had another weapon.

Fimi cried louder.

"Put one hand on its mouth and the other on its nose and pinch it shut," the man said.

Tara put one hand over Fimi's lips, mind racing. She couldn't kill her child, but she couldn't watch this man slit Kali's throat and kill Nanor. If she could stall, Cyril or Nate might arrive. She pinched Fimi's nose, but parted her fingers over the child's mouth so that she could breathe.

The man wasn't fooled. "Pinch it shut."

"I can't," Tara said. "Please. There must be another way."

The guard whipped his hand out from behind his back at the same instant the assailant's forearm jerked. The hand holding the knife swung to the side toward Nanor's face. The older woman reacted instantaneously, dropping to a bent-knee yoga pose, hands at her sides. The knife hit the doorframe. Nanor dove forward, landing on her stomach on the carpet. Kali flew to Nanor's left as if of her own volition. She yelled in surprise and pain, and the guard ran to her.

The legs of the man in the burgundy suit buckled. When he hit the ground, Tara saw the two men behind him. Thomas Stranyero held the knife in one hand and a crowbar in the other. Cyril tackled the assailant, held him down with a knee on his back, and with the help of the security guard handcuffed him.

Stranyero helped Nanor to her feet and turned to Kali, who stood panting. "I apologize for shoving you."

"Not a problem," Kali said. Her face was flushed.

Cyril flipped the man over.

Stranyero studied his face. "One of Evekial's. We'll leave him here for now."

"Should we call the police?" Kali said.

"After we're gone," Stranyero said. "We need to be quick in case more of Evekial's people are about. Or MacNeil's."

~

"I DON'T KNOW how many are after you." Stranyero unbuttoned his sport jacket and paced in the center of the new motel room.

Tara had called the detective who'd investigated Fimi's kidnapping, telling her what had happened, but she'd refused to say where she was now. She promised to come into the station the next day. She worried that might cause everyone trouble later, but she couldn't think about that now. She was more worried about whether Stranyero had noticed the boxes that held the urn and the vase or the list of ingredients on Nate's laptop. She'd done her best, with the guard's help, to get everything into the trunk of Cyril's rental car while Oni and Cyril had peppered Stranyero with questions.

"You think Evekial Adame sent that man," Cyril said.

"I do," Stranyero said. "Evekial's most devoted followers are known for their outrageous style. His theory is that it makes the outside world less likely to see them as a serious threat."

"How did he know where we were?" Tara said.

"The man probably spotted Kali and Nanor, much as I spotted him. There are others out looking for anyone connected to you."

"How many?" Tara said.

"I don't know," Stranyero said.

"Do they know our plans?" Kali said.

Tara hadn't told Stranyero what they were doing or their destination, and she didn't intend to.

Stranyero cracked the blinds and peered out at the parking area. "If they do, no one said so. They were told to scour the St. Louis and downstate Illinois areas for anyone associated with Tara. Either that man had the best luck in the world or there are a large number out searching and it was inevitable one of them would find one of you."

"Who else would there be?" Tara said.

"Evekial himself. Other than that, I don't know," Stranyero said. "Members of the Brotherhood who act against orders usually send only one person on such a mission, or go themselves, so there will be no witnesses. Much as Henrik Holmes did when he came after you. Or as I did for that matter. The Brotherhood disclaims responsibility if that person is captured or killed. If Evekial sent out a team, each one would know nothing of the other's existence. But that he has a team at all I suspect would surprise MacNeil and several others in the Order. I knew only because of the bug Sophia planted."

"Or everyone knows, and you've been kept out of the loop," Cyril said.

"Possible." Stranyero perched on the arm of a threadbare armchair near the window. "My involvement with Sophia made them doubt me. But the way I left her tended to support my claim that I am and have always been a loyal Brotherhood of Andrew member."

Tara studied Stranyero. He appeared alert yet relaxed, and his words came easily, not like those of someone thinking through every phrase to form a calculated lie. But if he'd been a loyal Brotherhood member for decades and still was, that meant nothing. Practiced lying must be a skill the Order prized.

"And it made us doubt her," Nanor said. "I cannot help but wonder if that was your intent."

"It was not," Stranyero said, "but I can see why you might believe that."

"That man was trying to make me kill my daughter," Tara said. "Why? Not why did he want her dead, but why try to get me to do it?"

"Many in the Brotherhood believe that once a child is born, the cycle can only begin again if the child dies of the mother's hand or of a natural disaster. The official word is that it must be the mother's choice to kill the child. So Rima Petrosyan allegedly suffocated her baby to save the infant from burning to death."

"I wouldn't exactly call that by choice," Tara said. She thought of the vision at the center who'd tried to persuade her to kill her child. What Stranyero was saying suggested Nate was right. That had been a first attempt to trick her. She wondered if Stranyero knew about it. If he'd taken part in whatever had been done to cause it.

"True," Stranyero said. "Personally, I believe the whole story is a fable to give members justification for murder."

Nanor had been sitting on one of the beds braiding Kali's hair to help calm both of them. Now she stood. "How do we know, Mr. Stranyero, that you did not send that man yourself so you could burst in and save the day?"

"You don't. There's no way I can prove I'm on your side. If you asked my advice in a similar situation, I'd tell you to be wary."

"And do you believe this ritual to force pregnancies, that is a fable too?" Nanor said.

"It may be or it may not. Somehow the pregnancies continue to occur."

"But why is it such a big deal that my child is a girl?" Tara said.

"You pose a threat. Both of you. You show the world a new path. It doesn't matter if it might be a good path, it's not the Brotherhood's. And so these stories arose about why it's justified to harass, threaten, and ultimately kill. If you're preoccupied simply trying to survive, you can't very well preach from the mountaintop."

Tara eyed him, unsure whether to believe him, and afraid to ask more for fear he'd realize she meant to try to perform the ritual. "So it never ends. The harassment. The persecution. The danger."

"It does. It can," Stranyero said. "You are gathering items, I assume for the ritual you must do." Tara forced herself not to glance out at the parking lot where the items were still locked in the trunk. "That will end it. Not only for you, but forever. It will change the world, or so I've been told."

Nanor crossed her arms over her chest. "I suppose you want to help us do that?"

"I do. You might say I've had a revelation, that I've been converted. But before I explain that, there are things you need to know."

# 31

"Sophia told us you killed Maya. My daughter. And any chance for her child to be born." Nanor's shoulders sagged, and her arms hung at her sides. She looked toward Stranyero as she spoke, but seemed to be looking past him at the window, though the blinds were drawn, so she couldn't see out.

"I may as well have," Stranyero said. "I was in the car when she was killed. I didn't try to take the steering wheel when I realized what he intended to do. I didn't try to change MacNeil's mind. I accepted that it must be done. That it was the right thing to do."

Tara lifted Fimi and held her child against her body. Despite having heard this already from Sophia, hearing him say it turned her insides to ice. If he'd been sure murder was right all those decades ago, if his strong convictions had told him it was justified, nothing would stop him from taking similar actions today. He might have shared with Sophia out of a genuine desire to confess, to clear the slate and give them all the chance to reject him because of his past. Or it might be to set them off guard.

Nanor moved toward Kali again, putting her hand on her granddaughter's shoulder. "The beliefs of men."

"That is so," Stranyero said. "And there are vengeful goddesses who cause death and destruction. Your granddaughter was named for one."

Nanor put her hands on her hips, elbows jutting out. "The goddess Kali is about far more than that."

"Yes, she is. And so I believed my mission, and the Brotherhood of Andrew, was about far more than that. When I allowed your daughter's death to happen, I believed she was an agent of the Beast. Not Satan incarnate, but one who would serve evil's purpose and lead the world into chaos."

Tara licked her lips, which had gone dry. "And now?"

"I believe her purpose, and yours, must be different. Perhaps to lead the world out of chaos. To bring a different kind of order. If any part of the Bible is true, men in power, whether the members of the Brotherhood of Andrew or not, have tried imposing our beliefs through fear and violence for millennia. It's time for something, someone, new."

Tara bent to rest her chin on Fimi's head. "But I'm not a savior. Or a messiah or teacher or prophet."

"No," Nanor said. "You are a good person. Who has healed others, including me, and the earth, at great cost to yourself. You inspire others to change, to become their best selves. Such as your old friend Roger. And Cyril. And this man—" the older woman gestured to Stranyero— "if what he says now is true. Imagine if you could reach the world."

"I don't know how to do that. When I tried, it made everything worse." Tara thought of her interview on the talk show, which had led to the meeting with the Pope, who'd died suddenly that very night, and about Sophia's neighbor so long ago who'd been killed in an explosion meant for Tara, and about Jeremy hurtling to his death.

"Don't blame yourself for the Brotherhood's crimes," Stranyero said. "Those of us who belong bear responsibility. You have the potential to offer a different image of the divine. Some are desperate to stop that. I want to continue to help you."

"Exactly what are you proposing?" Nanor said.

"To continue what I've been doing only with more direct communication with you. I'll maintain my cover as long as I can to stay as informed as I can about MacNeil, Evekial, and any other factions. I'll tell you what I learn—in fact, I'll call MacNeil now on speakerphone so you can hear."

Tara didn't see any downside to Stranyero making the call within her hearing. He knew where they were now and could share that with MacNeil regardless, and she didn't plan to stay here long. She looked at Nanor. "Are you okay with this?"

"I am not 'okay.' But while he helped kill my daughter long ago, he may have saved my granddaughter today, as well as you and your child. So I am not against this plan, so long as we tell him nothing of *our* plans."

Tara nodded. "Agreed. Who are you calling?"

"Fenton MacNeil. The man whose library you visited."

Tara searched the name and found the man's biography as Stranyero dialed. MacNeil was a retired CEO from a Fortune 500 company and he had numerous business holdings of his own. She hoped it was a good sign that Stranyero had shared his name.

The phone was on speaker. Stranyero put his finger to his lips as MacNeil answered. Tara recognized the booming voice from hearing it in the library.

"I've got eyes on our target," Stranyero said. "She and the others are in Belleville, Illinois. Someone else from the organization found them as well, but I stopped him before he could act contrary to our plans."

Tara stiffened for a moment at the mention of Belleville, then remembered they were far from there now. The many moves had become a blur.

"Who was it?" MacNeil said.

"Didn't recognize him," Stranyero said. "But he wore a burgundy suit, so I can guess."

"And I'll guess you're correct. Our target, is her objective as we thought?" MacNeil said.

"I believe so, though I haven't confirmed. Cyril is still with her, as are her women friends. I've lost track of her family."

"Others have eyes on them. How close is she to her goal?"

Tara's stomach tightened. She'd hoped her parents and siblings had split up and become hard to find.

"She and her team appear to be gathering items. So far, herbs and incense from a Chinese acupuncturist's shop."

Tara's hands began to ache, and she realized she'd been clasping her hands together too hard and possibly squeezing Fimi too tight, though Fimi hadn't complained. Despite Stranyero saving her, she had no way to know if he'd done it for her or for the Brotherhood, and his words weren't helping that. Though if he was using code to pass on information, she couldn't spot it, and she didn't know what that information would be.

"The phenomena are spreading," MacNeil said. "There was a quake this morning centered near Geneva, Illinois, and another in Milwaukee. It's time to renew your relationship with the lovely and erudite Sophia. The location where the target is headed is almost certainly the Arch, where her child was born, but you need confirmation."

Tara's heart skipped a beat at the mention of the Arch. She struggled to keep her face blank.

"I'll do my best," Stranyero said.

"I don't want your best. I want it done. It *must* be done. Or it'll be the end of everything."

Stranyero ended the call and returned his phone to his pocket. "I won't ask if you know what he was talking about, or whether you're going to the Arch. I'll simply warn you that he may have guessed I'm helping you and said everything for your ears. But that doesn't mean it's not true. He may well be focusing on the Arch and know where your friends and family are. I suggest whatever you're planning, you do it as soon as possible."

TWENTY HOURS LATER, Fenton MacNeil stood facing the other three men, his back to the wall that surrounded the rooftop deck and outdoor bar area of the downtown St. Louis Hilton. Behind him, the St. Louis Arch shone above the Mississippi River, more striking because of the contrast to layers of slate gray clouds beyond it. A neon pink and gold billboard flashed, advertising the casino in the Four Seasons Hotel.

"Thanks to excellent inside work by Stranyero, we received new information.

The subjects will have a vase with them. Break the vase and the ritual fails," MacNeil said. "You know who your partners are. Stranyero's team goes in first."

It was a four-person operation: MacNeil, Stranyero, and two other men Stranyero had never met. They must be new recruits. To his eyes, they looked about fourteen years old—rail thin with smooth, baby faces—which he guessed put them in their mid-twenties. All four men wore loose-fitting camouflage print cargo pants and khaki-green T-shirts, a field uniform designed for ease of movement while carrying small weapons and supplies and not drawing excessive attention. With the dark clouds threatening more thunderstorms and the threat of aftershocks, Stranyero doubted many people other than the Brotherhood men and Tara Spencer and her cohort would be on the streets.

The weather also had kept tourists and casual diners away from 360, the rooftop restaurant. MacNeil was certain that their mission, ordained as it was by God, would keep them from earthquake devastation. Stranyero was more practical. This building had been designed to shift and sway in an earthquake or high winds, much like the Willis Tower in Chicago and the St. Louis Arch itself.

"Why the vase?" The taller, heavier young man said. "Why break it?"

"It belonged to the very first guardian. We believe it was meant to commemorate the birth of the first girl mistakenly believed to be a messiah. She lived only a few days, then perished at her mother's hand. The guardian, aunt of the young mother, blessed it in her honor. Or, from our perspective, cursed it. Once it's broken," MacNeil said, "its power is lost. Tara Spencer can do nothing against us then. Her power comes from being a mother, and once the symbol of her motherhood is gone, and she stands on the ground where she gave birth, she'll become the perfect target."

"We need better weapons," the shorter, skinnier new recruit said. He had thick, bushy hair and thick sideburns, a look Stranyero couldn't reconcile with the Brotherhood's mission. "Guns."

"You're nowhere near good enough marksmen for that," MacNeil said. "We're not here to injure bystanders, however culpable they may be. We have two targets who can be dispatched only after the vase is broken, and they are the only two targets. We've heard they may have hired security guards with them. You're to neutralize the guards, not kill them."

MacNeil ordered the tall recruit to search everyone for phones and communication devices. He did so thoroughly, confiscating everything.

"But how will we monitor the girl?" the bushy-haired recruit asked.

Stranyero had been wondering the same thing. He also wondered if MacNeil was still uncertain whether to trust him not to communicate with Sophia or Tara and if that were the real reason for the embargo. But it didn't matter. After this mission, MacNeil would have no doubt where his loyalties lay.

"A team based in another city is monitoring her," MacNeil said. "She's about five miles from the Arch, riding in a silver panel van."

"Will you keep in touch with that team?" asked the other young guy.

"No. From this moment on, I'll be dark, too. We can't risk our communications with one another being intercepted," MacNeil said. "That's why I've ensured all of us—including myself—will not be tempted to use any device. Our plan is set. There is no back up."

Stranyero doubted that was true, but it was good motivation. If these recruits believed others would surge in behind them if needed, they'd be less motivated.

"We live or die on our own efforts, as does the Brotherhood," MacNeil said. "As does the world."

# 32

Stranyero retrieved his car from the parking garage. The short recruit with the big sideburns had been assigned to him. He road shotgun without speaking, probably still bent out of shape about MacNeil's disparagement of his shooting skills. When assigning teams, MacNeil had said to Stranyero, "Their job is to break the vase. It's up to you or me to kill the girl."

They could have walked the mile to the Arch, but the path ran across expressways, and rain had started sputtering. Also, unlike MacNeil and his recruit, Stranyero needed to be under the Arch near the museum entrance, ready to intercept Tara if she appeared from that direction or to surprise her if she approached from the outdoors.

He parked in the underground lot.

"Loosen up," Stranyero told the recruit. The ramrod posture and extreme vigilance—including swiveling their heads in all directions to check for threats or opportunities—made all the new recruits stand out from crowds. Particularly these days, when most people their age, most people for that matter, meandered and stumbled when they walked, dividing their attention between the electronic devices they relied upon and the real world, with the world coming in a distant second.

The recruit nodded, his thick curly hair bouncing, and stopped looking around so obviously. His eyes still scanned first the garage and then the Museum of Westward Expansion once they entered. It, too, was deserted. It smelled of old paper and must. Most people had a visceral reaction to being underground when earthquakes and aftershocks threatened. Stranyero wasn't immune to that type of claustrophobia, but he had other things to worry about.

The ticket lines were empty. Robotic automatons that normally spoke and moved and gave history lessons stood frozen at the entrances to many exhibits.

"We'll wait over there." Stranyero pointed to the sliding glass doors that opened to an outdoor ramp leading to the open area beneath the Arch. The comment was for the benefit of the guards and the ticket seller who might wonder why the two men stood in one place rather than exploring. Stranyero expected no one other than Tara and her friends. MacNeil and his recruit were hiking to the Arch and would station themselves on the concrete walkway along the river.

The recruit nodded. Now his obvious youth worked to their advantage. He took out a deactivated smart phone that from a distance appeared functional. He plugged in ear buds and pretended to both listen and type on the phone. Stranyero easily feigned the impatience most people in their fifties or sixties felt when trapped with a young companion who ignored their presence in favor of the virtual world.

Stranyero scanned the exits and entrances as if watching for the rest of his party. He expected Tara soon. Or someone connected with her, as she, too, might have split her party.

~

Evekial, it seemed, had been hiding quite a lot. Stranyero and MacNeil might both believe they had the Cardinal's ear, but it appeared to Sophia the man actually favored Evekial. That didn't mean, though, that Evekial followed the Cardinal's instructions, including the directive to delete all the communications between him and the Cardinal. He'd saved them. Based on his highlights, Sophia guessed he wanted to keep the positive comments fresh in his own mind as he pursued a promotion.

Evekial agreed with everything the Cardinal said, at least to his face, and praised him as brilliant, while MacNeil and Stranyero both argued with the man at times. Those two also ran covert missions and spied on one another and other Brotherhood members. Evekial wasted no time focusing on the competition. He directed his every effort at currying the Cardinal's favor. By appearing almost as a buffoon, he'd caused Stranyero and MacNeil to discount him, but he'd ensured the Cardinal knew how serious and dedicated he was. Every success he had, he made sure a Brotherhood member who served as the Cardinal's not-so-covert eyes and ears learned of it. As best Sophia could tell, he spent more time trumpeting his success and wining and dining the Cardinal and his men than doing anything else.

She sat back in the chair. So the Brotherhood wasn't much different from most secular organizations. Whoever crowed the loudest was rewarded the most, and those who toiled late into the night were perhaps thanked in the moment but later forgotten.

That the man lacked brilliance was shown by his poor security. But because no one thought him important, Sophia guessed no one had taken him seriously enough to monitor him carefully until recently. Even Stranyero had bugged his office the first time not to learn about Evekial, but to learn about those people with whom Evekial dealt.

She decoded the next few pages, stifling impatience. Unfortunately, the man also lacked intellectual curiosity. His efforts went not toward understanding his work but toward ferreting out what image to project and what effort would make him look the best. He suspected he'd taken part in a Spark of Life ceremony, but he didn't care if it had been that or something else, so long as the Cardinal knew he'd done it.

Later communications, though, provided hints. In the middle of a long passage, Evekial had asked if the ceremony might short circuit everything by tricking Tara into killing her child. The Cardinal denied that, but in such a way that she felt sure he disagreed with Evekial's choice to put the intent into words, not with the interpretation.

She let out her breath. She'd spoken to Tara earlier that evening when she'd taken a break, and she'd learned of the attack on Kali and the attempt to make Tara kill Fimi. Put together with what she'd just read, she felt certain Tara's brother Nate had been right about the vision Tara experienced at the center. It hadn't been divine or from on high. It had been created by Fenton MacNeil, with aid from Evekial, Thomas, and others. Which must be why Evekial, after it failed, had sent someone else, thinking that if he could make Tara kill Fimi, he'd be celebrated. Not grasping that there might be a subtle difference between trickery and force. The vision had played on Tara's own fears and guilt, pulling her darkest thoughts from her mind and offering her the worst possible solution. Had it worked, it would have meant she'd been persuaded to sacrifice her daughter, not forced into it by a knife at her friend's throat. Sophia shivered. Either approach was morally bankrupt.

The Cardinal referred to information from a source he trusted. Sophia smiled, certain it must mean Thomas and happy his cover had held. The smile faded quickly, though. If she believed Thomas was that successful fooling the Cardinal, it might mean Sophia and Tara were the real fools.

The next passage she translated chilled her. The Cardinal advised that if Tara couldn't be persuaded to do what was best for her child and the world, which Sophia took to mean to kill her daughter, there was one place where she and the child might be vulnerable before the 700 days ran out.

The gateway where she'd given birth.

"I DON'T SEE ANYONE." Cyril alternated peering into the rear and passenger side mirrors and checking the smartphone display he'd hooked to the vehicle's navigation system. The vehicle had been borrowed from the sister of Tara's family doctor. Dr. Lei had stayed in touch with Tara since she'd awakened from the coma and had offered to help in any way she could. If she'd been surprised to be asked for a vehicle, she hadn't shown it.

"Good." Oni kept her eyes focused on the road. Cyril, Tara, and Fimi had rendezvoused with her five miles outside St. Louis.

Tara rode in back with Fimi secured in a seat next to her and the vase belted in between them. She had half the anointing oil in a slim plastic test tube in her front jeans pocket. The urn was at her feet, packed into a box.

Nanor and Kali were traveling separately in a rental car with Lynette and Tara's sister Kelly. They had the other half of the anointing oil. Nate drove a third vehicle, one borrowed from one of Kelly's friends. He had with him one of the other vases from the cloister. It was meant to be a decoy.

Cyril glanced over his shoulder at Tara. "You're sure about leaving Bailey and your dad out of this."

"Yes," Tara said. She'd insisted that her littlest brother, Bailey, stay safe at her dad's house in Edwardsville. She wished they could be with her, and she'd seen them in her vision, but she couldn't bring herself to risk it. The last time Bailey had been under the Arch he'd been shot. "If there is a force for good in the Universe, it couldn't possibly require terrorizing Bailey another time."

*I hope.*

"Especially with what Sophia told us," Cyril said. "They really do want us to go to the Arch."

Tara's stomach flipped. She'd considered abandoning their plan after hearing from Sophia. But unless she wanted to create a fortress using Holmes' money and never let Fimi out of it, they'd never be safe. That was no kind of life. And she couldn't let other women in the future be subjected to forced pregnancies and face horrible deaths when there was a way to stop it.

"Not sure I trust her decoding skills," Oni said. "She's a former nun, not a cryptographer. But I agree, we'll have company. Those security guards better do their jobs."

"It fits with what that guy Fenton MacNeil said to Stranyero," Tara said.

Though the rain wasn't coming down in droves, large drops splattered the windshield, and heavy black clouds obscured the sun. It looked more like midnight than three in the afternoon. The local weather report warned people to stay near basements or cellars, as conditions were ripe for a tornado, and to shelter under sturdy tables and in doorways due to the aftershocks. Tara shut her eyes, breathing deep to calm herself, one hand resting on Fimi's foot. They still had seven more days after today, but the weather forecasts looked no better for any of that time.

"We're here," Oni said. She buzzed open the window and waved a fob over the pad at the entrance to a parking garage. While the others had been gathering supplies, Pete Spencer had borrowed the fob from a colleague who worked in the building next door, then met Oni when she'd retrieved the car from Dr. Lei. The garage was four blocks from the Arch. More important, it was a place no one would expect them to be.

They walked toward the Arch. Tara hoped the security guards were nearby but out of sight, as they'd been paid to be. Without speaking, Tara, Fimi, and Cyril veered toward the Arch's parking garage, the urn packed into a knapsack over Cyril's shoulder. Wind, heavy with humidity, smacked their faces.

Oni and Nate took the vase and circled through the park.

"Time to get out of sight," Stranyero said. The guard making a loop around the museum had completed his perimeter walk and disappeared into the Lewis and Clark exhibit. The ticket sales agent had vanished from the window. "Anyone who enters will see us right away."

"But where to?" the recruit said.

Stranyero couldn't believe the recruit hadn't been looking for hiding places. He'd heard the Brotherhood of Andrew was having trouble interesting qualified young men these days. Too few believers among the twenty-something generation, and even fewer who had police or military training.

Stranyero nodded his head toward the glass double doors. "Outside. We'll stand at the base of the ramp beyond the information booth."

Normally a Park Service employee was stationed inside the booth, but Stranyero had noticed it was empty today. The Service had probably determined, and rightly, that it was a waste to pay too many staff.

They stood where they'd be blocked from the view of anyone inside, wind whipping in their faces. They could see a small section of the platform under the Arch.

"Watch that," Stranyero said, pointing. "I'll keep an eye on the doors." By standing a step up and angling his body, he could see the far edge of one of the sliding doors. If it moved, he'd know someone was on the way out.

The museum was deserted and silent except for a single guard at the edge of the Lewis and Clark exhibit, who nodded to them, and one of the security guards Tara had hired. He browsed the displays opposite the entrance.

They saw no one near either set of the sliding doors leading to the outside. Cyril bought the tickets.

"Only a half hour until closing," the ticket taker said.

Tara checked her phone. A text from Nate said he was two blocks from the Arch. He'd spotted two more of the security guards and no one else. Oni texted that she and Nanor were approaching the river.

"That's all right," Cyril told the woman. "We're meeting someone out front, then we'll all take a quick look around and go."

"Oh, that man and his son? Or grandson maybe?" The woman peered at the sliding doors to the outside. "They were there a few minutes ago."

Tara saw no one.

"That's them," Cyril said. "You didn't see where they went?"

"No, I'm sorry," the woman said.

Cyril nodded. "It's all right. We'll find them."

"Brotherhood?" Tara said once they'd moved away from the booth.

"I can't imagine anyone else would be out today."

Tara texted Nate to warn him. Her phone buzzed a second later.

*No one near the river but Nanor and Oni*

They'd agreed to meet in the open, grassy area under the Arch, above the concrete steps leading down to the Mississippi River. They'd circle Oni so she could fill the vase with river water, consistent with the bookmark's design. There, water flowed into the vase the woman held.

Tara picked up Fimi and took the diaper bag with the urn packed inside it from the stroller's lower rack. The stroller looked eerie standing alone and empty in the stroller parking area. Cyril kept watch, eyes scanning the entire museum and the steps outside.

"If Nate can't see them and we can't see them," he said, "they must be hiding behind the information booth."

Tara turned at the sound of footsteps. Her mom and Kelly had arrived through the back entrance. She motioned them to stay inside with the security guard, who'd joined them.

Cyril stepped in front of Tara. She glanced behind to be sure no one snuck up on them.

The doors swooshed open.

STRANYERO HEARD the glass doors slide open. He turned to the bushy-haired recruit, only to discover the man had disappeared. Out of instinct, he reached for his phone and found an empty pocket. He edged sideways, out of the sight of anyone entering from the museum, and scanned the area. The recruit had stationed himself higher on the ramp and now motioned to Stranyero to join him. Stranyero reached him in an instant.

"Visitors," the recruit said.

Nanor and Kali Kerkorian and Nate Spencer stood on the concrete walkway near the river, each looking a different direction, their backs to a dark-skinned, dark-haired young woman Stranyero had never seen before. She crouched near the river. She had an object—the vase, he guessed—next to her and a hose in her mouth. It took him a moment to realize she must be inhaling to draw water from the river into the hose in the way that in his youth he'd once or twice siphoned gas from another car's tank. Why she was doing so made no sense, but he didn't stop to consider it.

"Get those people out of the way," Stranyero said. "And watch for guards—Spencer might very well have the place crawling with them, though MacNeil ought to be managing that. I'll break the vase."

The young man's eyes lit up. He'd probably been expecting, as the new person, to be given what he thought was the less challenging goal of breaking the object. Which worked perfectly, as Stranyero wanted the most important task reserved for himself.

# 33

Tara scanned the ramp as she followed Cyril. She had the urn in the diaper bag over her shoulder, one arm wrapped around it. With her free hand, she held Fimi's hand and led the toddler up the ramp.

Fimi moved slowly, her short legs struggling. Cyril reached the open air ahead of them.

"No," he said.

Tara bent, lifted Fimi in her arms, and hurried to his side.

Below, near the water, a bushy-haired guy in camouflage clothing rushed toward Kali, Nanor, and Nate. He shoved Nate into Nanor, and the two stumbled, barely avoiding plunging into the river. Now Tara could see Oni, who knelt holding the vase. Her hair, drawn into a ponytail, whipped about in the wind, and the waves from the river smacked against the bank. The man punched Kali, who went down.

Thunder rumbled. Oni stood, spun, and slugged the man in the jaw. His head snapped back, but he recovered quickly and hit Oni in the stomach. She doubled over.

A silver-haired man dressed in camouflage like the younger one darted as if from nowhere.

*Stranyero?*

Tara gripped Cyril's arm. "Get the vase."

He ran down the steps. Tara debated running inside for the security guard who was with her mom and sister, but she didn't want them unprotected or that method of reaching the Arch unguarded. She didn't see any of the other guards she'd hired anywhere along the river.

Nanor and Kali regained their feet, and Cyril motioned to them to join Tara.

Nate and Oni double-teamed the bushy-haired man, but his arms and legs lashed out, sending Nate sprawling again as Cyril reached them.

Nanor had a small vial of the blended oil in her hand that matched Tara's. Kali took Fimi while Nanor poured the oil into the urn Tara held. The scents of the anointing oil—fragrant, musky, and cinnamon—mixed with the smells of mud and grass and filled Tara's nostrils as she tried to see what was happening below.

Stranyero grabbed the vase and spun toward Cyril as Oni fought with the younger man. Cyril lunged. Stranyero jumped aside, yelled something, and held out the vase. Tara blinked in surprise. Cyril recoiled as if he'd been struck, then straightened and took the vase. He and Stranyero pivoted toward Oni. She'd just punched the younger man in the side of the head. He swayed but kept his footing.

Stranyero grabbed one of the bushy-haired man's arms, spun him about, and wrenched the other arm behind the man's back, shouting something at Oni. She helped Stranyero shove the young man, still struggling, onto the bottom concrete step, as Cyril bent over Nate, who lay motionless. The man got free, throwing himself from the step. Cyril abandoned Nate and the vase and lunged after him. Nate sat, holding his head in his hands.

Oni, Cyril, and Stranyero subdued the man. Stranyero pulled something from a side pocket of his cargo pants. Oni shifted position, blocking Tara's view, but a moment later Stranyero stepped back, and she could see again. The man sat with his arms tied behind him, shouting and stamping his feet, but unable to break free of the ropes that bound him.

Nate got to his feet and waved at Tara to let her know he was all right. Tara let her breath out. Lynette and Kelly had joined her under the Arch, and Lynette started to run for Nate, but Nanor pulled her back.

"He is fine. We must get the ritual underway for when Oni brings us the vase."

Below, Oni rubbed her shoulder as if it had been hurt, but she turned and bent to pick up the vase. Her foot slipped and slid out in front of her. She fell, and her struggle to right herself pitched her further backward and into the river.

Cyril shouted something and dove in after her. As he launched himself from the concrete walkway, his foot hit the vase. It skidded sideways toward the bound man. He reacted immediately, stamping on it and breaking it to pieces. The water Oni had siphoned into it streamed in all directions.

# 34

Lightning flashed and the ground shook. Tara ran down the stairs to the broken vase. Three large fragments and a handful of smaller ones lay on the pavement. Rain poured down, drenching every piece and washing away any trace of the river water.

Tara's heart raced. She stared into the river, where she saw no sign of Cyril or Oni. In the distance, two more men in cargo pants and T-shirts with knives in their hands ran toward her.

Stranyero clapped his hand on her upper arm. "Do what you can. I'll deal with them."

The man on the bottom step laughed. "Too late."

The river raged, sending waves washing onto the steps. Tara gathered the broken pieces, her breath coming in gasps. Nanor had to be right. The ritual couldn't turn on technicalities. But if it did work, if it stopped the cycle forever, Tara had no idea if it could save Oni and Cyril or stop the men from hurting her and Fimi if they got past Stranyero. The ground shook again, vibrating Tara's whole body. Far from shore, waves swirled into a funnel and rose from the water.

Tara hurried up the steps, aware of Stranyero and the men from the corner of her eye. Stranyero went down and the skinnier of the two men kicked him in the ribs and stomped one of his hands. The older, bulkier man stepped over Stranyero and charged in Tara's direction, knife drawn.

The water whirling over the river had spiraled higher. Its dank, fishy smell filled Tara's nostrils. She stared at it, mesmerized, remembering the moment she'd rested her hands on Nanor and had smelled the earth and imagined the grass and trees turning green after the fire. Now, without thought, she shut her eyes and imagined the whirlwind of water, and the debris within it, shifting closer to the bank and onto the land between her and the men attacking Stranyero. When she opened her eyes again, the column of water had widened and moved onto shore. It separated her from them, blocking their path.

The man on the step, trapped on her side of the water funnel, screamed, his face white. "Devil," he said.

Tara ran up the stairs, clutching the vase fragments, holding the image of the vast funnel of water in her mind's eye.

Rain poured down on the women and Nate, who'd joined them and held Fimi. Kali, Lynette, and Kelly cupped their hands, catching rainwater. Nanor gave Tara the urn, took the vase pieces, and broke them into smaller fragments so each person could hold one. Lightning flashed. Its reflections off the Arch's legs created a strobe effect as Tara poured scented oil onto her right thumb.

Lightning struck the stairs Tara had just ascended, and they cracked into two.

Tara pressed her thumb to Fimi's forehead, then Kali's, Nanor's, Lynette's, and Nate's, stopping twice to pour oil. As each person's forehead was anointed, he or she tipped their hands to spill the rainwater over their piece of vase and onto one another's feet. Fimi cupped her hands, too, imitating the others.

The funnel cloud of water kept expanding, drawing from the Mississippi River until its sandy bottom appeared. At the top, the funnel became one with the clouds.

~

STRANYERO ROLLED ONTO HIS SIDE, pain searing through his mid-section where one of the Brotherhood men had stabbed him. His left hand lay flat on the concrete, fingers splayed. He couldn't move them.

MacNeil and the tall recruit stood frozen in front of the funnel cloud of water as it rose to the heavens.

Stranyero coughed. The coppery taste of blood filled his mouth. Hot, it dribbled onto his chin and was rinsed away an instant later by the rain. A jag of lightning hit the Arch. All the lights of downtown St. Louis popped off. The Arch itself plunged into darkness.

~

TARA POURED the last of the oil over her thumb and pressed it to her own forehead, inhaling the spicy, earthy fragrance. As she did so, a lightning flash illuminated everyone on the platform, bathing them in clear, bluish light.

Time seemed to freeze the moment into a tableau of Fimi smiling with her hands out, Nate holding his niece solidly against his body, spots of fragrant oil gleaming on their foreheads; Lynette draping one arm around Tara's shoulders, her other hand gripping Nanor's; Nanor and Kali side-by-side and hand-in-hand, Kali's long black hair glistening with rain, and Nanor's black hair threaded with white, her face wrinkled but glowing; Kali's hand in Nate's, and Nate's in Tara's, completing the circle.

Beyond them, the water spun like a dervish. Tara's anger surged at the thought of the two Brotherhood men standing beyond it.

*I could let it go, let it wash over them.*

She knew Stranyero lay on the ground near the men. In that moment, though, she felt sure she could stop the rush of water and debris before it reached him, even as the waves swept the others—men who wanted to kill her and her daughter and who belonged to an Order that had been murdering women for thousands of years—into the river. It would be like the Red Sea drowning the Egyptians and their horses in the Biblical story.

Her mom's arm felt warm around Tara's shoulders. Across the circle, Fimi and Nate smiled at her. Tara studied Nanor's and Kali's faces, filled with love for her and each other, and she knew she couldn't drown anyone.

In her mind, she gradually released the water. Her perception of time passing returned as the funnel dispersed and the waves eased down into the riverbed. The earth stopped shaking. The rain ceased, and the clouds broke apart.

Oni and Cyril appeared one behind the other, drenched and panting, climbing up a ladder near the boat docks.

Sophia stood under the archway in St. Peter's. The electric candles in the alcove where her aunt's Bible still sat trembled. The church had begun to shake about ten minutes after the last text she'd received telling her Tara had reached the Arch. She'd heard nothing more from Stranyero. The cool air conditioning and the thought of her aunt soothed her, as did the silence, until it was broken by the glass candle cups rattling against one another and rain drumming on the eaves. Her cell phone blared a flash flood alert for the entire Midwest.

The Virgin Mary statue in the alcove shook. It was a statue Sophia liked more than most of the Virgin Mary, as it depicted her looking like the Jewish, Middle-Eastern woman she must have been, not as a blond-haired, blue-eyed Eastern European woman. The side wall blocked the view of the altar with its giant crucifix. Despite Sophia's love for this particular church, the emphasis on the suffering Jesus had always bothered her. She preferred the focus on the resurrection rather than the death of Jesus. Not only that, its central place, with the images of Mary relegated to the sides, spoke so eloquently of the place of men versus women that it reminded her of her initial doubts about whether she truly belonged in the Church.

A Franciscan friar, the friend of Sophia's from her convent days who'd placed the Bible, joined her in the doorway. He'd seen her come in and wanted to be sure she was all right. He wore the standard black Cossack of the Franciscan with a rosary around his waist, its hood pushed back.

The shaking stopped. The church stabilized, and the rain ceased.

In the silence, the statue of Mary glowed as if lit from inside. The light was so faint at first that Sophia thought it was reflected sunlight filtered through the stained glass windows. But the statue brightened until it illuminated the entire alcove, overpowering the tiny electric candles. All the statues of women saints throughout the church did the same. The intensity of them was nearly blinding.

"Do you see it?" she asked the Franciscan standing beside her.

"I do," the priest said.

# 35

Sun beat down on Stranyero, but he shivered as he watched the water drop down and flow into the river. The knife MacNeil held clattered to the pavement, and he and the tall, skinny recruit sank onto the concrete. They sat, staring first at the water as it dispersed, and next at the people gathered under the Arch. Stranyero saw with relief that Cyril had somehow gotten out of the riverbed, as had the young woman with him.

Three men in camouflage ran from the park area downriver from Stranyero. They headed for the Arch. But as they started up the steps toward the circle around Tara, their knees buckled, and they fell to the ground. One flung a knife in Tara's direction, but it stopped mid-air and fell as if it had hit an invisible wall.

Stranyero smiled. The ritual had worked. No one could harm Tara and Fimi now.

He coughed again. Hot pokers stabbed his insides. He guessed a rib had broken. Spots danced in front of his eyes. His flattened hand throbbed, and he wondered if that meant anything, that he could now feel it.

*Good thing I went to confession.*

At the very least, Sophia and Tara would both know that he'd truly been on their side. He closed his eyes.

A hand on his shoulder brought him part of the way back.

"Hold on, my friend," a deep, resonant voice said. It sounded like MacNeil, but that man hadn't called Stranyero a friend in a long time.

Another hand, a smaller, cooler, one rested on his shoulder.

*No. I'm not worth it. Don't risk it.*

The words wouldn't come out.

"It'll be all right," Tara said. He heard rustling as she moved, and he smelled cinnamon and an earthier, more pungent scent, along with olive oil.

Warmth and iciness flooded him, as if a soothing, cooling gel were being applied to his skin and a warm, healing balm to his insides. His muscles relaxed. There seemed to be more room in his ribcage. His hand stopped throbbing.

The hands withdrew. Stranyero opened his eyes, flexed his hand, and sat. Tara sat cross-legged next to him. Cyril stood behind her, holding the little girl.

Stranyero covered Tara's hand with his. "Thank you."

Behind Tara stood Cyril and the young woman, who introduced herself as Oni.

"I'm glad you're all right," he said to Oni. "I'd hoped to help you, but I didn't succeed."

"I'm fine. As I was telling him—" Oni gestured at Cyril— "I'm a strong swimmer. There was absolutely no reason to dive in after me."

"I didn't know if you knew how to swim," Cyril said.

She put her hands on her hips. "Why would you think I'd train for every possibility except a water emergency?"

MacNeil sat on the concrete stair next to the recruit with the bushy sideburns whose hands were still tied. The tall, sticklike recruit sat on MacNeil's other side.

As if all were waiting for someone to come for them.

> WASHINGTON DC—Members of houses of worship throughout the United States reported that statues and portraits of female saints began to glow, lighting the entire areas where they stood at 4:15 p.m. Eastern Time yesterday. People attending religious services in places of worship that featured no images of deities or saints reported visions of women bathed in light appearing in their midst. The timing corresponded with a fluvial event in the Mississippi River near the St. Louis Arch, as well as with the final aftershock from Tuesday's earthquake, and the end of another in a series of violent thunderstorms in the St. Louis area.
>
> Over a thousand religious leaders have since reported plans to remodel their institutions to include representations of the divine that show female, male, and gender-neutral images. Input from congregants is being taken into account.

"I went to confession," Thomas said. "But I didn't feel forgiven."

It was their first meeting since they'd talked on the Riverwalk. It had been a month since the incident at the Arch, which had come to be known as The Illumination. During that time, Thomas' lawyer had finally approved him speaking candidly with Sophia, or at least hadn't insisted he not do so. Thomas had entered into a plea bargain where he cooperated in identifying and testifying against other Brotherhood members in exchange for all charges other than misdemeanor theft being dropped. He'd been sentenced to paying Nanor restitution for the damage to Maya's grave, two years of community service, and two years of intensive probation.

They sat on the patio of Sophia's townhome. She'd abandoned her cane for good, and though her ankle still throbbed at the end of the day, it did so less each week.

"Why do you think that is?" Sophia said.

"I haven't believed for a long time that priests were needed to mediate between God and man. I was hedging my bets, I suppose. But the greatest challenge isn't laying one's soul bare to the Almighty. If you believe in that sort of God, he already knows. It's honestly confessing our sins not to any sort of God, but to those we love."

Sophia's mouth felt dry, her lips and throat parched, as if she were the one who'd revealed her sins and now needed to justify them or at least explain. She sipped her iced tea. She felt both curious to hear more and afraid. He'd told her he loved her in so many words. Yet if what he said next didn't aid her in getting past the things he'd done, this might be their last conversation as a couple.

He shifted his chair to face her and took her hands in his. "My choices over the years must seem appalling to you."

"You're not appalled?"

"You must understand that until the last two years, I viewed my life's work in black and white, one of the only black and white issues I believed existed in the world. A war between good and evil." He let go of her hands and straightened his back. "I apologize. There is no 'must.' You may very well not understand, but I hope you will."

"I'll try. Because I love you, too, Thomas."

Her heart pounded. She'd wanted to say those words for months, but she hadn't. She'd needed to see how she felt about Thomas after Tara awoke. She'd needed to know if he was being honest with her. She'd needed to know if he'd truly make the changes he wanted to make.

But now, with the warm late summer night and the last few cicadas singing, with the possibility that they might never be together again, it didn't matter. He was about to open his soul. She wanted him to know how she felt now, at this moment, regardless if it changed an instant from now.

Thomas shut his eyes. When he opened them again, they appeared bright with tears.

"Thank you. I hope you won't choose to retract that. And I love you. Whatever else you believe about me or don't, I hope you'll believe that."

"I do," she said.

"The first virgin pregnancy the Brotherhood of Andrew became aware of during the time I belonged was Maya Kerkorian's. I didn't learn until this year that the Brotherhood had actually caused these pregnancies. As best I can tell, there have been anywhere from a dozen to two dozen Spark of Life ceremonies since the time of Christ."

"And does the Brotherhood claim credit for him?"

"Not that I know of. I found nothing in MacNeil's library or the archives about the stories of Mary and Jesus beyond those also known to the rest of the world. The records predating Christianity were sparse, and it's unclear whether some form of the Order existed then. When Maya Kerkorian became pregnant, it was historic. For me, for everyone in the Brotherhood."

Part of Sophia wanted to tell him to stop. To tell him it was enough that he was sorry, that she didn't need to know. But she did. Forgiveness was one thing, but foolishness another. She owed it to Tara to hear the truth, and to herself.

"And your role?"

"We didn't have DNA testing then," Thomas said, "so we couldn't determine scientifically whether her child was the one we'd waited for. But we had other methods, and I was sent to get a sample of her hair. Easy enough. Like so many women, she kept a comb in her purse. At our second meeting, I obtained a few strands."

"If you didn't have DNA testing, what could you learn from that?"

"There were some scientific tests available. As to the rest, there was a holy man, or so I was told. That wasn't my jurisdiction."

Sophia shifted in her chair, repositioning her ankle to ease the aching. "So however it happened, Maya Kerkorian died because some holy man said she was going to have a female child?"

"Put that way, it sounds horrendous. It is horrendous. But remember that her fetus was determined to be female after her death, so the holy man wasn't wrong. And it wasn't that she was female. It was that she didn't meet the prophecy."

"So it's not that she was female, it's that she wasn't male."

"It's that if she didn't meet the prophecy, she'd either lied about a virgin pregnancy or—"

Sophia stared at him. "And that lie required a death sentence?"

"Let me finish. I told her she was not carrying a messiah, that her pregnancy was not divine."

"Because you knew that."

"I believed I did. Not I, but the Brotherhood," Thomas said. "So I tried to convince her to admit she'd been mistaken about her pregnancy. That she'd conceived the usual way. When she wouldn't recant her claims, I represented to her that she'd be better off terminating the pregnancy."

Sophia blinked, surprised. "To encourage abortion contradicts every teaching of the Catholic Church. And you were still Catholic despite your Brotherhood membership."

"Which is why I never went to confession about it. Women who had abortions were excommunicated. There was no forgiveness, regardless of repentance or remorse, no path for reconciliation. Whether I would have been excommunicated, I don't know. But I stopped receiving communion and, eventually, stopped attending mass. I felt I was doing what was right, but I also felt I should respect the Church's laws."

A neighbor passed on the sidewalk carrying an overloaded cloth bag from a grocery store. Sophia nodded to him and waited until he was out of hearing distance to speak again.

"So Maya's failure to do what you told her to do justified—in your mind—killing her?" Sophia said.

"No. I believed it justified because she was the opposite force to the Brotherhood, to Christ. The Antichrist, able to live forever by perpetually reproducing herself. You must understand—I hope you'll understand—that based on those beliefs I agreed with my superiors that we couldn't take a chance."

"Because what is one woman's life against a folk tale?"

"You became a nun, Sophia. You didn't see the Catholic Church's stories as folk tales. You saw them as myths that revealed a deeper truth regardless of their literal accuracy. You set your life's path according to those myths."

Sophia shook her head. "I never killed anyone because of them."

"Are you sure you wouldn't have? If you believed it required?"

"Yes, I'm sure. I never rested my ethical choices on what the leaders of the Church told me, even when I was a nun."

He sighed. "Which is no doubt part of why you didn't stay a nun very long. But I did, in a metaphorical sense. I believed what I learned. I believed in a great and real danger to the world from Maya Kerkorian and anyone like her. My part in her death has haunted me ever since, but I never strayed from the mission until you, though I did try to modify it."

"For the Brotherhood's sake, though, correct?" Sophia said.

"Yes, in part. Maya Kerkorian's death gave rise to Nanor Kerkorian's convictions about her daughter, which led her to become a minister, found Willow Springs, and begin watching for the next woman like her daughter. She now had a platform to preach from, and a constituency to preach to. That convinced the Order to try less extreme measures with Tara."

Somewhere in the distance, brakes squealed and horns blared. No impact sounds, though, so perhaps a collision had been averted.

"So the Brotherhood changed its approach not for moral reasons but for practical ones," Sophia said.

"Yes. But I encouraged it in part for moral reasons, particularly as I advanced in the Order. I never forgot that night in the car, never reconciled myself completely to what we'd done. It was the first chink in the armor of my faith. Not in God, but in the Brotherhood."

"And that makes you a better person than the rest of them?"

"It doesn't. And it's self-serving to say all this now. Perhaps I'm rewriting history and my place in it to make myself look better in my own eyes. So I'll say that I fully accept responsibility. My later regrets don't change anything."

"They don't." Sophia looked beyond him at the trees hanging over the street, and the brick townhomes lit in rose tones by the setting sun. "But they might have saved Tara's life."

She couldn't claim surprise at Thomas' actions and the reasons for them. She'd let him into her heart knowing, if not that he'd been in the car that killed Maya Kerkorian, that he was an integral part of an Order that had almost certainly arranged her death. She had eased into the relationship, counting on her ability to forgive if necessary, aware that the relationship might fail of its own accord given all the conflicts between them. She'd almost convinced herself that he'd been forced into his part in Maya's death, and in the later actions against Tara, but he'd made his own choices, and on some level she'd always known that was so. Thomas wasn't a man who let others dictate his life.

At least he had done all he could to aid the prosecutors, and he'd helped persuade Fenton MacNeil to do the same. MacNeil had pled guilty to numerous felonies, entering a blind plea, which meant a judge would decide his sentence. The information he and Thomas had provided was expected to lead to quite a few additional convictions.

"I need to think," Sophia said. "I'm grateful you came through for Tara in the end. But I need to think."

# 36

ROME— The Vatican announced today the formation of a commission to consider the ordination of women and transgendered persons as priests. This announcement comes exactly a year after numerous persons in churches, synagogues, mosques, and other places of worship all over the world reported visions of female deities and saints, while others saw portraits and statues of women illuminated by what they believed was a divine light.

Soon after these events, which have come to be known collectively as The Illumination, groups of all genders began petitioning the governing bodies of their religious institutions for greater gender diversity. A spokesperson for the Vatican claims, however, that the impetus for the commission was the widespread acceptance of women as lectors and extraordinary ministers over many years.

In politics and business, the United States has seen a dramatic shift in leadership demographics. In January, 2017, 80% of United States Senators, 80.6 % of Members of the House of Representatives, and 73% of sitting judges were men. Today, men account for 53%, 54%, and 42% respectively. Similarly, men accounted for 95.6% of CEOs of Fortune 500 companies and 67% of upper level management in 2016. Today, those numbers have shifted to 75% and 55%.

Many people believe that the publicity surrounding Tara Spencer, currently a resident of Chicago, Illinois, helped shape these changes. Spencer claimed to have had a virgin pregnancy. She and her child, Sophia Fiona Spencer, known as Fimi, sparked controversy among conservative religious figures who doubted Spencer's claims and denounced the possibility that the child might be a messiah. Regardless of the validity of her claims, Spencer helped bring to light a shadow religious organization, the Brotherhood of Andrew, whose wrongdoings are alleged to include the murder of Pope Matthew I.

Miss Spencer, now a first-year medical student, could not be reached for comment.

Tara set her backpack on the floor just inside the door of the apartment in Berwyn where she and Fimi had been living with Nanor and Kali. All the furniture had been moved the day before to a four-floor multi-family home in Chicago. The first floor apartment had been reserved for Nanor, the third floor for Tara and Fimi, and the fourth floor attic studio for Kali.

Kali bounced into the hallway, carrying an open cardboard box. "You've arrived in time!"

"I have," Tara said. "What's left?"

"Whatever's in the bathroom. I thought we might want it separate so we know quickly where to find it."

"Thank you. I owe you big time whenever any of us moves again." Kali had done much of Tara's packing, as her school year hadn't yet begun. She was now a junior at UIC.

"No worries. Grandmother and I are quite invested in your doing well in medical school. It's always good to have a doctor in the family."

Tara peered into the dining area that had morphed into being Fimi's playroom during the last year, feeling a trace of the old anxiety at its emptiness, though no one had tried to harm her or her daughter since that day at the Arch. "Fimi?"

"Your mom and dad picked her up an hour ago. She's probably settled in already playing with her toys."

"Great."

Tara's parents had driven from St. Louis to Chicago to help with the move, and they were staying at Sophia's old townhome, which was vacant for two weeks until the closing. Lynette and Pete had moved back into the updated and refurbished family home in Rock Hill last month with Bailey and Nate, who'd taken over Tara's old studio apartment in the attic. Kelly had her room back, too, at least officially, though she lived at college during school years.

Tara and Kali stowed the boxes of bathroom and kitchen supplies and clothes in the two-year-old Toyota that Tara had bought when she'd moved to the Chicago area permanently.

Traffic was backed up on the Eisenhower Expressway, so the drive to the South Loop took over an hour, but Tara didn't mind. She and Kali hadn't had much time to talk since Tara had started med school, so she told Kali about it.

"Sounds exciting," Kali said. "If a bit scary."

"Compared to the rest of life over the last few years, not so much," Tara said. "And it's a good thing I'm getting started, since it looks like that's the only way I'll be healing anyone."

She'd tried a few times to heal others without any success. It seemed like saving Stranyero had been her last healing. Whether Fimi had any ability remained to be seen, but so far Tara hadn't seen any evidence of it.

They'd planned to park in front of the four-story home, but more cars than usual lined the street. They were a level below Roosevelt Road, and sound barriers blocked the traffic noise. The low hanging trees, green patches of lawn, and kids riding tricycles on the sidewalk reminded Tara of home, though the tall, narrow homes with little space between them and the occasional rumble of the L trains reminded her she was in the city. She pulled into the side driveway.

Sophia popped out from the garage. She wore a long, loose-fitting tank top over flowered leggings. Her hair hung long down her back. She looked more relaxed than Tara had ever seen her.

"We'll take those," she said. Stranyero appeared behind her, and between the two of them they relieved Kali and Tara of the boxes. He and Sophia had bought the building and were living in the second floor apartment.

When Tara started to climb the back stairs, Nanor exited her apartment and blocked their way. "It is quite a mess in my kitchen. Come around front instead. Your parents and Fimi are in your place."

The request seemed odd. The stairs did provide a view through windows into each apartment, but Nanor had never minded Tara seeing her kitchen in disarray. But Kali shrugged and trooped toward the front, so Tara followed. Maybe Nanor was worn out and cranky with the move.

The common area entryway had four separate mailboxes. Fresh lilies in a green glass vase stood on one of Nanor's side tables. Tara wasn't going to miss being crowded into Nanor's and Kali's apartment as she and Fimi had been for the past year, but they'd had good times there, too, and she was glad to see this reminder of her first peaceful year with Fimi and her friends in the entry of their new home.

At the third floor, Tara pushed open the door.

"Surprise!"

Too many voices to count joined in the chorus. Tara's little brother Bailey ran forward from his spot near the antique bookcases and wrapped his arms around her waist.

She hugged him. "Hey, squirt."

He was fifteen now, a head taller than she was, and starting to protest her nickname for him. But this time he allowed it, saying only, "Happy new home."

Everyone converged on her. Her sister Kelly, her mom and dad, Sophia, Stranyero, Nanor, and Kali. And after them, Vicki, Zavia from the cloister in Pennsylvania, and Oni, all the way from London where she was living again, now with Cyril. He hugged Tara, too, and returned to Oni's side.

Alma Duttenhaver, on a release from the halfway house where she was living, came forward. She wore jeans and a bright pink T-shirt and her long blond hair shone. Tara hugged her, too. "I hope you're feeling better."

"Getting there," Alma said.

"Where's your baby?"

"Staying with my dad and his wife. He heard what happened to me and got back in touch. He's been a huge help."

"I'm glad," Tara said.

She excused herself a few minutes later to talk with Dr. Lei, who stood near the dining table talking with Cyril and Oni. She wore black jeans and a red blazer over a white T-shirt, and her hair hung straight and long down her back.

"It's so good to see you," Tara said.

"This is the first weekend of my vacation," Dr. Lei said. "I couldn't think of a better way to spend it. How's school going?"

From the first, her doctor had taken Tara's claims about her virgin pregnancy seriously, and she'd tried to help in any way she could. Tara felt like she'd burst, she felt so happy to see everyone in her life.

Lynette scooted up next to Tara and nodded toward Cyril and Oni. "He certainly got over you quickly," she said.

"Yeah," Tara said. "Isn't that great?"

The living room's bay windows faced Dearborn Street. A warm breeze drifted through, and the ceiling fan whirred overhead. Everyone settled onto the couch, love seat, and dining chairs. Plates of appetizers and drinks sat on a built-in buffet in the dining room, which was full-sized and overlooked the garden.

Fimi, held in Nanor's arms, clapped her hands together. "Welcome home, Mommy."

Everyone else raised their glasses and said, "Welcome Home."

Tara smiled at them all as sun streamed in through the windows.

If you enjoyed this book, please leave a review where you purchased it to help other readers find it.

To receive bonus materials about The Awakening Series, including deleted scenes and author's notes, join the author's email list.

# ALSO BY LISA M. LILLY

**The Awakening Series:**

The Awakening

The Unbelievers

The Conflagration

The Illumination

**Standalone Stories:**

When Darkness Falls (a supernatural suspense novel)

The Tower Formerly Known As Sears And Two Other Tales Of Urban Horror

**Writing as L.M. Lilly:**

How The Virgin Mary Influenced The United States Supreme Court: Catholics, Contraceptives, and Burwell v. Hobby Lobby, Inc.

Super Simple Story Structure: A Quick Guide to Plotting and Writing Your Novel

# ABOUT THE AUTHOR

Lisa M. Lilly is the author of the best selling four-book *Awakening* supernatural thriller series. All four books, *The Awakening*, *The Unbelievers*, *The Conflagration*, and *The Illumination* are now available.

Lilly also is the author of *When Darkness Falls*, a gothic horror novel set in Chicago's South Loop, and the short-story collection *The Tower Formerly Known As Sears And Two Other Tales Of Urban Horror*, the title story of which was made into the short film *Willis Tower*. Her stories and poems have appeared in numerous publications.

A resident of Chicago, Lilly is an attorney and a member of the Alliance Against Intoxicated Motorists. She joined AAIM after an intoxicated driver caused the deaths of her parents in 2007. Her book of essays, *Standing in Traffic*, is available on AAIM's website.

*Connect with the author:*

www.lisalilly.com
lisa@lisalilly.com

Made in the USA
Coppell, TX
20 May 2021